WHEN WISHES COME TRUE

WHEN WISHES COME TRUE

by

Joan Jonker

Magna Large Print Books
Long Preston, North Yorkshire,
BD23 4ND, England.

British Library Cataloguing in Publication Data.

Jonker, Joan
  When wishes come true.

A catalogue record of this book is
available from the British Library

  ISBN 0-7505-2134-1

First published in Great Britain in 2003 by Headline Book Publishing

Copyright © 2003 Joan Jonker

Cover illustration © Hulton Archive (Background)
Colin Thomas (Girl) by arrangement with Headline Book Publishing

The right of Joan Jonker to be identified as the author of this work has
been asserted by her in accordance with the Copyright, Designs and
Patents Act, 1988

Published in Large Print 2004 by arrangement with
Headline Book Publishing Ltd.

Magna Large Print is an imprint of Library Magna Books Ltd.

Printed and bound in Great Britain by
T.J. (International) Ltd., Cornwall, PL28 8RW

To Clare Foss, Sherise Hobbs and the staff at Headline, and to Darley Anderson and the staff at his agency, for their kindness, friendliness and encouragement over the years.

A big hello to my readers and friends

I hope all is well in your world.

There is a treat in store for you with *When Wishes Come True*. It's a little different from my other books, but I promise you will love it. Our heroine is a young girl who will capture your heart, as she has mine.

With a mother who shows her no love and thinks she is a cut above their neighbours, Milly's life is far from perfect. Then she is befriended by the woman next door and her two mates, who bring love and laughter into the young girl's life. There are a lot of surprises ahead for Milly, her new friends and for my readers. I suggest you hurry through your housework, make yourself a cup of tea, choose the most comfortable chair and put your feet up. But don't forget to have a box of tissues handy. I went through two while I was writing this book.

Take care.

Love

Joan

Chapter One

1925

'Just look at this one, walking up the street as though she owned it.' Aggie Gordon was standing on the bottom step of her two-up-two-down house, talking to her next-door neighbour, Rita Wells, when she saw a familiar figure turn into the street. 'Miss Hoity-Toity ... she gets on my bleeding nerves!'

'Ah, come on, Aggie, she doesn't do us any harm,' Rita said. 'I don't know why yer feel so strongly about her, she can't help it if she's down on her luck. She's in the same boat as all of us, without two pennies to rub together.'

Aggie pulled a face and folded her arms under her bosom. To say she was well endowed in that department would be understating it, she was enormous. 'Aye, but we don't all walk down the street with our noses in the air, do we? Stuck-up madam! She wants taking down a peg or two. And if she ever looks sideways at me, I'll clock her one.'

Rita turned her head to see a slim, attractive young woman who walked with a straight back and an air of confidence. She'd lived in one of the houses opposite Rita and Aggie for a few years now, but hadn't made any friends. Her seven-year-old daughter Amelia wasn't allowed to play with the other children in the street either, which caused most of the neighbours to say the woman was a stuck-up cow who thought she was too good for the likes of them. 'If she wants to keep herself to herself, Aggie, then that's up to her, she's not hurting anyone. It's the young girl I feel sorry for, she hasn't got one friend in the street. She's a nice little thing, too!'

'How d'yer know that when she's not allowed to speak to anyone 'cos her bleeding mother thinks we've all got fleas?' Aggie shook her head and her many chins danced. 'Ye're daft, you are, Rita Wells, yer never see the bad in anyone.'

'While you, Aggie Gordon, are never happy unless yer've got someone to pull to pieces. Yer haven't spoken more than ten words to Mrs Sinclair, but yer can't stand the sight of her. I'm glad I'm a friend of yours, 'cos I'd sure as hell hate to be an enemy.'

Aggie's head wagged from side to side, sending her layers of chins flying in all directions. 'And why haven't I spoken more than ten words to Her Ladyship? Because every time I see her she looks down her nose at me, as though I'm a bad smell.'

'That's probably because she knows ye're always pulling her to pieces. Yer've got a voice like a foghorn, Aggie, they should use you when there's a fog over the Mersey to guide the ships in. Unless Mrs Sinclair is deaf, she must hear yer calling her fit to burn and wonder why. The poor woman lost her husband in the war so yer should have some pity for her, having to bring her daughter up on her own. She's never done you or me no harm, so for heaven's sake leave the woman alone and pick on someone who can stick

14

up for herself.' Rita chuckled. 'Me, for instance, 'cos I could hit yer back.'

Aggie's laughter was loud. 'You! I could knock yer into the middle of next week with just one of me fingers.'

At that moment the woman who was the target of Aggie's criticism happened to turn her head before inserting her key into the lock. When she saw Rita nod her head, she nodded briefly in return before opening the door and stepping inside. Once the door was closed behind her, Evelyn Sinclair leaned back against it and sighed. How she hated this mean little house in the mean little street, where most of the neighbours were coarse and vulgar. Particularly the little fat woman opposite, whose language was that of a fishwife. The only person in the street she ever had any conversation with was the woman next door, Bessie Maudsley, and on the odd occasion she had exchanged nods with Rita Wells opposite.

Evelyn pushed herself away from the door and hung her coat on a hook in the tiny hall before entering the living room. There, she pulled out one of the wooden chairs from the table and sat down. With her chin cupped in her hands, she took a deep sigh. Just looking around the room filled her with despair. There were no mirrors on the walls, no pictures, and no ornaments on the bare sideboard. When she went into the kitchen to make herself a cup of tea, she would find the pantry almost bare. It wasn't because she was lazy, and spent her days gossiping like a lot of the women in the street. She had found herself a job in the office of a firm of solicitors in the city

15

centre, and worked there five hours for four days a week. But her job was really a junior's: running errands, making cups of tea and filing the correspondence of the two solicitors who shared the practice. The wages were low, barely enough to pay the rent on this house and buy what food she could to feed herself and Amelia. New clothes were out of the question, and a fire in the grate a luxury.

Evelyn dropped her head into her hands. What a far cry this was from what she had been used to. Then, as she often did, she closed her eyes and let her mind go back over the years to when she was nineteen. She was an only child, and lived with her parents in an eight-roomed house. Her father ruled her and her mother with a rod of iron. She wasn't allowed to invite friends to the house, nor accept invitations to visit theirs. But on her nineteenth birthday her father reluctantly agreed that she could go to an afternoon tea dance to celebrate, on the understanding that she was to refuse any requests from strange men to take to the dance floor. She had thought how stupid it sounded to say she could go to a dance but must not take part, but daren't voice her thoughts or she would have been sent up to her room and told to stay there until Father said she could come down for her meal. So she promised she would not dance, and that she would be home by six o'clock. She would have promised him anything, just to get out of the house and be able to act her age.

Her office friend, Gwen, had loving parents, and as a result was more sure of herself and more outgoing. When they met up that Saturday afternoon, she linked Evelyn's arm and grinned. 'First day of freedom, eh?'

'Hardly a day, Gwen, it's two o'clock now and I've to be home by six.'

'You'll not set any hearts on fire in that dress, Eve, it's positively old maiden auntish! Have you nothing more glamorous in your wardrobe?'

Evelyn shook her head. 'You don't know my father, he's so old fashioned. I'm lucky to be here at all, never mind worrying about my dress.'

'Then I'm going to put powder, rouge and lipstick on your face, and I'll do something with your hair. Otherwise you'll never be noticed.'

So the Evelyn who walked out of the ladies' powder room of the Adelphi Hotel was very different from the one who'd walked in. Not that she wouldn't have attracted many a roving eye without the make-up because she was tall and slim with dark brown hair, enormous brown eyes and a flawless complexion. But whether it was the make-up or not, the friends barely had time to sit at one of the small round tables before a man appeared in front of them, his hand outstretched, and addressed Evelyn.

'May I have this dance?'

She looked scared. She was about to stutter that she had never been to a dance before when Gwen said, 'Of course you may, my friend would be delighted. Go along, Evelyn, I will be all right, I can see some of my friends waving to me.'

So Evelyn, for the first time in her life, found herself in the arms of a man. And what a handsome man he was! Tall, slim, well dressed, with jet

17

black hair and laughing eyes that were constantly changing colour from hazel to dark green. When he spoke his voice was that of a well-educated person and very pleasing to the ear. 'Are you always so shy? You don't have to be afraid of me, I won't eat you.'

'I'm not afraid of you, I'm afraid of standing on your toes! You see, I've never been to a dance before and I'm nervous in case I make a fool of myself.'

'No one as beautiful as you could possibly make a fool of themself.'

And that was how their romance began. After the dance was over and Evelyn could see Gwen was with company, she agreed when her partner asked her to sit with him at another table. She may as well make the most of this opportunity, she thought, there may never be another. When he asked she told him her name, where she lived, and about the father who was very strict but who provided a nice comfortable home for her and her mother. Then the man, oozing confidence and looking at her with more than interest in his eyes, told her his name was Charles Lister-Sinclair. With a smile, he said, 'I work for my father who is far from strict and keeps me in the lap of luxury. He is also very generous in allowing me as much free time as I wish. So I hope to see much more of you in the very near future.'

Because she was smitten, Evelyn took a chance and arranged to meet him in her lunch hour the following Monday. She had never dared defy her father before, but she did so want to see Charles again, and if she had to tell lies to do so, then so

be it. When she met up with Gwen in the cloakroom later, she was so excited the words poured
from her mouth. 'I'm meeting him on Monday,
Gwen, and he's taking me to lunch. I find it
unbelievable I've met such a handsome and
charming man on my first day of freedom!'

Gwen raised her eyebrows. 'You do know who
his father is, don't you?'

'No, except that Charles said his father spoiled
him.'

'You are so innocent, Eve! Don't you know
anything about the social life of this city? Charles
is one of the most sought-after, eligible young
men in Liverpool. There are literally dozens of
mothers chasing him for their daughters. He
would be quite a catch for any girl, with his good
looks and charming manner, quite apart from the
fact that his father is one of the richest men in the
city.'

Evelyn gaped. 'He never said! Except that his
father was good to him.'

'No, he wouldn't brag about his wealth, that's
what is so refreshing about him. Not like some of
the young bloods I've met at parties who think
because their families are well heeled they should
be welcome in any virgin's bed.' Gwen grinned
when she saw the look of horror on her friend's
face. 'Don't worry, Charles isn't like that, he's a
perfect gentleman. And if you can hook him, Eve,
then you'll be the envy of every young female of
marriageable age, and that includes myself.'

'I didn't know you knew him? You never said
when he came over to ask me to dance.'

'I've seen him around many times, even been to

19

parties where he's been a guest, but I wouldn't profess to know him well enough to introduce him. Anyway, it's time for you and me to go our separate ways, so I'll say "Sweet dreams", and I shall look forward to hearing what happens on Monday. I presume you will not be telling your father?'

'You presume right, Gwen, I'm not going to say a word. If I did, I wouldn't be allowed out of the house.'

Sitting at the dining table later with her mother and father, Evelyn was praying that her father would question her about the dance. But it was her mother who, unknowingly, came to her aid. 'Were there many at the Adelphi, my dear? Do tell us what type of person frequents these places?'

Evelyn nodded. 'Yes, quite a few people, Mother, and some of the dresses on the young ladies were absolutely delightful.' She saw the familiar frown crease her father's forehead and hoped her little plan would work. 'I only knew Gwen, of course, but she did introduce me to one of her male friends.' She turned her head. 'I wonder if you know the Lister-Sinclairs, Father? Gwen said they are a very well-known family.'

The frown disappeared like magic, and his eyes widened in surprise as he lowered his knife and fork. 'I don't know them personally, but everyone locally has heard the name. They are a very well-known family, wealthy and much respected in the business world. Cyril Lister-Sinclair has many interests, and is probably the richest man in the city of Liverpool.' He coughed behind one curled fist before asking, 'And the son was at the dance,

20

you say?'

'Yes, Father, and seemed very personable.' Evelyn could tell her father had taken the bait. 'Quite friendly with many of the people there.'

Herbert Wilkinson looked across at his wife. 'Perhaps I have been doing our daughter an injustice, Gertrude, by not allowing her to attend these dances. Don't you agree?'

'Oh, yes, Herbert, now we know the cream of local society attends them, we can rest assured she is in good company. Would you like to go next Saturday? If your father gives his permission, of course.'

Evelyn's plan was working beautifully. She had bargained on this being the reaction from her parents, who were both tight with money and would be delighted if their daughter married a rich man. 'Oh, I don't think I want to go again, Mother, I would feel like a poor relation. You see, I couldn't compete with the fashionable dresses and high-heeled silver shoes all the ladies were wearing. I really felt like a wallflower in this drab dress, and wouldn't want to go through that again.'

'Oh, I'm sure that, under the circumstances, and because we want you to mix in the right circles, your father would give you an allowance to buy suitable clothes. We can't have our daughter looking less attractive than the other ladies. Aren't I right, Herbert, when I say you will give Evelyn an allowance for some new clothing?'

'Of course, my dear.' Herbert Wilkinson was what you would call a sombre man who seldom smiled, and had never been known to laugh aloud. But right now he was positively beaming. He had a good job and was well paid, but he was a greedy man; not content with being well off, he wanted to be wealthy. And now, perhaps, through his daughter and her newfound connections, he could well find himself on the way to riches and social acceptance. 'When we've finished our meal we can discuss what is needed so that Evelyn can mingle with the best in society as an equal.'

True to his word, if against his better judgement, Herbert handed over four white five-pound notes. That it pained him to do so was obvious from the length of time he held on to them before Evelyn finally whipped them out of his hand. 'I need at least two dresses, Father, I'd be ashamed to wear the same one week after week. Then there are silk stockings, shoes, a band to wear around my forehead and some jewellery...'

'Your mother has plenty of jewellery you could make use of. It's only lying in a box on her dressing table, it would be an absolute waste of money to buy more.'

'I'll see, Father, when I go to the dance on Saturday. I will take more notice of what is in fashion then, but meanwhile I can get advice from Gwen. She is very up-to-date on fashions as she attends many dances and parties.'

And so Evelyn's social life began. She had never known such freedom and, dressed to kill, was thoroughly enjoying herself. Wherever she went, Charles Lister-Sinclair went too. They saw each other every day and visited each other's houses. Herbert Wilkinson and his wife made a great fuss of Charles, but on visiting the Lister-Sinclairs,

Evelyn found that while Charles' father was friendly with her, his mother was distant and didn't even try to hide the fact that she wasn't pleased with her son's choice. When Evelyn mentioned this to Charles, he laughed and said any girl he took home would not be made welcome by his mother who doted on him. Her only child, she wanted to keep Charles under her wing until he was older, and only then would she find a suitable wife for him. Evelyn continued to be pleasant to Mrs Lister-Sinclair. It didn't bother her that her friendliness wasn't reciprocated because she knew Charles was besotted with her, as she was with him.

A rattling against a pane of glass in the window brought Evelyn down to earth. It took her a few seconds to get her thoughts together, then she jumped from her chair. This was her daughter home from school and she hadn't even thought about what they were going to have for a meal. It wouldn't be much because there was nothing in the house.

'I've been knocking for ages, Mother.' The seven-year-old girl hadn't inherited many of her mother's features, but she had learned to copy her expressions and mannerisms. 'I was beginning to think you had gone shopping or were working late.'

'I was tired after a busy day, Amelia, and must have dropped off to sleep. I've nothing in for our tea because all I have in my purse is a sixpenny piece, and that has to last until I get my wages on Friday.'

Amelia knew they were poor, her mother was always telling her so, and it made the young girl too old for her years. She didn't worry, though, because all the girls in her class at school were poor, and some of the boys in the street had no shoes on their feet. 'I could go for a pennyworth of chips, Mother, and we could make sandwiches with them. We could do the same tomorrow, that way your sixpence would last until Friday.'

'You need bread to make sandwiches, dear.' Somewhere at the back of Evelyn's mind a little voice was telling her she shouldn't burden her young daughter with their money worries. But another little voice, a trouble-maker, was saying that if Amelia had never been born then Evelyn would still be living a life of luxury, being waited on hand and foot by servants. And it was this voice that made her so bitter inside because her life had been reduced to living in this two-up-two-down house, with no money for the fine clothes she was used to. Not even enough to buy food or provide ha'pennies for the gas meter. So she found it hard to feel any sympathy for the little girl who wouldn't remember the good times, and who, if she was allowed, would be happy to associate with the common-as-muck people in their street.

'You could try the baker's, they usually sell it off cheap when it gets near to closing time. It's probably bread from the day before, and stale, but it would be filling and better than nothing. Perhaps you could get a small loaf for a penny, and with a pennyworth of chips we could make sandwiches and keep the hunger at bay.'

'Ooh, that's a good idea, Mother, I'll go there first.'

Evelyn passed the small silver coin over. 'Keep tight hold of that, in case you lose it. And if any of the women in this street are in the baker's, don't let them hear you asking if they have any stale bread. Come out of the shop and wait outside until they've gone. I don't want the whole street to know our business.'

'Yes, Mother.' Amelia placed the silver coin in the centre of her palm and closed her fingers over it. 'I'll keep tight hold of it. And if there's no one in the shop that I know, I'll give the woman behind the counter a big smile when I ask if they've any stale bread. You never know, Mother, I might get a large loaf for a penny if I'm nice to her.'

'Make sure you speak correctly, and don't run down the street, it isn't ladylike.'

'Yes, Mother.' The girl turned towards the door. She was mixed up inside because the other children at school made fun of her for talking so 'posh'. She didn't know about the children in this street because she wasn't allowed to play with them.

As soon as the door closed on her daughter, Evelyn held her head between her two hands and she went back to her memories of days gone by.

Chapter Two

It was 1914 when war with Germany broke out, and Charles wanted to join the Army right away. He said it was the duty of every able-bodied man to fight in defence of his country. He wouldn't be persuaded by Evelyn not to be hasty, but much to her relief Mr Lister-Sinclair pulled a few strings and Charles was classed as being involved in important war work. He wasn't happy about it, thinking he would be thought a coward, but gave in to his father's wishes and his mother's tears. So he and Evelyn continued to enjoy dances, theatres and eating out in the best hotels. Charles still had feelings of guilt, though, and every time he saw a man in uniform felt like a coward. He couldn't live with that. So when the war had been raging for eighteen months, without telling his parents first, he enlisted in the Army. With his education and background, he entered as a Captain and was sent for training in a camp just north of London so was able to get home regularly. Then, after a few months, he came home on a three-day pass to tell his parents and Evelyn that talk in the camp was rife that they were being sent overseas very soon, and he didn't know when he would see them again.

Cyril Lister-Sinclair showed no emotion, but there was fear in his heart for his son. Every day there was news of thousands upon thousands of young men being killed. As for Charles' mother, she wailed uncontrollably, and as there was nothing Charles could tell her that would calm her, he took Evelyn's hand and they stole away to find somewhere quiet and peaceful where they could have some privacy. This was impossible in either of their homes, so Charles suggested they take his car and drive out to one of the nearby country lanes. There was little petrol in the car because it was very hard to come by, but he felt sure that what he had would take them a few miles.

Dusk was falling as they sat with their arms entwined, wondering if they would ever see each other again. Charles rained kisses on Evelyn's face and promised to write to her every day, but that was little comfort to her, and tears trickled slowly down her face. 'Don't cry, my dearest darling.' Charles pulled her closer. With her body pressed against his, he could feel a stirring inside him. He tried to resist the urge, but need took him beyond the point of no return. Evelyn was taken by surprise at first and tried to pull away, but the thought that in a few days he would be going off to war caused her to cease her resistance. If she spurned him now, he would go away thinking she didn't love him, and she couldn't bear that.

When his passion was spent, Charles was full of remorse. 'Oh, I am so sorry, my dearest, what have I done to you? I have disgraced myself and am so ashamed I throw myself on your mercy. You will forgive me? Remember, I love you so much I couldn't help myself. But we'll get married on my

27

first leave, I promise. In fact, I travelled up today with another officer and he told me he was getting married tomorrow by special dispensation. Apparently if a soldier is being sent overseas, he and his fiancée can be married by special licence...'

'But I can't get married so quickly,' Evelyn protested. 'I haven't a wedding dress to get married in!'

'My darling sweetheart, you don't need a wedding dress to be married in a registry office! All you need are two witnesses, and I'm sure that will be no problem.' Charles was warming to the idea. 'I'll drive you home now and ask your father for your hand in marriage. If he gives his consent, I'll go and tell my parents. My mother will probably have a fit of the vapours and faint, and I don't think Father will be too pleased. I'm sure both of them would like a big, extravagant, high-society wedding for their only child, but I'll remind them there is a war on and many people are doing things they wouldn't normally do. I'll bring them around, I always do, then I'll meet you in the city centre tomorrow and buy you the engagement and wedding ring of your choice.'

Evelyn's parents were delighted. What a feather in their cap for their daughter to have landed such a good catch! And they didn't mind at all that the wedding was going to be a registry office affair, for, as Charles said, there was a war on. When their future son-in-law had left to break the news to his own parents, Mr Wilkinson was so full of good will towards his daughter he pulled her chair nearer the grate and, taking the

28

tongs from the companion set, placed three extra pieces of coal on the fire before rubbing his hands with glee.

However, the news wasn't so well received at the Lister-Sinclairs' home. As Charles had predicted, his mother reacted by falling back in her chair and lifting the back of one hand to her forehead. Her other hand was holding a fine, soft linen hand-kerchief edged with lace, which she waved at her husband while in a tearful voice demanding her bottle of sal volatile fearing she would faint. With a deep sigh, Cyril rang for the maid. He loved his wife, but did wish she had some backbone instead of always behaving like a child. He wasn't too pleased with the news his son had brought either, having always thought that when his only child married it would be the wedding of the year in their social circle. But the sight of Charles looking so handsome in his Captain's uniform, and the knowledge that in a few days his beloved son could be facing the enemy, was enough for him to keep his views to himself.

'Father, would you make some enquiries on how to go about obtaining a dispensation and special licence?' Charles asked. 'You're so much better at getting things done quickly than I am. And I'm meeting Evelyn in town tomorrow to buy the rings.'

Cyril nodded. 'I'll make a few phone calls in the morning and get what information I can. But you will only have two full days, and I can't imagine having the necessary papers completed in that time.'

'Two days and a half, Father. My train doesn't

leave until one o'clock on Thursday.' Both men turned their heads at the tinkling of the silver bell which Mrs Lister-Sinclair kept on her side table. They watched the maid enter the room, and heard her being told her mistress would like to retire as she was feeling quite light-headed. When his wife had left the room, leaning heavily on the maid's arm and sobbing as though her heart was breaking, Cyril asked if there was anything else he could do to help his son.

Charles leaned forward, resting his clasped hands on his knees. Gazing down at the floor, it was a few seconds before he spoke. 'This is frightfully forward of me, Father, and I would understand if you refused. But I would be so grateful if you would buy a house for Evelyn and me, as a wedding present. While I'm away she could be making it into a home for when the war is over and I'm back with her again. I really would like to know we had a place of our own, it would give me something to look forward to.'

Cyril was thoughtful for a few seconds, then sighed. This was a far cry from what he'd wanted for his son. 'I know there are one or two suitable houses empty in Princes Avenue. This confounded war has caused many people to move to the country. If that's what you want, I will certainly set the wheels in motion. You know I love you dearly and would move heaven and earth to make you happy. Everything I have will be yours eventually, and I'll be so proud when you take over the reins.'

'Thank you, Father, you are very kind and I admire and love you in return. When the time comes for you to retire – which I trust will not be for a very long while – I will do my best to make you proud of me. But if meanwhile you could settle Evelyn in a house, and look after her welfare, it would take a weight off my shoulders.'

Again Cyril was thoughtful for a few seconds before saying, 'I will purchase a house, furnish it, and make sure Evelyn has everything she needs. But I do think it would be best if I had my name put on the deeds. Only as a precaution, in case you came home and found you didn't like the house. You would have no ties to the property then and could look for another you think you would be happy in, and where you would like to raise your children.'

Charles lowered his head to hide the flush of guilt. 'Thank you, Father.'

So the following day, while Charles and Evelyn strolled down Church Street towards the jeweller's, their arms linked and their eyes gazing lovingly at each other, Cyril Lister-Sinclair was trying to arrange their wedding. After many phone calls, and taking advantage of his standing in the city, he managed to extract promises that the papers needed would be ready at five-thirty on Wednesday. Then, making a telephone call to the registry office, he was told they were booked solid for the whole week. However, when he mentioned his name and used a little persuasion they agreed to fit his son and fiancée in at half-past-eleven on the Thursday morning. No amount of coaxing would make the registrar's secretary change her mind about this. There were so many servicemen wanting to be married, she had to be fair to them all. Mr Lister-Sinclair was

31

lucky she'd managed to fit his son in at all.

Charles didn't let his disappointment show, for he knew he was lucky being able to marry before going back to camp. But it would give them only an hour and a half in which to get married and then head for the train station where he would catch the one o'clock train. There was no time to invite friends or even let them know, and both sets of parents declined to attend on the grounds that the whole affair was too rushed. Charles' mother said wild horses wouldn't drag her there because it was so degrading that a son of hers was being married in a registry office – oh, the shame of it! And when the Wilkinsons heard the Lister-Sinclairs were not attending, they made the same excuse. If Charles' parents had been going, they would have jumped at the chance of meeting the man who would soon be almost like family to them, and who they were hoping would help them up the ladder to social acceptance and wealth.

So the young couple were married with Evelyn's friend Gwen, and Oscar, a friend of Charles, acting as witnesses. They made a handsome bridal pair, with Charles looking handsome in his Captain's uniform and Evelyn in a fashionable short beige coat, a lighter beige cloche hat, and carrying a posy of flowers. It was a quarter-past twelve when they came out of the registry office, leaving them tight for time. Charles hailed a taxi and they reached the station with just enough time for last embraces, tearful kisses and vows to love each other for ever. Then Evelyn, accompanied by Gwen and Oscar, was waving goodbye to Charles through the steam and noise of the train taking him away.

Charles' father kept his promise to his son, and two weeks after the wedding Evelyn received a telephone call from her father-in-law asking her to meet him at the house in Princes Avenue which he felt sure she would like. And he was right, because she loved the wide avenue, with its three-storey red brick houses. The one he'd bought was handsome with an imposing entrance hall and a wide, curved staircase. Magnificent furniture graced the rooms on the first two floors of the house. What excited Evelyn the most, was that this was her means of getting away from her grasping parents. Cyril said he would give her a very generous monthly allowance and would also pay for the services of a live-in maid as the house was far too big for her to live in alone. In the days that followed, Evelyn had never been so happy in her life with her newfound freedom and very comfortable life style. The allowance from her father-in-law was three times what she'd earned at the office, and as he paid all the bills, too, she saw no point in working and gave in her notice.

Gwen was the only visitor to the house, for Evelyn discouraged her parents from visiting. But she didn't feel lonely, she revelled in the unaccustomed luxury and in being waited on by the maid, Eliza. Charles had been gone eight weeks, and although he had written to her from the camp before his unit was shipped out, she hadn't heard from him since. She wasn't particularly worried because Gwen had told her letters were taking months to get through, and because Evelyn was so content with her life of luxury, she gave little thought to anyone but herself and how lucky she was. Until the morning she experienced a feeling of nausea, followed by vomiting. It was only then she thought back and realised she'd missed the last two periods.

She took to her bed, telling Eliza she had a headache and would ring if she needed her. That she was with child she never doubted, but she didn't want a child, not now when she was enjoying the good things in life. Then, gazing up at the decorative ceiling in the huge, richly furnished bedroom, an idea formed in her head. She didn't want a child, she didn't feel in the least maternal, but perhaps that was the very thing that would make her mother-in-law warm towards her. If Evelyn was carrying her son's child, surely they would become closer – friends even? Of course they would, a grandchild would put a different complexion on their relationship. Feeling light-hearted in anticipation of now being taken into the bosom of the wealthiest family in Liverpool, Evelyn slipped her legs over the side of the bed and reached for the telephone on the ornate bedside table.

With the ear-piece in one hand, she was ready to dial when she gave a low cry and quickly changed her mind. Her face drained of colour, she sat back on the bed. How could she tell Charles' parents she was expecting his baby when officially they had never slept together? And she couldn't lie to them about it because they knew the young couple, with their friends, had gone straight from the registry office to the train station. Evelyn would have lied through her teeth if it would have got her out of this trouble, but no amount of lying would help her now. It was all Charles' fault, she should not have let him have his way with her. Her temper high now, Evelyn had no one to take it out on but the maid. So she pulled on the velvet bell cord. When Eliza entered the room she was ordered to draw the curtains as her mistress had a headache, then she was to fetch up a pot of strong tea.

It was Gwen who first remarked on Evelyn's expanding waistline and fuller face. 'Would I be right in saying someone has been doing things no respectable woman should?'

Evelyn's face turned crimson, but she tried to talk her way out of an embarrassing situation. 'Are you not forgetting I'm a perfectly respectable married woman?'

'Come off it, Eve,' Gwen drawled. She was quite happy to see her friend looking uncomfortable because she was tired of hearing how rich the Lister-Sinclairs were, and how wonderful life would be when Charles came home, and how they would always be giving lavish parties. 'Don't forget it's me you're talking to, and I know you too well to fall for any balderdash. If you are pregnant, then Charles can't possibly be the father. So come on, out with it, who have you been dallying with?'

Evelyn knew it would be no use pretending, she was in trouble no matter which way she turned. 'It *is* Charles' baby! I was stupid for allowing him to have his way with me before we were married.' She had the grace to blush. 'I felt sorry for him with him being sent overseas, and now I don't know which way to turn. I never see my parents, which is the way I want it, but what am I going to say to my father-in-law when he comes? He's due any time now with my monthly allowance, and you were quick enough to notice so he's bound to.'

'I imagine you'll meet some hurdles, Eve, because how can you prove it's Charles' baby? Mrs L.S. doesn't like you to begin with, so she's bound to cause problems.'

'Charles will soon put them straight when he comes home. And I hope that's soon because it's very embarrassing for me. Do you think I should explain to my father-in-law when he comes, tell him the truth? Or should I wear something that doesn't make it obvious and hope that the war will soon be over?'

Gwen shrugged her shoulders. 'That's up to you, Eve, I can't advise you.' She got to her feet. 'I'll have to go, I'm off to a cocktail party with Oscar. His parents are almost as wealthy as the Lister-Sinclairs, but I don't think I'll be letting him have his wicked way with me. Not until I have a wedding ring on my finger.' She swaggered towards the door. 'You take care, darling, and I'll call next week for the latest news.'

Evelyn eyed her coldly. She would have expected at least some show of sympathy or helpful suggestions from her friend. 'I'll let Eliza show you out.'

When her father-in-law called a few days later, Evelyn was wearing a loose dress, and as Cyril passed the money over without making any comment, she thought her weight gain had slipped his notice. He never stayed long to chat so there was nothing unusual in his making an excuse not to sit down. But as Evelyn followed him down the wide hall, she ventured to say, 'I've been expecting a letter from Charles, I thought I would have heard by now.'

He turned to face her. 'Any letters, or correspondence of any kind, would come to me. You see, when Charles joined up, he wasn't thinking of getting married and put me down as next-of-kin. There has been no word from him since he left, but I will inform you if there is any news.' He reached the front door, smiled at Eliza who was holding it open for him, then placed his hard high hat on his head and walked down the path to where a horse and carriage stood waiting for him. Without a backward glance he climbed into the carriage and gave his groom instructions to move away. His mind was very disturbed on the journey home as he hadn't failed to notice the loose-fitting dress which wasn't his daughter-in-law's usual style. That combined with the filling out of her face were signs of a woman with child. But it couldn't be, he was being bad-minded. However, in the weeks that followed doubt niggled at the back of his mind. If she was with child, it couldn't be his son's. She must have cheated on Charles.

Cyril waited another four weeks before calling on Evelyn again with her allowance. The door was opened by Eliza, whose usual smile was missing. The girl looked uncomfortable. 'The mistress asked me to apologise for her absence, Mr Lister-Sinclair, but she is feeling unwell and has taken to her bed. But she did say you could safely leave any messages with me and she would see you next month.'

Cyril stepped into the hall and handed his hat and gloves to the wide-eyed maid. 'Tell your mistress I insist upon seeing her, and will wait in the drawing room. And please ask her not to keep me waiting as I have an other appointment.' The maid did a little bob, placed his hat and gloves on the huge carved hallstand and scurried up the stairs while Cyril made his way to the drawing room. He didn't have long to wait for Evelyn was afraid of displeasing him. As soon as she walked through the door he knew his fears were well founded. Despite her loose-fitting dress, the filling out of her breasts and face were a sure sign. Although Evelyn had a large silk handkerchief trailing from her hands, it couldn't hide the swell of her stomach or the apprehension in her eyes.

'I won't beat about the bush, I have an appointment and can't stay long.' Cyril nodded to the hands vainly trying to cover her stomach. 'I think you have some explaining to do. It is very obvious you are carrying a child, and it is also obvious my son can't be the father. So I think an explanation is in order.'

'But it *is* Charles' baby!' Evelyn lowered her head in shame as she told him what had happened three nights before she and Charles were wed. 'I am telling the truth, Mr Lister-Sinclair, and Charles will verify that when he comes home. I should not have succumbed to his advances, I know that now, but he was going away so soon I couldn't deny him.'

Cyril reached into an inside pocket and brought out an envelope which he placed on the table. 'I will continue to pay you until my son comes home. If you are telling the truth I will be saddened by the actions of both of you. If you are telling lies, I will have no pity for you or your child, and you will leave this house as you entered it. There would be no further allowance and no further communication between you or any member of my family. I won't, for the time being, discuss the present situation with my wife as she is longing for her son's return and I will not add to her worries.' He nodded curtly and walked towards the door. 'I will in future hand the envelope in to Eliza. I will not enter this house until my son comes back from the war. If you take my advice, you will be more frugal with your money for the time being, and save what you can. The day might not be far off when you will have need of it.'

Evelyn was afraid now of a time coming when all this wealth and comfort was snatched away from her, so she became miserly with money. If she was thrown out of here she would have nowhere to go, her parents would disown her. But still she clung to the hope that the war would end soon and Charles would come back home and put things right. However, it wasn't to be. When she was seven months pregnant, Cyril came to tell her he'd had a telegram from the War Office to say Charles had been killed in battle. 'As I told you, Charles had put my name down as next-of-kin, and that is why the telegram was sent to me. My wife is absolutely distraught and

I must get back to her.'

'But what about me?' Evelyn cried. 'It is his child I'm carrying, you've got to believe me! You can't throw me out on the street, not in my condition.'

'You may stay until the baby is born, then you must look elsewhere for a house. Anyone could be the father. Please send a note a few weeks after it is born and I'll come and check that you have made arrangements to move. I might possibly allow you to take some of the smaller pieces of furniture and other items. Send the letter with Eliza and impress upon her that she must not hand it over to anyone but myself.' With a curt nod, Cyril was gone.

When Evelyn went into labour she would have been lost if Eliza hadn't run for her mother, who had delivered several babies in the street where they lived. Evelyn had not dared attend a hospital, nor had she booked the services of a midwife. All because of her pride, in case word had gone around that the woman calling herself Mrs Lister-Sinclair was carrying another man's baby.

She may have been unlucky in many things, but she struck lucky with Eliza and her mother. They were very efficient, and the mother in particular seemed to know exactly what to do. Evelyn was in labour for only five hours, there were no complications. She screamed throughout the birth. Afterwards there was relief on her face, but no thanks on her lips. She was used to being waited on by now and could not see why she should thank a servant who was being paid to look after

40

her. Eliza's mother didn't like her at all, thought she was a proper snob, but because she was her daughter's boss, she kept these thoughts to herself. Besides, she was being paid a pound for delivering the baby and that would keep her family for a week. So as she placed the baby in Evelyn's arms, she kept her voice pleasant. 'What are yer going to call her, Mrs Lister-Sinclair? Have yer got a name for her?'

'I've always liked the name Amelia, so that's what I intend to call her.'

Eliza, who would have loved to cuddle the baby, said, 'Oh, that's a nice name. She'll get called Milly at school.'

Evelyn nearly bit her head off. 'Her name is Amelia, and woe betide anyone who calls her Milly.' She looked down into the child's wrinkled face, then pushed the sheet aside. 'Take her away now, I'm quite exhausted and wish to rest.'

Eliza's mother was named Dora, and right now Dora was looking at Evelyn with disgust on her face. 'That baby needs to be put to yer breast. It needs feeding.'

'Feed a baby?' Evelyn looked at the woman as though she'd gone mad. '*I* am not going to feed the baby. Now take her away. Perhaps tomorrow when I feel a little stronger.'

'That baby needs feeding at once, yer can't feed her just when it suits you.' Dora didn't care whether her daughter got the sack, she wasn't going to stand there and listen to this selfish bitch. 'If yer won't feed her, yer'll have to get a wet-nurse to do it or I'll bring a doctor in to yer. I brought that baby into the world and I'll not

41

stand by and see it die just because you can't be bothered. Make up yer mind before me and Eliza walk out and leave yer to get on with it. And then it would be God help you and the baby!'

One look at the angry face looking down at her had Evelyn asking, 'What is a wet nurse?'

'It's a woman who has just had a baby herself, but who has enough milk to feed another. There's a few of them around here.'

Evelyn found this thought distasteful and shuddered. But one look at Dora's face told her she would be well advised to take heed of this woman; the last thing she wanted was to have a doctor call. A doctor who would perhaps know her in-laws. 'How would I go about getting one of these wet nurses, and would she be clean and decent?'

Dora shook her head. For all her posh talk, this woman was as thick as two short planks. If it wasn't for the baby she would have walked out and left her to get on with it. She'd soon learn the hard way, when the baby began screaming with hunger. Besides, Dora wasn't about to leave without a pound note in her hand. 'She would be as clean and decent as you are, madam. And the need is pressing, so yer'd better make yer mind up quick.'

'What would this person charge, and how often would she come?'

Dora wasn't going to let this spoiled woman off lightly. If she couldn't be bothered even to hold her new baby, let alone feed her, then she could pay handsomely for someone else to do it. She was living in the lap of luxury, while the wet nurse would be selling her milk to put food in the bellies of her family. The usual price was twopence for feeding a child three times a day, but there was nothing usual about the circumstances here. 'It will be two pence a time, and yer'll need her three times a day. During the night yer'll have to feed the baby yerself, and that'll get yer used to it. If yer have the nurse for a week, yer should be used to the baby by that time and be able to manage for yerself.'

Evelyn's eyes narrowed. She dreaded the thought of having to feed the baby herself, but she didn't want to part with any money to pay someone else to do it. 'But that is sixpence a day – three shillings and sixpence for the week! Surely if the woman is desperate for money she'll do it for less?'

Dora was really getting on her high horse now. Who the hell did this woman think she was? 'If yer don't like the terms, then forget it. Wet nurses are in great demand, they're not crying out for work. So I'll leave yer to sort something out yerself.'

'No! I would be grateful to you if you would arrange for one of the nurses to call as soon as possible. And as I'm sure you're wanting to get home now, I won't keep you.'

Dora's jaw jutted out. 'I'm not leaving here without the pound yer owe me for delivering the baby. And the wet nurse will want paying in advance, so have the money handy.'

At the end of the second day, the wet nurse, Minnie, waited until she had the sixpence in her hand before telling Evelyn she wouldn't be coming back. She made an excuse about someone in her family not being well, but it was a different

43

tale when she called at Dora's.

'I'm not going to be treated like a piece of dirt by anyone, I'd rather starve first. God help the baby, 'cos she's a lovely little thing and doesn't deserve to be lumbered with a mother like that. She's an unwanted child, that's sticking out a mile, and will never know a mother's love. The only one that stuck-up bitch thinks about is herself. She treats your Eliza like a slave. Sent the poor girl into town today to buy a cradle so she won't have to have the baby in bed with her. And she wrote down on a sheet of notepaper that the cradle must be of the best dark mahogany, with carving. But what's the good of a lovely cot when there's no love for the baby in it? Her own flesh and blood and anyone would think it had leprosy.'

Dora nodded. 'She's a stuck-up bleedin' cow, that's what she is. But I'm worried about the child. D'yer think I should get another nurse for her?'

Minnie pulled a face. 'That's up to you, queen, but if yer take my advice yer'll leave her be. Left on her own, she's going to have to feed the baby because her breasts are full of milk and she'll be in agony if she doesn't. It may take her a while to realise that, I don't think she's got a bleeding clue about being a mother, but she'll soon catch on when the baby's screaming and she's in pain. That's when she'll start putting two and two together.'

And Minnie was right. Evelyn hated the task, and at times hated the baby for making it necessary, but for her own comfort she fed Amelia whenever both felt the need.

Four weeks after the birth, Eliza was sent with

a letter to inform Mr Lister-Sinclair. It was another two weeks before he visited, and he spent several minutes gazing down into the cradle before asking, 'Have you been successful in finding a new house for yourself and the baby?'

'I haven't been out since Amelia was born, I haven't felt strong enough.' Evelyn didn't want to leave this beautiful house and the allowance that went with it, so she begged. 'Please believe that Amelia is Charles' baby. I swear that is the truth.'

Once again Cyril looked down into the child's eyes. They seemed to be looking straight at him. 'This baby bears no resemblance whatsoever to my son. Not in colouring, not in one single feature. In my eyes she was conceived out of wedlock and is therefore an illegitimate child, thanks to the immorality of her mother.'

He sighed, for he was not a cruel man at heart. But he was hurting so much from the loss of his son, and this woman was adding to the hurt by tarnishing the dead man's reputation and bringing discredit to the Lister-Sinclair name. And she had never loved his son, Cyril knew that now. His mind went back to the day he'd called to tell her he'd received a telegram saying Charles had been killed in action. She didn't even flinch, just stared at him as though the person he was talking about was a stranger to her. No tears, no outpouring of grief, no word of sorrow for the man she had married and professed to love. She hadn't even asked where and how her husband had been killed. Her only thought was of what was going to happen to her. She didn't even go into mourning, wearing widow's weeds, but was always colourfully dressed when he called. Nor had she ever expressed sympathy to him and his wife for their loss. It was as though Charles had never existed in her life. The only person Evelyn cared about was herself. No, she'd never loved his son, it was his money she'd loved.

'I do not want this child to bear my son's name,' he told her now, 'and if I find you have put Charles' name on the birth certificate as being the father, I will take legal action against you.' He turned, hesitating momentarily before walking away. 'There is a property letting office in Moorfields. They are a good firm and I suggest you try them.' He nodded curtly. 'Goodbye.'

The next day, after feeding the baby, Evelyn left Eliza in charge and went into the city. She soon found the letting office in Moorfields and asked for information on six-roomed houses. The clerk gave her a list of addresses, saying the rent of each depended on the area in which it was situated and the condition of the property. After listening to Evelyn's cultured voice, he recommended two that she should try first. They were in a good area, and as they were in sound decorative order, she could move in straight away.

From there, Evelyn went to order a pram to be delivered the following day. Then it was time to head for home before the baby started screaming to be fed. Once satisfied, Amelia settled down and would sleep for at least two hours, so Evelyn set off to look at the two houses. She wasn't very happy about having to move to such a small place, but was afraid the Lister-Sinclairs could make her life unpleasant if she didn't agree. One of the houses had a small front garden, and looking through the letter box and the windows, it seemed clean and bright. So she took the tram down to the letting office, was told the house was three shillings and sixpence a week, and was asked to pay two weeks in advance. She told the clerk she was a war widow and that her name was Mrs Sinclair. When the forms were filled in, she received a rent book and a set of keys.

Evelyn hated the house. It seemed so poky after the one she had grown used to. Nevertheless, having had to give Eliza notice, she found it impossible to clean and feed the baby, and keep up with the other washing and ironing, shopping and cooking. As she had no idea of the value of money, she bought the best of everything, even though she had no money coming in. It didn't take her long to fritter her savings away. When she'd been in the new house a year she had to pay her first visit to a pawn shop. Over the next year, all the expensive ornaments, pictures and mirrors, brought from the house in Princes Avenue, found their way into that shop. She was too naive to realise the pawnbroker was only giving her a fraction of what the items were worth, and she would never have the money to redeem them. She lived from day to day in a dream world, thinking that somehow she would be taken back to the riches and wealth she loved so much and which she thought she deserved. She never blamed herself for her situation, it was always the baby who had ruined her life.

One day as she sat at the bare table, she thought of the empty larder and her empty purse.

There was nothing left for her to pawn except the rings on her finger. She knew they were very expensive because she'd been with Charles when he bought them. The wedding ring she'd have to keep or people would think she was an un-married mother, and common sense told her the engagement ring would be better sold to a jeweller than to a pawnbroker. It was a beautiful ring with a huge diamond in a claw setting. She had to get a good price for it because the money would have to last a long time. She couldn't take it back to the shop it was bought from because they had known Charles. So she found another well-known jeweller's, and for once stood her ground and refused the fifty pounds she was initially offered for it.

'My husband paid four hundred pounds for that, and you offer me fifty? That is nonsense and you know it! I shall try elsewhere and am sure I'll get what the ring is really worth.'

She was right, of course, as the jeweller was well aware. 'What price were you expecting to get for it, madam?'

'At least half what my late husband paid for it.'

The man removed the glass from his eye. 'I'm sorry, madam, but you won't get that from any jeweller. It is after all secondhand which lowers its value considerably. I would be prepared to give you one hundred and fifty pounds for it, which would leave me a very thin profit margin.' He passed the ring back over the counter. 'But perhaps you would like to try one or two other shops?'

Evelyn didn't have time to try other shops,

she'd left Amelia playing with a rag doll in her bedroom. The child was three now, and sensible for her age because Evelyn was very strict with her. She had been warned not to leave the room, and wouldn't dare disobey her mother. They never had visitors, nor were they friendly with the neighbours. The women to either side had held out the hand of friendship to Evelyn the day they'd moved into the house, offering to mind the child while she got her furniture sorted out and was settled in. But all they had received in reply was a frosty stare, for she regarded them as being of a lower class than herself. They'd shrugged their shoulders and given up on her. Even now, after three years, she would pass them in the road without a glance. They felt sorry for the little girl because she was seldom taken out for a walk in the fresh air, even though there was a park nearby with swings which all the local children used. Except Amelia Sinclair.

'I'll take what you are offering, and would like to complete the transaction quickly, as I really must get home to my child.'

As Evelyn pushed the white five-pound notes into her handbag, her mind went back to the time she was getting as much money in her monthly allowance from Mr Lister-Sinclair. And she'd had no bills to pay out of it so it mostly went on clothes. She sighed as the tram came to a halt and she stepped on board. She would have to be very careful with this money, it would have to last until Amelia was old enough for school and she herself could look for work in one of the offices in the city centre. She had thought many times that she

49

should be entitled to a pension from the Army; with Charles having been a Captain it would probably be a decent one. But she was afraid that with his father being down as next-of-kin, he would probably be notified if she put in an application. It was years now since she'd had any contact with the Lister-Sinclairs, or her own parents who had disowned her for blackening their name. Nor had she seen Gwen or Oscar, but that didn't worry her because she'd hate them to know of her drastically reduced circumstances.

Amelia was holding the rag doll to her chest when Evelyn opened the bedroom door. 'I'm hungry, Mother, can I have some bread, please?'

'Yes, and I've got a treat for us. I bought some boiled ham, tomatoes and a nice crusty cottage loaf. And we'll have real best butter on the bread.' Evelyn found nothing strange in talking to her three-year-old daughter as if she were a grown-up, or that in return she was called 'Mother', not Mammy or Mummy. 'I've also bought a cream sponge cake for dessert, so we are eating well tonight. But it's only because it's a special occasion, so don't expect it every day. I'll have to be careful with money.'

Despite her good resolutions, with money in her purse Evelyn could not resist the finer things in life, and in eighteen months the money she'd got for her engagement ring had dwindled to a few pounds – not enough to send her daughter to a high school in six months when she'd be five. The thought of any child of hers attending a corporation school filled her with despair. Neither could they stay on in this house because the rent had

50

gone up over the years to four shillings a week, and it was such a draughty place it took two bags of coal a week to keep it warm. So once again Evelyn had to lower her sights, and was forced to move to a working-class area, with street after street of two-up-two-down houses occupied by families who were lucky if they saw a square meal once a week. There was a lot of unemployment there, dozens of men chasing after every vacancy. They would turn their hand to anything to put food on the table for their families, but life was hard and poverty was rife. Evelyn, with her knowledge of another lifestyle, hated it, and looked down her nose at everyone. The only person she felt sorry for was herself. Her misfortunes were not her fault, she decided. They were the fault of Charles for going away to war when he didn't have to, and of Amelia for being born.

Once again a knocking on the window had Evelyn shaking her head to clear it of the memories. She pushed her chair back and, wiping her eyes with the heel of her hands, opened the front door to her daughter. There was no smile or greeting for the child, she just turned on her heels and walked back to the chair she'd vacated.

Amelia's face was aglow as she followed her mother in, forgetting to close the front door behind her in her excitement. 'Mother, you'll be very pleased with me!' She put the newspaper-wrapped parcel containing the chips on the table, plus a large tin loaf. 'I walked up the street with Miss Bessie from next door, and she said I was very clever for getting a large loaf for a penny.'

51

The slap was delivered so quickly, and with such force, it shocked the young girl who looked bewildered as she let out a cry before putting a hand to her cheek. The cry of pain was loud enough for Bessie Maudsley to hear as she rooted in her bag for her front door key. Bessie was a small, wiry woman, who seemed to do everything at the double. A spinster, she'd lived alone in the house next door since her parents had both died in their fifties. She had a job as a seamstress and worked five and a half days a week. The pay wasn't much, but there was only herself to worry about and she managed fine. She was fond of her young neighbour who, to her mind, was too old in the head for her years, and wasn't allowed to enjoy her childhood like the other kids in the street. And if she thought for one minute that Lady bleeding Muck was going to give the girl a thrashing, she'd be in next door like a shot. So she stood with her door key in her hand and listened.

Unaware that the front door was still open, Evelyn raged at her daughter who couldn't understand why she'd been smacked for doing what her mother had asked her to do. 'How dare you discuss our affairs with the neighbours when I have told you so often that you must not have anything to do with them? They are not our kind and I will not let you bring us down to their level.' Poking a finger in her daughter's chest, she growled, 'Now do you understand what I'm saying, or do I have to knock it into you?'

Over my dead body, Bessie thought, rushing to knock on the open door. But she remembered to be careful what she said in case young Amelia suffered for it. 'Is everything all right in there?'

It was then Evelyn noticed the front door was still open, and hissed, 'You stupid child, you didn't close the door behind you!' Then her expression changed from one of anger to one of sweetness and light which didn't sit well on her face because it was so obviously false.

'Oh, hello, Miss Maudsley! Of course everything is all right. My clumsy daughter here bumped into the table and hurt herself, but it was nothing serious.'

Bessie stared her out. 'I'm sorry if she hurt herself 'cos I'm fond of yer daughter. I'll no doubt see her tomorrow and I can ask her meself how she is.'

With that veiled warning she turned back to her own front door. She'd be keeping her eyes and ears open in future, for she wouldn't trust that two-faced villain as far as she could throw her. Apart from thinking she was better than anyone else in the street, she had that sly look about her and obviously wasn't to be trusted. Now Bessie didn't care what her neighbour did, she could pretend she was the Queen of England if she wanted, it was no skin off Bessie's nose. But when it came to a child being ill treated, well, that was a different kettle of fish. She'd not stand by and see any youngster punished when they'd done nothing wrong. She'd mention it to Rita over the road, ask her to keep an eye out during the day while she herself was at work. The queer one next door was sly and needed watching.

53

Chapter Three

Rita Wells happened to glance out of her front window and saw Bessie Maudsley standing on her front step with her arms folded. The table had been cleared after their meal, the dishes washed and the two boys were out playing. Her husband Reg was reading the *Echo*, which was a ritual with him every evening and the one luxury he had in life beside his pint every Saturday.

'Bessie's standing at her door watching the world go by. She's probably glad of the fresh air after being stuck behind a sewing machine in a noisy factory all day. So, seeing as I've cleared up and everywhere is tidy, I think I'll go over and have a natter with her.' Rita jerked her head back and tutted. 'Don't look at me like that! Anyone would think I was Cinderella and had told yer I was going to a ball in a glass carriage, the sour face on yer. I wouldn't care if it was a case of yer missing me to talk to, but yer never open yer ruddy mouth until yer've read the paper from front page to back page. All I ever see is the top of yer head, and that's not interesting enough to keep me in. So whether yer like it or lump it, I'm slipping across to wile away half-an-hour with Bessie.'

Reg lowered the paper to his knees and spread his hands. 'I haven't opened me flaming mouth! If yer want to go and have a talk with Bessie, then by all means do so.' He was a tall, broad man with black hair who loved his wife and kids dearly. He had a sense of humour too. 'As long as ye're back in time to make me a cup of tea and put me slippers on.'

Rita patted the top of his head. 'I'll be back long before yer bedtime, sunshine, I'll only be half an hour. Unless Bessie has some exciting news for me, and then yer can make yer own tea and put yer own flaming slippers on.' She got to the door and turned with a puzzled expression on her attractive face. 'Ay, yer haven't got no pair of slippers.'

'I wondered when the penny would drop.' He gazed at his wife's bonny figure, curly mouse-coloured hair, and round happy face. It was a lucky day when she'd come into his life. 'Go on, love, yer deserve a break. But give us a kiss first.'

'Pucker up then, don't leave me to do all the work.' Rita bent to kiss him and found herself being pulled down on to his knee. 'Ay, now come off it, Valentino, don't be going all he-man on me. Not when I could be missing some juicy gossip.'

'How can Bessie have any gossip for yer when she's been out at work all day? You and Aggie see more of the neighbours than she does.'

'I know that, soft lad, it was supposed to be a joke. Anyway, I'm off, and I'll see yer when I see yer.'

As Rita crossed the cobbles, she was hoping her next-door neighbour Aggie wasn't watching through her window. She liked Aggie who had a heart of gold and was always the first to help in time of trouble. Her only fault was she couldn't

55

control her tongue. If there was anything on her mind, she came out with it, regardless of the consequences. If she took a dislike to anyone, she let them know in no uncertain terms. But if she took a liking to yer, she'd move heaven and earth to do you a good turn.

Bessie smiled. 'Hello, girl, where are you off to?'

'Nowhere, I've just come to keep yer company and have a natter.' It was Rita's turn to smile. 'And if yer believe that, sunshine, then yer'll believe anything! I'm here because I'm nosy. No, I'm not going to call meself nosy! Let's say I'm curious about what was going on next door.' She kept her voice low. 'I saw yer going to the door, and I heard yer shouting in, but I couldn't hear what yer said. Has Her Ladyship been up to something or were yer just being neighbourly?'

Bessie stepped back into her hall. 'Come in, girl, before the whole street gets nosy about what ye're doing standing on me step.'

When Rita followed her friend into the living room, she nodded. 'Yeah, yer still keep it like a little palace. Yer should have got married, sunshine, and had a load of kids, 'cos yer'd have made a wonderful wife and mother. Still, yer know the old saying: If yer've none to make yer laugh, yer've none to make yer cry. There's times I wish I'd never got married, even though I love the bones of my feller and the two boys.'

'Go 'way, yer'd be lost without them.' Bessie waved to a chair. 'Sit down and take the weight off yer feet.' She sat down opposite. 'This is to go no further, girl, especially to Aggie. Not that I've

56

anything against her, she's a good mate, but yer know she can't keep a thing to herself. And knowing how she feels about Mrs Sinclair, this would be right up her street. So, least said, soonest mended.

'Anyway, I walked up the street this evening with young Amelia, who was really excited 'cos she'd gone to the baker's and they'd let her have a stale loaf for a penny. God love her, she said her mother would be very pleased with her.' Bessie shook her head sadly. 'Her mother was pleased with her all right ... so pleased she gave her a smack across the face that I could hear as I was looking in me bag for the door key. So yer can imagine it must have hurt the poor lass if it was loud enough for that. Anyway, Her Ladyship mustn't have known the front door was open, and gave the girl down the banks for telling the neighbours their business. It went something like this.' Bessie put on a posh accent, looking comical as her mouth did contortions. '"How dare you discuss our affairs with the neighbours when I have told you time out of number that you must not have anything to do with them? They are not our kind and I will not let you bring us down to their level. Now do you understand what I'm saying or do I have to knock it into you?"'

Rita gaped. 'Well, the cheeky sod! There isn't a woman in the street who isn't a better person than she is. They mightn't have much money, and their clothes might be threadbare, but by God, they love their kids. They have a happier life than poor Amelia, 'cos it's sticking out a mile her mother has no love for her.' She tutted. 'The cheek of the woman to say we're on a lower level than her! Who the hell does she think she is?'

'I was blazing meself,' Bessie said, 'but because I thought she might give the girl another smack, I kept me face all innocent like when I knocked and asked if everything was all right. And yer wouldn't have thought she was the same person, she was all smiles then. Well, what passes as a smile for *her*. I think a good belly laugh would kill her! Anyway, I felt like having a real go at her, the two-faced so-and-so, but I thought better of it because of the girl. I wouldn't want to get her into more trouble. The queer one made an excuse, said her clumsy daughter had bumped into the table and hurt herself. Well, as I've told yer, I didn't want to cause any bother because I could hear the child sobbing. I was as polished as Her Ladyship, said I hoped her daughter hadn't hurt herself badly but no doubt I'd see her tomorrow and could ask her then meself how she was. That was by way of a threat, and I hope it sank in 'cos I'd be in there like a shot if I thought the kid was being ill treated.'

'D'yer think she's all right in the head?' Rita asked. 'I mean, what makes her think she's better than any of us? Oh, I know she talks and acts posh, but that could all be put on! If she's from monied people, she wouldn't be living in a two-up-two-down, would she? I've always thought there was a bit of a mystery about her, ever since she moved into the street. I wouldn't say that in front of Aggie, I always stick up for the woman when me mate's pulling her to pieces, but I can't

58

help thinking there's something weird about the airs and graces she puts on. And she wants reporting for the way she treats her daughter. The poor kid has no fun at all, she's missing her childhood years.' Rita let out a deep sigh. 'God knows, they're not children for long, they should be allowed to enjoy every minute of it while it lasts. And playing rounders or tag or going on the swings doesn't cost nothing, so why doesn't Mrs Sinclair let Amelia be her age and play out with the other kids?'

'I haven't got no answer for yer, Rita, 'cos I've spent hours trying to puzzle her out meself. The clothes she wears are years old, but yer can tell they were very expensive when she bought them, and she does look after them.' Bessie gazed up at the ceiling before coming to a decision. 'I'm going to tell yer what I know about her, but yer have to give me yer word that it isn't repeated to anyone, not even your Reg, although I know men don't tittle-tattle like women.'

Rita made a cross on her chest. 'On my honour, sunshine.' A smile crossed her face. 'Anyway, me and my Reg don't spend our time in bed telling tales, we've other things on our minds.' The smile became a chuckle. 'And it's not what ye're thinking either, Bessie Maudsley. Our conversation before turning our backs on each other usually consists of me asking him what he'd like for dinner the next day, and him telling me to blow the candle out.'

'Yer've got a good man there, Rita, he's one of the best in the street. But let's get back to Her Ladyship next door. You won't have noticed this because she always uses the back door but she's forever on the cadge. It's bread, tea or milk, things like that, and it's usually twice a week. It's been going on since the week she moved in, and she doesn't come herself, she sends Amelia. I got fed up with it after a while, thought she had a bloody cheek and felt sorry for the kid who looked terrified. So when I was asked to lend them sugar one day, I wouldn't give it to the girl, said I'd carry it for her and give it to her mother myself. I followed her up the yard and into the kitchen. That's how I came to go in the house and found she had little in the way of furniture but what she had was pure solid mahogany, the likes of which you and I would only ever see if we walked up Bold Street and looked in the windows of the posh shops there. She's only got a couple of pieces, mind, but enough for me to think that somewhere along the line she's known a better life.'

Rita leaned forward, her eyes wide and her voice angry. 'Are yer telling me that she's been borrowing off you all these years? You, who has to work hard to keep yer own head above water? She's got some nerve, she has. All la-di-dah, but she sends her kid out the back way to scrounge off yer?'

Bessie shook her head. 'Not now she doesn't, girl, 'cos the day I took the sugar to her, I told her straight that anything she borrowed must be paid back, in full, every Saturday when she'd her wages. So, while she still borrows, I make sure I get it back. If I didn't, I'd tell her to find herself another sucker. But I'm fond of Amelia, she's a

60

good kid with a lovely nature.'

'It's a shame,' Rita said. 'The kids all make fun of her because of the way she speaks, and there's nothing she can do about that now. I know it's not her fault, but yer can't blame the other kids because she's different from them.'

'Nobody is blaming them, girl, certainly not me. But before I go and put the kettle on to make us a cuppa, let's finish off the business with next door.' Bessie laced her fingers together. 'Now all the information yer've had off me tonight came with a price attached. I've never told anyone before, and you know, girl, I'm not a gossip. But I told you because I want a favour off yer, and that is, will yer keep yer eye out for Amelia? I know yer can't see right into their living room, and I know her mother won't let her play out, but with yer living opposite yer might just see something that makes yer think the girl is being badly treated. And if yer do, I want yer to tell me. Oh, I know it's none of my business, but the kid has nobody else with her welfare at heart so I intend being a busybody and keeping an eye on her. Obviously I can't do it while I'm at work so that's why I'm asking you to do it as a favour for me.'

'Of course I will, particularly now I know that woman's capable of hitting the child for nothing. She certainly wouldn't get away with it if I saw her. I'm on nodding terms with her, much to the disgust of Aggie, so I might try and take it a bit further, to where we pass the time of day. I'm not saying she'll co-operate, or that we'll become bosom pals, but it's worth a try. In any case, I'll keep an eye out, sunshine, yer have my word on

61

it. And now, if it's not asking too much, will yer go and put that ruddy kettle on? Me tongue is hanging out!'

Next door, Evelyn was still seething. Betrayed by her own daughter! Now everyone in the street would know their business and be laughing because they were living on stale bread. She had worked hard to teach Amelia how to act like a lady, to enunciate her words and be careful not to associate with the poorer class of people who lived in the street because one day they would be back where they belonged, with people of their own class. She never told her how or when this would happen, and would never admit to herself that it was only a dream. She was so wrapped up in herself, it hadn't occurred to Evelyn that while she could keep Amelia away from the children in the street, she had no control over her during school hours. Never once had it entered her head that, for all her teaching and dire warnings, she couldn't control every one of her daughter's waking moments. Nor had she sensed that her child was very confused and unhappy. She was forced to have one personality at home to please her mother, then to become someone different at school. The one she attended was for the children of working-class parents, some of them living in abject poverty, and Amelia quickly learned she must speak like them if she didn't want to be pushed around and laughed at. At school she spoke with a working-class Liverpool accent, while at home she spoke as her mother wished her to.

Now and again, in her head, Amelia questioned her mother's attitude towards her. She knew Evelyn wasn't the same as the other mothers in the street, who hugged their children as they set off for school, and laughed as they played games with them. She wouldn't say what she thought out loud because it would only bring forth a tirade from her mother, but inwardly she wondered why she was never kissed, or loved like all the other children. She did try to do everything she was told so her mother would love her, but no matter how hard she tried, she never received a word of praise or affection. Young as she was she knew this wasn't fair, and wished she was allowed to mix freely with other children instead of having to be careful of every word that came out of her mouth.

'Well, young lady, are you going to apologise?' Evelyn bent to poke the girl in the chest. 'I want you to say you are sorry over and over again until I say you may stop. Now do as I say.'

The injustice of it brought tears to the back of Amelia's eyes. 'But I haven't done anything wrong, Mother, so I don't understand. I only did as you asked, why should I be punished for it?' She rubbed the cheek that was still tender from the smack she'd received. 'You hurt me.'

'Don't you dare answer me back! If you continue to disobey me then I shall have no alternative but to smack you again. And I can assure you it will hurt you much more this time. Now, I want to hear you saying you are sorry.'

Amelia had never answered her mother back, nor questioned anything she was told to do. But a little demon in her head was telling her now

63

that if she didn't stick up for herself she'd never be like the other children in the street. 'Miss Bessie thought I was very clever, and I think I was too! I told her you would be pleased, and she said she would be if someone got her a loaf for a penny.'

The mention of their neighbour's name had a sobering effect on Evelyn. She relied on Miss Maudsley to help her out when she was desperate, without a penny in her purse. And she hadn't forgotten the little woman's remark about seeing Amelia herself tomorrow, and asking her daughter if she was all right. But she wasn't going to give the child the satisfaction of seeing her weakening or she would soon become out of control. 'I am tired – too tired to argue. So instead of the chastisement I had in mind, I will instead send you up to your room where you will stay until the morning.'

Amelia was glad to get out of the room and away from a mother she could no longer understand, and who, more and more, was beginning to frighten her. So she took the stairs two at a time. Instead of going into her own little room, which was at the back of the house, she entered her mother's and went straight to the window to look down on the street where boys and girls were playing, shouting to each other and having a fine time. Oh, how she wished she could join them. She pulled aside the net curtain for a better view, just as one of the boys on the opposite pavement looked up. He stared at her for a while, then smiled and waved. There was no return smile or wave because Amelia had quickly dropped the curtain. She would really be in trouble if her mother knew she was looking out of the window, never mind having one of the street children smiling and waving at her. But when her mother didn't come running up the stairs to give her another ticking off, the fear subsided and Amelia felt a warm glow. That was the first time since she'd lived in the street that one of the other children had smiled at her. Mostly, when she was going and coming home from school, a gang of girls would walk behind her and shout and make fun of her.

Stepping over the floorboards she knew would creak, Amelia made her way to her own bedroom and lay on the bed staring up at the ceiling, which was badly in need of attention. It had once been white, but now was a dirty colour, with cracks everywhere and plaster peeling off and falling like snowflakes on to her bed and the lino-covered floor. But although she was staring at the ceiling, she wasn't seeing it. She was thinking about the boy who had waved and smiled at her. He lived opposite, next to the house where the fat woman lived. The woman her mother said was the most common, ill-bred person it had ever been her misfortune to meet. But Amelia thought the woman looked a warm and happy person, who always had a smile on her face. She did talk loudly but there was no harm in that. It didn't matter how noisy you were, if you had a smile on your face. The boy's mother was nice, she always let on when she saw Amelia. There were two boys. The one who had waved was the smallest, so he must be the youngest. He was a big lad, though, and Amelia guessed he'd be about nine or ten. They were lucky to have such a nice mother who was always hugging them, even in the street.

Amelia sighed. She was seven now, but it was her birthday in a few weeks and then she'd be eight. Not that her mother would even mention her birthday, she never did. Not even a card to celebrate a new year of her life. She'd never had a birthday party, never even been to one because she wasn't allowed to have friends. Another deep sigh. If she ever got married and had children she'd love them to bits, would always be hugging them and kissing them better when they hurt themselves. But that was a long time off, and until she was old enough to look after herself she'd have to put up with the life she had.

It was Evelyn who opened the door to Bessie the following day. 'I've just called to see if Amelia is better? You know, after the accident she had?'

'Oh, she's fine, Miss Maudsley, a storm in a tea cup. She banged herself, but she was as right as rain half an hour later.'

Evelyn was standing four-square in the centre of the step, and Bessie thought, Oh, aye, she doesn't want me to see the girl. Which only made her more determined. 'Let's have a look at her then, I'm not going to eat her.'

Grinding her teeth, and wishing she was in a position to tell this nosy little woman to go away and stay away, Evelyn called, 'Amelia dear, come and say hello to Miss Maudsley.'

'Hello there, sweetheart,' Bessie said. 'I was

66

expecting to see yer in bandages, like a wounded soldier. But yer look fine to me, as pretty as a picture.' She raised her eyes to Evelyn. 'She seems to get taller every time I see her. How old is she now?'

Amelia saw her chance and took it. 'I'm seven now, Miss Bessie, but in three weeks I'll be eight.'

Bessie pretended to look surprised. 'Well, I never! It's my birthday in three weeks as well! What date is yours on?'

A smile lit up Amelia's face. She knew she had an ally in their neighbour. 'Mine's on the eighteenth, when's yours?'

'I don't believe it! Talk about coincidence isn't in it! Mine is on the eighteenth, too! Except, of course, I'm forty odd years older than yer. Well, well, how about that!' Bessie beamed at a very irate Evelyn. 'Ay, would yer let Amelia come to me for a birthday tea? Just her and me, like, for a little celebration. I've never got anyone to celebrate me birthday with, being on me own, so if yer've no objection, Mrs Sinclair, can I expect her to come to mine for tea on the eighteenth? It would give me something to look forward to, and I can make some fairy cakes and jelly creams.'

Evelyn was trying to think up an excuse for refusing, but Amelia could see how her mother's mind was working and begged, 'Please, Mother, say I can? I've never been out on my birthday before.'

Afraid of any more home truths coming from her daughter, Evelyn gave in. 'Just this once, Amelia, and only because it's Miss Maudsley.'

Bessie kept the smile on her face, but inside she

was thinking that this woman must think she was stupid if she expected her to fall for that. There was no way she would have agreed to the request if she'd had nothing to hide. She was a queer one, all right, but now she'd agreed to Amelia having a birthday tea with her neighbour, then that's how it would be. Mind you, she'd had to tell a white lie because her birthday was months away. But to see the pleasure on the girl's face was worth the prayers she would say in bed tonight.

Reg Wells watched his wife run her hand over the maroon chenille cloth she'd just put on the table. There was an affectionate grin on his face as he saw her stand back, her head tilted, to run a critical eye over the cloth and make sure it was perfectly straight before taking a glass bowl from the sideboard and setting it in the middle of the table. 'Yer should have been in the Army, love, yer'd have made a good sergeant.' He himself had served a year in the Army when the war was on, and was one of the lucky ones who'd come home. 'Mind you, ye're nicer-looking than any sergeant I've ever seen, and yer don't put the fear of God into me.'

'It'll take me a while to figure out if that was a compliment or an insult.' Rita tapped her chin with one finger and looked thoughtful. 'Is it a compliment to say I'm nicer-looking than a man, and that I'd have made a good sergeant? Oh, I need help from another woman on that, so I think I'll nip over to Bessie's and ask what she thinks.'

'Over to Bessie's again! Why don't yer take yer

bed over there?'

'It's yer own fault, sunshine, yer asked for it.' Rita turned her head to hide a smile. 'If yer'd said I was nicer-looking than any woman yer'd ever seen, well, I think I'd have been suggesting we had an early night in bed. But being likened to a man ... it's just put me off.'

'Excuses, excuses! Ye're a fine one for wriggling out of things, Rita Wells. But if this nipping over to Bessie's for a natter becomes a regular habit, I'll start thinking yer've got a fancy man and yer make that yer meeting place.'

Rita's head went back and her chuckle was loud. 'I should be so lucky, sunshine! And wait until I tell Bessie that yer think she's running a brothel, she'll die laughing.'

Reg's chair was creaking as he rocked back and forth. 'Tell her if she is, love, I'll be one of her customers, as long as I can choose me own wife to slink into one of her bedrooms with. At least I wouldn't have to beg, or wait until yer were in the mood.' The creaking of the chair grew louder. 'I don't think good-time girls ever have headaches.'

His wife pretended to be outraged. 'Well, it just shows the way your mind works, that does. Anyway, clever-clogs, good-time girls get paid, or haven't yer thought of that? And if yer were to pay me, well, I'd make yer the happiest man in the street. Yer'd be guaranteed to go out of this house every morning with a spring in yer step and a smile on yer face.'

Rita placed her arms straight and stiff by her sides, then spread her hands out to give a short exhibition of the dance she'd heard was all the

69

rage in the dance halls: the Black Bottom. She'd never seen it, and was only going by hearsay, but whether she'd got it right or wrong it was enough to please her husband.

'See how lucky yer are, sunshine, being married to a good-time dancing girl?' She reached into the glass bowl for the front-door key. 'Entertainment over now, I'm off to see me mate what lives across the street. I won't stay long.' She reached the door, then turned. 'I'll mention to her about her letting the house be used by women of the street – she might think it's a good idea. If it took off, she'd soon be rolling in money and could pack her job in.'

There was no surprise on Bessie's face when she opened the door because she'd seen her friend crossing over. 'Come in, girl, I've got a bit of news for yer. But yer probably saw me talking to next door, did yer?'

Rita plonked herself on the couch, then put a hand to her heart. 'I cannot tell a lie, sunshine, 'cos God might be listening. Yeah, I did see yer, and yeah, I'm glad yer've got a bit of news 'cos I could do with something to liven me day. And when I've heard your news, I'll tell yer the idea my feller has for yer making yerself a bit of money so yer can retire.'

Bessie's eyebrows shot up. 'If he's got an idea how to make money, why doesn't he make some for himself?'

'It doesn't work like that, sunshine, I'm afraid. But you start and I'll explain later what Reg has in mind. It won't half surprise yer.'

'Ooh, er, yer've got me wondering now. Why don't you go first?'

'I couldn't stand the excitement, that's why, sunshine, me heart would give out on me. So, off yer go.'

'I hope God isn't listening because while I was standing next door I committed two sins. I told a bare-faced lie, and I had bad thoughts. Still, they were in a good cause, and I'm sure God will take that into consideration. Anyway, I knocked next door on pretext of asking how Amelia was after she'd hurt herself. It was Her Ladyship who opened the door, and she tried to get rid of me quick by saying her daughter was fine. But I wasn't going to be fobbed off, so I asked if I could see Amelia.

'She called the girl to the door and yer'll never guess how devious I was! I said Amelia seemed to get taller every time I saw her, and asked how old she was. Then, although I could tell the queer one was wishing I'd go and drown meself in the Mersey, Amelia took advantage of what I'd said, and told me she was seven now, but would be eight in a few weeks' time. That's when I started to lie me head off. I asked her when her birthday was, and when she told me the eighteenth of next month, I made a great fuss by pretending that was my birthday as well. Honest, Rita, I deserved a prize for me acting. I invited Amelia to come and have tea with me on her birthday, saying I'd never had company to celebrate mine with before.'

Bessie pushed a hand through her greying hair. 'Honest, girl, I've had a ruddy good laugh about it. While I was frying meself an egg for me tea, the tears were blinding me I laughed so much. Anyone would think me and the girl had rehearsed what we were going to say. I could see her mother was blazing, but she didn't have a leg to stand on when her daughter said she'd never been out for tea on her birthday before. And when I said I would make some fairy cakes, and jelly creams, I bet Her Ladyship was wishing I choked meself on them.'

Rita was sitting on the edge of the couch by now. 'Yer don't mean to tell me that Miss High and Mighty agreed to let the girl come here for a birthday tea?'

'There was no way she could refuse without insulting me, was there? If she had refused, I'd have asked her if my house wasn't good enough for her.'

'Well, that certainly is a piece of news. They must have lived in the street for three or four years now, and that's the first time she's allowed the girl to mix with us riff-raff. Yer've worked wonders there, sunshine, and I'm glad for Amelia's sake she's got you to look out for her.'

'It's a start, isn't it, girl? Who knows what will happen in the future? Yer know they say big trees from little acorns grow, all yer need is patience. So, we'll just have to wait and see what happens.'

'I'll get a birthday card for her,' Rita said. 'I'd buy her a present, but yer know what the money situation is, we're living from hand to mouth like everyone else in the street. I'm just about keeping our heads above water.'

'There'd be no point in buying her a present

anyway, girl, 'cos she wouldn't be able to take it home. Her mother would make her throw it right in the bin, then wash her hands thoroughly before touching anything. A card would be nice, though, she could leave it here if she thought she'd get into trouble.' When Bessie sat back in a chair, she was so small her feet didn't touch the floor, and as she couldn't wait to hear what Rita's husband's idea was, she wriggled to the edge of the chair and leaned forward. 'Well, yer've heard my news, so what was it Reg told yer to tell me?'

'Will yer promise not to throw that cushion at me?'

'Why would I do that? Ye're not expecting me to get a cob on over what your Reg said, are yer? When have yer ever known me to really lose me temper with you? Other women in the street, yeah, but never you.' Her eyes narrowed. 'D'yer think I won't like it?'

'Like it? I hope yer laugh yer ruddy head off, Bessie, same as I did. Yer see, it all started when I told Reg I was coming over here, and he asked me why I didn't bring me bed 'cos I was spending a lot of time here and he was beginning to think I had a man on the sly, and your house was our meeting place. Anyway, that's how it started, and I'll tell yer the rest as long as yer promise we'll still be mates afterwards?'

Children playing in the street, and neighbours standing at their door having a jangle, all looked over to Miss Maudsley's house when the roars of laughter began. The children stopped playing, and the women stopped talking, as wave after wave of merriment reached their ears. And,

73

laughter being contagious, it wasn't long before everyone else had a smile on their face too. Bessie Maudsley's mood was contagious. It cheered them up, and brought a little sunshine into their lives.

Chapter Four

Evelyn stopped briefly outside the building in Castle Street where she worked, and glanced at the gold lettering on a first-floor window which read 'Astbury and Woodward, Solicitors'. Then she mounted the steps, pushed open the heavy door and hastily climbed the flight of stairs facing her. She was a little late this morning as she'd missed the tram she usually caught, and unless she could sneak in without meeting either of the partners she would receive a glare to reprimand her for her tardiness. But she was lucky. The only person she saw was Miss Saunders, secretary to the senior partner, Mr Astbury.

'I'm sorry I'm late,' Evelyn said, hanging her coat on the carved coatstand. 'I'm afraid I missed the tram and had to take a later one.'

Mildred Saunders, a woman in her late-fifties, had been with the firm since she was eighteen years of age. She was plain, a spinster who still lived with her aged mother, and although always neat, to Evelyn's mind she was dowdy. 'You're only minutes late, and I'm sure that on this rather special day, Mr Astbury would excuse you.'

'Why is this a special day? Is it Mr Astbury's birthday?'

'No, but he has made up his mind that at the grand old age of seventy it's time for him to retire. He will be staying on for two weeks for the new

75

partner to acquaint himself with the clients he will be taking over.' Mildred Saunders was usually prim and proper, always working with quiet efficiency and seldom indulging in conversation with Evelyn or the other female member of staff, Janet Coombes, secretary to the younger partner, Mr Woodward. But today she seemed different, and was wearing a smile as she spoke. 'As I've worked with Mr Astbury for so many years, and am used to his ways, I feel I'm too old to begin with a new partner and have decided to retire at the same time.'

'Is there someone ready to take over?' Evelyn asked. 'And if so, do you know him?'

Mildred nodded. 'Mr Astbury's nephew is taking over. He's coming in today so you will meet him. He is also an Astbury, Philip, and is leaving his present firm to take up the position here. I have met him, he seems very pleasant.'

Evelyn couldn't help herself from asking, 'Is he a young man, then?'

'I would say mid-thirties, but I'm not very good at guessing a person's age. He has several letters after his name, which takes years of exams, so he's certainly no younger.' Mildred fixed her gaze on Evelyn for a few seconds. She had never taken to the woman somehow, but couldn't put a finger on why. There was little known about her except that she was a widow, her husband having been killed in the war. One really should make allowances for her, and help her if it was possible. 'I believe you told me once that before you married you worked in an office and were skilled in shorthand and typing?'

'I did some secretarial work, like shorthand and typing, yes, but that was some years ago. I would be very rusty at it now.'

'It wouldn't take you long to get your speed up,' Mildred said. 'You'd be surprised how quickly it comes back to you. I only mentioned it because they will be taking on another secretary when I leave, and I thought you might be interested. It would mean a rise of five shillings a week which should be an incentive. I'm sure it can't be easy living on an Army pension.'

'No, it isn't.' While Evelyn spoke slowly, her brain was working overtime. An extra five shillings a week ... just think what she could do with it. The only drawback, was it meant she would have to work an eight-hour day for five days. The office didn't open on Saturdays. It would be awkward with Amelia, but she couldn't say this because she had never told anyone here that she had a daughter. 'Thank you for telling me, Miss Saunders, and for considering me suitable. I will certainly give it some thought, and if I think I can make up for all the lost years, and not be a hindrance, then I would love to apply for the position.'

'Why don't you slip into my office while I'm taking dictation from Mr Astbury? I'll be with him for half an hour, and in that time you could practise your typing. If anyone asks for you, I'll say I've asked you to do some filing for me.'

'You are very kind, Miss Saunders, and I'll definitely take you up on your offer.' Evelyn had already made up her mind she wanted the job if only for the rise in status it would bring. She'd manage somehow with Amelia, the girl was quite sensible and reliable. She could have a key and let herself in after school and make herself tea and sandwiches. 'May I use some of the office paper?'

'Yes, of course.' Mildred was wondering now whether she should have kept the news to herself for a while longer, as Mr Woodward's secretary Janet had already met Mr Astbury's nephew at a social event and taken quite a fancy to him. In fact, she'd talked about nothing else for a week afterwards. He was good-looking and a bachelor, which made him fair game for the unattached Janet. If she knew there was a possibility of gaining the position of secretary to a young man with film-star looks, she would move heaven and earth to secure that position. Janet had told Miss Saunders he'd gone out of his way to smile at her, but neglected to add that he'd smiled at every woman in the room. At least all the young and pretty ones. 'Please don't discuss our conversation with anyone, Mrs Sinclair. I only mentioned it to you because I thought you would be interested in the promotion,' said Mildred nervously.

'Which I appreciate. And I assure you it will not be mentioned elsewhere.'

Sitting at Miss Saunders' desk later, with the typewriter in front of her, Evelyn felt a little nervous. Not about the fact that she would be leaving her daughter on her own for a couple of hours every night, she would get around that somehow. The girl was quite capable of looking after herself and surely wouldn't come to any harm. Besides, she would benefit from her mother working full-time as they wouldn't go hungry any more. No, Evelyn was nervous about passing the interview if she applied for the post. She would surely be asked about her speeds at both shorthand and typing, and it wasn't something she could lie about. It would be almost impossible to get them up to the required speed within two weeks. The shorthand she might manage perhaps, for this she could do at home every night by asking Amelia to recite poems or repeat what she'd been up to at school that day. But how could she hope to impress at an interview if she could only have half-an-hour's practice on a typewriter two or three times a week?

Evelyn sat up straight and shook her head to clear it. She had a chance now to try her hand again at something in which she was once very proficient. Why not take full advantage instead of wasting precious time? After fifteen minutes her fingers were losing their stiffness and she was remembering how the letters were placed on the keyboard. When Miss Saunders came into the office later, she raised her eyebrows in surprise for the keys were clicking away quite quickly.

'Very good, Mrs Sinclair, I'm quite sure that within the two weeks available, you will be well up to speed.'

Evelyn smiled with pride at the compliment. It made her more determined than ever. After all, a new job could quite possibly change her whole life. Get her out of the rut she was in and back amongst people of her own class.

'I hope you won't think it very forward of me,

Miss Saunders, but I would be grateful if you'd allow me the use of your office, and typewriter whenever possible,' she said. 'I would need to practise very hard to make a suitable applicant for the position which you say will soon be available.'

'My office will be free after our lunch break, Mrs Sinclair. Mr Astbury is writing to all the clients who have retained him over the years. He wishes to let them know personally that he will be leaving and to thank them for their loyalty over the years so I imagine his dictation will take at least an hour. You are more than welcome to make full use of my office then.'

Mildred Saunders hadn't realised until now how happy she would be to retire. She would have more time to devote to her mother, and even enjoy a limited social life herself. She would never have retired while Mr Astbury still worked, but both of them now deserved a more leisurely kind of life, and she could see herself sitting in the garden on a sunny afternoon, with her dear mother, enjoying a pot of tea. How blissfully happy she would be.

Evelyn tutted when her finger landed on the wrong key and the word on the paper came up as 'would' instead of 'could'. 'I really am very stupid,' she muttered. 'I should know better by now.'

'We all make mistakes, even the best of us.'

She spun around, her face crimson. 'I'm sorry, I didn't hear the door open and you've taken me by surprise.' The man standing inside the door was tall and slim with pale brown hair and bright blue eyes. He was dressed in a suit of the finest tweed, an expensive shirt and silk tie, and wore an air of confidence that was so obvious you felt you could stretch out your hand and touch it. It was a long time since Evelyn had seen a man dressed in such fine attire, or one who was so very attractive. She pushed her chair back. 'If it's Miss Saunders you wish to see, I'm afraid she's taking dictation from Mr Astbury. If you will tell me your name, I will let her know you are here.'

'There's no need, I've just come from my uncle's office where he is keeping Miss Saunders very busy dictating dozens and dozens of letters.' Philip Astbury leaned against the frame of the door, a man at ease with himself. 'I was on my way to see Mr Woodward when I heard someone in here calling themselves stupid. I wasn't listening at the door, it was ajar and I couldn't fail to hear. I was rather curious to see this stupid person.' He moved away from the door and approached her with hand outstretched. 'Philip Astbury, delighted to meet you.'

Evelyn took his hand. 'Evelyn Sinclair.'

'I will be joining the firm as of today, but will not be taking over completely from my uncle until he retires in two weeks. In the meantime I shall be looking and learning, and making myself familiar with the files of our clients. And you, Evelyn Sinclair, what is your position here? Oh, and is that Miss Sinclair?'

She shook her head. 'I'm a widow, my husband was killed in the war. And I'm more or less the junior here because I do the menial chores. I

81

came back to work to give my life some meaning. I was wallowing in self-pity for too long and allowed myself to lose contact with all my friends. Consequently my social life was non-existent. At least coming here every day gives me a reason for getting out of bed. I don't work full-time at present, but that may change in the near future.'

'And would it be presumptuous of me to ask why you think you are stupid?'

Evelyn lowered her eyes coyly, remembering how Charles had found this habit very endearing. 'It's a while since I sat behind a typewriter and I was calling myself stupid for having forgotten the position of all the keys. I had no idea the door wasn't closed properly or that I would be overheard. I'm not actually stupid, just finding it rather strange. But that's something I can easily overcome, and I am determined to do so.'

Philip had an eye for a pretty face, and found Evelyn very pleasing to look at. A bachelor of thirty-three, he had many women friends, but with him it was a case of love them and leave them. He led a very enjoyable life as a single man and no woman had yet been able to lure him away from it. 'I hear Miss Saunders is leaving the same time as my uncle, and haven't had time as yet to ask if they have found a replacement for her?'

'I really don't know.' Evelyn didn't want to pass on any information in case he repeated it to Miss Saunders. If she lost the trust of the older woman, she may also lose the chance of filling the vacancy. 'I only found out an hour ago that Mr Astbury was retiring, and it came as a great surprise. It was an even greater surprise to hear Miss Saunders was retiring too, but having been secretary to your uncle for so long, and being so used to his ways, I imagine it would be difficult at her age to adjust to starting afresh with a new partner.'

'So with whom am I going to have the pleasure of working? I hope it is someone pretty, and not an ogre with two heads.'

Evelyn thought it would be to her advantage to leave the room before this conversation became too personal, and questions were asked that she would have difficulty in answering. 'It's time for our morning break so if you're going to see Mr Woodward, I will bring in an extra cup of tea for you. And would you prefer a digestive biscuit or a cream?'

'That rather sounds as if I'm getting my marching orders.'

'Not at all!' Evelyn was beginning to think that here was a man who was so sure of himself he expected every woman to fall at his feet. But she felt sure this wasn't the way to attract his attention. 'I am not in a position to give anyone their marching orders. This is Miss Saunders' office, lent to me only until she has finished taking dictation.' She took the paper out of the typewriter, folded it in two then pushed her chair nearer to the desk. 'I really must make the morning tea, I'm sure the partners and their secretaries are feeling thirsty.' She squared her shoulders and held her head high as she passed an astonished Philip, who wasn't used to being dismissed in such a manner. 'I will see you in Mr Woodward's office. It has been most pleasant talking to you.'

'Yes,' he agreed, 'a pleasure indeed.'

Philip and his uncle were having their lunch in the State Hotel when the younger man asked, 'Uncle Simon, have you anyone in mind for my secretary?'

Simon Astbury raised his thick white eyebrows. 'I presumed you would be bringing your present secretary with you. I'm used to hearing you singing her praises.'

'She is very efficient, I must admit.' Philip decided a little white lie was called for. 'However, the other two partners feel she will be needed for the new man they are bringing in to fill my position as she is familiar with our clients. And as I have given so little notice of my departure, I felt it would be unfair of me to deprive them of such an efficient worker. You must admit, Uncle, a good secretary is jolly hard to find.'

'Then we must be quick about finding a replacement for Miss Saunders as we are both leaving in just two weeks. I'll have a word with her when we get back, perhaps she knows someone who would fit the bill.' Simon picked up the heavy linen napkin and patted his lips. 'Miss Coombes is very punctual and efficient, but she is settled in with James and I'm sure he wouldn't want to share her.'

'What about Mrs Sinclair? I was talking to her while you were busy and she seems to have had a decent education. She is certainly articulate.'

His uncle showed surprise. 'Mrs Sinclair is an office clerk, she does not have the qualifications

84

to be a secretary.'

'You do surprise me,' Philip said. 'I walked into Miss Saunders' office after leaving yours because I heard the click of a typewriter and wondered who could be in there. I found Mrs Sinclair sitting at the desk, typing. She stopped immediately so I couldn't say for sure how fast she was. But I'm surprised you didn't know this, Uncle Simon? She's obviously far too intelligent to be a mere clerk.'

Simon looked at his nephew under his thick eyebrows. 'And of course she is very attractive too, is she not?' He shook his head. 'Don't you tire of constantly moving from woman to woman? Would you not like to settle down with a good wife and raise a family?'

'Good heavens, Uncle Simon, are you trying to spoil my lunch for me?' Philip laughed, for he and his uncle were very close and dear to each other. 'I ask a question about a member of your staff who is, I admit, very attractive, and it leads directly to my settling down and getting married. Oh, *and* raising a family.'

'You are incorrigible, Philip,' Simon Astbury said, a smile on his thin, lined face. 'Anyway, I know very little about Mrs Sinclair apart from the fact that she's a war widow. Perhaps Miss Saunders would be the best person to whom to direct your questions. She probably knows more about the woman's qualifications than I do. And in the meantime, could we forget the office and enjoy our meal in peace? It isn't often I have a companion to talk to over a decent meal and a glass of excellent claret. So indulge an old man

85

and forget your pursuit of the opposite sex for the next half-hour.'

Philip feigned shock. 'Half an hour, Uncle Simon, surely not! That's an eternity.'

'You mark my words, young man, the day will come when one of the pretty girls you pursue will trap you in her net. And I hope I live long enough to see it, it would give me great pleasure.'

'I'll see if I can arrange it, Uncle, but didn't you suggest a while ago that we should eat our meal in peace? It will soon be time to return to the office.'

'Miss Saunders, may I have a word with you in your office?' Philip knew that Mrs Sinclair was in his uncle's room filing away some correspondence and wanted to take advantage of her absence. 'I won't keep you long from your work.'

'That's all right, Mr Philip, the letters I have to type practically all read the same so I don't have to keep checking my notes.' Mildred led the way into her office, and when Philip was inside, closed the door. 'How can I help you?'

'It concerns my secretary.' He sat down and crossed his legs. 'Uncle Simon was under the impression I was bringing my own, but two of us leaving the firm at once is a little too much. It would be inconsiderate of me to leave my previous partners short-staffed. After all, I've been there for ten years, and we have always worked in harmony. I would not like to walk out leaving any bad feeling. Which means I have to find a new secretary before my uncle retires.' Forever the ladies' man, he added, 'Of course, you would have been ideal, but alas you too are leaving. Which leads me to ask for your help. I do hope you don't mind my taking advantage of your experience?'

Mildred was old enough to want to retire, but not too old to succumb to the charm of such a handsome young man. 'Not at all, Mr Philip! If I can help then I will be more than happy to do so. What had you in mind?'

'I met a young woman in your office this morning. Her name, she told me, is Mrs Sinclair. She was busy at the typewriter at the time, and I took her to be a senior secretary. But Uncle Simon tells me she is merely a clerk and not experienced enough to take over from you. In fact, he was of the opinion that she was unable to type. So I thought I would seek out someone who has the welfare of this firm at heart and ask for her opinion.' His lopsided grin, as he'd expected, had her going weak at the knees. 'Do you think Mrs Sinclair, given a little time, is capable of following in your footsteps?'

'Oh, I couldn't say with any certainty, Mr Philip, that wouldn't be fair to you. But she worked in an office before she was married, and was qualified then in both shorthand and typing. She admits she is rusty now, after so long, but I allowed her to use my office this morning, and was quite pleased with her speed on the typewriter. Not up to the standard required, mind you, but she could well pass a test in a few weeks.' Mildred thought she'd better include the other female member of staff in this conversation too. 'Miss Coombes mentioned that she would be happy to serve both you and Mr Woodward for the time being. And she suggested that as your uncle has the heavier workload, with her experience, it would be best if she stayed with your uncle and his replacement, and the new secretary could work for Mr Woodward.'

There, Mildred told herself, no one could accuse her of not passing on the message as she'd promised. But she hadn't promised anything else. 'I don't think that would work, frankly. I believe a new member of staff would be better placed with a new partner, so they could learn together how the office has been run under Mr Simon. We had a system, understood each other, and have worked in harmony for more years than I care to remember.'

Philip remembered flattery always worked for him. As he was intrigued by the very attractive war widow, he now flashed his best smile. 'It would solve all our problems if you could stay on, Miss Saunders. My troubles would be over then, I think we would work well together. But I understand your desire to retire, and am in agreement that you have earned the right to enjoy some freedom now. You have served my uncle well, our whole family agrees, and we are grateful to you.'

Blushing like a schoolgirl, Mildred was indeed delighted by such praise. 'It has been a pleasure to serve Mr Simon. In all the years we have worked together there has never been a cross word. I shall miss him, and miss coming to this office every day too. But no one can go on for ever, Mr Philip, age catches up with us all eventually.'

'Nonsense, Mildred! You don't look a day older

than you did ten years ago. I have watched Uncle Simon grow older, but you never seem to change.'

It was the first time the blushing woman had been addressed by her first name since she came to work for the firm, and she lowered her head to hide her embarrassment. 'Now you know that's not true, Mr Philip, the mirror in my bedroom tells me otherwise. But it's nice to be flattered by a handsome young man.'

Philip left his chair and sat on the edge of the desk. 'Sit down, Mildred, and let's discuss this further. I want the take-over from Uncle Simon to go smoothly so that our clients are not inconvenienced. In other words, in the next two weeks I have to learn everything I need to know. Now, can we go back to Mrs Sinclair? I know she is at present filing away copies of letters to and from clients which I hope means she is familiar with the filing system and able to put her hand on any correspondence I may need? Am I correct in thinking this?'

Mildred nodded. 'Oh, yes, she is very competent. You will never find a file or a letter out of place. She is always able to put her hand on anything she is asked for. And she is familiar with the working of the office, which it would take a newcomer several months to get used to. There are many points in her favour, I have to say. She is always neat, never a hair out of place, and quite capable of answering the telephone politely and welcoming clients to the office. In fact, several clients have commented on her style and deportment.'

'Both qualities which are an asset to the firm,

would you not say?' His uncle's secretary was eating out of Philip's hand by now, and nodded enthusiastically. So he pressed the case he was quite sure he would win. Mrs Sinclair's looks and manner had appealed to him, and he intended to become better acquainted with her. Miss Saunders was being very cooperative, and he was sure she would add her weight to his intention of making Mrs Sinclair his secretary. If she didn't, then he would seek permission from the uncle who would deny him nothing. One thing he was certain of: Janet Coombes would never get close to him. She may be an excellent worker, but he didn't find her in the least attractive. He'd only met her once socially and then she'd been all over him, practically drooling. Philip liked a challenge, he didn't want an easy conquest, there was no thrill or fun attached to it.

'Well, what do you think, Mildred?' he asked, knowing it made little difference what the older woman said for his mind had been made up since Evelyn had walked out of the office, saying indifferently, 'It has been most pleasant talking to you.' He had immediately told himself that this was a challenge he couldn't resist. 'I think we should give her a chance, rather than taking on a new member of staff. After all, she has been here for a couple of years and deserves to be considered. And I'm sure that while you are here, you will continue to offer her all the help you can.'

'You have my promise that my office will be at her disposal for at least an hour in the mornings and an hour in the afternoon.'

Philip stepped away from the desk and ran his

fingers down the immaculate crease in his trousers. 'I don't think Mrs Sinclair should be approached by me or your good self. Uncle Simon is the obvious one to interview her. That's if she's interested in taking up the position, of course. Perhaps she has a private income and doesn't need any extra money?'

'Oh, I'm sure she will be interested, Mr Philip, I don't think she has any private income. She is as careful with money as she is with her clothes. She never mentions a family, so I have always presumed she lives alone. Never talks about her dead husband either, but of course the reason for that may be that she finds it too painful.'

'Then I'll ask Uncle Simon to go gently with her. On such a delicate subject as her late husband, I'm sure he will be very understanding.' Philip put a hand on each of Miss Saunders' shoulders, sending shock waves down her spine. 'You are a brick, Mildred, and I am indebted to you for your help. I hope our plan works, for I would hate to take over from my uncle while working with a secretary who knows nothing of the firm or its clients. At least Mrs Sinclair can hold my hand and show me where everything is.'

Mildred was wishing she was twenty-five years younger. She hadn't been bad-looking then, and might have stood a chance with Philip. Then she mentally shook her head. He was a playboy, not likely to be content with a nice, down-to-earth girl who would keep a good house for him. He would find that far too dull. Playing the field was more in his line. 'I won't say anything to Mrs Sinclair, I'll wait until she tells me, and then I'll act as though the news is a complete surprise.'

Philip squeezed her shoulder again. 'How lucky my uncle has been to have you to care for him all these years. Never a worry about correspondence going astray or words mis-spelt. He has been truly blessed.'

And Philip's words were sincere, for he was very fond of his uncle and had been told over the years how this dear lady made sure his working life was made easy. Always a hot drink when he arrived at the office on a winter's morning, and never a draught allowed to reach his desk. Philip bent to kiss her forehead. 'Thank you.'

After leaving a tearful Miss Saunders, he made for his uncle's office. He rapped on the door with his knuckles and called, 'It's only your beloved nephew, Uncle Simon, so you don't have to hide your snuff box.'

Simon Astbury tried in vain to hide a smile. 'You cheeky young whippersnapper. Wait until you reach my age, then you too will have to make do with whatever pleasures remain to you.'

Philip pulled out a chair facing his uncle across the shiny dark mahogany desk. 'Thank you for the warning, Uncle. I shall have to make hay while the sun shines, don't you agree? I intend to experience as much of life as is humanly possible, and I reckon I have at least thirty years left to do it in.'

'And with the grace of God you may, my boy. But try to pack everything into the time allotted to you and you may find yourself worn out before you reach the age of fifty. You can never have your cake and eat it.'

'I intend to do my damnedest, Uncle, but I will remember your words when I reach the grand old age of fifty. For now, I want to talk to you about engaging a secretary. Do you have the time to spare?'

Simon took off his spectacles and laid them on the desk. 'I will always make time for you. What have you in mind?'

Chapter Five

'Well, Mrs Sinclair, in two weeks' time you will be working as my secretary. Meanwhile I hope to find out a little more about how my uncle's office has been run so efficiently for the last twenty or more years.' Philip had caught up with Evelyn as she was leaving Miss Saunders' office after telling her why Mr Simon had asked to see her. 'I am quite looking forward to the experience, as I hope you are?'

'Like yourself, Mr Astbury, I have quite a lot to learn in the next two weeks, and think perhaps I would rather answer your question after that. If I wasn't so out of practice in taking dictation, I would feel much happier about my abilities. As it is, I have to admit to being a little apprehensive.'

Evelyn was feeling quite flustered by the way he was staring her out, but she was determined not to show it. He was very sure of himself, almost cocky, and she didn't intend to add to his inflated ego. 'I am not used to this feeling, I am usually so sure of myself. But I'm going to put that down to the surprise your uncle sprang on me. The last thing I expected was to be offered the position of secretary. It's a position I last held before I was married and, without wanting to sound boastful, I really was very good at my job then.'

She didn't want him digging too deeply into her past, and tried to step around him. But he was quick to put himself in her path. 'Oh, and where was this job you were so good at? In the city centre, was it?'

'I'm a private person, Mr Astbury, not one to gossip about myself or other people. My private life is my own, and I wish to keep it that way. I hope you will understand and respect my wishes?'

'Ah, well now, Mrs Sinclair, that has made me very curious. Two or three children hidden away, and a man friend perhaps? Or is it one child and two men friends? I am really very intrigued now.'

'I live alone, Mr Astbury, and that is through choice. After my husband was killed in the war I became a recluse. Over a period of time my friends dropped off one by one, and for the last couple of years my social life has been non-existent.' Evelyn liked the sound of the life she'd just created, and almost came to believe it herself. But she mustn't let herself be carried away. 'May I pass now, please? If I want to be proficient by the end of two weeks, I am really going to have to work hard on both my typing and shorthand speeds. Miss Saunders has kindly offered the use of her machine, but shorthand I'll have to practise at home. Something we shall both benefit from.'

He watched her take her coat from the stand and said, 'I forgot, you only work until four o'clock.'

Evelyn slipped her arms into the sleeves of the coat. 'Just for today and tomorrow. On Monday I start working full-time.' She was fastening the buttons as she walked towards the door. 'I'll see

95

you tomorrow, goodbye.'

Philip stood still for a few minutes after she'd disappeared through the door. And under his breath, he muttered, 'It's going to be fun breaking *her* in.'

He might have thought differently if he could have read Evelyn's mind as she skipped lightly down the stairs. For while he saw her as an attractive woman whom he would eventually add to his long list of conquests before moving on to the next, she saw him in an entirely different light. She saw him as a way out of the rut she was in, and a way back to the life she believed she deserved. A wealthy husband and a life of luxury. She'd known it would happen some time.

Evelyn's spirits were high, her mind filled with excitement and pleasure as she sat on the tram on her way home. She had no doubt it was Philip Astbury who had talked his uncle into offering her the position of secretary, which meant he was more than a little interested in her. In fact, he hadn't hidden the fact he found her attractive. But he was so sure of his ability to charm any woman, she knew he was the love them and leave them type. Because of this, and because she really needed him in order to change her life, she'd decided the way to keep him interested was to play it very cool. And she would do, until she had him just where she wanted him. She didn't want a short fling, she wanted a lasting relationship which would lead to marriage and her step back up the social ladder to all the trappings that went with wealth.

It was only when she turned into her own street that her spirits fell and she stared reality in the face. How could she ensnare a rich man when she lived in such a poor neighbourhood, amongst people of the lower class? Philip Astbury would take one look at the street and turn tail and run. And what about Amelia, how could she hide the fact that she had a daughter? And how was she to manage working full-time when it would mean the girl being on her own for two hours every night when she came home from school?

As Evelyn walked down the street, looking neither to left nor right, she began to have dark thoughts about her daughter. If it wasn't for Amelia, she wouldn't be living like a pauper. She would still be a member of the Lister-Sinclair family, enjoying the sort of lifestyle that only their sort of money could buy. She would have had to pretend she was heartbroken over Charles being killed, of course, and gone into mourning for a few months. It would have been a small enough price to pay for a lifetime of being waited on hand and foot. The truth was, she hadn't mourned him at all. She was sorry he was dead simply because it had cost her so dearly. But she could be a good actress when necessary, and it would have been worth it for the reward. It could well be that with Mr Philip she'd have a second chance of the good life ... if only she didn't have the drawback of a daughter nobody knew about.

When Evelyn reached her house she could see the two women who lived opposite out of the corner of her eye, but was in no mood to acknowledge their presence. If they had nothing better to

97

do than stand jangling all day, what a sad life they led. They'd never know what it was to walk into the Adelphi on the arm of one of the wealthiest men in Liverpool, wearing clothes that were the height of fashion and had cost a fortune. Well, she was going to do her very best to get away from this tiny house in this narrow street full of common people. How she'd do it, she didn't know right now, but she vowed that as soon as Mr Philip began to woo her – as she had no doubt whatsoever that he would – then she would manipulate him until he was so crazy about her he'd do anything to keep her happy.

After hanging her coat up Evelyn sat at the table, wanting to clarify things in her mind. That her daughter would be in from school any minute meant little to her. She never cooked a proper meal anyway, it was only ever egg on toast, a sandwich or a pennyworth of chips from the chip shop. And for that they'd consider themselves lucky, for many a time all they had to eat was bread and dripping. Even if she'd had enough money to make dinner, though, she would have turned her nose up at the thought of soiling her hands peeling potatoes.

A knock on the door brought a frown to Evelyn's face. The girl was home. She would have to go to the chip shop again, there was nothing to eat in the house. When Amelia looked up at her mother she was met with a hostile glare. There was no greeting, but then she didn't expect something she'd never had. She was left to close the door after herself, and when she entered the living room her mother didn't even meet her eyes as she said, 'Sit down, I have something to tell you before you go to the chip shop for our tea.'

Always afraid of doing something to upset her mother, Amelia pulled a chair out from under the table, taking care to keep the legs clear so they didn't get scratched. 'Yes, Mother?'

'I had some very good news at the office today, Amelia, which I am sure will make you feel proud of me. I was offered the position of private secretary to one of the partners. It is a promotion, which is an honour, and also brings with it an increase in wages.'

'Oh, Mother, that's wonderful news. When will you start this new job?'

'I am to begin learning on Monday, and start the job proper in two weeks. But I am in a dilemma, Amelia, and need to ask your advice.'

Her daughter was not used to being spoken to so softly, and young as she was, sensed her mother was putting on a show because she wanted something. 'I don't see how I can advise you, Mother, when you are far more clever than I am.'

'Perhaps advice was the wrong word, I should have said I need your help. You see, I would be working full-time, which means you would be back home from school two hours before I was home from the office. That is the only thing that stands in the way of my taking up a position of importance which would bring in enough extra money to make a difference to our lives. We wouldn't have to borrow any more, and there would be a vast improvement in the meals we eat and the clothes we wear. We wouldn't be rich, not by any stretch of the imagination, but we would be better off.'

'Mother, I can look after myself for two hours, you know I can! You need have no fear, I'll not come to any harm. Is that all that is worrying you, my being left alone for two hours?'

These weren't the words of a young girl, nor did she sound like one. But that was how Amelia had been brought up. She acted and spoke differently at school, knowing the girls in her class led a very different life from her. But she was too young to be in any position to change her lot. 'You can trust me, Mother, you know you can,' she said eagerly.

'Yes, I know I can trust you, but what are the neighbours going to think if they know you are left on your own for two hours, especially in the dark nights of winter? They will think I am a very wicked mother.'

This gave Amelia food for thought. She had forgotten the winter nights, and the prospect of sitting in the dark for two hours every day filled her with dread. She wasn't allowed to light the gas and there would be no fire in the grate to give out light so it would be pitch black. 'Could I not go into Miss Bessie's to wait for you? I think I would be afraid in the dark nights, Mother, with no fire to see by and not being allowed to light the gas.'

'What a silly child you are. Once you are in your own house, with the curtains drawn, what harm can come to you?'

'I am afraid of the pitch dark, Mother, which is what it would be.'

'How silly! The street lamp isn't far away,

100

there'd be light through the curtains. I do *not* want the neighbours knowing my business, so if I am to take advantage of this opportunity you will have to learn that one can't have everything one's own way. If we are to have a more comfortable life, it will have to be earned – by you as well as by me. Now, do you understand me?'

Something in Amelia made her rebel. 'I do understand, Mother, but I don't want to be in a dark house on my own 'cos I'd be frightened. I'd rather stand outside and wait for you, then I wouldn't be scared because there're always children out playing.'

Evelyn was about to scold her daughter when a thought entered her head. If Mr Philip were to ask her out, something she confidently expected in the very near future, she couldn't refuse by making her daughter the excuse because she had no intention of telling him about Amelia. On the tram journey home, she'd made her plans very carefully. She would take things slowly, charm him into wanting more than she would give him at first. She needed him to become besotted by her, to desire her so much he would do anything for her. But all her dreams and desires would come to nought if he knew where she lived, and that she had a seven-year-old daughter. So she had to lead a double life, and for that she would need help.

'I'm surprised at your being scared, Amelia, but we'll have to find a way around it. What time does Miss Bessie get in from work?'

A smile crossed the girl's pretty face when she saw a glimmer of hope, but she quickly hid it for fear it would displease her mother. 'I'm not sure because she sometimes goes in at seven in the morning and finishes at four o'clock. I think she told me it depended on whether they have an urgent order to finish or not. I'm not sure what she meant by that, and I didn't like asking.'

'I wonder if she would be kind enough to mind you for two hours every night, if I were to pay her a shilling?'

The girl's eyes nearly popped out of her head. 'A whole shilling! That's a lot of money, Mother. I'm sure Miss Bessie wouldn't ask you for that much just to let me sit in her house for two hours each night. I could pay her back by running messages for her, or helping her with the dishes.'

'I think we should ask her first before we discuss it any further. She could possibly refuse point blank. If so, I would have to reconsider the situation.' Evelyn shook her head as though to dismiss the possibility of being turned down. She knew Miss Maudsley had a soft spot for Amelia, and it was to this she would appeal. 'I heard the front door closing a few minutes ago so I know she's home. If you will go to the chip shop for a pennyworth of chips and a pennyworth of scallops, I'll slip out the back way and put my request to her.'

Amelia jumped from her chair and stood by the table waiting to be given the two pennies. Chips and scallops, that was a rare treat. Being offered a promotion must have made her mother very happy. As soon as she had the two coins in her hand, she skipped out of the door and down the street. She could hear the other children out playing, but tonight she didn't envy them. And all the way to the chip shop she kept on praying that Miss Bessie would agree to mind her each day until her mother got home from work. If she had to choose between having a nice meal from the chip shop tonight, or Miss Bessie agreeing to what she was now being asked, then Amelia would starve tonight and live on the thought of the pleasure she'd have every night thereafter. For in their neighbour, she knew she had found someone who really liked her and would enjoy her company. And she wouldn't have to watch every word that came out of her mouth in that house, or be afraid to laugh out loud. Oh, it would be lovely.

As Evelyn walked up next door's yard, the smell of bacon frying wafted towards her. But although it made her empty stomach rumble, she wasn't jealous. In the not-too-distant future she would enjoy food only the rich could afford, things which Miss Maudsley and her cronies had probably never heard of. But of course she mustn't say anything to annoy her neighbour, she needed her now.

When Bessie opened the door she showed no surprise, she'd seen her neighbour pass the window. She wasn't particularly pleased to see Evelyn. She'd not long got in from work and was longing to sit down and eat the bacon, the smell of which was making her mouth water. She was wearing a floral wrap-around pinny that almost reached the floor, and which she'd been promising herself for months that she'd put a hem on to save her tripping herself up. But she wasn't a snob and didn't care whether her neighbour wrinkled her nose at the sight or not. 'Yer've just caught me making me dinner, Mrs Sinclair, so can yer make it quick before me bacon burns?'

'I'm sorry to call at an inconvenient time, Miss Maudsley. If you like I will call later when you are more prepared?'

Bessie pushed a strand of hair out of her eyes. 'Was it something important?'

'Yes, it is really.' Then Evelyn played her trump card. 'Important for me, and for Amelia. But I can see you're busy so I'll call back later.'

Had it not been for the mention of Amelia's name, Bessie would have told her to come back. Instead she opened the door wider. 'Come on in. I don't want me bacon to be ruined, but I'll make a butty of it and yer'll have to put up with seeing me eat it. I can't afford to waste good food.' She waved Evelyn through to the living room. 'Make yerself comfortable, I won't be a minute.'

While she was waiting, Evelyn looked around the room. She had to admit it was clean and polished, like a new pin. But the furniture wasn't up to her own standards, far too cheap-looking.

Bessie bustled through with a plate in one hand and a cup and saucer in the other. 'I won't offer yer a drink 'cos I know yer'll be having yer dinner soon.' She sat at the table and lifted the butty, which was very substantial and which her neighbour was mentally comparing to a doorstep. In fact, she was having trouble trying to stop her nose from wrinkling, which Bessie noted and found hilarious. What a snob Evelyn Sinclair was!

Before taking a bite from the butty, she said, 'I don't mind yer talking while I'm eating, Mrs Sinclair, so don't let me stop yer. I'm too hungry to be polite and wait until yer've gone.'

These people were not brought up to be genteel, they had no manners whatsoever. This was the thought running through Evelyn's head, followed by one that said she must make sure her neighbour's lack of manners didn't rub off on Amelia. But right now it wouldn't do to offend the woman she was going to ask for help.

'Please don't think me forward, Miss Maudsley, and please don't hesitate to refuse what I am about to ask you if it is something you wouldn't want even to consider. But I'm going to ask a big favour of you.' She thought a little craftiness would help her cause. 'At least, it was Amelia who put the idea in my head for, as you know, my daughter is very fond of you.'

Bessie's eyes narrowed as she took another bite. This one was after something, the two-faced, stuck-up article. And she didn't have the nerve to come straight out with it, had to pretend she was asking for her daughter. She must think I was born yesterday, Bessie told herself. That I'm green around the gills.

'Yer can only ask, Mrs Sinclair, and I can only say yes or no. Which I will do, if yer'll tell me what it is?'

Evelyn laced her fingers and put her hands on her knees. 'I was pleasantly surprised today when one of the senior partners in the office where I work asked if I would like the position of private secretary to a new partner who is starting with the firm next week. It is obviously a great honour and brings a not insignificant increase in salary. It was only after the interview that I realised it would mean my working full-time, which would leave Amelia to come home from school and be alone in the house for two hours each night. That is something I couldn't even contemplate. The girl is only seven, after all, and couldn't be expected to stay in the house on her own on dark nights. So I was intending to tell my boss tomorrow that, sadly, I am not able to take up the position...'

Bessie could see what was coming, but she certainly wasn't going to make it easy for a woman who looked down her nose at everyone in this street. It was a wonder she'd sat down on the couch without flicking her handkerchief over it in case it was dusty. So let her sweat it out for a while. 'Ye're not taking the job then?'

'That is what I was telling Amelia when she surprised me by saying perhaps you would mind her for those two hours every night? I pooh-poohed the idea at first, but Amelia was so taken with the idea, she wanted to come and ask you herself. Of course I wouldn't let her do that, so I'm here instead. There would be recompense for your trouble, I wouldn't expect you to do it without payment. I thought a shilling a week would be appropriate.'

Bessie didn't reply for a while as she stared down at a tea leaf floating on top of her cup. Of course she would have the child, she would love to. And she knew jolly well the girl would be overjoyed. But although her first instinct had been to tell her neighbour to stick her shilling where Paddy stuck his nuts, a voice in her head told her she would be stupid not to take the money. She could use it to buy treats for Amelia because she had never seen the child with a bag of sweets in her hand in the three years she'd lived next door.

'I'm not always home before Amelia, it depends whether I start at seven or half-past. We sometimes have to pack orders, yer see, and they need to be on the cart by eight. Mind you, some of the women go in at seven all the time, so they can be home for their kids coming in from school. I could do the same thing.' She pretended to give the idea some thought, but it was only to keep the queer one in suspense for a while. Then she said, slowly, as though she wasn't really keen, 'I suppose we could try it for a week to two, see if it works out. I mean, I'm not used to having children in the house, and on the other hand, Amelia might not like sitting with an old woman every night.' Then she felt like a little bit of devilment, and came out with something she knew would fill her neighbour with horror. 'She would be better playing out in the street with the other children. I could keep me eye on her through the window, make sure she came to no harm.'

The colour drained from Evelyn's face, and Bessie, who held conversations with herself as people who live alone often do, told the frying pan later that night as she was washing the dishes that her neighbour looked so shocked anyone would think a doctor had just told her she dying, and only had minutes to live.

'Oh, I can't allow Amelia to play in the street,

107

Miss Maudsley, not under any circumstances. Heaven alone knows what sort of diseases those children could be carrying, not to mention head lice. It is entirely out of the question. I will not subject my daughter to their lack of hygiene or their ignorance. And I must insist that you do not allow her to play in the street.'

How Bessie kept her temper she would never know. There wasn't a woman in this street wouldn't lay down her life for her children, and many of them were going hungry to give food to their families but never moaned about going without themselves. Family always came first. But if Bessie told Miss High and Mighty what she really thought of her, she'd be cutting off her nose to spite her face. The stuck-up snob might take the huff and say she had decided it wasn't appropriate to leave Amelia in her care, which would mean Bessie and the girl losing out on something they would both enjoy.

'If that is the way you want it, Mrs Sinclair, then of course that's the way it shall be. She is your daughter after all. So shall we start our trial period on Monday and see how it goes?'

Evelyn kept her sigh of relief silent. Although she'd meant what she had said about her daughter playing in the street, she knew she needed Bessie more than Bessie needed her. She hadn't the slightest intention of telling Mr Simon she wouldn't be taking the job, for his nephew was at the forefront of all her plans. And she wasn't letting the welfare of her daughter get in the way of those plans. If all else failed, the girl would have to be in the house on her own for two hours each night, whether she was frightened or not. In her twisted mind, Evelyn put the blame on Amelia for everything that had gone wrong in her own life.

'You are very kind, Miss Maudsley,' she said now, 'and I'm sure we shall both benefit from it. And Amelia, of course, will be delighted when I tell her the result of our conversation.' Evelyn got to her feet. 'I must go now, Amelia will be waiting for her tea. I want you to know I am very grateful, and hope our little arrangement is of mutual benefit. And I do apologise for calling when you were about to have your meal.'

'I'll see you out.' Bessie pushed her chair back and began to walk towards the front door with her. 'Tell Amelia I'm looking forward to seeing her. Oh, and remind her it's only two weeks on Saturday to our birthday party.'

But as Evelyn pulled on Bessie's arm it was herself she was thinking off, no one else. 'I'll go out the back way, Miss Maudsley, I don't want to be seen by the neighbours. Especially those two from opposite, who seem to spend their whole lives gossiping in the street. It's a pity they haven't got anything better to do. I do not want them knowing my business so, if you don't mind, I'll go out the back way.'

'Please yerself.' Bessie followed her through to the kitchen, and when she'd closed the door after her, muttered, 'Good riddance to bad rubbish.'

Then she went back to the table for the remains of her sandwich, and a conversation with the fireplace. 'I don't know whether to laugh or cry, I really don't. There's something wrong in the head with that bleeding woman. She's definitely not normal, yet the silly bugger thinks we're all mad and she's the only sane one! I mean, how does she think I can have her daughter coming here every night straight from school, and not one of the neighbours will see her and start asking questions? Is the silly bugger going to give everyone in the street a ruddy blindfold and insist they wear them?'

Then Bessie chuckled. 'She'd do her nut if she knew Rita is coming over tonight, and seeing as she's me best friend in the street, it's only natural I'll tell her me bit of news. She's bound to find out, living opposite, and she'd think me a fine friend if I hadn't let on. In fact, she'd think it was sneaky, and I'd agree with her. So Rita will be told of our little arrangement when she comes tonight, and sure as eggs is eggs she'll tell Aggie first thing in the morning. I'll tell them to keep it to themselves, of course, but I can't help it if they can't keep a secret. But I'd better not mention what her Ladyship said about the other kids having diseases and head lice, 'cos then they'd lynch her. I think Rita might laugh and see the funny side, but not Aggie. Aggie Gordon has a good sense of humour, but not when someone is saying her two children are diseased and lousy. She'd be over there like a shot, with all guns blazing, and if she didn't get an answer, she'd boot the ruddy door in. I don't want no trouble, so I'll be careful what I say and make sure me tongue doesn't run away with me. I don't like the woman, it's no use saying I do, she gets up me bleeding nose with her airs and graces – but I'd hate to see her getting her hair pulled out and losing her front teeth.'

Bessie chuckled and pointed a finger at the fireplace. 'That's the best thing about having a conversation with you, yer never repeat it. And yer don't use no bad language either.' She'd picked up her cup and saucer, put them on the plate and was carrying them out to the kitchen when she turned and looked back at the grate. 'Don't start getting big-headed, 'cos I'll still be taking me poker to yer in the morning to rake out the ashes. So behave yerself, and don't be spitting no live coals on to me hearth rug either.'

'Don't die of surprise, will yer,' Rita said, passing Bessie on her way in, 'but I've got a few biscuits to have with the cup of tea I know ye're going to insist on making. I hopped in lucky when I went to the corner shop for a gas mantle, and Sally was sorting the biscuit tins out. She was emptying the crumbs into a bag ready to put in the bin when I spotted that the tin next to the one she was emptying was the broken biscuit one, and there were some decent ones in there. So I acted daft and pretended I thought she was going to throw them away too! And although she said she wasn't mad enough, nor rich enough, to throw out nearly good as new biscuits, she did take pity on me eventually. God love her cotton socks, she picked a few of the best out and put them in this bag.' She waved a small paper bag in the air. 'So when we're having our cuppa, we'll raise our cups to Sally.'

'You're me second visitor since I got in from

work, I'm getting to be very popular.' Bessie waited until her friend was seated. 'Only I didn't ask the other one if she wanted a drink 'cos I knew she wouldn't drink out of one of my cups in case it had a crack in it. And I bet she's never heard of broken biscuits in her life.'

As Rita passed the bag over, she said, 'I don't need three guesses for this one, sunshine, I'll lay odds it was the queer one next door?'

'Right first time, girl. But I'll bet yer'd never guess in a month of Sundays what she came to see me about.'

Rita rolled her eyes. 'She was on the cadge for something?' When Bessie shook her head, her mate racked her brain for inspiration, then said, 'Ooh, don't keep me in suspense, sunshine, me heart won't stand it. Come on, I'm all ears.'

Bessie pushed her chair under the table before striking a pose. She straightened her back, stuck her nose in the air, then laced her fingers across her tummy. And only being the size of sixpenny-worth of copper, she looked so funny Rita was laughing before the little woman opened her mouth.

'I was honoured today when one of the senior partners in the office asked me if I would like the position of private secretary to a new partner who is starting on Monday. It is a great advance and brings a not insignificant increase in my salary.'

Unable to keep up the pose, Bessie burst out laughing. 'It's all right for you, Rita Wells, but I had to keep me face straight while she was going on, in that posh voice of hers, about how delighted she was. And d'yer know what was going through me head as she went on about it? Well, I was thinking that while not one soul in this street likes her, she doesn't see it 'cos she's too busy loving herself.'

'I'm surprised she told yer, sunshine, 'cos she never talks to anyone else. None of us knows the first thing about her, so how come she's suddenly opening up to you? She must be after something, so I'd watch out.'

'Oh, she was after something all right. I knew that as soon as I saw her passing me kitchen window. But what she was after suited me, so while I dragged it out for a while, I knew she was going to get her own way.' Bessie pulled the chair back out and sat down. 'I may as well sit while I tell yer the whole story. But before I start, I want yer to know I only let her carry on because of young Amelia. I'm very fond of that girl and think she leads a lousy life. Otherwise I wouldn't have let Lady Muck over the doorstep.'

Rita listened wide-eyed, clicking her tongue a few times. But she didn't interrupt until Bessie had finished. When she did open her mouth to give her opinion, she was asked to wait until they had a pot of tea on the table. Then they sat facing each other across the table with cups of tea in front of them and some biscuits in the saucers.

'She's done me a favour, girl, 'cos since they moved in I've wanted to make friends with Amelia seeing as she doesn't have any young friends. Not that I'm young, like, but at least I talk to her as I would a young girl, not as if to an adult like her mother does. I think we'll both

113

enjoy being together for a few hours each night. It'll be a change for me to have young company, and I'll be able to take her to the park or round the shops, something her own mother never does. And she can't say she hasn't got time, 'cos she's in from work about the same time as me. Anyway, that'll all change on Monday 'cos she's working full-time then, and what the eye don't see, the heart don't grieve over.' Bessie put her cup down on the saucer. 'It goes against the grain with me, taking a shilling a week off her, and I almost told her what she could do with it. Then I thought of how I could spend it on Amelia, buy a few books I can keep in here for her to read, and a game of Snakes and Ladders or Tiddly-winks. She'd like those. I'd rather she had it than the mother who doesn't show any love for her. No hugs or kisses, no sign of affection even.'

'That's because there isn't any, sunshine,' Rita said. 'I can see a lot from our house, and it's not because I'm nosy but yer can't help noticing that she never sees the girl off to school, never stands at the door to give her a kiss or shout after her to tell her to hurry home. They'd only been living there a couple of months when I started to notice those things. I've never said anything to anyone 'cos it's not my worry, but I'd say that woman has no feelings, no emotions, and no love to give her own daughter. In fact, I doubt if she has ever known what true love is.'

'I've noticed all those things too!' Bessie was thinking of Amelia's happy expression when she'd been able to get a loaf for a penny. She'd been so sure her mother would be pleased with her, yet her only thanks was a smack across the face. 'That's why I want to show the kid all women aren't like that. I want to try and show her the love, affection and fun that every other kid in this street knows. They might not have any shoes on their feet, but by God, they know what love is. And laughter too.' Bessie looked surprised that she'd only just thought of this. 'D'yer know, Rita, I've never once heard laughter coming through the wall of that house. I think Amelia is afraid of her mother, afraid to look as though she's enjoying herself.' She banged one clenched fist on the table. 'By God, I'm going to change all that, starting on Monday. I don't care if I have to lie to the stuck-up snob, I'm determined to show that young girl what a real home is like.' She grinned. 'I'll keep God informed every night, and I'm sure He will be on my side.'

'Yer can count on me to be on your side as well, sunshine, I'll help all I can. And yer can take it from me, I'll be doing it willingly. And I'll have a word with God too, 'cos yer never know, an extra voice might add more weight.'

Chapter Six

It was Monday morning. Rita was waving her sons off when the front door to the next house opened and Aggie's eleven-year-old daughter Kitty stepped down on to the pavement, followed by her brother, ten-year-old Kenny. Close behind came Aggie, who never missed seeing her children off.

'The start of another week, eh, girl? The flaming time just flies over.' Aggie held on to the door frame for support as she carefully lowered her eighteen stone down the steps. 'You two better get a move on 'cos ye're a bit late this morning. Too bleeding lazy to get out of bed.'

'It was your fault, Mam, yer never called us.' Kitty wagged her head from side to side, a habit she had acquired from her mother. She also had her mother's features, plus her quick tongue and sense of humour, and was already showing signs of being plump. But woe betide anyone who dare mention this. 'It was you what slept in, so don't be trying to get out of it.'

Her brother pulled on her arm. 'Me mam made us a bit late, but it's you what's making us very late. Shut up and come on, otherwise the school gates will be closed by the time we get there.' As he dragged his sister down the street, he turned his head and appealed to Rita, 'Why do girls and women talk so much? They'll have the last word if it kills them.'

'You're a fine one to talk,' Kitty growled, trying to tug her arm free. 'When ye're out with yer mates, it's always your mouth what's going fifteen to the dozen.'

When Aggie let out a roar and pretended to run after them, shaking her fist in the air, her two children ran hell for leather. But they were both laughing, for they loved the bones of their mother who was warm, loving, and very funny. There was never a dull moment in their house for she never ran out of funny tales. Most of them she made up, but that didn't matter if it made them laugh. 'See yer tonight, Mam,' they both shouted, waving their hands over their head.

'God love them,' Aggie said, 'if they get the cane for being late, it's not because they overslept. It was the ruddy alarm clock, it's away to hell. I'll have to see if Sam can fix it tonight 'cos I can't afford to buy a new one.'

'I can always give yer a knock on the wall,' Rita told her. 'Our alarm clock has never let us down.' She crossed two fingers. 'It's bad luck to speak too soon, so forget I said that. But I'll give yer a knock, if yer want.'

'I'll wait and see if Sam can fix the clock. If he can't, I'll let yer know.' Aggie folded her arms which disappeared under her mountainous breasts. 'Ay, her over the road, Tilly Mint, she was out early this morning. I don't know what the time was, what with the bleeding alarm letting us down, but it can't have been more than eight o'clock, ten-past at the latest. That's early for her. And when the girl came out later, I felt

117

sorry for the poor lass, she had a hell of a job closing the door. She tried pulling it with her two hands in the letter box but that was no good. Then she stood on tip-toe to reach the knocker and that failed. I'd have gone out to her if I hadn't been at sixes and sevens, trying to make the kids some toast before they went to school. I wouldn't let them go out on an empty tummy.' The bosom was hitched up higher. 'Anyway, Mr Bleasedale from the top of the street gave the door a good bang for her.'

'Aggie, I've got something to tell yer,' Rita said, 'although I really shouldn't.'

'Then leave it until later, eh, queen? There's half a pot of tea on me table, and I want to drink it before it gets cold. I can't afford to throw good tea away.'

'It's to do with Mrs Sinclair, and I thought yer'd be interested. So when yer find out, don't call me a dark horse for not letting on.'

It didn't take long for Aggie to decide, and she decided she didn't want to miss her pot of tea *or* the news her neighbour had. So she grabbed Rita's arm and pulled her up the steps. 'I think there's enough tea in the pot for two cups. And that way I've got the best of both worlds.'

'I suppose yer know yer nearly pulled me arm out of its socket?' Rita bent over and then straightened the arm in question. 'The trouble with you, Aggie Gordon, is yer don't know yer own strength. Yer'd make a ruddy good prize-fighter.'

Aggie wasn't even listening, she was too busy laughing at what she had in mind. Opening a door in the sideboard, she brought out a china cup and saucer, and with a flourish put them down in front of Rita. Once she saw her good china was out of harm's way, she began to shake with laughter. 'Nobody has ever drunk out of that cup before, I've treasured it for the last ten years. But I suddenly had a flash, like lightning, of Her Ladyship's face. She was looking down her nose at someone as though they were the lowest of the low. And I thought that's how she'd look if yer were pulling her to pieces while drinking out of a mug what had dozens of cracks and chips in it. So tell me what the news is, and because of the dainty cup and saucer, I expect yer to speak proper posh.'

'How long did yer say yer'd had this cup and saucer, sunshine?'

'Ooh, easy ten years, maybe a bit more. It's the first and only time I've ever had anything so delicate, and I wouldn't use it in case it got broke.'

'And have yer ever washed it in all those years?'

'Of course I haven't. I've been frightened to touch the bleeding thing, never mind wash it. And you'd better be careful 'cos I'm never likely to get anything else so fragile and dainty.'

'Oh, I won't have to worry about being careful, sunshine, 'cos I've no intention of drinking out of a cup that hasn't been washed in ten years. It's probably thick with dust, and has had creepy-crawlies walking all over it.'

'Ay, ye're not half a fussy blighter, Rita Wells.' Aggie was laughing inside as she picked up the delicate white china cup that was decorated with tiny pink flowers. 'I'll give it a rub with me pinny

119

if that makes yer feel better.'

Rita gasped. 'What! I'd rather take a chance on the creepy-crawlies than your pinny. God knows what yer've spilt on it, let alone wiping yer hands down it after yer've cleaned the grate out and scrubbed the step. So I certainly ain't going to drink out of a cup that yer've wiped on that filthy pinny, I'm too young to die. Put the flaming thing back where it's been for the last ten years and get me a mug with chips and cracks in.'

The cup and saucer were put back in the dark depths of the sideboard, and probably wouldn't see daylight again for another ten years. 'Fussy bugger, that's what yer are. And just because ye're afraid of creepy-crawlies, and yer've kept on about it for the last ten minutes, the ruddy tea in the pot is stone cold now. So whatever it is yer have to tell me, queen, after all that, it had better be good.'

Rita suddenly remembered she'd left her front door wide open. 'You put the kettle on and boil enough water to warm the tea up, while I go and close me front door. I haven't got anything worth pinching, but what's mine is mine and I don't want no one else having it.'

She was back within seconds and Aggie was just carrying the kettle through. 'I only put enough water in to cover the bottom but the tea will be weak. So long as it's wet and warm I don't care, it's better than a slap in the face.' She put milk in the mugs, poured the tea out and then plonked herself down heavily on a wooden dining chair. 'Well, go on, queen, tell me what all the mystery is about? Make it as interesting as yer can so it'll give me something to think about all day while I'm doing me housework and then when we're out shopping.'

'I'm afraid there's no mystery about it, sunshine, but I believe yer will find it interesting. And it's for your ears only. Is that understood?' Rita waited for her friend's reluctant nod for Aggie was hopeless at keeping things to herself. 'It's about Mrs Sinclair – she's got another job and it's full-time. That's why she was going out early.'

'Oh, aye, what sort of a job is that, then? How come she can get a job and half the men in the street are out of work? And it's not for the want of trying. They're out at the crack of dawn down to the docks, hoping to get a day's work in.'

'She's been promoted to private secretary to one of the big nobs at the office she works in.' Rita could see that didn't go down well with her mate, who couldn't stand Mrs Sinclair. 'And if yer start making fun of her, I won't tell yer any more.'

Aggie put a hand to her mouth and muttered behind it, 'I promise I won't laugh, girl, at least not until yer've gone. Then I'll laugh me bloody head off. She was a snob before, so what's she going to be like now? Will she expect us to curtsey to her and pull our forelock?' Her eyes narrowed to slits. 'How do you know all this anyway?'

'She asked Bessie if she'd mind Amelia for two hours each night, 'cos working full-time she won't be home until after six.'

'Bessie didn't agree, did she?' Aggie tutted when she saw Rita nod. 'She wants her bleeding bumps feeling! She does all the hard work while Miss Hoity-Toity walks around as though she owns the place? I know what I'd have done, I'd have told her to get lost and then thrown her out.'

'Oh, and would yer have thrown young Amelia out as well?'

'Of course I wouldn't, she's only a kid. Yer can't blame her for having a stuck-up madam for a mother. I feel heartily sorry for the poor blighter.'

'So does Bessie, and that's the only reason she's agreed to mind her. She really loves that kid, and she's not half looking forward to having her for those two hours. Don't forget, Bessie hasn't got no family. She'll show that girl more love than her own mother does. Already she's talking about playing Snakes and Ladders and Ludo, and taking her to the park so she can have a go on the swings. That will have to be kept quiet, though, 'cos the queer one doesn't like the girl to play with the children round here. As yer say, Aggie, she's a bloody snob, but that doesn't mean we have to take it out on young Amelia whose life is miserable anyway.' Rita knew how to bring her friend round to her way of thinking. 'Anyway, I told Bessie I'd give her all the help I can, 'cos I've felt really sorry for the poor mite since the day they moved in across the street. That will be my good deed, and I'm sure God will chalk it up to me.'

'Ye're a crafty sod, Rita Wells, yer must think I'm as thick as two short planks. I'm supposed to say now that I'll be delighted to help, aren't I? Just so I'll get in His good books up in heaven.' Aggie pressed her thumbs into the fat around her

122

elbows, leaving deep hollows. 'The way I look at it, we've lived next door to each other in this street for about fourteen years or thereabouts and never really had a falling out. So what I say is, if yer've got good neighbours then hang on to them. Which boils down to me saying I'll help with the young girl, as long as I don't have to get involved with her mother, 'cos I know that sooner or later I'd end up flopping her one. Yer can tell Bessie I'm here if she wants me, and yer can also tell her I'll keep me gob shut. And now that little matter is settled to our mutual satisfaction, can I ask if yer have any influence in heaven?'

'No more than anyone else, sunshine, I just do the best I can in life. The only sin I ever commit is telling a little white lie, and I'm sure I won't have that held against me. I believe God is very fair-minded.'

Aggie wrinkled her nose and swung her head from side to side, her chubby cheeks wobbling. 'It doesn't sound very promising, that, girl, 'cos it means yer can't put in a good word for me. What yer *could* do for me, and it won't cost yer nothing only a little breath, yer could casually bring my name up in yer prayers each night. That way He would get to know me.'

'Why don't yer say what yer want to in yer own prayers each night? It would be in your favour to do it personally.' Rita saw a blush spread across Aggie's face. 'Aggie Gordon, yer don't say any prayers, do yer? Well, shame on yer, that's all I can say.'

'I do say prayers, queen, cross my heart and hope to die. It's just not every night, like what you do.' Aggie put on the woe-begone expression which to her friend was a sign that excuses were on the way. 'Yer see, I'm so worn out by the time me head hits the pillow, I'm fast asleep before I know what's happening. It's hard going looking after a husband and two children, and doing the washing, ironing, cooking and shopping. I never seem to have a minute to meself.'

Rita tutted. 'It's no good moaning to me 'cos yer won't get any sympathy. Yer seem to forget I've got a husband and two kids, the same as you!'

Aggie injected a whine into her voice, which she was very good at and did for fun. 'Well it's like this, yer see, queen. You don't moan, so how can anyone give yer sympathy if they don't feel sorry for yer? Me now, I can put on a miserable face and a crying voice, and before yer can say Jack Robinson, folk are asking what they can do to help. Yer should try it, 'cos it never fails for me.'

Rita knew this was a load of rubbish, and thought she'd throw in some of her own to even things out. 'And you're daft enough to think people like yer and feel really sorry for the hard-done-by Aggie Gordon? That only shows how stupid yer are! Yer should hear what they're saying behind yer back. Calling yer fit to burn, they are.'

'Ye're only making that up, Rita Wells, 'cos yer know the neighbours like me more than they do you, and ye're jealous. And there's nothing worse than jealousy. I can't help it if I'm more popular than you are.'

Rita looked at the clock. Another five minutes of this comedy and then she'd better be on her way and get some housework done. But she'd make good use of the five minutes, she couldn't let her mate get the better of her. 'Yer live in a dream world, Aggie, a little world of yer own. If yer'd heard what Mrs Sloane said about yer in the butcher's last Thursday, it would have brought yer down to earth. Her and Mrs Johnson called yer for everything.' Rita spread her hands. 'I stuck up for yer though, sunshine, 'cos I couldn't stand there and let them pull me best mate to pieces.'

Aggie's arms appeared like magic from beneath her bosom to press upon the table. 'When did yer say this was, queen?'

'It was last Thursday morning, about half-eleven. I'm so sure of the day and time, 'cos I remember wondering how I was going to manage two days on the tanner I had in me purse.'

'Oh, yeah, I remember that now, 'cos I had a penny more than you did!' Aggie rubbed two fingers on each of her temples and closed her eyes, imitating the actions of a gypsy who came to the street about once a year to ask if she could read their fortunes for a penny. The women in the street had got together and said if she would only charge a ha'penny, then they'd all have their fortunes told.

Aggie began to groan. 'Oh, yeah, it's all coming clear now, I was standing next to someone – I can't clearly make the face out, but I think it's my neighbour and best friend ... Rita Wells. We were in the butcher's together waiting to be served.'

She frowned as though deep in concentration. 'But I can't see Mrs Sloane or Mrs Johnson, and I can't feel their presence. Oh, it's all fading now, my mind is going blank.' She fell back in the chair, seemingly worn out by the experience. 'Oh, I do feel drained.' Then a smile spread across her chubby face. 'That was good, that, wasn't it, girl? Passed a bit of time away.'

'Anybody listening to us would think we were two sheets to the wind, yer know that, don't yer?' Rita pushed her chair back. 'I'm glad I got someone as daft as meself for a neighbour 'cos it adds a bit of spice to me life. But I'm going to love yer and leave yer now, and get me dishes washed and the grate cleaned out. The washing has been steeping all night in the dolly tub, so the worst of the dirt will be out. I'll have a bash with the dolly peg for a few minutes, then rinse the clothes, put them through the mangle and have them on the line in no time. There's a bit of a blow out, so they should be ready for ironing tonight.'

Aggie put her hands flat on the table and pushed herself up. 'What time will yer be ready for the shops? Say half-eleven?'

'That's fine, sunshine, I'll give yer a knock as near to that as I can. And don't sit down again when I'm gone, get cracking on yer housework.'

Aggie stood to attention, as did her bosom, and saluted. 'Aye, aye, sir! Three bleeding bags full, sir!'

Over the years since her fall from grace Evelyn had made the most of the clothes she had. No one would have guessed on the Monday morning when she entered the office that her coat and dress were years old, and that she'd spent the weekend sponging and pressing them. She was an attractive woman, with an eye-catching figure. Buoyed up with newfound confidence she walked with the air of a woman who knew what she wanted in life and intended to have it. And adding to her feeling of well-being was the news that Mr Simon had decided that as Miss Saunders would be spending a lot of time in his office over the next two weeks, making sure that everything was up-to-date for his nephew to take over, her office could be assigned to Mr Philip and his new private secretary. He would, of course, have to spend some time with his uncle, familiarising himself with those clients who were important to the firm, but several hours a day could be spent getting his secretary used to his way of working. Although Evelyn kept her cool exterior when told the news, she was gloating inside.

Philip Astbury was already in his temporary office when Evelyn opened the door. He was sitting in a leather swivel chair, smartly dressed as usual and wearing a satisfied grin. He jumped to his feet when she entered and waved to the chair on the opposite side of the desk. He was congratulating himself on being so lucky in having been handed such a stunning-looking woman to work for him. He was sure they were going to get on very well together. 'Good morning, Mrs Sinclair. My Uncle Simon has kindly given us the use of this office until such time as he and Miss

Saunders finally retire. Jolly thoughtful of him, don't you agree?'

'Extremely generous.' Evelyn placed her handbag at the side of the chair, took her time over sitting down, and once seated crossed one slender leg over the other. It was done deliberately to catch his attention, and she smiled inwardly as she saw his eyes following the movement. 'We must show our gratitude by taking full advantage of his kind offer.' She bent down to take a notepad from her bag. 'I have been practising my shorthand over the weekend and feel I have made real progress. Perhaps you would like to dictate a letter to an imaginary client, to test my speed?' She lowered her eyelids seductively and said softly, 'You see, I aim to please.'

'Oh, I have no doubt I shall be well pleased, Mrs Sinclair.' Philip sat up straight and leaned his elbows on the desk. 'So, this letter to an imaginary client. Shall we begin?'

Evelyn had her pencil poised in readiness. 'May I crave your indulgence, Mr Philip, and ask that you do not dictate too quickly? Otherwise I shall become very embarrassed and my hand will shake. Now, can I have the name and address of the client, please?'

His eyes shining with laughter, Philip said, 'How about my writing to a certain charming lady by the name of Evelyn Sinclair, to ask if she would do me the honour of having lunch with me today? I'm sure Uncle Simon would not be too upset if he were to lunch alone at his club, and it would give you and me a chance to get better acquainted?'

Although her heart was fluttering, and she would indeed be delighted to dine with such an attractive man, Evelyn let her head rule. To rush into anything would be completely the wrong thing to do with a man who was obviously very fond of getting his own way with the female sex. The thought of a nice meal in one of the finest restaurants was tempting, but Evelyn was aiming higher than a few stolen moments.

'I really don't think so, Mr Philip.' She met his eyes and held them. 'I think we should keep our relationship on a strictly boss and secretary basis.' Head bent slightly, and eyelids fanning her cheeks, she said softly, 'At least, for the time being.'

'Oh, and how long is for the time being? It could be anything from a moment to a year or more. Would you really be so cruel to your new boss?'

'That is the problem, Mr Philip, don't you see? It is because you are my boss that I must not be seen to be taking advantage of you by flirting. Perhaps when we know each other better we will be able to meet away from the office and the gossiping.'

'Is that a promise I can hold you to, Mrs Sinclair?'

Evelyn was very sure of this because she had lain awake in bed last night planning the whole operation. And so far it was working just as she had planned. 'Yes, Mr Philip, that is a promise you can hold me to. And I'll see if it can be arranged in the not too distant future.' Lifting her pad, she said, 'Now, can we proceed with the

129

letter to the imaginary client, please?'

That evening, as she sat on the tram on her journey home, Evelyn told herself she must somehow find the money for new clothes if she was to make a real impression on a man-about-town like Mr Philip. His family were almost as rich as the Lister-Sinclairs, very well known in the higher social circle. The dress she had on today was dark blue, knee-length, and showed off her figure to perfection. It had cost a fortune when new, and she had certainly had her money's worth out it. She also had a deep maroon one, also well-cut and fitting her very well. But two working dresses were not enough; she really needed another two, at least. Her mind went to the large trunk in her bedroom which was filled to the brim with fine silk dresses, long and short, several silk and satin shoulder capes, feather boas, costume jewellery, shoes made of the softest leather, and several wide-brimmed hats. None of these had been out of the trunk since Charles had gone off to war, for with his death had come an end to her social life. Nothing in that trunk was any good for day wear, but she was sure there would be something suitable that she could wear to go out for an evening meal with Mr Philip. She'd go through the trunk tonight, after Amelia had gone to sleep. Thinking of her brought a frown to Evelyn's face. How could she get ahead in life when her daughter would always be holding her back? For Evelyn was under no illusion about her new boss. The admiration and desire in his eyes would soon disappear if he found out she had a seven-year-old daughter.

Evelyn saw her tram stop looming up, and made her way down the aisle to the platform. As she waited for the tram to come to a shuddering halt, she reminded herself that her daughter would be eight a week on Saturday, and was having tea with Miss Maudsley then. This gave birth to an idea of how she could manage an evening being wined and dined by Mr Philip. Stepping down on to the pavement, Evelyn told herself it would be simple enough to find an excuse for asking her neighbour if she would allow Amelia to stay with her until ten o'clock. After all, there would be no school the next day so the girl could have an extra hour in bed. Oh, there would be a way around it, she was sure. There had to be if she were ever to get out of the working-class rut she was in.

While her mother was thinking of ways to off-load her daughter on to her neighbour, Amelia was in Bessie's kitchen helping to dry the dishes. Her pretty face was flushed with laughter. Oh, the last two hours had been the happiest of her life! Miss Bessie was so funny, and it was a nice change not to have to worry about what she said. 'I can come tomorrow, can't I, Miss Bessie? We can play Snakes and Ladders again, and you won't have to let me win 'cos I know how to play it now.'

'Of course yer can come, sweetheart, it's been a pleasure having someone to talk to and laugh with.' Bessie handed a plate over to be dried. 'I usually talk to the fireplace, and though we get on fine, there's not much fun when yer never get an answer to a question.'

Amelia's chuckle filled the tiny kitchen. 'You don't really talk to the fireplace, do yer, Miss Bessie?'

She kept the smile on her face, but groaned inside. Already there were signs of a Scouse accent creeping into the girl's voice, and her mother would not be very happy about that. But Her Ladyship couldn't put all the blame on Bessie, for the girl had been telling Bessie about the friends she'd made at school, and how she played with them in the playground. It was a dead cert they all had accents you could cut with a knife. 'Don't lose that nice way of speaking yer have, sweetheart, or yer mother will think it's my fault and have me life. It's no good saying I'll learn to speak posh, 'cos I'm too old to change the habits of a lifetime even if I wanted to, which I don't. I believe everyone should be natural, and not try and change themselves to please other folk.'

'My friends all speak like you, Miss Bessie, and I do when I'm in school. Only not in front of my mother because she's very strict.'

Bessie took her hands from the soapy water and pulled the plug out of the sink. As she watched the water running away, she thought what a sad life this young child had. In a roundabout way, when they were playing board games, she had asked what games Amelia had at home. Her face as innocent as a new-born babe's, the child had answered that her mother didn't believe in games, they were a waste of time. She was set homework to do by her mother apparently, and

132

not allowed to leave the table until it was completed and every question right.

'I think I heard the latch on the entry door open, sweetheart, so yer mother must be here for yer,' Bessie told her now.

The expression on Amelia's face changed completely, from a happy little girl's to that of someone afraid they are going to be reprimanded for doing something wrong. 'Don't forget to tell my mother I've been good, and ask if I can come again tomorrow?'

This was all that could be said before the knock came on the door. 'Come in, Mrs Sinclair,' Bessie called. 'Your daughter has been helping me wash and dry our dishes. I hope yer don't mind me giving Amelia some dinner, do yer? It just means me cooking a bit extra, but if you have any objection then I'll just give her a cup of tea and she can wait until you come home for her meal.'

No matter what Bessie had asked, Evelyn would have agreed. She needed this little woman, for she had no friends she could call on to mind her daughter. 'That is extremely kind of you, Miss Maudsley, and I do hope Amelia was gracious in her thanks.' Her voice was so sickly sweet, Bessie turned her head away. If it weren't for the girl, and her affection for her, she would have told this false, lying snob to go to hell.

'Amelia has been a pleasure to have as a guest. She is very polite, doesn't answer back or give cheek, and we get on very well together.' And for good measure, she added, 'And her table manners are impeccable.' That was a big word for Bessie, who felt like sticking out her tongue and

133

telling Her Ladyship she wasn't the only one who could get her tongue around big words and know the meaning of them. 'If you still want me to mind her for two hours every night I'll be delighted, and I'll give her a meal.'

'You really are too kind, Miss Maudsley, and perhaps one day I will be in a position to repay your kindness.' For the first time, Evelyn acknowledged her daughter. 'You are a very lucky girl, Amelia, and I'm only agreeing to Miss Maudsley having you each night on the strict understanding that you behave yourself and do exactly as you are told. Do you understand?'

In a tiny voice, devoid of any emotion, she answered, 'Yes, Mother.'

Chapter Seven

It was eight o'clock when Evelyn told her daughter it was time for her to go to bed. Amelia didn't object. She was longing to lie quietly and go over all the things Miss Bessie had said and done, and the way they'd laughed at silly things her mother would only have frowned at. There had never in her life been a goodnight kiss or a hug, so after saying, 'Goodnight, Mother,' the girl climbed the stairs. She didn't run up them, even though she wanted to, for that would have brought a sharp rebuke, and she didn't want anything to spoil the day. And tonight she didn't shiver when she slid in between the cold sheets, for she had a hand over her mouth so her mother wouldn't hear her giggles. It had been so funny when Miss Bessie had told the fireplace to keep quiet and not to interrupt. And then she'd pretended it answered back, and said, 'Don't be so flaming cheeky, I won't tell yer again. Anyone would think yer owned the house, the way yer carry on.'

Downstairs, Evelyn told herself to wait half an hour to give her daughter time to go to sleep. Amelia wasn't allowed in her bedroom, and although she may have seen the trunk through the open door, had no idea of its contents. That was the way it would stay. The less the child knew about her previous life, the better. She had been

135

told very bluntly that her father had been killed in the war and wasn't encouraged to ask further questions. What she didn't know she couldn't pass on, and that was how Evelyn wanted it. So, while Amelia was reliving every second of the time she'd spent next door, her mother was making plans for a future that would take her back to the good life she had known, and which she longed to regain.

Exactly half an hour after her daughter had gone to bed, Evelyn lit a candle and placed it in the middle of a saucer. Then she made her way quietly up the steep, narrow stairs, lit by the flickering flame. She stood on the landing for a few seconds, her ear to the door of her daughter's room. Satisfied the child was asleep, she entered her own bedroom and closed the door. Then she put the saucer on the floor near the trunk before taking a large, rusty key from the top drawer of the tallboy. At first she thought she wasn't going to be able to open the trunk, for over the years the lock had rusted inside too and she couldn't turn the key in it. It would have been easier if she'd knelt down to do it, and shown a little patience.

But patience was not one of Evelyn's virtues, and there was much tutting and clicking of her tongue before the key finally turned. 'Confounded thing,' she muttered when she lifted the lid and it creaked loudly. The smell of dampness was another irritant which had her wrinkling her nose. Not for a second would she take the blame for not having opened the trunk before now, so the clothes could be aired. But then, nothing was ever her fault. In her mind there were two people responsible for her present plight: Charles for being killed, and Amelia for being born. But she intended to turn her life around as soon as possible. And to do that she must put on a front. She had never allowed herself to become friendly with the staff of Astbury and Woodward, and they knew nothing of her circumstances, which was fortunate. So as far as Philip was concerned, she wasn't poor but a well-to-do widow who had the means to live comfortably without a man in her life.

The candle was too low to give much light out, so Evelyn carried a wooden chair from the side of her bed and placed it by the trunk. Then she set the saucer on it, and nodded as if to say that was much better and she could see what she was doing now. The first thing she touched when she put her hand in the trunk was a feather boa, and as she shook it out memories came flooding back. It was one of the first things she had bought with the allowance her father had given her. This, and much of the clothing in the trunk, had been paid for by him as he saw Evelyn as his passport into the higher echelons of Liverpool society. But things hadn't gone the way anyone planned when Charles was killed in 1917. That in itself hadn't upset Herbert and Gertrude Wilkinson too much, for their daughter was now a member of the Lister-Sinclair family and could still be their means of joining the ranks of the very rich. However, when they found out she was pregnant, believing her marriage to Charles had not been consummated, they blamed her bitterly

137

and disowned her. She hadn't seen them since. Not that it worried her, for she'd never had any love for her penny-pinching parents. She had never made the connection, but now she was treating her daughter exactly as they had treated her.

Evelyn laid the feather boa on the lino and leaned into the trunk to see if there was anything fit for her to wear on an evening out with Philip. Fortunately she had kept her slim figure, so the clothes would fit, but were they good enough? Were they still fashionable or would they look dated? She hadn't been to a social gathering for eight years and didn't know if the fashions had changed greatly. She hadn't noticed much change in everyday wear, except in the length of day clothes. Nowadays women wore them anywhere between knee and ankle-length. Cloche hats were still in vogue, though, and she knew there were two or three in the trunk. But would they be fit to wear or would the moths have eaten into them?

Delving into the darkness of the trunk once more, Evelyn came up with a dress that brought a smile of triumph to her face. It was a long blue gown in the finest silk which was a joy to the touch. It had full-length sleeves which were slit from the shoulder to be gathered together into a cuff at the wrist. It was low-cut to back and front, to reveal her spine and the cleft between her breasts. She held the dress to her, as though welcoming an old friend, and whispered, 'Please don't let the moths have got to you.' She draped it carefully over one arm while with the other she reached into the trunk to search for the cape

138

which had been bought to match the dress. When she felt the material in her hand, she felt like shouting for joy. It was impossible in the candlelight to tell if there were any moth holes in it, but light enough to see it was a beautiful, knee-length cape in the same material as the dress with a diamante clasp at the neck.

Evelyn sat back on her heels. If these garments had stood the passage of time, they would certainly pass the most critical eye. She remembered walking down Bold Street with Charles and seeing them in the window of the most expensive shop in the city. She had stopped to admire them, and of course the outcome was the one she'd hoped for. Charles insisted he'd buy them for her, and half an hour later she was walking down the street with the cord of a square silver dress box over her wrist, and her head in the clouds. Charles had offered to carry the box but she would have none of it. The name on the box and its shape were exclusive to the only shop in the city to have a uniformed man standing outside to open the door for customers, and then wave their carriage or automobile down.

There was a deep sigh from Evelyn as she remembered the heady feeling of buying only from the best shops and dining in only the best hotels and restaurants. Having a man admiring you across the table, and knowing there wasn't another woman who could beat you for looks or style. And she could make it happen again if she had the right clothes to wear, and a good address to invite prospective suitors to. She smoothed the soft material of the dress and cape draped over her arm, and decided: I'll take them downstairs to try them on and see if they still fit. If I raise the gas, it may give me enough light to check for moth holes. If fate is kind, and the clothes are wearable, I'll put them on hangers and hang them outside the wardrobe in the hope of getting rid of the smell. Then at least I will have one stylish, attractive outfit to wear. And who knows what else the trunk may produce?

So many years had passed she couldn't remember what she had packed into it, and it was too dark now to have a really good clear out. Perhaps she could get up half an hour early tomorrow and begin her search, before her daughter was awake. She'd do it a bit at a time, when Amelia wasn't around.

Evelyn shivered as she slipped the dress over her head. The material was cold, and the smell of damp sickening. It still fitted her, though, and as she ran her hands down the sides, she prided herself that it clung to her figure. If there was no moth damage, the one way of treating it so it would come up like new, and without the smell, was to have it cleaned at the Chinese laundry. It would probably cost a few shillings to have both dress and cape cleaned, but that was a small price to pay. The increase in her salary would start from Saturday, and although she had to pay Miss Maudsley a shilling a week, she would still be a few shillings better off. More even, as her neighbour was going to give Amelia a dinner every night. And she had asked if she could do it, it wasn't as though she was doing it out of pity for them. No, it was more likely they were doing her a favour, for, after all, it must be a lonely life not having any family.

When she finally climbed the stairs to bed, Evelyn felt younger than she had for years and in a more pleasant frame of mind. She had decided on her new future, and not for a second did she think she would fail.

At the precise moment Evelyn was climbing the stairs, Philip was lying in the arms of a very pretty young woman, paying her sugary compliments and claiming she was the most wonderful girl he'd ever had the pleasure of meeting. And the young girl blushed at his compliments for, at nineteen years of age, she had never met up with a charmer before, and believed he was sincere in what he was saying. Had her parents known where she was, and with whom, they would have been horrified. Philip was at least eleven or twelve years her senior, and although he didn't have a bad reputation, he was well known by his close friends for playing the field. But the girl's parents would not find out, for although she was young and inexperienced in the ways of romancing, she wasn't stupid enough to tell them; she knew what their reaction would be. And she did so want to see Philip again, he was so interesting, amusing, and a real man of the world.

'And what is my lovely Charlotte thinking now?' he asked, his finger running down a cheek as soft as silk. They'd met at a soiree in the home of one of his friends, and as Charlotte was the youngest and prettiest female there, Philip had lost no time in making her acquaintance. With

141

the drink flowing, and the many conversations going on in the room becoming louder, it was almost impossible to hear each other. So Philip had taken her hand, and making sure they weren't seen, had led her to the study where he knew it would be quiet and there was a very convenient and comfortable chaise-longue. Charlotte wasn't worldly enough to know that going into an empty room with a strange man might not be the thing to do. Philip had in fact no intention of going beyond the bounds of decency. His trouble was, he was a born womaniser and couldn't help flirting with a pretty young girl. Had she been older, or married but available and willing, then he might have been more daring and taken his chances. But he wouldn't deliberately court trouble, especially in the home of one of his best friends.

'My father is sending the car to pick me up at half-past ten,' Charlotte said. 'I don't want to go, but I'm afraid I must. But will you promise we'll meet again soon, Philip, so I have something to look forward to? I really would like us to be friends.'

As soon as a female began to get serious, he backed away. He had heard the phrase 'shotgun wedding', and he was looking for fun, not a married life of so-called bliss. 'I'm sure we'll meet up again, my love, we're bound to. Most of my friends know your parents, so I have no doubt we will see each other again in the very near future.' Philip swung his legs off the chaise-longue. 'It's almost ten-thirty now. I'll walk with you to the front door and see you safely into the

142

car. We'll pick up your coat on the way.'

On the front step of the large house which was now brightly lit, Charlotte reached for Philip's hand. 'Promise you'll see me again very soon?'

'I'll try, my love, but I am not a free agent. I have a job to go to every day, and apart from the time I spend at the office, I often have to take work home with me. I still live with my parents and feel duty bound to spend some time with them. But I do have some free evenings, of course I do, and I'm sure that the next party I go to, you will also attend. Anyway, my lovely Charlotte, you are so pretty you will always be sought after by men nearer your own age and far more suitable than myself. I promise that if we meet again at a mutual friend's house, and I see you with a very handsome Romeo, I will not try to steal you away from him. So go now, my love, don't keep the chauffeur waiting any longer. And do give my kind regards to your parents.' He waited until she was safely in the car, waved her off, then breathed a sigh of relief when he went back into the house.

In the wide hall, brightly lit by a huge scintillating chandelier, Philip was met by his friend and host Nigel, who raised his brows and shook his head slightly. 'You're sailing close to the wind, old boy. She is far too young for you, and her father is very protective. So take care, my friend.'

'Nigel, my dear boy, I may be many things but stupid I am not. Nor am I a rotter. I didn't lay a finger on the girl, didn't even kiss her goodnight although she stood with lips pouted in readiness. And despite her pleas, I have not promised to see her again. Like yourself, I prefer someone nearer my own age who is responsible for their own actions.'

'Don't compare us, Philip, I happen to be a very happily married man. If Marigold had heard you say that, she would have raised hell with me and never let me out of her sight again.' Nigel grinned. 'And I would never leave you alone in a room with my wife, even though you profess to be my best friend.'

'Have no fear, old boy, I have my sights set on a very attractive older woman. She has worked for Astbury and Woodward for several years, and as Uncle Simon's secretary is retiring too, luck was on my side and I acquired this lovely vision for my personal secretary. She hasn't fallen for my charms yet, but it's early days. She may be testing me, playing hard to get, or maybe she genuinely doesn't fancy me. Which would be quite a let-down for me. She's tall, very attractive, with dark hair, liquid brown eyes and a curvaceous figure. So while I have Mrs Sinclair in my sights, I am not really interested in any other female.'

'Mrs Sinclair? You mean you intend to pursue a married woman?' Nigel was taken aback. 'Shame on you, Philip.'

'You have it wrong again, dear boy. Mrs Sinclair is a widow. Very little is known about her at the office, apparently, she's not the talkative type. All that is known is that her husband was killed in battle in seventeen, not long after they were married. I find the aura of mystery surrounding her both thrilling and challenging and have made a vow to woo her, solve the mystery and claim the prize.'

Nigel again raised his eye brows. He was very fond of his friend, who was always good company and very loyal. But with the best will in the world, no one could say Philip was not a terror for a pretty face. 'And providing she allows you to woo her and win her, what then?'

Philip flashed the grin no woman could resist. Both old and young were captivated by it. 'Ah, well, I'm not looking that far ahead, old boy. At the moment I'm attracted and intrigued, but once I've won the chase, who knows?'

Nigel's wife Marigold came looking for him then. She was very much in love with her husband, but could see why so many of her friends fell head over heels for Philip. He really was an attractive devil. 'Oh, and what are you two cooking up? We have guests, Nigel, and mustn't neglect them.'

'I'm coming now, my love, but would you kindly lock all the good-looking, available women in the study, please, where Philip can't get at them? I'm just giving him a lecture on his womanising. It really is time he settled down and gave his parents the grandchildren they long for before they grow too old to appreciate them.'

'Now you go too far, Nigel.' Philip feigned horror. 'In one fell swoop you would have me married off to a sensible little woman who would set to and bear several children to keep my parents happy.' He put a hand to his forehead. 'The mere thought is enough to bring on a headache. Come on, be a good host and give your guest a glass of champers before he faints.'

Marigold linked his arm. 'I'll look after you

while Nigel fetches you a drink. I'll introduce you to a merry widow who has pots of money and is looking for someone to lavish it on.'

Philip pretended to draw away. 'Oh, no, not another merry widow! Why do all my friends wheel me out whenever they're a man short? And I don't know why you use the phrase "merry widow", because they're usually wearing thick make-up to hide the fact that they're ancient. I know some young men have no objection to being kept by a woman old enough to be their grandmother, as long as the money and expensive presents keep coming their way. But I do not need the money or expensive gifts, nor am I a kind enough person to flatter an elderly woman by telling her she looks twenty years younger than she actually is. Let them grow old gracefully, that's what I say. So, Marigold, my darling, I'll have the drink but not the woman.'

'Why don't you tell her you already have a beauty in your sights, Philip?' Nigel said as they made their way towards the loud laughter and voices coming from the drawing room. 'I'm sure Marigold would love to pass on that piece of information, and revel in the disappointment on the face of every female guest.'

She squeezed his arm. 'Oh, do tell, Philip, is what Nigel said true?' Again she squeezed his arm. 'Can you hear the noise of laughter and people shouting to make themselves heard? Well, if I repeat what my darling husband has just said, the female voices will all fall silent and the men will have smiles on their faces as they gloat over the fact that at last someone has stolen your heart

146

and you are no longer a threat to their wives, lovers and sweethearts. Oh, I can't wait to tell them.'

'I think that would be a little premature, my dear Marigold, and the day may come when you are forced to eat your words. So I think silence would be a virtue right now, and perhaps for the next few weeks. I've a feeling Mrs Sinclair is not going to be an easy conquest.'

The next morning Philip was no further advanced with his secretary for her face showed no emotion whatsoever. She most certainly wasn't outgoing, didn't speak unless it was necessary, nor did she smile much. Her greeting to him when he arrived at the office didn't hold much warmth. Still, he told himself, it was early days yet. He would take things slowly, so she wouldn't be put off.

Little did Philip know that every movement and every word was calculated to heighten his interest and admiration. When Evelyn crossed her legs it was done slowly, for effect. She sat upright in the chair, shoulders back to emphasise her breasts in the well-fitted maroon dress. Her eyelashes were used to great effect, and her words spoken softly, in a husky voice. To an onlooker, it would be difficult to say which one was the hunter in this room where there was an unmistakable atmosphere.

'Mr Philip, would you be kind enough to dictate a little faster this morning? Just to see if my speed has improved at all. I did spend an hour on it last night, and feel I have improved a little.' Evelyn's big brown eyes held his as she took a gamble. 'I realise it must be troublesome for you to have been landed with a secretary who isn't up to speed. I would understand if you thought I wasn't up to the job and would perhaps prefer to find someone more suited to your needs?'

'Good gracious, Mrs Sinclair, do you see me as so hard-hearted? I wouldn't dream of replacing you with someone else. I am sure you are more than capable and we will get along very well together.' Then came the grin that usually brought results. 'Besides, where am I likely to find another woman as lovely as yourself? No, from the first time I saw you, I had no doubts that we would suit each other beautifully.'

'You are very kind, Mr Philip.' Evelyn thought it was now time for her to pay compliment. 'There are not many men who would be as patient as you, and I hope you realise I am most appreciative of your understanding. I promise I will repay your kindness, patience, and the faith you have in me. I will not let you down.'

Philip leaned his elbows on the desk. 'Now it is getting interesting. I wonder how you will repay me, Mrs Sinclair? Would it be by returning favour if I were to ask for one?'

Pretending to be shy, Evelyn lowered her head. This was an opening, but she didn't want him thinking she was going to be an easy catch. If she gave in too quickly to a man like Philip, he would soon tire of her. 'Really, you do put me on the spot, Mr Philip. Of course I would be happy to do you a favour, but that would depend upon what it was you were asking of me.'

148

He chuckled. 'There's no reason to look so serious, Mrs Sinclair. I wouldn't ask you to rob a bank or murder someone. No, it would be a favour we could share and enjoy. Does that not make you curious, not tempt you?'

'It makes me curious, certainly, but how can I be tempted when I know nothing of your intentions?'

Philip decided to take the plunge. 'Would dinner at the State Hotel not be tempting? I can assure you they serve excellent food to a very select clientele.'

Evelyn nodded. 'Ah, yes, the State. It is many years since I was last there, but I do remember they serve excellent food. I also remember the atmosphere there was always pleasant and never noisy.'

'In that case, would you not like to sample the fare there again, Mrs Sinclair? Just for a couple of hours one evening, when you are free.'

'I have plenty of free time, Mr Philip, because I have absolutely no ties whatsoever. It is not lack of time that would stop me, but the fact that you are my boss. It might appear to some that any association between us, outside the office, would be inappropriate. I'm quite certain that tongues would wag.'

'And that would be your only concern, that tongues might wag?'

'Oh, the concern wouldn't be for myself, Mr Philip, for I only have myself to consider, and I never listen to gossip, anyway. It is you for whom I would be concerned.'

As he swung the swivel chair from side to side,

Philip laughed heartily. 'My dear Mrs Sinclair, I can assure you that there is, and always has been, lots of gossip about me. Why am I not married, for instance? Thirty years of age and still a bachelor! Oh, I could recount many things I've heard said about myself, mostly behind my back. But I am my own person, it is my life, and I really don't care what opinion people hold of me. I have a lot of true friends, who know the real Philip Astbury, and along with my parents they are the only ones I care about. As for office gossip, well, if anyone dared, I would laugh first, then give them a week's notice.'

Evelyn allowed herself a rare smile. She wasn't to know, but when she allowed that her face was transformed and she looked years younger. 'Oh, that's very drastic, Mr Philip, I really will have to watch myself. I enjoy working here and would not like to be given a week's notice for bad behaviour.'

'Then you had better keep on the right side of me, had you not?' Philip's tone was teasing. 'So, is it to be dinner at the State one night, or do I serve you with a week's notice?'

'I am sure I would find it very pleasant, and also sure you would be an entertaining escort. But I must admit to being afraid of what your Uncle Simon would say if he knew? Would he perhaps think me a gold digger?'

'Good grief, Mrs Sinclair, my uncle is well used to my taking lovely ladies out for meals. So too are my parents. And as I have said, apart from family and close friends, I really don't care what anyone else thinks about me. So forget all this tosh, and say you will do me the honour of allowing me to take you out for a meal one night? To cement our friendship, shall we say?'

Evelyn pondered as she tapped her pencil on the note-pad on her knee. 'And no one in this office would ever find out about it? As I am a very private person, that is important to me.'

'You have my word.' Philip was so pleased at the way things were going, he would have promised her anything. 'The office staff, my uncle, even my parents, won't be told. Now does that meet all your demands?'

'They are not demands, Mr Philip, I'm merely making sure my private life remains private. Anyway, I'm not sure I have a dress grand enough for the State, I will have to look through my wardrobe tonight. It is sadly depleted, unfortunately. After my husband died, I lost my zest for parties. But I'm fairly sure I can find something that won't embarrass you.'

'And how long am I going to have to wait for this night I am already growing excited about? This week, perhaps?'

Evelyn knew exactly when she would be going out with him, but had to make sure of her clothes first, and also work out what to do about Amelia. 'If not this week, then definitely next. Although I have to say, I am still not sure that this is a good thing. We have only known each other a week, and after two hours in each other's company may end up finding we have absolutely nothing in common. I may even find myself out of a job.'

'I think along different lines, my dear Mrs Sinclair. I believe we are going to get on wonderfully well together.'

151

Evelyn was in high spirits when she stepped off the tram. Before she'd fallen asleep last night, she had divided her plan into three phases. The first was to captivate Philip Astbury. For once he was hooked, she would never release him. The second phase was to sort herself out with the right clothes. And the third, and perhaps hardest, phase was to find a way of having Amelia minded on the night she wanted to be free. It wouldn't only be for one night either, she had high hopes of returning permanently to the good life. She couldn't abandon her daughter completely for if the neighbours found out the girl was in the house on her own they would create ructions. The only person who might be of help was Miss Maudsley. How fortunate the woman was fond of Amelia. But what excuse could she make? It could be tricky. Her neighbour was uneducated but not stupid by any means.

Evelyn loitered by a block of shops. It was part of the plan for her to be a little late tonight. She wasn't seeing anything in the windows, her mind was too full of all she was greedy for. A good life for herself. It could come about, but she must tread carefully or Philip would find out she was a liar and a fraud. She dawdled for a further five minutes, then turned the corner into her street. Reaching Bessie's yard door via the entry, she paused to force a smile to her face.

'I'm sorry I'm a little late this evening,' she said when Bessie opened the door. 'But I had the most marvellous surprise while I was waiting in Lord Street for my tram home. Standing at the

152

same stop was a girl I went to school with. I haven't seen her for fifteen years.'

'Come in.' Bessie closed the door behind her neighbour and waved her to the living room, where Amelia was playing with a board game. 'Say hello to yer mother, Amelia.'

The girl lifted her head, the dice in her hand ready to throw. 'Hello, Mother.'

Her greeting was answered by a nod as Evelyn sat down and carried on with the lie she had rehearsed. 'Oh, it was truly wonderful! We were both so happy to see each other again after all those years. Her name was Elizabeth Donaldson then, but she's married now and Mrs Waterson. She has two children, both at boarding school, and had been shopping in the city. Her husband was picking her up in his car, they'd arranged for her to be at the tram stop. As Elizabeth said, she could have got a taxi home but her husband wouldn't hear of it. So we had much to talk about, too little time.'

Bessie had taken a seat next to Amelia. She leaned her elbows on the table and cupped her chin in her hands. She listened without interrupting, but many thoughts were running through her head. Her usually stuck-up neighbour was being very friendly tonight, too friendly for Bessie's liking. There was something in the wind, but she was in no hurry to find out what, just let her neighbour carry on. They say if you give liars enough rope they will hang themselves, so this should be interesting. Bessie would bet a pound to a pinch of snuff Mrs Sinclair was lying through her teeth at the moment.

153

Putting Bessie's silence down to the fact that she was interested in her news, Evelyn carried on with her make-believe. 'She asked me to visit her one night so we could talk about our school days and the friends we had. And our teachers, of course, who were very strict and very old-fashioned! But, although I said I would try to visit her, I really don't see how I can. It would mean leaving Amelia in the house on her own...'

Bessie wasn't falling for that. And she'd just remembered another saying her mother used to have. It went something like: liars always get found out in the end 'cos they forget who they've told lies to. Yes, that was it. She could see her mother's face now in her mind, saying, 'Yer need to have a good memory to be a liar.' And Mrs Sinclair was certainly coming out with some whoppers. 'Oh, that's a pity, it would have been nice for yer, talking about yer school days with yer friend.'

Evelyn was growing irritated. She needed to sort something out tonight. Otherwise, if she told Philip tomorrow she hadn't got a definite date in mind, he'd think she was messing him around, or else hiding something from him. As she was. 'I wonder if I could go to visit her next Saturday, since you have kindly offered to have Amelia for tea? Would you mind?'

'It's got nothing to do with me what yer do, ye're old enough to make yer own decisions. I'm having Amelia for tea, so what you do in that time is yer own business.'

'Oh, you are so kind. I will really look forward to catching up with Elizabeth's news as I don't

154

get out very often. And would you mind if I was a little late getting home? I should hate to just rush in and out, we have so much to catch up with.'

Oh, so that's your game, is it? Bessie thought. We're getting to the root of your lies now. Ten to one there's no such person as your old school chum Elizabeth. More likely it's a bloke yer've got a date with. Well, if it is, more fool him. He doesn't know what he's letting himself in for. 'Oh, I can't have Amelia until late, Mrs Sinclair,' Bessie said, enjoying every second of it. 'Yer see, I've invited Rita Wells and Aggie Gordon for eight o'clock, just to have a birthday bottle of milk stout with me. I thought Amelia would probably have gone by then. And I can't put Rita and Aggie off now, they'd be upset 'cos they're me best mates.' Then, because she was so angry at the way this stuck-up bitch treated her daughter, Bessie rubbed salt in the wound.

'If it weren't for that, I'd say Amelia could stay later, even sleep here if it comes to that, 'cos I've got a single bed in the back room. But it's out of the question because I know yer don't like her to mix with the neighbours or any of the kids in the street in case they've got a disease or nits in their head. So I can't help yer out there, I'm afraid. Perhaps yer could visit yer friend another night, when I can keep Amelia for an extra hour or so?'

Evelyn's nostrils flared and she felt like hitting out at this silly old woman who would spoil her chances in life, just for the sake of a bottle of milk stout with her common-as-muck friends. But although she was seething, Evelyn didn't forget

155

the fact that this woman was her only chance, and without her she could say goodbye to all her hopes and dreams. With a huge effort she was able to say, 'I have no objection to Mrs Wells and Mrs Gordon. I'm sure they would behave very properly with Amelia in their company. And I'm sure my daughter would be very happy to stay until I get home. You really are most kind, Miss Maudsley, I am very lucky to have you as a friend and neighbour. So I accept your offer with deep gratitude.'

Although Amelia had her head bent as if studying the board game, Bessie could feel the tension coming from the girl. It was for her sake that Bessie replied, 'Well, in that case, Amelia might as well sleep here. I will send her to bed when I think it's time, or she tells me she is tired.' She put her arm across the girl's shoulders. 'Is that all right with you, sweetheart? Here's me and yer mother making plans without even asking what you want to do.'

The face that turned to her was aglow. Amelia's eyes were full of excitement and a smile creased her whole face. 'Oh, I'd love to sleep here, Miss Bessie.'

'That's settled then.' She got to her feet and gave Evelyn no option but to follow suit. The little woman had had enough of the lying and the high-handedness. 'Yer may as well go and see to yer meal, Mrs Sinclair, while me and Amelia finish our game of Snakes and Ladders. I'll send her as soon as the game is over.'

Evelyn was propelled towards the kitchen door. 'Thank you once again, Miss Maudsley, I will always be indebted to you.' She was feeling very relieved that the first date with Philip could be set and could see no reason why her neighbour would refuse to help in future. How fortunate it was that she had mentioned the bed in her spare room. 'It is definite for next Saturday then, is it? You see, I must write and tell my friend I shall be coming, and what time.'

Bessie stood as tall as her four foot eleven would allow. 'I do not tell lies, Mrs Sinclair, nor do I disappoint a young girl who is looking forward to her birthday celebration. I'll say goodnight to yer now, and get back to our game of Snakes and Ladders.' She was never rude or impolite unless she was pushed too far, but this was one time Bessie had gone past the stage where she would try to be polite. But for the sake of the girl she wasn't going to start a slanging match. Instead, she closed the door in her neighbour's face.

Chapter Eight

When the knock came on the door of his office, Cyril Lister-Sinclair took off his pince-nez spectacles and laid them on his huge mahogany desk. 'Come in.'

It was his secretary, Miss Williams, and she was carrying a sheaf of letters in her hand. 'I have these ready for signing, will you do them now or shall I leave them on the desk and you can ring for me when you have read and signed them?'

'Yes, leave them on the desk if you will, Miss Williams, and I'll attend to them shortly. I'm afraid this is one of those days when I really don't have the energy or the will, for work.'

When his secretary had closed the door behind her, Cyril let out a deep sigh. It was seven years now since Charles had been killed in action, and those years had not been kind to him. He had aged considerably, both physically and mentally. He had never come to terms with the loss of his son, and not a day went by when he didn't grieve for him. Charles had been the reason Cyril had built up a successful business, and become one of the wealthiest merchants in Liverpool. He loved his son dearly, and wanted to make sure he would never lack for anything in his life. He'd been Cyril's reason for living, and when he was killed there didn't seem any point any more. Why carry on making more money, or take a pride in his

158

business like he used to, when there was no one to leave it to? No one to take up the reins when he retired.

And at home there was no one who understood his grief, and his need to talk about his son. There were photographs of Charles everywhere, but no one mentioned him and that wasn't natural. It was his wife's doing. She'd wanted all the photographs removed because she'd said it broke her heart to look at them. It was one of the few times in his married life he'd put his foot down. His wife refused to mention her son's name, and said she'd lost the will to live. She was so full of self-pity she didn't notice her husband needed to talk about Charles, wanted to keep the boy's memory alive. Most of all he wanted the arms of a loving wife to comfort him. Even the house didn't seem like a home any more. Once it had been a place where Charles had brought his friends for partying, and the place rang with music, dancing and laughter as they dined on the very best of food and wines. Now the house was silent; even the servants talked in hushed tones. Never any laughter or the hubbub of conversation. Everything changed after Charles was killed.

Cyril's eyes rested on the sheaf of letters, and he was just reaching for them when a knock came on the door that he recognised. 'Come in, my boy, I know your knock by now.'

The face that came around the door had a mop of black hair, flashing brown eyes and a friendly smile. Just the sight of it lifted Cyril's spirits for this was Charles' best friend, Oscar Wentworth. The one person who loved to talk about his son,

159

who had been his school chum at five and was still his best friend when they were twenty-five. He missed him as much as Cyril did. He had been best man when Charles married Evelyn at the registry office on the day he'd left to fight in the war from which he never returned. A year later Oscar had married Gwen, Evelyn's friend and bridesmaid, and they now had two children.

'Sit down, my boy, and I'll ring for a pot of tea.' Just a few seconds after the bell on his desk tinkled, Miss Williams opened the door. She had worked there long enough to be able to say, 'The kettle is on the boil, just give me five minutes.'

'Miss Williams, what would I do without you?'

'Find another secretary who would put her foot down and say, "Please sign those letters, Mr Lister-Sinclair, so they can catch the lunchtime post".'

Cyril smiled, something he could do when Oscar was there. It brought a blessed release from tension. 'They will be signed by the time the tea arrives, Miss Williams, I don't want to be scolded.'

When they were alone, Oscar said, 'You are lucky with Miss Williams, Cyril, she's perfect. Friendly without overdoing it, and not afraid to smile. My father's secretary is like a little mouse, I've never seen her really smile in all the years she's worked for him. She shuffles along with her head down, and even one of my famous jokes doesn't light up her face. I tried for years, but I've given up now. Father is quite happy with her, her work is faultless. But I would prefer a spelling mistake that came with a smile.'

Cyril signed the correspondence, and pushed it

160

across the desk when the tea was brought in on a silver tray. 'There you are, my dear, signed and sealed.'

'Thank you.' Louise Williams smiled at the boss who was so kind and thoughtful she would go to the ends of the earth to please him. When she caught him looking sad, she was saddened, too. 'I'll be mother and pour. Then I'll leave you in peace and make sure those letters get to the post on time.'

While she was pouring, Cyril looked from her to Oscar, the two people who had helped him keep his sanity. Particularly Oscar who, since the day the telegram had arrived to say Charles had been killed, had seldom missed a day without visiting Cyril either at the office or at home. He was the one who snorted with derision when Cyril said he was thinking of selling off his business interests and retiring, for he had lost the competitive thrust needed to stay ahead of his rivals. But his son's friend wouldn't allow him to. He'd come into the office every day for a year and willed Cyril to reawaken the interest he'd always had. He knew that if his dear friend's father was at home all day, he would slowly fade away through lack of companionship, stimulating conversation and love. There was also the need to talk about Charles. Oscar was fond of Mrs Lister-Sinclair but thought her selfish, a little childish, lacking in humour and with no interest in her husband's businesses or what was going on in the world. And Oscar had been very straight about telling Cyril that if he was at home all day he would go crazy.

161

The tea poured, Miss Williams made her exit, saying over her shoulder, 'I've left room for .a touch of the whisky you have hidden in the side drawer.'

Oscar chuckled. 'She really is a treasure.'

'Clever, too,' Cyril said. 'She knows as much about this business as I do. If I were to absent myself from the office for a month, everything would still run smoothly.'

'If you want to take a holiday, Cyril, I could always come and work with Miss Williams to keep the wheels oiled. You could do with one, you know.'

'Who would I have for a companion? I would be as alone on holiday as I am here.' Cyril opened the side drawer and took out a bottle of whisky. After pouring a small measure into his cup, he handed it to Oscar. 'How is the family, my boy? Mother and father keeping well?'

'Both fine! Dad doesn't seem to grow any older for all he works hard. I'll swear he has more hairs on his head than I have. And Gwen and the children are well, although my wife has her hands full with the two boys. Charles is nearly six, and Richard just a year younger.'

'I was grateful to you and Gwen for calling your first-born Charles, it was very thoughtful of you.'

'Nonsense! Charles was my friend, the best anyone could have, I never considered any other name for my first son. And it was Gwen's wish too, not mine alone.'

Cyril looked down into his empty cup for a while, then asked, 'Gwen was friendly with Evelyn, wasn't she? I believe they were together

162

when Evelyn first met Charles.'

'Yes, I believe they were. I'd known Gwen for a while at that time, but there was nothing between us but friendship. The seeds of romance were sown at the registry office the day Charles and Evelyn were married.'

'Does she still see Evelyn?'

Oscar looked surprised. 'No, I think she only called to see her once after the baby was born. Amelia, I believe the child was called.'

'Yes, I saw the baby, and she was called Amelia, but whether she was ever christened I do not know. Over the years I've many times wondered if I was wrong about Evelyn. You know the story she told me, and I didn't believe her because I didn't think my son capable of treating the woman he wanted for his wife in such a shabby way. The child bore no resemblance to Charles at all. Colouring, features, nothing that would lead me to think she was my son's child. And on top of that there were no tears of sorrow when I told her Charles had been killed, she never went into mourning. In fact, what really sickened me was the way she failed to ask what the telegram said, or where or how Charles died. There was not one tear shed. The only words she uttered, were, "What's going to happen to me?"' He placed the cup and saucer on the silver tray. 'But always at the back of my mind I'm asking myself, did I do right? I don't worry about Evelyn because I never did like her, she was shallow and selfish. But what if Charles was the father of the baby, and for seven years I've never bothered to find out about the child? I've left it so long now, I wouldn't know where to start. But I'd hate to go to my grave wondering if I had made my son's child an outcast.'

'There must be some way of finding her if that's what you want, Cyril. I'll have a word with Gwen, see if she has any way of finding where Evelyn disappeared to.'

'When I asked her to vacate the house in Princes Avenue, I did suggest she tried the property letting office in Moorfields. Whether she ever went there I don't know, but it's the last thing I remember saying to her. Oh, and I told her to take whatever items of furniture and bedding she would need. That is all I can tell you.' There was a plea for help and understanding in the eyes searching Oscar's face. 'What are your thoughts, Oscar? Was I wrong in the actions I took? Too quick to judge? Was I perhaps hitting back at her for not being heartbroken, as I was?' Cyril ran a finger across his forehead. 'I know you are the one person I can rely on to tell me exactly what you think. So, in my place, what would you have done, then and now?'

'Acted as you did at the time, Cyril, without any doubt. Evelyn's actions would have hurt and angered me. But they would not have surprised me, I was never an admirer of hers. Never thought she was good enough for Charles, but he was besotted and wouldn't listen. However, since it means such a lot to you, I will be perfectly frank. Over the years, like yourself, I have had doubts niggling at the back of my mind. Was Charles the father of the child? Could he have lost control because he was going away to a foreign country to fight in a bloody war that was claiming the lives of millions of men? If he did act out of character, who are we to blame him? I for one would not think badly of him, for he was a good man and a friend I was proud to have.' Oscar leaned forward to put a hand on the teapot. 'Talking is giving me a thirst, and this tea is still warm enough to be drinkable.'

'I'll ring for a fresh pot,' Cyril said, reaching out to press the bell. 'I feel quite thirsty myself.'

Oscar covered his hand. 'No, don't ring. Why don't I finish what I have to say, then we can adjourn to the club for lunch and a drink? We can spend an hour going over what we've discussed and see where we want to go from there.' He grinned. 'It's nice and quiet there, and although I am partial to a drop of whisky, my favourite tipple is claret.'

'Good thinking, my dear boy. The chairs are more comfortable there, too!'

'I forbid you to fall asleep in them, Cyril. My imagination is fired now, and I want an answer to the question that has plagued both of us for seven years.' Oscar sank back in his chair. 'One thing you should perhaps know is that at the age of one month, all babies look alike. Mine both had blue eyes and mousy hair. At eight months their eyes were brown and their hair dark. Then we could see baby Charles gradually taking on my features, when his nose became the shape of mine. And the same thing happened a year later with Richard. Blue eyes, mousy hair at birth, then six months later the spitting image of me. So you really wouldn't have been able to make any judgement

165

on baby Amelia, she was far too young for anyone to say who she resembled.' He went to push himself out of the chair. 'Shall we make our way to the club now?'

'Can we just go a little further here first, my boy, and then smooth the details out at the club? The main question I want to ask is, do you think it's too late to try and solve the mystery or shall I begin to search for Evelyn and her daughter? I could hire a private investigator, that would speed things up. I wouldn't know where to start myself.'

'I think we both know the answer to that in our hearts, Cyril. If we don't try, we will always wonder what the truth is. I definitely think we should waste no time, enough has been lost already. We may be disillusioned at the end of our search, but at least we will have tried and will not be burdened with guilt for the rest of our lives. But rather than hire a private detective, I would like to start the search myself. I would feel I was helping Charles. I could start at the property letting office in Moorfields. I know that many years have passed, but they must keep records. Have you any recollection of the date Evelyn left Princes Avenue? That would be a help.'

Cyril rubbed his chin, his brow furrowed in concentration. 'I remember the baby was born on the eighteenth of September, the maid brought a note to inform me. That was in seventeen. Evelyn and the baby left the house one month later. That means her daughter will be eight next week.' A catch came to his voice, and an unwelcome tear to his eyes. 'What a stupid, blind fool I've been to have left it so long! If she is Charles' daughter, I have missed seven years of my granddaughter's life.'

'Come now, Cyril, this is no time for self-pity. If we find the girl, and find proof that she is your granddaughter, then think of the happiness it will bring you and your wife. It would change your whole lives, give you something to live for. It will also give you back a part of your son. If we are not successful in finding mother and daughter, then you will have lost nothing. But let's think positive, it's half the battle.'

'Are you sure you want to take such a task on, my dear boy?' Cyril asked. 'I would willingly hire a detective.'

Oscar shook his head. 'I want to do it to put your mind at rest, and my own. But most of all, I want to do it for Charles.'

The following morning Oscar entered the premises of the property letting office in Moorfields. He was well dressed and had an air of authority about him, so one of the two men behind the counter came over to him immediately. 'Can I help you, sir?'

'I hope so, my good man, but my quest is not an easy one. I am trying to trace a woman who may have rented a house from you in October nineteen seventeen. Rather a long shot, I know, but I would be grateful if you could assist me. It's important to a friend that we should trace this woman and her child.'

'We keep records of all our tenants, sir, and they go back some twenty years. If you can give me the family's name, I can certainly look it up for you.'

'The lady in question is a Mrs Lister-Sinclair, and she was a widow with a new baby.'

The man's face showed his surprise, for the Lister-Sinclair name was known by most business people in the city. 'Oh, I don't think I can help you, sir. I've worked here since the office opened, twenty years ago, and know all the names of the people who rent our property. I can safely say I would have remembered if anyone of that name had registered with us, it is a name well known in the city.'

Oscar's heart sank for a second, then he had an idea. 'It is possible the lady married again, so could I crave your indulgence and ask to look in your tenants' book for a name I might recognise? I am prepared to pay you a pound for your time.'

The man's colleague left the person he was talking to and came down the counter. A pound was almost a week's wages, and he wanted his share. Particularly as he was the senior clerk. 'Bring the book out, Watson, and let the gentleman look through himself to see if any of the names rings a bell.' He gave Oscar his best smile. 'We are always willing to help, sir.'

The large, hardbacked book was well thumbed, and as the clerk opened it a sprinkling of dust rose from its spine. Although he was seeing it upside down, Oscar could see the first dates were in January, and said, 'Could you start at the October entries, please? I believe that would be nearer the time she would have applied to you for rented accommodation.'

The clerk turned the book around so Oscar could read the entries. 'If as you say, sir, the lady may have married again, then she would have registered under her new husband's name. But if you wish to check, then you are very welcome.'

Oscar was beginning to think he was on a wild goose chase. He had lost the feeling of optimism he'd had when he'd walked into the shop. It all seemed pretty hopeless if the two clerks didn't remember a name that would stick in most people's minds. Still, the man had been kind enough to take the trouble of rooting the book out, the least he could do was take a look. He went down the list of names, and was about to admit defeat when the name Mrs E. Sinclair seemed to jump off the page. He tried not to let his excitement show, he didn't want to divulge any of Cyril's private business.

'This is a possibility – Mrs E. Sinclair. There was a slight tiff in the family and to alter her name was probably her way of getting her own back. All over a silly quarrel, she was just cutting off her nose to spite her face. Anyhow, it's worth a try, so if you would be good enough to give me her address, I would be most grateful.'

'Oh, I couldn't give you her present address, sir. She is no longer a tenant of ours. She handed in her rent book several years ago. I can remember her vaguely, an attractive woman. A bit standoffish, if my memory serves me right, but a good looker.'

'When she left, did she leave you a forwarding address, or give you any idea where she was moving to?'

The senior clerk had finished with his customer and came down the counter. 'I remember her, too, sir, she rented from us for about four years. When she came in with her money for the week's notice, I did ask why she was leaving and where she was going. But she was reluctant to talk, merely said she had found somewhere more suitable.'

'Would you be allowed to give me her old address, then, and I can try the neighbours there, see if she was more forthcoming with them?'

The older man nodded. 'Get the books out, Watson, and help the gentleman. If I am not mistaken, Mrs Sinclair rented a property in Bedford Road. But if you go through the books, you can give him the correct address. And please be quick about it, Watson, I'm sure the gentleman hasn't got time to waste.'

The clerk disappeared into a back office and was away for ten minutes. When he returned he had a look of triumph on his face and dust all over his jacket. 'I've got it, sir. I'll write the address down for you when I've wiped some of the dust off my hands.' The pound note he'd been promised would now have to be shared with his senior, which he felt was a bit unfair, but still, ten bob was a lot of money and his wife would be over the moon when he handed it over to her. They'd be able to have a roast dinner on Sunday, with a large joint of meat. 'I do hope you are successful, sir,' he said, handing over a piece of paper with an address on. 'Bedford Road is easy to find, it's off Stanley Road and the trams stop on the corner.'

170

'That is exceedingly kind of you, you have been most helpful. But I know where Bedford Road is, and I have my own transport.' Oscar dipped his hand into his waistcoat pocket and brought out the pound note he'd carefully folded before entering the office. 'Here you are, my good man, this is for your co-operation which I can assure you was most appreciated.'

He placed the note on the counter and out of the corner of his eye could see the senior clerk edging his way towards it. He knew that as soon as the door closed behind him the two men would argue over how the money should be shared.

Once out of the property letting office, Oscar walked the few yards to his car. Sitting behind the wheel, he glanced at the slip of paper, made a mental note of the address, and slipped it into his jacket pocket. Then as he switched on the ignition, he said aloud, 'I can but try. For Cyril's sake, and my own, I pray I have some success.'

It wasn't a great distance from the city centre to Bedford Road, and soon Oscar was sitting outside the house where Evelyn and her daughter had lived. It was a come-down from what she was used to, but nevertheless it was a nice road with plenty of greenery in the gardens, and the houses looked solid and well cared for. He decided not to knock on the door of the address he'd been given but instead to knock at a neighbour's house and ask if the tenant had been living there at the time Evelyn lived next door. It was to be hoped the person wouldn't think he was up to no good and slam the door in his face. But he assured himself that, although he wasn't gifted with film-star looks, he didn't look disreputable enough to be a beggar.

Oscar failed to notice, as he opened the iron gate, that the net curtain in the front window was already twitching. The woman watching him was asking herself who this swank was, coming to her house. He wasn't a canvasser, and certainly not a rag and bone man. His clothes were expensive, and there was the car parked outside her house. She'd never had a toff like him walking up her path before, and she'd never known anyone who had a car. Perhaps she shouldn't open the door to a stranger, 'cos her Ted would go mad if she let herself be talked into anything. Only last week she'd bought some pegs off a gypsy because she believed it was bad luck to refuse, and her husband called her for all the silly buggers going. But she couldn't not open the door to this man 'cos she wouldn't sleep tonight for wondering what he'd wanted. So, when the knock came, Sarah Higgins straightened her pinny and patted her hair before opening the door. She mightn't have much money, but she did have her pride.

'I'm sorry to bother you,' Oscar said, 'but I've come to see if you can help me trace someone for a friend of mine. Her name was Evelyn Sinclair, and I believe she was once a neighbour of yours?'

Sarah nodded. 'She used to live next door, yes.' The thought entered her head that if she did tell this toff what she thought of her former neighbour, then she didn't want the neighbours to know. And remembering she'd given the parlour a good dusting and polishing this morning, she thought she may as well show off. 'Would you like to come in?' she asked in her very poshest voice. 'I'm not one for standing at the door nattering, I think it's common.'

Oscar was amused, but didn't let it show in his smile. 'That is most kind of you, and also very trusting. After all, you don't know me and I could be a bogeyman.'

'I'm a pretty good judge of character,' Sarah said, holding the door open and hoping all the neighbours were watching. 'The parlour is the first door on your left. I'm sorry there isn't a fire going, but my husband and I use the living room in the winter.' She congratulated herself on speaking in her best accent. 'Unless you are cold, of course. If so we can go through to the living room and I can make a pot of tea.'

'That's jolly good of you! Yes, I would like that. A cup of tea is always welcome.'

Ten minutes later he was sitting facing her across a table covered by a maroon chenille cloth, with an aspidistra plant standing square in the centre.

'This is really very kind of you, Mrs, er, Mrs...?'

'Mrs Higgins – Sarah Higgins. And can I ask your name, please?'

'Oscar Wentworth, Mrs Higgins, and I have to say I am quite overwhelmed by your hospitality.'

Sarah, who had used her best china cups and saucers, waved the compliment aside. 'I would never keep anyone on the step, especially someone as respectable-looking as yourself. And about Mrs Sinclair – did you say a friend of yours was trying to find her?'

Oscar had no intention of bringing Cyril's name into the conversation, so he chose his words carefully. 'Yes, he is quite elderly, and met her many years ago. He knew she had a daughter and was wondering how they were faring. It's not desperately important that he find her, mind you, but I took it upon myself to try, as a surprise to him. That's if I can trace her, of course.'

'Well, much as I'd like to help you, I'm afraid I can't tell you a lot about her, or where she is now. She wasn't a very friendly person, not the neighbourly type at all. I did offer to help when she was moving in, and so did the neighbour on the other side of her, but she turned us down. Several times in the winter I knocked to say I'd mind the baby while she went to the shops, but no, she refused point blank. If the weather was bad she'd leave the baby in the house alone while she went shopping. And she didn't turn you down in a nice way, she didn't even have the grace to thank you for offering. So after that I didn't bother because she was a cold person and very stuck-up. Thought she was too good for the people round here.' Then Sarah decided she'd better watch her tongue in case she landed herself in trouble. 'The baby was a lovely little thing, though, very quiet and good. I used to feel sorry for her 'cos she seldom went out. And for a child of her age, she was very well spoken. She sounded more like a grown-up than a child, but that's 'cos she never mixed with other children.'

'Did she take after her mother in looks?' Oscar asked casually. 'My friend said Mrs Sinclair was an attractive woman.'

174

Sarah pursed her lips and frowned as she tried to bring pictures of the couple to mind. 'Mrs Sinclair had dark hair, but the girl's was much darker, almost jet black. And their eyes were different, if my memory serves me right. The mother's were dark brown, but the girl's were more of a greeny-hazel. She had her mother's way of speaking and walked like her, with her back as straight as a rod. I can still hear Mrs Sinclair's voice coming through the wall, saying, "Straighten your back, Amelia, and hold your head high." I often said to myself that she'd make the girl into an old woman before she'd had her childhood.'

Oscar felt his heart pounding as memories of Charles' face flashed into his mind. His friend with his green eyes lit up with humour and a lock of black hair falling on to his forehead. The images seemed so real he felt he could reach out and touch the man who had been his friend for years, and for whom he still grieved. He mentally shook away the memories, for he could see Sarah watching him. 'Was she a good mother to the child?'

'She thought she was, but you wouldn't find any neighbours who would agree with her.' She caught and held Oscar's eyes. 'I don't know you from Adam, and I'm probably talking out of turn, but so help me God, I'm speaking the truth. There was no love in that house while Mrs Sinclair lived there. Far from being a good mother, she didn't seem to have any affection for that poor child. And although it's a few years now since they left, I often think about them. Not the

175

mother, I couldn't care less what happens to her, but I'd like to know if the girl is being well treated. Trying to look on the bright side, I keep telling myself she'll be going to school now, and will probably have made friends of her own age to play with. I certainly hope so, she deserves better than she was getting when she lived here.'

Oscar sighed. 'And Mrs Sinclair gave no hint where she was moving to?'

'Mr Wentworth, she didn't even tell us she *was* leaving. And no one saw her going, so she must have had the removal cart or van here when it was dark and we were all in bed.' The memory was too much for Sarah, who started to feel angry. 'You will have to excuse me, Mr Wentworth. I'm ashamed of what I'm going to say to a gentleman like yourself, but I've got to get it off my chest. Mrs Sinclair left here without so much as a wave, a goodbye or a kiss my backside! She thinks she's the whole cheese, but she is the most ignorant woman I have ever met. And there you have it in a nutshell.'

'She doesn't sound like a pleasant person, I must say.' Oscar was feeling really let down. 'My friend spoke so highly of her, but it seems he is not the judge of character that you are, Mrs Higgins. Oh, dear, I am glad I didn't tell him what I was up to. It would have given him false hope. My best bet is probably to keep quiet and then he won't have lost anything. It does seem strange, though, that a woman and her child can live in a house for four years and not get to make friends with one single human being. One would have thought Mrs Sinclair would have been glad of company and someone to talk to. It must have been a very lonely life for her and the young girl.'

Sarah averted her eyes before saying, 'Oh, she did talk to one person – and that's the man in the pawnbroker's shop. Very often you would see her leaving the house with a wrapped parcel under her arm. I was only one of many who saw her going into the pawn shop with that parcel, and come out five minutes later without it.'

'A pawn shop?' Oscar looked stunned. 'You do surprise me. I thought the lady was comfortably off.'

'I wouldn't lie to you, Mr Wentworth, I'm a regular churchgoer and live by the Ten Commandments. The odd swear word slips my lips occasionally, but only very mild ones.'

'You are a good woman, Mrs Higgins, and a kind one. I am very grateful for your help and your friendliness. Now I will leave you, I have taken up far too much of your time. But before I go, I would like to ask one more favour from you. While I am in the area, I think I may as well call in to the pawnbroker's shop to see if he knows the whereabouts of Mrs Sinclair. Could you tell me where I might find it?'

'It's in Stanley Road, Mr Wentworth, not five minutes' walk from here. If you drive back to the junction of Stanley Road and turn left, you'll find it's in the second block of shops. You can't miss it, there are three brass balls hanging outside.'

Oscar pointed to a framed picture standing proudly on the sideboard. 'Are they your grandchildren?'

Sarah was off her chair like a shot to fetch the

picture to him. There was real pride in her voice when she said, 'That's Bobby, he's ten in two months, and the girl is Theresa, she's eight. They're bonny kids, and me and my husband love the bones of them.'

'I have two sons, Mrs Higgins, and I love the bones of them!' It was an expression Oscar had never heard before, but he liked it, it sat well on his tongue and in his heart. 'Yes, indeed, I love the bones of them.'

While Sarah was replacing the photograph on the sideboard, and standing back to make sure it was arranged just right, Oscar took a wallet from his inside pocket. He took out two pound notes and returned the wallet quickly before she turned around. He had thought of putting the notes under the plant pot on the table to save any embarrassment, then decided that wasn't quite the thing to do. So when Sarah was showing him to the door, he asked, 'Would you be offended if I gave you a few shillings to buy some sweets for your grandchildren? It would give me great pleasure if you would accept.'

Sarah's brows shot up when she looked down at the notes in his hand. 'I can't take two pound off you, that's a lot of money!'

'Mrs Higgins, you took a total stranger into your home and treated him with warmth and friendliness. The only way I can repay that kindness is through your grandchildren. So please take it, and make me and them happy. What I am giving you doesn't match up to what you have given me.' He placed his black bowler hat on his head, patted the top of it, then smiled. 'Thank you again, Mrs

178

Higgins, and who knows but we may meet again some day?'

Oscar walked down the path leaving Sarah staring down at the two pound notes in her hand. And as he opened the gate, he heard her say, 'Well, did yer ever! Just wait until my Ted comes in, I bet he won't believe the day I've had.'

Chapter Nine

Oscar came out of the pawnbroker's shop feeling
despondent. He was no better off now than when
he'd walked into the shop. The man behind the
counter had been less than forthcoming. Yes, he'd
admitted, he remembered Mrs Sinclair, but
would give no other details as they were con-
fidential. And no, he hadn't any knowledge of her
present whereabouts. He had looked genuinely
surprised when Oscar mentioned that she had a
daughter, and it was very obvious he was sincere
when he said he didn't know there was a child.
But as to the transactions between himself and
Mrs Sinclair, he was not in a position to divulge
the affairs of a customer.

As he sat behind the wheel of his car, Oscar was
in a dilemma. Should he tell Cyril what he'd
heard from Mrs Higgins, or should he lie and say
he was unable to obtain any facts about Evelyn
and her daughter? At first he thought that would
be the kindest thing to do, and then perhaps
Cyril would put the ghost of the past behind him.
But, on reflection, Oscar decided he couldn't lie
to a man he admired and was very fond of.
Besides, he himself didn't want to put the past
behind him, he couldn't. Not after he'd been told
a child, who might be Charles' flesh and blood,
was unloved and being badly treated. Another
thing he couldn't ignore: hadn't Mrs Higgins

said Amelia didn't take after her mother in looks, and also mentioned jet black hair and green eyes? The woman wouldn't just make that up, there must be some truth in it. And if so, then all the more reason to trace the child who could make a difference to so many lives. It would bring such happiness to Cyril and his wife Matilda. It would give them a new lease of life, something to live for, and hopefully bring them closer together. And as for me, Oscar thought, I would spend the rest of my life happy in the knowledge that if Charles is looking down, he can be at peace, knowing those who have never stopped loving and thinking of him, are there for his daughter.

As he neared the offices of Cyril Lister-Sinclair, Oscar cursed himself for being so sentimental. But he couldn't help being the way he was, nor could he help the tear that rolled down his cheek as he switched the car's engine off. And he knew worse was to come. If he repeated everything he had found out, it was bound to have Cyril in tears.

Without giving himself any more time to think, Oscar locked the car, strode through the double doors and ran lightly up the flight of stairs. He managed a grin at the surprise on Miss Williams' face. 'I know I'm not expected, and if Mr Lister-Sinclair is engaged, I will come back later.'

'He's had a busy morning with meetings, but he's alone now. I've just taken him a cup of tea through. I'll tell him you're here then make a fresh brew.'

'Don't get up, Miss Williams, he knows my knock by now. And I'm going to talk him into

181

coming to the club for an hour so he can see some of his friends. He doesn't get out nearly enough, and needs some male company. If I come out carrying him over my shoulder, don't be alarmed. It just means he's made an excuse not to go out, and I refuse to take it. He needs fresh air and he needs company.'

Miss Williams grinned as she nodded. 'I'm glad you come so often to see him, Mr Wentworth, because you're good for him. His business associates are kind, but they're here to work while you come as a friend. That makes a big difference. Give him a knock, he'll be glad to see you.'

Oscar rapped on the door with a knuckle, waited until he heard his friend's voice, then walked in. 'I've been told by your irreplaceable secretary that you've had a hectic morning, old boy, so I am here to whisk you off to the club for a couple of drinks. And some interesting conversation, of course. There would be no point in leaving here just to sit there looking at each other.'

'I'm afraid I have nothing of interest to talk about,' Cyril said, 'my life is a very dull one and I'm not the most interesting of companions.'

'Have no fear, I shall keep the conversation flowing, my good man, as long as you keep the claret flowing. Am I not noted for being articulate and amusing?'

Cyril chortled as he picked up a stack of papers and put them in one of the deep side drawers. 'How can I resist such an invitation?' But he wasn't fooled by Oscar's jovial manner. He had grown to know the younger man very well over the years, and although he was always happy and talkative, there was something different about him today. It was as though he was bubbling with excitement inside, and trying to contain it. 'You seem in a good mood this afternoon, Oscar, is there a reason for it?'

'All shall be revealed later, when I have a glass of claret in my hand. But don't think I have any earth-shattering news to tell you, I'm afraid that's not the case. Still, there is a topic we can talk about, and that should give us something to mull over while sampling the excellent wines from the club's cellar. So, after giving Miss Williams instructions that if anyone calls you will not be back in the office for the rest of the day, we shall be on our merry way.'

Cyril leaned forward from his deeply sprung leather chair and raised his glass. 'A toast to our friendship, what say you?'

Oscar nodded. 'To our lasting friendship, I say.' He was giving every appearance of being his usual chatty self, without a care in the world. Yet inside he was still full of doubt. He wanted to do what was best for the older man, say what would make him the happiest. But deep down he knew Cyril Lister-Sinclair was a man who would want to know the truth, not a lie that was supposed to make him feel good. 'Now, I don't quite know whether I'm doing the right thing here, Cyril. I have spent an hour going over the pros and cons. However, I have reached the conclusion, rightly or wrongly, that you would prefer the plain unvarnished truth.'

Cyril's hand began to shake around the glass he was holding. 'You have found Evelyn and the girl?'

Oscar shook his head. 'No, I'm afraid this story does not have a happy ending. But one day it will, and that is my promise to you.' He took a deep breath. 'This morning I visited the property letting office in Moorfields.' He held up one hand as Cyril went to speak. 'Don't say anything yet, Cyril, wait until you hear everything I have been able to unearth about Evelyn and Amelia.' He lifted his glass. 'This is to give me courage and to loosen my tongue.' After drinking deeply, he set the glass down and began his tale. He left nothing out, and gave it word for word. He did try to keep it light, though, even repeating Mrs Higgins' remark: 'Mrs Sinclair left here without so much as a wave, a goodbye, or a kiss me backside'.

Nevertheless a sigh came from deep within Cyril. 'That is a heartbreaking story to listen to, my boy, especially as it is possible this child is my granddaughter after all. To think I have left her with a woman who appears to have a heart of stone! This neighbour of hers, Mrs Higgins, appears to be a kind and truthful person. I think we can believe what she says.'

'Oh, without a doubt! I believed her when she said she offered to help with the baby many times, that is the type of person she is. I was a total stranger knocking on her door, yet she took me in and made me feel right at home.'

'We have to find them, Oscar. I couldn't live

184

with myself, knowing there is the possibility of the girl being Charles' daughter. I will hire the best private investigator there is. If necessary I will bring one from London.'

Oscar gazed down at his shoes for a few seconds, then raised his head. 'Cyril, I'm going to ask you to let me find them. It would be quicker, perhaps, with a detective, but think what sort of private matters he may unearth in the course of his work. There may be skeletons in the cupboard, Cyril, that you wouldn't wish to become public knowledge. Evelyn used the name Sinclair to both the letting office and to her neighbours, but she could easily revert back to Lister-Sinclair and cause trouble for you.'

Cyril shook his head. 'I never told you because I didn't think it was important at the time. When I believed the child was illegitimate, and because I was so sad at losing Charles and angry at Evelyn for blackening his name, I told her the marriage was to be annulled on the grounds it was never consummated, and if she put Charles' name down on the birth certificate as the father, I would take legal action against her. What a stupid man I was! Why didn't I let more time pass before making a judgement? I pray to God Amelia is my grandchild, but will God think I am worthy of her after the way I treated her mother?'

'Never have any regrets for the way you treated Evelyn, because from what I knew of her, and from what I've heard today from someone who lived next door to her for several years, she is not a nice person. She's selfish, without any capacity to love anyone but herself. I agree we must find her, not for her sake but for the girl's. Now I'm going to ask you again, please let me be the one to seek them out? I need to do it, Cyril, so I can remember my best friend with a clear conscience. It may take me a while, because Liverpool is a big city with many suburbs, but I promise you I will never give up until they are found.'

'You have my blessing, Oscar. All I ask is for you to keep in touch and update me with your findings.'

'I will still call in every day, my dear friend, and keep you informed. I have already begun to make plans in my head. I think a good start would be the schools. I realise there are hundreds of them, if not more. As I said, Liverpool covers a very wide area. But one has to start somewhere, and as Amelia must go to a school, then that is where I shall start.' Oscar lifted his glass. 'A toast to success.'

At the same time the two men were drinking to their hope of finding her, Amelia was running down the street on her way home from school. She was wearing as big a smile today as she wore every day now. Those two hours with Bessie each night had brought about a radical change in the girl. While she was still quiet and polite with her mother, she was vastly different with their neighbour next door. Bessie gave her the hugs and kisses she had never had before. Amelia had come to love the little woman, and in return was loved back. For the first couple of days she had followed her mother's instructions and reached Bessie's house down the back entry, but Bessie put a stop to that. And she did it in a way that had the girl doubled up with laughter.

'Yer'd better start using me front door if yer know what's good for yer, sweetheart, 'cos I got a good telling off over you. "Aren't I good enough for her?" That's what me door said, and it was in a right temper, I can tell yer. In fact, I thought it wasn't going to let me in. "I'm as good as any door in this street, in fact I'm better than some what have got no brass knockers, so you tell her from me I am not a bit happy about her deciding that the dirty old yard door is better than me".'

Amelia had run and put her arms around Bessie's waist then. 'Oh, you *are* funny, Miss Bessie. It was my mother who told me to use the entry, but I think I'd better apologise to the door, don't you? I mean, it might not open and close for me if it doesn't like me.'

'Oh, worse than that, sweetheart, you don't know my door. Because I keep it well washed and polished, and the brass shining enough to blind yer, it thinks it's the pig's ear. And if it thought for one moment that yer didn't think it was the most handsome door in the street, well, it would bang in yer face to let yer know who's boss.'

And so Amelia never used the entry after that. Her mother thought she did, but as she'd never asked, the girl didn't have to lie to her. It was a source of fun to Amelia, and every afternoon she would have something to say before she knocked on the door. Today she said, 'You look very posh today, Mr Door, I think you've been given a good polish. The most handsomest door in the street, I bet.'

Rita Wells had been told the joke about the door, and when she saw Amelia's lips moving gave a satisfied smile. The girl had changed so much in such a short time, Bessie was to be congratulated. As it was the birthday party on Saturday Rita was looking forward to getting to know Amelia better, and wanted her to know that if Bessie was ever late getting in from work, she could always cross the road to the Wellses' house.

Just then the door opposite opened and Bessie appeared with her arms held wide and a smile of welcome on her face. The girl didn't hesitate to walk into them. It was a happy sight, and Rita sniffed up to keep the tears back. She prayed this story would have a happy ending and her best mate's heart wouldn't be broken.

'Hello, sweetheart.' Bessie held Amelia from her for a moment. 'Yer cheeks are as red as the rosy apples on Tommy Flannigan's fruit cart. Have yer been running?'

'I always run home, Miss Bessie, 'cos the sooner I get home, the more time I have to sit with you and listen to you talking to the fireplace.'

Bessie noted the word 'home', and although it gave her a lovely warm glow inside, she was afraid that if Mrs Sinclair heard she might perhaps put a stop to the arrangement, for she looked the type who didn't like to see people happy. 'Oh, I've already had a row with the grate, sweetheart, and believe me it needs taking down a peg or two 'cos it's getting too cocky for my liking. Yer see, when I was walking home from work I thought I felt a nip in the air, and decided to light a fire so

188

we wouldn't be cold. So I laid the paper and wood down, then struck a match to light the paper. I had the shovel of coal all ready, nice-sized cobs what looked as though they'd catch easy. But, blow me, every time I struck a match, a gust of wind came down the chimney and blew it out. And because yer can't see wind to tell it off, or give it a good hiding, I put the blame on the grate and we had a real set-to. And talk about cheek! Well, I've never heard the likes of it. If I'd talked back to my mam like that, God rest her soul, then I'd have had me backside tanned.' They were in the living room by this time, and Bessie nodded towards the fireplace where a small fire was struggling for survival. Shaking her fist, she said, 'If yer don't pull yer socks up, I'll not be cleaning you out in the morning. Yer can wallow in yer dirty ashes till I come home from work.'

As though a magic wand had been waved, a single bright flame shot up, and when it began to flicker it looked as though it was dancing. 'Look, it's dancing, Miss Bessie! I bet it's trying to say it's sorry and it won't be naughty again.'

'Oh, a belly dance won't get it back in my good books, so it needn't bother. When I see flames going up the chimney, then I just might consider forgiving it. Only might, like, that's not for certain.' Bessie put her arm across the girl's shoulder. 'It's only poached egg on toast for tea tonight, sweetheart, 'cos I'm not long in and haven't had time to do potatoes. But I scrounged a few bacon ribs off the butcher, so tomorrow night we'll have potatoes mashed with the top of the milk, and lovely bacon ribs.' She rubbed her tummy. 'Ooh, I can feel me mouth watering at the thought.'

There was a frown on Amelia's pretty face. 'What are bacon ribs, Miss Bessie? I know what ribs are 'cos we've all got them and I can feel mine. But I've never heard of bacon ribs that you can eat.'

Bessie ground her teeth. What on earth had this child and her mother been living on? Never heard of bacon ribs, indeed. 'Then ye're in for a treat, sweetheart, 'cos they are delicious with cabbage and mashed spuds. The best way to eat them is to hold them between yer fingers and bite the meat off the bone. Sweet as honey, it is.'

Amelia's eyes were wide. 'I'm learning a lot from you, Miss Bessie. Things I've never heard of before.' Her green eyes sparkled. 'Like ribs that are as sweet as honey, and you eat them with your fingers. And a talking door and fireplace. I bet none of the girls in my class have doors and fireplaces that talk.'

'Ah, well, they're our secret, sweetheart, and you mustn't tell yer friends or they'll be jealous.' Mentally Bessie added that if anyone knew what they were on about, they'd think her and Amelia were ready for the loony bin.

The girl nodded. 'I won't tell Mother, either, or she'll tell me not to be so silly. But it's not silly, is it, Miss Bessie, not when it's only in fun?'

At that very moment, Evelyn couldn't have cared less what her daughter did. In fact, she very seldom gave a thought to Amelia during the day.

190

Particularly today. She was feeling very pleased with herself. She'd asked Philip if it was possible for her to leave half an hour early as she wanted to pick up an outfit she'd put in to be cleaned and the shop closed at half-past five. As Saturday was drawing near, and he intended to use their date to find out if she was really as cold as she seemed, he agreed to her leaving early so long as she made the excuse of not feeling well to the rest of the staff.

Evelyn hurried down the entry with her head bent. The precious dress and cape were wrapped in tissue paper, and she carried them carefully. She wanted to look stunning on Saturday, and her dress must be free from creases. She had it all planned in her head. On Saturday night she intended to be cool with Philip, but a little coquettish to keep his interest roused. If she played her cards right, she'd have him eating out of her hand before the night was over. The only problem she had was meeting him. He wanted to pick her up in his car, but she'd kept her air of mystery and shaken her head, saying she would take a taxi and meet him inside the State Hotel. The only way she could think of doing this was to leave her best clothes in one of the left luggage boxes in Exchange Station on Friday night, take the tram down on Saturday and change in the ladies' lavatory. Not the best way of doing things, but she couldn't risk letting him see where she lived, nor could she let the neighbours see her walking down the street in her finery.

After opening the entry door, Evelyn crept quietly up the yard. If Miss Maudsley heard her,

191

she'd wonder why she hadn't called for Amelia first. Then she tip-toed upstairs to hang the dress and cape on a hanger. She was delighted it had cleaned up so well and looked almost new. Even the dreaded smell of damp had gone.

In the space of a few minutes she was knocking on her neighbour's door. And because her day had been fruitful, and her future looked bright, tonight she actually smiled at her daughter. 'I hope you've been good for Miss Maudsley? And you do realise how kind she is, looking after you for two hours every night? You and I would be lost without her.'

Just before the knock had come on the kitchen door, Amelia had been shaking with laughter and looking happy and care-free, as any girl her age should. Now she was standing straight-faced, her body as stiff as a board. 'Yes, Mother.'

Bessie had seen the change come over the girl and was boiling inside. 'Your daughter is very well behaved, Mrs Sinclair,' she commented quietly. And because she wanted to get a jab in at her neighbour, she added, 'Her manners are so perfect, they are a gift. She must have been born with them because they come so natural, yer can tell she didn't need teaching.'

Evelyn would have taken issue with her over this slur, but with Saturday looming she was in the hands of this little woman who really wouldn't know what good manners were. Why, if she went into the Adelphi or the State, she wouldn't know where to turn. She wouldn't have the least knowledge of which knife and fork to use, or how to conduct a conversation. But right now she did have her uses, and it would be prudent to keep on the right side of her. 'Yes, I agree, Amelia is very little trouble.'

But Bessie wasn't finished with her yet. 'Oh, by the way, while I think on, has Amelia got a frock she can wear on her birthday? I've only ever seen her in her school clothes, but I'm sure she has a pretty dress at home.'

Evelyn was caught unawares and didn't immediately have a reply. And this was so obvious that Bessie mentally chalked one up for herself. After a moment's thought, Evelyn concocted a lie. 'It was going to be a surprise, but if it puts your mind at rest, Miss Maudsley, I'll have to let the secret out of the bag.' She did this grudgingly for she was stretching every shilling she had so she looked the part for Philip on Saturday. But this stupid little woman had backed her into a corner. 'I am buying Amelia a new dress for her birthday. She will have it on when she comes to you on Saturday.'

Bessie chalked another one up for herself. The lying so-and-so hadn't had any intention of buying anything for her daughter until she'd been shamed into it. Still, never mind if the dress would be begrudged, Amelia would be delighted, and that was what counted. 'Oh, aye, sweetheart, ye're going to be proper posh on yer birthday. I'll have to pull me socks up or yer'll be putting me in the shade.' She thought of something then and began to laugh, for she knew Mrs Sinclair would find it in bad taste. 'Ay, I'll have to tell Aggie to make sure she washes her neck properly. We can't have you and me all dressed up and Aggie with a ruddy big tidemark what yer could sail a ship on.'

Evelyn's lip began to curl in disgust, until she saw Bessie watching her out of the corner of her eye. Then she tried to force a smile to her lips, but it came over more like a snarl and made her look ugly. 'Shall we go now, Amelia? I feel very peckish. Not everyone is as lucky as you, having a meal put down in front of them every night.'

The girl stood on tip-toe to reach her coat which was hanging on one of the hooks near the door. She answered without any trace of animation in her voice. 'Yes, Mother, I know I am very lucky.'

'Then come along, don't dally.'

Bessie looked down at the lino and counted to ten. She and Amelia had been really happy and enjoying each other's company until Misery Guts came on the scene. God certainly slipped up when he'd made this woman a mother, she didn't deserve the child she'd given birth to. And it wasn't only motherly feelings she was lacking, it was all the others too. Selfish to the core, without love or compassion, and a whopping great liar into the bargain was Evelyn Sinclair.

'I'll see you tomorrow, Miss Bessie.' Amelia wanted to kiss her friend goodbye, but knew she'd suffer for it when she got home. 'Sleep well.'

Bessie ruffled the girl's thick mop of black hair. 'You too, sweetheart. And don't forget, it's only two days to our birthday. Yer've got yer nice new dress to look forward to.'

Evelyn was unable to raise a smile as she pushed her daughter towards the back door. She had been forced into saying she would buy Amelia a dress, but where was the money going

194

to come from? She needed every penny to make herself so attractive on Saturday that she would stand out and Philip would be proud of her. Their first night out together. He would either fall head over heels for her and be trapped, or so disillusioned he would step back. 'Goodnight, Miss Maudsley, I'll see you tomorrow,' she said briskly.

Bessie stood on the kitchen step watching mother and daughter walk down her yard and into the entry. All because one stuck-up woman thought she was too good to be seen coming out of her neighbour's front door. 'Silly bugger,' Bessie muttered. 'I feel sorry for her 'cos she doesn't know what it's like to have a good belly laugh with her neighbours. And she needn't think she's pulling the wool over my eyes by saying she's going to see this old school friend of hers on Saturday, the one what turned up out of the blue, 'cos I don't believe it for a minute. Not that I care what she does, as long as the girl doesn't get hurt.' She closed her kitchen door, still talking to herself. 'If I ever hear she's laid a finger on Amelia, she'll rue the day. I'll have her guts for garters.'

Bessie walked through and sat at the table in the living room. Her eyes on the grate, she began talking to it. 'There's some bad 'uns in this world, and our Mrs Sinclair is one of them. May God forgive me if I'm saying things about her what aren't true, but I've always thought there was something fishy about her, even from the first week she moved in, 'cos it isn't natural for a woman to ignore her neighbours and look down

195

on them as though they're muck. Yer never know when yer might need them to help yer. Even dirty Annie, her what lives at the top of the street whose house is filthy and her language enough to make yer hair curl, would knock spots off her next door, 'cos at least she loves her kids.'

Banging her fist on the table, Bessie pushed the chair back and got to her feet. 'I can't spend me night talking to a fireplace what can't talk back to me, so I think I'll nip over to Rita's for half an hour for a natter.' She wagged a stiffened finger. 'Don't you dare go out 'cos I don't want to come back to a cold house. I don't mind yer dying down a bit if I'm out a long time, but leave a couple of flames to warm the cockles of me heart.' She reached the door, saying over her shoulder, 'And behave yerself. No spitting sparks on to me rug for spite.'

Chapter Ten

'Oh, don't you look pretty!' Bessie smiled down into the laughing face of her neighbour's daughter. 'That's a lovely dress and it really suits yer.' Silently, she was telling herself it was far from being a new dress, you could tell it had seen the dolly tub many times. But who cared if it was second-hand, so long as it made Amelia look like a ray of sunshine? 'Are yer coming in, Mrs Sinclair, or are yer off out now?'

'I may as well be on my way, Miss Maudsley, save being under your feet.' Evelyn was a bundle of nerves, knowing she had so much to do in so little time. And she was painfully aware that at any minute she might be found out. First there was the journey by tram to the railway station, then changing the clothes she had on for the ones she'd yesterday put in a box at the left luggage office. At any time she could be seen by someone who knew her – a person who worked in the office perhaps or a neighbour. Even, heaven forbid, by Philip himself. Still, these were chances she had to take. 'Be good for Miss Maudsley, Amelia, and go to bed when she tells you. I hope you both have a very enjoyable birthday party.'

'Oh, we will!' Bessie held the door wide. 'Come in, sweetheart.' She waited until the girl had passed through to the living room, then said to the woman who wasn't looking at all at ease with herself, 'I hope you have a lovely evening, too, but don't do anything I wouldn't do.' This was a remark anyone would make to another person and it would be taken as a joke. But the tell-tale blush it brought to her neighbour's cheeks told Bessie she was right in thinking there was more to this night out than visiting an old school friend. 'Give a knock on the wall tomorrow when yer want Amelia to come home.'

'What time would you like me to knock? Are you an early riser?'

Bessie shook her head. 'I sometimes go to church, but I won't be going tomorrow, I'll be having a lie-in. So Amelia can stay as long as yer like. But I'll have to go in now, 'cos I've got to put the custard on the jelly creams before it sets. I'll see yer tomorrow.' She closed the door quickly. She'd only just remembered that before the knock came, she was halfway through putting the custard on top of the jelly she'd set previously in white pleated paper cases. She wasn't changed yet, either, and she wanted to look respectable when Rita and Aggie came over. Not that she'd look like a film star no matter what she wore, but a girl had her pride and should make the most of herself, even if she did have a face that resembled the back of a tram.

Amelia was waiting for Bessie to come back into the living room. 'Do you really like my dress, Miss Bessie? And does it suit me?'

'It looks lovely on yer, sweetheart, and yer look as pretty as a picture.' Bessie grinned. 'Guess what that cheeky front door's just said to me? It said I have a face like the back end of a twenty-two tram.'

Amelia hurried to put her arms around the little woman's waist. 'You've got a lovely face, Miss Bessie, and I've a good mind to give that door a smack.'

'We'll leave it till tomorrow, eh, sweetheart? We don't want to be fighting on our birthday, do we? We're going to have a really good time and enjoy ourselves. But first I've got to see to the cakes and then change meself before me mates come. It won't take me five minutes, then I'll be ready. You sit yerself down so yer don't dirty yer new dress.'

Amelia lowered her head. 'It isn't a new dress, is it, Miss Bessie? You see, I can tell because it doesn't feel new, and there's a little tear at the back, near the hem.'

'Oh, sweetheart, what difference does it make whether it's new or not! It's new to you, and that's the main thing. Perhaps yer mother didn't have enough money for a new one, 'cos times are hard now and lots of people don't even have enough money for food, never mind new clothes. I bet there isn't a girl in this street who wouldn't envy you if they could see how pretty yer look in it. D'yer think they'd worry about whether it was brand-new or not?' Bessie shook her head. 'Not on your life they wouldn't. And, anyway, I haven't got a new dress, and I'll lay odds that neither Mrs Wells nor Mrs Gordon will walk in here dressed up to the nines in brand-new clothes.' She dropped a kiss on Amelia's cheek. 'Ye're a lucky girl, sweetheart, compared to some, believe me.'

'Yes, I know, Miss Bessie, 'cos I've got friends

at school who sometimes don't come in because they haven't any shoes to wear. So I know I'm very lucky. But my bestest piece of good luck is having you for a friend.'

'Oh, well, that's a piece of good luck we share, sweetheart, 'cos I look forward to you coming so much my eyes never leave the clock.' Bessie's jaw dropped. 'Oh, my God there's Aggie knocking at Rita's door. They'll be over in a minute and here's me not ready. You let them in, love, while I do a quick change. If yer can think of a joke to keep them amused, they'd be over the moon.'

Amelia was taken aback. 'I don't know any jokes, Miss Bessie.'

Bessie was halfway up the stairs when she shouted down, 'Tell them about the door saying I have a face like the back of a tram.'

When Amelia opened the front door, she stepped aside to let Mrs Wells and Mrs Gordon enter. She was in a predicament. She didn't want to let Miss Bessie down, but she couldn't bring herself to say what she'd been told to say. However, her problem was solved when Mrs Wells told her, 'We heard what Bessie said about that ruddy door of hers, and if I was in her shoes I'd stop polishing its knocker for a while. That would take it down a peg or two.'

Feeling relieved, Amelia told her, 'Me and Miss Bessie are going to leave it until tomorrow, Mrs Wells, because we don't think we should fight on our birthdays.'

'Quite right, too, sunshine, it's a day for yer both to be happy. And seeing as it's a party, don't yer think it sounds unfriendly to call me Mrs

Wells? Just for tonight, wouldn't yer like to call me Auntie Rita?'

Amelia frowned, thinking her mother would be angry about that. Then the frown was replaced by a smile when a voice in her head said her mother need never know. 'That would be nice.' Her curls bounced up and down as she nodded. 'Yes, I'd like that, Auntie Rita.'

Aggie Gordon hadn't spoken so far, but she'd been taking all this in with narrowed eyes and decided she wasn't going to be left out. 'If we're going to be pally, queen, yer can call me Auntie Aggie.'

Amelia clapped her hands. She had never had a birthday party before, and she had never had any aunties. She would have to keep them secret, of course, but she was thrilled. 'I've never had an auntie before, now I've got two!'

Bessie almost fell down the stairs in her haste. 'No, yer haven't, sweetheart, yer've got three. Yer wouldn't leave me out, would yer?'

When the girl ran to put her arms around Bessie's waist, and told her she would never leave her out for she was her best friend, Rita and Aggie exchanged glances. Rita wasn't surprised, she'd always felt sorry for Amelia and had a soft spot for her. But Aggie Gordon was having her eyes opened. For the first time she was seeing a young girl who was friendly and affectionate. She certainly didn't take after her stuck-up mother. And Aggie admitted to herself that she'd been wrong, for the child shouldn't be blamed for the faults of the woman who had given birth to her.

'I hope there's going to be food at this here

201

party,' Aggie said, letting her large frame drop on to the couch. There were a few twangs as the springs complained at the sudden weight but Aggie didn't turn a hair. Any chair or couch that couldn't stand her weight was obviously cheap and badly made. After all, she wasn't that heavy. Well, perhaps a bit heavier than most, but not so much you'd notice. She wasn't a flaming giant. 'Did yer hear me, Bessie, 'cos I'm starving. I didn't have no dinner 'cos I thought if I did I wouldn't be hungry, and I'd hate to insult yer by refusing food what yer'd spent hours getting ready for us.'

Bessie and Rita looked at each other and roared with laughter. 'You refuse food, Aggie Gordon? Never in yer life. And I'll bet any money that yer didn't go without yer dinner either, 'cos yer love yer belly too much.'

'I hope ye're not too hungry, Aggie,' Bessie said, ''cos I've only made jelly creams, and they won't fill yer. I didn't bother with sandwiches or anything like that, I was sure yer'd have had yer dinner before yer came.'

Amelia's wide eyes were going from one to the other. She wasn't used to being in a room with more than one person, and had never before heard a conversation going on between three grown women. She'd heard groups of children in the school playground, of course, and she'd always joined in. But she couldn't join in here, for she was at a loss to know why Miss Bessie had said she only had jelly creams when there were sandwiches and a large sponge cake in the larder.

'Some bleeding party this is going to be.' Aggie tossed her head back then turned it sideways so

202

she could wink at Amelia. 'Nowt to eat, and I bet she hasn't even bought a few bottles of milk stout so we can get drunk and forget how hungry we are.'

'Ay, ay,' Bessie said. 'Yer were warned to watch yer language in front of Amelia, 'cos she's not used to women what swear.'

'I'm sorry, queen, and I'll watch me tongue from now on.' Once again she winked at the birthday girl. 'But yer must admit that coming to a party what's got nothing to eat, and not even a bottle of milk stout, well, it's enough to make a saint swear. I'm no saint, mind yer, but I will promise it won't happen again.'

Amelia had never been so close to the big woman before, in fact she was a little afraid of her because she had such a loud voice. But she wouldn't be afraid any more, for she could see laughter lurking in the bright eyes that were almost hidden in the woman's chubby face. 'That's all right, Auntie Aggie, I'll forgive you.'

Aggie was so chuffed she leaned forward, giving the couch false hope that she was about to remove her weight elsewhere. But it wasn't to be, and the largest spring passed the word around to all the smaller ones that it wasn't worth creaking, it would be a waste of energy. 'Ooh, that sounds nice, that does, queen!' Her bosom grew two inches. 'Auntie Aggie!'

Rita tutted. 'D'yer know what would sound nicer? If we wished Amelia a happy birthday and gave her the birthday cards.'

Aggie slapped an open palm to her forehead. 'Oh, stupid Aggie! D'yer know, queen, I'd forget me head if God hadn't had the sense to screw it on. Pass me bag over, Bessie, there's a good girl.'

'Ay, who was yer servant before I came along?'

'I'll get it for her, it'll be quicker.' Rita picked the bag up from the side of the couch and passed it to her neighbour. Then she opened her own bag and took out an envelope. 'Here yer are, sunshine, it's from me and the rest of me family. Have a very happy birthday.'

Amelia was beside herself with happiness as she opened up the card to see 'Mr and Mrs Wells' written inside, and underneath the names of the two boys, Billy and Jack. Aggie's card wished her a happy birthday and was signed by her and her husband and the two children, Kitty and Kenny. 'Oh, they are lovely, thank you very much. I've never had a birthday card before – and look at all the names on them. I am a very lucky girl.'

'There's mine to come yet,' Bessie told her. 'It's on the sideboard, sweetheart, you get it while I start to set the table before Aggie dies of hunger.' Once out in the kitchen, she leaned her hands on the draining board, and bit on her bottom lip to keep the tears away. Eight years of age and never had a birthday card. Even the poorest family in the street wouldn't let their child's birthday go without buying them a ha'penny card, even if it meant sitting in the dark with no money for the gas meter. Oh, that girl's mother had a lot to answer for, and if there was any justice in the world, then a day of reckoning would surely come for her.

Evelyn's heart and stomach were all of a flutter as

she walked out of Exchange Station under the gaze of people waiting for trains. They must have thought she was mad, parading through the station dressed to kill. She couldn't go through all this rigmarole again, her nerves were shattered. It was a good job it wasn't far to the hotel, she felt so conspicuous. She couldn't tell either if her appearance was perfect. There was only a small mirror in the ladies' cloakroom in the station. She had done the best she could with her hair, but of course, unlike the old days when money was no object, she hadn't been able to visit a hair salon to have it Marcel-waved. But the velvet band around her forehead looked attractive, she hoped.

As she neared the hotel, she stopped for a while to compose herself. The last thing she wanted was to look flustered and unsure of herself. So she took several deep breaths before smiling at the uniformed doorman who held the door open for her. 'Good evening.'

'Good evening, madam, and what a pleasant evening it is.'

Evelyn had barely stepped into the foyer before Philip was standing by her with a smile on his face and a look of admiration in his eyes. 'My dear, you look delightful.' He took her hand and kissed it. 'I think I can safely say you will be the most beautiful woman here this evening, and I'll be the envy of every one of my friends.'

Evelyn allowed him to take her cape which he handed to a nearby page. 'I hope I haven't kept you waiting?'

'If you have, I can assure you it has been worth the wait. I have booked a table for two, my dear, in a quiet alcove where we can talk without interruption.' He had found her attractive from the moment he'd set eyes on her in the office, but tonight she looked more than attractive as she walked with her back straight and her hips swaying gently. She looked positively regal, and Philip was conscious of men turning their heads as they followed the maître d'hôtel past tables catering for larger parties, to the alcove where their table was set with shining silverware, sparkling glasses, a flickering candle, and to add that bit extra to a table set for a lavish meal, a beautiful white and lilac orchid at the side of one of the place settings.

'Oh, how sweet!' Evelyn picked up the delicate flower and held it to her face. Its soft perfume took her back over the years to when one of these expensive flowers was always presented to her by Charles when they were dining out. 'It is really beautiful, Philip, and very thoughtful of you.'

'It matches your beauty, my dear, and my aim in life is to please you.' He waved to the maître d'hôtel who was hovering in the background. 'A bottle of your finest champagne, Alfonso, my companion and I wish to celebrate. We will order our meal later, but first I wish to make a toast.'

Alfonso bowed. 'I will choose the wine myself, Mr Astbury, and it will be the best.'

'What are we toasting, Philip?' Evelyn asked, feeling relaxed now, and very much at home in a room where the women were richly dressed and you could almost smell the wealth. 'Is it your birthday or a special event?'

'A very special event, my dear Evelyn. Our first

evening out together socially, which I'm hoping will be the first of many.'

She lowered her eyes and her dark lashes fanned her cheeks. Now was the time to put her plan into action. And because what she was tasting this evening was something she wanted very much for her future life, she had to be word perfect. No more scraping along each week with not enough money to live on, no more living in a poky two-up-two-down house with common people for neighbours. To get what she wanted more than anything in her life, her acting had to be faultless.

'I'm afraid it would have to be the odd occasion for me, Philip, even though I wish it were otherwise. You see, while I am not penniless, I really don't have enough money to buy the sort of clothes I would need for many social outings such as tonight's.' When Philip would have spoken, she silenced him with a raised hand. 'I manage quite well, and am not complaining or looking for sympathy. And I really don't want to have to explain my position, or any part of my past life. That would benefit no one. I would love to see you again, but, as I said, it would only be on the odd occasion, and not often as you suggest. I do not want to lie to you, I prefer to tell you the truth. And the truth is, I have to be very careful with what money I have. I can't afford expensive clothes, nor can I afford taxis every time I go out. My life was very different years ago, but now I must live within my means.'

Much to the irritation of Philip, Alfonso arrived at that moment with a silver bucket half-filled with ice on which rested the bottle of champagne. With an exaggerated flourish, the waiter popped the cork and poured a little into Philip's glass. 'Would you care to taste, Mr Astbury?'

'If it is your choice, Alfonso, then I'm sure it is splendid. Please pour then leave the bottle in the ice. I will attend to it myself and indicate when we are ready to see the menu.'

The only thing that was spoiling the evening for Evelyn was the thought that she might meet up with someone who knew her from the early days, and remembered her connection with the Lister-Sinclair family. 'You appear to be well known here, Philip, is it a favourite haunt of yours?'

'One of them,' he answered briefly, wanting to turn the topic back to Evelyn's situation. 'Let us drink to our friendship, and then I want to know more about you. You see, you intrigue me.'

She sipped the wine, then gave an appreciative nod and giggled as the bubbles tickled her nose. 'I always did like champagne, and I would say this was a very good year.'

'You are a woman of mystery, Evelyn Sinclair,' he said. 'And I very much want to unravel that mystery.'

Again Evelyn's lashes fanned her cheeks. 'There is no mystery, I am what you see.' She raised her eyes to gaze into his. 'My husband idolised me, put me on a pedestal and gave me everything my heart desired. Then came the war, he was killed, and suddenly I found I had to fend for myself. I had little money, and although for the first year after he died I tried to keep in contact with friends, I had to come to my senses eventually, and settle for a comfortable unexciting life.'

Philip reached across the table and covered each of her hands. 'Oh, you poor darling! I can well understand your husband idolising you, it would be very easy to do so. But we can't allow you to hide yourself away, it would be a sin! I want you to let me help you be happy and bring you pleasure. Someone as beautiful as you should not be hidden away.'

Her brain was scheming, but the large brown eyes that stared into his were as innocent as a baby's. 'That is very good of you, Philip. You really are a kind man. And I would like to meet you socially now and again, but that is as far as our relationship can go. I have my pride, and unless I could afford to be fashionably dressed, with my hair waved by a specialist, and able to take a taxi to our meeting place, I would feel most uncomfortable.'

He topped up their glasses. 'Come along, my love, there's nothing quite like champers to cheer one up.' While he drank, his eyes were glued to the face he thought so perfect. Eyes you could swim in, sculpted cheek bones, excellent complexion and a set of perfect white teeth. As well, of course, as a figure any woman would envy. 'I am more than comfortably off, Evelyn, and so are my parents. I don't need to work, I only do so because I would get incredibly bored playing tennis all day and every day like some of my friends. So I am in a position to help you enjoy a pleasurable life.'

Pretending to be naive, she asked, 'What do you mean, Philip? You're not suggesting I should become your mistress, are you?'

209

He chuckled. 'You say that as though you couldn't bear to be near me! Surely I am not so ugly?'

'You are not a bit ugly, Philip, you are a very attractive man. And I'm sure if I let myself I could fall head over heels for you.'

'After that compliment, my dear, I am determined to help you. And you needn't feel under any obligation to me, as I will explain if you will give me the chance.'

'May we order our meal first? I do feel a little peckish.'

When Evelyn smiled shyly, Philip wasn't to know it was contrived. He felt his heart would surely burst. 'Your wish is my command, my love.' He raised a hand and within a couple of seconds Alfonso arrived with large menu cards. 'Give my companion and me ten minutes to make our choice, my good man, then we will order.'

Evelyn's eyes ran down the menu. She could almost hear her tummy's reaction. It was over eight years since she'd set eyes on such a fine selection of food. But she didn't want to appear too eager as she passed her menu across to Philip. 'I'll have the consommé, and then the fillet of salmon.'

Philip decided he'd have the same, plus another bottle of champagne, and chuckled when Evelyn asked him if he was trying to get her drunk. 'I wouldn't dream of it, my love, but if by some unforeseen circumstance you did become slightly merry, my bachelor flat is just two minutes' walk away.'

'Oh, that's interesting.' Things seemed to be

going her way, and Evelyn was prepared to help them along. 'Do you use it often to entertain your lady friends?'

'Not an awful lot, I prefer the comfort of my parents' house. Plus the fact they have a wonderful cook whose pastry melts in the mouth.' Philip sat back in his chair, glass in hand. 'Why do you ask? Do you think that's where I keep my harem?' He was teasing her and also trying to find out more about her. 'Do you object to a man having a mistress?'

'I have never really thought about it,' she told him. 'I imagine there are situations where it would suit a wife for her husband to have a mistress, and in those circumstances I imagine I too would have no objection.'

Philip was digging for her opinion on such subjects, and as he swirled the wine around in his glass, asked, 'What about a young bachelor with no ties? And a young widow who also has no ties? What are your views in these circumstances?'

'Really, Philip, I do believe you are teasing me! You are making me blush, and that's something I haven't done publicly for a long time.'

'It suits you, my dear, you look quite enchanting. And it is so refreshing.' Philip saw two waiters approaching with their first course. 'Ah, we will have to continue our very interesting discussion later.'

'Perhaps, when we resume our conversation, we can keep it less personal? Don't you agree, Philip?'

'I disagree, I'm afraid,' he said with a charming smile. 'Things were just getting interesting. I told you I was intrigued by you, and I am determined to get to know the real you, not the small part of yourself you allow strangers to see.'

It was impossible to talk while the waiters were there, dedicated to seeing the thick, white linen napkins were covering their laps at just the right angle before the consommé was served. And having been told by Alfonso that Mr Astbury and his companion must be given the very closest attention, they would have stayed by if Philip hadn't dismissed them, saying he would signal when they were ready for the next course.

'Do they always make such a fuss of you, Philip?' Evelyn had taken a spoonful of the delicious soup and was finding it hard to keep a look of bliss from her face. Oh, what she wouldn't give for a life like this again. 'I think you are spoilt.'

'Alfonso knows he will be handsomely tipped, my dear, and also knows I like the best service in return.' Philip laid down his spoon and patted his lips with the napkin. 'I'll let you into a secret which of course you must not relate to my good friend Alfonso, who would be deeply wounded. I would much prefer being spoilt by you than by him.'

Two glasses of champagne and her plan seemingly on course had the effect of loosening Evelyn's tongue. 'Ah, but I cannot make such delicious consommé, or pastry that melts in the mouth, nor do I have the money to tip you handsomely.'

'All things I could live without, my dear Evelyn.' Philip hadn't failed to notice how relaxed she had become, and wondered if he was making headway. There were so many things he would like to know, but if he rushed her he could scare her off. For instance, she must have parents of her own somewhere, and what about the family of the man she'd married? Why was she so alone in the world? Was there a simple explanation? 'Another glass of bubbly, while we are waiting for the next course?'

Evelyn nodded. Why not make the most of tonight and enjoy herself? 'Thank you, Philip, I think I'm safe with one more glass.'

But an hour later, after the most delicious meal she'd had in years, Evelyn threw caution to the wind when he refilled her glass. 'If I start to giggle or lisp, Philip, then please don't offer me any more drink. I am not used to it these days, and wouldn't like you to see me tipsy and making a fool of myself. Not that I ever have, but I'm relying on you to see I remain sober enough to make my way home.'

'I would not allow you to go home on your own in an inebriated state, my lovely Evelyn, especially in the dark. Have no fear, I will take care of you.'

'I don't want this evening to end, Philip, I'm really enjoying myself. You are very good company. But I want you to promise that you will see me into a taxi when the evening draws to a close?'

'I have another suggestion to make but I don't want to offend you. So listen carefully before you answer. First, would you like to do something to please me?'

Evelyn's brain wasn't too fuddled to know that this could be make or break time. She didn't know what Philip was going to ask, but she had to be prepared. Did she want to stay in her two-up-two-down house for the rest of her days, or would she take whatever terms he offered if it got her out of the rut? 'Why would I not want to please you when you have been so kind to me? Anything within reason, Philip, I will happily agree to.'

'Then let us leave here after our coffee. Come back with me to my bachelor flat. I promise I have no ulterior motive, I will be the perfect gentleman.' He leaned across the table and caught her hand. 'I would like you to see it, and then if you are agreeable, and as eager to see me as I am to see you, we can use it to meet whenever we like. On Monday I take over my uncle's office and you will be my full-time secretary. It will be difficult for us to talk privately there for I would not like there to be a whiff of gossip that would embarrass you. So please come with me now to my flat where we can finish our discussion on how I can help you improve your life. But always remember you are a free agent and can do as you wish. So it's for you to decide, my dear, do you come back to my flat or shall I call you a taxi from here to take you home?'

'I would love to see your flat, Philip. As long as you promise to call a taxi for me when it's time for me to go home.' Evelyn lowered her eyes to hide her look of triumph. 'Even if it's the middle of the night when we finish talking and getting to know each other, you must call a taxi to take me home.'

Philip also felt a sensation of triumph, but warned himself to tread carefully for the time being, he didn't want to frighten her off. 'You have my solemn promise, my dear. I intend to take good care of you.'

Chapter Eleven

'Well, yer did us proud, girl, I'll give yer that.' Aggie Gordon ran the back of one chubby hand over her mouth as she looked across the table to where Bessie sat next to Amelia. 'A feast fit for a king, that was.'

'Aggie's right,' Rita Wells said, her head nodding in agreement. 'And yer made those pies yerself, did yer say?'

'Yeah, I made them last night and put them between plates in the larder,' Bessie said, looking pleased with herself and the world in general. 'I knew it would be too late to make them when I got home from work today, what with shopping and all, so I thought I'd get stuck in last night and get them off me mind.' She chuckled, 'I knew Aggie would have something to say if there wasn't a good spread and she went home hungry, I'd never have heard the last of it.'

Amelia, sitting next to Bessie, couldn't keep still for excitement. This had been the best day of her life and she'd never forget it. 'The pies were lovely, Auntie Bessie, and so were the sandwiches and cakes. I've never had a birthday party before, but I bet this was the bestest anyone ever had.'

'But yer must have been to a party sometime, sunshine, surely a friend's or a relative's?' Rita asked. 'Even if yer've never had one yerself.'

'No, I haven't, Auntie Rita.' It wasn't just the

food and the fact it was her birthday that was making Amelia feel so happy. It was being spoken to by adults, and being able to answer them without having to think before speaking. And she had never laughed so much in her life, for Mrs Wells and Mrs Gordon were so funny the way they pretended to be mad with each other and then ended up laughing so much the tears rolled down their cheeks. 'No, I haven't, honest! I haven't got any relatives, you see.' A cheeky grin came to her face as she added, 'Well, I never used to have, but I have now, I've got an Auntie Bessie, Auntie Rita and an Auntie Aggie.' She rocked on her chair with laughter that brought smiles to the faces of the three women. 'There's not many girls get presents like that for their birthday.'

'And the day's not over yet, sweetheart.' Bessie winked knowingly at her two mates who were listening with interest. 'After the table's been cleared and the dishes washed and out of the way, we're going to have a few party games.'

Amelia's eyes nearly popped out of her head and she clapped her hands with glee. 'Ooh, what sort of games, Auntie Bessie?'

'You'll soon find out, sweetheart, after yer've helped me clear the table.'

'I'll help yer with the dishes, Bessie,' Rita said, pushing her chair back. 'Amelia can keep Aggie company.'

It was while the two women were at the sink washing and drying the plates, that they heard Aggie say, 'How come yer always get yer full title, queen?'

Bessie took her hands out of the soapy suds and

cocked an ear. 'Oh, God, I hope she doesn't say something she shouldn't. I wouldn't like anything to get back to the queer one in case she stops the girl from coming here.'

'Aggie's not soft, sunshine, she wouldn't do that. Just listen.'

'What do you mean by my full title, Auntie Aggie?'

'Well, queen, I know a lot of women what were christened Amelia, but they always get Milly 'cos it's easier and more friendly. And that's whether they like it or not. It's a case of like it or lump it.'

The girl pulled on a lock of her black hair while giving the matter some thought. 'There's two girls in my class at school called Amelia, and they get Milly. But my mother has told me I must never answer to anything but my proper name, which is Amelia.'

In the kitchen, Bessie tugged on Rita's arm. 'Oh, my God, I hope Aggie doesn't put her foot in it, yer know how outspoken she can be.'

Rita put a finger to her lips. 'Don't look for trouble before it hits yer in the face, sunshine. So far Aggie has been on her best behaviour, only one swear word all afternoon and that's a record for her. But she's taken a fancy to the girl, and I'm positive she'll not say anything that would upset her.'

Bessie's fears were unfounded, for it wasn't Aggie who spoke next but Amelia. 'You know, Auntie Aggie, I would really like to be called Milly, I think it's a nice name. It's just that I don't want to upset Mother, she's very strict. But I could be Milly in Auntie Bessie's house couldn't

217

I, and Amelia everywhere else?'

'That's good thinking, that is, queen, it could be our little secret. And me and me mates wouldn't snitch on yer and get yer into trouble.' Then Aggie said something that sent Bessie and Rita into fits of laughter. 'We'll be the soul of discretion, queen, you'll see.'

Rita poked her head around the door. 'Ye're going up in the world, aren't yer, Aggie? Soul of discretion, where did yer dig that one up from?'

Aggie's laughter was so loud her whole body shook. Her bosom bounced up and down, her tummy pushed the table back, and her chins parted company to go in opposite directions. 'The bloke in the pawnshop said it to me one day when I took Sam's suit in. I was short of a few bob and told him I'd be taking it out again on Saturday before my feller knew it was missing. And 'cos he knows Sam by sight to say hello to, I warned him if he breathed a word to my feller I'd break his bleeding neck. And that's when he said that in his business it paid to be the soul of discretion.' The chair creaked and the table was lifted from the floor as the memory of that day came back to her. 'I've been waiting for an opportunity to use it, and this is the first time it fitted in.' She winked at Amelia. 'I'm sorry about the swear word, queen, but it slipped out, like, before I had a chance to stop it. I don't suppose yer hear swear words in your house, do yer?'

The girl's eyes were alive with devilment. 'No, Auntie Aggie, my mother doesn't swear, she says it's very unladylike. But some of the girls in school do, they get it off their mothers, so I know some bad words.'

The dishes put away now, Bessie and Rita came into the room. 'It doesn't mean because some of yer school friends swear that it's all right, sweetheart,' Bessie said. 'Because while it's bad for older people to use swear words, it's even worse for children. So we'll have to make sure Mrs Gordon doesn't lead yer astray, or yer'll get into trouble with yer mother.'

'I'll not lead her astray, no fear of that!' Aggie was on her high horse now. 'But the girl needs to know a bit more about what life is really like, otherwise when it comes to her leaving school and finding herself a job, she won't have a clue how to mix with other people. And she's bound to hear plenty of very ripe swear words 'cos not everyone she meets will speak as though they've got a ruddy mouthful of plums.'

Amelia's face was glowing and her childish laughter, so seldom heard, was loud, 'Oh, you are funny, Auntie Aggie.'

But Bessie wasn't so sure. 'It's up to her mother to say how she's brought up, not us,' she said, taking a seat on the couch. 'We all have different ideas and think we know what's best for other people, but when it comes down to it, it isn't really any of our business and we have no right to interfere.'

Amelia ran to sit beside Bessie and slipped an arm through hers. 'It doesn't matter how I speak, Auntie Bessie, or what sort of a job I get. Even when I'm grown up, and a young lady, I will always come and see you 'cos you're my very best friend.'

Rita thought it was a sad scene and turned her head away, silently cursing the woman whose child only asked for the one thing that didn't cost anything, and was so easy to give. And that was someone to love her.

'I hope you do, sweetheart.' Bessie squeezed the girl's shoulder. 'I'd be really sad if I ever lost touch with yer. I'm hoping yer live here long enough to grow into a lovely young lady and find the man of your dreams. That would make me very happy.'

Aggie banged a closed fist on the table. 'Before the front of me bleeding dress becomes sodden wet with tears, can we start on these games yer were talking about, queen?'

Bessie shook herself. She knew she shouldn't become too attached to her neighbour's daughter for she could be letting herself in for a lot of hurt and heartache. But she couldn't help herself, no matter what her head told her. For what had started off as liking had turned to fondness and now to love. There wasn't a thing she could do about it. Love wasn't something you could turn off as easily as a tap. 'Right, what about a game of "I spy with my little eye"? Only we'll have to stick to easy words for them what can't spell.'

Aggie took umbrage at that. 'Are you hinsinuating that I can't spell, Bessie Maudsley? I'll have yer know that when I went to school I was always top of the class for spelling.'

Rita chuckled. 'Oh, aye, Aggie, yer've never mentioned that before, yer've been hiding yer light under a bushel. Go on, tell us what the longest word is that yer can spell?'

Without a hesitation, she answered, 'Bleeding,' and she was laughing so much her next words was just about audible. 'And bugger.'

Although Bessie didn't approve, Aggie's laughter was so contagious she couldn't keep a smile at bay. 'Neither of those words will be acceptable in our game, Aggie Gordon, so stick to words with three letters.'

Aggie spread out one of her chubby hands and started ticking the fingers off. 'That's all right then. So I'll be the first one to go, and yer can try and guess my first word which starts with the letter S.'

'It's got to be something in this room, Aggie,' Rita said. 'And it's got to be something we can all see.'

'I know what I'm doing, queen, I'm not thick.' Aggie leaned her chubby elbows on the table. 'Go on, get yer brains working.'

Ten minutes later, and flummoxed, Bessie said, 'We'll have to give in. We've said everything beginning with S in the room, but I'm blowed if there's anything with only three letters in. So shall we give in, Rita and Amelia? Otherwise none of us will get a turn.'

'I give in, Auntie Bessie, 'cos all I can see is the shovel and the sideboard,' Amelia said. 'But they've got more letters in.'

Bessie looked to Rita. 'Do you give in, sweetheart?'

Rita nodded. 'I give in, but there's something fishy here, I can tell by the smirk on Aggie's face. She's having us on, I know.'

'No, I'm not! It's you what's stupid and can't

221

see something what's right in front of yer.'

'Okay, Aggie,' Bessie said, 'we all give in, so what's the word?'

Aggie was gloating. 'S-o-d, sod.'

Rita and Bessie spoke as one. 'Sod! Yer can't use that, it's got to be something in this room!'

Her head wagging nonchalantly from side to side, Aggie asked her next-door neighbour, 'What did yer call me yesterday afternoon, queen, when I spilled a cup of tea on yer?'

Rita looked perplexed for a second, a frown creasing her forehead. Then she slapped a hand on her cheek and said, 'You silly sod!'

Aggie looked as though she'd been cleared of committing a crime. 'That's it, queen, that's what yer called me. A three-letter word, beginning with S, and right in front of yer eyes.'

The first one to laugh was Amelia, and it was as much at the expressions on the faces of Bessie and Rita as the craftiness of Aggie. 'Does that count as a word, Auntie Bessie?'

'No, it flaming well doesn't!' Bessie was red in the face. 'A sod is a piece of earth, it can't be a person or a piece of furniture.'

'Now don't be getting yerself all worked up, queen,' Aggie said, her chins nodding to show they agreed with her, 'or yer'll be having a heart attack. And it would be real thoughtless of yer to have a heart attack and spoil Milly's birthday party.'

While Aggie's two mates roared with laughter, Amelia didn't think it was a bit funny. Her chin jutted out as she said, 'Auntie Bessie isn't going to have a heart attack, so there!'

'No, I'm not, sweetheart, Aggie was only joking. And I think we'll change the game and have another one, so we don't have some silly beggar wasting our time.'

'Oh, no, don't do that, please!' Amelia begged. 'I wanted it to be my turn and I've got a word all ready for you to guess.'

'Of course yer can have a turn, sunshine,' Rita told her, 'after all it is your birthday. Without you we wouldn't be having no party, so go on, what's the first letter? Oh, and before we start, it is something we can see, isn't it?'

Amelia pursed her lips and nodded. 'Yes, and it begins with the letter A.'

Bessie got in first. 'I've got it, it's me aspidistra plant.'

The girl shook her head, looking very serious. 'No, it's not, Auntie Bessie, and you are not even warm.'

Rita's face lit up when she thought she'd guessed the word. 'Armchair! It's the ruddy armchair!'

Again the girl shook her head. 'Wrong, Auntie Rita! And there's not just one of it, either, in case yer say I'm cheating.'

'Got it, got it, got it!' Aggie was over the moon. 'Don't any of yer ever say again that I'm as thick as two short planks. It's the ashes in the grate! I got it as soon as she said there was more than one.'

'Uh-uh,' Amelia said, her face aglow as she swayed back and forth on the couch, her hands clasped between her knees. 'That's not right, either.'

A quarter of an hour later the three women had

gone over every item in the room with a fine tooth comb. 'There's nothing else here beginning with A,' Rita said. 'Are yer sure yer've got the spelling right, sunshine?'

'Oh, yes, Auntie Rita, I'm top of the class for English and spelling.'

'What d'yer say then, girls?' Bessie looked from one of her mates to the other. 'Shall we throw in the towel?'

They both nodded. 'May as well,' Aggie said, 'or we'll be here all night.'

'Okay, sweetheart, yer've got us beat, we'll give in.' Bessie raised her brows. 'What's the word that beat us?'

Amelia sat up straight, her hands on her knees. 'It's Aunties! There's more than one of you and you can all be seen. So I haven't cheated, have I?'

Even if she had cheated, there wasn't one woman in the room who was going to tell her and take that radiant smile off her face. 'I think yer've been very clever, sweetheart, I would never have thought of that.'

'Me neither,' Rita told her. 'It took one young girl like yerself to beat three grown-up women. It just goes to show how clever yer are.'

'Aye, and how thick we are.' Aggie was being gracious in defeat. 'D'yer know why I think we didn't get it? Well, it's new to us, isn't it? We're not used to being Aunties. And if anyone in this room contradicts me, I'll clock them one.'

Amelia glanced at the clock on the mantelpiece and saw it was half-past eight. It was past her usual bedtime. But she didn't want the best day of her life to end, not yet. 'Auntie Bessie, I don't have to go to bed yet, do I? I'm not a bit tired, and you said we had another game to play.' Then a picture of her mother flashed through her mind. 'I'll go if you think I should, though, I promised to do as I was told.'

'Of course ye're not going to bed yet, it's yer birthday and that makes it a very special day. A day when ye're allowed a few treats.' Bessie wouldn't have let her go to bed now even if the girl had begged to for there was still a treat in store for her. 'When yer eyes begin to close, then yer can go to bed. But right now we're going to have a game of Pass the Parcel. Which means we'll all have to sit around the table.'

Amelia's hands came together and she held them to her chest. What an exciting day it had been for her. 'How do you play the game, Auntie Bessie?'

'It's easy, sweetheart, yer just pass the parcel on to the one next to yer as quick as yer can, so ye're not caught with it. Anyone caught with it has to pay a forfeit. They either sing or say a piece of poetry.' Bessie pulled a face. 'The only trouble is, there's usually someone who stands with their back to the players and gives a shout when to stop. If one of us does it, there'll only be three playing and it's not worth it.'

'I'll go and get one of the lads if yer like, Bessie?' Rita volunteered. 'They won't be in bed yet, and it'll only be for fifteen minutes at the most.'

So ten-year-old Billy, much to his disgust at having to be at a girl's birthday party, was roped in to stand in front of the window and shout out

225

every few seconds to catch whoever was holding the parcel. There was so much laughing and screaming, he began to enjoy himself, and was surprised to find that the girl who lived opposite with her stuck-up mother wasn't as quiet as he thought, she was really very funny. He for one wouldn't be shouting names after her when she was coming home from school. He couldn't stop himself from cheating by taking sly glances at her when he thought no one was looking, 'cos he wanted each one to have to pay a forfeit.

The first time Billy shouted 'Stop!' Aggie was caught with the parcel. She tried to shove it towards Rita, but calls of 'Cheat' by the others caused her grudgingly to agree to pay a forfeit. Her choice was the song sung in most of the corner pubs at throwing-out time. It was 'Sweet Nellie Dean', and God help the man who wrote that song for Aggie had a voice like a foghorn and murdered it. But the contortions of her chubby face caused much hilarity and even Billy clapped her at the end. His second victim was Rita, who strongly objected to singing on the grounds that she had a worse voice than Aggie, if that were possible. She opted for the nursery rhyme 'Three Little Pigs'. It didn't go down as well as Aggie's but was worth a round of applause because Rita had at least tried.

Billy timed the third intervention nicely, shouting 'Stop' just as Bessie was handing the parcel to Amelia. The girl was screaming with laughter as she looked down at the parcel in her hand. She had no way of knowing that this was the moment the three women had been waiting for. 'What shall I do, Auntie Bessie? Shall I sing a nursery rhyme?'

'You do what yer want, sweetheart, but remember, the one who is judged to have given the best forfeit gets to keep what's in the bag.'

'Ooh, er, I'm not very good, but I will try.' Amelia took a deep breath and began to sing in a sweet, clear voice.

'Georgie Porgie, pudding and pie, kissed the
    girls and made them cry,
When the boys came out to play, Georgie
    Porgie ran away.'

The three women made a lot of noise by banging on the table and shouting 'Hurray'. Even Billy clapped and whistled. 'That's the best so far,' he surprised himself by saying. Usually he gave all girls a wide berth.

Amelia gave him a stern look. 'Auntie Bessie hasn't had her turn yet, and I bet she's the best of the lot.'

'No, I think we'll leave it at that, sweetheart, or me mates will be dying of thirst. I can see by their faces they're ready for their bottle of milk stout. Besides, seeing as it's my house, I can't be the winner or they'll say it was rigged.' Bessie ran her hand over the girl's hair. 'We'll vote now, sweetheart, and if there's a tie Billy can be the judge.'

And of course it was rigged, that was the intention. All hands, even Billy's, shot into the air when Amelia's name came up. 'Go on, queen, open it up,' Aggie said. 'Put us out of our misery. But don't forget, I came a close second.'

'Don't expect too much, sweetheart,' Bessie told her. 'It's only a small token.'

Amelia's hands were shaking with excitement. Never had she dreamed of having a day like today, with so many people being nice to her. Normally her birthday passed without even a mention. 'Can I tear the paper, Auntie Bessie?'

'Of course yer can, sweetheart, but don't be too rough with it in case I want to use it again some time.'

Billy came closer to the table, not wanting to miss anything. And when the paper had been carefully torn and spread open to reveal a doll, instead of jerking his head in disgust as he usually did over girls' sloppy toys, he joined the women in their loud exclamations of surprise. Amelia herself didn't make a sound. She sat wide-eyed, looking down at the first doll she'd ever had in her hands. It was a rag doll, with a pretty china face, long blonde hair tied at the back with a pink ribbon, and dressed in a long dress of pink and white cotton, trimmed at the cuffs and hem with white lace.

Bessie exchanged glances with her two mates before asking, 'Don't yer like it, sweetheart?'

Amelia lifted her head, her eyes wet with tears. 'Is it for me, Auntie Bessie?'

'Of course it is, sweetheart, it's yer birthday present.'

The girl lifted the doll from the paper, stroked its hair, and held it to her chest with one hand while wiping away the tears with the other. Then she pushed her chair back and ran to throw an arm around Bessie's neck. 'She's lovely, Auntie

Bessie. She's the first doll I've ever had. You are very kind to me, and I do love you.'

Rita was beginning to understand why Bessie loved this girl so much, no one could help it. Except her mother, of course, who must be heartless. 'You can go now, Billy, we won't be playing any more.'

'Ah, ay, Mam! Can't I stay for a bit, just a few minutes?'

'No, yer can't, sunshine, me and me mates are going to have a drink now.'

'Thanks for helping us out, Billy,' Bessie said over Amelia's head. 'I appreciate it.'

Amelia was feeling happy and sad at the same time, but she didn't forget the manners she'd had drummed into her. 'Yes, thank you, Billy.' Then she had a thought, and giggled. 'It was a good job you stopped at me, otherwise your mother or Auntie Aggie might have ended up winning the doll.'

'Yeah! That would have been funny.' He was chuckling as he stepped into the street. His mother had opened the front door for him, and he grinned up at her. 'She's all right, that girl, not like her stuck-up mother.'

'I don't want to hear yer saying that to anyone else, Billy, d'yer hear? None of us can help the mothers we get, but you just thank yer lucky stars that yer ended up with me.' She watched as he crossed the cobbled street. 'Yer'll be in bed when I get home, so goodnight and God bless, sunshine.'

'Goodnight, Mam.'

Rita closed the door and went back into the living room. Amelia was sitting on the couch next to Bessie, inspecting the doll's clothes. Bessie had bought the doll for sixpence and made the clothes herself on the old Singer hand-machine she kept in her bedroom. She didn't use it much, for she spent her working life behind a sewing machine and never felt like starting again when she got home. 'Ay, sunshine, yer made a good job of that dress, it looks smashing,' Rita said. 'Yer could make a few bob taking sewing in, 'cos that looks really professional.'

Amelia lifted the dress on the doll. 'Look, Auntie Rita, it's got knickers on as well, and they've got lace round the legs.' She held the doll to her chest. 'I do love it, and I'll always love it and always look after it and keep it safe.' She glanced at Bessie. 'Can I keep it in my bedroom here, please, Auntie Bessie? 'Cos my mother thinks dolls are childish and she might not let me play with it.'

'Oh, go 'way,' Aggie said. 'Yer mam won't stop yer playing with the doll, that's what little girls do. Even if it's only for half an hour a night before yer go to bed.'

'Please let me keep it here, Auntie Bessie, please! It can sleep on my bed when I'm not here, and it won't be in your way.'

Bessie could see the girl was agitated and wasn't going to spoil the day for her. 'Of course she can stay here, sweetheart, she'll be company for me as well as keeping the bed warm for you.'

'Aren't yer going to give her a name?' Rita asked softly. 'She'll have to have a name so yer can talk to her.'

Aggie added her twopennyworth. 'And as she's

230

a pretty doll, queen, with a pretty dress and lace on her knickers, yer'll need to give her a nice name.'

The girl looked very undecided, as though she didn't really believe what she'd been told. 'You won't make me take her home, will you, Auntie Bessie, promise?'

'I've said she can stay here, sweetheart, and I never tell fibs or break a promise. So, now can you think of a nice name you would like for her? Or shall we all make suggestions until yer come to one yer fancy the best?'

'I know what name I want to give her, Auntie Bessie. As soon as I opened the paper and saw her lying on my knee, I thought she looked as pretty as a flower and the name Daisy came to me. I've seen daisies growing in a garden near our school, and they're yellow and bright and look cheerful. So I'd like that to be her name.'

'Then so be it, sweetheart, because she's your doll and it's only right you should call her what you want to. Besides, I think Daisy is a lovely name.' Bessie appealed to her mates, 'Don't yer think so, ladies?'

Rita nodded. 'Whenever I see a daisy, it always reminds me of sunshine. There are usually some growing wild in the park by the swings, and they always cheer me up.'

Aggie was nodding her agreement. 'And what about the song, "Daisy, Daisy, Give Me Your Answer Do"? That's not half a cheerful song, I always have to sing along to it.'

Amelia's face was a picture of happiness as she held the doll to her cheek. It was the first toy she'd ever had to call her own, and her pleasure knew no bounds. 'I'm going to sing her to sleep tonight. And I'll wrap my nightie around her, so she won't be cold.'

'There'll be no need for that, sweetheart,' Bessie said, pushing her chair back and making for a cupboard in the sideboard. 'Daisy's a very posh doll, she's got her own blanket.' She held a square piece of pink blanket aloft. 'I knew yer wouldn't want her to get cold.'

As the three neighbours were to say later, when the girl was in bed and they had their glasses of milk stout in front of them, they couldn't remember seeing anyone so happy. Amelia had wrapped the doll in the blanket, cuddled her to her chest, then rocked her for a while before saying, 'I think me and Daisy would like to go to bed now, Auntie Bessie, because we are both very tired. But we want to thank you for bringing us together, and we both love you very much. And you too, Auntie Rita and Auntie Aggie.'

She'd kissed everyone, told Daisy to be a good girl and kiss her aunties, then she'd made her way up the stairs, cuddling the doll as though it was the most precious thing on earth. And, needless to say, left behind three women whose tears kept their glasses topped up.

Chapter Twelve

Philip had his hand on the small of Evelyn's back as they stepped through the doors of the hotel and into the cool night air. He felt her shiver. 'Oh, you are cold, my dear, let me put my overcoat across your shoulders, I can't have you catching a chill.'

'I'm not really cold, Philip, it was coming out of the warm atmosphere that caused me to shiver. And there is a feel of autumn in the air.'

Philip was being very gentlemanly and draped his fine wool overcoat across her shoulders. Cupping her elbow, he said, 'We'll be at my apartment in a few minutes and you'll soon be warm, I left a fire burning.' Then he asked, 'Did you come to the hotel by taxi?'

'Yes, I could hardly come by tram in this attire, I would look so out of place. And I'm relying on you to arrange a taxi to take me home later, if you will be so kind?'

'Don't let's talk of you going home, my love, I hope you will stay for a while. After all, there is no one at home expecting you, is there?'

Evelyn felt no guilt about continuing the lie, nor did she give any thought to her daughter. That was something she would sort out later when she knew Philip better and he was well and truly under her spell. She shook her head. 'No, I live alone, as I told you.'

233

'Then the night is ours, my love. There is so much I want to know about you.' He pulled her to a halt outside a building. 'This is where my apartment is.'

Evelyn's surprise could be heard in her voice. 'But I thought all these buildings were business premises!'

Taking a key from his pocket, Philip placed it in the lock of a door set slightly back from the building's frontage. 'The ground floor consists of three offices. My apartment covers the whole of the second floor, and as you can see has a private entrance.' He pushed open the door, waited for her to enter, then followed her, closing the door behind him and switching on an electric light. 'It's just the one flight of stairs, my lovely, and don't look so frightened, there are no bogeymen.'

'I'm not afraid,' Evelyn told him, thinking a few compliments wouldn't go amiss. 'Not when you are here to protect me.'

When they reached the top of the stairs, Philip led her towards one of the four doors she could see leading off the landing. 'In here, my lovely, and I'm happy to say the fire is still glowing.'

It took all of Evelyn's willpower to stop her jaw from dropping at the sight of the luxurious furniture in the huge room. She knew Philip's family must be well-to-do because of his clothes and his air of confidence, but had never expected to see such opulence in the apartment he said he seldom used. 'It seems a large place for one man,' she said. 'Or do you share with another person?'

'Good heavens, no!' he said, taking her cape from her. 'I could never share with anyone,

234

certainly not a man anyway. Besides, I have no need to. My father owns the whole building.'

'You are very lucky, Philip.' Evelyn lowered herself on to the huge brown leather couch. 'I'm surprised you haven't been snaffled up by now, you must have had plenty of chances.'

He chuckled as he walked towards the massive mahogany sideboard where there were four bottles standing on a silver tray. 'Many, many chances, my dear Evelyn, but the right one never came along. Now, what would you like to drink?'

'You choose,' she told him, while crossing her legs and making sure she showed more than a little of her slim ankles. 'But not a full glass, please, Philip. I have to find my way home, remember.'

'Not for several hours, my lovely Evelyn, for I intend to start unravelling the mystery that surrounds you. And I need my senses intact to do that.'

'There is no mystery surrounding me, Philip, I promise you. What you see is what I am.'

He sat down beside her and handed her a glass half filled with deep red wine. 'I like what I see, my lovely, but surely there is more to your life than you admit? Perhaps something too hurtful for you to talk about?'

'I have told you about my husband and how he was killed. What I haven't told you is that although we had courted for a year or two before the war, I only saw him a few times after he joined the Army when he was allowed home on leave. When he learned he was being shipped out, he was given three days' leave and we were

235

married by special dispensation on his last day. I never saw him again after he went back to join his unit.'

Philip placed his glass on a mahogany side table before putting an arm across her shoulders. 'Oh, you poor darling, how very sad. It must have been heartbreaking for you, and I can understand why you have no wish to talk about something that must still cause you great pain and sadness.' He pulled her close. 'And has there been no one else in the years since then? No one to hold you close and soothe your aching heart?'

'I didn't want anyone else. Oh, there were chances, several suitors came along after my hand in marriage, but I could not feel anything for them.' Evelyn was lying so well she actually thought that what she was saying was the truth. So she stretched her made-up story further, for she had an idea Philip was going to delve deeper into her past. 'In fact, because I turned away several men my parents approved of, and they were eager to get me off their hands, it caused a rift between us and I am no longer in touch with them.' Her wide brown eyes stared into Philip's and he could feel his heartbeat quicken. 'How could I marry a man who didn't excite me or make my heart flutter at the sight of him? No, I preferred spinsterhood to marriage to a man I didn't love.'

And Philip believed every word she said. She had solved, for him, the mystery of why she had no family, and he never thought for one second she wasn't telling the truth. 'Oh, my poor darling Evelyn.' He pressed her head to his shoulder and kissed her brow. 'D'you think the time could come when the sight of me might cause your heart to flutter?'

'We hardly know each other, Philip.' She was clear enough in the head to keep to her plan. And that didn't include giving in to him quickly. Anything easily obtained is quickly tired of. 'I am fond of you already, it would be hard not to be, but it would be silly to jump into saying things one might regret within weeks. We will be working together every day from Monday, and that will be the testing time. You may find I am not the sweet woman you obviously think I am. So shall we give it a couple of weeks, Philip, and see what our thoughts are then?'

He raised his eyebrows. 'I am looking forward to seeing you each day, I will walk to the office with a spring in my step. But I want to see you outside work as well. We can work together as diligently and efficiently as ever my Uncle Simon and Miss Saunders did. I have every intention of applying myself to my new job with the same zest and energy I did in my previous firm. But I can't for the life of me see why we shouldn't meet as friends outside the office, can you?'

Evelyn ran a finger down his cheek. 'You are very forceful, my dear, and obviously used to having your own way. But I too am quite stubborn, so our relationship should be a very interesting one. I will give in to you as far as seeing each other outside work, but only for the next two Saturdays. As I have told you, my wardrobe is not what it used to be, and it will take me a while to save for suitable clothes.'

'I have already decided to increase your wages by a pound a week. That should help a little until we come to some other arrangement.'

'I can't take an increase in pay beyond the one I have already received, which is what a qualified secretary is entitled to. Any extra and the other staff would not be happy. Apart from the fact that it would set tongues wagging and they would see me as a painted lady.'

Philip chortled. 'A painted lady! Oh, I do like that description of you. If only it were true we would not be sitting here all sedate and respectable, we would be much more intimate.'

Evelyn slapped his hand playfully. 'I can see I'm going to have trouble keeping you in order, Mr Astbury. Now, you can be a good host and show me around this bachelor flat of yours which I find most interesting.'

He pulled her to her feet. 'Your wish is my command. We shall start off with the kitchen.'

It contained every modern appliance possible, and was an eye opener to Evelyn after her own tiny kitchen with its huge chipped sink and only one cold water tap. She found the sheer luxury of the bathroom breathtaking. Of course the electric lighting was a novelty to her, for she was only used to gas. 'Very nice,' was her only comment. She was determined not to let him see how surprised she was, and would be bitterly ashamed if he ever saw where she lived.

However, when he threw open the bedroom door she couldn't help but gasp. It was magnificently furnished, and the huge bed with its rich drapes and covers was the largest she had ever seen as well as being the most luxurious. But what struck her most forcibly was the masculine style which had been so noticeable in every room. Not a trace of anything female here. 'You have a very beautiful apartment, Philip, I feel quite jealous,' she said softly.

'My dear, the apartment is at your disposal whenever you feel the need of privacy. When you decide you would like our friendship to progress further, we can spend many a pleasant night in each other's company here.' He squeezed her shoulder and smiled down into her face. 'You have no need to pull away from me, my love, for I spoke in hope, not as a threat.'

'I didn't pull away from you, why should I? I would only pull away from someone I was scared of, and I have no fear of you.'

'Come, let us go back and relax on the couch with our glasses refilled. We can talk until the wee small hours of the morning, then I shall see you safely into a taxi before returning to this room which will hold no pleasure for me without you to grace it.'

Evelyn was feeling the effects of drink by now, and though she was not quite tipsy enough to be careless of what she was saying, she was happy to appreciate the compliments and the nearness of this very handsome man who also happened to be very rich. It was so long since she'd been flattered and pampered, she could feel herself basking in the attention. 'You are spoiling me, Philip, and while I should resist you, and start on my journey home, I feel too snug and warm to move.'

'Why should you move when you have no reason to? No one is watching the clock, waiting for you to come home. No one will be there to welcome you, and no fire to greet you. Make me happy and stay for a while, I want you by my side. Close enough to touch, to smell the sweetness of you.'

A lock of Philip's hair had fallen over his forehead. Evelyn reached up to push it back. 'Oh, you are very tempting, dear, but I'm trying to control myself. This is not the time for flattery. I have had far too much to drink to think clearly.'

He caught her hand and held it to his cheek. 'Are you saying that when Monday comes, and you are stone cold sober, perhaps you will find me unattractive?'

'Good grief, no! I was stone cold sober the first time I saw you in the office; and even at first glance I found you a very attractive man. Never for one second did it enter my head that you were a bachelor, not with your good looks.'

'And not for one second did I think I would ever be sitting in my lounge with the beautiful creature I first saw tapping at a typewriter. Fate has stepped in, my lovely, so let us take advantage of our luck.'

Wrapped in Philip's arms, Evelyn didn't want the evening to end as she revelled in the luxury of her surroundings, and the sweet words being whispered in her ear. They talked and kissed, and never once did Philip overstep the mark. He wanted to – oh, how he wanted to – but he was afraid of frightening her off. After all, hadn't she told him she was only married for one day before her husband was sent overseas? And she'd implied there had been no other men in her life, so she would be a novice when it came to love making. He would have to be patient until the time was right, and she came to him of her own free will. Then he would need to be gentle and tender.

It was the grandfather clock on the wall striking the hour of four that brought Evelyn out of her dreaming. Pushing Philip gently away from her, she said, 'I really must be going, my dear, or like Cinderella my coach will turn back into a pumpkin.' She kissed his lips with the softness of a butterfly. 'Ring for a taxi for me, Philip, please.'

This wasn't to his liking. He was besotted with her and wished she was as free with her favours as some of the other women he knew. But he dismissed that thought before it took root; he didn't want her to be like the other women, he wanted her to be special. 'I will ring now, my love, although it will break my heart. I would like you to stay here with me forever.'

Evelyn was fastening her cape. 'The easiest and quickest way to tire of someone is to be in their company too often. And I don't want you to tire of me, Philip, not when we are just getting to know each other.'

'You promise you will come here again, very soon?'

'I promise. Now ring for a taxi, please.'

'What address will I tell him to take you to?'

She tapped his nose with a forefinger. 'There are some mysteries I would like to retain, my dear. I will give the driver the address when he comes.'

241

Philip dialled a number, gave his address, then after replacing the receiver, told Evelyn the taxi would be there in ten minutes. He reached for his coat which had been casually thrown over the back of a chair. Taking a wallet from the inside pocket, he slipped his hand inside and brought out a five-pound note. 'This will help towards your taxi fares. I will instruct the driver to make sure you reach home safely.'

'Philip, I can't take money from you!' Even while she was speaking, Evelyn was thinking what she could do with so much money. 'Besides, the driver wouldn't be able to change that, he'd think I was mad. I have a few shillings in my purse, that should be enough to cover the fare.'

Philip folded the five-pound note three times then slipped it down the front of her dress. 'I insist you take it, my darling. I cannot allow you to pay for spending an evening with me, especially when you have delighted and charmed me with your presence. Please take it, my lovely, and put it to whatever use gives you pleasure. If you need anything ... new clothes, jewellery, perfume, or anything else you desire ... you only have to ask.'

Evelyn knew she had him in the palm of her hand now, and felt safe in saying, 'That would make me feel like a kept woman, Philip, and I'm afraid that wouldn't sit well on my shoulders.'

He shook his head. 'Not at all, I would never think that of you. I have had many fleeting romances, none of which were serious, and have always been generous with the women concerned. I can assure you, not one of them has complained about my generosity. I wasn't buying them, I was merely giving them a gift because I like to please the opposite sex. There is nothing sinister in that.'

As though on impulse, Evelyn kissed his cheek. He wasn't to know it, but the kiss was to thank him for enabling her to accept his money. 'How could there be anything sinister in anything you do, my dear? I will keep the money in the spirit it was given. Thank you sincerely, and I apologise if I have displeased you.'

Philip was all smiles again. 'I think we must go downstairs now, the taxi should be waiting for you. I will count the minutes until I see you in the office on Monday, and we can arrange to meet here again next week.'

Evelyn turned to wave to Philip out of the back window then leaned towards the glass partition that separated her from the driver. 'I need to pick up something from Exchange Station, driver, so would you kindly take me there first, please?'

'There'll be no one there this time of the morning,' the driver growled in a husky voice. 'The place will be deserted.'

'I have a key to a left luggage locker so I don't need the services of station staff. You can drive into the station and I'll be less than five minutes.'

'Yer'll have to pay extra for the waiting time.' The driver couldn't stand these poncey people who had more money than they knew what to do with while thousands of families in Liverpool were living below the poverty line. 'It'll cost yer an extra tanner.'

'You will be paid for your time, my good man, have no fear.' Evelyn stepped out of the taxi and

243

shivered. The station was deserted and eerie. She lost no time in opening the locker and taking out the bag with her working clothes in it. She got into the back of the taxi with it, placing it on the seat next to her. When she spoke next it was an order, not a request. 'Take me to Newsham Street, driver, and drop me off halfway down. And please be as quiet as you can, I don't want my neighbours complaining.'

There was a look of disgust on the driver's face as he set the taxi in motion. She must be a good-time girl, this one, been out to make herself a few bob. She was dressed to kill, but her clothes didn't go with the address she'd given him. He knew the area well, and they were two-up-two-down houses. Not that there was anything wrong with living in a two-up-two-down house, for he lived in one himself and his neighbours were the salt of the earth. They never put on airs and graces and pretended to be something they weren't. Not like the one he had in the back of his cab now, giving orders as though she was the Queen of bloody Sheba. She must think he was born yesterday, telling him not to make a noise 'cos she didn't want her neighbours complaining. More likely she didn't want them to see her all dressed up like a scarlet woman.

As the taxi turned into her street, Evelyn asked, 'How much is that, driver?'

'I'll tell yer when I've stopped the cab, and checked the mileage and the waiting time.'

'Stop here, please.'

The tone of her voice rubbed him up the wrong way and he carried on past several more houses.

When he heard her knock on the glass, he growled, 'If I'd pulled up sharp, the brakes would have woken the whole bloody street, missus, so yer can't have everything yer own way.' Normally the driver was a pleasant man who would jump out of his taxi to help a passenger. But not this one, talking to him as though he'd crawled out from under a stone. She could get out of the cab under her own steam. 'That'll be three bob, missus.'

That was all the money Evelyn had in her purse, and it would leave her without any change to buy food from the corner shop for her and Amelia. Still, she comforted herself with the thought of the five-pound note nestling between her breasts. The corner shop wouldn't be able to change it, but she could borrow on the strength of it from her neighbour. 'Here you are, and please try not to make a noise as you drive away.'

Evelyn's mistake was in not closing the passenger door behind her. She tutted angrily when she heard the driver slam it shut before driving away. She got herself in so much of a dither, trying to open the front door quickly in case any nosy neighbour had been woken, that her hand was shaking and she had a problem fitting the key into the lock. Once inside, she leaned back against the door and breathed a sigh of relief. She'd got away with it, thank God, but she couldn't go through that again, she'd have to make other plans in future. Far better to stay the night at Philip's and come home at a respectable time when she wouldn't be so noticeable. That could easily be arranged if she was able to leave several changes of clothes at his apartment. The only thing that stood in her way was her daughter. But she'd find a way around that when she'd had a few hours' sleep and her head was clear. At least she hadn't been found out.

However, the banging of the taxi door, and the noise of the engine, had been heard by Evelyn's next door neighbour. Bessie hadn't been able to drop off to sleep, had spent hours tossing and turning. The reason for this unrest was her neighbour, and the manner in which she treated her daughter. Also, Bessie hadn't believed the tale Evelyn had told her about visiting an old friend she hadn't seen since school days. The words didn't ring true. And while Bessie didn't care what her neighbour got up to, she worried it might in some way affect Amelia.

So the slamming of the car door, in the silence of the night, was enough to take Bessie from her bed to the window. The gas lamp in the street didn't throw out much light, but it was enough for Bessie to catch a glimpse of Mrs Sinclair, and that short glimpse was sufficient to make her gasp in surprise and wonder. She thought she was seeing things at first, but the few seconds her neighbour spent fiddling to get her key in were enough to tell her her eyes weren't playing tricks on her. She'd never seen anyone dressed like that before, not in her whole life. The sight certainly confirmed the doubts Bessie had about Evelyn visiting an old school friend. The woman looked as though she'd been to a fancy dress ball, or, more likely, been spending time with a rich fancy man.

Bessie went back to her bed and sat on the side of it. She shook her head, not knowing what to think about the whole set-up. It should be interesting tomorrow when her neighbour came to pick up Amelia. Whatever she said would be a pack of lies, for she was good at that. Still, it would be interesting.

She slipped between the sheets and lay on her back staring up at the ceiling. She wouldn't say anything to Amelia's mother about seeing her coming home at half-past four in the morning in a taxi. No, she'd act daft and ask Evelyn if she'd enjoyed visiting her old school chum. Pretend to be interested, like. The answer she got would be a web of deceit and lies, but it wouldn't be dull and she'd have a good laugh afterwards. And they did say that if you gave a liar enough rope, they would hang themselves. Not that Bessie wished that on the woman. God forbid, she was still Amelia's mother.

Telling herself there was no point lying there wondering what was going on when she would be told tomorrow exactly as much as Evelyn Sinclair wanted her to know, Bessie snuggled down and made a determined effort to go to sleep. Her last conscious thought, as she pulled the blanket up over her shoulders, was that the stuck-up so-and-so wasn't worth losing sleep over. And very soon after that, the room was filled with the sound of her even, gentle snoring.

In the next bedroom Amelia lay dreaming with her rag doll pressed close to her chest, the one thing the child had ever been able to call her very own.

It was eleven o'clock when Evelyn walked up Bessie's back yard. Amelia, who was sitting on the couch with the doll on her knee, heard the latch clicking back into place, and a look of fear came over her face. 'Don't let Mother see Daisy, Auntie Bessie, or she'll take her off me.'

'Run upstairs, sweetheart, and we'll keep her a secret.' Bessie stood at the bottom of the stairs until she heard the girl reach the landing, then put a smile on her face and went to open the kitchen door. 'Oh, hello, Mrs Sinclair, I wasn't expecting yer until about twelve o'clock, I thought yer'd be enjoying a lie-in.' She stood aside to let Evelyn pass and told herself to be as polished as her neighbour. 'Amelia is upstairs, she won't be a minute. Sit yerself down while ye're waiting and tell me how the visit to yer old school friend went. Did yer enjoy catching up on old times?'

'Oh, yes, it was lovely, talking about all the girls in our class, and wondering what paths their lives have taken. Elizabeth has seen a couple of them over the years, and tells me they married well and have good lives.'

'That's nice for yer, I'm glad yer enjoyed yerself.' Bessie was waiting to see if Amelia's mother would ask how her daughter's party had gone. Surely she wouldn't let it pass without a word? But so far, nothing! 'Would yer like a cup of tea? It won't take me a minute, and Amelia can have one before she leaves.'

'I would love one, thank you so much.' Evelyn laced her fingers together when Bessie went out to the kitchen. How was she going to ask to borrow some money for food? What excuse could she use? Telling her about the five-pound note was out of the question because people in Miss Maudsley's position had probably never set eyes on one in their lives. And Evelyn needed some money, even if it was only a shilling, for there was no food in the house and she was starving. Nor did she have any coal to light a fire, and the house was freezing.

Amelia came down the stairs and stood sedately in front of her mother. 'Hello, Mother, did you have a nice time with your friend?'

'Yes, I did. Have you behaved yourself for Miss Maudsley?'

Waiting in the kitchen for the kettle to boil, Bessie could feel herself getting mad. Couldn't the woman ask her daughter if she'd had a nice party, instead of asking if she'd behaved herself? Was she so selfish she'd never given a thought to whether her daughter enjoyed her birthday? The kettle started to whistle and Bessie poured the boiling water into the dark brown teapot. Then she walked to stand in the kitchen doorway. 'I'll let it brew for a few minutes, I can't stand weak tea.' She watched as Evelyn put a hand in the pocket of her coat, shook her head, then put a hand in her other pocket. 'Have you lost something, Mrs Sinclair?'

Evelyn's acting was perfect. With a look of panic on her face, she tried each of her pockets again. 'Oh, dear, I had two shillings in my pocket when I was on the tram last night, now I don't seem to have them. I must have dropped them getting off and didn't hear them fall.'

Bessie felt like applauding. If she didn't know

249

the woman better, she would have believed what she was being told. Dropped them on the tram indeed? What a ruddy liar! But she'd go along with her neighbour, just for the hell of it. 'Oh, dear, that's a shame. It's a lot of money to lose.'

'It's worse than you think, Miss Maudsley, for I intended to send Amelia to the corner shop for a bag of coal and some food. There's nothing in the house for our dinner.' Evelyn wrung her hands. 'Oh, dear, what am I going to do?'

Bessie was watching Amelia's face and it spoke volumes. She showed no emotion at all. It was as if she wasn't involved and had no worry that there wasn't going to be any dinner. This told Bessie that the child was used to her mother telling lies, and felt no pity for her. And, the little woman asked herself, why should the child pity someone who never touched her, kissed her, or told her she loved her?

It was for Amelia's sake that Bessie said, 'I can lend yer a couple of bob, but I would have to have it back before the rent man comes. I don't miss my rent money for anyone.'

'I will give it back to you tomorrow, definitely.' There was relief in Evelyn's voice, she didn't like having hunger pains. Anyway, her life would be changing for the better very soon and then she wouldn't have to cadge off this insignificant little woman. 'You are very kind and I promise to repay you when I call for Amelia tomorrow night.'

'She can stay here for a few hours, if yer like,' Bessie said, noting the happiness she'd seen in the girl's eyes all morning had now turned to sadness. 'It would give yer a chance to put yer feet up for a while.'

'No, I need her to go to the corner shop for bread and whatever meats they have. And a bag of coal.' And while Evelyn stood waiting for Bessie to get the two silver shillings out of her purse, she silently added, that her daughter could also light the fire and wash any dirty dishes. For in the new life she intended for herself, she couldn't be seen with broken, dirty fingernails. She'd have to be perfectly groomed at all times if she was to regain the luxurious lifestyle she'd once had.

As Evelyn held her hand out for the money Bessie was passing to her, she caught sight of her daughter out of the corner of her eye. And for a second she was brought down to earth. But it was only for a second, because she had no intention of letting Amelia stand in her way. How she was going to get around that she didn't know, but she would do it. For to tell Philip now that she had an eight-year-old daughter would be to say goodbye to all her dreams.

Chapter Thirteen

Evelyn wasn't a bit shy about meeting Philip in the office on Monday morning. Nor was she embarrassed, for she felt there was nothing to be embarrassed about. She wasn't a child, at twenty-nine years of age, and they hadn't done anything improper, though she wasn't stupid enough to think it would always be so. The prospect didn't worry her, she was willing to do anything to get what she wanted. Although she was a little concerned about her inexperience in love making. There was only ever the once with Charles, and that was in the confined space of his car. She couldn't remember much about the actual deed, except the slight discomfort at first. This wasn't the case for Charles, though, for the moans and sighs coming from him had told her he was finding great pleasure in the act. She, on the other hand, was left unmoved.

She was going through the large three-drawer filing cabinet, making sure the correspondence was correctly filed and familiarising herself with the names of clients, when the office door opened and Philip breezed in with a huge smile on his face. 'Good morning,' he said, then closed the office door before adding, 'my lovely.'

'Good morning, Mr Philip.' Evelyn wagged a finger at him. 'Please be careful, anyone could walk in.'

He was grinning as he hung his coat on the ornately carved coat stand. 'There is no one to walk in, my darling. I could hear James dictating to Miss Coombes, and the young lady taken on in your place, Grace Carr, is now making us a pot of tea. And I did tell her that she must never enter either office without knocking.' He walked over to where she stood, kissed her cheek, then sat in his swivel chair. 'Are there any letters awaiting a reply?'

'The post has arrived, but I left it for Miss Carr to sort out. That was one of my duties and I thought it should be left with her. If it pleases you, I will go and collect it from her.'

Philip shook her head. 'It pleases me that you stay here, where I can feast my eyes on you. We can deal with the post later.' He crossed his legs and raised his brows. 'You obviously arrived home safely on Sunday morning, so I won't bore you by asking. What I am interested in is, did you enjoy your time in my company? Did I pass the test?'

Evelyn was leaning her elbows on the cabinet, and smiling up at him. 'Did you really think there was any chance of not passing the test?'

'You are a woman of mystery, my love, so I am not taking anything for granted.'

Evelyn glanced towards the door. 'Please can we keep to "Mrs Sinclair" while we are in the office, Philip? If they knew of our relationship I would feel quite embarrassed and it would sour our friendship.' The words were barely out of her mouth before there came a tapping on the door. 'This will be Miss Carr.'

Philip jumped to his feet to open the door. 'Ah, refreshment. There's nothing better than a cup of tea to charge the brain cells. Leave the tray on my desk, Miss Carr, Mrs Sinclair will bring it out when we're ready.'

As soon as the door closed, Evelyn said, 'That's very high-handed of you, Philip! We only ever have one cup of tea first thing in the morning, not a pot full. If Mr Woodward receives the same treatment, he's in for a shock. He may not like changes being made without his consent.'

'James Woodward is the least of my worries at the moment,' Philip said. 'My main concern is that I am your first priority in this office. Anything that goes amiss outside these four walls, I will deal with. Inside them I want your undivided attention. So now, woman, I want you to pamper me by pouring out the tea.'

Evelyn knew he wasn't being serious, but she intended to show him she wasn't going to be an easy catch. He appeared to get everything he wanted in life very easily, and she decided he would appreciate her more if he had to do some running. 'I'm going to collect the post from Miss Carr, so perhaps *you'll* be good enough to pour the tea while I'm away. There is work to be done, Mr Philip, we need to earn our wages.'

'Have your cup of tea first, the post will wait for ten minutes.'

But Evelyn was already opening the door. 'I can drink it while I'm opening the post, to save time.'

Philip was more subdued for the rest of the morning. As Evelyn opened the letters and passed them across the desk to him, he read each

254

one carefully, making a mental note of its contents before setting it aside ready to dictate a reply. Neither of them spoke again until all the envelopes had been opened and the letters stacked in front of Philip. Then he said. 'You are a slave driver, Mrs Sinclair.'

She shook her head. 'As you know, Mr Philip, I'm not particularly quick at taking dictation, and a couple of those letters are urgent and need to be in the lunchtime post.' She gave him the benefit of her coy smile. 'Besides, I thought if we got through the post quickly, it would give us more time to talk.'

'When you look at me like that, I will forgive you anything. Now, I believe there are four letters that need to be answered right away, so if you will get your pencil and pad, I will start to dictate. And I will speak slowly and clearly, so you can keep up.'

Evelyn left her chair to pick up the tray. 'I'll take this out and ask Miss Carr if she will be kind enough to make us two more cups of tea. Once we're refreshed, we will sail through those four letters – I hope! My typing isn't much better than my shorthand, and it will take me all my time to have the letters ready for the noon post.'

'Don't upset yourself if they are not ready for the lunchtime post, my love. If they're posted by five o'clock they will still arrive by tomorrow's first delivery.'

'Let us stick to the routine of the office, Mr Philip, at least until my speed has improved. I'm afraid that any diversion from that would be put down to my inexperience. The last thing I want is an irate client storming into the office complaining he has not received a reply to his letter. It is I who would have to shoulder the blame, not you. Miss Saunders ran this office like clockwork for your Uncle Simon, I want to do no less for you.'

Philip's cheeky grin reappeared. 'I bet Miss Saunders didn't boss Uncle Simon around, as you seem intent on bossing me.' He held a hand to his heart. 'But I won't complain, for you are much more beautiful than Miss Saunders.'

Like giving a child a sweet to keep them happy, Evelyn blew him a kiss before she opened the door. 'Thank you, my dear. And now I will collect my pencil and pad, and work shall commence in earnest.'

Philip was very fluent in his speech, and spoke clearly and slowly until he found Evelyn was more than keeping up with him. He dictated the last two letters at his normal speed. When he had finished he complimented her. 'Very good, Mrs Sinclair, you can now go to the top of the class.'

'Thank you, kind sir, I am pleased you are happy with me.'

'I am more than happy with you, my dear, and will remain so as long as you remember it is my class you are in, and I am your teacher.'

Evelyn closed her note pad and pushed her chair back. 'Ah, it will be interesting to know which lessons exactly you have in mind.' She was feeling secure in the knowledge that his interest in her hadn't dimmed, but was taking no chances until she had him in the palm of her hand. To do that she had to show she shared his feelings. 'I wonder when I will find out?' Without waiting for a reply, she left the office to type the letters ready for the lunchtime post.

Philip sat for a while staring into space. He couldn't help himself where Evelyn was concerned, he was besotted with her. His only worry was that she didn't feel the same about him. Was she just a tease? he asked himself. Then a voice in his head told him not to be stupid, a woman her age wouldn't be childish enough to tease him. But he wasn't entirely convinced. Only time would tell. So, trying to put her from his mind, he picked up the letters still to be answered, and as he read them composed the answers in his brain, ready to dictate later, probably after lunch. And thinking of lunch, Evelyn was back in his mind. They had an hour, and his apartment was only minutes away...

While Philip's mind was on her, Evelyn was intent on typing the letters ready for the early post. While her hopes and the stakes were high, her feet were still on the ground. If an affair with him didn't materialise she would need this job. Especially now when her salary had been increased. So she typed as quickly and as accurately as possible, and as she finished each letter asked Grace Carr to check them for errors. There was only one, and Evelyn was in high spirits to hear it. 'Thank you, Grace, that is very good news. I'm getting back my speed now, thank goodness.'

As Evelyn left her chair, Grace asked, 'How are you getting on with Mr Philip? He's very good-looking, isn't he?' She giggled. 'I know I could fall for him.'

'Mr Philip is a gentleman, and very easy to work with.' Evelyn stiffened. The last thing she wanted was for a young girl to be making cow's eyes at him. 'But I rather think he's out of your league, dear, so I wouldn't waste your time.'

'You never know your luck,' Grace called after her as she walked towards the office. 'If you don't try, you won't get anywhere.'

Evelyn lifted her hand to show she'd heard before opening the office door to find Philip swivelling in his chair, fingers pressed together to form a steeple shape. She placed the letters before him, saying, 'All ready for your signature, my dear. I have had Miss Carr check each one for spelling errors, so unless you really feel you ought, there is no reason for you to read them.'

'Then I shan't.' He signed each letter with a flourish and handed them back to her. 'Ask Miss Carr to attend to posting them, I want you back in here. There's something I would like to ask you.'

Curious though Evelyn was to know what he had in mind, she didn't want to delay the letters. 'I'll be back before you've had time to miss me.'

True to her word, in less than a minute she was sitting before him. 'Now you can have my undivided attention, sir.'

'Come to the apartment in our lunch hour. If you are afraid of being seen with me, we can make our way there separately. But I want a little time alone with you.'

'Oh, Philip, I'm going shopping in my lunch hour! I'm sorry, but there are some things I need.

258

Also, I have to change the five-pound note you gave me, otherwise I'll have no coppers for the tram fare home tonight.'

'That is a very poor excuse, my love. I can give you small change for your fare, and surely there is nothing so important that you need from the shops it can't wait another day?'

He looked so disappointed, Evelyn found herself feeling guilty. She also realised for the first time that he was getting to her, she was really beginning to like him. 'I was going to use the money you gave me to buy myself something nice to wear when I'm meeting you. Over the years I'm afraid I haven't been able to afford the pretty satin underwear I was used to, nor the fine pure silk stockings and up-to-date shoes. There is little in my wardrobe that is modern and attractive, and I do so want to look my best for you. It will take me a while to get back to where I was a few years ago, but I'm determined to. I want to look my best for you.'

'I wouldn't care if you were dressed in sackcloth, my love, I find you very beautiful. But because spending an hour in your company would make me so happy, perhaps I can come up with a solution. Why don't I give you some small change for your fares and any foodstuffs you may be in need of for the week, and then, if you are agreeable, it would give me great pleasure to buy the satin underwear I'm sure you would look wonderful in. I would delight in choosing it for you, and will have it at the apartment next time you come. Please don't say no, my love, indulge me.'

Evelyn was stunned, her brain trying to take in too many things at once. One part of it was telling her to agree. This way she would be getting the best of both worlds. Money to last her the week, her satin under garments bought for her, and she would still have the five-pound note. On top of that, she knew that anything Philip bought would be far more expensive than the clothes she could afford for herself. But there was a niggle in the back of her mind that stopped her from answering him straight away. If she let him give her so much, what would he want in return? Oh, she knew he would expect sexual favours, she had never thought different and the idea didn't bother her. But would he tire of her sooner if he thought of her as his mistress?

She sighed. 'I don't know, Philip. I feel torn between wanting to please you, and worrying that the time will come when you lose your respect for me because you believe I am only after your money. I would agree to your offer only if it is understood that I keep part of the life I have that makes me feel secure. My own home, although I don't own it, my work here, and to retain what you call my air of mystery. If you agree then I would be happy about the financial arrangement, and would love to spend my lunch hour with you in your apartment.'

A slow grin spread across his handsome face. 'And would you love to spend Saturday evening in my company? We don't need to go out for a meal if you don't wish to, I can arrange for one to be delivered. Whatever you would like to do, I will agree to. You see, my lovely Evelyn, I am completely captivated by you.'

'It is still early days, Philip, let us not rush into anything.' Evelyn could see the time coming when he would ask her to live with him, and she wasn't ready for that yet. There was Amelia to consider, and that would be one piece of news that would put an end to any relationship if he found she'd lied to him. 'We haven't known each other long, let us take things slowly and enjoy getting to know each other. Like a courting couple, except it must be kept a secret during office hours.'

When Evelyn called for Amelia on Monday night, she was filled with the joy of living. And her expression wasn't lost on Bessie. She had never known her neighbour look so happy, or be so pleasant and talkative. More than ever she was convinced there had been a great change in Evelyn's life over the last few weeks, and from the brightness of her eyes, that change wasn't anything to do with her old school chum. More likely it was a man who had brought it about.

'Here's the two shillings I borrowed from you yesterday, Miss Maudsley, and I owe you a debt of thanks, I don't know what we'd have done without your help. You really are most kind. To me and to Amelia, who has grown very fond of you.'

'And she's a treat to have in the house,' Bessie said, smiling at the girl who was looking from one to the other with apprehension. She was still afraid her mother would find out about the doll and forbid her to have it. 'She's company for me,' Bessie went on, 'someone to talk to instead of the four walls.' Then she set a trap, wondering if her stuck-up neighbour would walk into it. 'Yer can leave her any time, if yer want to go somewhere. To visit yer old school friend, like.'

Evelyn was hoping for this and gushed, 'Oh, that is thoughtful of you. I'm sure Amelia would like that, I can tell she's happy here. But I can't allow you to feed her six days a week for a shilling, that would be most unfair. I'm expecting another raise in my salary soon. The man to whom I am private secretary is so pleased with my work he has intimated I will be receiving an increase in the next week or so. I am able, therefore, to give you two shillings a week, which should help you out.'

'I like having the child here, I don't do it for money. But an extra shilling would come in handy with the winter coming on and me needing extra coal. As I say, though, I would mind Amelia for nothing, she's a mate to me.' Bessie tilted her head. Her neighbour had walked into one trap, for there was no boss living that would give a worker a raise in pay twice within three weeks. Still, it was no skin off her nose if the woman lived in a fantasy world and was a compulsive liar. But would she walk into another? 'She can stay here any time yer like, Mrs Sinclair. Perhaps when yer visit yer old school mate yer could sleep there overnight, save coming home in the dark?'

These words were music to Evelyn's ears. 'Well, if you wouldn't think I was taking advantage of your good nature, it would be lovely to stay over-night at Elizabeth's. I will write to her tonight, she'll be really pleased.'

Amelia knew better than to show she was

262

delighted. Her voice was soft when she asked, 'Does that mean I'll be sleeping here on Saturday night, Mother?'

'Yes, it does. And I hope you realise what a lucky girl you are.' Evelyn pushed herself off the couch feeling everything was going her way. The future looked very bright, except for the problem of her daughter, but she'd worry about that when the time came. Until then she intended to live the good life and take everything that Philip offered. 'Come along, Amelia, I'm really quite hungry tonight. I have brought something in for our tea.'

Bessie opened her mouth to say the girl had enjoyed a meal only an hour ago, but closed it before the words came out. The most she'd be offered by her mother would be a sandwich, and she could manage that. It was funny that Bessie had never thought about it until the last few weeks, but never once had she smelled cooking coming from the house next door. It was no wonder the girl cleared her plate every night. When she'd finished her meal it was always as clean as a whistle.

Half an hour after Evelyn left with her daughter, Rita was knocking on Bessie's front door. 'I haven't got me bed with me, so yer don't need to worry about me taking root in yer house. But you are the only bit of social life I get, sunshine. If it weren't for our little chats I'd go round the bend with boredom.'

'Sit yerself down, girl, yer know ye're always welcome. And although I haven't got any earth-shattering news for yer, I do have a tit-bit that

263

might give yer something to think about. I'll put the kettle on for a cuppa first, though, 'cos I always seem to find more to talk about when me whistle is whet.' Bessie turned when she reached the kitchen door. 'D'yer know, Rita, at one time I couldn't stand women who had nothing better to do than jangle. Now I'm getting to be as bad as them. Not that I stand in the street gossiping, I don't have time for that with going to work, but yer'll see what I mean when I've made the tea and we can talk in peace.'

'How is Amelia?' Rita asked as she took the cup and saucer Bessie was holding out to her. 'Still thrilled with the doll, is she?'

Bessie held the saucer steady while she lowered herself on to a chair. 'If I'd spent a pound on a present for her, she couldn't have thought more of it than she does that doll. She talks to it all the time, and sings to it when she pretends to be getting it to sleep. And when I'm in the kitchen, and she thinks I can't hear her, she talks to it like her mother must talk to her. I can hear her saying, "Now, Daisy, what have I told you about keeping your dress clean? Just look at that mark, made with a dirty hand. I haven't got money to buy you new clothes, so do as I say and make sure you wash your hands before touching anything. Don't make me have to tell you again or I shall have to punish you. And remember, cleanliness is next to Godliness."'

Rita shook her head and tutted. 'She's got the poor kid like an old woman, so serious and old fashioned. The only time I've ever heard the girl laugh was here on Saturday for her birthday. And she looks so pretty when she's acting her age, any mother would be proud to have her for a daughter. I know I would.'

'Oh, she knows how to laugh, don't worry. She has me in stitches sometimes when she's taking off one of the girls in her class. We get on like a house on fire, me and her.' Bessie tapped a finger against the side of her forehead. 'She's all there, Rita, believe me, and the more I see of her, the more I realise the poor kid learned from a very early age that the way to stay out of trouble is to do everything she's told. She never answers her mother back, just keeps quiet and does as she says. But she's a clever kid and must know that she doesn't get the love and attention most children get from their mother. I've never seen the queer one give her a smile, never mind a kiss. Yer want to be here at night when it gets near the time for her mother to come and pick her up. She changes from a happy, laughing child to one who is a bag of nerves, terrified in case she says the wrong thing. It's a crying shame, for she's a girl crying out for love and attention.'

'Mrs Sinclair doesn't deserve her.' Rita stretched forward to put her cup on the table. 'But yer want to watch yer don't get too fond of the girl, Bessie, 'cos if yer do, yer'd only be heading for a load of heartache. I can't see them staying in this street for much longer, it's not posh enough for Her Ladyship.'

'Ah, well, now, I think there's something in the wind.' Bessie lifted the corner of her pinny and wiped it across her mouth. 'Nothing's been said, but I think our posh neighbour is up to no good, and I'd lay odds there's a man involved.'

Rita sat forward, her eyes wide with interest. 'A man! Oh, go 'way, what makes yer think that, sunshine?'

'Intuition, girl, that's all. I might be miles out, but I'm not very often wrong. I know it's going to make me sound like a nosy so-and-so, but I set two little traps for her tonight and she walked into them. Not that it proved anything beyond doubt, and I really don't care what she gets up to as long as Amelia doesn't get hurt in the process, but I'll be interested to see how things go in the next few weeks.'

'If yer think yer can get so far with yer story and then not tell me the rest, yer've got another think coming, Bessie Maudsley!' Rita sat back. 'I'm not moving from this chair until I've heard the lot. And another thing, didn't we agree that in this house we'd call the girl Milly and not Amelia? She's only a kid and she's got such a lovely, cheeky smile, she'd suit being called Milly.'

'Yeah, I do call her Milly when we're on our own. But when it comes to six o'clock she's Amelia. Anyway, back to what I was telling yer. I don't know anything for sure, so it might only be me imagination. But whichever way, I don't want yer to pass anything I say on to Aggie. If the queer one got to know I'd been telling tales about her, she'd have me ruddy guts for garters and I'd never be allowed to have Milly again.'

'If yer don't get on with it, sunshine, it'll be midnight and my feller will be out looking for me. Or he might even decide to teach me a lesson and lock the front door and go to bed!'

Bessie pictured Rita's placid husband and chuckled. 'That'll be the day, when Reg Wells puts his foot down with you! He started off the wrong way when yer got married, by being too soft with yer. It's too late for him to change now. Anyway, yer don't know when ye're well off, having such a good husband.'

Rita nodded her head vigorously. 'Yes, I've got a husband in a million and I love the bones of him. He's got one fault, though, and that is he's dull! He never comes home from work with any juicy bits of gossip for his wife who has had a bloody miserable, boring day. And that is why I rely on you, and why I'm sitting here waiting for you to put some interest back into my life. But trying to get it out of you is like getting blood out of a stone. So instead *I'll* give *you* a piece of gossip that will have yer falling off yer chair.'

It was Bessie's turn to sit forward in anticipation. 'Go 'way! What have I missed?'

Rita puckered her lips and slowly nodded her head. 'Keep tight hold of the arms of the chair, sunshine, 'cos ye're in for a shock. D'yer know Doreen Brown, her from number sixteen at the top of the street?'

'Yer mean, the nice-looking blonde woman?'

'Yeah, that's her. Blonde hair and a smashing slim figure. Well, didn't she go and run off with the milkman this afternoon! The whole street saw them. Running like hell they were.'

'Ooh, I can't believe it! She seemed such a nice girl. And she's got two young children and a very handsome husband, too!' Bessie looked genuinely shocked. 'He's the man who delivers our milk in

267

the mornings, isn't he?'

Rita let a smile appear. 'That's right, but yer don't need to worry, yer'll get yer milk in the morning as usual. Him and Doreen were only running for the twenty-two tram to take them to the Atlas.'

'Well, I'll be blowed!' Bessie said, chortling. 'I must be getting slow on the uptake, 'cos I fell for that hook, line and sinker.'

'Ye're not only getting slower on the uptake, sunshine, ye're getting a damn' sight slower on the out-take! I've been here half an hour and still haven't heard enough to whet me appetite for a bit of excitement. So come on, Bessie, tell me why yer think there's dirty works at the crossroads regarding yer neighbour?'

'Okay, sweetheart, but don't blame me if nothing is going on. It might just be me bad mind. Anyway, here goes.' Bessie crossed her thin legs, making sure to pull her pinny down over her knees. And she told an enthralled Rita all that had been said in conversation with the woman next door. How she'd casually offered to mind Milly if Evelyn wanted to visit her so-called old school chum on Saturday. And if she wanted to stay overnight, well then, Milly was welcome to sleep in Bessie's spare room.

'And did she accept yer offer?' Rita asked, sitting so near the edge of the couch she was in danger of falling off. 'Is she staying out on Saturday night?'

'Oh, she accepted all right, it was what she'd been angling for. Nice as pie she was, I've never seen her smile so much. And I'll tell yer another thing, she's a bloody good liar. She told me about two weeks ago that she'd been offered this job as a private secretary, and because it meant a rise she would pay me a shilling a week to look after Milly for the two hours each night. Well, now she says her boss is so pleased with her work he's going to increase her wages again, so she's going to give me two shillings a week to look after Milly.' Bessie shook her head. 'And the woman thinks I'm stupid enough to believe every word she says!'

'But what makes yer think there's a man involved, sunshine, has she ever mentioned having a man friend?'

'No, she's always been very brief with her words until a week ago. Never said anything except "hello" and "goodbye". And she was always so dead bloody miserable, with a face like a wet week, she used to give me the willies. But these days she's all sweetness and light. She even looks happy, in her own way, contented like, and that's what makes me think there's now a man in her life.' Bessie pulled a face and held her hand up. 'But don't take that as gospel, I could be wrong.'

'Yer mean, there's no old school friend?' Rita asked. 'That's a lie as well?'

'We'll just have to wait and see what develops over the next few weeks. If she has got a man, and he makes her happy, then good luck to her. As long as she doesn't stop Milly from coming here.'

But Rita still wasn't satisfied. 'Surely if she had a man friend she would have brought him to the house by now, to meet her daughter?'

'Unless he's rich, and she'd be ashamed to bring him here.' Bessie got up to poke the fire and put some life back into it. 'It might be me being bad-minded, Rita, and in that case I should apologise to the woman if I'm wrong. But it'll all come out in the wash, and then we'll see if I'm right or a foolish, bad-minded spinster. Only time will tell.'

Rita glanced at the clock and jumped to her feet. 'I'd better go, I haven't done my feller's carry-out yet. But I'll be looking forward to the next instalment, sunshine, so keep me informed.'

Bessie saw her to the door. 'I'll let yer know if anything exciting happens, girl, but keep it under yer hat in case I'm making a fool of meself.'

Rita turned as she stepped off the pavement. 'My money's on you, sunshine! And if yer turn out to be right, well, that'll be enough excitement to keep me going for a couple of weeks.' She waved her hand as she crossed to the opposite pavement. 'Goodnight and God bless, sunshine, see yer tomorrow.'

'Goodnight and God bless!' Bessie waited until her mate was safely in her own house before closing the front door. And once in the living room, she told the grate, 'She's a good mate, is Rita. And so is Aggie, except she doesn't think before she opens her mouth. No secret is safe with her, especially when she's had a couple of milk stouts.' Grinning to herself, Bessie put the fireguard in front of the fire. 'This is in case you heard everything I told me mate tonight, and yer decide to spill the beans to the wallpaper. Ye're as bad as Aggie, yer can't be trusted.'

Chapter Fourteen

Evelyn could hear Bessie's footsteps climbing the stairs and wondered what she would do without her neighbour. She was a blessing, and it would be wise to keep her sweet. Future prospects looked very rosy, and the time might come when Miss Maudsley would be asked for more help than she was giving now. She would be paid well, of course, for Evelyn would have plenty of money to spare. And the little woman next door wasn't the kind to ask awkward questions, she was too naive. So far she'd believed everything she'd been told.

Turning on her side, Evelyn drew her knees up and wrapped her arms around them. She couldn't sleep, but then she didn't want to. She wanted to relive over and over in her head the hour she'd spent in Philip's apartment. In all the time she'd gone out with Charles, and he'd kissed and cuddled her, he had never sent a thrill down her spine the way Philip did when he held her. The first time she felt it, it was so strong it took her breath away. He only had to stroke her face, or kiss her, and her whole body tingled. He was very experienced where women were concerned, that was obvious, but Evelyn didn't care. She'd never had these feelings before, and even now, lying in bed in the cold room, the very thought of them sent a warmth through her whole body. They

271

hadn't made love, although Philip had begged her. But as she explained, if their first act of love making had to be rushed, over in fifteen minutes so they could go back to work, then it wasn't for her. She would feel no better than a woman kept solely to service his sexual needs, and she had more pride than to sell herself like that.

Evelyn smiled and clasped her knees tighter. Philip had been full of apologies. He hadn't meant it to seem like that, but told her he couldn't control his feelings when she was close to him. And to please her, he said he was taking a long lunch hour tomorrow when he'd go shopping to buy the clothes he'd promised. And when she asked how he would know her size, he tapped his nose and said to leave it to him, she wouldn't be disappointed. They were going to the apartment again on Wednesday lunchtime, so Evelyn could see what he had bought for her, but then she insisted they shouldn't meet outside the office until Saturday, when she would be spending the night with him. And when Philip had held her tight, nibbling her ear, his whispered words left her in no doubt that on Saturday she would be taught her first lesson in how to satisfy his sexual needs. And she wasn't afraid, she was looking forward to it. Even the memory of his hand running down her back brought a thrill which caused her to shiver. When she finally closed her eyes in sleep, there was a smile on her face.

Evelyn reached the apartment a few minutes after Philip on the Wednesday and found he had left the door open for her. She could hear him in the kitchen. When she called his name, he called back, 'Go straight to the bedroom, my darling, and you will find some presents on the bed.'

He was right behind her, and in time to see the pleasure on her face as she looked down at the array of cream-coloured satin underwear. There was everything she would need from brassieres to cami-knickers, short underskirts, long underskirts with matching lace insets, and several pairs of pure silk stockings. Next to them, laid out on the huge bed, were two nightdresses, one pale blue, the other a deep red. And beside them were matching satin dressing gowns.

'Oh, Philip, they're beautiful. But you shouldn't have bought so much, I feel quite embarrassed now.'

He slipped his arms around her and pulled her tight. 'There's no need to feel embarrassed, my darling, it gave me a lot of pleasure choosing things for you. And I can't wait to see you wearing them.'

Evelyn was more excited than she would let him see. She didn't want him to think she'd never known what it was like to be rich and wear such fine clothes. 'You are very clever, Philip, they're all my size! How did you guess?'

He knew that the truth, that this wasn't the first time he'd been in the lingerie department of George Henry Lee, wouldn't find favour, so said what he thought she would be happy with. 'I chose an assistant I thought was your size, and she was very helpful.'

Evelyn stroked the fine satin of the red dressing gown, then turned her head to ask, teasingly, 'I believe the women in houses of ill repute wear this colour?'

Philip's head tipped back and he roared with laughter. 'In that case, my lovely, when you wear it I shall pretend I am in a house of ill repute. I have it on good authority that the women there are very knowledgeable when it comes to making men happy.'

'Then I feel sorry for you, because I am only a novice and will need lessons.' The lovely lingerie had put Evelyn in high spirits, and she found herself being more outspoken than she'd ever been before. 'Would you like me to visit a brothel to learn the tricks of the trade?'

Philip pulled her even closer. 'I'll let you into a secret, my darling. I have never wanted anything in my life as much as I want to make love to you. I want to pleasure you as much as I am certain you will pleasure me. And now, my love, if we don't make a move, we will be late back at the office. Difficult as it will be, I shall have to keep my feelings in check until Saturday.'

Evelyn was still in very high spirits when she called for Amelia, and her good mood wasn't lost on Bessie. 'Ye're looking very well lately, Mrs Sinclair. Happy, like, as though yer've had good news or something nice has happened to yer.'

'I must say, I am feeling very well, Miss Maudsley. It must be the satisfaction of my new job, that's all I can put it down to. I have a very good boss, and he's really pleased with my work. Oh, I shall be getting my raise in pay from this week, so I'll be in a position to give you the extra shilling from this Saturday.'

Bessie nodded and smiled in a friendly way. 'It's nice when yer get on with the people yer work for. Makes going to work each day a bit easier, doesn't it? You seem to have a very good boss, is he elderly or young?'

Evelyn dampened her enthusiasm. 'Mmm, I really wouldn't know. If you were to ask me to guess, I would say somewhere in the region of fifty-five or thereabouts. He has children in their twenties, so that might give you an idea.'

How well you lie, the voice in Bessie's head was saying. It would take more than a fifty-five-year-old married man to put that sparkle in your eyes. But it hasn't anything to do with me, so good luck to you. 'So I'll know about food for the weekend, is Amelia still sleeping over on Saturday night? And d'yer want me to give her a dinner on Sunday? It would be no trouble, just a few extra roast potatoes.'

Evelyn averted her eyes as her brain ticked over. Oh, how tempting the offer sounded. It would mean she could lounge around that luxurious apartment with Philip until the afternoon. Then she sensed her daughter standing nearby, waiting for her reply, and didn't want her neighbour to think she was neglecting the girl. 'Oh, it's kind of you, Miss Maudsley, but I don't think I should leave Amelia so often. You'll be thinking you have no mother, won't you, dear?'

As usual the girl kept her face straight and her voice flat. 'I don't mind, Mother, if you want to stay at your friend's house. Miss Bessie looks after me very well. She plays cards with me, and

Snakes and Ladders.'

'So you would prefer to stay with Miss Maudsley, would you?' Evelyn managed to keep the eagerness from her voice, but her fingers were crossed. 'I told you she'd taken a fancy to you, Miss Maudsley, but you mustn't let her put on you, it wouldn't be fair. I am quite prepared to come home on Sunday morning and cook a meal for us both.'

Bessie shook her head. 'No, we'll leave it that she has dinner with me. I enjoy her company. So you come home when yer like. Yer may as well enjoy yerself while yer can.'

'I must admit I am enjoying the first bit of freedom I've had in eight years,' Evelyn said. 'And it's thanks to you.' She stood up, and for the first time in Bessie's presence, reached for her daughter's hand. 'Come along, Amelia, I'm sure Miss Maudsley is sick of the sight of us. Let's leave her in peace.'

When mother and daughter were going out of the kitchen door, Amelia turned to say, 'Thank you, Miss Bessie, I'll see you tomorrow.' And gave a wave with her free hand.

Bessie watched through the kitchen window as they walked down the yard. She was glad she was going to have the girl overnight on Saturday, and probably until Sunday afternoon. She was really good company for a woman who had lived a lonely life for so many years. Rita was only being sensible when she'd told her not to get too fond of Milly, and Bessie appreciated her mate's concern. But how could she not be drawn to a child who hugged her tight while gazing up with wide green eyes that were crying out for affection? Oh, she might be storing up heartache for herself, as Rita said, if Mrs Sinclair ever decided to move away from the street. Bessie had warned herself about this on several occasions, and each time, a little voice in her head had told her that at least the girl would leave knowing what love and affection were. And another thing, she would be old enough by then to come and visit. As Amelia grew older, she would have a mind of her own and Bessie had a feeling they would always be in touch with each other.

Reg Wells lowered the evening paper to watch his wife hopping from one foot to the other as she kept watch through the window. 'In the name of God, woman, what's the matter with yer? Anyone would think it was a matter of life or death, instead of you just being nosy.'

Rita grinned at him. 'It *is* a matter of life or death, sunshine, but I don't expect you to understand, 'cos ye're too busy reading the ruddy paper to notice that yer poor wife is bored rigid. It's the same every night! Yer come in from work, have yer dinner, then all I see of yer for the next few hours is the top of yer flaming head. Yer never think of asking yer dear wife what sort of a day she's had. Oh, no, the *Echo* comes first. Then, when yer've finished, if it's not bedtime, yer might condescend to notice I'm still here.'

He grinned back. 'If yer feel that way inclined, love, I can always fold the paper, put it under the cushion, and we can have an early night. D'yer think that would bring a bit of excitement into

277

yer life? Make yer more content, like?'

Still keeping an eye on the house opposite, Rita told him, 'I'm waiting to nip over to Bessie's, sunshine, and if she hasn't anything of interest to tell me then I'll come back and take yer up on the offer. That's if yer've had a shave. Otherwise ye're not on 'cos that stubble of yours isn't half rough on my delicate skin.'

Reg rubbed a hand across his chin. 'I'd have a shave if I was sure I was on a real promise, otherwise I'll leave it till in the morning.'

Rita, who loved her husband dearly, pretended to be giving it some thought. 'Ooh, er, decisions, decisions. Ooh, heck, it's a hard one. I'll tell yer what, sunshine, you have yer shave and work yerself up into a state of excitement while I ask Bessie if she's got any news. And if she has, I'll tell her to speak quickly 'cos my feller is on a promise and the waiting won't be doing him no good.'

Reg chortled. 'Bessie's a spinster, yer shouldn't be putting those sort of thoughts in her head. She probably doesn't know what it means to be on a promise.'

The clock told Rita it was ten minutes now since Bessie's visitors had left, and as she reached for the coat hanging on a hook behind the door, she said, 'Yer think Bessie's education's been lacking, do yer, Reg? Shall I ask her if she'd like yer to tell her about the birds and the bees? Ye're very good at explaining things, you are.'

He knew his wife was quite capable of repeating what he'd said for a joke, and shook his fist at her. 'You do that, Rita Wells, and I'll never be able to look the woman in the face again. Now get over there and don't spend too much time jangling. Just remember, I'll be having a shave for your benefit, and one good turn deserves another. I'm on a promise, and if ye're not back by the time the kids are in bed, I'll come over and carry yer home. This is one promise I won't let yer break.'

Rita bent to cup his face in her hands. 'Ooh, I do like masterful men, yer've got me heart all of a quiver. The strong silent type ... yer remind me of Rudolph Valentino. Remember that picture we saw him in, where he picked his women up and laid them down on satin sheets in the big tent in the desert? Ooh, it wasn't half romantic.'

Reg's rich chuckle filled the room. 'While you had yer eyes fixed on the screen, with yer mouth wide open, thinking how wonderful he was, I was busy trying to figure out how he never used to get sand in his eyes. And where the hell he could get satin sheets from in the middle of the ruddy desert! Not a shop for hundreds of miles, but he had everything to hand.' Again he chuckled. 'You women are daft enough to fall for anything.'

Rita pulled a face. 'Yeah, I know, we'd fall for the ruddy cat. We tell lies, too, which yer forgot to mention. Tell lies and break promises, that's us women.'

He was off the chair like a shot. 'Give me yer hand, love.'

'What d'yer want me hand for?'

He made a grab and caught her wrist. 'Come on, I'm taking yer across to Bessie's.'

'Don't be daft, I can take meself across there.' Rita was still protesting when her husband opened the front door and pulled her down the

279

steps. Her two sons were playing with their mates, and they all stood like statues as Reg dragged Rita across the cobbles and knocked on Bessie's door.

There was a look of surprise on the little woman's face when she saw Reg with Rita in tow. She'd been washing some clothes in the sink, and wiped her wet hands down the side of her pinny. 'Well, this is a surprise. When I heard the knock I thought it would be Rita, but I never expected you, Reg.' She stood back. 'Come on in.'

'No, I won't come in, Bessie love, but thanks for asking. I've just brought the wife over, and in half an hour I want yer to remind her not to forget the promise she made. She's got a head like a sieve, and she'll forget all about it if someone doesn't remind her.'

Now Bessie might be a spinster, but that didn't mean she was totally out of touch with married life. Although she kept her face straight, she was shaking with laughter inside. 'Oh, I won't forget to remind her. On a promise are yer, Reg?'

The man didn't know where to put himself. The only face-saving thing he could think of was that the boys were on the other side of the street with their noisy mates, and wouldn't have heard. His face the colour of beetroot, he dropped Rita's hand and hurried back across the cobbles with his wife's laughter ringing in his ears. But as he was stepping on to the top step, he heard her call, 'Half an hour, sunshine, I promise.'

It was then he forgot his red face and embarrassment for he had more pressing things on his mind. First he would bring the boys in and make them a hot drink before seeing they gave themselves a good wash. Left to their own devices they'd be going to school tomorrow with a huge tidemark round their necks and dirt behind their ears. Then, when they were settled in bed, he would set about giving himself a very close shave. He would hate to be rough on his wife's delicate skin.

Bessie closed the door, tittering to herself. 'Your feller will kill yer when yer go home. His face was like thunder. And me putting me foot in it didn't help. I should have had more sense.'

Rita knew her husband too well to be afraid. He'd never really lost his temper with her in all the years they'd been married. And she had to admit there were many times she'd given him cause to. 'It was a bit thoughtless of yer, sunshine, especially as I'd asked him if he'd explain to yer about the birds and the bees, and he didn't refuse. So, yer see what yer've missed, eh? I'd have sat in on that conversation meself, 'cos I'd love to hear Reg trying to explain how babies are made. It would have been hilarious.'

'Oh, aye, and I'd have been expected to sit here with me eyes open in amazement and acting the picture of innocence! Oh, yeah, that and cut me throat would be the last thing I'd be doing.' Bessie pointed to the couch. 'Sit yerself down, sweetheart, but don't expect me to make a cup of tea, not while your feller is pacing the floor waiting for yer.'

'Nah, he's just called the boys in, and it'll take him half an hour to get them ready for bed. But I won't have a drink, anyway, 'cos it wouldn't leave us much time to talk.'

'Sorry to let yer down, Rita, but there's not a lot to tell yer. Except Mrs Sinclair is going to her old school friend's again on Saturday and sleeping over. And I've told her she needn't rush home on Sunday, I'll give Milly her dinner.'

'Ooh, er, Bessie, yer might not have much to tell me, but think how much we can read into those few sentences. I mean, d'yer still think she's telling fibs about the old school friend? If she is, then where is she going to spend Saturday night, and who with?'

'I have no way of finding that out,' Bessie told her. 'She's more open than she used to be, more pleasant, like, but she still doesn't give anything away. If yer were to ask me to guess, I'd say she has a man friend, and he's a wealthy one. I am to get an extra shilling a week from this Saturday for having Milly more often, and she must be getting the extra money from somewhere to pay me so much.'

'It's a good help that, two bob a week. But it's not the money ye're doing it for, sunshine, is it? I bet yer'd mind Milly even if yer didn't get paid for it.'

'Of course it's not the money I do it for, I can live very comfortably on me wages. I've always paid me way and never owed anyone. But I'm not going to refuse the two bob a week, that's for sure. I'd be daft to when she's out enjoying herself. Anyway, I can spend it on Milly. I don't think she's ever been into town, so I might take her down on the tram on Saturday to look around the shops. It'll be an outing for me as well.'

Rita tilted her head. 'Would yer like another companion? It's years since I've been into the city, I've never had the money. Yer don't mind me asking, do yer, don't think I'm being pushy?'

'Of course I don't, yer daft ha'porth, I'd be glad of yer company. And Milly will be over the moon, walking between the two of us.'

'Ooh, that hasn't half cheered me up, it's something to look forward to. And tonight is a very good time to scrounge the two pence tram fare off my feller. If I get him at the right time he'll promise me anything.'

'That sounds like blackmail to me,' Bessie said, with a shake of her head. 'A married man is entitled to his rights, yer know, he shouldn't have to pay for them.'

'Bessie, I feel in such a good, generous mood now, thanks to you, my feller will think he's got a strange woman in his bed. By the time I've finished with him, he'll be thinking two pence is a small price to pay.' Rita pushed herself to her feet. 'In fact, when it's over and he's got his breath back, he'll probably ask when we're going into Liverpool again.'

'Have you no shame in you, woman?' Bessie followed her mate to the door. 'I feel really sorry for Reg.'

Rita stepped down on to the pavement. 'No need to, sunshine, 'cos in half an hour's time my feller will be the happiest man in this street. And that is my solemn promise.'

'Oh, I believe yer, sweetheart,' Bessie said. 'Just remember, though, he has to go to work tomorrow.'

It was only after Rita had left that Bessie realised it might not be possible to take Milly into town on Saturday afternoon after all, for she didn't know what time Mrs Sinclair would be going out. If she was meeting a man, it would probably be in the early evening, and that would dash any hope of Bessie and Rita taking Milly into town. Bessie felt really disappointed because she'd been looking forward to giving Milly a surprise, and Rita would feel let down, too! But there was no point in waiting and wondering what Saturday was going to bring, she may as well come right out and ask her neighbour. She could always tell a little white lie and say she was thinking of taking Milly to the park. Yes, that's what she'd do, she'd ask her neighbour tomorrow night and get it over with. After all, the woman couldn't expect an eight-year-old girl to spend all her time in the house, it wasn't healthy.

Bessie was late getting in from work the following night, and found Milly sitting on the kitchen step waiting for her. 'I'm sorry I'm late, sweetheart, we had an order to get out in a hurry and there was nothing I could do about it. Come on in, yer must be freezing. I'll put the kettle on and put a light to the fire. It won't be long, I'll soon have you warmed through.'

'I'm not cold, Auntie Bessie, I folded my arms across my chest and put my hands under my armpits, and they're nice and warm.'

Bessie smiled down at her with affection in her eyes. This girl was one in a million, never gave any cheek, kept herself clean and tidy and was always well mannered. Her mother didn't appreciate how lucky she was. 'I've brought some sausages in, we'll have them with an egg. How does that sound to you?'

Milly giggled. 'My tummy says it sounds very good, Auntie Bessie, and when it arrives it will be made really welcome.'

Bessie threw her coat on a chair and knelt in front of the fire which she'd set ready for lighting this morning before she went to work. After striking a match, she held it to the balls of newspaper laid out under the firewood. 'I'll give it a minute to catch, then I'll pull the damper out and we'll have a roaring fire in no time.' She felt the girl's arms coming round her neck and then soft lips kissing her cheek. 'Oh, that's nice, sweetheart, but what have I done to deserve it?'

'That's 'cos I love you, Auntie Bessie, you're my very bestest friend.'

'Well, I think you must be a mind reader, sweetheart, because I was just thinking the same thing. That you are my very bestest friend. And you know they say great minds think alike, so you and me must be very clever.' Bessie disentangled herself from Milly's arms and used her closed fists to push herself off her knees. 'Now, while I'm frying the sausages and eggs, you can help me by setting the table. Like your tummy, I'm famished.'

When Milly had set the table, she went into the kitchen to where Bessie was standing by the stove, leaning as far back as she could to escape the spitting fat. 'Why are the sausages spitting, Auntie Bessie? Is it because they are angry?'

Bessie chuckled. 'No, they're not angry, sweetheart. It's not the sausages that are spitting, it's the fat. So don't come too close, 'cos yer might get burnt, and then what would I say to yer mother when she comes?'

'She wouldn't know, Auntie Bessie, 'cos I wouldn't tell her. But she wouldn't shout at you, she would scold me for being careless.'

Not wanting to criticise her mother, Bessie changed the subject. 'Dinner is ready now, so go and sit at the table, sweetheart. I'll cut us a round of bread each, to dip in the egg yolk.'

The fire was established now, and the bright, dancing flames gave the room a nice warm glow. And with Milly relating a funny incident in the school playground, and her infectious laughter ringing out, Bessie was feeling really contented. She'd taken on a new lease of life since the girl had been coming into her home, and not for the first time she was questioning the decision she'd made all those years ago when she'd told the boy she was courting that she couldn't leave her ailing parents to marry him. She'd said it was her duty to care for them, and when in anger he'd asked if she didn't have a duty to him after courting him for several years, her heart had been torn in two. She was an only child, born when her mother was forty years of age. By the time Bessie was courting, both her parents were old and frail. She chose them over the boy who'd wanted to marry her. Now, looking at Milly's happy face, she wished she could have married her boyfriend *and* cared for her parents. Perhaps if she had she would have had a family of her own now.

'That was lovely, Auntie Bessie, and my tummy said to thank you very much.'

Bessie shook her head to empty her mind of thoughts of what might have been. 'I'm glad you and your tummy enjoyed it, sweetheart.' She patted her own. 'And I have to admit I've had an elegant sufficiency.'

'Ooh, those are big words, Auntie Bessie!'

Bessie chuckled. 'Yes, I know, I frightened meself 'cos I don't know where they came from. I'll have to try them on yer Auntie Aggie some time, I'd love to see the expression on her face.'

Milly's laughter rang out. 'I bet she'd use some words back at you.' Her deep green eyes rolled. 'And I bet they'd be naughty ones, too!'

'Aggie means no harm, sweetheart, she's got a heart of gold. But I admit she uses some words she shouldn't. Not in front of children anyway.' Bessie reached for the girl's empty plate and put it on top of her own. 'I'll wash and you can dry. Then when the place is tidy, you can play with Daisy for half an hour before your mother comes.'

The girl scrambled from her chair. 'I'm going to tell her about the three bears tonight.'

Bessie grinned. 'And I bet she'll enjoy it. In fact, I might just listen in meself and yer'll have an audience.'

When Evelyn called for her daughter later, Daisy was tucked up in bed in the spare room and Milly's face had lost its sparkle.

'The weather has turned very cold,' Evelyn said, shivering. 'I won't sit down, Miss Maudsley, thank you, I want to get in and light the fire. Get your coat, Amelia, and don't dawdle.'

Bessie decided to strike while the iron was hot. 'Before you go, Mrs Sinclair, there's something I'd like to ask yer. Do you know what time yer'll be going out on Saturday? Yer see, I thought it would be nice if I took Amelia to the park for a walk. I don't like her to be indoors for so long, I think we both need a little fresh air. But it depends on what time you will be going out. If it's late afternoon, then it will be too late and we'll leave it for another time.'

Evelyn stared at her. This woman is either a mind reader or my guardian angel, she thought. Only this morning Philip had asked her why she couldn't come early on Saturday morning, so they could spend the day together? He would take her for a run to Southport in the afternoon, and they could stroll along famous Lord Street with its many exclusive fashionable shops. He would buy her anything that took her eye, he said. And what she did want was another day coat, so she could have one at home and one in the apartment. She had promised to think about it without knowing how she could wangle it. She'd never dreamed this opportunity was going to fall in her lap. But although she was cheering inside, she didn't want to appear too eager. She gave a deep sigh and closed her eyes as though deep in contemplation.

'You have been so kind to Amelia and me, I really can't let you down. So what I'll do is write to Elizabeth tonight, and tell her I find myself with Saturday free and could she possibly put up

288

with me for a few extra hours. I'm quite sure she'll be agreeable.'

Bessie didn't know how she kept her head from shaking and her tongue from clicking. This woman was the best liar she'd ever known. There was always an answer to everything, and it appeared she made a career out of telling the most exaggerated fibs Bessie had ever heard.

'Oh, no, don't do that!' she said, to put the wind up Evelyn. She knew there was now no doubt that Milly would be going into town on Saturday with her and Rita, but she could play games as well as Mrs Sinclair with her posh voice. 'I wouldn't dream of putting you or yer friend to any trouble. We'll leave it until another time.'

Amelia had been standing quietly by, taking it all in. Her face had lit up when she'd first heard about the walk in the park, then when her mother hadn't seemed too keen her spirits had dropped. They'd been lifted again for a short while. Now, listening to her Auntie Bessie, she looked really crestfallen. This gave Evelyn the way out she'd been looking for.

'Don't look so sad, Amelia, I won't do anything to upset Miss Maudsley's plans. I insist on making myself invisible on Saturday, come what may. And I hope you appreciate what a lucky girl you are, having Miss Maudsley for a friend. I too am lucky in that respect.'

Wearing the look of someone who has generously put herself out for the sake of others, Evelyn gave a slow, sideways nod of the head to Bessie. The little woman didn't know whether to

289

laugh in her face or curtsey. But she was prepared to put up with her neighbour's shenanigans for Milly's sake. She gave a wide smile while inwardly calling her all the polished buggers under the sun. 'Oh, that is kind of yer, Mrs Sinclair. You enjoy yerself on Saturday now, and don't worry about Amelia 'cos I won't keep her out too long.'

The wink Milly gave her as she followed Evelyn out of the house told of her pleasure. And Bessie also wondered if it was a wink of victory. If it was, then good for her.

Chapter Fifteen

Bessie had told Rita not to call for her until two o'clock on Saturday, in case her neighbour had had a change of plan and was at home. Milly still hadn't been told they were going into Liverpool, she was excited enough at the prospect of going to the park. 'Will I be allowed to go on the swings, Auntie Bessie?'

'Of course yer will, sweetheart, there's no charge, the swings and see-saw are free.'

Bessie looked into the girl's shining eyes and thought it was time to tell her the truth. There'd been no sight or sound of Evelyn, so it was safe to presume she had kept to her word. 'Me and Auntie Rita have got a surprise for yer, sweetheart, but I won't tell yer what until she comes.' She heard a door bang and, looking through the window, saw her mate crossing the cobbles. 'Here she is, and I think yer'll like our surprise.'

Milly couldn't think of anything more exciting than going to the park and having a turn on the swings. 'I would like to go to the park, Auntie Bessie, you don't need to do anything special just for me.'

'We'll see, sweetheart, you might have a choice of two options. But open the door for Auntie Rita, there's a good girl.'

Rita came in bright and breezy. It was a rare treat to be going into the city on the tram, for she

291

had to stretch her housekeeping like a piece of elastic to make it last the week. But her feller had come up trumps with sixpence for her to pay her fares and buy a cup of tea in a cafe. She patted Milly's cheek. 'Hello, sunshine, all ready with yer coat on, eh? Looking forward to seeing the sights with yer aunties, are yer?'

Milly's brow creased as she wondered what sights they'd see in the park, and Bessie was quick to notice. 'I haven't said anything to her yet, Rita, except that we had a surprise for her. But I said she had two options, and we'd let her choose where we go.'

Rita's heart sank. Surely she hadn't gone through all that with Reg just to go to the swings?

Milly also looked downcast. 'I thought we were going to the park, Auntie Bessie, that's what you said?'

'Yes, I know that, sweetheart, and that's what I told your mother. But since then, me and Rita have had a little talk and we thought perhaps yer might rather go into town than go to the park? We could get the tram from the top of the street to take us into the city centre, and spend some time there looking in the shops. But it is entirely up to you. Me and Rita will fit in with whatever yer want to do.'

Milly's mouth was wide open and her eyebrows nearly touched her hair-line as she gazed from one to the other of them. It was a few seconds before her voice came out in a squeak. 'Go into town on the tram?' She knew Liverpool was a big city, but she'd never been there. 'Are you pulling my leg, Auntie Bessie?'

'Am I heckerslike! I don't get all dolled up to pull no one's leg. This is your day, and me and Rita want you to choose where we go. But if you don't decide soon, all the shops will be closed before we get there.'

Rita put her hands behind her back and crossed her fingers. Please don't say you want to go on the swings, sunshine, please!

'I'd like to go into town on the tram, please. I've never been there, but some of the girls in my class have, and they've told me about the shops that are as big as the Queen's palace.'

'Well, not as big as Buckingham Palace, sweetheart, but ten times bigger than the shops around here. I think your friends were bragging a bit. But yer can put them straight when yer go to school on Monday.'

Milly's chest seemed to swell with pride as she held out a hand to each of her adopted aunties. 'You are very kind to me, and I do love you.'

Over her head the eyes of the two women met, and it wouldn't have taken much more for the tears to appear. 'Come on, let's be on our way and make the most of the time we have,' Bessie said gruffly.

They walked down the street with Milly between them, each holding one of her hands, and she smiled at the other children who stopped in their play to watch the girl they knew by sight but had never spoken to or played with. Rita's youngest son, Jack, skipped alongside them, his socks crumpled around his ankles and patches of dirt on his face.

'Why can't I come with yer, Mam?' Jack was

skipping backwards now, so he could see their faces. 'Go on, I'll behave meself.'

'Some other time, son, not today.' When Rita saw the disappointment in his eyes, she felt so guilty. Her boys, like all the other kids in the street, didn't get much out of life because of the shortage of money. But, like Jack now, they didn't whinge when they were told they couldn't have everything they asked for. Nevertheless, he must be feeling a bit jealous, and she couldn't blame him. 'Yer can't come now, sunshine, just look at the state of yer. Yer knees and face are as black as the hobs of hell. But next time I have the chance to go into town, I'll make sure I take you and Billy with me.'

They'd reached the top of the street by now and Jack grinned. 'I don't mind, Mam, 'cos yer'd only make me wash me neck. I'll go back to me mates and me game of marbles.'

Milly's heart went out to the boy, for she knew what it was like to be left behind. She still remembered hearing the key turn in the lock of the room she was confined to while her mother went out shopping. Still remembered the feeling of fear at being left alone in the house. 'I'll tell you about it when we come home, Jack, and if Auntie Bessie ever takes me out again, I'll ask her to let you come. I know she will, she's very kind.'

Jack grinned, then turned to run hell for leather back to his mates with his mother's voice following him. 'Pull yer socks up, for heaven's sake, yer make a holy show of me!'

'Leave him be, Rita,' Bessie said. 'He's only a lad, yer can't expect him to be spotlessly clean all the time.'

'Bessie, I'd settle for him being clean for half an hour. Sometimes he's got that much grime on his face, I don't recognise him! A while back I passed him in the entry and wouldn't have known it was him if he hadn't said, "Hello, Mam".'

Milly thought that was really funny and she was still giggling when the tram came trundling along. She begged to be allowed to go up to the top deck, and when Bessie nodded ran up the stairs with the speed of a whippet while the two women pulled themselves up by the rail, fighting to keep their footing while the tram rattled from side to side. When they finally reached the top it was to see Milly sitting in a seat by the window, her smile bright enough to bring out the sun in a sky that was overcast with dark clouds.

'Can I sit by the window, please, Auntie Bessie, so I can see all the people rushing in and out of the shops? They look really small when you look down on them, like little diddy people. They look cold, too, but I don't feel cold at all.' Milly fingered the beige scarf Bessie had wrapped around her neck. 'This is keeping me nice and warm.'

Bessie sat beside her, while Rita sat in the seat in front. 'It is cold out today, sweetheart, it seems winter is coming early.' She heard the conductor coming, clicking the handle of his ticket machine and calling, 'Fares, please. And try to have the right money ready if yer can.'

Rita was opening her bag to get her purse out, when Bessie tapped her shoulder. 'I've got the fare ready, girl, so put yer purse away.' She took sixpence from her pocket which she handed to the conductor. 'Two tuppenny returns to Church Street, and one child's fare.'

Milly was intrigued to see the conductor turn the little handle at the side of the machine which hung down from a wide leather strap over his shoulder. And when three tickets came out from a slot in front, she thought it was magic. 'Ooh, isn't that clever, Auntie Bessie? I'd like to be a conductor when I grow up, and have one of those to give people their tickets.'

The conductor passed the tickets to Bessie before smiling at the young girl. 'You wouldn't like it, love, not when the novelty wore off. In the winter months yer've got to fight against the wind to get up the stairs, and yer hands get so cold yer expect yer fingers to fall off.' He leaned towards her and lowered his voice. 'And yer get some ruddy awkward passengers, as well. I had one this morning. Some bloke fell asleep and missed his stop. He blamed me, said I should have woke him up, and now he was late for work he'd have his pay docked. Anyone could see why he'd missed his stop, he'd been out boozing last night and was bleary-eyed. He was so bad-tempered and shouting the odds, everyone on the tram could hear him. But we all had a laugh when he went to punch me 'cos he wasn't quite sober. He could see three of me and missed by a mile.' The conductor was chuckling at the memory. 'To top it off, I went to help him off the tram 'cos he wasn't capable of walking straight, but he pushed me away and fell down the ruddy step! It had passed the time away for other passengers, and they all jeered and clapped. I don't know where the bloke worked, but this is one day his boss won't be getting his money's worth. It brightened my day, though, it's not often I get a drunk taking a punch at me.'

Bessie and Rita were shaking with laughter. The man was a good storyteller; doing all the actions as he told the tale. Milly had a hand over her mouth while her eyes glistened with happiness. Oh, this was going to be the most exciting day of her life!

While her daughter was sitting on a rickety tram, swaying with each movement and shudder, Evelyn was sitting back in Philip's luxurious car with a travelling rug covering her knees. She was revelling in the smell of its leather seats and the comfort all around her. It was over eight years since she'd been in a car, and without warning she remembered the last time. It was in Charles' car that she'd become pregnant with Amelia. She shivered at the memory, and Philip was quick to lean sideways to tuck the rug closer, thinking she was cold. 'Tuck it in the other side, my lovely, I can't have you catching a chill.'

'I'm not cold, my dear, it's very warm and comfortable in here. It was just someone walking over my grave, as the saying goes. I've no doubt it has happened to you at some time. No one seems to know the reason for it.'

They were driving down country lanes, and some of the properties they passed were lovely, beautiful big houses with large, well-kept gardens. 'How peaceful it is here compared to the city,'

Evelyn said. 'The only problem would be shopping. We haven't passed any shops to speak of.'

'My darling Evelyn, everything in the way of foodstuffs and coal is delivered. The only shopping local residents do is for clothes, and then they drive to the city, either by car or horse-drawn carriage.' Philip turned his head briefly. 'I remember my father having a horse and carriage when I was younger, before automobiles became fashionable. I actually prefer to ride in a carriage because I love horses and am glad there are still so many of them on the streets of Liverpool. They're loyal, trustworthy and hard-working, and it would be a sad day indeed if man ever forgot their strength, loyalty and courage.'

Evelyn patted his arm. 'I can't see horses disappearing, dear. Without them there would be no milk or coal deliveries, and of course no furniture removals. That's apart from the haulage companies down at the docks, who wouldn't survive without horses and carts.'

Houses were becoming more frequent now as they drove through the lush areas leading into Southport. There were no streets of two-up-two-down houses here; only people with money could afford to live in this affluent area. Every property was large, and built to accommodate maids, housekeepers, gardeners, and cars or carriages. Although she couldn't see them, Evelyn was sure there would be stables at the back of the houses.

'I'll drive into Lord Street and park the car in front of the hotel,' Philip said. 'Then we'll have some refreshment, I feel quite peckish.'

'Yes, I would appreciate a drink myself, I'm

thirsty.' Evelyn was never free from the fear of bumping into someone from her past, if not Cyril or Matilda Lister-Sinclair themselves then one of their acquaintances who would be only too eager to spread the news that she had surfaced and been seen on the arm of a man. Worse still, they could accost Evelyn while she was with Philip, then the truth would come out and he would be so horrified he would walk away. She had altered her hairstyle in an attempt to make herself less obvious, but there was little else she could do except pray.

Philip parked the car in the forecourt of the Prince of Wales Hotel, the grandest in Southport. He opened the passenger door and helped Evelyn from the car. 'We'll have something light here, my love, to ease the pangs of hunger. But we won't dine here. I have ordered a very lavish meal to be delivered to the apartment at eight o'clock. It will be piping hot, served by waiters from the hotel.' He tucked her arm under his as they walked together into the foyer of the large hotel, and while his eyes searched for the most discreet table he whispered in her ear, 'I am secretly wishing the time away, my lovely Evelyn. I can't wait until the afternoon is over, and we have dined in the apartment on a delicious meal accompanied by excellent wine to give you that lovely warm glow. The waiters will be encouraged to clear away quickly then and leave us alone. And I can take you in my arms and show you how much I need you, and what you have been missing by keeping me at arm's length for so long.'

Evelyn could feel herself colour as she looked around her to see if anyone was close enough to have heard. 'Really, Philip, see how you have made me blush?'

He chuckled as he led her to a table in an alcove. 'That is what I love about you, my very dear darling. You are so innocent. And while I hope you do not remain so for ever, I would be very sorry to see you change too swiftly.' He held her hand as she lowered herself into a chair. 'Besides, if you look around, people are far more concerned with their own affairs than they are with listening in to ours.' He sat facing her, ran two fingers down the perfect crease in his trousers, then leaned forward. 'But none of them have as much to look forward to as I have, especially with such a beautiful woman.'

Evelyn was secretly lapping up the compliments she'd been starved of for so long. To be treated like someone special was boosting her confidence. 'Really, Philip, I think such talk should be reserved for when we have complete privacy.'

He had never met a woman so retiring before, and found it refreshing. And she didn't use a lot of make-up on her face either, didn't need it with her colouring and complexion. Some young women looked like painted dolls, but not Evelyn. Tonight he was hoping to find that she had not been with any man since her husband was killed. He caught the eye of a waiter and beckoned him over. 'A pot of Earl Grey tea, my good man, and a selection of sandwiches and cakes.'

When the waiter retreated, Philip asked, 'Tell me, my love, have you ever smoked?'

Evelyn looked surprised. 'What a curious question, Philip! Yes, I smoked when I was younger, in my late-teens, but it is many years since I've held a cigarette. It was quite the rage at one time. I remember one was thought to be quite a frump if one didn't walk around at parties with an ebony or silver cigarette holder.'

'I'm glad you don't, my love. There is nothing so off-putting as kissing a woman who smells of smoke.'

'You sound as though you are very experienced in the ways of women,' Evelyn said, crossing her shapely legs to remind him she could compete with the best. 'I am not a jealous person, or at least I hope not, but I'm wondering whether I should be a tiny bit jealous of you or not? Do I have reason to be?'

'Good heavens, my love, no! No woman has ever come near to having the qualities you possess. I consider myself very lucky to have found you.'

Conversation ceased then as two waiters appeared bearing trays of tea, a variety of thinly cut sandwiches and cakes. Evelyn sighed, 'They look delicious.'

While Philip and Evelyn relaxed in the comfort and luxury of the Prince of Wales Hotel, the child he didn't know existed was sitting in a cafe in a little side street with her two new aunties. There were no tablecloths on the wooden tables, and a cup of tea and scone cost only threepence. The customers were all working-class, not used to luxury but quite content with their lot. Milly was more than content. All this was new to her and

301

she was finding pleasure in everything. Her green eyes were wide as she gazed at the people around her, and listened to them talking loudly and cracking jokes. Some of them wore black knitted shawls over their shoulders and their hair was plaited into buns, either at the nape of their neck or one by each ear. They were a few of the well-known Mary Ellens who brought colour to the Liverpool scene as they went about the business of selling their wares. Having sold out of flowers early today, they had nipped into the cafe for a cuppa before making their way back home with their empty baskets balanced on their heads. Milly was intrigued by them. Two had gold teeth, and when they smiled the metal flashed, causing the young girl to stare, mesmerised.

Rita leaned sideways to whisper in Bessie's ear, 'It's to be hoped a certain person doesn't tell another certain person about what she's seen today. That would really let the cat out of the bag, and it would be goodbye to future outings.'

'If you knew a certain young person as well as I do, you would give her credit for having more brains than that. I've told yer before, sweetheart, Milly has more sense than any of us. And though I shouldn't say it, she's got more on top than her own mother gives her credit for. She knows what's at stake. I am so sure of her, I'm not even going to mention that she should keep today's outing a secret.'

'I'm surprised she's never been into town before, aren't you? To hear her mother talk yer'd think they were used to living like rich people.' Rita tutted. 'I can't stand people who think they're better than anyone else, sunshine, they get on me nerves. God made us all equal, and money doesn't make one person better than the rest.'

Bessie nodded in agreement. 'Ye're right, Rita, definitely. Yer hit the nail right on the head. But Milly is going to have the last laugh, for she will have known both worlds by the time she's older. She'll never be a snob like her mother.'

Rita sighed. 'Let's hope not. Anyway, let's settle up before we leave here so I know I'm out of debt. How much have yer paid out altogether, sunshine?'

Bessie made sure Milly was still listening to the conversations going on around her before answering. 'This is my treat, Rita, so don't be making a fuss. If the truth were known, it's really Mrs Sinclair's treat 'cos it's her two bob I'm using. So she's come in handy and done us a good turn, after all the times we've called her fit to burn.'

'Yer don't get the two bob for nothing, Bessie, yer earn it. So don't forget that, and let me pay me way or I won't come out with yer again.'

'I was living all right before Tilly Mint started paying me, and for what it costs to give Milly some tea each day, well, it's not worth talking about. So I'm really two bob a week better off than I was. And in bed last night, I dreamt up an idea of how you can give me a hand, and in return we'll make sure all the kids have a Christmas party this year and get a present off Father Christmas.'

Rita folded her arms and leaned her elbows on the wooden table. 'That sounds just up my street,

303

sunshine, but where do I come into it?'

'You and Aggie, sunshine, 'cos we can't leave her out. I felt mean not asking her to come with us today, but I'll make it up to her. And what I thought up in bed last night was a way to help us all to a better Christmas than we've had for the last few years, with so many men out of work. But I can't tell yer more now, for it's a well-known saying that little pigs have big ears.'

Milly happened to turn towards them just in time to hear the last few words. 'Who has big ears, Auntie Bessie?'

Bessie gave her mate a kick under the table. 'You wouldn't know her, sweetheart, she's a woman lives in the next street. But don't think I was saying anything bad about her, 'cos I wasn't. And her ears haven't anything to do with it anyway, that was just a chance remark I made.' She felt like cupping the lovely little face and kissing it. But she had to refrain from getting too close to the child, or letting the child get too close to her. It could end in heartbreak for both of them. 'Well, have yer enjoyed yer afternoon in the big city?'

Swinging her legs under the table, Milly gave a big sigh. 'I have had a wonderful time, Auntie Bessie. All those big buildings, and big shops it would take a week to walk around. And I've never been in a cafe before, so I feel like the girl in *Cinderella*. Except she had two ugly sisters, while I have two lovely kind aunties.'

'Well, all good things come to an end, sweetheart, and we've got to be making tracks for home. If we leave it any longer, we'll have a devil

304

of a job getting on a tram 'cos the queues will be miles long with women wanting to get home to make tea for their families.'

'That goes for me too, sunshine,' Rita said. 'If my feller doesn't get his tea by six o'clock, the people down at the Pier Head will hear his tummy rumbling. It's been known for people in the street to think it was thunder. And one old lady, terrified that thunder doesn't come without lightning, didn't she take a chair and sit under the stairs for an hour until her son convinced her it wasn't thunder at all, only Mr Wells letting his wife know he was hungry.'

Milly had learned many things since spending time with her Auntie Bessie, and one of those things was that it wasn't bad manners to laugh out loud, like her mother had always told her. When you laughed, you made other people feel happy. So now she let her head drop back and her childish giggles filled the air, causing people to turn and smile indulgently. 'Oh, you are funny, Auntie Rita, you do make me laugh. I wish I could think of funny things like you do, things that would make people happy.'

'Oh, you do, sweetheart! You make me very happy indeed!' There was affection in Bessie's eyes. 'I lived all alone until you came along, and even though my friends the front door and the grate were company for me, they're not the same as having someone real who can answer me back. I'm really glad your mother lets yer come to me, yer've cheered my life up no end.'

'Are yer going to tell yer mates in school about coming to town today, sunshine?' Rita asked. 'I

305

wonder if any of them have been in this cafe?'

'I will ask them, Auntie Rita, but the first one I'm going to tell is Daisy. I'm going to sit her on my knee and tell her every little thing that's happened.' Milly giggled. 'I bet she'll laugh when I tell her about the conductor on the tram, he was very funny.'

'Yeah, he was a corker, he was,' Bessie agreed. 'It's no joke running up and down those stairs in bad weather, 'cos they're open to all the elements. It's certainly not a job I'd thank yer for, not when it's blowing a gale or snowing.'

'It's not the best of jobs,' Rita agreed, 'but there's thousands of men in Liverpool who'd be glad of it. They'd put up with the bad weather and the drunks, just to bring a wage packet home to their wives every Saturday. I feel sorry for the poor buggers who go out every morning and traipse around begging for a few hours' work.'

Milly's eyes rolled. 'You said a bad word, Auntie Rita.'

Rita looked surprised. 'Did I?' Then she remembered. 'Oh, yeah, I did, it must have slipped out.' Her eyes narrowed. 'How d'yer know it's a swear word? Yer mother doesn't swear, I'm sure, and neither does Bessie. So how come yer know a swear word from any other word?'

'Because one of the girls in my class got three strokes of the cane for using it in the playground. Teacher sent her to the headmistress, and as well as getting the cane, she had to write out fifty times. "Nice girls do not swear".'

Bessie bit on the inside of her bottom lip to stop herself from chuckling. This young girl knew far more than she was letting on. And what a shock it would be to her mother if she ever found out! 'The headmistress was right, sweetheart, 'cos nice girls shouldn't swear. It's bad enough for a grown-up to use bad language, but it's ten times worse coming from the lips of a child. So don't you forget that, young lady.' Bessie picked her bag up off the floor at the side of the table. 'Come on, let's make our way to the tram stop in Lime Street. And stay downstairs this time, Milly, 'cos it's murder climbing those stairs with this wind blowing.'

As Rita slipped her arms into her coat, she said, 'I might nip over tonight, Bessie, about eight, after the meal's over. I can't wait to find out what thoughts yer came up with when yer were in bed.'

Milly took hold of Bessie's hand as they left the table. 'Auntie Bessie talks to the wallpaper in her bedroom, Auntie Rita. I know, 'cos I've heard her.'

And the three of them walked through the cafe door roaring with laughter.

Chapter Sixteen

Milly was sitting on the couch with Daisy propped up on her knee, telling the doll once again about the wonderful time she'd had in the city and the sights she'd seen. It was half-past eight, way past the girl's bedtime, but she was still so excited Bessie didn't have the heart to insist she went to bed.

When Rita arrived, she raised her brows in surprise. 'I thought yer'd have been in bed ages ago, sunshine, tired out with all the walking yer did?'

Milly smiled at her. 'I'm telling Daisy about the shops, and the cafe, and she really is interested. She said she wants to come with me next time.' She looked across at Bessie. 'Do you have to pay to take a doll on the tram, Auntie Bessie?'

'No, sweetheart, they don't charge for a doll.' Bessie saw the query in her mate's eyes and shrugged her shoulders. 'There's no sign of sleep, she's wide awake.' But knowing Rita had come for a purpose, Bessie decided firmness was the order of the day. 'I think yer should go to bed now, though, Milly. You can talk to Daisy while ye're laying down, nice and warm, and me and Rita won't be interrupting yer story.'

The girl didn't argue, for she saw the sense of talking to her doll in bed. 'All right, Auntie Bessie, I am beginning to feel a bit tired.' She held the doll close to her face. 'I've still got a lot to tell you, though, before we go to sleep.'

'Don't forget to tell her about the conductor on the tram,' Rita reminded her. 'I know she'll enjoy that. I told my family and they were in stitches.'

Milly's childish giggles rang out again. 'I was saving that until the last, Auntie Rita, so me and Daisy could go to sleep with a smile on our faces. She does know what I'm saying, you know, I can tell by the way she looks at me.' She kissed the two women, but Bessie was also given a special hug and a whispered, 'I love you, Auntie Bessie.'

'And I love you, sweetheart. But poppy off now so me and Rita can talk about the day, too! Ye're not the only one who enjoyed themself, yer know. It was a treat for me and me mate, for we don't often get the chance to go into the city.'

The two women listened as Milly scrambled up the stairs, and when they thought she was out of earshot, Rita said, 'I'd give anything for a daughter like her, she's a little gem.'

'Same here, girl.' Bessie heaved a deep sigh. 'She's a beautiful child to look at, and her beauty doesn't stop at looks, she's got a beautiful nature too. I'd be the happiest woman alive if she was mine.' She gave a few shakes of her head to clear away such longings. 'What's the good of wishes and dreams? We should be thankful we're alive and have got our health. There's many a one would swap places with us.'

'Ye're right there, sunshine, that goes for half the people in this street. All they've got to look forward to, week after week, is scrounging enough money to keep body and soul together.

We've nowt to complain about.' Rita slipped her shoes off and swung herself round so she could stretch her legs out on the couch. 'Anyway, don't let's start feeling sorry for ourselves, not after having such a nice afternoon. Tell me about the idea that came to yer in bed last night? If it's any good, I'll tell yer what came to me in bed last night. The trouble with that, though, is yer might be too embarrassed to look Reg in the face again.'

'Rita Wells, I'll have yer know I have no interest in what happens in your bedroom.' Bessie feigned disgust, but she was chuckling inside. 'I wish yer'd remember I am a spinster, as innocent and as pure as the driven snow.'

'We've only got your word for that, sunshine, but once again we're getting away from the matter in hand. What is this idea yer've come up with? If it means a better Christmas for the kids, then I'm all for it.'

Bessie leaned back in the fireside chair, her fingers gently tapping on the wooden arms. 'Well, yer know I changed me working hours when I started minding Milly? I go in at seven now so I can finish at four, whereas I used to go in from eight till five. They're always asking me to work longer hours, 'cos although I say it as shouldn't, I've been doing the job so long I get through twice as much work as the younger ones. I used to work all the hours they wanted me to until Milly came on the scene. But what I was thinking, which will help out with the money, is that if you and Aggie have Milly for an hour each night, so I can work until five, it would give yer a few extra coppers every week. It would only be a tanner a week each, but if you and Aggie did help me out, I could put that shilling a week to the two bob I get off Mrs Sinclair, and that would be three bob a week I'd put away until Christmas. I'd still give Milly her tea every night, so it wouldn't cost you or Aggie any money, and we're just into October now which means we've at least twelve weeks to Christmas. That would be enough for a party for the kids and a present each. There might even be enough over for a few drinks for us grown-ups.' Bessie took a deep breath and blew out slowly. 'Well, sweetheart, what d'yer think?'

Rita swung her legs around and put her feet on the floor. 'And what do you get out of this, sunshine? Sweet bugger all from what I can see. Yer've got no kids, while me and Aggie have four between us, and yer've got no family! No, I wouldn't be happy with that, it wouldn't be fair. It would be you doing all the giving, and us doing all the taking. No thanks, Bessie, I couldn't go along with that. I'll mind Milly for an hour every night for yer, but I don't want paying for it. I'd be tickled pink to have her, I've always wanted a girl in the house.'

Bessie tutted. 'Don't be so ruddy quick off the mark, Rita Wells, just wait until yer hear the whole story. I went a lot further in me plans last night before I went to sleep. I'd never drop off unless I had it all sorted. So listen to what I think, and hope, might happen. And I've a feeling it's more likely to happen than not.'

'Ye're getting me all mixed up with yer mights

and might nots, sunshine, so give it to me in plain English.'

'Well, I think it's quite likely that I'll have Milly over Christmas. I'll lay odds Mrs Sinclair has got herself a man, and I'll also lay odds she hasn't told him she's got a daughter. If she had, it would be only natural he'd want to see the girl. Even this imaginary school friend of hers, Elizabeth, wouldn't she wonder why Milly never came with her mother on a visit? No, the whole situation is cock-eyed, and the queer one is lying through her hat and taking me for a sucker. At least, she thinks I'm a sucker, and I'm happy for her to go on thinking so for as long as it suits my purpose. When it gets nearer the time, I can actually see her, in me mind of course, sitting in that chair trying to find the right excuse so as I'll have Milly and she can spend Christmas with her man friend. And I'll admit to yer, Rita, that if she gets all flustered and finds it hard to make an excuse that sounds plausible, I'll help her out! I'll be as nice as pie and encourage her to go out and enjoy herself. She's selfish enough to take me up on it.'

Bessie grinned ruefully. 'I don't usually think badly of people, Rita, and it's got nothing to do with me what Mrs Sinclair gets up to. She can walk Lime Street picking men up for money for all I care. It's what happens to Milly I'm concerned about. What sort of a Christmas would she have if there was nowhere for her to go except be with her mother? Whether it was to the boyfriend's, or the old school chum's, she'd have a miserable time because she wouldn't be wanted. And they wouldn't be having the same

312

sort of Christmas we have because snobs don't know how to let their hair down like we do. I can't stand the thought of Milly sitting in someone's house, watched over by her mother in case she spoke out of turn or put a foot wrong, and being unhappy. I'd crawl to the stuck-up snob next door rather than have that happen.' The look in Bessie's eyes begged for her mate's understanding. 'So, yer see, Rita, I might have a child over Christmas after all. I'm going to say so many prayers, God will give in just to shut me up.'

'It would be wonderful if it turns out that way, sunshine. Milly would have a lot of fun with my two and Aggie's. But don't pin yer hopes on it, Bessie, 'cos I'd hate to see yer let down. And it wouldn't only be you disappointed, it would be Milly, too. I know she'd rather be with you than with her mother.'

'I'm not even going to consider her not being here, Rita, I'm going to be positive and work on the assumption she's going to spend Christmas with me. And that's not because I'm selfish in wanting to keep her away from her mother, it's because I know she gets more love while she's in this house than she does anywhere else. So, are yer prepared to help me out if I take an extra hour's work on? If yer are, yer can mention it to Aggie if yer would, see if she's agreeable to what I've suggested. If it turns out I can't have Milly, it won't make no difference to you or Aggie, the kids will still have their party and presents, I'll make sure of that.'

Rita clicked her tongue on the roof of her

mouth. 'Yer should have had half a dozen kids of yer own, Bessie, 'cos yer'd have made a marvellous mother. And I hope to God things work out as yer want them to. But, that aside, you go ahead and work the extra hour, me and Aggie will look after Milly. It'll do the girl good to mix with other kids.' She suddenly took a fit of laughing. 'But I have to say, neither me nor Aggie will take any responsibility if the girl's mastery of the English language suffers a severe set back. It's too late in life for either of us to go back to school to learn how to speak properly. I will ask Aggie to try and control some of the more colourful words she comes out with, but I can't guarantee success.'

Bessie chortled. 'I'd be more afraid of Milly teaching Aggie some new words. The girls in her class must hear their parents cursing to high heaven.'

'My kids don't hear me swearing often, I try to control meself in front of them. Yer can't expect children not to repeat things they hear in their own homes, they're not to know some of them are bad.' Rita slipped her feet into her shoes. 'I'll have a word with Aggie in the morning, sunshine, and tell her what yer've got in mind. She'll be more than agreeable to helping, she'll be over the moon. If it means a halfway decent Christmas for the family, she'd walk to Timbuctoo and back. But, so she doesn't think we're making plans behind her back, I'll come over with her tomorrow night, after Milly's gone to bed. Aggie will feel better if she's involved, and it'll give her something to look forward to. Like meself, she doesn't get any social life because of lack of

314

money, and this scheme of yours will be just the job to keep the pair of us going. And if it turns out as you think it might, then it will take a lot of the worry of Christmas off our minds and we'll be yer friends for life.' She patted Bessie's arm. 'We'll be that anyway, sunshine, 'cos we couldn't have asked for a better mate over the years. Yer've always been there when we were in trouble, and yer know that even if we've never told yer, we've always appreciated yer kindness.'

Bessie nodded and followed her friend to the door. 'Make it half-past eight, then Milly will be in bed. I'll make us a pot of tea, which is more than yer got tonight. I've been that busy talking I forgot me manners. It won't happen again, sweetheart, I promise.'

Rita waved when she reached the opposite pavement. 'Goodnight and God bless, sunshine, and go straight to sleep, no more laying awake, d'yer hear? Yer've given me enough to think about, but it won't stop me from getting me beauty sleep.'

'Goodnight and God bless.' Bessie blew a kiss before closing the door.

As Bessie was closing her front door, Philip was holding his apartment door open for the two waiters to pass through. They were carrying boxes filled with crockery, glassware and cutlery used in the meal they had served earlier. The food had been delicious, and the serving of it faultless. This was much appreciated by Philip who, as they passed him at the door, gave them a pound note each to show his gratitude. Then with the door closed behind them, he rubbed his hands in satisfaction. Now he and Evelyn were alone, and from their conversation over dinner he was sure she was aware he was no longer going to be satisfied with kissing and petting. He wanted to possess her, and teach her the ways in which she could please and satisfy him. That wouldn't happen in one night, and he wasn't a cad who would force her into doing things she objected to. But his passion needed satisfying tonight, he could wait no longer.

Evelyn turned her eyes to meet his when Philip entered the room. 'I must say, dear, that the meal was absolutely perfect in every way. I thoroughly enjoyed it.'

'I agree, my lovely, it was far better to dine in comfort here than going out to a restaurant. I feel quite full, though, and think we should change into something not quite so restricting. Do you wish to use the bathroom first, or shall I?'

'You go first, my dear, I'll relax here until you return.' Evelyn wasn't afraid of what she knew was going to happen, it was inevitable if she was to keep him. But she wasn't quite sure what was expected of her now. What did he mean by changing into something not quite so restricting? She wasn't about to show her ignorance, nor make a fool of herself by asking, so she'd wait and see what Philip was wearing when he came back. 'Hurry, my dear, I shall be lonely without you by my side.'

Her words were like music to his ears. 'I shall be ten minutes at the most, my dearest Evelyn, I am loath to leave you for even such a short time.'

With that he turned on his heels and left the room, humming softly to himself.

Evelyn sat back in the comfortable couch feeling happy and contented. It had been a lovely day and Philip the perfect escort. He had walked with her down Lord Street, stopping when she spied anything in a window that caught her eye. She could have had anything her heart desired, but she refused all the evening and party dresses, saying what she really needed was a coat to wear for work. She only possessed the one, and it needed to be cleaned. So without further ado, and giving her no chance to object, Philip cupped her elbow and marched her into one of the elegant shops. To the assistant who hurried forward to help, he said, 'My fiancée would like to see a winter coat. Would you bring several out for her inspection while we take a seat?'

Against Philip's wishes, Evelyn chose one of the least costly coats, and nothing he said would make her change her mind. She would have loved several of them, but she couldn't walk down her street in a coat that was obviously expensive nor would she feel comfortable wearing it to the office. So she chose one in a deep plum colour, in pure wool, that came with a matching scarf. She was delighted with it, could never have afforded one so fine with the money she had left from the five-pound note. And when she told the assistant she would like to leave the shop in her new coat, Philip was so delighted that she liked it so much she wanted to keep it on, he instructed the assistant to see his fiancée's wishes were carried out. So they had left the shop with her

317

old coat in a very exclusive shopping bag, and in her purse she still had money left from the five pounds he'd given her.

The opening of the door brought Evelyn's thoughts back to the present. Although she was surprised to see Philip walking towards her in a deep maroon, heavy satin dressing gown, she didn't let her feelings show. 'You have been quick, my dear, and I really have to say you look extremely handsome.'

He bent to kiss her, then took her hand and pulled her to her feet. 'Thank you, my darling, for the compliment. And I am sure that when you return from doing what women do, you will look very beautiful. Now, make haste, my love. I am eager to hold you in my arms.'

Evelyn took off her dress and hung it in the wardrobe, then stood for a while, not knowing quite what to do. She hadn't seen any sign of pyjamas under the dressing gown Philip was wearing so presumed he was naked. This brought a blush to her face, and set her heart beating faster. What would he be expecting her to wear? Perhaps she should take herself to the bathroom to wash herself thoroughly with his beautiful perfumed soap, and brush her hair until it shone. She really did want to look her best to please him. Perhaps the red satin nightdress would be the most suitable item of clothing to wear. Or, like Philip, should she just wear the dressing gown to cover her nakedness? She shook her head. No, it would have to be the nightdress to spare her blushes. After all, it would be the first time any man had seen her naked, for her husband never had.

Having decided, she moved a little faster. She knew Philip would be impatient and she didn't want him to come looking for her. She wanted to go to him, not the other way round.

Fifteen minutes later, a faint smell of the perfumed soap pervading the air, her face glowing and hair shining, she stood framed in the doorway of the lounge. She had no idea how appealing she looked. The satin and lace nightdress did little to hide her firm breasts, slim waist and curved hips. Philip sat drinking in every inch of her, until she became uncomfortable under his gaze. Her voice timid, she asked, 'Do I pass inspection, then?'

He jumped up from the couch and crossed the room in a few strides. 'My dearest darling, I have never wanted anyone so much in my life as I want you.' He bent down, lifted her off her feet and carried her through to the bedroom where he laid her down gently on top of the bed. There was a look of trepidation on her face and her body was tense, which he didn't fail to notice. 'It's all right, my darling, there is nothing to fear. If you don't want it to happen, then it won't. Please relax, we'll lie together under the bedcovers.'

Her eyes averted, Evelyn felt him move his naked body closer. 'Would you allow me to remove your nightdress, my darling?' he asked. 'Or would you rather not?'

She nodded, curious now that they'd gone so far to know what it was that Philip so desperately craved. 'Yes, please.' She raised herself from the bed to assist in the removal of the nightdress, and

319

as it slipped over her head could feel her bare flesh next to Philip's. A tingle ran down her spine. Then he lowered her gently before covering her body with his, whispering huskily, 'Don't be afraid, my darling, I want to teach you the pleasure that comes from love making.'

Evelyn could feel her body being caressed, and gradually it awoke in her a passion she had never experienced before. She gave low cries of pleasure as her body arched to meet Philip's. And when he asked softly, 'Am I pleasing you, my darling?' she sighed and murmured, 'Oh, yes, my love.'

Then she felt the weight of his body leave hers as he rolled away and lay next to her, his breathing heavy. 'What is it, my love?' Evelyn thought she had disappointed him in some way. 'Am I not satisfying you?'

'I don't want what we have now to be over too soon, so let me rest a while. But you are the most lovable, adorable creature imaginable, and you possess a passion I was not prepared for. I want this feeling of ecstasy to last, my darling, therefore I must let my passion subside for a short while.'

Evelyn was too inexperienced fully to understand the meaning of Philip's words, and in her naivety turned on her side and put an arm across his waist. As she was kissing his shoulder, she let her hand stroke his chest and heard him sigh. 'Please take it easy, my love, I can only stand so much.'

'Shall I bring us a drink in?' Evelyn asked. 'We left a bottle on the table and our glasses, I'll go

320

for them while you get your breath back.' She was reaching for her nightdress when Philip stayed her hand. 'No, go as you are, my lovely Evelyn. Seeing you naked is like seeing a dream walking.'

She knelt on the bed and kissed him, showing no sign of embarrassment or shyness at seeing him naked. 'Yes, my master, I shall do your bidding.'

Philip watched her walking towards the door, delighting in the sway of her hips and long shapely legs. She really was a beauty, and he would hazard a guess no other man had touched her. For although she had lost her shyness and aloofness, and was perfectly at ease with him, she couldn't understand why he had suddenly halted the love making. Any woman experienced in the ways of men would have known without having to be told. For him this added to the attraction she had for him. He had never felt like this about any other woman, and there had been plenty. Evelyn satisfied him in every way, and tonight he'd proved to himself, beyond a doubt, that he had fallen in love with her. But he wasn't going to tell her so, she might not have the same feelings for him although he didn't think it was just in his imagination that she was drawing closer to him. She'd amazed and delighted him tonight when she hadn't tried to hide the pleasure she'd experienced as he'd fondled her. What was happening was something new to her, and he couldn't even imagine the heights they could reach when she'd learned all he had to teach her.

Evelyn came through the door with a bottle of wine in one hand and two glasses in the other. The fact that she was naked seemed not to affect her at all. 'Here you are, my love, your favourite wine. Sit up and I'll hand you a glass. I'll have mine sitting on the side of the bed. We can chat, and say nice things to each other.'

Philip sat up and plumped the pillows at his back before taking the glass of red wine from her. He watched as Evelyn poured her drink before sitting on the side of the bed and lifting her glass. 'A toast, my dear, to a lasting friendship.'

As he sipped the wine, Philip couldn't tear his eyes away from her breasts. So full and ripe, and so near he couldn't resist the temptation to fondle them. As he did so, he felt a stirring in his loins and groaned. He couldn't hold out much longer. 'Put the glass down, my lovely, and get back into bed. My need is desperate and I can no longer ignore it. I'm sorry, it's out of my control. I will do my best to be gentle, but tell me if I hurt you.'

The pain Evelyn experienced was sharp, but it lasted only seconds, and soon she was lost in a world she had never known, writhing in ecstasy with Philip panting above her. Wave after wave of the most thrilling pleasure she had ever known overtook her. She cried out while her hands clasped his shoulders. It was a wonderland for her of sheer sensuous pleasure. When Philip stopped, wanting to see on her face the pleasure he was able to bring about with his love making, she begged, 'Don't stop, my darling, please!'

He rolled away from her. 'I am sorry, but to lose

my head and carry on would be foolish. That is how babies are made. But I can satisfy your needs in other ways.' He threw all the bedclothes on to the floor, then his hands began to stroke and explore her body as Evelyn, with her eyes closed, reacted to his touch by stretching, and arching as her passion reached peaks of pleasure she had never thought possible. In the end, she could take no more and begged, 'Please, my darling, no more for now.'

He took her in his arms. 'Am I right in saying you have never been made love to before? Never known what a wonderful thing passion is?'

'You are right, my darling, I have never been made love to before. My husband was a good man who I had been courting for a while, but I never lay in bed beside him for he went away to war the day we were married.' This was the first time she had talked of her husband to anyone since her parents and the Lister-Sinclairs had refused to believe that Charles was the father of the baby she was carrying, and had disowned her. She was left with nothing, except a baby who wasn't born out of love, and a heart full of bitterness.

'I don't want to rake up the past, it achieves nothing. You know now as much as you need to know, and as much as I am prepared to tell you, for talking of it is painful. Let us leave the past in the past, and talk of more pleasant things.' She stroked his cheek. 'Thank you for being so gentle and understanding, and for showing me what I have been missing all these years. And most of all, thank you for making me into a woman who is complete. The last hour or so has been absolute bliss, unbelievably thrilling and very fulfilling.'

'It is I who should be thanking you, my darling Evelyn. Last week in the office I said you were a slave driver. Well, you may be a slave driver in the office, but you are an angel in bed, and I adore you. Did I really please you?'

'Oh, how can you ask that, my dear, when it must have been very obvious I was lost in a passion I didn't even know I was capable of? If you had told me a few weeks ago that one day I would be walking around your apartment naked, or lying next to you in bed, I would have said you had lost the run of your senses. If you had tried to explain passion, and the delights it can bring, I would not have believed you. Oh, there is so much I have to thank you for, Philip, I really don't know where to begin. You have taught me so much.'

'Not everything, my darling, there is more for you to learn. And that is the way in which you can please me, and take me to the heights you have just come down from. Give me your hand, my love, and I will show you.'

Chapter Seventeen

Philip walked across the bedroom floor carrying a tray set with a pot of tea, a plate of pale golden toast, pot of marmalade, and the appropriate crockery and cutlery. He stood by the bed, gazing down at the sleeping form of Evelyn, and felt a quiver of excitement run down his spine at the memory of the joy she'd given him last night. He placed the tray on a small table near the bed, then gently shook her shoulder. 'Evelyn, my lovely one, I have brought you some tea.'

She stirred, turned on her side, then after a few seconds opened her eyes. 'Oh, Philip, for a while I couldn't make out where I was.' Her eyes caught sight of the tray, and she was pushing herself into a sitting position when she realised she was naked. She made a grab for a sheet to cover herself, but Philip anticipated her move and took hold of her hand. 'Would you spoil a day which I am sure is going to be such a happy one for both of us?'

It was then she noticed that once again he was wearing no clothes beneath the dressing gown. 'Pass the tray, my dear, then get into bed and we will enjoy breakfast in each other's company.' She was wide awake now, and felt a tingle as the memories came flooding back. 'How thoughtful of you to bring me breakfast in bed. I will have to watch you don't spoil me. I do believe it should

325

have been me waiting on you.'

He placed the tray carefully on her lap, then slid into bed. 'I want to spoil you, and go on spoiling you. What man in his right senses would not spoil a woman who is so beautiful and passionate?'

Evelyn was pouring the tea into small china cups. 'Please be still, my love, otherwise the tray and everything on it will spill over. I think we should drink a cup of tea first, put the empty cups on the table, and have our toast. We can always have another cup of tea later.'

'Oh, there won't be time for a second cup of tea, darling,' Philip said, a twinkle in his eye.

There was surprise on Evelyn's face, and a look of disappointment. 'But I thought I wasn't going home until this afternoon? That is what we arranged.'

'If I can bear to part with you, then yes, it will be this afternoon when you go home. But, my wonderful lover, I am hoping for several repeat performances of last night before then. That is if you are agreeable?'

The anticipation started with butterflies in her tummy and accelerated with her racing heartbeat. She held on tight to the tray while she closed her eyes. At twenty-nine years of age, she was just finding out the real meaning of happiness and pleasure, and she wasn't going to throw them away. 'I find I am not so hungry after all, so shall we just have one cup of tea and one slice of toast?'

Philip nearly sent the tray flying when he put his arms around her and kissed her cheek. 'You, my very darling Evelyn, are the most adorable woman I have ever met. And one slice of toast will be ample. I have an appetite, but it is not for food.'

Evelyn searched his face. 'Talking of food, how is it you always have a well-stocked kitchen? Does your mother shop for you?'

'Good grief, no! The person who does my shopping for me is the same person who keeps the apartment clean and attends to my washing and ironing.'

There was a look of horror on Evelyn's face. 'Then she must wonder who owns the ladies' clothes in the wardrobe, and satin underwear in the drawers. Does she know you have a lady friend, or does she think you have a mistress?'

'Keep calm, my love, keep calm.' Philip began to chuckle. 'I don't know, though, they say anger is excellent for enthusiastic love making.'

'Philip, please be serious. I do not want anyone thinking I am your mistress or that I am a paid paramour. It would spoil our relationship for ever.'

'My maid of all work is a woman in her fifties, with a husband and four children. She is an excellent worker, doesn't ask questions, just gets on with what needs doing. I stole her from my mother who has never forgiven me. Annie had worked for her for ten years. Now, does that explanation satisfy you?'

Evelyn raised her brows. 'And she will never be here when I am due?'

'Certainly not!' Philip was enjoying this. 'I could never attend to two women at the same time, I haven't the stamina for it.'

This brought a smile to Evelyn's face, another indication of how she had changed. 'Oh, from

327

what little I have seen of you, my dear, I would say you are perfectly capable of attending to two women at the same time. But I would not advise it, as I have a very jealous streak.'

'You would be prepared to fight for me, then, my darling? What a very lucky man I am. Now shall we partake of a little sustenance to give us the strength for the very pleasant task ahead of us? I should hate to fall by the wayside before lunch.'

Their love making became more playful, each teasing the other and both filling the room with laughter. It was perfect heaven for Evelyn who had never known what it was to be so happy. She felt contented, taking the love Philip was giving her and giving it back in return. She was shocked to realise she had never before known what true love was. For her parents weren't loving or even affectionate towards her. She couldn't remember ever once being kissed or hugged, and never a word of endearment.

Evelyn gave a start as Philip cupped her chin and turned her face towards him. 'You look so serious, my darling, what thoughts were in your head to bring a frown to that beautiful face?'

'They weren't pleasant thoughts, my dear, but they have helped me understand why I have never known any real happiness until the last few weeks when you came into my life. Oh, I thought I loved my husband, and if he hadn't been killed perhaps our love would have blossomed. But it was not him I was thinking of, it was my parents and the miserable existence they lived.' Evelyn felt Philip pull her close to comfort her, and opened a little of her heart to him. 'My parents were never loving towards me. All they cared about was money, it was their only topic of conversation. They were very frugal, almost miserly, and I was never given pocket money or allowed to bring my school friends home. There was never any laughter in the house, it was frowned upon. On my nineteenth birthday I was allowed to go to my first dance with a girl I knew from school. And because my mother bought my clothes, ones in the style she liked, I was the frumpiest girl at the dance.'

Philip was shaking his head in disbelief. 'How could they treat you like that? They should have been so proud of you!'

'I could have understood if money had been scarce, but it wasn't! Father had a decent position and earned a good salary, but he and Mother hated parting with a penny.' Evelyn felt she had said enough now about her past, but hoped what she had told Philip would help him understand why she might have appeared aloof and secretive. He had been drawn to her by her air of mystery, and it was vital she should keep back the most important part of that mystery, her daughter Amelia. If he became aware of her existence, it would surely have him walking away ... their association at an end. She realised now that would break her heart, for she had fallen in love with him.

'In a few short weeks, you have brought me out of my shell and shown me how loving a person can bring happiness,' she told him. 'Especially last night. You were so understanding, so gentle and loving. I will always love you for that.'

'My poor darling.' Philip pressed her head to his shoulder and stroked her hair. 'Never again will you be without laughter or love, I shall make sure of that. From now on, my main priority in life will be to protect you, take care of you, and love you. In fact, my darling, I think it would be a good idea if you were to move in here permanently and then I can take care of you, properly. If you would agree, my life would be complete.'

A cold hand clutched Evelyn's heart. There was nothing in the world she would like more than to be with Philip every day, but she knew that could never happen. At least not for the forseeable future. 'No, Philip, much as I would love to live with you, I think we should have more time to get to know each other. It's barely a month since we met for the first time.'

'I know all I want to know about you, my love.' He looked disappointed. 'I know every part of your body, as you know mine. And, little by little, I am finding out what you have done so far in your life. I really see no reason to wait.'

'But what about me, Philip? I would have to get used to being a kept woman, and even though I do love you, that wouldn't sit easy on my shoulders. I do not want to give up my job, I enjoy it and it makes me independent. The staff at the office would soon notice the difference in our relationship, too, and I'd feel they were talking about me behind my back.'

'Hang the office staff! Who cares what they

think? I wouldn't want you to live here as my mistress but as my wife! And under no circumstances would I permit a wife of mine to go out to work.'

Evelyn was stunned. For a brief moment she listened to the voice in her head which was saying, If only your life wasn't such a mess... But it was a mess, and although she would like nothing better than to be his wife, that could never be. 'Philip, I feel very honoured, and I know your intentions are good. But I don't think you have had time to consider what you are saying, or what the consequences would be if I were to encourage you into asking me to be your wife. For your sake I suggest we carry on as we are for a few more months, to give us both time to find out if getting married is what we both want.'

'I don't need time to consider.' Philip's expression mirrored his stubborn streak. 'I know without any doubt that I want you to be my wife. We may only have known each other a short time, as you point out, but I think I knew from the second I set eyes on you that I wanted you. I admit that in the beginning, when you were so cool and off-hand with me the attraction was more of a challenge.' He managed a grin. 'I was going to stalk you, like a tiger stalks its prey, until I got what I wanted. But as each new day came, and you walked into the office, I could feel a pounding in my heart which went beyond lust.' He gazed at her naked body, the firm breasts jutting out so proudly, and stroked a finger over a taut nipple. 'I have opened my heart to you, my lovely, now it is your turn to tell me your thoughts.'

'Let us snuggle down under the clothes,' Evelyn said, 'and we can hold each other close. I want to feel you near me.'

With a soft feather eiderdown over them, they snuggled up close. 'The way I feel about you now, Philip, I would marry you tomorrow. I have truly fallen head over heels in love with you. But in my life so far I have been dealt some hard blows and have learned to be cautious. That is why I am going to ask you to wait a few months, until we know each other inside out. Our good points, and our bad. I am considering your welfare, not just my own. It's Christmas soon. Why don't we carry on as we are until the festive season is over, see how we feel then? It is not an eternity, my love, just a matter of weeks.'

'And we'll see each other as often as possible in those weeks, won't we?' Philip pushed a lock of dark hair back from her forehead. 'I won't agree to your terms unless we continue to meet as often as possible.'

'Yes, I promise.' Evelyn had something on her mind that was troubling her. 'What about your mother? Does she know about me, and my visits to your apartment?'

'No, she doesn't. Until last night your visits have been on a friendly basis, remember. But I am going home today. When you are ready to leave, I shall leave with you. Mother rang this morning while you were still asleep, to ask if I had forgotten where I live. So I'll have my evening meal and sleep there for the next two or three nights. That will keep my parents happy. Which means, apart from Annie coming in to clean, the apartment won't be used until we meet for our tryst at lunchtime on Wednesday. I shall leave a note asking her to have a light lunch set out for us.'

'I'm going to request, Philip, that my name is not mentioned while you are at home. Promise you won't tell your parents about me? If your mother knew I visited you here, unaccompanied, she would be entitled to think I am not the sort of woman she would welcome as a wife for her son. So you would do our relationship no favour by discussing our friendship.'

A sheepish grin crossed Philip's face. 'You are far more practical than I am, my love. I want to tell the world about our romance. But that would be foolhardy of me. My parents are quite strait-laced and I haven't always lived up to their standards. But being free from any tie, old enough to know what I'm doing, attending parties several times a week where the girls were practically throwing themselves at eligible males ... well, my parents must have known I wasn't living the life of a saint! And I have never pretended to you that I was inexperienced, have I? I have had several affairs. None of them has lasted longer than a week or two. I find myself getting short-tempered with females who cannot conduct an intelligent conversation, whose only interest in life is having the most fashionable clothes and being invited to the best parties. They make very dull companions.'

'But not too dull to go to bed with?'

Philip wasn't in the least embarrassed by the question, and didn't see why he shouldn't be truthful. 'With the light out, my lovely, they all look the same. Those were not acts of love on my part, but acts of necessity. I can honestly say that last night was the first time I made love to someone I was in love with. The other women served their purpose, over in a short time and forgotten immediately I was outside the bedroom door. Last night was a miracle for me. You transported me to a place I had never been before, and I shall never make love to anyone but you for the rest of my life.'

Evelyn had felt her jealousy rising as he spoke about the other women he had bedded, but quickly pushed the thoughts out of her mind. They were in the past, and best forgotten.

'Considering you are my first lover and I am twenty-nine years of age, I didn't do too badly, did I?'

Philip frowned. 'I only have a vague recollection of the night's events, my love, so could you please give me a repeat performance?'

Evelyn was learning fast, and surprised herself by asking, 'You mean, on my own?'

He chortled. 'Oh, I think I will join in somewhere along the way. In fact, even talking about it has my heart pounding, so I think I will start off the proceedings and you can just lie still and enjoy yourself.'

Evelyn walked down the entry with her head bowed, deep in thought. On the journey home, as the tram rattled and lurched, she had taken stock of her life and been surprised and shocked by some of the things that occurred to her. She had told Philip how her parents had never shown her any affection, no hugs, kisses or endearments. And suddenly it had come to her that she had treated her own daughter in the same way. She had never kissed Amelia, even when she was a baby. The wet nurse and the maid had taken care of the child's needs. And when the wet nurse had left, Amelia was put on a bottle. So did Amelia hate her, as Evelyn had hated her own parents? She really hadn't been fair to the child, blaming her for everything that had gone wrong in her life. Still, she couldn't honestly say she loved her daughter, for she didn't. She felt sorry now for the way she'd treated her, and wouldn't hurt her or wish her harm, but she couldn't conjure up these maternal instincts she'd heard people refer to. And it was going to be difficult putting Philip off after Christmas, he wasn't stupid enough to keep on believing her lies and excuses.

What a mess my life has become, she thought. And all because no one would believe that Charles could be such a cad as to get me in the family way before we were married. Even Gwen, her best friend, hadn't believed her. And because they wouldn't believe the truth, she'd been left without family or friends. But she'd put all that behind her if she could marry Philip. She was besotted with him. And Amelia was the only obstacle in the way.

Evelyn sighed as she stopped outside Bessie's entry door. She knew it would be on the latch, they would be expecting her, so pressed it down and entered the yard. As she walked over the uneven, broken tiles, she decided fate had a lot to answer for. Miss Maudsley loved Amelia and

335

would make a wonderful mother, naturally kind and loving as she was. And the girl certainly loved the little woman, you could see it in her eyes. That look was never there when she was talking to her mother.

Bessie had the kitchen door open before the knock came. 'Come on in, Mrs Sinclair, and get a warm by the fire.' She steered her neighbour into the living room. 'Say hello to yer mother, Amelia.'

'Hello, Mother, have you had a nice weekend?'

'Yes, dear, really nice. It's been a real treat for me over the last few weeks, quite a change from just bed and work.'

'D'yer fancy a cup of tea, Mrs Sinclair?' Bessie asked. 'It'll warm the cockles of yer heart. And I made a batch of fairy cakes, which are nice and light. I'll put one on a plate for yer.'

'Thank you, Miss Maudsley, it's very good of you. A cup of tea and one of your fairy cakes will be much appreciated.' Evelyn was seeing her neighbour in a new light now. Instead of looking down on her for her lack of education, her Liverpool accent and lack of social skills, she now saw her as a woman to be envied. She had so much Evelyn herself was lacking in. A warm and happy nature, a ready smile and sense of humour, and real friends. And, judging from the way her daughter was looking at their neighbour, she also had Amelia's love. 'I'm afraid I'm hopeless at baking, my cakes always turn out like rocks,' Evelyn said.

'I'll put the kettle on. And I would much prefer you to call me Bessie, that's what my friends call me.' She ruffled Milly's hair as she passed, and was on the threshold of the kitchen when she heard her neighbour reply.

'You're right, it is more friendly. But if I'm to call you Bessie then I must insist you call me Evelyn.' Remembering how badly she had treated this little woman, who had only ever been good to her, Evelyn sounded humble. 'That's if you don't mind?'

Bessie turned and grinned. 'That's fine by me, sweetheart, I can't be bothered with people what stand on ceremony. Now, Amelia, you can help get the cups and saucers ready before yer mother dies of thirst.'

It was while they were having their tea and Bessie's light-as-a-feather fairy cakes, that she asked, 'Was yer friend all right, Evelyn?'

'Yes, she was as bright as ever.' Evelyn lowered her eyes. She no longer found it easy to lie to this woman, but there was little else she could do if she wanted the freedom to meet Philip. 'She has a lovely house, a husband who spoils her, and well-mannered children.'

Milly was sitting quietly taking it all in. She could sense the change in her mother, and was pleased she was being so friendly towards Auntie Bessie. But the child had lived long enough with her mother to know she wasn't always truthful, and that her mood could change quickly, for no reason at all. Still, Auntie Bessie wasn't soft, she wouldn't be taken in by lies. And Milly didn't really care what her mother did, as long as she never put a stop to her coming here every night. She couldn't bear it if that happened. She looked

337

forward to coming home from school each day now, knowing she would have a couple of hours where she could say what she liked, laugh when something funny happened, play with her doll, and hug and kiss Auntie Bessie. And she had Auntie Rita and Auntie Aggie now, too, and Jack. She thought he was lovely, even though he always had dirty knees and socks round his ankles.

Milly's lips clamped together as these thoughts ran through her head, and felt a rebellious mood coming on. If her mother ever said she was moving to another house, far away from this street, then she wouldn't go. She'd run away and hide somewhere until her mother had left, then come back and live with Auntie Bessie. Such were the thoughts running through the head of the eight-year-old-girl who in the last few months had found a love and happiness she'd never known. The prospect of living with her mother, away from the new friends she'd made, filled her with dread.

Evelyn touched her daughter's knee. 'Amelia, I want you to stay here for a while until I get a fire going next door. The house will be very cold, so be a good girl and stay with your Auntie Bessie until I knock on the wall.'

'Yes, Mother.'

'You are sure you don't mind, Bessie?' Evelyn asked. 'I always seem to be asking favours of you. But just for half an hour, while I get a fire going.'

'Poppy off, sweetheart, Amelia is all right here for as long as it takes. It'll be flipping perishing in your house with not having a fire lit for two days.'

When her mother had left, Milly ran upstairs for

her precious doll. Clutching it tight, she sat on the couch. 'It was cold upstairs for her, Auntie Bessie, so when Mother knocks for me, will you let Daisy stay down here with you so she's warm?'

'Of course she can stay down here, sweetheart, she'll be company for me. And when I go to bed, I'll wrap her in her blanket and she can sleep on the couch. It stays warm in this room with having had the fire burning all day.'

'I wish I could stay here with her,' Milly said, wistfully. 'We could keep each other warm. She told me this morning that she misses me when I'm not here.'

'Well, that's only natural, isn't it? I mean, you're her mother and you look after her. I bet she loves the bones of yer.'

The girl smiled. 'I know she loves me, she tells me every day. She's never said she loves the bones of me, but if she loves me, then she must love all of me, mustn't she?'

Bessie nodded. 'That means yer bones, yer arms and legs, pretty face and yer lovely smile. There's lots more, of course, but I'm hopeless about the names of some parts of me body. I couldn't pronounce half of them, let alone spell them. Still it wouldn't do me any good if I did know them, would it? Imagine Rita if I asked her where her hepaglotis is, she'd think I'd gone barmy.'

'Where is her hepagots, Auntie Bessie?' Milly looked suitably impressed. 'You must be very clever, 'cos I've never heard of it.'

'Neither have I, sweetheart, but don't tell my mate if she says anything to yer. Let her carry on thinking I'm a genius.' Bessie chuckled. 'I'll get it

339

into the conversation tomorrow, and I can't wait to see her face.'

'Ooh, I hope I'm here, Auntie Bessie. But I'll have to be very careful not to let her see me smiling or it'll give the game away.'

Bessie bent down to take the poker from the brass companion set, and then rattled it between the bars on the grate. There was a sudden flare, with flames dancing, and she nodded as she put the poker back in its place. 'There, that's better. Yer can't beat a good fire on a cold night.'

Milly waited until Bessie was seated, then said, 'My mother looked very different tonight, didn't she? She must have really enjoyed being with her friend. It must be a long time since she'd seen her, 'cos I've never heard of her before.'

It ran through Bessie's mind that although this girl was only eight, she didn't miss anything. Then again, there would have had to be something wrong with her eyesight if she hadn't noticed the change in her own mother. 'Well, they lost touch with each other when they left school, Milly, and only met by accident a few weeks ago. But it's nice for yer mother to have a friend, 'cos we all need one. I'm very glad about it because it means I get to see more of you.'

Milly seemed satisfied. 'I'll never stop coming here, I know I won't. So you and me will both be very happy, Auntie Bessie.'

'We sure will, sweetheart, we sure will.'

Chapter Eighteen

It was half-past three on the Monday afternoon when a flustered Rita knocked on her neighbour's door. 'Ay, Aggie, I'm in a bit of a dilemma. Milly is supposed to be coming straight to me today, but I don't think Bessie realised that when she gets home from work there'll be no fire lit. And it's too cold for her to take Milly over to a house what's freezing. But Bessie left me her key in case Milly wanted to go in there for her doll, or to go to the lavvy, and with her doing the extra hour in work to help us all out for Christmas, I was wondering if I should go in and put a light to her fire.'

Aggie's head and chins agreed. 'Oh, that would be nice of yer, queen, I'm sure she'd be grateful to yer. And when it's my turn tomorrow to have Milly, I'll do the same. Be nice for Bessie to walk in to a roaring fire.'

'That's what I had in mind,' Rita said. 'But I'm worried she might think I'm only being nosy, and going in there to snoop.'

Aggie pooh-poohed the idea. 'Away with yer, Bessie's not bad-minded. Anyway, she's only got the bleeding same as we've got in our houses, so why should she mind?' Aggie's laugh was more of a hoarse cackle. 'Mind you, hers is a damn' sight cleaner than mine. Yer can see yer face in her sideboard, it's that highly polished, where mine is

341

full of finger marks. Still, I'm not a proud woman.'

Rita mentally compared her house, and Aggie's, to Bessie's, and shook her head. 'You and me aren't in the same league as her, sunshine, she's got her house like a new pin. Mine looks passable until the boys come in from school, then it looks as though it's been hit by a bomb.'

'My old ma, God rest her soul, had the same problem. I remember her saying, time and again, that if it wasn't for me and me brother, her house would be a little palace, and she wouldn't be afraid to invite the Queen for tea.'

'Well, that's settled then,' Rita said, with a determined nod of her head. 'I'll walk up to the top of the street to meet Milly coming home from school. I'll take her in to Bessie's while I light the fire, then bring her to mine for a hot drink. I'll nip back home now and put me coat on, it's too cold to be hanging around.'

When Milly saw Rita waiting for her at the top of the street, her face lit up. And not for the first time, Rita thought what a beautiful child she was: a heart-shaped face with high cheek bones, green eyes that changed colour by the second, and a smile to melt the hardest heart.

'Are you waiting for me, Auntie Rita?'

'Yes, sunshine, I'm minding yer for an hour, like yer Auntie Bessie told yer. But 'cos she's left me her key in case of emergency, I thought you and me could light the fire for her and give her a nice surprise.'

Milly reached for her hand. 'That really would be nice for her, Auntie Rita, you are kind. Are we walking down the entry?'

Rita reached a quick decision. Sneaking down the back entry like a couple of thieves – blow that for a joke. The sooner this girl got used to mixing with her neighbours the better. 'No, me and you are going to walk down the street with our heads held high and our backs straight. We'll pretend I'm a queen and you are a princess.'

Milly put a hand over her mouth while her eyes brimmed with laughter. 'Oh, you do say some funny things, Auntie Rita. I'll like pretending I'm a princess, yes, I will. I'll put my nose in the air and wave to everyone.'

'Oh, I wouldn't go that far, sunshine, or they'll send for an ambulance to take us away to an asylum.'

They began to walk down the street, Milly's hand clasped in Rita's. 'What is an asylum, Auntie Rita? Is it somewhere not nice?'

All her life, Rita had objected to people making fun of people who were mentally ill. When she was a young girl, there had been a woman living in their street who'd acted strangely and everyone used to make fun of her. Except Rita's mother, who had once clipped her around the ear for saying the woman was doolally. And her words had stayed with her daughter all her life. 'Never mock people who can't help themselves, queen,' she'd said. 'Remember, there but for the grace of God go I.' Rita was too young at the time to understand what her mother had meant, but she had never forgotten her words.

'An asylum is for people who are sick. Some people who are physically sick go into hospital to be made better, but those who are sick in their head, they go in to an asylum until they are better.' While she was talking, Rita could see the looks directed their way. It was very unusual for Milly to walk down the street, never mind walking down it clasping Rita's hand. But it would only be curiosity on the part of the neighbours, there would be no ill-feeling against the child. They weren't keen on her mother, who they saw as being a snob who believed she was too good even to pass them the time of day, but none of that animosity would be aimed at the young girl.

When they reached Bessie's house, Rita slid the key into the lock. 'Come in with me until I've got the fire going, sunshine, then it's across to mine for a nice warm cup of tea.'

'Can I go upstairs for Daisy?' Milly asked. 'She would like to come with me.'

Rita pursed her lips and blew out. 'Well, it's like this, sunshine, I've got two boys in my house, and I think they'd pull yer leg soft if they saw yer nursing a doll. They're not like girls, they like games where they play with balls, or marbles, and get their knees dirty. It's up to you, though, sunshine, as long as yer don't mind getting laughed at.'

'In that case, boys aren't fair, are they?' Milly's chin jutted out determinedly. 'Girls don't laugh at them for playing football or marbles and getting themselves very dirty, so why should they laugh at the games girls play? At least we don't get filthy.'

Rita struck a match and held it to the newspaper balls Bessie had set under the sticks of firewood. 'I wish I was as organised as Bessie is. She left the house at half-past six this morning to go to work, but the fire's set and everywhere neat and tidy.' She grinned at Milly, who was kneeling down beside her. 'Yer won't find my house as tidy as this, sunshine, and I've been at home all day! Lazy beggar, that's what I am.'

Milly wasn't going to agree with that. After a lifetime of living with just her mother, and never even having one visitor crossing their front door step, she wasn't going to hear a word against her newfound aunties. 'You are not a lazy beggar, Auntie Rita, you must work very hard with a husband and two children to look after. Especially when both of them are boys, and play marbles in the gutter.'

Rita saw the firewood was now alight, and took the tongs from the companion set to pick out some small cobs of coal from the scuttle at the side of the hearth. 'Oh, my two are no different from any of the other children. They're only kids once, so let them enjoy themselves while they can.' She turned her head to study the girl's face. 'I bet you get dirty sometimes, as well?'

'Oh, no, Mother wouldn't allow it, she would get very angry. She won't let me sit at the table if my hands are the least bit grubby. And if we have no soap, then I have to wash them in cold water and use the scrubbing brush. I don't like having to do that, it hurts, but Mother stands over me and makes sure I do it properly.'

Rita lowered her eyes to hide her anger and shock. There was no self-pity in the girl's voice, no whingeing, so it was obvious she believed all children were treated the same way by their mothers. It wasn't Rita's place to tell her different. She wasn't going to set daughter against mother. But, oh, dear, wouldn't she like to give Mrs Sinclair a piece of her mind? A lovely daughter like this, and to treat her so badly, it just wasn't right.

The flames were licking the coals now, it wouldn't be long before there was a fire roaring up the chimney. 'I'll put the fireguard in front of it now the coals have caught, just in case any sparks fly.' Rita used her curled fists to push herself up. 'I want Bessie to come home to a nice, warm welcoming fire in her grate, but not her house on fire. D'yer know where she keeps the fireguard, sunshine?'

Milly nodded and made for the kitchen. 'I'll get it, Auntie Rita, it's in the larder.'

The guard safe in front of the fire, Rita looked around to make sure everything was as they'd found it, then held out her hand. 'Come on, sunshine, I'm dying for a cuppa, me mouth feels as though it's full of feathers.'

Aggie was standing at her door when the two crossed the cobbles. She smiled at Milly. 'Are yer all right, queen?'

The world was opening up for Milly who had never known such happiness. 'I'm fine, thank you, Auntie Aggie. We've lit the fire for Auntie Bessie, so won't she have a lovely surprise when she gets home?'

'She will that, queen, she will that. And tomorrow it will be my turn to light it, so will yer give me a hand? Help me out, like?'

'Oh, I'd like that, Auntie Aggie! I'll get the fireguard for you, just in case some sparks fly out and set fire to the place. Auntie Bessie wouldn't be a bit happy if she came up the street and found her house on fire.'

Aggie kept her face straight and told her chins to stay put. 'Oh, yer think she'd be upset, do yer, queen?'

'Oh, yes, Auntie Aggie, she would be very upset. In fact I believe she would be so upset she would cry.' Then the girl had a horrible thought. 'Oh, and Daisy would get caught in the fire! She's upstairs and there would be no one rescue her.'

Rita gave her neighbour a look that said she should knock it off, she was frightening the girl. 'There won't be no fire, sunshine, we've put the fireguard in front to keep it safe. So Daisy won't come to any harm, today or tomorrow.' She glared at her neighbour, daring her to say different. 'Isn't that right, Aggie?'

If Aggie hadn't nodded of her own free will, her chins would have done it for her. They didn't want to see a young girl frightened. But Aggie came up trumps. 'I'll tell yer something, queen, I've lived in this street for nigh on eighteen years, and there's never, ever been a fire in any of the houses. Not in any of the streets around either, so yer've no need to worry, the odds are stacked against it.'

Milly looked confused and turned to Rita. 'What does Auntie Aggie mean, about the odds being stacked against it? I don't understand.'

Rita put an arm across her shoulders. 'That's

nothing, sunshine, 'cos I've lived next to Aggie for eighteen years and I still don't understand her. But I'll have a guess at this one. I think that, roughly translated, she was telling yer there isn't a snowball's chance in hell of there being a fire in Miss Maudsley's house, or any other in the street. Am I right, Aggie?'

'As near as damn it, queen, as near as damn it.' Aggie folded her arms and hitched her mountainous bosom. 'Now go and make the girl a cup of tea before I come out with another of my gems that yer'd have to explain.' She gave a broad wink to Milly. 'I'll see yer tomorrow afternoon, queen.'

Milly nodded and took Rita's hand, just as her two sons put in an appearance. The eldest, ten-year-old Billy, jerked his head and let out a sigh when he saw Milly. Why did his mam have to mind her for an hour every night? Girls were nothing but trouble, always crying before they were hurt. They talked too much, and most of the time it was a load of rubbish. 'Did I hear yer were making a cup of tea, Mam? I'll have one with yer before Tommo calls for me. We're having a competition tonight, to see who's the best at playing marbles.'

Milly shook her head and tutted, just like she'd seen Bessie doing a few times. 'That means you're going to get your knees all dirty, and your socks. Why don't you play a game where you don't have to kneel in the gutter?'

Billy glared. 'And why don't you mind yer own business? I can get dirty if I want to, it's got nowt to do with you.'

'That's enough now, in the house all of yer.' Rita

348

thought it time to intervene. 'And while Milly is with us, we'll have none of yer cheek or sarcasm. Get inside and wash yer hands if yer want a cup of tea.'

Nine-year-old Jack was looking on with a grin on his face. He waited until his brother went into the house then winked at Milly. 'Take no notice of our kid, he's like that with all girls. If yer ignore him, he'll soon get fed up of being sarky.'

Milly followed him up the steps. 'Why doesn't he like girls? And how can he be sure whether he likes them or not if he doesn't know any?' They were in the living room when she said, 'I know why your brother doesn't like girls, it's because we are more clever than boys.'

Billy was at the kitchen sink, about to put his hands under the running tap when he heard Milly's words and flew into the living room. Once again he glared at her. 'What makes yer think ye're more cleverer than boys? The only thing girls are good at is whingeing. They run crying to their mother at the least thing. And if the boys won't let them play footie with them, they tell fibs and say we hit them.'

Rita was standing in the kitchen waiting for the kettle to boil, and wondered whether she should put a stop to her son's protests. Then she decided to wait and see whether Milly was capable of sticking up for herself. When the girl started to speak, Rita moved to peep through the gap at the side of the door. The sight she saw had her clamping her lips together to keep the laughter back.

Milly's head was jutting forward and there were

sparks coming from her green eyes. 'That shows how wrong you are, Billy Wells. I do not tell fibs, and I don't go running to my mother every time I don't get my own way. And I'm certainly not stupid enough to kneel in the gutter and play with little glass balls.'

Billy was so taken aback he just stared. He'd never for one moment thought this girl, who lived opposite and never came out to play, would answer him back. He was so dumbstruck, he was lost for words. All he could think of, which even to his own ears sounded daft, was, 'I've left the tap running, ye're not worth bothering about.'

Rita would have loved to take the mickey out of her son. He was rude to all the girls in the street, and it was about time he got his comeuppance. But if she said too much, it would be like pouring oil on troubled waters. And she thought Milly had done a good job of cutting him down to size. Still she couldn't resist a little taunt when she looked at him with raised brows. 'I think yer've just met yer match, sunshine. But do us a favour and don't keep picking on her while she's here. She's a nice kid if yer'd give yerself time to get to know her.'

'She's still a girl, isn't she?' he grunted as he turned the tap on. 'But if she doesn't come out with any more of her wisecracks, I'll keep out of her way.'

Rita ruffled his hair. 'That's my lad! It shows ye're growing up.' These few words worked wonders, and while he sat across the table from Milly as they drank their tea, he didn't speak to her. But he couldn't help noticing those green eyes. He'd never seen eyes that colour before. And her jet black hair, heart-shaped face and winning smile brought him to the conclusion she was all right as far as girls went. Then he became disgusted with himself for finding things to like about her, and starting looking for faults. He found one. It wasn't really true, but it was the only one he could think of. She was not as pretty as Doreen, who lived at the top of the street. He'd bet she wouldn't like it if he told her that! But he wasn't going to say anything to her, and when she came over every night, he'd keep out of her way so his mam wouldn't be at him all the time. Oh, and so she wouldn't have anything to criticise him for, he'd wash his hands as soon as he came home from school.

Billy looked across the table to where Jack was sitting next to Milly, laughing and joking with her. He was even laughing at things that weren't funny. Billy was disgusted. He'd have a word with his brother later and tell him he'd looked a right cissy. When they were in bed tonight, he would tell him not to be making such a fuss of the girl 'cos it looked daft. If she was made so welcome, she'd never be away from their house. And *that* would mean them getting washed so often they'd have no skin left.

When Bessie got in from work her face lit up when she saw the fire roaring up the chimney, a pot of tea made and Milly sitting on the couch playing with her doll. 'Oh, I wasn't expecting yer to do this, Rita, it wasn't part of the deal. But, by golly, I'm glad yer did. I'm perished right through to me marrow, and me fingers are like ice.'

Milly rushed over to put her arms around her waist. 'Why didn't you put gloves on, Auntie Bessie, then your fingers wouldn't be cold? And your face must be cold too, it's bright red.'

'Let me take me coat off, sweetheart, so I can feel the heat from the fire.' Bessie slipped her arms out of her coat and handed it Milly. 'Hang it up for me, there's a good girl.'

Rita came through from the kitchen. 'Sit down, sunshine, and I'll hand yer this cup of tea. We'll have yer as warm as toast in no time.'

'Ooh, it's not often I get spoilt, so I'm going to make the most of it.' Bessie took a sip of the hot tea and could feel it going right through her body. 'The best cup I ever tasted, Rita, ye're an angel. It's murder working in that factory in winter. The sewing room is freezing. The only heating we've got is a small black stove in the middle of the huge room, with a pipe going up through the ceiling to let the smoke out. And the boss is so tight with his flaming money, he goes mad if one of the women puts more than a small shovel of coal in every few hours. He watches from his office window, and I'll swear he counts the pieces of coal that go in. The miserable bugger doesn't even buy the decent sort, there's more slate in the bags than there is coal.' Bessie was warming up now, and stretched her legs towards the fire. 'He's not so mean with himself though, he's got an electric fire in his office.'

Milly was kneeling down at the side of her chair, Daisy tucked under one of her arms. 'He's a very naughty man, Auntie Bessie, sitting in a nice warm office while the workers are freezing cold. Why don't you ask him to let you put more coal on?'

Bessie chuckled at the child's innocence. 'Anyone who was brave enough to do that, sweetheart, would find themselves without a job. Yer see, a lot of the women there are sole breadwinners with their husbands out of work. Their wages just barely keep the wolf from the door. Same with me, I couldn't do without me wages coming in, I'd really be in Queer Street then.' She pulled herself to her feet. 'I'll see to our meal, it won't take long 'cos I peeled the spuds last night. And you, Rita, you poppy off home and see to the family's dinner. And thanks a million for lighting me fire and looking after Milly, I really appreciate it.'

Rita reached for her coat off the hook behind the door. 'It's Aggie's turn tomorrow. She'll have the fire lit for yer, and she'll see Milly has a warm drink when she comes home from school. So, yer see, sunshine, we've got yer whole life planned out for yer.'

Bessie walked to the door with her. 'I'm lucky to have friends like you and Aggie, I'd be in a right fix without yer. Not a soul to call me own.' She pretended to be playing on a violin. 'Is this music sad enough for the occasion, d'yer think?'

Rita grinned as she stepped down on to the pavement. 'Oh, yeah, sunshine, it certainly adds to the melodrama.' She hurried across the cobbles. 'See yer tomorrow some time, but until then, don't do anything I wouldn't do.'

'I'll try, sweetheart,' Bessie chortled, 'but it's

353

going to be hard with all the men beating their way to me front door.'

'Split them into groups, sunshine, and divide them between yerself, me and Aggie. I think the three of us could manage them between us.' Rita was shouting by now from the opposite side of the street. 'Mind you, they'd probably take one look at our faces and run like hell for cover.'

'You speak for yerself, Rita Wells, there's a bloke at work thinks I'm a cracker. He said he would ask me to marry him but his wife might object.' Bessie gave a last wave before closing the door. 'Now I'll get cracking with something to eat, sweetheart, or yer mother will be here before we've had our meal.'

Milly followed her in to the kitchen. 'Why are these men beating a way to your front door, Auntie Bessie? And why does the man in work say he'll marry you, when he knows he's already got a wife?'

Bessie put a light under the pan of potatoes, then blew out the match before grinning at Milly. 'Not a word of truth in any of it, sweetheart, it's all wishful thinking on my part.' She could see the puzzlement on the girl's face and cupped it between her hands. 'What I mean is, it was all said in fun. Grown-up fun, what young girls wouldn't understand.'

Milly hugged her tight. 'I'm going to have a word with the front door, just to be on the safe side. I'll tell it that if any men come along and start hitting it with sticks, it must tell them to go away, you don't want to see them. And if I'm here when they come, I'll chase them with the yard brush.'

Bessie pictured it in her mind. 'The stiff brush or the soft one, sweetheart?'

Milly pursed her lips and drew her brows down in thought. Now that was a poser, she didn't know there were two brushes. 'Which one do you think, Auntie Bessie?'

'Oh, the stiff brush would cause more damage, sweetheart, without a doubt. And now you go and play with Daisy while I get a move on.'

Bessie had just finished washing up when Evelyn passed the kitchen window. She hadn't been told about the new arrangement with Rita and Aggie because Bessie was of the opinion she would definitely disapprove. Although she hadn't told Milly not to mention it to her mother, she was confident the child would know without being told. So, no one was actually telling lies, and what the eye didn't see, the heart didn't grieve over.

'Come in, Evelyn, I'm just drying me hands.'

She came in, shivering and bringing the cold air with her. 'If today is anything to go by, we're in for a long, hard winter. I'm sure it couldn't be colder living in Iceland than it is sitting on our trams with the wind blowing right through.'

Bessie steered her to the living room. 'It's not too bad if yer get one of the new trams where they've filled in the staircase, but with the old ones, open to all the elements, yer get blown off yer feet.'

'Oh, what a lovely fire! I feel warmer just looking at it.' Evelyn held her hands out to the flames. 'If I had three wishes right now, one of them would be that when Amelia and I open the living-room door, there would be a fire like that in our grate. And the second wish would be to find a tray with a pot of hot tea on it, and several rounds of toast.'

Bessie waited for a few seconds than asked, 'And the third wish?'

'Oh, I'd have to think carefully about the third and last wish. I wouldn't want to waste it on something so trivial as a fire and a pot of tea. It would have to be something important, something that would change my life so I could live happily ever after.'

'That's a miracle ye're looking for, Evelyn, and miracles don't happen in Walton. At least not to my knowledge they don't.' Bessie held out a hand. 'Give me yer coat and sit near the fire. I'll make a fresh pot of tea, then yer'll be warm enough to face the icebox next door.' On her way to hang the coat up, she tilted her head at Milly. 'Have yer said hello to yer mother, Amelia?'

'Not yet, Auntie Bessie, I was waiting for her to be settled.' The girl walked to the side of the couch. 'Hello, Mother.'

And to the surprise of Bessie and her daughter, Evelyn patted the seat beside her. 'Sit here and tell me what you've done in school today.'

There was suspicion on the girl's face, and it was obvious to Bessie that her mother being so friendly was something new to Milly. It was a while before she answered. 'I've got my exercise book, Mother, you can look in that and see how I'm getting on in class.'

'The kettle's boiling now,' Bessie said, in a bid to avert embarrassment, 'so let yer mother have a hot cup of tea and she can look through the book later, when ye're in the comfort of yer own home. After the fire's lit, of course, 'cos there won't be much comfort while ye're sitting there like blocks of ice.'

She poured a cup of tea out and carried it through to Evelyn. 'I got a nice surprise when I got home from work today, I was over the moon. Rita had been in and lit the fire for me so the room was lovely and warm to walk into. *And* a pot of tea into the bargain. I was so pleased, I felt like kissing her. She's always had a key to the door, ever since I moved in and we became friends. It's so she can let the coalman into the yard, otherwise there's many a time I'd be without coal. I thanked my lucky stars for her today, there's nothing worse than working all day then coming home to a cold, cheerless house.'

There was a little bit of snobbery back in Evelyn's voice when she asked, 'Do you not mind letting strangers loose in your house?'

Her tone got Bessie's back up, but she did her best not to ruffle any feathers. 'Good grief, no! I've known Rita for fifteen years, she's as honest as the day is long. Besides, what harm could she do?' Bessie shook her head vigorously. 'I would trust Rita Wells with me life, and Aggie Gordon, too! Like meself, they're ordinary working-class people, struggling to make ends meet. There's no shame in that.'

'Of course not!' Evelyn's brain had been at work when she'd heard Rita had lit the fire for Bessie. Now she was worried she may have spoiled her own chances. 'What I said was out of curiosity, not a reflection on the honesty of your friends, Bessie, please believe me. You are indeed very lucky to have such thoughtful neighbours. I only wish I was so lucky. It must have been a wonderful surprise, and relief, to come home to such a warm welcome.'

Bessie's brain was also at work. She's a devious one all right, this one is, and she's angling for something. Well, I too can be devious, especially when it comes to my two mates. 'Oh, I wouldn't let her do it every night, not without some reward. So I'm going to give her a shilling a week for lighting the fire every night. Until the weather improves, that is.'

'Do you think she would like another shilling a week to light my fire for me? I can afford it now I'm better off, and it would be such a relief to come home to a warm house, both for Amelia and myself.'

Bessie could hear applause in her head for her own ingenuity, but kept her face straight. 'I couldn't possibly answer that, Evelyn, I'd have to ask Rita first. But if you want me to, I'll put your request to her tomorrow and see what she says. That's all I can do, I'm afraid, I can't speak for her.'

'If you would put in a good word for me, I'd be really grateful, Bessie. It would make my life so much easier.'

And a shilling a week would make life a lot easier for Rita, Bessie thought. She'd share with Aggie, doing a night each, which would mean an extra tanner every week. They could spend it if they were stuck, or add it to the money she was putting by each week so the three families would have a really happy Christmas. 'I'll have an answer for yer when you call tomorrow night. But it would mean yer leaving yer key with them. Would that suit yer?'

'I'll leave the key here, so Amelia can let Mrs Wells in. I would have no objection to that. Please do your best for me, it would help enormously.'

Bessie nodded, and followed mother and daughter to the door. Once it was closed on them, she hurried back to the living room, pulled her chair nearer the fire, and let her chuckles out. Ah, well, she thought, rubbing her hands in glee, life is full of surprises. Wait until her two mates heard they were in for a tanner each, every week. Well, it would be enough to send Aggie running to the corner pub for a bottle of milk stout to celebrate.

Chapter Nineteen

Oscar Wentworth looked across the breakfast table at his wife Gwen, and sighed. 'I have visited twelve schools in the area around Aigburth and the Dingle, all to no avail. To cover the whole of Liverpool, into Lancashire, will take me almost a year. I'm becoming quite despondent, losing faith in ever finding Evelyn or her daughter. She just seems to have vanished off the face of the earth. I mean, neither we nor any of our acquaintances have set eyes on her. Never bumped into her in the city, never even heard her name mentioned.'

Gwen indicated to the maid that she could leave the room and they would serve themselves. She disliked holding a personal conversation in front of staff. 'Evelyn could have married again, have you thought of that? Which means the child's name will no longer be Sinclair.'

Oscar nodded. 'I have thought of that, of course I have, but I can't let such a possibility stop me from doing what is important to me, and more so to Cyril. He is blaming himself for not giving Evelyn the benefit of the doubt, at least until the child was old enough to show a likeness. And I don't come out of it very well. As Charles' friend, I should have thought things out more clearly, instead of jumping to conclusions.'

'I am to blame for that, my love, I was the first to call her a liar. And don't think I haven't asked myself a thousand times why I didn't believe her. We'd been friends since school, and I was almost certain she had never been out with any other man but Charles. Yet I could have been wrong about that. Maybe she wasn't the innocent little goody-two-shoes I thought she was. We are still not certain Charles is the father, but like you and Cyril, I believe if we don't try and solve the puzzle, it will haunt us for the rest of our lives.'

'If I am to be honest, darling, it is not Evelyn I am interested in. I would feel guilty if it turns out she was telling the truth, but I will never really forgive her for her lack of emotion when told of Charles' death. She was cool and remote, as though he'd meant nothing to her. She never even visited his parents to offer condolences or comfort and help them in their hour of need.'

'I'm afraid Evelyn was always lacking in emotion, even when she was young. But that was due to her parents. They were dreadful people who never should have had a child. She didn't know what it was to get a goodnight kiss, or be tucked up in bed and have a story read to her. I was her only real friend, but I was never allowed to visit her. When I called for her to go to school, I was never invited in. That says a lot about her parents.'

Oscar sighed. 'From what little I've heard, she is treating her daughter as she was treated. That's why I must try and find her. Charles would expect no less from me.' He wiped his mouth on a damask napkin then laid it on his plate. 'I'll call and see Cyril, then try the next three schools on my list. I keep telling myself that one day I'll walk into the office of a headmistress and be told that, yes, they do have an Amelia Sinclair attending their school.' He walked to the other end of the long dining table and kissed his wife's brow. 'How lucky I am to have you, my darling. A wonderful wife and mother.'

'I wish you well today, love, and please don't give up hope. Patience and endurance will pay off in the end. And give my love to Cyril.'

Cyril Lister-Sinclair was lost in reverie when the knock came on his office door. He quickly gathered himself together and called, 'Come in.' He smiled when he saw Oscar, and waved his friend to a seat facing his across the desk. 'I was lost in thought when you knocked. It happens very often these days.'

'You should get out more, old man, you're too young to live the life of a hermit. Why don't you and Matilda come to us for dinner one night, we would be delighted to have you.'

Cyril tapped his fingers on the desk. 'It is very kind of you, my boy, but I wouldn't be very good company, I'm afraid. And, as you know, my wife goes out very little. If she needs a new dress or whatever, she gets a taxi to her favourite shop, has the driver wait for her, and when she's bought what she wants, it's straight back home again. Actually she spends most of the day on the chaise-longue, fast asleep. Nothing seems to interest her any more, and I'm at a loss to know how to change her for she refuses to hold a sensible conversation. Her maid is the only one who can get through to her. I don't know what I'd do if it weren't for her.'

'If Matilda refuses to visit friends, it shouldn't stop you. It's not as though she needs you, there are enough staff to attend to her.'

Cyril shook his head. 'No, I would never go out socially without her. I come down to the office each week day because I need to keep an eye on my business affairs so she is without my company on those days. I know Matilda is not the easiest woman to get along with, has no interest in business or politics and subsequently no real conversation. Also, she can be quite childish and demanding. But I fell in love with her the moment I set eyes on her at a mutual friend's house, and I still love her.'

There was affection in Oscar's eyes as he gazed at the man who had always made him welcome whenever he'd called for Charles. Cyril was like a second father to him, and Oscar loved him dearly. 'I'm afraid I've had no success with the schools so far, Cyril, but I've got another three to visit today so I'm keeping my fingers crossed. If I'm not successful I shall just carry on until I've covered every school across the city. It is possible, however, as Gwen pointed out his morning, that Evelyn may have remarried, and then the child will no longer have the name Sinclair.'

'I've been considering all the possibilities too,' Cyril told him. 'In fact, the matter is seldom far from my thoughts. The easiest and most sure way of finding them is to go to the police or put a notice in the local evening paper so that, if she didn't see it herself, it would at least be seen by a neighbour. But either way could have its drawbacks. The notice might send Evelyn into hiding

363

and then we would never find her or the girl. Although I toyed with the idea of a private detective at one time, I agree with you now that it is not the right way.' He sighed and swivelled his chair. 'If we make a song and dance about it, the whole thing would become public knowledge and perhaps alienate Evelyn completely. If she was telling the truth, she has just cause to hate us. Or, I should say, hate me, it is I who turned her out of the house. She would have no cause to hate you or Gwen.'

'If she is a fair-minded person then she will understand the reasons why you acted as you did. Any father who had just lost a son would have found it very difficult to believe her story.' Oscar was saying this after years of heart-searching. 'At the time, I would have found it hard to believe it of Charles. But on reflection, he knew he was shortly to be shipped abroad and perhaps lost his head for a while. Who are we to say we would have acted differently? None of us is a saint.'

'That is very true, war changes people. So the sooner we find Evelyn and the girl, the sooner my heart will be at rest and we can put the whole sordid affair behind us. I wish you well today, Oscar, but if it isn't to be the day we must continue to be patient.'

'I second that.' Oscar got to his feet and stretched his tall frame. 'I won't share a pot of tea with you this morning, Cyril. I want to visit two of the schools on my list before lunch. Then I'll call to see my father and spend some time in the office with him so I can keep abreast of business affairs. Later, I will visit the third school on my list.'

'You shouldn't let my problems interfere with your work or home life, Oscar,' Cyril told him. 'I don't want to poach you from your family business.'

'Not at all! My father has an excellent staff, plus my brother, and his office runs like clockwork.' Oscar looked at his friend. 'It must be a while since you and Father met. Why don't I pick you up in the morning and take you to see him? I know he would be delighted, he never fails to ask about you. And the two of you could talk shop for an hour, after which I'd be free to run us down to the club for some lunch.' He could see Cyril was uncertain, and waved a hand. 'No excuses, old man, I'm sure your excellent secretary can rearrange your diary to enable you absent for a few hours. In fact, I will have a word with the very efficient Miss Williams on my way out, and tell her you are not to be allowed to change your mind under any circumstances. I shall also ask her to have a pot of tea sent in now. After all, what is the point in being your own boss if you can't do as you wish?' He leaned across the desk and shook the older man's hand. 'I will see you at eleven-forty-five tomorrow.'

The following day was Wednesday. As Oscar and his father Richard, with Cyril walking between them, strolled down Castle Street towards their club, little did they know that about thirty yards from them, Evelyn was letting herself into Philip's apartment. Had they seen her, they would have hurried towards her, filled with relief. Had she seen them, she would have fled in the opposite direction, afraid of the consequences. But they didn't see each other, and a golden opportunity was lost.

Evelyn went straight to the kitchen to make a pot of tea to go with the delicious sandwiches and cakes Annie would have left ready for them. She had never met the cleaner, deliberately keeping away when the woman would be at the apartment. The fewer people who knew of her business the better. Evelyn lived in fear of being caught out, and losing the man she had fallen deeply in love with. He was the only person who could bring her to life, appreciate all the emotions that come with being in love. The very thought of him sent a shiver down her spine as she carried a tray through to the lounge. Hearing his key in the door, she put down the tray and ran to meet him in the hall. They had spent the morning together in the office, but even though their relationship had moved on away from work, Evelyn still insisted they remain businesslike in front of their colleagues. Not that Philip was as strict about it as she was, for if he couldn't resist a kiss then she was well and truly kissed. He derived great pleasure from seeing her blush with embarrassment in case anyone walked into the office. He would be quite happy for everyone to know of their relationship, for he was deeply in love with her and very proud. He couldn't understand why she wanted to keep it secret for the time being, but went along with it. After all, she'd said that after Christmas she would discuss the subject of marriage, and he could wait that long.

Philip cupped her face. 'Now, when we are married, that is the sort of welcome I'll expect every night when I come home from the office.' And to bring a blush to her cheeks, he added, 'I would expect you to be wearing less than you are now, though.'

'You are incorrigible, Philip, I really don't know what I'm going to do with you. And I am a fool for allowing you to make me blush.'

'Do I have a power over you, my lovely Evelyn? Do I really?'

'Of course you do, my love, and well you know it.'

'Oh, I am not so sure, my darling.' They were still standing in the hall, their arms around each other. 'I would like to test this power you say I have over you. Would you permit me to try?'

Evelyn tutted. 'You are like a child who is over-indulged by his parents. But if it makes you happy, then you may.'

'Good!' Philip moved out of her arms and cupped one of her elbows. He proceeded to walk her towards the bedroom. 'Well, so far my magic seems to be working.'

Inside the bedroom, Evelyn stared at him in bewilderment. 'What are you up to, Philip? Remember, we don't have much time.'

'Sshh! Don't break the spell! Just slip your coat off, my lovely, and lie on the bed like the Sleeping Beauty. I will waken you with a kiss.'

'Philip! I have made a pot of tea and our lunch is set out on the tray…'

He put a hand over her mouth. 'I am using my magic powers on you now, my beauty. The tea can wait, my desire cannot. It is two whole days since I held you in my arms and made love to you. Two whole days and nights of longing for you. Even my parents noticed I was preoccupied and asked if I was sickening for a cold. Having you so close to me in the office, and be unable to touch you, it is agony.' While he was talking, Philip slipped the coat off her shoulders, then scooped her up in his arms and laid her gently on the bed. 'I will disrobe in the bathroom, my darling, please be ready for me when I return.'

Even if she'd had the willpower to resist him, Evelyn didn't want to. Her own body was crying out. She undressed quickly and slid between the sheets. She was eager to have him hold her and thrill her with his love making, but remained clear enough in the head to remember she had to be back in the office for two o'clock. Philip wouldn't remember because he didn't care. If they were late, they were late, that was all there was to it. After all, there was no one above him to tick him off. But Evelyn wanted to keep her job as a safety net, and couldn't afford to ruffle feathers or cause gossip.

Philip lifted the sheet and gazed lovingly at her naked body. 'You are so beautiful, my darling Evelyn, I could spend my life making love to you.' He ran a hand over her breasts, tummy and thighs, and smiled with pleasure when he heard her gasp. Then he climbed into bed and lay on top of her. 'This, my darling, is as close to heaven as it gets. I want to marry you, to have you all to

368

myself forever, please don't keep me waiting long.'

She put a finger to his lips. 'Make love to me, my darling.'

On Tuesday it had been Rita's first night to have Milly for an hour, and also light Bessie's and Mrs Sinclair's fires. Everything had gone to plan. When Bessie's fire had caught, Milly had taken Rita next door and let her in with the key. She'd stayed with Rita until the fire was well and truly lit. She hadn't told anyone that the night before her mother had sat her down and given her a good talking to. She'd been given strict instructions that under no circumstances was Mrs Wells to be left on her own in the house. Amelia must stay with her the whole time, and when they left she must make sure the door was locked and that she kept hold of the key. And Milly had done as she was told, although she couldn't understand why it was necessary, not when she could be playing catch with Jack. Anyway, Tuesday went off without a hitch, and Bessie and Mrs Sinclair were delighted to walk into rooms that were warm and welcoming.

Wednesday started off all right, with Aggie having a cup of tea ready for her two children, Kitty and Kenny, and Milly. She didn't usually make tea for her children, but as this was her first night with Milly, she wanted to make a good impression. But it aroused suspicion in her two children.

'What's this in aid of, Mam?' Kitty asked. 'Are yer sickening for something?'

369

'She must be,' Kenny said. 'Either that or she wants us to go on a message for her. I bet she wants us to go to the corner shop for a loaf or summat on tick. Well, I'm not going for nowt on tick, I feel a right lemon with the shop packed and me trying to whisper.'

Aggie gave him a light slap across the face. 'I don't want yer to go on no message, so there, clever clogs. And will yer remember we've got a visitor, and behave yerselves?'

It was then Kitty saw the light. She looked across the table at Milly, who was sitting very quietly taking it all in. 'So, this is in your honour, eh? In that case ye're very welcome 'cos a hot drink is just the job when it's so cold. What do we call yer anyway, yer must have a name?'

Milly began to swing her legs under the table. 'My name's Amelia, but you can call me Milly as long as my mother doesn't hear. She doesn't like me being called that.'

Kenny huffed. 'Pity about her, isn't it? My proper name is Kenneth, but I don't mind being called Kenny. That's 'cos I'm not a snob.'

That remark would usually have earned him a thick ear, but before Aggie could reach him, Milly spoke. 'Are you saying me and my mother are snobs? Well, perhaps you can explain to me what a snob is, 'cos I don't know?'

Kitty gave her brother a sly kick on his shin. 'Yer asked for that, our kid. Now explain to her what a snob is.'

Kenny gave her daggers. 'Everyone knows what a snob is, soft girl. It's someone what walks round with their nose stuck in the air, and talks funny.'

Milly's green eyes were flashing. 'Oh, you think I talk funny do you? That means you can't understand me. So I won't talk to you any more because I'd only be wasting my time. I'll talk to your sister instead.'

Kenny wasn't going to be beaten by a girl, especially one younger than him. He had his pride. 'I never said I couldn't understand yer, I said yer talk funny, an' yer do, so there!'

Aggie thought they'd carry on for ages if they were let, so she said, 'Drink yer tea up, Milly, then yer can come to Bessie's with me while I light her fire.'

Rita was standing at her front door to make sure Aggie did her fair share. And it was Rita, watching her neighbour and Milly crossing the cobbles, who saw Aggie's fleecy-lined bloomers showing below her skirt. 'Ay, sunshine, I see yer've got yer blue fleecy-lined ones on today, eh? Giving the neighbours an eyeful, are yer?'

Aggie stopped when she reached the opposite pavement and looked down. She shook her head and tutted. 'Bloody things, I'll pull them up when I get in Bessie's.' But she was only on the second step when she nearly tripped over. The elastic had snapped on the waist of her bloomers, and the whole lot was around her ankles. 'Oh, bloody hell! The elastic's gone, I'll have to take them off.'

Rita gasped. 'Not in the street, Aggie! Wait until yer get in Bessie's!'

'I can't walk in the bleeding things, d'yer want me to break me bleeding neck?'

'No, I don't want yer to break yer neck, Aggie,'

Rita said, dying to laugh. 'And I don't want yer to make a spectacle of yerself either. Ye're letting the tone of the street down.'

'Sod the tone of the street, that's what I say!' Aggie bent down and lifted one foot after the other to climb out of the offending bloomers. Holding them aloft, she shouted, 'I've only got the same as every other woman in the street, so to hell with modesty.'

Milly's face was a picture no artist could paint. She had never seen anything like it in her life, and although she knew her mother would be disgusted, she herself thought it was very funny. When she saw Rita doubled up, it was a signal for her own infectious giggle to make itself heard. And Aggie's son and daughter, not surprised or ashamed of anything their mother did, were in stitches. 'Oh, Mam,' Kitty croaked, the tears running down her face, 'wait until we tell our dad, he'll laugh himself sick.'

'If either of yer say one word to yer dad,' Aggie warned, pointing the hand holding the bloomers at them, 'then I'll separate yer head from yer body.'

Rubbing the tears from her eyes, Rita ran across the cobbles. 'I'll light Bessie's fire, sunshine, you go and put another pair of bloomers on.'

'No can do, queen, 'cos I haven't got another pair to put on,' Aggie said, stuffing the bloomers into her pocket. 'I'll go without, no one will be any the wiser.'

Rita managed to look horrified. 'Yer can't walk around with no bloomers on! How would yer feel if yer got run over and yer were laying on the

372

ground, a crowd of people around yer, and you with no knickers on? I'd have to pretend I didn't know yer, I'd be that mortified.'

Cool as a cucumber, Aggie asked, 'Oh, aye, queen, how long have the trams been running down this street then?'

'Well, it wouldn't have to be a tram or a car, sunshine, it could be the coal cart or the rag and bone man. It could even be the milkman with his pony and trap.'

'Ooh, ay, queen, yer've given me a belting idea.' Aggie thought if she was giving all her neighbours a laugh, she may as well have one herself. 'If the rag and bone man does happen to come down the street while I'm in Bessie's, will yer ask him to hang on a minute while yer give me a knock? I could give him the pair of bloomers in exchange for a goldfish. Then that would be my feller's dinner sorted out, 'cos he's partial to a bit of fish is Sam.'

'And yer don't think he'd notice it was a goldfish on his plate?' Rita asked, while telling herself Aggie had more to do than stand and talk, there were two fires to be lit. 'I don't think there's anything wrong with Sam's eyesight.'

'Nah! I'll smother the plate with chips and he'll tuck in without a word. It'll be a nice surprise for him when he gets a taste of fish.'

'Ye're past the post, you are, Aggie.' Rita held out her hand to Milly. 'Give us the key, sunshine, and I'll light Bessie's fire while my mate runs home to make herself presentable.'

But Aggie was quick to intervene. 'Not on yer bleeding life, Rita Wells, I'll light the ruddy fire if

373

it kills me. And I'll do it without bloomers on.' Her chins anticipated movement and nodded in unison with her head. 'And I bet the grate won't notice nothing. If it does, think of the treat it'll get.' She nodded to Milly. 'Go on, girl, open the door and let's get on with it.'

'Yer better had get on with it, Aggie Gordon,' Rita told her retreating back. 'Bessie will be in soon and yer haven't even made a start. And yer've got Mrs Sinclair's to do as well.'

Aggie's laugh reached the few neighbours who were watching through their windows. 'I was going to say don't get yer knickers in a twist, queen, but as bloomers and knickers are a delicate subject right now, I'll say don't be getting yerself all het up, it's not worth it. Life's too short to spend it worrying.' She grinned into her mate's face, then said to Milly, 'Come on, queen, let's get this here fire lit.'

As Milly sat on the couch watching Aggie light Bessie's fire, she was thinking how lucky she was now, with all these friends. They were always so cheerful, and they were really funny, especially Aggie, who always seemed happy even though she only had one pair of bloomers. Mind you, she was right when she said no one would know the difference. As she knelt in front of the grate, you could see the top of her stockings, but that was all.

'There yer are, queen, that should be roaring up the chimney by the time Bessie gets home.' Aggie didn't find it easy to get to her feet because of her size, so she shuffled her bottom along the floor until she was by the couch, then pulled herself up. 'Straight to your house now, queen, and get the fire lit for yer mam. She doesn't come in until after six, so the place should be warmed through by then. I'll have it done in no time, you'll see.'

Unfortunately for Aggie, she couldn't have been more wrong. She was expecting the grate to be cleaned and the fire laid out ready for lighting, like it was in Bessie's. So she got an unpleasant shock when Milly let her into the living room and she found the grate with the remains of the night before's fire. It was full of ashes and they'd spilled over on to the hearth. The bars were grey with it as well. Aggie was taken aback. 'Ay, queen, doesn't yer mam clean the grate out before she goes to work?'

Milly shook her head. 'No, Auntie Aggie, she cleans it out when she gets home, then sets it for a new fire.'

Aggie got very uppity, and so did her bosom, tummy and chins which all quivered in unison. 'Well,' she bridled, 'no one told me I'd have to clean the ruddy grate out. Wait until I get me hands on that Rita Wells, I'll marmalise her for lumbering me with this.'

'But Auntie Rita had to clean it yesterday,' Milly said. 'I know 'cos I was here with her. She got a surprise, like you, but she soon raked the ashes out and wiped the hearth down. It didn't take her long.'

'Well, she might have said something to me. I mean, I don't know where the ashes go, or where there's a floor cloth.'

375

'Shall I do it, Auntie Aggie? I know what to do 'cos I've done it for my mother.'

But Aggie wasn't going to let a young girl show her up. 'No, queen, I'll do it. I see there's a poker on the companion set, I'll rake the ashes down into the ashcan, then carry it to the midden.'

The first mishap occurred when Aggie was being too rough with the poker and brought down a fall of soot. It went on her hair and face, and her hands and arms were black. When she tried to wipe it away, she only made matters ten times worse. As she turned her head, an open-mouthed Milly could only see the whites of her eyes. 'Don't worry, queen, I'll get a good wash down when I get home. Everything is under control. I'll take these ashes out, then set the fire ready for lighting,' Aggie told her.

Trying to be helpful, Milly pointed to what looked like a small poker. 'If you put that in the handle of the ashcan, Auntie Aggie, it will be easier to carry out to the yard.'

'Yes, queen, we've got one of them and they're very handy.' With all the ashes now in the ashcan, Aggie got to her feet with the help of the coal scuttle at the side of the hearth. And all would have gone well if she hadn't tripped over the fireside rug, fallen flat on the floor and sent the ashes flying everywhere.

Milly put a hand over her mouth, closed her eyes and pictured her mother's face if she could see what was happening in her living room. There was soot and ashes on the sideboard, the mantel-piece, the couch, the table, the chairs. Not to mention the whole floor and in the air of the room. 'I'll try and help you up, shall I, Auntie Aggie?'

'Yer'll never make it, queen, and I'll never be able to get meself up. So will yer take the ashcan out to the yard, and then run for Rita? She's very good in a crisis, is Rita, never gets flustered or nothing like that. And hurry, queen, 'cos we don't want yer mam coming in to this.'

Milly's feet didn't touch the ground. Fear of her mother coming home to the house in such a mess lent her wings. She was out of breath when she knocked on Rita's door. 'Come quick, Auntie Rita, 'cos there's been an accident.'

'Oh, my God, what sort of an accident, sunshine?'

'Auntie Aggie is lying on the floor, and the room is full of ashes and soot.'

Rita didn't even bother to close her door, she was over the road like a shot, followed by Milly. She stood in the doorway of Evelyn's living room and didn't know whether to laugh or cry. I'll do neither, she thought quickly, there's no time. Crying won't help, and I'll leave the laughter until tea time, then all the family can join in. 'What the hell d'yer think ye're doing, Aggie, lying on the floor instead of getting some of this dirt washed off? Mrs Sinclair will have a fit if she comes in to this.'

'Oh, I'm having a little nap, queen, what d'yer think I'm doing?' Aggie's mountainous bosom was beneath her, and it wasn't very comfortable. 'Don't just bleeding well stand there, give us a hand up! And none of this would have happened if Mrs High and Mighty had cleaned her bloody

377

grate out before she went to work, instead of leaving the dirty work to some other poor sucker.'

Rita stood astride her. 'Let's talk later, eh, when ye're standing upright. Now if yer can press the palms of yer hands into the floor and raise yerself a little, I'll try and get me arms around yer tummy. While you're pushing, I'll be lifting.'

She'll never do it, Milly said silently as she looked on. She'll never lift Auntie Aggie, not in a million years. But much to the girl's surprise and admiration, after one big heave Rita had pulled her mate to her knees. 'I'll give yer a hand to get to yer feet, Aggie, but yer'll have to help yerself as well, 'cos I'm not Man Mountain. But for heaven's sake, don't put yer hands on anything, the room's bad enough without you making it worse.'

After a struggle, Aggie was standing upright, her eyes blazing out of a black face. 'If yer so much as grin, Rita Wells, so help me I'll strangle yer.'

'Oh, I've no intention of laughing now, sunshine, there's too much to do. I'll do me laughing with Reg and the kids while we're having our meal. They'll think I'm exaggerating 'cos this is like a slap-stick Laurel and Hardy film, but they'll get a good laugh.' Rita surveyed the room. 'I think the best thing is for you to go home and clean yerself up, Aggie, 'cos ye're covered in soot and yer'll only make things worse here. I'll put the kettle on for hot water, and while I'm waiting for it to boil, I'll get Milly to show me where the brush is, to clear the worst of the top dirt off. Then I'll mop out.'

'I'm not leaving yer with this lot,' Aggie said. 'I'll nip over and give me face and arms a good swill, then I'll be back. But I'll tell yer something for nothing, queen, I ain't clearing this grate out again. If she wants her fire lighting, then she'd better set it before she goes out.'

'Get moving, Aggie, we'll talk it over after. In fact, I'll have a word with Bessie, and if this fire isn't set for lighting each day, then I'll do here and you can do Bessie's. Yer can't get up to any mischief in Bessie's, all yer need to do is strike a match.'

While Aggie was at her sink trying to get the worst of the soot off, Bessie was walking up the street on her way home from work. She was looking forward to a warm house and to seeing Milly. She was surprised when Kitty Gordon came running over to her. 'Me mam fell over in Mrs Sinclair's house, Auntie Bessie, and she's come home black with soot.'

Bessie's heart sank. Just when things were going too well, something was bound to come along and spoil it. Giving a deep sigh, she passed her own house and entered the open door of her next door neighbour's. The room was a hive of activity, with Rita on her hands and knees washing the hearth down, and Milly brushing the floor as best she could. 'Oh, dear, what's happened, Rita?'

The story didn't take long, and the way Rita told it, it sounded so funny Bessie was laughing as she took her coat off. 'Another pair of hands won't go amiss, sweetheart, I'll get the mop and bucket ready. We've got three-quarters of an hour at least, so we should make it. We'll leave the front and back doors open so the lino will dry before Mrs Sinclair arrives.'

When Aggie came back over, most of the work had been done. There was still a smell of soot in the air, but with back and front doors wide open, that should disperse pretty soon. 'I'm sorry I had to leave yer to it, but I couldn't get the bleeding soot off meself. Me hair is still thick with the ruddy stuff, but I'll give it a good wash tonight. And I had to take me dress off and put it to soak in the sink.' She pulled at the skirt of the dress she was wearing. 'This was the only one to hand.' Her eyes were taking in all the work that had been done since she'd gone home. 'I feel bad leaving yer to do the dirty work, Rita. And you, Bessie, yer've put in a full day at work, as well.'

Bessie tried to keep a straight face. 'Well, Aggie, yer did very well for yer first day, I must say. There's not many could bring about a fall of soot, then trip up and spread the ashes over everything in the room. I wonder what trick yer've got in store for us tomorrow?'

'Now, now, queen, there's no need to get sarky with me, anyone can trip over a ruddy rug what's curled up at the corners. And the fall of soot must have been an act of God, 'cos I didn't do nothing to cause it. Milly is my witness, she'll tell yer I didn't do nothing.' Then she saw the unfairness of it, and got her dander up. 'Anyway, I'm giving me notice in, I'm not having anything to do with lighting that fire no more.'

Rita chuckled. 'That's good, sunshine, it saves us giving yer the sack.'

'Giving me the sack! Well, the bloody cheek of

you! You ain't giving me the sack 'cos I won't let her!'

'Yeah, we agreed to sack yer,' Bessie told a disbelieving Aggie. 'But the minute we gave yer the sack, we had another job lined up for yer. Same pay, less work.'

Aggie looked suspicious. 'Oh, aye, pull the other one, it's got bells on.'

'Leave it if she's not interested, Bessie,' Rita said. 'I'll do both jobs.'

'Sod off, Rita Wells, and mind yer own business. Now, Bessie, what did yer have in mind for me?'

'You light my fire, and Rita lights this one. How does that suit yer?'

'Suits me fine, Bessie.' Aggie was grinning from ear to ear. 'I'll take the job.'

Chapter Twenty

Each Wednesday before their tryst in Philip's apartment, to allay suspicion Evelyn would leave the office at one o'clock and Philip would follow a little later. Then she would be back at her desk dead on two o'clock, while he strolled in ten or fifteen minutes later. After all, he could please himself what he did, there was no one to question his movements or time-keeping. He would have been quite happy for them to leave and return together, and to hell with what the rest of the staff thought, but Evelyn wasn't prepared to have her name bandied about. So far no one had made any comment on the regular pattern set for each Wednesday lunchtime.

But the regularity of their timing hadn't gone unnoticed by one member of staff, and that was Mr Woodward's secretary. Janet Coombes had watched the comings and going of the pair, and was convinced they were having an affair. Secretly she was consumed with jealousy. She had made several advances towards Philip, to whom she was very attracted, waylaying him whenever the opportunity arose. But although he was very polite, he made it perfectly clear he wasn't interested. The attention he paid to Mrs Sinclair was like a slap in the face for Janet, who was much younger than Evelyn, and considered herself much prettier and more modern in her dress. And she had never been married, so wasn't second-hand goods.

Her jealousy was like a festering sore that wouldn't go away. She strongly suspected that although they left the office separately each Wednesday, they met up somewhere and spent the lunchtime together. But where? Consumed with jealousy and bitterness, she determined to find out.

When Evelyn left the office on this particular Wednesday, she made her way to the apartment feeling happy and looking forward to having Philip to herself for an hour. Little did she know she was being followed.

Janet kept back at a safe distance, with an excuse ready if Evelyn should turn her head and see her. She stopped when Evelyn stopped, and watched with mounting interest as her target let herself into a door between two office blocks. There's something underhand going on here, she told herself, but is Philip Astbury involved? The only way to find out was to wait in a doorway opposite for ten minutes to see if he turned up. If he didn't, then what was the snobby Mrs Sinclair up to? Perhaps she had another fancy man, Janet wouldn't put it past her. She'd wheedled her way into Mr Philip's heart. How many others had she done the same to? It would be worth watching that door, even if it took up the whole of her lunch hour.

So Janet crossed the busy road and stood in the entrance of another office building. She was careful to stand back in the shadow so she wouldn't be seen. Her feet were cold from

383

standing still, and she did some on the spot walking to warm them up. She popped her head out to see if there was any sign of anyone she knew, and when she saw the familiar figure of Philip striding down the pavement quickly drew back into the shadows. From where she was standing she had a really good view. She saw him stop outside the door opposite, feel in his pocket for a key, insert it in the lock, open the door and disappear, all in the space of one minute. It left Janet blazing and bitter. Just showed she'd been right all along. They were definitely having an affair, and were very keen to keep it quiet from the sly way they were going about it. Apparently, while she wasn't good enough for Philip Astbury, Evelyn Sinclair was. She was probably giving him what he wanted, which was why he was interested in her. It certainly couldn't be for any other reason because there was nothing so special about his private secretary. She wasn't bad-looking and had a decent figure, but she was nothing out of the ordinary. And with his looks and money, Philip would only have to snap his fingers and dozens of women would be falling at his feet.

Janet's imagination was running wild. Evelyn Sinclair could be doling out her favours to several men, in return for gifts or even money. And to look at her, you'd think butter wouldn't melt in her mouth! But all this didn't explain what went on behind the door opposite. Was it an office, and Philip and his secretary had legitimate business there? Or was a room in the office block hired out for clandestine meetings? Oh, how she would love to know. She would like nothing better than to expose Mrs Sinclair in front of the rest of the staff.

Time was ticking by, and Janet realised if she waited to see Evelyn or Philip come out, her whole lunch hour would be gone. She couldn't go all day without a bite to eat. Best to nip to the little cafe in Dale Street for a sandwich and pot of tea. While she was sitting, she would put together a plan on what to do about the secret she'd found out today. For she fully intended to bring the high and mighty Evelyn Sinclair down off her pedestal. And it would have to be done in such a way it wouldn't cost Janet her job.

She ordered a toasted teacake and a cup of tea, and while she was waiting glanced at the people seated nearby. She was the only person sitting on her own, the other tables were occupied by two or three people, mostly men, all of them deep in conversation. She could hear snatches of what they were saying, and it was obvious they were work colleagues. This gave her food for thought. Perhaps she could suggest to Evelyn that they should have lunch together one day. But as quickly as the idea entered her head, she dismissed it. That would surely make the woman suspicious.

The waitress came with her order, and for a short time Janet was busy pouring herself a much-needed cup of hot tea. The teacake, oozing with butter, looked so appetizing she couldn't resist folding it in two and sinking her teeth into it. It wasn't until the cup and plate were empty that her thoughts returned to the subject that plagued her: Philip Astbury and Evelyn Sinclair. Not that she had bad thoughts about Philip, she didn't. She wanted him for herself and was sure she could prove to him that she was more his sort than Mrs Sinclair, if only he would let her. In fact, if Evelyn was out of the picture, Janet was convinced he would take more notice of her.

The clock on the wall of the cafe said it was a quarter to two, and Janet told herself if she hurried she might catch Evelyn coming out of that door in Castle Street. She could hang back until the door opened, then catch up with her prey and pretend she was surprised to see her. Yes, that was a good idea. So she picked up the bill the waitress had left and counted out the right money from her purse. Then, hoping that being generous would bring her good luck, she left a penny tip on the table for the waitress.

Standing outside the cafe, Janet could feel the cold wind coming off the River Mersey, and shivered as she pulled on her gloves. She'd walk slowly up Castle Street, and if she was lucky and Evelyn came out of the door on cue, that would be marvellous. But if it wasn't to be, she wasn't going to hang around, it was too cold.

Evelyn pulled the door closed behind her, then tucked her handbag under her arm while she put on the warm, fur-lined soft leather gloves which Philip had surprised her with this morning. He'd said her old ones had well served their purpose and she should put them in the bin. This was one time she'd thrown caution to the wind and kissed him for being so thoughtful. Winter had certainly come with a vengeance, and people were saying it was the worst for many years. So as she stepped into the street, she was thanking him mentally for the warmth of the expensive kid gloves. He really was an angel, and she was falling more in love with him every day.

She had only covered a few yards when she heard running footsteps and her name being called. She turned her head and felt her heart miss a beat when she saw Janet Coombes. Had she been spotted coming out of the apartment? She hoped not, for Janet was the one person in the office she couldn't take a liking to.

'I thought I recognised you.' Janet was smiling in a friendly manner when she caught up. 'You've just come out of one of those offices, haven't you?'

Evelyn quickly pulled herself together and decided to brazen it out. She ignored the question. 'You gave me quite a scare, calling my name so loudly. I thought something dreadful had happened.' Without giving Janet time to answer, she went on, 'Have you been out for lunch? You need to get something warm inside you this cold weather.'

Janet nodded. 'Yes, I've been to that nice little cafe in Dale Street. They do wonderful toasted teacakes.' She couldn't let this opportunity pass, she may never get another one. 'I did see you coming out of one of the offices, didn't I? Have you a friend in there?'

As calm as could be, Evelyn, who was several inches taller than Janet, looked down with her eyebrows raised in surprise. 'I haven't just come out of an office, you must be mistaken.' Then she added, 'Oh, I understand now, how silly of me. I had stepped into a doorway out of the wind while I fixed my scarf. It had worked itself loose and my neck was freezing.'

Janet was lost for words. At least there were plenty of words wanting to tumble out of her mouth, but they weren't the right ones. If she came right out and called Evelyn a liar, she knew she would bring down on herself Philip's wrath. She was also sure she would lose her job. So she bit her tongue. There were many ways of skinning a cat, and Evelyn wouldn't be allowed to get away with making a fool of her.

'It's a lovely warm scarf.' Janet had to force herself to speak in her normal tone of voice as she kept in step with the woman she disliked intensely. 'And I do love your gloves, they look like real kid.'

They were nearing the office when Evelyn answered, 'Yes, they are. They were a gift from a very good friend.'

Janet couldn't keep the sarcasm out of her voice when she said, 'Lucky you to have such a generous friend. He must be a man of means.'

They walked up the three steps to the office door, and with her hand out ready to push it open, Evelyn drawled, 'And what, pray, makes you think they were a present from a man? You should never pass a remark like that unless you have your facts right.' She pushed the door open. 'And now it's back to work, and reality.'

'Yes,' Janet said between gritted teeth. 'I wish I could meet a really rich man who would take me away from all this.'

'They are few and far between, Miss Coombes, but I wouldn't stop wishing if I were you. You might just be one of the lucky ones.'

Being addressed so formally enraged Janet. She felt like a child being put in its place. 'Is that what you're wishing for, Mrs Sinclair? To be one of the lucky ones?'

'Good heavens, no!' Evelyn slipped her arms out of her coat. 'I am more than content with my lot in life, there's nothing more I could wish for.'

Evelyn was sorting the second delivery of mail with Grace when Philip strolled into the office. 'Any post for us, Mrs Sinclair?'

'Half a dozen letters so far, Mr Philip. When Grace and I are finished sorting them properly, I'll open those which are addressed to you and file them in order of importance. Give me half an hour and I'll bring them to you.' Evelyn averted her eyes, afraid Grace would see the special look she reserved for him. 'There are two letters on your desk needing your signature. If you could attend to them, Grace will put them with Mr Woodward's letters to be posted later.'

When Evelyn carried the post through to Philip's office later, he jumped to his feet as always. 'Sit down, my love, I've missed you.'

She sat facing him. 'It's been about half an hour, Philip, if that! But it pleases me to hear you say you've missed me, for I've missed you.' She crossed her legs and pulled her skirt down. 'I missed something else as well.'

'Oh, and what was that, my lovely?'

389

'I just missed getting caught coming out of the apartment. In fact, I was caught, but I think I got out of it by telling lies.'

'Why was it necessary to lie? You were coming out of my apartment as you have every right to if you wish. Surely there was no reason to pretend?' He leaned his elbows on the desk and leaned towards her. 'Who was it you found it necessary to lie to?'

'Janet. I believe she's noticed the regularity of our Wednesday meetings, and today set out to find if we meet up outside the office. Whether she followed me and saw me going in the building, I don't know, but she pounced when I left.'

'Surely you don't care what Janet thinks, do you? She is insignificant, of no consequence. Did she dare to question you?'

'No, of course not.' Evelyn wasn't about to tell him more or he would surely bound out of his office and into James Woodward's to confront Janet. 'I told her I was standing out of the wind while I fastened my scarf. It was a lie, of course, and I really do not like to be in a position where I have to lie to the likes of Janet Coombes. So all I'm asking is that we are more careful in future.'

Philip was angry. 'How stupid all this secrecy is! I love you and want to marry you. And I am of the opinion that you love me. Why should we hide it?'

'For my sake, my darling. Look at it from my point of view. We haven't known each other very long, I know that matters little when we adore each other, but think what a field day the rest of the staff would have. Me, a widow, throwing myself at you. That is what they will think, and what they will say behind my back. I am not so thick-skinned it wouldn't hurt me.'

Philip was becoming impatient. He could not understand why Evelyn was so insecure she allowed his partner's secretary to have this effect on her. The girl was an employee, nothing more. And if Evelyn was to become his wife in the very near future, there was no reason on earth for her to fear anyone. 'I'm going to ask you a question, my darling, and I want you to answer truthfully. Do you really love me?'

'Philip, I love and adore you! And that is the truth.'

'Then I will bear with you, as promised, until all the Christmas and New Year festivities are over. After that I will accept no delay or argument about our future. This is what I have planned.' Philip wished they were in the privacy of the apartment so he could hold her in his arms, for she was looking at him now with apprehension in her eyes. 'You will give in your week's notice here on the day we return to work after the New Year break, and when you have served your notice you will move into the apartment until we are married. I will tell my parents tonight that I have met you, fallen in love, and that you are the girl of my dreams. I will add that in the near future I will be asking you to be my wife. I will take you to meet them when you are no longer an employee of this firm, and will also take you to meet my best friend who, with his wife, already knows about you. When that is done, we shall set a date for the wedding. That is how it will be, my darling, for I love you too much to listen to any further excuses for delay.'

'You will have to be a little more understanding, Philip, and try to see things from my point of view. Your life is easy, always has been, but I haven't been so lucky. There are many things I'm afraid of that you appear not to have given any thought to. First, I am a widow of twenty-nine. I have no money or assets to bring with me, and how are your parents going to react when you tell them that? Or your friends?'

'They will love you as I do, and they'll be very happy that at last I have found someone I truly feel for. Of this I am certain, I know my family and friends. But if I am wrong, and my parents object to our marriage, it will not alter my feelings for you, or stop me from marrying you. I would be sad, but it is my life and I have at last found someone I want more than anything in the world. Nothing, and no one, can change my mind.'

Philip smiled as he leaned across the desk and took her hand. 'Don't look so afraid, my lovely, I won't let anything happen to you. And now that we have a timetable set for the events that will lead to the happiest day of my life, and yours, I hope, then let us put it from our minds for now. We will continue to meet as often as possible, I have become addicted to you. And you must bear in mind that I expect you to spend time with me in the apartment over Christmas. In fact, I not only expect you to, I demand it. I couldn't live a whole week without seeing you.'

Evelyn's mind was in a turmoil. She would give anything to be able to round the desk, hold him in her arms, kiss him soundly, tell him she idolised him and agree with everything he'd said. For what he was offering her was nothing short of life in paradise. But it would not be right to agree to it for what he was asking was also impossible. She was living a lie, and he would hate her when she was forced to tell him the truth. But for now she would enjoy what little time they had left. She would take and return his love, and when it was over, as it surely would be over when he knew she'd been lying, she would at least have the memory of that love to cherish forever.

'As always, your wish is my command, Philip. We will continue to meet, as often as it pleases you, and to hell with what people think. And with regard to Christmas, I will try to fit in with your plans.'

Her words pleased Philip. His mischievous grin appeared. 'You will be my Christmas present. And if you would give me an inkling what you would like, it would be of enormous help. I want to buy something that would please you. Will it be French underwear, my darling, or jewellery perhaps? A hint would be very useful.'

'As I can't buy you an expensive gift in return, I would prefer an inexpensive present. I am not complaining, but the facts are that I am on a very tight budget. I have a couple of people I need to buy presents for, neighbours who have been good to me, and I have to be careful. So please don't embarrass me by giving me a present that costs the earth.'

This was the first time Evelyn had mentioned

anyone else in her life, and Philip was interested. 'You have good neighbours then?'

'Yes, they are very kind. One lady in the street does little jobs for me, which I pay her for. When I get home every night there's a fire lit and it makes the house seem more lived in.'

'Then I have an idea,' he said. 'Let me pay for the presents you want for your neighbours. If they are good to you, then they are good to me. Let me reward them, please, it would make me happy.'

'Oh, I shall only be buying them some small items, just to show my appreciation. Something for their children, perhaps, because they are quite poor and will have little money to spare for Christmas presents.'

'Then let me be their Father Christmas.' Philip had taken to the idea. He would enjoy helping poor families, and could certainly afford to. 'Yes, I would like that. But as I don't know the age or sex of these children, I will have to leave the buying of the presents to you.'

'I can manage to buy their presents, Philip, I'm not exactly a pauper.'

'But I would like to! Many of my friends give to organisations who help the needy at Christmas but I've never even given the matter any thought, been too busy enjoying myself. So you see how you are changing me, my lovely Evelyn, by reminding me there are people who are not as fortunate as myself.'

'If it will make you happy, my love, then so be it. I know the ages of five children, three boys and two girls. Although I am reluctant to take money from you, in this instance it will be in a good cause.'

'I don't have much ready cash on me today, but tomorrow I will give you an envelope with money in. And nearer Christmas, I will give you an afternoon off work to do your shopping. I will mention it to James, and if he is agreeable, we will give each member of staff an afternoon off to do their shopping too.'

'You are kind, thoughtful, and I love you very much. How lucky I am that you love me in return. My life is so much happier since you became part of it.' There was a shaky smile on Evelyn's face, but tears in her heart. How was she ever going to be brave enough to walk away from this man?

'Yer look a bit off colour tonight, Evelyn,' Bessie said when her neighbour called to pick her daughter up. 'I hope ye're not sickening for a cold, there's a lot of them around. Sit yerself down and I'll pour yer a cup of tea. It is fresh, I've only just made it.'

Bessie's kindly face, and honest concern, had an effect on Evelyn. How she had lied and used this little woman for her own ends, when all Bessie had done was offer the hand of friendship! Right now Evelyn needed a shoulder to cry on. 'I will have a cup of tea, Bessie, thank you. And if you're not too busy, I would like to talk to you in private. Can you spare the time?'

'Of course I can.' Bessie saw Milly sitting at the table, her coat on ready to go home, and wondered if by saying she wanted to talk in private her neighbour meant that what she wanted to say was not for her daughter's ears. Well, if she was going to tell a secret, then Bessie would get hers in first. 'Oh, Evelyn, before I pour yer tea out, I've been meaning to tell yer for a week or two, but I keep forgetting. I bought Amelia a doll the other week, then wondered if I should have asked you first. But yer don't mind, do yer? After all, there's no harm in a young girl having a doll. I had one when I was young, I still remember it.'

'I have no objection to Amelia having a doll.' A few weeks ago this would not have been true, but Evelyn's head and heart were going through major changes. 'Where is it?'

'It's upstairs on the bed I sleep in on a Saturday night, Mother.' Milly couldn't believe her luck. As Auntie Bessie had said, perhaps her mother wasn't feeling very well. 'And her name is Daisy.'

Bessie jerked her head towards the stairs. 'Go and get it, sweetheart, and perhaps yer mother will let yer take it home to play with while me and her have a little talk.'

When Milly had gone, clasping the doll to her chest and looking so happy to be taking Daisy home, Bessie pulled her chair nearer the fire. 'I could tell there was something bothering yer as soon as yer walked through the door, Evelyn, so whatever it is, get it off yer chest. It'll do yer no good to bottle it all up. And anything yer say will go no further than these four walls.'

Evelyn dropped her head. 'I'm afraid you're not going to like me by the time I've said what I feel

396

I must. You have never been anything but kindness itself to me and Amelia, and yet I've lied to you since the day I first became your neighbour. In fact, I have lied to everyone I've come into contact with for the last eight years. But someone has come into my life who has made such a difference, made me see myself for what I am – and that is not a very nice person.' She raised her eyes to Bessie's. 'I know I don't deserve your friendship, not after the way I've treated you, but I need to talk to someone who will not judge me too harshly, and you are the only one I can turn to. So I'm going to ask you to listen while I take you back more than eight years, to what my life was like then and how I have lived since.'

'Look, I can see ye're distressed. Why go over old ground and make yerself worse?' Bessie asked. 'Just tell me what ye're upset about now, and yer might feel better once yer've got it off yer chest.'

'No, I have to tell you all I've gone through for you to understand. I need to go back to the year I was nineteen years of age and still living at home with my parents.' Evelyn dropped her head as she gathered her thoughts together, then began by describing her parents and how, for her nineteenth birthday, she was allowed to go out with a girl friend for the first time. Then the meeting with Charles, the whirl of social activity that lasted for a year, how he gave her everything she wanted. Then the day he told her he had joined the Army. She said he came from a very wealthy family, but gave no name. She raced through the episode before they were married, when they'd sat in the car and she had allowed him to take liberties with her because he was going away and she felt sorry for him.

Evelyn stopped then to try and clear her throat of the lump caused by unshed tears. And Bessie, who had been enthralled by what she was hearing, didn't know whether to offer words of comfort, or leave her neighbour to get what was troubling her out of her system.

'I'm sorry, I needed to breathe for a while,' Evelyn said, her face pale and drawn. 'I don't want to upset you with my troubles, but I'll go mad if I don't tell someone so please bear with me, I won't keep you much longer.' Then she took up the story again. When she reached the part where Charles' family wouldn't believe it was his baby, and she was disowned by her own family and friends for having an illegitimate child, she was shaking and sobbing so much she couldn't continue.

Bessie crossed the room to sit beside her, and put an arm around her shoulders. She couldn't see anyone in such distress without trying to comfort them. 'I think yer should leave it for now, Evelyn, if it's going to affect yer so much. You can tell me the rest when ye're feeling up to it.'

Evelyn became more agitated. 'No! I have to tell you everything! I've lived with this for so long because I've never had anyone to confide in. If you won't listen, I have no one to turn to. Please hear me out, then with you seeing things from a distance, you may understand them more clearly and tell me what you think I should do.'

Bessie patted her shoulder then stood up. 'Okay. I'll go and sit in me own chair, and as yer say, I'll hear yer out. But as for telling yer what I think yer should do, well, I don't feel as though I'm in a position to do that. But anyway, go ahead, sweetheart, it's better out than keeping it in and making yerself ill.'

Evelyn took a deep breath and let it out before taking up her story. 'When my father-in-law came to tell me Charles had been killed in action, he said I was no longer their responsibility and that I must be out of the house in two weeks. I moved from a beautiful, grand home to a six-roomed house. Then I slid further down the scale and could only afford a house in this street.'

Bessie couldn't keep quiet. 'May God forgive them, the miserable rotters! Fancy throwing you and the baby out!'

'Don't think too badly of them, Bessie, I don't. I did at first because I was selfish and wanted to keep the life I had become used to. But I wasn't a very nice person then. I didn't even mourn my own husband, so I could never really have loved him. I refused to wear black, as I should have being a new widow, and did nothing but complain and whine to his father. Never once did I think how he and his wife must have suffered, losing the son they adored. I was too busy feeling sorry for myself. And I was childish enough to put the blame on Amelia, always thinking if it wasn't for her, I'd still be living a life of luxury. I have made that child suffer for my own mistakes. It is only since a certain man has come into my life that I can see what a dreadful mother I've been. He has helped me realise that the problems I've had and dreadful life I've led for eight years, were all due to my feeling sorry for myself. Now I see myself as others see me, and I don't like what I see.'

'Oh, I'm glad yer've met someone, sweetheart, that will make up for all the bad years. Are yer serious about each other?'

'He loves me very much, and I can honestly say he is the only person I have ever loved in my whole life. He makes me feel special, and I'm a different person altogether from the one I was a few months ago.'

'Is he coming to your house to meet Amelia? She'd be over the moon to have a dad.'

Evelyn closed her eyes. This was the part that would take the concern from Bessie's face and replace it with dislike. 'I haven't told him I have a daughter. He is my boss at the office, and at first there was no reason to tell him any of my business. He knows nothing of my past, nothing at all. Then there was a spark between us, we both felt it. I should have told him about Amelia then, but I was afraid of losing him. Now it's too late. He wants to marry me, and he will think I've lied to him if I tell him now. He'll walk out of my life, and I couldn't bear that.'

'So what are yer going to do? Yer wouldn't put him before Amelia, would yer?'

'Bessie, I'm out of my mind with worry. I haven't been a good mother to Amelia, I know that, I don't have any maternal feelings towards her. It's something I can't help. Maybe I'm not normal or maybe it's because of the way I was treated.'

'Is Amelia illegitimate?' Bessie couldn't help but ask.

Evelyn shook her head. 'No, Charles was her father. Anyone who knew him would recognise that straight away, the resemblance is remarkable.'

Bessie felt a little of her anger drain away. Thank God for that. 'Then why don't you go to see your late husband's parents? They have a right to know, and would probably be over the moon to see her now. She is part of their son after all.'

'I have thought about that, Bessie, but after the way they treated me, I don't think I would be very welcome.'

'You might not be, but their granddaughter would, I'll bet! As I said, sweetheart, there were wrongs on both sides, but that should not be allowed to keep Amelia from a family she doesn't know she has.'

Evelyn glanced at the clock and jumped to her feet. 'I forgot she'd been left in the house on her own, I'll have to fly. But can I talk to you again, Bessie? I do feel a lot better for having got so much off my chest.'

'You're welcome any time, Evelyn. And we'll let Amelia go and play with Rita's kids next time, save her being in the house on her own.'

'Yes, we'll do that, as long as Mrs Wells doesn't mind.' Evelyn reached the door, then put her hand on Bessie's arm. 'Thank you for being a friend in need. I don't deserve your friendship after the way I've treated you in the past. I have been short with many of the neighbours, and I'm really sorry about that. I'll be a better person from now on, I've had my eyes opened.'

Evelyn was turning the key in the door when Bessie remembered Aggie's disastrous trip over the rug. The place had been cleaned and all traces of ashes and soot been removed. But when Bessie was in there, there was still a smell of soot. 'Oh, before I forget, sweetheart, yer need yer chimney sweeping. There was a fall of soot when the fire was being lit, but it's all been cleaned up. I thought I'd better tell yer in case yer can still smell it. Yer know how the smell stays in the air for a while.'

'Do I need to get the sweep in, then?'

'Nah, I think it'll be all right until after Christmas. Yer've got enough on yer plate.' She waited until she saw her neighbour open the door. 'Goodnight and God bless. Get a good night's sleep, it'll do yer the world of good.'

Chapter Twenty-One

Bessie lay awake till the early hours of the morning, going over in her mind all that Evelyn had told her. What a story it was, almost like sitting in the pictures watching a drama unfold. She was at a loss what to make of her neighbour now. There were times in the story-telling when she'd felt sorry for her, then others where she would like to have given her a good shaking. But when it came down to it, it wasn't Evelyn she worried about. The woman was old enough to take care of herself, and make up her own mind what she wanted to do with her life. But Milly couldn't, and this was what Bessie was fretting over. She was eight years of age, a little angel, but she hadn't had much pleasure or love in her life, and God knows what was going to happen to her in the future. She had grandparents she didn't even know about, and who would probably love her to death given the chance. Perhaps they had been hard on her mother, but as Evelyn had admitted herself, she'd deserved it, after behaving badly. Whichever way it was there was no reason why the child should suffer for it, and next time her neighbour came for a heart to heart, Bessie would tell her so in no uncertain terms.

It was with this determination to protect Milly's interests that Bessie turned on her side and counted sheep until she fell into a deep sleep.

Meanwhile, next door, Evelyn was tossing and turning. She was glad she'd unburdened herself to Bessie, although she still hadn't told her that Philip was expecting her to spend time with him at Christmas or that he wanted her to give her job up and live in the apartment until they'd fixed a date for their wedding. And she hadn't the strength of character to tell the truth: that she would like nothing better than to walk away from everything in her life now, and go to the man she loved. But there wasn't much point in talking about something that wasn't possible.

Evelyn sighed deeply and turned on her side, wiping a tear away. How was she to face Philip and see the hurt on his face when she shattered his dreams? Her own dreams, too, but she had known all along their love was doomed, and he'd hate her for leading him on. The only other option, which Bessie had brought up, was to go and see Mr Lister-Sinclair. But what if he still wouldn't believe her, even though Amelia was the spitting image of his son? She would be totally humiliated then and made to feel worthless. No, she didn't think she could face that. Then she asked herself if it wouldn't be worth a try? Anything that would lead to her being free to marry Philip would be worth it. But she began finding obstacles to put in the way. What if she told Mr Lister-Sinclair who had asked her to marry him, and it came about that Philip's family were well known to them? This was very likely, for the wealthy people of the city usually mingled in the same circles, frequenting the same parties and social events.

404

Once again Evelyn turned over in bed, this time telling herself there was no way out. The best thing she could do would be to make the most of the next couple of weeks with Philip, and then either pluck up courage to tell him the truth or just disappear out of his life.

When Evelyn called in the following night she didn't accept Bessie's invitation to sit, saying she was hungry and urging Amelia not to dawdle and put on her coat. She felt she couldn't sit and go over her troubles again, last night had left her drained. 'Come along, Amelia, I'm really starving.' She thought Bessie would take the hint, but her neighbour had other ideas.

'Rita was asking me if yer were satisfied with her work. Was the room left clean and tidy enough for yer?'

'Oh, yes, I am well satisfied. Please tell her so.'

'I can see ye're eager to be away so I won't keep yer long,' Bessie said. 'But I was wondering about Saturday. Will yer be going to yer friend's and staying overnight? It doesn't matter to me, yer can please yerself, Evelyn, but I need to know if Amelia will be staying over so I'll know what bread and milk to get in?'

Evelyn's eyes darted towards her daughter, putting her coat on. She hadn't expected this, not after telling Bessie about Philip. But from the sound of things her neighbour hadn't taken it for granted that she was sleeping with him. 'I thought perhaps you wouldn't want me to stay at my friend's, not after our heart-to-heart last night. I was under the impression it may have changed your opinion of me?'

'Not at all!' Bessie said. 'It's not for me to judge, or tell yer how to run yer life. If yer want to go to yer friend's, I'll be more than happy to have Amelia.' She smiled when she saw the girl's eyes light up. 'We get on like a house on fire, don't we, sweetheart?'

'In that case, I'll be delighted to go to Elizabeth's.' Evelyn nodded to her daughter. 'You have the key, Amelia, you run and open the door while I have a quick word with Bessie.'

'If yer starving, Evelyn, why don't yer go home and have something to eat? Amelia's had a meal, so yer've no need to worry about her. But I bet you haven't had much since yer left the house this morning.'

'Only a sandwich, and that wasn't very filling.' Evelyn laid a hand on Bessie's arm. 'Thank you, you are a friend indeed. I'll go and make myself something warm, then I'll come back, for I have something to tell you that I hope will please you.'

When Evelyn knocked an hour later, she had Milly with her. 'Bessie, Amelia asked if she could go over to Mrs Wells, to have a game of cards with one of the boys.'

'The boy's name is Jack, Mother, and he's very good to me. We play together.'

'Will Mrs Wells mind?' Evelyn looked up at her neighbour, who was standing on the top step. 'Shall I go and ask?'

'There's no need,' Bessie assured her. 'Like me, Rita doesn't stand on ceremony.'

Milly didn't wait to hear any more, she was

across the road like a flash and knocking on the Wellses' door. It was opened by Jack, whose dirty face beamed when he saw her. 'Hi, Milly, come on in.' His greeting was missed by her mother, who had deliberately been ushered quickly into Bessie's living room out of earshot. She and Evelyn had come a long way in the last few days, but giving her daughter a change of name might not go down too well. 'Yer've no need to worry about Amelia, she's in good hands over there.' And for good measure, with a silent chuckle, she added, 'Two well-behaved boys they are, and yer'll not hear bad language in there either.'

Evelyn sat down without waiting for Bessie to ask her to. She was feeling a little happier now she knew she had the weekend free, and wanted to give a little happiness in return. 'I won't bore you with my tales of woe, Bessie, at least not tonight. But I have some good news for you, and hope you will take it as such.'

Bessie was thinking Evelyn must have had a good education, her English was perfect. Still, the little woman thought, it's too late in life for me to remember to sound me Gs and me Hs.

'I could do with a bit of good news to cheer me up, Evelyn, we don't get much chance in work for telling jokes. If our machines stop for a minute, the boss is down on us like a ton of bricks. The only time we get a smile out of him is when he's got a rush job on and he's coaxing us to work either later or faster. And then he's a smarmy toad.'

Evelyn smiled, hoping the news she'd come with would indeed cheer Bessie up. 'I want you to

407

believe me when I tell you that every word out of my mouth tonight will be true. I have lied before, not only to you but to everyone around here and I am not proud of myself. Tonight is different, I come with the blessing of another person's generosity. So please hear me out before judging me. And please don't take this as an insult, or think it's given out of pity, it is far from that.'

'For God's sake, Evelyn, will yer get on with it! Yer've got me on pins now, so get a move on before I throw a wobbly.'

'Well, you know about my relationship with Philip, and this is his doing. We were talking about Christmas presents, and I said how some people couldn't afford to buy their children presents because there were so many men out of work, and even those who worked were on very low wages. He asked me how I knew, and although he doesn't know where I live, I did say I had seen for myself that some boys and girls were running around barefoot.' Evelyn was watching Bessie's face for any sign of indignation, but her neighbour's face remained expressionless. 'He said many of his rich friends give to charities at Christmas, but he never has because he'd never really given it thought. Then he insisted I take some money from him to help anyone I thought was in need. So will you help me, Bessie, and tell me who is most in need in this street? I don't want anyone to know where it comes from or think it's been given out of pity. That would rob them of their pride. I've seen boys at the top of this street running around without shoes on, and I would like to help them.' She was worried that her neighbour hadn't yet said a word. 'You're not happy about it, are you, Bessie?'

'Not happy! I'd be over the bloody moon if I could help some of the families hereabouts afford a proper dinner over Christmas, *and* get shoes for the kids. They needn't be new shoes, they could be good secondhand ones from the market. I could easy do it without them knowing it was charity. I could always say the shoes came from the Wells boys, and they'd grown out of them. And Kenny Gordon, he's always growing out of shoes according to Aggie. Her and Rita could take the shoes up and the women wouldn't think anything about it, they'd be that glad to see their kids shod. It breaks a woman's heart if she can't afford to feed and clothe her children, but there's nothing they can do if their husbands are out of work.'

Evelyn bent down to pick up her handbag from the floor at the side of her chair. 'I have the money in an envelope. I would like to buy presents for Mrs Wells and Mrs Gordon, and also for their children so they can open them on Christmas morning. And it would be nice if you could buy books and games for Amelia, you will know what she likes better than I do.' She handed over the large envelope. 'I will be buying her a nice dress and a new coat, so she will have a lot to make her happy over Christmas. And if you won't be insulted, I would like to buy you something for your kindness, if you would give me an idea of what you would like?'

Bessie looked down at the envelope which was sealed. 'Don't worry about me, Evelyn, I'll be all right for the holidays, I've got clubs in most of the shops. I put a few coppers in each week and it soon mounts up. I'm lucky I can do that, with me working and only meself to worry about.' She waved the envelope. 'Would yer mind if I opened this in front of yer? I'd feel better if yer would watch me and we agree what's inside.'

'By all means, go ahead, Bessie. But it isn't necessary, I would trust you with anything. You are the only one I have spoken to about the last eight years of my life. I wouldn't have done so if I didn't trust you implicitly. However, I understand why you would want me to see you open the envelope. So please do.'

Bessie ran her thumb along the inside of the flap and took out the contents. Her mouth gaped and she looked as though she couldn't believe what she was seeing. She thought the white paper was wrapped around the money Evelyn had mentioned, but it was a five-pound note! She'd never had one in her hand before. And when she opened it up, she found it had been wrapped around a further three. 'Oh, my God, Evelyn, there's twenty pounds here! I've never had so much money in me hand at one time in me whole life! I can't keep this, it's a fortune!'

'It's not my money, Bessie, it was Philip who gave it to me. And believe me, he can well afford it. He is so happy knowing he is helping children who are not as privileged as he has been. He didn't do it to look good, he will never meet those he's helped and is not a snob. He would treat anyone the same, be it a king or a tramp.'

Bessie couldn't keep her eyes off the notes in

410

her hand. She'd never thought the day would come when she'd have one of those white ones, never mind four! She was shaking her head in disbelief when she gazed across at Evelyn. 'Are you sure about this? Do yer not want to keep some to buy Amelia's coat and dress? And something for yerself to wear over Christmas?'

Her neighbour shook her head. 'I have enough for Amelia's clothes, and I'll only be wanting an inexpensive dress myself. Please help as many of the poorer people as you can, Bessie, and you mustn't say where the money came from. Not a word, please, even to Mrs Wells and Mrs Gordon. Oh, you can tell them I paid for their children's presents as a thank you for lighting my fire every night and leaving the house neat and tidy, but nothing else.'

'I feel as though it's Christmas Eve, and Father Christmas has just come down the chimney.' Bessie grinned. 'I'll really get a kick out of buying shoes for those children at the top end, because when I was going to school I remember a lad in our school coming barefoot, and the other kids didn't half make fun of him. I can still remember the look of shame on his face. But he had someone come along like your Philip has, only his benefactor was one of the teachers. And she didn't make a show of him by giving them to him in front of the class, she took them to his home. I can still see that lad's face when he came to school the next day, he didn't half swank. He walked across that playground as though he was ten foot tall.'

'You're a good woman, Bessie, and it's a pity I

didn't have the sense to see that years ago. We could have been friends. I'm sorry I won't be able to help you with buying the presents, but I will help you wrap them up when Amelia's not around. And tomorrow I will tell Philip how his money is to be spent. He will be really pleased, he's quite tender-hearted.'

Bessie was beginning to grow excited. 'He has been very good, and yer can thank him from me. With this money, I can help so many people in the street who are on their uppers. I'll make a list of names and presents. He has a right to know where his much-appreciated money has gone. There's not many people give this much away, I'll bet. He must be a very special man.'

'Oh, he is, Bessie, a very special man indeed.' Evelyn pushed herself to her feet. She didn't want to talk about Philip for she was in danger of crying. 'I'll knock for Amelia, and then go home and sit on the couch with my feet up in front of the nice warm fire. I'll see you tomorrow night and you can tell me what thoughts you've had on how to make best use of the money. Perhaps you could write a list of those most in need? But of course you don't need me to tell you what to do, you are a very sensible lady.' She shivered as she opened the front door. 'Tell Mrs Wells I bless her every night when I open the door and see the flames flickering in the hearth. It makes that house feel like home, which it never has before.'

As soon as she'd closed the door on her neighbour, Bessie was so eager to start making a list she moved too fast and banged her shin on the sharp corner of the sideboard. 'You bloody nuisance,' she said, rubbing her shin, 'why don't yer get out of the way!' Then as she opened one of the drawers she burst out laughing. 'I'm talking to the ruddy sideboard now. It's the sight of so much money what's gone to me head.' She took a notebook from the drawer, then rummaged through the bits and bobs in there until she found a pencil. 'One of these days I'll get down to cleaning the drawers out, I should be ashamed of meself.'

The fireside chair was pulled closer to the hearth and Betty sank back, telling herself she felt like the Man Who Broke The Bank At Monte Carlo. Then she hugged herself before licking the pencil, hand poised ready to start writing. 'Now, let me see,' she said aloud, 'I can think of four families at the top who badly need help. Mrs Roseby ... her husband's been out of work for ages, and the whole family look half-starved. So it'll be shoes for the two boys, and if I can wangle it somehow and she won't wonder where it's coming from, I'll make them a box of food up for Christmas. And the same goes for the Summerhill family, father out of work and a boy and a girl needing shoes. Then the Andersons and the McCarthys, all in the same boat. Shoes for the kids, and a box of food for Christmas. I'll think of some way to give it to them without it looking suspicious.'

Bessie licked the end of the pencil again and began to write. The names of the families went in a column at one side of the page, and she jotted down all that they needed beside these entries. That was the worst off accounted for. There were others who could do with help, but she wanted to do the job properly, and take her time. She looked up at the ceiling, hoping for help from above. 'I could sit here all night staring at this ruddy book, but that wouldn't get me anywhere. So here goes, I'll try and price them. Secondhand shoes from the market, in good nick, would cost between a shilling and two bob a pair, and there are eight kids so that could come to sixteen shillings at the most. I could make up a good food hamper for seven and six which would see them a few days over Christmas. So for those four families, it would come to, let me get me thinking cap on, two pounds, two shillings. That's not bad, and the families would be made up. It would make all the difference to them. I'd still have nearly eighteen pounds left ... that's a lot of money.'

The notebook open on her lap, Bessie stared into the fire. She'd promised Evelyn not to tell anyone where the money came from, but couldn't get away with buying things for everyone without them wondering what she'd been up to. What was she supposed to say to her best mates? Rita and Aggie weren't soft, they wouldn't fall for any cock and bull story she came up with. Anyway, how could she carry boxes of food to the women at the top of the street without being seen? No, she couldn't do it on her own, she'd have to tell too many lies, and Him up there wouldn't take kindly to her telling fibs on His birthday. He'd know it was in a good cause because He knew everything, but still she wouldn't feel right about it. 'No, I'm going to have to let me mates in on it,' she told the

414

poker in the companion set. 'I'll tell Evelyn tomorrow night, then have Rita and Aggie over on Saturday afternoon and explain everything to them.' She nodded to the hearth. 'They'll get the shock of their flaming lives. I can't wait to see the look on their faces. I bet Aggie will say they're fake notes, but seeing as she's never seen a five-pound note in her life, like meself, she wouldn't know the difference.'

Bessie put a hand in the pocket of her pinny and brought out the envelope. She fingered the notes. To look at, you wouldn't think just one of them was more than five men earned for a week of hard work. And the rent would have to come out of that, plus food and clothing, coal and gas. There wouldn't be any luxuries, not even enough to go to the pictures one night or a bag of sweets for the kids. But that was the way of the world. The rich got richer and the poor got poorer. But even though Evelyn's man friend was one of the rich ones, Bessie still thought he was a good man to want to help others. She wouldn't let him down. She'd use the money wisely, and make it stretch to help as many poor folk as she could. With Evelyn's blessing, she'd have her two mates to help her.

She was getting a headache now with the excitement and the calculations, so Bessie left her chair to put the money away. 'I'll have to find a safe place to hide it,' she told the sideboard, 'where can I put it?' As though she'd been given an answer, she nodded. 'Yeah, I'll do that, it's a good idea.' So she pulled a drawer out of the sideboard, pushed the envelope to the very back, then fitted the drawer back in. Then she rubbed her hands together as though dusting them, and went back to her chair with a smile of satisfaction on her face. All in all it had been, as Evelyn would say, a remarkably good day.

On the Friday evening, Milly walked over with Rita when she went to light the fire. This was their routine now, as she had the front-door key. She would sit on the couch and watch as the fire was lit, then wait with her Auntie Rita until the fire was burning brightly. But Milly was fidgety that Friday night, and her eyes kept going to the stairs. She'd always known about the trunk in her mother's bedroom, but had never been close to it for she was afraid her mother would catch her and give her a telling off. But she had always been curious about what would be inside, and had made up her mind that tonight she would try and sneak a peep in it.

'I'm just going upstairs to my bedroom for a few minutes, Auntie Rita, is that all right?'

'Of course it is, sunshine!' Rita was kneeling in front of the hearth placing the sticks of wood carefully in a criss-cross pattern on top of the screwed-up pieces of newspaper. 'It's your home, yer can do as yer like.'

'I won't be long, call me if you need anything.' Milly took the stairs two at a time, but hesitated outside her mother's room. It had always been out of bounds to her although she could never understand why. There was nothing in there she could break; besides she was always very careful and never broke anything. And she was only going to look anyway!

She tip-toed across the room and stood in front of the trunk. It looks very old, she thought, I bet it's a hundred years old. It looked as though it was locked, for there was a big rusty bar coming down from the lid, and it had a slit in it which fitted over a rusty ring in the front of the trunk. Milly wasn't expecting to be able to open it, but when she played with the bar, it came out of the ring and dangled between her fingers. Afraid she'd done something wrong, and her mother would know she'd been in her bedroom, she let the bar fall. But it didn't fall back into the ring, it rested on top. And this was too much of a temptation for the young girl. She gently lifted the lid.

There wasn't much light in the bedroom for it started to get dark early these nights, and Milly couldn't hold the heavy lid up and at the same time have a proper look at what was inside. With her free hand, she touched something, and after feeling it carefully, knew it was a big hat. Then her hand fumbled around and she could feel feathers. Not just one or two feathers, but a long string of them. They felt lovely. She wanted to pull it out and see what it was, but was afraid her mother would know if anything had moved. And then the matter was decided for her.

'Are yer coming down now, Milly?' Rita shouted from the bottom of the staircase. 'The fire is lit and the guard in front. Let's go to mine and have a hot cup of tea.'

Milly closed the lid very softly, put the bar back in the ring, then tiptoed on to the landing.

'Coming, Auntie Rita! I'll bring Daisy over with me.'

'On yer own head be it, sunshine, 'cos yer know what our Billy's like for pulling yer leg.'

'I'm not coming to play with him, I'm coming to play with Jack. So your Billy can take a running jump. Anyway, I haven't got dirty knees like him, and I'll tell him so.'

Rita grinned. She was becoming very fond of this girl, and was surprised at her spirit. She always appeared to be shy, and quiet, but she could certainly hold her own if anyone rubbed her up the wrong way. And that someone was usually Billy, who thought girls were nothing but a ruddy nuisance. There was a young girl lived a few doors away, Polly, who dogged his footsteps everywhere he went. No matter how much he shouted at her, and told her to vamoose, she was never far behind him. When Rita pulled his leg about it, he swore he'd never have a girl friend, and he'd never get married. He was going to stay at home with his mam, 'cos she was the only one who didn't talk the ear off you. Poor Polly. According to Billy she was as thick as two short planks. When she told him, truthfully, that she'd come second in class, he'd snorted and told her not to tell so many lies.

Rita let Milly pull the front door behind her, for she knew it made the girl feel important. Also because she guessed Evelyn had given strict instructions that she must never let anyone be alone in the house, but must stay with them.

Sure enough, there was Billy kneeling in the gutter with his mate Tommo. The concentration on both faces was enough to bring a smile to Rita's face. Anyone would think there was a lot of money riding on who won this game of marbles for neither boy lifted his head, afraid the other would cheat.

'I'm making a pot of tea, son,' Rita said, 'are yer coming in for one?'

His eyes fixed on a blue and white glass marble, Billy said, 'I'll come in when this game's over, Mam, I'm winning right now.'

'You flippin' fibber!' Tommo actually took his eyes off the prized marble, he was so angry. His mate was showing off because he didn't like Milly, but Tommo had a mind of his own and thought she was nice. 'I'm a game ahead of him, Mrs Wells, he's only saying that to show off. If I win this shot, that marble will be going in my pocket and coming home with me.'

'Take no notice of him, Mam, it's him what's showing off 'cos yer've got a girl with yer. The daft beggar always does the same thing.'

'I'll thump yer if yer say that again,' said a very vexed Tommo. 'The trouble with you is ye're not a good sport. Yer can't stand losing, and ye're like a big soft baby.'

Milly thought that was a very good description, she couldn't have done better herself. Her infectious laughter filled the air. It also fuelled Billy's embarrassment. 'Take her in the house, Mam,' he growled, 'she's spoiling our game. And I won't bother with a cup of tea, I'll wait until the nuisance has gone over to Auntie Bessie's. If I lose this game, it'll be her fault for putting me off.'

Milly tugged on Rita's arm. 'Come on, Auntie

419

Rita, let's leave the baby alone before he starts crying. He'll blame us if he loses. Not like your Jack, he's a good sport. I bet we won't hear him moaning when I win the game of Snakes and Ladders we're going to have.'

Rita chuckled as she followed Milly up the steps. This was one little lady who wouldn't be pushed around. Perhaps her mother's strictness with her would pay dividends in the end. Or was the change due to someone else? The girl had certainly come out of her shell since she'd been coming to Bessie's. That's what a little warmth and love did for you, it gave you confidence.

Chapter Twenty-Two

Bessie came home from work on the Saturday at one o'clock, and spent the next hour and a half drumming it in to herself that she had to put her foot down and be firm. Never mind what reasons Evelyn came up with, they had to be brushed aside. But being firm in your head, and full of good intentions was a different kettle of fish to being as firm when the time came to face your problem. When a knock heralded the arrival of her neighbour and her daughter, Bessie's heart did a double somersault as she went to open the door.

However, part of her problem was solved by young Jack Wells, who was standing outside his house, opposite, leaning against the wall. He waved to Milly, and called, 'Can yer come over for a game of Snakes and Ladders, Mill – er, Amelia?'

Evelyn shook her head and was about to push Milly up the step when Bessie barred her path. 'Let her go over to Mrs Wells' for half an hour. I want to have a few words with you and I'm sure Amelia would be bored stiff.' The look in her eyes told her neighbour it was a matter of importance.

'You may go over, Amelia,' Evelyn told her daughter. 'But you must come back here when Miss Maudsley tells you to. And mind you don't lose the key or I shall be very annoyed.'

Milly was off like a shot. Last night, for the first

time, Jack had beaten her at the game, and she intended to get her own back. 'Yes, Mother,' she called over her shoulder, 'I won't forget to do as I'm told.'

Bessie waved to the couch. 'I won't keep you long, I know yer'll be eager to be off to yer friend's, but I've been thinking things over very carefully, and although I'm more than delighted with the money given so generously by your man friend, I don't feel easy in my mind that you and me are the only ones who know about it. No matter which way I look at it, I can't give food and clothes out like Lady Bountiful without it looking suspicious. Mrs Wells and Mrs Gordon aren't stupid, they'll know I'm not paying for everything out of me own pocket. And being me mates, they're bound to ask where the money is coming from. If it was only a few bob then it would be fine, but it's twenty pounds and that's a fortune to anyone living in this street.'

'But I was under the impression you were really pleased, and knew who you could best help with the money,' Evelyn said. 'Why have you changed your mind?'

'Oh, I haven't changed me mind, Evelyn, or me gratitude, but to do it alone would be impossible. I've made a list of all those I would love to help, and I can show it to yer if yer like. The kids going round barefoot would get shoes, and the poor families would get boxes of food to see them over Christmas. I know you and your generous friend would be more than satisfied that the money was being used to help those most in need. But I can't go round giving boxes of food out without

422

someone asking where the hell I got the money from. Besides all that, it would be physically impossible for me to do it all on me own. So I'm going to ask yer to let Mrs Wells and Mrs Gordon in on the secret. I promise that they will not be told any more than they need to know, and I swear on my life that yer can trust them. Like meself, they may be rough and ready, but they're as honest as the day is long. With their help, it would be so much easier. Any shoes and clothes we get from the market, we can say their children have grown out of or we got them off a relative. And boxes of food I can explain away by saying I'd heard a Good Samaritan was helping the poor, and I'd been to see him. People will be so happy to have food for the table over Christmas, they're not going to ask too many questions. Not when there'll be three of us giving the hampers out.'

Evelyn heard her out, then nodded. 'Of course it would be too much for you to do on your own, I should have realised that. Please ask your friends for help, but I beg you to protect my privacy.'

Bessie nodded her head vigorously. 'I would never discuss your affairs, you need have no fear of that.' She put her hand under the cushion of her chair and brought out the notebook. 'I know you are eager to be on yer way, but just cast yer eyes over the list and yer'll see how many I have down as being in desperate straits. Every family on that list is worthy of help, but a few more so than others. There are women in this street walking round with hardly any flesh on their bones, 'cos whatever money they get they spend on food for their kids. I promise you they will be blessing you and your friend when they sit down to a proper meal on Christmas Day.'

Evelyn studied the list. She'd been shaken by Bessie's words, and would repeat them to Philip. There were no addresses in the notebook, so she wouldn't be giving herself away by showing him the list. 'Would you let me take this to show to my friend? I'm sure he would be very touched by what you intend doing with the money.'

'Ah, not today, Evelyn, it took me ages to go through this street from top to bottom, both sides, and write the names down. I could write it out again tonight, and give it to yer tomorrow, would that do?'

'Yes, it would.' Evelyn got to her feet. 'Thank you for showing it to me, Bessie, I'm sure you and your friends will do a good job. I would give you a donation myself if I was able, but unfortunately I am not in a position to do so.'

Bessie went to the door with her. 'Yer've done enough, Evelyn! If it weren't for you, we wouldn't have this money. It's me what should be thanking you, not the other way round.'

She watched her neighbour walk up the street, her back ramrod straight. What a difference there was in her over the last month or so. Just went to show what love can do.

Bessie shivered with the cold, rubbed her arms briskly, then went inside and closed the front door. When she'd had a warm through, she'd nip over and ask Rita to come over for an hour tonight, and bring Aggie with her. Oh, and because little pigs have big ears, it would have to be an early night in bed for Milly. Not that the girl would mind, she was quite happy to go to bed at half-eight as long as Daisy went with her.

Milly had something on her mind and lost the game because she wasn't concentrating. This made Jack whoop for joy. 'That's two games I'm up on yer. D'yer want another game, yer might get lucky next time?'

'No, I'd better go over to Auntie Bessie's, she'll be lonely without me.' Milly pushed the chair back under the table then went out to the kitchen where Rita was rinsing some clothes through. 'I'm going in my house for a minute, Auntie Rita, before I go to Auntie Bessie's. Is that all right?'

'Of course, sunshine, yer don't have to ask me. Yer mam's let yer have a key, so she must think ye're old enough to look after yerself.'

'I only want to fetch something, then I'll go to Auntie Bessie's.'

'I'll come with yer, if yer like?' Jack offered. 'In case yer might get frightened being in the house on yer own.'

Rita walked through from the kitchen, wiping her hands on a small piece of towelling. 'No, yer can't go with her! Anyway, why should she be frightened in her own house? Let Milly do what she wants, and you go and play with the lads.'

As Milly skipped across the cobbles, in her mind's eye she could see the trunk. She couldn't wait to have a proper look inside. It wasn't dark yet so she would be able to see instead of feeling. Once inside the house, she made sure the door was firmly closed before tripping up the stairs

425

and turning into her mother's room.

Minutes ticked by as Milly gazed at the trunk, willing herself to open it. But she was nervous after letting her imagination run away with itself. It was very old, perhaps a hundred years or more, and there might be nasty things inside, like mice or creepy-crawlies. Then she began to tell herself off for being stupid. Of course there wouldn't be nasty things inside, her mother wouldn't allow that. And besides, the hat and the feathers she'd felt the other day were real enough, and it was the feathers in particular she wanted to see. So with her lips clamped together and a look of determination on her pretty young face, she lifted the lid before she lost her nerve. She let it fall back against the wall, and this gave her the freedom to use both hands in her search for the feathers. She found the hat which was right on top. Looking mischievous she placed it on her head. It was a very grand hat, in dark blue, with a wide brim trimmed with a lighter shade of blue lace. But as it was too large for her, it came down over her forehead and her eyes rolled upwards, filled with laughter. Afraid to make a sound in case Auntie Bessie would hear her, she covered her mouth with one hand. She'd bet her auntie would love to see her, but best not to let her in case it got back to her mother.

The next item Milly picked out was the feather boa, and she was filled with delight when she put it around her neck and felt the soft feathers next to her skin. The girl began to think how lovely her mother must have looked in this finery. Milly had only come to the house with the intention of looking for the feathers, wanting to know what they were. Now the temptation to look further was so great she couldn't ignore it. So with the hat falling over her eyes, and the feather boa hanging over her thin shoulders, she began to explore the contents of the trunk. But she was very careful to remember exactly where each item was when she'd first opened it. A satin dress caught her eye and she took it out for a better look. She knew it wasn't an everyday dress, for it was in blue satin, had no sleeves and was cut very low at the back and front. Milly rubbed the satin against her cheek and thought how lovely it would be to wear a dress like this one. With the feather boa and the hat, of course. And the shoes she'd seen pushed down the side of the clothes. They were in silver, with narrow straps and heels higher than she'd ever seen before.

More curious than ever now, Milly hung the dress over the side of the trunk and delved down the side of the clothes to find the shoes she'd spotted. When I'm older, I'll wear shoes like this, she told herself. And satin dresses, hats like this one, and a scarf made of feathers. Then a mischievous little voice in her head asked why she didn't try them on? No one would see her, and she could put everything back the way it was. So she quickly took all her school clothes off except her vest, it was too cold to take that off. Five minutes later, with the dress trailing on the floor, the feathers on the boa tickling her nose, and wobbling on the high heels, she stumbled her way over to look in the wardrobe mirror, and smiled at what she saw. Why had her mother never shown her the contents of this trunk, and why had she never worn them? To a child's mind, it seemed a shame to have such beautiful clothes and never put them on. She wasn't to know there were many reasons why the clothes had been locked away for the last eight years.

'I'll go and show Auntie Bessie before I take them off,' Milly told her reflection in the mirror. 'I bet she'll get a surprise. It's only next door and no one will see me.' Then she remembered something else she'd seen in the trunk, next to the shoes. It was a silver evening bag, although the girl wasn't to know that. To her it was just a pretty handbag which matched the shoes.

Lifting the dress, Milly turned away from the mirror, forgetting the shoes were miles too big for her. As she turned, the high heels gave way and she would have fallen if the bed hadn't been there. 'Oh, dear,' she said aloud, 'I'll never get down the stairs in them, I'll fall and break my neck. I'll carry them until I get to the front door, then I'll put them on.' She was carrying the shoes by the straps, with the silver handle of the bag over her wrist and her other hand holding the dress off the floor. She got on to the landing when she suddenly remembered the front door key. She thanked her lucky stars for if she locked herself out she wouldn't be able to get back in until her mother came home, and then there'd be ructions.

Jack had been waiting for Milly to come out. When he saw her hanging on to the door for support, with this large hat on her head, a dress that was now trailing on the ground and a feather thing around her neck, his jaw dropped open while his eyes couldn't believe what he was seeing. 'Eh, Billy, look at the state of Milly.'

Billy and his mate thought they were seeing things. Then when they realised there was nothing wrong with their eyes, they started to point at the girl and laugh. This upset Jack who gave his brother a shove. 'Don't you be laughing at Milly, she looks lovely.'

'Ay, who d'yer think ye're pushing!' Billy gave his brother such a push, Jack ended up on his backside. He scrambled to his feet, with fists flying, and landed a couple of blows on his brother's back before Billy knew what hit him. Then a couple of boys from up the street came to see what was going on, and those who laughed and poked fun at Milly were set upon by a very irate Jack. Now Billy didn't like being hit by his brother, but he wasn't going to stand by and watch Jack being thumped by two bigger boys. So he gave his mate Tommo the eye, and they both got stuck in.

While all this was going on, Milly was standing with her eyes popping at the scene before her. Boys fighting, and girls laughing and making fun of her. But not all the girls were laughing. A couple came over to her and stood admiring the dress, the feather boa, the shoes and handbag. 'Are these yer mam's clothes?' One girl was fingering the satin. Neither she nor any of her friends had ever seen such a dress, although it was miles too big for Milly and they didn't think you were supposed to wear a vest with it. Still, it must have cost a lot of money. And the feather

429

boa was given the thumbs up by all the girls. They swore they'd have one when they grew up and started work. Milly was wishing they would go away, in case they left fingermarks on the dress. But this was the first time any of them had spoken to her and she wanted to be friends with them. Her biggest worry was the boys fighting, though. She knew it was all her fault, but couldn't really understand why. She hadn't done anything wrong, hadn't said anything to start a fight. She hoped Auntie Bessie wouldn't be upset by it all.

Rita was in the kitchen and could hear a racket going on in the street, but Reg was sitting in the living room and she was sure he'd have said if anything untoward was going on. After a few minutes, she put the potato knife down and walked through. She had to make sure her two boys were all right. 'Are yer deaf?' she asked her husband, half-asleep in the chair by the fire. 'Can't yer hear the rumpus?' She didn't wait for an answer, it would be a waste of time. Reg had been working all morning and had probably dropped off in the warmth from the fire. Men didn't half have an easy life.

When Rita opened the front door the first thing she saw was a gang of lads beating hell out of each other. And two of them were her sons! 'Ay, come on, break it up now.' She collared Billy, who was the nearest. 'What started this off, yer stupid nit? Yer should have more sense at your age.'

Rubbing his chin, he growled, 'It all started because of the soft girl across the street. Just look at the state of her, she's barmy!'

Rita glanced across to the group of girls on the opposite pavement. One of them moved, and she saw Milly in all her glory. 'Oh, dear God in heaven, what does she think she's doing!' The girls heard Rita and scarpered quick, in case they got the blame for the boys fighting. By the time she'd crossed the cobbles, they were hot-footing it home. 'Milly, sunshine, where did yer get those clothes?'

'None of this is my fault, Auntie Rita, I didn't say anything. In fact, I never opened my mouth to anyone. The first I saw was Jack and Billy fighting. That wouldn't be Jack's fault, it would have been Billy that started it. And it wasn't anything I said, for I haven't said a word to either of them. I was just going to Auntie Bessie's to let her see me dressed up, and then some boys and girls were laughing at me, and the fighting started.'

'I thought yer were in Bessie's,' Rita said. 'Have you been in yer own house since yer left ours?'

Milly was feeling guilty now. But she wasn't going to lie, her teacher was always telling the class that it was a sin to tell lies. 'Yes, I have, Auntie Rita. I didn't mean to stay so long, but I was looking at some of my mother's clothes and thought I would put some of them on and show Auntie Bessie how I looked. I thought she would enjoy seeing me all dressed up. But I didn't get the chance to get as far as her house before the boys started fighting. I don't mind being laughed at because I know I look funny in my mother's clothes, but why the boys started to fight, I don't

431

ow. Boys are silly, aren't they?'

Rita felt like hugging her. In fact she wished they owned one of those camera things what took photographs. It would be lovely to have a photograph of Milly as she was now, with a satin dress trailing the ground, heels so high she was swaying to balance herself, a hat that must have been bought for a wedding, and a feather boa. She looked funny, but at the same time vulnerable and lovable. 'I'm surprised Bessie hasn't been out, unless she's in the kitchen and didn't hear the commotion. But I'll tell yer what we'll do, if yer want to surprise her. You stand behind me while I knock on the door, and when she opens it, I'll step aside. Just imagine the surprise on her face. Would you like that, sunshine?'

'She won't be upset with me, will she?'

'Bessie Maudsley be upset with you? Never in a million years, sunshine, 'cos she loves the bones of yer.'

'Will you let me link you, Auntie Rita, because I can't walk in these shoes. I'll topple over if I try.'

Rita held out her arm. 'Stick yer arm in, sunshine, and I'll help yer on yer way.'

Bessie smiled when she saw Rita. 'Ooh, yer've saved me a journey, I was coming over to your house later.'

Rita stepped aside. 'I've brought someone to see yer.'

Thinking it was all a joke that Rita was part of, and that she would be expected to show surprise, Bessie lifted her hands and cried, 'Oh, my, who is this little lady?'

Milly's green eyes shone. 'It's me, Auntie Bessie,

432

can't you tell?'

Bessie pretended to fall back in astonishment. 'Well, I never! I'd have passed yer in the street and not known it was my little sweetheart.' She looked over the girl's head to Rita. 'Where did yer get the clothes from?'

'Ah, well, I think Milly will have to explain that. And I'll come in with her 'cos we'll both catch pneumonia if we stand out in this cold much longer.' Rita winked. 'Will yer give Milly a hand, 'cos she's not very safe on her feet?'

As soon as she was in the living room, Milly kicked the shoes off and made straight for the warmth of the fire. She wasn't looking forward to telling her Auntie Bessie what she'd been up to. It wouldn't have been so bad if the boys hadn't seen her and started fighting, then nobody would have known. She could have had a laugh with the woman she had grown to love, then put the clothes back and no one would have been any the wiser.

Rita had been replying to Bessie's silent questions by pulling faces and rolling her eyes. She wasn't sure herself how Milly had got hold of the clothes, so couldn't have told her mate anything even if she'd wanted to. Then, knowing the girl was playing for time by standing warming her hands by the fire, she mouthed, 'Ask her!'

Bessie nodded before saying, 'Sit down, Rita, and take the weight off yer feet. I'm sure Milly will solve the mystery of the clothes when she's ready.'

'Oh, there's no mystery, Auntie Bessie.' Milly turned to face the two women. 'They belong to my mother. I've been naughty, though, because I didn't ask her if I could wear them.' She lowered her head so she didn't have to face them. 'I've been naughty two times over, because the clothes were in a big trunk in Mother's bedroom, and I only knew they were there, yesterday. I knew the trunk was there, 'cos you can't help but see it, but I never knew what was in it, and I didn't like asking my mother. As far as I know, she never opens it.'

'Oh, it was very naughty of yer to look in the trunk without asking your mother. There may be things in there that are important to her, like memories from the past.'

'I only wanted to put these things on to show you.' Milly fingered the dress and the feather boa. 'I was going to be very careful with them, and put them back exactly as I found them.' She was close to tears now, couldn't bear to think her actions had upset her Auntie Bessie. 'If the boys hadn't started making fun of me, and then fighting, I would have got here without causing any trouble. I'm sorry I've been naughty, Auntie Bessie, I won't ever do anything like this again.' Then, her lips quivering and eyes wet with tears, she asked, 'You won't stop me from coming here, will you?'

That did it for Bessie. She pushed herself off the couch and put her arms around the trembling girl. 'Of course not, sweetheart, why would I do that? I know yer didn't mean any harm, even though, as I've said, yer shouldn't have touched anything in the trunk without asking yer mother first. But everyone does things they shouldn't when they're young. I was no angel meself at your age.'

'Me neither!' Rita didn't like seeing the girl so upset. What she did was nothing compared with what her two sons got up to. 'And our Billy and Jack get in more trouble in one day than you will in a lifetime, sunshine. They'll both get a thick ear when I get home, fighting in the street like hooligans.'

Milly was biting on her bottom lip, for laughter was fighting with the tears, and she didn't know whether this would be the proper time to laugh. But it came out regardless. Peals of infectious laughter filled the room. 'It was funny, wasn't it? I was standing there, holding the wall so I wouldn't fall over in those shoes and at the same time trying to hold the dress up off the ground, when the next thing I know there's about six boys pushing and punching each other.' But the girl never forgot where her loyalty lay. 'It wasn't Jack that started it, though, Auntie Rita, I'm sure it wasn't.'

Rita chortled. 'Yer've got a soft spot for our Jack, haven't yer, sunshine? And he's got one for you, 'cos *that's* how the ruddy fight started. From what little I've heard, our Billy was laughing at yer, with Tommo, and Jack thumped him one. It started off with just the two of them, then before they knew it, a gang had joined in. But I'll get it all out of them later and let yer know the ins and outs. Anyway, right now, don't yer think yer should take those clothes off before yer do any harm? If yer rip that dress then yer mother will be very annoyed.'

435

A smile was lurking behind Milly's eyes when she said, 'I can't take them off because I've left my clothes on top of my mother's bed. I thought I would only be away for about five minutes, and then I was going to sneak back home, change into my own clothes and put Mother's things away neatly, so she wouldn't know I've been naughty.'

Bessie held out her hand. 'Let me have the key, sweetheart, and I'll go and pick up your clothes. Then, when yer're dressed, and yer look like my little sweetheart once again, I'll help yer with those very posh clothes ye're wearing. Yer could pass for a proper princess in them, and we'd all have to curtsey to yer.'

In her auntie's good books once again, Milly regained her sense of fun. She had a very vivid imagination and it was up and running now. With green eyes shining with devilment, and her cheeky grin, she held up the back of her hand to Bessie. 'You needn't curtsey, Auntie Bessie, because you are my friend. You may kiss my hand instead.'

'Oh, aye, Miss High and Mighty.' Rita pretended to get on her high horse. 'If Bessie is yer friend, what does that make me? An enemy?'

'Oh, no, Auntie Rita, you're not an enemy.' Her childish laughter ricocheted off the walls and brought a smile to the faces of the two women. 'You may kiss my other hand.'

'While you two are deciding how to address each other, I'll nip next door and get yer clothes, sweetheart, so hand the key over.' Bessie lifted her coat down from a hook. 'It'll be freezing in there with no fire lit, and I don't want to come down with a cold. Keep Milly company till I get back, Rita, there's a pal.'

'Don't be long, Bessie, 'cos my feller will be wondering where I've got to. Unless he's still asleep, of course, and that wouldn't surprise me. Stick him in front of a fire and he's away in no time. The only thing that would wake him would be his tummy, and I imagine it'll be starting to rumble any minute now. So get yer skates on, kiddo.'

Bessie was in and out of her neighbour's house in less than a minute. She grabbed Milly's school clothes off the bed, ran down the stairs and out of the front door. She didn't give a second glance to anything in the bedroom or living room, feeling as though she was trespassing. She wouldn't like a stranger wandering around her house, and was sure Evelyn wouldn't either.

'Blinking heck, that was fast!' Rita said. 'I asked yer to be quick, but I didn't tell yer to fly.' She stood up from the couch. 'I'll get over to my feller. Probably see yer tomorrow, Bessie.'

Her mate tried to send a message with her eyes. 'Oh, I was going to ask you and Aggie to come over tonight, I've something to tell yer.'

'Ooh,' said Rita, who had received the message, 'what time would yer like us?'

Bessie rolled her eyes towards Milly. 'Not until about half-eight, if yer get me meaning.'

'I'll be glad to get out of the house for an hour,' Rita said. 'Me and Aggie will be over around eight-thirty then, sunshine. Ta-ra for now. Ta-ra, Milly.'

Chapter Twenty-Three

'I think it's time yer were in bed, sweetheart,' Bessie said, 'it's half-past eight and yer know I'm expecting me friends.'

'Ah, can't I wait up and see them?' Milly asked, running a comb through the doll's hair. 'I promise to go to bed when I've had a goodnight kiss from them.'

'That won't be long, 'cos they're on their way.' Bessie said, making for the door. 'I can hear Aggie's voice. It's like a foghorn, I bet the whole street can hear her.'

'I heard that!' Aggie said when Bessie opened the door. 'If I was the kind what got upset easy, I'd take the huff over that. A foghorn indeed, I'm surprised at yer. I'll have yer know I can beat a foghorn any day. If I put me mind to it, or someone says something what they shouldn't, then I bet they can hear me down at the docks, never mind just in this street.'

Rita let her neighbour go up the steps first, then jerked her head at Bessie. 'Fancy bragging about having a voice like a foghorn. Honest to God, she's as common as muck and yer can't take her anywhere for fear she makes a show of yer.'

Aggie took her coat off, threw it over the back of a chair, then winked at Milly. 'Hark at her, queen, yer'd think she was born with a silver spoon in her gob to hear her talking. But it's all put on, 'cos she forgets I live next door and can hear everything what goes on in her house. And although she's me mate, and I shouldn't be snitching on her, I'll let yer into a secret 'cos I know yer'll keep it to yerself. Sometimes her language is so bad I have to cover me ears. And because I haven't got no cotton wool, I make the kids put their fingers in their ears until the worst of it is over. Anyone who didn't know her would think she was as innocent as a new-born babe, but yer have to live next to her to know what she's really like.'

'Just listen to her,' Rita said, handing her coat to Bessie, 'talk about the kettle calling the pot black isn't in it. Everyone knows she invented most of the swear words, half of which I don't even know the meaning of. When she takes off in one of her tempers, I go down the yard and sit on the lavvy until I think she's finished, 'cos I don't know where to put me face with my feller sitting there listening.'

'She's got no flaming manners, either,' Bessie said, her hands on her hips and her jaw set. 'Just look at the way she's flung her coat down. Ye're not at home now, Aggie Gordon, so yer can just hang that coat up in a proper manner.'

Aggie gave Milly a very exaggerated wink as she picked up the offending coat. 'Miserable buggers, if they smiled their faces would crack. But I'd better hang me ruddy coat up or I'll be the talk of every wash-house from here to the Pier Head.'

Milly was rocking with laughter as Aggie ambled out to the narrow hall where the hooks were. She had never known anyone like these three women in all her life. She knew her mother would disapprove of their bad language, but coming from them it was funny and you couldn't help but laugh at the expressions on their faces. Her life had changed so much since the day her mother had asked Miss Maudsley if she would mind her. It was the luckiest day of Milly's life, for she had made new friends that day and found love and happiness with the woman who was now no longer Miss Maudsley but her Auntie Bessie.

When her two mates were settled, Bessie looked at Milly meaningfully. 'Get yer kisses, sweetheart, and then up the wooden stairs to dreamland. Me and me mates want to sit and have a good old chinwag.'

Milly pouted. 'Can't I stay up for a while? Not even if I promise not to listen?'

'God bless yer cotton socks, sweetheart, but it would be really hard not to listen with us three women talking fifteen to the dozen.' Bessie held her arms wide and the girl ran into them. She hugged her tight, then said, 'The reason I want yer to go to bed is that me and me mates are going to be talking about the Christmas party we're hoping to have. We don't want any of the children to know what's happening, we want it to be a surprise. And it wouldn't be fair to the other kids if you knew and they didn't. You can understand that, can't yer, sweetheart?'

Milly moved away a little so she could look up into Bessie's face. 'Will I be coming to your party, Auntie Bessie?'

I don't want her to go to bed feeling sad, Bessie thought, so I'll tell a little lie, it won't do no

440

harm. 'I'm not sure yet, me and yer mother haven't discussed Christmas. But I think I can safely say I'll be able to get around her. Perhaps her friend is having a party, most people do, so when I ask if yer can stay here, I'm pretty sure she'll be agreeable.'

She was rewarded by a big hug, and a muffled voice saying, 'I love you, Auntie Bessie, more than anything in the whole world.'

'After yer mother, sweetheart, for she must always come first.'

Green eyes gazed up at her. 'I do love my mother, Auntie Bessie, but I love you too.'

'And I love you,' Bessie told her as she gently pushed her away. 'Now give my guests a big kiss, and then take Daisy to bed with you, there's a good girl.'

Kisses and hugs exchanged, and then Milly climbed the stairs with her beloved doll. It was only when they were sure she was in her bedroom, out of earshot, that Rita said, 'It's to be hoped that kid's mother doesn't take her away to live somewhere else 'cos she wouldn't half fret. It would break her heart if she lost you.'

'D'yer think I don't worry meself sick about that? Every night when I go to bed it plays on me mind so much I lie awake for hours. But last night I made an early New Year's resolution, and that was not to worry about something I can't change. So I'm going to enjoy Milly for as long as I can, and pray to God she is never taken far from me.' Bessie bustled towards the kitchen. 'I'll make us a pot of tea, and yer'll be glad to know I've mugged you and meself to a cream slice. I didn't leave Milly out, she had hers with her tea.'

'What's the celebration,' Rita called, 'it's not yer birthday, is it?'

'I'm not telling yer what the celebration is until the tea's made and we can sit round the table while I tell yer me news. And yer'll be bowled over when I tell yer, but that's all ye're getting until we're all sitting comfortably.'

'In the name of God, Bessie, this is bleeding torture, this is.' Aggie plonked her cup down so hard on the saucer she even frightened herself in case she'd cracked it. Bessie was fussy about her crockery, didn't like cracks or chips in anything. And she never gave yer a drink in a cup with no handle. 'It's all right, queen, I haven't put no crack in it. But if yer don't tell us quick what yer news is, I might just break this over yer bleeding head.'

'I'm with Aggie on this,' Rita told her. 'I don't know what ye're keeping us in suspense for, 'cos if yer don't tell us soon we'll both have heart attacks.'

Bessie leaned forward and put both elbows on the table. Oh, how she was going to enjoy seeing their faces. This sort of luck didn't come their way very often. 'Well, how would yer like to be Father Christmas's helpers for two days before Christmas?' She laughed when she saw their blank expressions. 'I'm not pulling yer legs, I wouldn't do that to yer, not over something that will make a lot of poor people happy.'

'Yer'll have to tell us more than that, sunshine. Explain to us in simple terms – what and where, when and how?'

'Now I know we've all called Mrs Sinclair fit to burn over the years, but for the last few months she's been different, changed like. She's friendly with me and doesn't talk down to me like she used to. And although it's not her herself who's being generous over Christmas, 'cos she's not well off, it's through her in a roundabout way.' Bessie pushed her chair back. 'Hang on until I get me notebook out, and I'll show yer how I want us, me and you two, to give certain things to certain people through the goodwill of someone that Mrs Sinclair knows. He's very rich apparently, and wants to help some poor people who are in dire straits. When Evelyn heard this, she remembered the kids in the street who have no shoes, and those families where the father is out of work. She told this person she knew of people in need, and that's how come we are going to be Father Christmas's little helpers.'

Bessie took the notebook out of the sideboard drawer and threw it on the table. Then she took the whole drawer out and stretched her arm to reach the envelope at the back. She threw this on the table, too, so she could manoeuvre the drawer back in place. Then she sat down with the notebook and envelope in front of her. 'I've made a list of the families I think are worst off, so will you and Aggie look at it and see if I've left anyone off?'

Rita pulled her chair nearer to Aggie's, their faces expressing their doubt that Bessie could possibly have enough money to do all the things she said she would. It would cost a fortune, and no one in their right mind gave a fortune to strangers. After a quick glance down the list,

443

Aggie growled, 'I see yer haven't put me or Rita on the list. Is that because yer think we're rolling in money?'

'Don't start crying before ye're hurt, Aggie, just hold yer horses until we sort that list out. Can yer think of anyone I haven't got down, Rita?'

'Yeah, old Mrs Ponsonby, she's probably worse off than anyone in the street. She's still scrubbing steps, at her age, just to earn enough to pay the rent and keep the wolf from the door. She's had that coat she wears for at least ten years to my knowledge, and it's practically in tatters.' Rita ran her eyes down the page again. 'The money yer've got by each name will come to quite a sum. With the best will in the world, sunshine, yer'd never be able to cope with all this.' She waved the book before handing it back to Bessie. 'I bet if yer add it up, it would come to about six or seven pound, and no one is that generous with money.'

Bessie pushed the envelope over to her. 'I don't know the gentleman's name, so I can't tell yer, but take the money out of the envelope and yer'll see for yerself how generous he's been.'

Intrigued, Rita took the contents out of the envelope, Aggie's head on her shoulder. 'If yer got any closer, sunshine, yer'd be sitting on me ruddy knee! Move back a bit will yer, and stop breathing down me ear.'

'I'm just as keen to see how much there is as you are, so don't be getting narky with me, queen, 'cos ye're not the only pebble on the beach.'

'It's a five-pound note.' Rita turned her head quickly and found herself rubbing noses with her mate. 'It's one of those five-pound notes what

444

only the rich can afford. Ay, I've never had one of those in me hand before.'

'Let's have a feel.' Aggie went to snatch the note, so she could brag to her husband about it, and anyone else who would listen. Mind you, when Aggie spoke everyone listened, they were afraid not to. But Rita pulled her hand away quick. 'If ye're not careful, yer'll tear it, and then they won't take it off yer in the shops.'

'Open it up, Rita,' Bessie said, waiting with mounting excitement to see the look on their faces. 'Go on, it won't bite yer.'

Rita was very careful unfolding the thin white piece of paper which was more than her husband earned in a month. It had been folded four times to fit the envelope, and when she opened it up and saw there were four notes in all, the colour drained from her face. 'In the name of God, Bessie, I've never seen so much money in me life. There's twenty pound there!'

Aggie's mountainous bosom was hitched up, and her mouth was working but no sound was coming from her lips. She was dumbfounded. It was so unusual for Aggie to be lost for words, Bessie thought the shock might have been too much for her. 'Are yer all right, Aggie? Don't let it upset yer, it's only money.'

'Only money!' she croaked. 'Bleeding hell, queen, that's not only money, it's a ruddy fortune!'

'She's right, sunshine, it is a fortune. D'yer think it's true what Mrs Sinclair told yer, that it was given by a rich person to help the poor? There's nothing dodgy about it, is there?'

'Don't be daft, Rita,' Bessie tutted. 'How would

445 -

she, or anyone else, get hold of dodgy money? No, it's all above board, I can assure yer, 'cos there's no way I'd get involved in anything that wasn't honest. There's twenty pound there, and your two names are not on the list because Mrs Sinclair told me she would like you two to have something for being so kind to her, and I've reckoned on five bob each for yer.'

Aggie's bust went back on the table and her voice was restored to normal. 'She didn't say that, did she? Ooh, er, after me calling her for all the stuck-up cows going. It just goes to show yer should never pull anyone to pieces 'cos yer might be wrong about them. D'yer hear that, Rita, we're not going to call Mrs Sinclair bad names in future.'

Rita looked at her mate in horror. 'Why, you cheeky monkey! It's you what's been calling her fit to burn since the day she moved into the street! I've told yer off about it time and time again, but yer wouldn't have it. May God forgive yer, that's all I can say.'

'Oh, He will, sunshine, 'cos He knows I've done nothing to hurt her. I mean, a few words, even swear words, won't do her no harm, especially as she didn't hear them.'

'I don't know how yer can be so polished, Aggie Gordon,' Rita told her. 'And I don't know how yer keep expecting God to forgive yer for everything. Yer tell yer husband lies, and some of the swear words yer come out with would shame the devil. So if ye're expecting to go to heaven when yer die, yer can forget it 'cos yer stand no chance.'

Aggie began to laugh, and as her tummy lifted

the table up, her bosom pressed it down again. 'He will if you and Bessie give me a good reference. Seeing as the pair of yer live like saints, I'm sure ye're very well thought of in heaven. So on your recommendation, St Peter will let me go through the pearly gates with yer.'

Bessie chuckled, 'I don't think much of the odds on that, sweetheart. Are yer expecting us all to die on the same day?'

'For heaven's sake, can't we talk about something more pleasant?' Rita gave her mate daggers. 'Here's us, sitting at the table with more money in front of us than we've ever seen in our lives before, and all you two can talk about is what's going to happen when we die! I think we should look after ourselves in that department, as long as we keep in mind that wicked people don't go to heaven no matter how holy their friends are.'

'Ooh, er.' Aggie's brows almost touched her hair-line. 'She's only had that money in her hand for five minutes, and already she's talking so bleeding far back yer can hardly hear her.'

'Stop larking about and let's get down to business,' Bessie said. 'How many names are on that list, Rita?'

'D'yer want me to count Aggie and meself, in, sunshine?'

Bessie nodded, 'Yes, go on.'

Rita's finger went down the names. 'There's fourteen here, and yer mustn't leave Mrs Ponsonby out because if this was my list she'd be on top of it.'

'Right, now I'll tell yer what I've got in mind. I'd like to have a party and invite all the kids in the street who won't be getting much in the way of presents at Christmas. Which means all the kids who are on that list. We'll never have this much money again, so let's give the kids the best Christmas they've ever had. What d'yer think?'

'I think the idea is wonderful, sunshine, and it would be marvellous. But where would yer have the party? Ye're talking about eighteen kids, and these houses weren't built to cater for that sort of number.'

'We can try, Rita,' Bessie said softly. 'Where there's a will, there a way. And I've set me heart on it now. I could move as much out of this room as possible, with the help of your men, and I'd have to borrow one of yer tables. It would be a squash, I know, but d'yer think the kids would worry? I bet most of them have never been to a party. They wouldn't care if they were standing on each other's heads.'

'Ye're dead right there, queen.' Aggie's chins were having a field day as she nodded her head. 'And I think the man who gave that money would feel the same. Some of the kids in this street have never had a cake, never mind been to a party. The poor buggers don't know what it is to have a farthing for sweets. So yer can count me in, queen, I'm all for it. And my feller will help with the table, and anything else yer want doing.'

'Yeah, the more I think about it, the more I agree,' Rita said. 'The five bob yer said I was going to get, well, I'd rather it went towards the party. I'd be in me element to see the kids with smiles on their faces. It's a very good idea, sunshine, and only you would have thought about

448

helping others and leaving yerself out.'

'Oh, I'm not leaving meself out, sweetheart, how could yer think that? Won't I have all the kids here, and won't I be over the moon to see their faces when they see this room done up with paper decorations and balloons? That will be all the thanks I need. And when the party is over, and the kids have gone home, we can have a party for us grown-ups.' Bessie pulled the notebook towards her. 'I reckoned on twelve bob for the boys' shoes, and say seven and six for each hamper. So how much does that come to. Let's see, there's four five shillings in a pound, so say fifteen seven and sixes, how much does that come to?'

Aggie didn't even bother trying to figure that out. She could add two and two together, and that was her limit. So she sat and watched her mates counting on their fingers. 'As near as I can get without writing it down,' Rita said, 'is about six pound three shilling. But I must be wrong, it's bound to be more than that.'

'I get it near enough the same, Rita, so I'd better write it down and make sure.' Bessie licked the end of the stub of pencil and put a line under the fourth name. 'I'll split the list into fours, it'll be easier. Otherwise I might end up spending more than we've got, and then I'd feel a right nit.' So while her mates looked on, Bessie went over the sums four times to make sure. 'It's just over six pound, so we've got enough to give every name I've got down here an extra couple of bob so they can get coal in to last them over the holiday. Are yer both in agreement with that?'

'It's you what managed to get the money,

queen, so it's up to you,' Aggie said. 'But I'll go along with yer, 'cos I'm over the bleeding moon. Just to see those poor lads having shoes on their feet, and the mothers having food for the table at Christmas, well, if I knew the man what gave the money, I'd shake the hand off him.'

'Then can I ask a big favour of you both?' Bessie waited until her mates gave her the nod, then said, 'Could yer find out what size shoes the lads take? Yer could knock tomorrow and pretend your lads have outgrown theirs and so have the lads of yer mate's. And don't forget to say yer hope they won't be offended, because there's nothing worse than them thinking yer feel sorry for them. Just be casual and say the shoes don't fit any more, and they're too good to throw out.'

'Yeah, we'll do that, won't we, sunshine?' Rita grinned at Aggie. 'And we'll be very diplomatic, as well. No swearing or nothing, just friendly.'

'I'm going to be hard-faced, girls, and ask yer if yer'd take the tram down to Great Homer Street market, if yer've got time, and buy the shoes? With the weather what it is, the boys may as well be wearing them now as wait until Christmas. I'll give yer the money for the shoes and the tram fare.'

'Not one of those five-pound notes, Bessie.' Rita was shaking her head. 'I don't want the responsibility of carrying one of those around. Besides, the stallholder will think I've nicked it.'

'I wouldn't expect yer to take one of those, sweetheart, I'll give yer the money out of me own purse and get it back later.' Bessie smiled and gave a sigh of contentment. 'It will do me heart good to see those poor lads with shoes on their feet. And it'll be only the first of our good deeds. I won't be able to do all the shopping with me only having Saturday afternoon off, so I'm hoping you two will get most of it in. I'll write out a list of what is going in each food hamper, like dry goods, vegetables and a large chicken.' She looked from one to the other. 'Yer don't mind, do yer? The dry goods we can get any day now, but the veg and chickens will have to be ordered for Christmas Eve.' She pushed her chair back and went to the sideboard where her purse was in the large glass fruit bowl. 'I've only got about twelve bob now, but I think that'll be enough for the shoes, won't it?'

'More than enough, sunshine, yer'll have change out of that.'

'I'll take one of the fivers to work with me,' Bessie said. 'Ask the boss to change it for me. I'll tell him how I came to have it, and that I've got more I'd like him to change. He'll believe me, he's known me long enough to know I'm honest and don't tell lies.'

'Give us the money then, sunshine, and we'll be on our way. My feller likes a cup of tea before he goes to bed, and he'll have a cob on if I leave him to make it himself.'

Aggie used the table for leverage to get to her feet. 'We'll have good news for yer tomorrow night, queen, and there'll be a few lads blessing yer for being a guardian angel.' She grinned when she saw Bessie's mouth open. 'Don't worry, I know when to keep me mouth shut. As far as anyone will know, the shoes will have come from

451

us or one of our friends.'

Bessie stood at the door until her mates reached their own houses, then they all wished each other a goodnight and three happy women closed their doors.

A few miles away, Evelyn and Philip sat on the couch in a room which was warmed by radiators. It was a luxury for Evelyn not having to put pieces of coal on a fire to keep warm. With Philip's arm across her shoulders, she was happy and contented. Every now and again he would put a finger under her chin and turn her face towards him for a kiss. He was eager to go to bed, so he could hold her in his arms and make love to her, but Evelyn told him to be patient as she had something to show him. She left the shelter of his arms to fetch her handbag and from it took the list Bessie had given her. She had thought long and hard about showing it to him, but there were no addresses on it, only names, so the street could be anywhere in Liverpool.

'I've brought you a list of deserving people who will be the recipients of your very generous gift of money. There are a lot more people in need in Liverpool, of course, because there is so much unemployment as you well know, but one can only do so much. There are more names to go on the list, but my friend has put beside each name what the family is most in need of.' Evelyn pointed out the names where the word 'shoes' was written at the side. 'These are the children who are going around barefoot in this freezing weather. They will be getting shoes, and their

452

parents a food hamper so they won't starve over the Christmas period. My friend is being meticulous about where the money goes, and said to tell you that you have been the means of many people having the best Christmas they've ever had. There'll be almost twenty families helped, so I'm sure that must give you great satisfaction, my darling.'

Philip looked at her with eyes wide with disbelief. 'All those people! But I only gave you twenty pounds, surely that's a mere drop in the ocean? How can she possibly buy shoes and food for so many people on so little money?'

'My darling, when you have absolutely nothing then sixpence is a lot of money. I've learned a lot in the last few years, which you have yet to learn. My friend will make that twenty pounds go a long way. She will make sure the barefoot children are shod, and that every family has enough food for a Christmas dinner. The shoes won't be new, of course, but she assures me they will be good secondhand ones. And the food hampers will contain everything from a chicken to potatoes and vegetables, tea, sugar, milk and biscuits, plus a bag of coal delivered to each house so they will be warm over the holidays.'

'Who is this friend of yours? I would very much like to meet her.'

Evelyn folded the piece of paper over and reached down for her handbag. It was all to buy her a few seconds in which to compose herself. This afternoon, after she'd dropped Amelia off at Bessie's, while sitting on the tram into the city she had reached a decision. She could no longer put Philip off with lies, and wouldn't give him up without a fight. So she had made up her mind to seek out Cyril Lister-Sinclair and throw herself on his mercy. And she would take Amelia, she'd decided, for when he saw her, he would know she was his son's daughter. That was the only way she could see of standing a chance of keeping the man she adored.

'You will meet her one day, my love, but it won't be until after the holiday, she works every day. She has to earn a living, she's not a wealthy woman.' Evelyn stroked his cheek and smiled. 'She is a spinster of fifty who has lived alone since her parents died many years ago. And she is not your type, otherwise I wouldn't let her within a mile of you.'

'She must be a very caring person to go to all this trouble to help people less fortunate than herself. It reflects badly on me to say this, being too lazy to follow her example, but it's a good job there are people like her. If you think I can help ease her load with another donation, I will gladly give it. I have far more money than I need.'

Evelyn nodded. 'You are quite right, she is a very caring person. Someone who would give you her last penny. But I don't think you should offer more money, I'm sure she will manage very well on what she already has.'

Philip's eyes were twinkling. 'And what about your Christmas present? Have you given it any thought?'

She shook her head. 'I would rather you gave me a surprise. Not an expensive one, though, or you will embarrass me. Perhaps perfume. That is

454

a present I would appreciate for it is a long time since I had a bottle of French perfume on my dressing table.'

He pulled her closer. 'You need have no worry about what to buy me, my adorable Evelyn, you have it already.'

She raised her brows. 'But I haven't bought any presents yet!'

'You are my present, and there is nothing in the whole world that I would rather have. Two whole days alone with you will be like heaven. To wake up with you lying beside me, to make love to you before breakfast, before dinner, whenever we feel the need. For I believe your need is as great as mine.'

'It is, my darling, it is.' Evelyn was fervently hoping Bessie would come to her aid and have Amelia for the two days. She thought this very possible as her neighbour adored her daughter. 'More so now than ever.'

'Then why are we sitting here when there is a very comfortable bed awaiting us in the next room? I'll set a tray with bottle and glasses while you retire to the bedroom. But don't bother putting a nightdress on, my lovely, allow me to see what a beautiful body awaits me. And hurry, please. I'm eager to hold you and caress every inch of you. I love you so much, my lovely Evelyn, it hurts.'

As she undressed, she asked herself how she could possibly leave this man and never see him again? No, she couldn't, it would break her heart. There must be a way she could keep him, and she intended to find that way.

Chapter Twenty-Four

Bessie sat on one side of her table, her two mates opposite. 'I've made two lists out, one for each of yer, for groceries that will keep, like tea, sugar and tins of condensed milk. Oh, and I've put down a red jelly on each, and a packet of custard powder. We can get round Molly in the corner shop for some biscuits. She'll throw in a few broken ones if I ask her nicely, and I'm sure whoever gets the hampers will be too happy to worry about a few broken biscuits. Anything is better than nothing when ye're hungry.'

Aggie's chins and hitched-up bosom agreed. 'Ye're not kiddin', queen. There's many a time broken biscuits have been a luxury in our house while Sam was out of work. And the same goes for Rita, doesn't it, queen?'

She nodded. 'I can remember us having half a biscuit each and thinking ourselves lucky to get that! No biscuit ever tasted so good.' She grinned at Bessie. 'Are yer going to tell the families who are on the list what they're getting? It would take a load off their minds and stop them from worrying about not having anything for Christmas.'

It was Bessie's turn to nod. 'I've been in two minds what to do about that, but in bed last night I decided it would be best to tell them so they're not worried sick. I'll wait until yer've been to the market for the shoes, then I'll tell them.'

'We're going for the shoes tomorrow, aren't we, queen?' Aggie felt really important. 'We've found out the sizes we need, and the mothers almost kissed us to death they were so happy. We told them our lads had outgrown theirs, and one of Rita's sisters has a lad who can't get his feet into his any more. So that part of it is over and, please God, the kids will soon be able to go to school swanking with a pair of shoes on their feet.'

'I've changed one of the fivers so I can give yer enough money to cover the food on the lists and the shoes. How much d'yer reckon yer'll need?' Bessie took her purse from the pocket in the wrap-around apron which would have wrapped around her twice, it was so big. 'Add a bit on to what yer think, just to be on the safe side.'

'Yer haven't put how much tea or sugar,' Rita said, fingering the list. 'Is it two ounces of tea and half a pound of sugar?'

'No, the money will run further than that, sweetheart, so make it a packet of tea and a pound of sugar. Two ounces of tea in a sweet bag looks paltry, we may as well go the whole hog and give them a real treat. God knows, they deserve it. Most of the women on that list look twenty years older than they are because of the worry. Their faces are haggard and careworn, and there isn't an ounce of flesh on them. So while we've got the chance, let's do what we can for them.'

'I couldn't agree with yer more, sunshine, it breaks my heart just looking at them. It takes me and Aggie all our time to keep our families going, but we're not as badly off as some poor buggers. You, Mrs Sinclair, and the man who generously

457

gave the money, are going to make a lot of people happy. I take me hat off to all of yer.'

Aggie nudged her friend. 'I didn't know yer had no hat, queen! I haven't never seen yer in one in all the years I've known yer.'

'No, yer wouldn't, sunshine, 'cos I haven't got no ruddy hat. But if yer want me to be precise, I'll say that if I did have a hat I'd take it off to them. Now then, does that make yer feel better?'

Aggie put on a sad face and even made her lips quiver. 'No, it doesn't make me feel better, queen, it makes me feel sad. Fancy, a mate of mine with no hat. Well, that's really touched my heart. If I wasn't so bleeding skint, I'd fork out and buy yer one.'

'Oh, that is kind of yer, sunshine, but yer needn't worry about little old me. If the occasion arises, like say if our Jack ever decides to get married, I can always borrow yours.'

Aggie grinned. 'Yer'd have a ruddy job, queen, 'cos I haven't got no hat. But I have got a mobcap, and if yer stuck a feather in the side of that, it would go down a treat.'

Bessie banged her fist on the table. 'Ladies, can we get our business sorted out, please? If there's any money over, I'll buy yer both a ruddy hat!'

Rita giggled as in her mind's eye she could see herself and Aggie walking down the street in posh hats with huge ostrich feathers sticking up at the side. Oh, what a field day the neighbours would have! Her hat and feather were in two shades of blue, Aggie's was bright red. 'Aggie,' she said now, 'don't ever wear red, sunshine, 'cos it doesn't suit yer.'

Aggie frowned at Bessie. 'What's wrong with this one? She's not having a funny turn, is she, not in the middle of a business meeting.'

'If you two don't stop acting the goat,' Bessie told her, 'this business meeting will never get off the ground. Now tell me how much yer think the shopping will come to, and I'll give yer the money?'

'Lend us yer pencil, then.' Rita totted the money up in her head. 'I can't tell yer to the penny, sunshine, but I would hazard it's at least a pound. And I'm going to be very cheeky now, Bessie, and ask, if I see a cheap coat in the market, would yer let me get it for Mrs Ponsonby? I worry meself to death about that woman. She always looks starved of food and heating. Yer never see a coalman there, so she must never have a fire lit. And at her age, God knows, she deserves some comfort. She's out cleaning and scrubbing steps for people in all weathers, it's a wonder she doesn't catch pneumonia.'

Bessie nodded. 'You get her a coat if yer can, sweetheart, and a pair of gloves and a scarf. We've got twenty pound to play with, and she's as deserving as the rest. I'll put her down for the coalman to drop her a bag in before Christmas, and yer can tell her the same tale as we're going to tell all the others. That a very kind gentleman gave us some money to help people out, but wouldn't give his name. We'll all tell the same tale and then we won't get ourselves mixed up.'

'That's a good idea, queen,' Aggie said. 'Yer know what my mouth is like for running away with itself. But what yer've just said is easy to

459

remember, so I won't get meself in a muddle.'

Bessie opened the back compartment of her purse and took out some pound notes she'd folded over. 'There's two pounds to pay for what's on the list, the coat for Mrs Ponsonby, and the shoes.' She passed the notes to Rita. 'Seeing as ye're going to the market, would yer like some of the money I've been saving for you? Yer might see something yer like for yerselves, or something for the kids.'

'That would be marvellous, sunshine, 'cos both my boys could do with another pair of kecks. And I bet Aggie would be pleased, wouldn't yer, sunshine?'

Aggie's nod sent her chins swaying, her folded arms raised her bosom, and her tummy lifted the table off the floor. 'Ooh, I'll say I would! Our Kenny's got no backside in his kecks. He was moaning last night because the wind was getting inside the patch I put on a couple of weeks ago, and is only hanging on by a thread.'

'Well, I'll give yer what I've saved for yer. And d'yer want the five shillings Mrs Sinclair told me to give yer? Yer can have it now if yer want to buy things for the kids for Christmas.'

Rita shook her head. 'No! We want yer to keep that towards the party yer said we're having. You hang on to it, Bessie, there's a good girl.'

'Ahem!' Aggie put a hand to her mouth as she'd seen posh people do when they cough. 'Don't I get a say in this? You speak for yourself, Rita Wells, and let me do me own talking.' She smiled sweetly at Bessie. 'This is me what's telling yer to keep the money for the party. I haven't been to a real knees-up, jars-out party since me wedding, and I'm really looking forward to it.'

'You'll have the party even if yer take the money what I've got saved up for yer,' Bessie said. 'I've been doing a lot of working out in me head, and this money I've got will cover all I'm expecting it to, and a damn sight more. Yer have my word on that.' She pushed another pound note over the table. 'Take this, Rita, and if you and Aggie see something yer'd like for yerselves to wear at Christmas, then buy it. Yer might see some nice, decent, secondhand dresses, and yer can titivate yerselves up for the party. So spoil yerselves for once. It's not often yer get the chance.'

'And what about you, sunshine, what are you getting yerself for the party?'

'I'm making a dress for meself, when I get the time to nip into town for material. I won't leave meself out, don't worry. And I'm making a dress for Milly, as a Christmas present.'

'Will yer be having her over Christmas?' Rita asked. 'Or don't yer know yet?'

'It hasn't been mentioned, but I'm keeping me fingers crossed. Milly keeps asking me, but I haven't the nerve to bring the subject up with Evelyn. Not after she's turned out to be a much nicer person than we thought. I'll have to see how the land lies over the next few days. If she seems in a good mood when she calls one night, I might mention it to her.' Bessie hadn't told her mates anything about Evelyn's private life, and had no intention of doing so. She was told in confidence, and that's the way it would stay as far as she was concerned. As for having Milly for Christmas, her

461

hopes were quite high for she thought Evelyn would want to spend time with her man friend. But it wouldn't do to take anything for granted. To do that could mean heartache and disappointment, not only for herself but for Milly too. So best keep things close to her chest for the time being until she picked up the courage to ask Evelyn.

'Look, we know ye're rushed off yer feet, we can see that for ourselves,' Aggie told the very flushed and irate stallholder. 'Me and me mate aren't blind, and we're not bleeding well daft, either.' She nodded her head vigorously to add weight to her words. 'Of course yer think we are, otherwise yer wouldn't be trying to tell us those shoes are worth two bob! No one will give yer that much for shoes what are well worn.'

The stallholder thought it best to do business with the one who hadn't opened her mouth yet, for he knew he'd never win with the big woman. She was some size, and he wouldn't stand an earthly if she clocked him one. 'The shoes are not very well worn, missus,' he said to Rita, 'yer can see for yerself there's still plenty of wear in them. I'm not trying to diddle yer into paying more than what they're worth.'

'Oh, I'm going to let me mate deal with yer, 'cos the shoes have nothing to do with me.' Rita thought she'd go for the sympathy touch. 'Yer see, she's got a big family, her husband earns buttons, and she's only got so much to spend. After all, she wants eight pair of shoes, and her money will only stretch to eighteen pence a pair

462

at the very most. But if yer can't do a deal with her, don't worry, we'll try another stall.'

Aggie's mouth opened wide in surprise. What did her mate think she was doing? But a kick in the shin warned her to be quiet. It was a painful warning, and if anyone else had done it they'd have been flat out by now. But Rita had a way with people so Aggie told herself to go along with her. That was why, when the man turned to her, he thought he was looking at a different woman. There was no sign of the battleaxe of a few minutes ago. 'Is it right that yer've got a big family, missus, and yer want eight pair of shoes?'

'That's right, lad, but I don't want to plead poverty. It's my feller's fault we've got so many kids, but he doesn't have the flaming worry of trying to feed and clothe them.' When Aggie sighed her bosom almost touched her chin. 'Still, that's not your worry, lad, so we'll try another stall. There's one not far from here.'

'Hang on a minute, don't let's be too hasty.' The man was thinking if she bought eight pairs of shoes he'd still make a good profit even if he let them go for eighteen pence a pair. 'Perhaps we can reach a mutual agreement. If yer buy eight pair of shoes, then I'll let yer have them for the one and six a pair. Now I can't be fairer than that, can I? I'm robbing meself at that price, but I'm all heart when it comes to children, I've got four meself.'

Aggie could afford to grin now. 'Not as active as my feller, then? Mind you, ye're on yer feet all day, while my feller thinks the only reason we were born with backsides was to sit on them.'

The stallholder managed a smile. If he'd been a brave man, he'd have said she probably thought we were born with mouths so we could talk all bleeding day. But he wasn't a brave man, so he said, 'Have a look around and see if yer can find what yer want, but they must be children's shoes, not adults'.'

'God bless yer, lad, there'll be a place in heaven for you, that's for sure.'

Rita smiled at the man while pulling her mate away from the stall. If she hadn't, she'd have burst out laughing. When they were out of the man's hearing, she chuckled, 'What a two-faced cow I've got for a mate! Yer were on the point of clocking him one five minutes ago, now yer've promised him a place in heaven.' She doubled up with laughter. 'What a pity you won't be there to see him.'

'Ay, I wouldn't be too sure about that if I were you, queen, 'cos I think I'll have the last laugh when the time comes. God has a sense of humour, yer know, and He might think I'll brighten the place up.' Aggie had just had a thought that pleased her. 'Anyway, ye're always saying I tell lies. Well, what about yerself? It was you what told that man I had eight kids, queen, not me.'

Rita had a joker up her sleeve, which she now brought into play. 'I bet your feller will get a laugh when he hears that yer told the stallholder he was very active in bed.'

'Oh, I won't tell him that, queen, I'm not daft. He'd do his nut if he thought I'd been speaking to a man about ... er ... about ... well, you know, personal things.'

'You might not tell him, but that doesn't mean no one else will.' Rita saw a mound of shoes on one of the trestle tables, and was making her way towards it when she was pulled up sharp. She'd been expecting it, and quickly dropped the smile from her face. 'What was that for, sunshine? Yer frightened the life out of me.'

'A fine mate you'd be if yer snitched to my feller! Yer know he's got no sense of humour, particularly when if comes to what happens behind bedroom doors.'

'I was pulling yer leg, sunshine, I'd never tell Sam anything like that! And if anyone else told him in front of me, I wouldn't know where to put me face, I'd be wishing the floor would open and swallow me up.'

Aggie's smile was wide. 'Ye're not the only one who can pull legs, yer know, queen, so don't be getting those fleecy bloomers in a twist.' Her eyes lighted on the piled-up shoes. 'Ooh, eh, queen, let's get stuck into that lot. I've got a feeling we're going to have a lucky day today.'

Rita agreed. 'I was just thinking the same thing. If we get the eight pair of shoes, which I'm sure we will out of that lot, then fate is on our side and we'll find what we want for our kids, and ourselves. I'd like to get meself a nice dress to wear on Christmas Day, just to remind Reg what I used to look like when we were courting. It's years since I've had anything nice to wear.'

'Oh, yer'll have no trouble finding a dress to suit you. You're so lucky, if yer fell down the lavvy yer'd come up smelling of roses.' Aggie had a pair

465

of boy's shoes in her hand, joined together by one of the laces. 'Whereas I'm so bleeding fat I need a tent to fit me. And there's not much chance of finding a tent with sleeves in.' Then she saw the funny side, and grinned. 'Not in a colour that would suit me, anyway.'

Rita didn't like to hear her mate making fun of herself, for she knew that deep down Aggie would give anything to be thinner. 'We'll find you a dress, don't worry. There's lots of big-made women around, ye're not on yer own.' She changed the subject, but made up her mind that they would look for a dress for her mate first, then she'd try for one for herself. 'Let's get the shoes, and that'll be one job off our mind.'

Rita had brought a big, well-worn canvas bag with her, thinking it would be large enough to hold everything they'd be buying in the market. It took the shoes with room to spare. The two friends left the stall in a happy frame of mind. They'd got what they wanted at the price they wanted. The next priority was trousers for the boys. They were in luck at that stall as well, for they walked away with three pair of decent trousers for the grand sum of two shillings and threepence. The trousers were all in good nick and had plenty of wear left in them. A good pressing with a hot iron and a wet cloth, and they'd come up like new. The boys would consider themselves very lucky.

'I was going to say there's only our dresses to get now, but I've remembered we said we'd get a coat for Mrs Ponsonby.' Rita changed the heavy

466

bag over to her other hand. 'She's about my size, near enough, so what fits me should fit her.'

'We've passed a few stalls with coats on so yer should find something suitable.' Aggie put her hand on the handle of the bag. 'Give it to me, it's heavy and we'll take turns carrying it.'

Rita was glad to pass it over for the canvas handles were digging into the flesh of her palms. 'Anything would be better than the coat she's wearing now. It's nearly falling to pieces, and it's always so crumpled I'm sure she sleeps in it.' She sighed. 'We're not exactly well off ourselves, but yer can always find someone worse off than yerself.'

They reached a stall with coats spread out on top of each other, and Aggie stood the bag between her legs. 'You have a root, queen, and I'll keep me eye on the bag. If yer see anything exciting, give us a shout.'

It took Rita five minutes to find a really nice coat for Mrs Ponsonby. It was a heavy tweed with a trim fur collar, and although the cuffs were slightly frayed, they could easily be turned up a little. She tried it on to show Aggie, and they both agreed it was a bargain at two shillings. But it wasn't the only coat Rita spotted. There was a navy blue heavy winter coat which seemed in good condition from what she could see of it. So she handed the first coat to Aggie, and pulled the navy blue one from under the pile to hold up against her.

'That's no good, queen,' Aggie shouted, 'yer'd get two of Mrs Ponsonby in that, it's miles too big.'

467

'The coat yer've got over yer arm is for Mrs Ponsonby, sunshine, I was thinking this one would fit you.'

Aggie pulled a face. 'Nah, it wouldn't.' She was so used to not being able to buy anything to fit her, she shook her head. 'Yer need glasses, queen, if yer think that'll go anywhere near me.'

'There's nothing wrong with my eyesight, Aggie Gordon, and I'll bet yer a penny that this coat will go on yer.'

'Away with yer, and don't be acting the goat.'

Rita huffed and she puffed. Grabbing the tweed coat off her mate's arm, she pushed the navy blue one at her. 'I'm not asking yer to try it on, sunshine, I'm telling yer to. Now do as ye're told and don't be so ruddy stubborn.'

And didn't the coat fit Aggie like a glove, and didn't the smile on her face show how pleased and proud she was? 'Ay, queen, it feels as though it's been made for me. Do I look posh in it?'

'Only like a million dollars, sunshine, or else Mae West.'

'Ooh, I wonder how much it is?' Aggie asked the question, but in her mind was already telling herself that no one was going to separate her from that coat. She loved the colour, it was a thick, warm material, and she felt at home in it. 'You go and ask how much it is, queen, 'cos yer seem to have more luck than me.'

The stallholder was an elderly woman with white hair plaited into a bun at the nape of her neck. A thick black knitted shawl covered her shoulders, and her heavy black skirt reached down to her sturdy buttoned boots. She had been watching the two women, and when Rita approached, said, 'That coat fits yer friend like a glove. Good quality, too, and never been worn much.'

Oh, dear, thought Rita, it sounds as though she's after a good price for it. It was probably worth it, too, but could Aggie afford it? 'She loves it, and with her being so big it's unusual for her to get anything that fits her. She's conscious of her size, too, so I had to talk her into trying it on.' There was no way Rita could tell even little white lies to this stallholder who was no doubt having to work hard to keep body and soul together. 'It depends how much yer want for the coat, 'cos my mate doesn't have much money.'

Faded blue eyes moved from Rita to where Aggie was standing. 'I couldn't let it go for less than three shillings. It's worth a lot more than that, it hasn't been worn much. Came from a house where the people can afford to throw clothes out after wearing them only a few times. My son goes out with his cart to the rich areas in the city, and sometimes gets a real bargain like the coat yer friend has taken a fancy to. I hope she can manage the three bob. She looks good in it, and looking at her I'd say she was a warm-hearted woman.'

Rita couldn't believe her luck. She wanted to run to Aggie, but made herself walk as she normally did. But with her back to the stallholder now, she was able to let her wide smile show. 'Three bob, sunshine, and a real bargain if ever I saw one. But don't look too pleased or the price might be put up. In all honesty, though, Aggie, it's the bargain of a lifetime, and yer'd be crazy not to jump at it.'

'And I would bleeding well jump if I didn't have this ruddy bag between me legs.' She thrust Mrs Ponsonby's coat at Rita and waved like mad to where the stallholder was standing. 'Go and pay her for me, queen, and tell her I'm really happy. Go on, I'll settle up with yer when we get home and are sitting down with a nice hot cuppa.' She grabbed Rita's arm as her friend went to walk away. 'I'll tell yer what, queen, you are definitely my lucky mascot, and I ain't going nowhere without yer in future.'

The stallholder took the three silver shillings. 'Is yer friend keeping the coat on?'

Rita grinned. 'It would take a very strong, brave person to separate my mate from that coat. Tomorrow she'll be walking up and down our street, swaggering like Mae West, until she's sure every neighbour has seen it. She'll be like a child with a new toy. But I'm made up for her, it's not often nice things happen to people like us. So thank you, and we both hope yer have a very happy Christmas.'

The little woman smiled. 'And the same to you, girl, the same to you.'

'I'm not going home without something for meself,' Rita said, a determined expression on her face. 'How soft you are! Yer get the bargain of a lifetime, now yer want to go home! It's a case of I'm all right, so sod you! Well, we're not leaving this market until I get meself a dress to wear on Christmas Day. And seeing as I'm the one with

470

the purse what has the money in for the tram fare home, then it's just too bad on you, isn't it? Unless yer feel in the mood to walk home, like.'

'There's no need to be sarky, queen, I only said me feet were killing me and me corns were giving me gyp. That's all I said, and yer jump down me throat.' And Aggie was only telling the truth, for her feet had a very heavy weight to carry around. 'I'll stay with yer till the bitter end, queen, so march on and I'll follow.'

Rita felt sorry for her, but didn't fancy going home with everything they had on their list except something for herself. 'There's only one more stall what sells decent dresses, so can yer hang on for a bit longer?'

Aggie knew how to bring a smile to her mate's face. 'When yer've got yer dress, will yer give me a piggyback to the tram stop?'

Rita grinned. 'Oh, yeah, 'course I will! And all the shopping as well!' She spotted a trestle table with dresses, blouses and jumpers all jumbled up together. 'Ay, keep yer fingers crossed, sunshine, there's a good girl. And while ye're standing there like a miserable wet week, say a little prayer I'll find something for meself.'

Aggie rolled her eyes towards the dull sky. 'Of course I'll say a prayer for yer, it'll pass the time away. Now get a ruddy move on before my feet take off on their own.'

Fifteen minutes later Aggie saw Rita walking towards her with a smile on her face and a scruffy paper bag in her hand. 'Got one then, did yer, queen?'

Rita nodded. 'Yeah, I got what I wanted, and

471

the woman even put it in a bag for me. So we've had a very successful day all round, sunshine, don't yer think?'

'Well, let's see the ruddy dress, queen, unless ye're keeping it a secret?'

'No, there's nothing hush-hush about a sixpenny dress. I'm pleased with it though, and that's the main thing. I'll show it to yer when we get home, and you've got yer feet up on the couch.' Rita lifted the heavy bag from between her friend's feet. 'I'll carry this, sunshine, and those two coats, it'll take the weight off yer. If we're lucky with catching a tram, we'll be home in twenty minutes.'

Aggie held her arm out so Rita could take the coats. 'Did yer hear that, queen?'

'Hear what, sunshine?'

'Yer must be going deaf, queen, if yer didn't hear nothing. When yer said we'd be home in twenty minutes, me corns said, "Thank God," and me feet said, "It's the last time we come to this bleeding market with yer."'

'Oh, I see, yer've got yer feet swearing now,' Rita said. 'It's a good job ye're the only one what can hear them.'

Their luck stayed with them, for a tram came along just as they got to the stop. And the conductor was standing on the platform, which was a godsend. 'Will yer be a pal and take this bag off me, please?' Rita asked, holding out the heavy canvas bag containing all their shopping except the two coats. 'Then I can give me mate a hand getting on.'

The conductor put the bag down in the well under the stairs, then looked from Rita to a very downcast Aggie. My God, he thought, she's carrying some weight. 'Hang on a tick. If you get on first, missus, I'll get off and give yer mate a hand from the back.'

Despite feeling miserable, Aggie couldn't help but laugh. 'Yer'll need both hands, lad, one for each cheek.'

Rita turned towards the aisle down the centre of the tram when she heard the driver and the conductor laughing. That was all Aggie needed. A bit of encouragement, and she'd be in her element telling the kind of jokes Rita would find embarrassing in front of strange men. So best find herself a seat and keep out of it, even though she could see smiles on the faces of passengers in front. But before she reached her seat, Rita heard gales of laughter and was too curious not to turn. And what she saw was one of the funniest sights she, or the passengers on that tram had ever seen. The conductor was on the pavement trying to get his shoulder under Aggie's bottom, and the driver had hold of each of her hands, trying to pull her on board. But she was laughing so much, really enjoying herself, they couldn't manage to get her eighteen stone off the ground.

In the end Rita walked back and stood behind the driver. 'If yer don't want to be here all day, let go of her and I'll show yer how it's done.'

Aggie was still grinning. 'Ye're a spoilsport, you are, a real misery guts!'

'Put one hand on that rail, sunshine, and the other on that one. Like we always do. And if yer don't behave yerself, so help me, I'm going to tell Sam yer've made lewd suggestions to two men

473

today, and we'll see what he's got to say to that.'

Once on the platform, Aggie grinned down at her. 'Ooh, I wouldn't if I were you, queen, 'cos my feller is dead ignorant. He'd ask yer to explain what lewd means, and then where would yer be, eh?' She frowned. 'By the way, what does it mean?'

Chapter Twenty-Five

Aggie flopped on to the couch without even taking her coat off. One shoe after the other flew across the room. 'Thank God for that, me bloody feet are dropping off. That walk from the tram stop was murder.'

Rita put the shopping down on the floor. 'You sit there, sunshine, and I'll make us a nice cup of tea. And I'll put some warm water in the bucket, if yer like, and yer can put yer feet in to steep for half an hour. It'll do yer the world of good.' She grinned. 'And I'm sure yer feet would be grateful.'

'Ooh, ay, queen, that would be just what the doctor ordered. Me feet have bucked themselves up no end, and me corns are throbbing for joy. They can't wait to soak in some nice warm water.' Aggie jerked her head. 'Well, don't just stand there, droopy drawers, get cracking.' Rita had reached the kitchen door when Aggie called, 'While ye're waiting for the kettle to boil, yer can show me yer dress.'

Rita popped her head around the door. 'Stop giving yer orders, Mrs Woman, just one thing at a time if yer don't mind. When yer've got yer feet in water, and a cup of tea in yer hand, then I'll show yer the dress. So have a little patience.'

After filling the kettle and putting a light to the stove, Rita stood the bucket in the sink and ran some cold water into it. She'd add hot water when the kettle boiled. While she was waiting, she leaned against the wall near the living room. 'Don't forget, we've got to give those shoes out this afternoon, and go to the Maypole for the groceries on the list Bessie gave us.'

Aggie groaned. 'Ay, queen, there's no way I could walk to the Maypole and back, me feet really are in a terrible state. Couldn't we leave it until tomorrow, when I'll feel more up to it? Besides, one day isn't going to make any difference.'

'It is if ye're running round in bare feet in this weather. And we promised Bessie we'd let the lads have them today. But there's no need for you to bother, I can take the shoes up meself, it won't take ten minutes. All I need do is hand them in to their mothers, 'cos the lads will be at school. And once I've had a cup of tea and a little sit down, I'll be refreshed and ready for the walk to the Maypole. I know that could wait till tomorrow, but I want to try and have a word with the manager. We'll need some cardboard boxes to make up the hampers, and if I can get him in a good mood I'll ask him to start saving some for us. And I'll ask the corner shop, as well, 'cos all those boxes are not going to be easy to come by.'

The kettle began to whistle and Rita made haste to switch the gas off. She poured half the boiling water into the brown teapot, the other half into the bucket. 'Take yer stockings off, sunshine, I'm bringing it through.' She lifted the bucket out of the sink by the handle, and after testing the water wasn't too hot or too cold, was carrying it through to the living room when the

476

sight she met brought her to an abrupt halt. 'In the name of God, Aggie, have yer no shame? I can see everything yer've got!' Rita was shaking her head, wondering whether she dare laugh, for her friend was trying to cock one leg over the other, hoping by doing so she could reach down to pull her stocking off. But her knee kept slipping off, and her bosom and tummy were no help, they flatly refused to move out of the way.

Bright red in the face, and huffing and puffing, Aggie glared at her. 'I've got nothing you haven't got, queen, so don't be going all bleeding shy on me.' Her eyes narrowed. 'If yer so much as crack yer face, so help me I'll pour that bucket of water over yer.'

'I really don't think ye're in a position to make threats, sunshine, do you? Besides, I'm much faster on me feet than you are, yer'd never catch me.' Rita put the bucket down and doubled over with laughter. 'I'm sorry, Aggie, but if yer could see yerself, yer'd see the funny side of it.' She moved forward. 'Here, let me take yer stockings off for yer, then yer can have a nice cup of tea while yer feet are soaking.'

After a few seconds, when Rita was having no success, Aggie said, 'It would help if yer took me garters off first, queen, 'cos they're what's keeping me stockings up.'

'Yer can just sod off, Aggie Gordon, I'm not putting me hand up yer clothes. Yer can take yer own garters off, I'll see to the tea.'

Aggie grabbed Rita's arm before she could move away and with her free hand lifted the skirt of her dress to reveal a garter. It was a piece of well-worn elastic, tied in a knot, holding up her stocking. Only to the knee, though, for the top of the stocking was hanging loose.

'In the name of God,' Rita said, 'don't ever get run over when ye're out with me, sunshine, 'cos I'd either die of shame, or say I wasn't with yer.'

'Listen to me, queen. Let me tell yer that for me to get a garter on at all is no less than a ruddy miracle. If I sit down, I can't reach me bleeding feet, me chest and me tummy are in the way. And if I stand up, I can't even see me feet or me legs. I do what I can, but I'm not a ruddy contortionist. So think on that when I'm lying in the gutter and you're telling everyone that yer've never seen me in yer life before.'

'Oh, stop feeling sorry for yerself, Aggie Gordon, and let me get those stockings off yer. If yer carry on much longer, the water in the bucket will be cold and so will the teapot.' The stockings were removed in a flash and put on Aggie's knee. 'And if yer behave yerself, I might just have a nice surprise for yer.' Rita brought the bucket nearer to the couch. 'But one moan out of yer, sunshine, and I'll give it to the woman next door.'

'Ah, yer wouldn't do that, not to yer mate.' Aggie frowned. 'And what are yer playing at? You are the woman next door!'

Rita grinned. 'I know that, sunshine, and aren't you the lucky one, having me for a neighbour? Yer should be counting yer blessings, not moaning.'

It was three o'clock when Rita got back to Aggie's, but she was feeling very pleased with herself and wearing a wide smile. 'Oh, Aggie, yer missed a treat. Yer should have seen the faces on the women when I gave them the shoes. They were absolutely over the moon. They couldn't thank us enough. They'll tell yer themselves when they see yer. I said yer would have been with me but yer feet were tired. So stick to that story, sunshine, and don't forget the shoes were from us and a friend of ours.'

'How did yer get on at the Maypole? Did yer manage to have a word with the manager?'

Rita nodded. 'When I told him Bessie had been lucky to get a sum of money from a man who wanted to help some poor people, he was really pleased. And of course it helped when I said she would be buying the groceries from his shop. So, to make sure I got some boxes off him, I gave him the order and said we'd pick it up tomorrow. And he said he may have a few more boxes by the weekend.' Rita gave a sigh of contentment. 'So, sunshine, all in all, it's been a very rewarding day.'

There was no sign of the bucket now, and Aggie had a pair of scruffy slippers on her feet. 'I should have looked in the market for a pair of slippers for meself, 'cos these are Sam's and they're falling to pieces. I could probably have got a pair for two pence and they'd have been well worth the money.' Remembering the market, she remembered something else too. 'Ay, queen, what did yer do with the dress yer got? When yer'd gone, I looked high and low for the bag but I couldn't see it nowhere.'

'No, yer wouldn't, sunshine, 'cos I had a change of mind and took it with me. I knew yer wouldn't be able to keep yer hands off it. I thought we'd take everything over to Bessie's when she gets in from work, and she can see what we bought this morning. She has a right to know what we managed to get, and hear how much it cost, even though I know she trusts us not to diddle her.'

Aggie looked aggrieved at the mere thought. 'She knows we wouldn't do that, queen, not after she's been so good to us.'

'You should be going over to light her fire soon, so I'll come with yer,' Rita said. 'We can take everything over, including the coats and the children's things.'

Aggie's jaw dropped. 'I don't have to take me coat, do I? I was hoping I could start wearing that tomorrow.'

'Blimey, Aggie, ye're worse than a child! Can't yer let Bessie see it first? She can have a look-see at everything, then hide them away upstairs before Mrs Sinclair calls to pick Milly up.' Rita looked down at her friend's feet. 'I can take them over, sunshine, if yer feet are still sore. And I can light both fires, come to that, it won't kill me.'

Aggie wasn't having any of that. If there was anything going on, she wanted to be part of it. 'No, I'll do me whack, queen, as well as you, it's only fair. After all, I'm getting paid for it so it's like a proper job.'

'Yeah, ye're right, sunshine, we do get paid for it. So, 'cos ye're me mate, and not a bad old stick, I'll open the bag and let yer see me new dress.' Then Rita shook her head. 'No, I'll give you the privilege of opening the bag, and yer can tell me what yer think of me taste in high fashion.'

Grabbing the bag from her, Aggie chuckled.

480

'High fashion me backside, all for a dress what cost yer a tanner.' But her chuckle faded when she realised she was holding more than one dress. 'What's all this? How many bleeding dresses have yer bought yerself?'

'Only one, sunshine, I'm not greedy.' Rita felt very happy, the wait had been worth it to see her mate's face. 'There was one I thought would fit you, and I remembered your Kitty was the only one we hadn't got anything for, so there's one there for her as well. I hope they fit, it was just a case of guessing.' She leaned forward and pulled one of the dresses from Aggie's hand. It was a beige and brown short-sleeved cotton dress, more suitable for the summer than winter really, but it was very neat, and would look nice when it had been pressed. 'This is mine, and don't yer dare say it isn't high fashion because by the time I've finished with it, I could say I'd bought it at George Henry Lee and people would believe me. Now, don't sit staring down as though they're going to bite yer, and I don't think yer need me to tell yer which is yours and which is Kitty's.'

For a whole minute, Aggie was struck dumb. Then, in a tearful voice, she said, 'Honest, queen, this is the biggest surprise I've ever had. I'm not half bleeding lucky to have you for a neighbour.'

'Aggie Gordon, I do believe ye're going to cry! Well, don't yer dare let any tears fall on those dresses, not after paying sixpence and threepence for them.'

Rita had spotted the navy blue dress on the stall before she'd seen the one she liked for herself, and when she saw the size of it was sure it would fit her friend. 'Well, go on, sunshine, don't keep me in suspense. Have a look and see if it will fit yer. I know Kitty's will be all right, 'cos the woman on the stall has a girl her age and she picked it out for me.'

It wasn't often that Aggie prayed, but as she shook the dress out and held it against herself, she said a prayer. 'How does that look, queen?'

'I reckon it'll fit yer like a glove, same as the coat. But the only way to tell is to try it on. So come into the kitchen.'

Aggie put Kitty's dress down and lumbered to her feet. 'I ain't standing in no bleeding cold kitchen catching me death of cold, not when there's a fire in here. So if yer don't want to see me in all me glory, queen, I suggest you go and wait in the bleeding kitchen.'

'Have yer no modesty?' Rita asked as her friend pulled her dress up by the waist. 'I could no more get stripped in front of you than fly.' As the dress was pulled higher, an expanse of bare leg appeared, followed by blue fleecy-lined bloomers. 'Oh, I'm going to stand in the kitchen before I see any more of yer body.'

A muffled voice came from inside the dress. 'No, wait, queen, 'cos I need yer to help pull me dress over me bosom. And before yer start moaning, I know I have to do it meself every day, but it's murder getting the waist over these two bleeding big balloons I've got. So while you're here, yer may as well give me a hand. Just grab hold and pull, while I breathe in.'

The state of Aggie was such that Rita couldn't keep her laughter back. It wasn't so much the bulging tummy, or the rolls of fat on her legs, 'cos none of that could be helped. It was the huge safety pin keeping her bloomers up that was the last straw. Laughing as the tears rolled down her cheeks, Rita said, 'I'm sure if Laurel and Hardy could see yer, sunshine, they'd offer to make yer a partner. Laurel, Hardy and Gordon. Oh, what a scream it would be.'

'I'll give yer something to scream about if yer don't hurry up and get this bleeding dress off me. Ye're having the time of yer life while I'm suffocating. I can't get me breath.'

Rita gave one last tug, and Aggie's head appeared. She was bright red in the face and her chest was heaving. 'I'd have been a bloody sight quicker doing it meself,' she groaned. 'If me breasts weren't so firmly attached, yer'd have pulled the ruddy things off.'

Rita put a curled fist to the stitch in her side. 'It's a long time since I had such a good laugh, sunshine, but I wasn't making fun of yer, I think too much of yer for that. I know if yer could have seen yerself, yer'd have laughed louder than me.'

'I'll do a deal with yer,' Aggie said, keeping her face deadpan. 'If this dress fits me, I'll love yer till the day I die. If it doesn't go near me, I'll chase yer down the street with the stiff brush in me hand.'

Rita nodded. 'It's a deal, so let's be having yer. I really hope it fits yer, sunshine, 'cos it's a nice dress. But if it does, it's going over to Bessie's with the rest of the stuff. Nobody is allowed to have anything until Christmas Day. The kids have got to wait, otherwise they'll have nothing to wake up to on Christmas morning, and the same applies to us. So I want yer to say yer agree before yer try the dress on?'

Aggie made a grab for it and held it to her bosom. 'D'yer know what, Rita Wells, up till a minute ago I thought yer were as good as Cinderella's fairy godmother. But I've changed me mind, and now yer remind me of her wicked step-sisters.'

'That's too bad, sunshine, I'm sure I'll live. Now put that dress on, for heaven's sake, or Milly will be home from school and I don't want her to see anything. Not that there's anything here for her, but she might just let it slip to one of the kids. So put a move on, slow coach.'

The dress slipped over Aggie's head, over her bosom and then her tummy. She didn't have to tug or pull, and couldn't believe her luck. Even her chins were pleased for her when she shook her head in disbelief. 'I take every word back, queen, and once again ye're my fairy godmother. I'm beginning to think I'm dreaming and will wake up to a big disappointment. I'm not, am I, queen?'

'You are not!' Rita said, straightening the neat round collar on the navy dress. 'Right now yer look like a very attractive lady with a face like a film star and a figure like Mae West. Yer really look a treat, sunshine, and yer'll have your feller licking his lips when he sees yer on Christmas Day.'

Aggie's bosom swelled with pride. It was a long time since she'd heard compliments like that. Mind you, she wasn't daft, she knew her mate was only being kind, but she had to admit she did think she looked more than passable. And although it might be wishful thinking on her part, she'd swear it made her look thinner. Why, she could almost see her feet. She cast her eyes down again, then asked herself if she was seeing things. Was that her toes, or was it a dirty mark on the lino? Better not ask, 'cos ignorance was bliss.

When Milly came home from school she didn't need any persuading to stay in Rita's and play Snakes and Ladders with Jack. The girls in the street were more friendly with her now, and she could have played with them, but no, her best mate was Jack. So she was out of the house when Bessie came home from work to be greeted by a smiling Rita and Aggie.

'What is this, a welcoming committee?' Bessie walked straight to the fire to warm her hands. 'Yer both look like the cat what got the cream, so I presume yer've had a good day?'

'Well, we've a lot to tell yer, sunshine, but will have to make it quick because we've got our dinners on the go. Anyway, in a nutshell, we got the shoes for the boys and gave them to their mothers, who were absolutely delighted. I bet the lads are playing out in them right now.'

'Oh, that's grand, sweetheart, a job well done. And I bet the lads are blessing the pair of yer. Did yer manage to get them from the market, then?'

Rita nodded. 'We got everything we wanted from there. A lovely coat for Mrs Ponsonby, and Aggie got herself one which is a real smasher. Trousers for the three boys, a dress for Kitty, and

485

a dress each for me and Aggie. And I've ordered the foodstuffs from the Maypole. I left the list with the manager and am picking it up tomorrow. I've paid for it, as well. I told Mr Lacy you'd been given some money to help out a few poor families over Christmas, and he's going to save as many cardboard boxes as he can. I told him there'd be another big order for him Christmas week.' She shrugged her shoulders and added, 'I can't see him having enough boxes to spare, 'cos he'll have a lot of orders to be delivered. Still, we can ask the corner shop, I'm sure Sally and Alf will help out when they know what they're for.'

'Yer have been busy,' Bessie said. 'I'd have been lost without yer.'

'Ooh, ay, I can't take all the credit, it was team work. Aggie did just as much as me. In fact, she did most of the carrying. We work well together, don't we, sunshine?'

This compliment took Aggie's chubby cheeks on an upward journey which almost had her eyes disappearing from view. She was having some really nice things said about her today. 'Yeah, I bargained at the shoe stall, and Rita bargained at the next. We did really well, didn't we, queen?'

Rita nodded, knowing her mate would be tickled pink and feeling very important. 'We did that, sunshine, and next time we've got a few bob, we'll take a trip down there again. But now, down to business.' She passed two pieces of paper over to Bessie. 'One's the list of all the items we said we'd get – the prices are at the side. I couldn't get a receipt for anything from the market 'cos they don't give them. But the Maypole receipt is there,

486

so yer can check the prices, and I've got the rest of the money here.' She put a hand in her pocket and brought out a large amount of coppers and silver. 'I think yer'll find the money will tally with the lists, Bessie, except yer'll have to take our tram fares into consideration.'

Bessie shook her head slowly. 'Yer don't really think I'm going to sit down and check, do yer, Rita? If I can't trust you two, then I can't trust anyone. I think yer've done wonders to have any money left out of five pounds. The way you two are going on, we'll have enough to put quite a lot in the hampers.' She suddenly remembered something. 'Oh, I nearly forgot again. I didn't put margarine down on the list, or bread. And if yer'd be angels could you order eighteen chickens from the butcher, and ask him to have them plucked and cleaned. It'll save anyone having to spend Christmas Eve with their hand up the backside of a chicken.'

Rita frowned. 'I thought it was fifteen hampers yer were making up, so why eighteen chickens?'

'To use in sandwiches for the two parties. And ask the butcher how much a decent-sized bird will be so I'll know where I'm working. And tell Stan not to worry, he'll get his money. I'll pay him a few days before the holiday. And seeing as it's a bloody good order for him, ask him to put a piece of dripping in with each one.'

'Are yer sure yer've got enough money for all this, sunshine?' Rita sounded doubtful. 'Yer won't get a chicken under three bob.'

'I'll sit and do a list tonight, and if yer find out roughly what the chickens are going to cost, I can pretty much work it out to the penny. Potatoes and veg will only be coppers, I'm almost sure I'll have money over. Enough to put a tangerine and an apple in each hamper to make the kids happy.' Bessie looked at the clock. 'Don't yer think yer'd better be on yer way, before yer husbands come in from work?'

Rita jumped to her feet. 'Yeah, come on, Aggie, the men will want feeding. But before we go, Bessie, yer've had the good news, but I'm afraid there's some bad news for yer.'

She was crafty enough to know that if it was really bad news, they'd have told her straight away. 'Oh, aye, what is it?'

'Well, we wanted yer to see what we'd bought, but we didn't want anyone else to see it 'cos it would spoil things for the kids. So it's all on your landing for yer to look through. We haven't just dumped it there, it's all neat and tidy. But d'yer think yer could keep it here until me and Aggie get a chance to take our stuff? The dresses and trousers will need washing and pressing, but we'll have to do it while the kids are at school.'

'Don't worry yer heads about it, I'll sort it out. I can put it in the bottom of me wardrobe until ye're ready for it. Now get home and see to the family.'

Rita stepped down on to the pavement. 'The only big things that will take up a lot of room are the two coats, but I can take Mrs Ponsonby's tomorrow and that'll be out of the way. Aggie wants to wear hers now, but she's not getting it until Father Christmas brings it down her chimney. She's begged, and had a little weep, but

I've put me foot down. Christmas Day and not before.'

Bessie made sure the clothes were off the landing and in her bedroom before Milly came over for her dinner. She was afraid that if the girl saw the boys' trousers she wouldn't be able to keep it to herself. The temptation to tell her best friend Jack would be too great.

They were eating their meal and not a word had been spoken for a while. This was unusual as Milly was a real chatterbox, never stopped talking usually during a meal. When Bessie shot a quick glance her way, she noticed the girl seemed preoccupied, as though there was something on her mind. She was soon proved right.

'Auntie Bessie, can I ask you something?' Milly kept her eyes down, her hand gripping the fork which was chasing a potato around her plate. 'You won't get mad at me, will you?'

'Now, Amelia Sinclair, when have I ever got mad with you? You can always talk to me, and I will always listen, yer should know that by now. Whatever it is yer want to ask, do it now and give that poor potato a rest, 'cos it's worn out running around that ruddy plate.'

Milly giggled, put the fork down and addressed the potato. 'I'm sorry, Mr Potato, but you can have a rest now while I talk to Auntie Bessie.' She laid down the fork and leaned her elbows on the table. 'Will I be here on Christmas Day, Auntie Bessie? Jack said there's going to be a party, and I would like to be here for that.'

Bessie wiped the back of a hand across her lips.

489

'I'm afraid I can't answer you, sweetheart, because I don't know. I would love you to be here, yer know that, but it's not up to me. Hasn't your mother mentioned it?'

Milly shook her head, looking downcast. 'Mother hasn't said anything about Christmas, and I don't like to ask her. But she might go to her friend's, I'm sure she'd like that better than being just the two of us.'

'I really don't know what to say, Milly, but yer know I'd love yer to be here. It's up to your mother, though, there's little I can do about it.' But the sadness on the pretty young face was more than Bessie could bear. 'Look, I'll tell yer what, sweetheart, I'll have a word with yer mother when she calls for yer. I can't promise anything, but I'll do me best.' And hoping to put a smile back where it belonged, she added, 'I'll get me guardian angel to have a word with her, too, 'cos she can be very persuasive when she's asked nicely to help me out.'

This cheered Milly up no end, and she giggled, 'Yer could ask the door and the fireplace as well. I bet they'd help if they could, being good friends of yours.'

'The door won't help, I'm afraid, 'cos it blames me for leaving it out in the cold all the time. I'm fed up telling it that every door is out in the cold, but I may as well talk to the wall.' Bessie leaned across the table, her face one big smile. 'Ay, I forgot about the wall, so there's another one to get on our side. Oh, I don't think we can lose with so many friends, it'll be a walkover.' She reached across for Milly's plate. 'Come on, sweetheart,

490

let's get the dishes washed, 'cos yer mother will be here any minute.'

Evelyn's face was set when she came into Bessie's living room. She had made a decision and wanted to get it off her chest before she weakened. When she sat down, she addressed her daughter. 'Amelia, will you be a good girl and go home while I have a word with Miss Maudsley in private? I won't leave you on your own for long, and as the fire will be lit the room will be nice and warm. You could take the doll for company.'

'Yes, Mother.' Milly draped her coat over her arm. 'Shall I put the kettle on so you can have a cup of tea when you come in?'

Evelyn shook her head. 'I would rather you didn't light the gas, just in case of an accident. But I shan't be long.'

'Put that coat on, sweetheart, 'cos it's bitter out,' Bessie told her. 'I know it's only two or three steps, but yer could still catch cold.'

Evelyn sat nervously fingering her gloves as she waited for the door to close on her daughter. Then she wasted no time. 'I have thought over what you said about my late husband's family, Bessie, and intend doing what you suggested I should do. It is a drastic step for me, after eight years, and I risk being shunned. But I will not give Philip up without a fight. I love him dearly, and he returns my love. It remains to be seen if he will still feel the same when he knows I have lied to him about Amelia.' She screwed up her eyes and shook her head. 'No, I have not told him a deliberate lie, though I have acted one and that

491

is as bad. But I believe there might be a way of keeping his love. After the holidays, I intend to visit Mr Lister-Sinclair with Amelia. When he sees the likeness between my daughter and his son, I don't think he could or indeed would want to deny she is truly his granddaughter. For Amelia is so like Charles it is uncanny. And if he accepts Amelia, then the hardest part of my battle will be over.'

'I think it is the best thing to do for everyone's sake. Amelia's grandfather would probably welcome yer both with open arms.' Bessie's heart went out to the woman she'd once thought of as a stuck-up snob, but who now looked sad and vulnerable. 'Yer'd never forgive yerself if yer didn't try.'

'My hope is that this time my father-in-law will believe me. It would make it so much easier for me to be truthful with Philip. You see, Bessie, my one fear is that, like Mr Lister-Sinclair, Philip won't believe the man I married was the father of Amelia. After all, any man could have been, in fact, I could have been a woman who bestowed her favours freely.' Tears weren't far away, and she was quiet for a while until she composed herself. 'It doesn't automatically mean Philip will gather me to him and swear undying love for me. Rather than still wanting to marry me, he may turn me away for what he sees as my deceitfulness. But I love him so much I am prepared to throw myself at his mercy. And more than that I cannot do.'

'If he loves you as much as yer love him, then I'm sure he won't turn away from yer. Why should he? You are a married woman who had a baby by a husband killed in the war. Is there anything so terrible in that? Of course there isn't, and yer mustn't let anyone think you are ashamed. Keep that in mind and yer'll find the courage and the strength to do what yer have to do.'

Evelyn leaned forward and took both of Bessie's hands in hers. 'If I hadn't been so selfish all these years, thinking myself too good for anyone in this street, then what good friends we could have been. You would probably have talked sense into me years ago, making me confront Mr Lister-Sinclair with the truth. But then I would never have met Philip. I might have lived in luxury, and Amelia and I would have wanted for nothing. However, I would have missed two very important events in my life. One is meeting the man I adore, and the other is being brought down from my ivory tower to meet the most genuine people I'm ever likely to meet. I've been taught well by you and your friends, Bessie, and it's a lesson I will never forget. That money doesn't mean a thing if you haven't got good friends who are warm and compassionate.'

Bessie could feel a lump forming in her throat. 'I'm sorry meself that we left it so late to become friends, and I hope that now we are, we always will be. And I'm glad yer've decided to take the bull by the horns, for I do believe you will come through it a very happy woman. I hope so, for Amelia's sake. But I hope yer'll never stop me from seeing her? I have grown to love her very much.'

'That's a promise I will make, and which will be

493

easy to keep. My daughter would never forget you, or allow me to either.' Evelyn stood up. 'I'd better go, I don't like leaving Amelia on her own too long. But I do thank you for making me see sense, and will keep you informed every step of the way.'

'Tomorrow night, when yer've got five minutes to spare, I'll tell yer what we've bought so far with the money. A lot of poor people in this street will bless you and your friend for giving them the chance to enjoy Christmas with food and warmth.' Bessie told herself now was the time. 'Oh, speaking of Christmas, will I be having Milly? That's if yer want to spend the time with yer friend, of course. If you are, I'd be very happy to have her for the two days.'

'Thank you, Bessie, I'd love to be with my friend. And I don't think I'm being selfish, I know my daughter would much prefer to spend Christmas with you and your friends.'

Chapter Twenty-Six

On the Monday of Christmas week, Bessie spent her dinner break going into town to buy material for the two dresses she had to make for the holidays. If she didn't put a move on they wouldn't be made in time, and then she'd have no present for Milly or a decent dress for herself. There was no time for her to dawdle in the big store, so she headed straight to the material department. Thankfully there were few customers, for most people who were able to make their own clothes would have allowed themselves more time than she had. Still, she was working every day and couldn't be in two places at once.

As she approached the long counter covered with bales of material of all colours, her eyes lighted on a roll of crêpe in a lovely warm deep wine colour. That's for me, she said to herself, just what I had in mind. She beckoned one of the assistants over and asked her for three yards, which was ample for her with her small, slim figure. While the assistant was busy, she walked along the counter, eyes searching for a colour which would suit Milly. And then she spotted it. A soft green, the same colour as Milly's eyes. It was in a linen material, medium thickness, which would be suitable for wear in summer or winter. She could make a small round collar in white, which would set it off nicely. So the assistant was

495

asked to cut two yards off, and would she kindly wrap both materials together to make it easier for Bessie to carry?

Once out of the shop, she hurried to the tram stop. She'd be hard pushed to get back to her sewing machine before the buzzer sounded, but she wouldn't get into trouble for she was otherwise always punctual and never took time off. Her tummy was rumbling with hunger, but it would have to rumble until she got back to work. She'd brought two sandwiches in with her and had left them on her machine, covered by a roll of cloth. She'd have to wait until her boss had his back turned or was out of sight in his office before she could eat them. Anyway, she was feeling so pleased with her purchases she wouldn't be upset if she got told off.

Once settled on the tram, Bessie let her body sway from side to side with the movement, as her mind drifted over the latest events. Life was good right now with everything ordered for the hampers, which would be picked up by the very happy recipients on the morning of Christmas Eve, about ten o'clock, to give the butcher time to have them delivered. When Bessie had first told her neighbours in the street, a few days ago, their faces showed they didn't believe her. They took some convincing at first, for nobody had ever offered them a helping hand before. Then she'd been hugged and kissed so much she expected to be bruised all over. But it would have been worth it just to see a smile on the thin faces of these careworn women who had been dreading Christmas without even money for food, let alone presents for their children. And what mother doesn't want to see the happiness on their children's faces when they think Father Christmas has been and left them a present?

Bessie was brought out of her reverie by the conductor dinging the bell to warn the driver there were passengers wanting to alight at the next stop. When she glanced through the window she saw it was hers. She picked up the paper bag with the material in, and clung to the back of each of the seats between her and the platform. She swung herself down on to the pavement with a smile on her face when she remembered there were only five more days to go. She'd have to move fast to have the two dresses finished, but she'd get there. Once she started she'd go like the clappers.

Rita was taking a flat iron off the gas stove when she heard the entry door latch slotting into place. 'Oh, no,' she groaned aloud, 'I was hoping to get these finished and out of the way before the kids come in from school.' Putting the iron back on the gas ring, she lifted the net curtain and saw Aggie walking up the back yard. But it wasn't the same Aggie she was used to seeing, with untidy hair, stained pinny and stockings crumpled round her ankles. Oh, no, this Aggie was walking with the air of someone of note, her head held high and bust standing to attention. Rita didn't bother opening the door, she knew her neighbour would walk in without knocking. So she quickly picked up the iron, pretending she hadn't seen anything.

Aggie shut the door behind her and waited for her mate to notice her. 'Busy are yer, queen? I see yer pressing the boys' trousers.'

Rita didn't look up. 'Yeah, I want to get them out of the way before they come in from school. I've done the best I can with their shirts, and they look quite presentable, so that'll be them finished.' She was dying to look up, could imagine her mate getting all hot and bothered by this time. But Rita told herself to wait and see what Aggie would do to draw attention to herself.

'I've pressed Kenny's trousers and Kitty's dress, and put them away in the wardrobe so they won't see them. And I've done me own dress as well.' Aggie was indeed getting all hot and bothered. She'd gone to the trouble of dolling herself up to the nines, and her mate hadn't even looked at her! 'Have yer pressed your dress yet?'

'Yeah, I did mine first.' Rita didn't turn a hair, just kept on pressing even though she knew she wasn't making a ha'porth of difference to the trousers because the iron had gone cool. 'It's come up a treat, looks really nice on me.'

That did it for Aggie. 'Well, you miserable cow! I suppose yer've put yer dress away in the wardrobe without letting me see it on yer, have yer? That's dead mean of yer, that is, seeing as I've gone to the trouble of coming to show yer what mine looks like on.'

Rita was chuckling inside. 'It looks very nice on yer, sunshine, dead smart.'

'How would yer know that, smart arse, when yer can't even be bothered to turn yer head to see what I look like?'

'I heard the entry door go, sunshine, and lifted the curtain to see who it was. And, to my complete and utter amazement, I see a stranger walking up the yard.' Rita put the iron back on the stove. 'I had to look twice, and it was only seeing the blue fleecy-lined bloomers that I realised it was me mate and not Ethel Barrymore.'

Aggie bent down. 'My bloomers are not showing, clever clogs, 'cos I've put new elastic in the legs. So ye're not so smart, after all.'

'Take no notice of me, Aggie, 'cos I'm only jealous. Here's me, looking like a scullery maid, and you dressed to kill. I was taken aback, I can tell yer, jealousy eating at the very heart of me. In fact it was worse than jealousy, it was envy. And as yer know, envy is one of the deadly sins.'

'All right, all right, queen, yer've had yer twopennyworth of fun now so let's have a bit of honesty out of yer. How d'yer like me dress, and does it look nice on me?'

'Aggie, yer really look great. The dress suits yer, it fits yer curves as though it's been made for yer, and it makes yer look a lot thinner. Ye're never likely to get such a good bargain in yer life again. When yer go out in that, with yer new coat on, the neighbours will think there's a new family moved into the street.' Rita kissed her on the cheek. 'Just wait until Sam sees yer, his eyes will pop out of his head.'

Aggie's chuckle should have warned her neighbour. 'It's not his eyes I'm after, queen, my thoughts are a bit lower down.'

'Don't you say another word, Aggie Gordon, or yer'll be sorry.' Rita wagged a stiffened finger

499

under her friend's nose. 'Ye're likely to end up on yer backside in the yard, and that wouldn't do yer posh dress much good.'

Aggie managed to look aggrieved. 'I don't know what's wrong with you, Rita Wells. Ye're a married woman, like meself, have had two kids, like meself, and yer husband must have got the same parts to his body as mine has.' She stopped as a thought apparently entered her head, gave a little nod then went on, 'Mind you, your feller might have the same number of parts, but it doesn't mean his are the same size as my feller's. And I'm just beginning to see why yer haven't got no sense of humour, and never laugh when I tell yer a dirty joke. *That's* why there's never a smile on yer gob in the mornings when I come in full of the joys of spring after a night of passion.' Oh, how Aggie's thoughts ran ahead of her. She'd bring a smile to her mate's face if it killed her. 'Yer know, I always thought we were good friends, helping each other out in times of trouble. So it makes me feel really sad that yer have suffered in silence instead of sharing yer troubles with me.'

'What troubles?' Rita asked, while knowing full well she was walking into a trap. 'I haven't got no troubles, what are yer on about?'

'Yer can tell me, queen, yer know yer can trust me not to tell no one. And I'm the best person to ask about any problems ye're going through in the bedroom department. Yer shouldn't just lie there, gazing at the ceiling and thinking of England, when yer could be having the time of yer life. My feller sends thrills up and down me spine, has me crying out with desire, and takes

500

me on a journey to heaven and back. Yer just don't know what ye're missing, queen, yer really don't.'

'Ah, but that's the point, sunshine, I don't miss it. Not one tiny cry or scream, not one plea for more, not one creak or twang of the bedsprings. And many's the night me and Reg have lain there listening to Sam pleading, "Ah, not again, girl, I'm worn out! It's all right for you, sitting on yer backside all day, but I've just put in a day's hard work, I haven't got the energy. Now turn on yer side and behave yerself until Saturday night."'

But Rita should have known she couldn't get the better of her mate. For as Aggie stood there with a look on her face that could have been anger or horror, she was actually using the time to think of a really good answer. 'D'yer mean you and Reg lie there and listen to our private conversation? Yer have no right to listen in, queen, that's being nosy.'

'Aggie, sunshine, once you get in yer bedroom, nothing is private because yer've got such a loud voice. If yer don't want to be heard, keep it down.'

'Ah, is that why we never hear you and Reg enjoying yerselves? D'yer put gags in yer mouth, so we can't hear yer?' Aggie dropped her head. 'It just goes to show, yer never really know who yer bleeding friends are.' She began to click her tongue. 'Yer've really taken me by surprise, queen, I'm cut to the quick. I mean, fancy your Reg lying there, listening to me pleading and not coming to my aid.'

Rita chuckled, 'How could he come to yer aid

501

when yer were in bed with yer husband?'

'Yeah, I know all that, queen, but Reg knew my feller wasn't up to it, and knowing I was desperate, he could have come and taken over. I mean, he's a good mate of Sam's, he could have helped him out. Sam would have appreciated it.' Aggie saw Rita walking towards her with a very stern expression on her face, and tried to reason with her. 'One man is as good as another in a dark room, queen, and you would have gained from it, too! I've got a few tricks up me sleeve I could have taught Reg, and yer'd be surprised how much more exciting yer love life would have been. You and your feller wouldn't be lying there like dummies every night, listening to me and Sam enjoying ourselves, 'cos yer'd be too busy trying out the new tricks I'd taught him.'

Her face deadpan, Rita lifted the latch on the kitchen door. 'On yer way, sunshine, I've got too much to do to listen to what yer get up to in yer bedroom. So yer can just poppy off.'

Aggie's jaw dropped. 'Yer mean I get all dolled up in me new dress, comb me ruddy hair, and I don't even get asked if I want a cup of tea? Ye're taking yer spite out on me 'cos yer don't like hearing what goes on in me bedroom?'

Rita shook her head. 'No, that's not the reason I'm throwing yer out, sunshine, it's because yer were prepared to tell my Reg the secret of your fantastic love life, instead of telling me.' She couldn't keep her face straight any longer, her cheeks were aching. 'It's me what's supposed to be yer mate, not my Reg.'

Aggie pushed her friend aside and rushed into

502

the living room before Rita could stop her. 'For one cup of tea, with a spoonful of sugar in, I will sit here and tell yer everything yer want to know about how to make your feller a happy man.'

Rita closed the back door and faced her mate. 'Yer know I don't like bad language or crude words, don't yer? So before yer get a cup of tea, I want yer to promise that what yer tell me will be really romantic, with no crude words about body parts.'

As she looked up at her neighbour, Aggie was thinking to herself that this cup of tea was going to be hard come by. How could she explain what went on in bed if she was stuck with making it romantic, and no crude words about body parts? Blimey, there was only one body part needed to give yer thrills of excitement, so if she couldn't be crude, what could she call it? Oh, she'd think of something while the kettle was boiling. 'All right, queen, yer've got yerself a deal.'

Rita was doubled up with silent laughter as she put the kettle on the stove. Many's the night her and Reg, lying in bed, had been convulsed as they listened to the antics of their neighbours. Not so much Sam as Aggie, who didn't know how to keep her voice down. And how she was going to tell Rita now about making love, without using crude words ... well, she couldn't wait to find out. Particularly one part of Sam's anatomy that seemed to be Aggie's favourite, and for which she had several names.

The kettle began to whistle and Rita reached for a cloth to cover her hand from the steam as she poured the boiling water into the teapot.

Perhaps she shouldn't encourage her friend, she might hear more than she'd bargained for. And it wouldn't be fair to encourage her then tell her off if her language, natural to her, was objectionable to Rita. No, it wasn't fair to do that to a good mate and neighbour.

'Here yer are, sunshine, a cup of nice, sweet tea. And I managed to find two biscuits, so there's one in yer saucer.' Rita put the cups down on the table. 'And I've decided not to charge yer, seeing as it's Christmas week. And I don't mean charge yer as in money, but as in yer telling me the story of yer love life. So drink up and enjoy yerself.'

When Aggie's bottom hit the chair, her bosom hit the table at the same time. 'Oh, thank God for that, queen, 'cos I've been racking me bleeding brain on how to tell yer something without using any bad words. And if I'd tried to describe things by using me hands instead of words, I know yer'd have clocked me one.' She took a deep breath. 'I can enjoy me cup of tea now, and me biscuit, even though it is two halves of a broken one. I'm not fussy, queen, I'm dead easy to please. And I'm not going to dunk the biscuit for long in case a piece drops off, like it usually does with me. I don't want to get a stain on me good dress 'cos I won't have time to wash it again before the big day.'

Rita watched with her heart in her mouth as Aggie picked up half a biscuit in her chubby hand and held it in the hot tea. Please God, don't let her ruin her dress, she hasn't got another one. I know she's not always as pure as she should be, but she doesn't mean no harm, she's really got a good heart. Then came a sigh of relief as the biscuit was taken from the tea and carried to Aggie's mouth with one hand, while her other was held below in case of an accident.

Aggie chuckled. 'Yer can breathe now, queen, the mission was accomplished with no accidents. But I don't think I'll dunk the other one, it's not worth the risk. It would break me bleeding heart if I messed me dress up before my feller sees it. It's only once in a blue moon he sees me looking decent, and I can't wait to see his face.'

'I'll bet yer a pound to a pinch of snuff he'll grab hold of yer and hug yer so close yer'll be gasping for breath.'

'D'yer think so, queen?' Aggie lowered her head a little so her friend wouldn't see her lips twitching. 'Ay, I don't suppose yer'd do us a favour on Christmas morning, would yer?'

'Oh, I don't think so, sunshine, there'll be too much to do here. Can't it wait for some other time, like Boxing Day?'

'Not really, queen, the mood would have worn off by then.'

Rita pursed her lips and wagged her head from side to side. 'I don't know why I always give in to yer, sunshine, but yer never fail to get round me. What is it yer want me to do for yer, and how long will it take? Don't forget I've got the dinner to see to.'

'Twenty minutes should do it, and I'd be really grateful to yer, queen.'

'What do yer want me to do in that twenty minutes?'

'Mind the kids for us. They wouldn't be in the

505

way, they'd play with your two.'

'But where are you and Sam going? Yer didn't tell me yer were going out.'

'Oh, we wouldn't be going far, queen, only up the stairs to the bedroom.' Aggie banged the table so hard it lifted the cups out of the saucers. 'Oh, if yer could only see yer face, yer'd die laughing. And I can tell, without yer saying, that yer won't be minding the kids for us on Christmas morning. I'm surprised, really, 'cos I'd rather have twenty minutes with my feller, than the present yer've bought for me.'

'I haven't bought yer no present, Aggie Gordon, and well yer know it. Where would I get the money from to be buying you a present?'

Aggie spread her hands out as though asking for understanding, while inside she was having a good laugh. 'Yer couldn't buy me a better present than giving me twenty minutes alone with my feller. And it wouldn't cost yer a farthing either. Won't yer at least give it some thought? It would put me in a good mood for the rest of the day, and I'd go through me work like a dose of Andrews' Little Liver Pills.'

Rita looked in Aggie's cup to make sure it was empty before she spoke. Then she pushed her chair back and took her neighbour's elbow. 'I'll help yer up, sunshine, then let's see yer going through my kitchen door as fast as yer can, without the help of Andrews' Little Liver Pills. That'll get yer in practice for Christmas morning.'

With Rita helping her along, Aggie seemed to bounce across the living-room floor. 'Call yerself a friend! I bet I'd get more sympathy from her in number twenty-two.'

This statement pulled Rita up sharp. 'Mrs Finnigan? Yer can't stand the sight of the woman, yer call her all the names under the sun!'

'I know I don't like her, and I know I call her fit to burn.' Aggie was putting a fierce face on. 'But I bet if I asked her to do that little favour for me, she'd say she would.'

'Oh, I agree!' Rita glared back. 'She would say yes out of fear. The poor woman is terrified of yer.'

Aggie suddenly erupted. Her eyes receded into her cheeks, and her bosom and tummy shook with laughter. From between the folds of flesh, her eyes appeared for a second as she asked, 'So I take it yer won't have the kids on Christmas morning?'

Rita collapsed. Her arms went around Aggie's neck and they clung together, laughing so loud the neighbours could hear. The sound brought a smile to many faces. 'Aggie Gordon, what would I do without you?'

Between gasps, Aggie replied, 'Yer'd be bleeding miserable, queen, same as I would be without you.'

Bessie hurried up the street on her way home from work. But she wasn't on her own side, she wanted to ask a favour from Rita. When her friend opened the door, Bessie put a finger to her lips, telling Rita not to speak. If Milly heard her voice, she'd be out like a shot and that was what Bessie didn't want. 'I'm after a favour, Rita,' she said softly, holding up the paper bag. 'I've got the material in here for the dresses for Christmas and I don't want Milly to see it, I want it to be a surprise on Christmas morning. So will yer keep her here for a bit longer while I hide it?'

'Of course she can stay here, she's in the middle of a game with our Jack. But aren't yer cutting it a bit fine when there's only a couple of days to Christmas?'

'I know, but I don't seem to have had time to breathe the last few weeks. You and Aggie have sorted the hampers out, but I've had to keep check on the money every night, and by the time Evelyn calls and takes Milly home, I'm too tired for anything.' Bessie, red in the face from battling the wind, grinned. 'I'll not take long once I start. I can have Milly's dress cut out in half an hour. I'll do that tonight when she goes home. I don't need a pattern, 'cos it's something I do all day. I could cut a dress out with me eyes shut.'

'I wish I was that clever,' Rita said, 'but I'm ruddy hopeless. Anyway, yer'd better go before Milly hears yer. I'll keep her for half an hour, and perhaps yer can get her dress cut out in that time.'

'Ah, ye're a smasher, Rita, a real pal. I made a pan of stew last night, so I only have to put a match to the stove to warm it through slowly. And I can have the dress done while I'm waiting.' Bessie, as thin as a rake, was across the cobbles in no time. Rita would have sworn her feet didn't touch the ground. The two women waved to each other then disappeared into their own houses.

Bessie went straight through to the kitchen and lit a match under the pan. Then, still moving at the double, she went back to the tiny hall to hang up her coat. Without stopping for breath, she carried the plant from the centre of the table to the sideboard, whipped the chenille cloth off and folded it up. Then the green material was taken from the bag and spread on the table, and a pair of scissors and a box of straight pins brought out of one of the sideboard drawers. This was a job Bessie was used to and good at. She'd been doing it every day for about twenty years. With confidence and speed the scissors snipped away until the skirt was cut and folded to one side, followed by two parts of the bodice and the two short sleeves. The old saying that the hands are sometimes quicker than the eye was certainly true in Bessie's case. When Milly knocked everything had been tidied away and the makings of her Christmas present were lying on Bessie's bed, ready to sew when she was on her own later. As she prepared to put their dinners out, Bessie decided she would buy the small white collar, it would save her time. She'd seen one in a haberdashery shop nearby which would really set it off. It had a ticket on it saying it was sixpence, but Bessie thought it would be worth it because the white linen was edged with lace, and Milly would be over the moon with it.

There was a rush to get the table cleared and the dishes washed before Evelyn was due, and Milly giggled as the knock came when she was reaching up to put the last plate on a shelf. 'Just in time, Auntie Bessie, we were saved by the bell.'

Bessie gave her a big hug before hurrying through the living room to open the door. 'Come in, Evelyn, it's bitter out there. Winter has certainly come with a vengeance, I wouldn't be surprised if we have thick snow for Christmas.'

Evelyn shivered as she took her gloves off and went to stand near the fire. 'I don't mind if I'm indoors, I think snow looks so pretty seen through a window. It's when it turns to slush I don't like it. And I have to tell you that I don't know what I'd do if your friend didn't light my fire for me. It is such a pleasure to walk into a warm room. I often wonder how Amelia and I managed all those years of coming into a freezing cold house.'

Milly stood at the kitchen door, watching and listening. Her mother had changed such a lot in the last few months, and the girl was delighted that she and Bessie had become friends. But although Milly was pleased she was allowed to come to stay with Bessie so often, and her mother wasn't so distant with her, she knew she wasn't treated by her mother as Jack and Billy were treated by theirs. She saw there what a mother's love was, but had never experienced it for herself. Oh, things weren't as strict, and she didn't get told off so often now, but the girl knew that Bessie's love for her was genuine while her mother didn't show any love at all.

'Would you like me to go home and have a cup of tea ready for you, Mother?' Milly asked. 'I will be very careful striking a match.'

This suited Evelyn, so she agreed. 'Yes, that would be nice. But you must promise to be very careful.'

Milly threw her arms around Bessie and gave

her a big hug and kiss. 'I'll see you tomorrow, Auntie Bessie. It won't be long now to Christmas, will it?'

'No, sweetheart, only a few days now. And Father Christmas will be visiting all the children who have been good, and leaving them a present.'

'I've been good, haven't I, Auntie Bessie? I haven't been cheeky or naughty, and I always do as I'm told and say my prayers every night.'

'Oh, you've been very good.' Bessie felt uncomfortable talking to the child as though she was hers, when her own mother was sitting watching. But she couldn't force Evelyn into doing something that didn't come naturally to her. 'I think she's almost certain to get a visit from Father Christmas, don't you, Evelyn?'

'Oh, undoubtedly! And as you've been such a good girl, Amelia, I think we can safely say you will get a good present.'

Milly smiled, even though her mother still sounded distant, as though she was talking to a complete stranger. 'I'll go and put the kettle on.'

Evelyn listened to the door closing then said, 'I'm glad Amelia offered to make tea, I wanted to speak to you. I have bought her a new dress and coat for Christmas, but I don't want her to see them before. How am I going to manage that?'

'Where are they now?'

'Still in the shop. I've paid for them, they just need picking up. I can do that tomorrow when I leave the office, but if I take them home she's bound to see them.'

'Drop them off before yer come here. Put them

in yer wardrobe, and I'll get them after work on Thursday. Don't worry, Milly won't see them, I'll make sure of that.'

Evelyn got to her feet. 'That's a load off my mind, thank you. And now I'd better get in to her.'

'Are yer still going to see yer father-in-law, or have yer changed yer mind?'

'I haven't changed my mind, no! It's my one hope of clearing up this mess. Amelia is off school for a couple of days after Christmas, and I'll take her on one of those days. And have no fear that I will back out, for I am determined.'

'I thought you were leaving it until the New Year, when all the holidays are over?'

'That was my intention, but I really can't wait that long, I have to get it sorted after Christmas, and hopefully start the New Year with my prayers and wishes granted. I may not be lucky, it's possible my father-in-law will not be at the office on the days before New Year, he may take an extended holiday. But as Amelia is off school then, I intend to take a chance. If I am unfortunate and my father-in-law isn't in the office, I will have to keep her off school one day in the first week of January.'

'I wish you all the luck in the world, Evelyn, I really do.'

Bessie closed the door on her neighbour and sighed as she leaned back against it. She meant what she'd said to her neighbour, she did wish her well. But was the time drawing near when she would no longer be able to see the young girl she'd grown to love? She sniffed up and pulled herself away from the door. Crying wouldn't get her anywhere, she should have known from the beginning that one day Amelia would be lost to her. And it was no good being miserable with Christmas on top of them. She wanted to give the girl the best Christmas she'd ever had, so she'd never forget her Auntie Bessie.

Chapter Twenty-Seven

Bessie's kitchen was as busy as a market on Christmas Eve morning with all the neighbours coming at five-minute intervals to pick up their precious hampers. Rita and Aggie were there to help, and there were many tears of happiness shed that morning as the women gazed down at the packets of tea, sugar, margarine, fruit, potatoes, veg, bread, biscuits and chicken, complete with dripping. Oh, and a couple of colourful crackers for the kids to pull. Bessie had put a piece of paper on the top of each box with a name on, so there were no mistakes made and every person on the list got their hamper.

Next door, in her kitchen, waiting for the kettle to boil so she could get washed, Evelyn could hear the commotion in the yard next door, and being curious hurried up to Amelia's bedroom to look down from the back window, with her daughter following close behind.

'What is it, Mother?' Milly asked as she watched a woman walking down her Auntie Bessie's yard carrying a box and looking very happy. 'Look, there's another lady coming into her yard. I wonder what's going on?'

'Let's be quiet for a while, Amelia, and we might see the reason for these women visiting Miss Maudsley.' It was after she'd seen four of them arrive empty-handed and five minutes later leave carrying a box that Evelyn realised what was happening. It was easy to see the chicken on the top of each one. The sight made Evelyn feel very humble. She wanted so much out of life, always had done, and these people asked for so little. 'Your Auntie Bessie is a very kind person, Amelia, and so are Mrs Wells and Mrs Gordon. They're giving food to those women to help them give their families some festive cheer.'

'It must be costing them a lot of money 'cos, look, there's another lady coming in from the entry.'

'I did hear Miss Maudsley say that a very kind gentleman had given her a certain amount of money to help families who were very poor. I'm sure his heart would be warmed if he could see what was happening next door, and his own Christmas would feel extra special knowing he'd made so many people happy.'

'Won't Auntie Bessie tell him how happy the people were? I bet she will, 'cos I'm sure she'd like him to know.'

'Oh, she's bound to tell him,' Evelyn said, promising herself that as soon as she got to the apartment she would tell Philip of the scene she was now witnessing. And she would also tell him of the barefoot boys now wearing serviceable shoes that would see them through the winter. He would be so pleased. In her mind she could already see his smiling face.

'You can tell Miss Maudsley we saw the women and their hampers of food, and how much we both admire her, but you must not question her about where the money came from. Do you understand that, Amelia? You would be asking her to break a confidence, as the benefactor wishes to remain anonymous.'

Milly nodded. 'I won't ask her, Mother, but even if I did she wouldn't tell me. Auntie Bessie would never break a promise or tell a secret.' The girl was on pins, the time wasn't going fast enough for her. 'When am I going next door, Mother?'

'I said I would be leaving to go to my friend's at twelve o'clock and would call with you then so I could wish her the compliments of the season. I only have to get washed, I have my clothes all ready, so be patient for a little while longer.' A pang of guilt caused her to add, 'I have left Christmas presents for you, Amelia, I haven't forgotten you, but I'm not telling you any more, it would spoil the surprise.'

'Thank you, Mother.' Milly turned to leave the room. 'I'll get Daisy ready, she needs her hair combing.'

'Ta-ra, Sally, mind how yer go!' Rita closed the kitchen door and let out a long sigh. 'Thank God, that was the last one. Me feet are killing me, and I'm dying for a cuppa.'

'It's yer own bleeding fault, yer would insist on walking some of them down the yard in case they slipped.' Aggie turned the gas higher under the kettle. 'They would have made it under their own steam but, oh, no, yer had to do the job proper.'

'Stop moaning, the pair of yer,' Bessie said. 'Anyone would think yer'd done a day's hard work down a coal mine. Go and sit at the table and I'll bring yer a cup of tea through when the water's boiled. I'll have to put more water on, 'cos I've got thirty-six jelly creams to make.'

'Thirty-six!' Aggie put a hand to her cheek. 'What the bleeding hell d'yer want thirty-six jelly creams for?'

Bessie raised her brows. 'Don't yer like jelly creams, sweetheart?'

'Yeah, 'course I like jelly creams, queen, but not thirty bleeding six of them.'

'Have yer forgotten there's a kids' party here tomorrow afternoon, for eighteen kids what have probably never been to one in their lives? Surely yer don't expect to have a party without jelly creams, or trifle come to that.'

Aggie wasn't very good at adding up in her head, so she used her fingers. And when she found she ran out of fingers, she turned to Rita. 'Ay, queen, if the kids have one each, how many does that leave of the thirty-six?'

Rita gave Bessie a sly wink. 'Well, if they have one each there'll be eighteen over, sunshine, but they'll more than likely want two each. Which comes to thirty-six.'

'Well, the greedy little buggers! D'yer mean they'll eat 'em all, and there'll be none left over for us?'

'I thought yer weren't that fussy, sunshine,' Rita said. 'After all, yer seemed surprised when Bessie said how many she was making. And yer aren't wicked enough to pinch a jelly cream out of a kid's mouth, are yer?'

Aggie was going to nod her head, but her chins were disgusted with her and refused point blank to move upwards. Instead they swayed from side to side, which meant she meant one thing but was forced to say another. 'I wouldn't pinch one, no, but I'd ask in a nice way if they'd take their bleeding hands off and give someone else a chance.'

'I'll pour the tea out,' Bessie said, grinning at the hurt expression on Aggie's chubby face. 'Before you two come to blows.' She reached the kitchen, stopped, then turned around. 'Don't fall out, for God's sake, 'cos ye're supposed to be doing me shopping while I see to the jellies, trifles, make thirty-six fairy cakes, and on top of that get me veg done for tomorrow. I don't want to be running round like a scalded cat on Christmas morning getting the dinner on, when I've got eighteen kids coming at two-thirty.'

'Me and Aggie will be over to give yer a hand, sunshine, we won't leave yer swinging on yer lonesome. And while we're having a cup of tea now, yer can be making yer shopping list out. It won't take me and Aggie long to get round the shops.'

Aggie clicked her teeth. 'I bet she'll give us a list as long as me arm, and we'll be running round the shops like blue-arsed flies.'

Rita threw daggers at her mate. 'Yer know, sunshine, if ye're not that fussy on coming to help at the kids' party, and ye're also not fussy on the party for the grown-ups at night, then just say the word, and Bessie's shopping list will be a lot shorter.'

Aggie wagged a forefinger, inviting Rita to come closer. 'Why don't yer keep yer ruddy nose out of my business? And if yer insist on meddling, then make sure yer get it right. I didn't say I wouldn't help at the kids' party, and I didn't say I didn't want to come to the one for the grown-ups, either. I am dying to help with the party, 'cos yer know I love kids, especially eighteen of the little sods. And I'm looking forward to the company of grown-ups, too, and even more the company of six bottles of milk stout.' She tapped the side of her nose. 'So keep this out of it in future, queen, 'cos a black eye wouldn't go with the colour of yer new dress.'

While they were enjoying their well-earned cup of tea, Bessie had her notepad in front of her and the stub of pencil between her fingers. 'I think I'd better get three large tin loaves, to be on the safe side. It should be ample 'cos everyone will have had a big Christmas dinner.' She wrote that down at the top of the sheet of paper. 'I've already got the margarine in, and tea, sugar and connie-onnie. The milkman is filling me big jug, and that will well see me through.' She put the pencil between her teeth and rolled her eyes. 'If yer get twenty-four sausage rolls, Rita, that should be enough 'cos I'm going to cut them in two. But what to put in the sandwiches, though ... have yer got any ideas?'

'Jars of paste are always handy, sunshine,' Rita said. 'There's salmon, chicken and meat. A jar of each would go a long way. Don't forget there'll be the jelly creams, the big trifle and fairy cakes. I don't think yer need much more.'

Bessie was busy writing. 'I've put down two jars of each of the pastes, 'cos I've got to think of

519

feeding you and the men in the evening. I think I'll push the boat out and get a quarter of boiled ham too, it won't hurt to go mad and spoil ourselves for a change.'

'Is this yer own money ye're using, sunshine, 'cos if it is then yer can cut out the likes of boiled ham. Yer work hard for yer money and I don't want yer spending it on us.'

Aggie turned her head and glared at her neighbour. 'Speak for yerself, queen, 'cos I'm very partial to a nice boiled ham sandwich. Partickerly with a bit of mustard on.'

Rita returned her glare. 'Oh, and do yer often have boiled ham in your house? And is it partickerly spread with mustard?'

Aggie scratched her head. 'Well, I can't remember exactly when I had it last, queen, but I do remember how much I enjoyed it.'

'Perhaps I can jog yer memory, sunshine, wasn't it at yer wedding reception?'

'Ooh, er, was it that long ago, queen? It just goes to show how time flies when ye're having fun.'

'Well, since yer partickerly like it with mustard, I'll have to put a small jar of that on me list.' Bessie licked the end of the pencil. 'How do yer spell partickerly, sweetheart?'

Aggie snorted. 'How the hell do I know? I want to eat it, not spell it!'

Rita kept her face straight. 'D'yer think it's spelt the same way as particularly? Or is that a different word altogether?'

Aggie got the last word. 'Oh, it's a different word altogether, queen, and I wouldn't partickerly like it spread on me boiled ham sandwich.'

Bessie was thinking of all the work she had to do. She'd finished Milly's dress, but still needed to do some work on her own. 'To get to the question yer asked, Rita, I still had three pound left of the money I was given. So last night I took two pound notes to the corner shop and asked Alf to give me some two-shilling pieces. Every hamper that went out of here this morning had a two-bob piece in it, wrapped up in a piece of me notepad so it couldn't be missed. The rest is buying lemonade and food for the kids' party and ours, and I'm paying for drinks for the grown-ups' party. That, I think, takes care of everything, and I hope it answers your question, sunshine.'

'I think yer've done wonders, Bessie,' Rita said. 'I couldn't have organised things the way you have, I'd have been out of my mind.'

'I'll go along with that, queen, because if anyone had given me that much money I'd have spent the lot on meself.' Aggie had her arms folded under her bosom and for once was serious. 'Well, perhaps not all on meself, but I would have spent some on me house. And that's why I'll be needing a reference from both of yer to give to St Peter if I ever make it up that pathway to the pearly gates. At least I'm not lying. I would have been tempted by seeing so much money, and I'd have given in to temptation.'

Rita patted her arm. 'I think most people in our situation would have been tempted, sunshine. Trying to stretch the money every week, robbing Peter to pay Paul, and yet never quite managing to make ends meet. But when push came to

521

shove, Aggie, yer wouldn't have used that money for yerself. I know yer well enough to know that. Tough on the outside yer may be, and a big mouth yer may have that puts the fear of God in most of our neighbours, but a thief, never!'

'I know what I would have done, though, queen, I would have sat up all night looking at it.'

'What!' Rita exclaimed. 'You what loves yer bedroom so much?'

Bessie held a hand up for silence. 'Right, that settles it. When the word bedroom is mentioned in Aggie's presence, then it's time to split up. Here's the list, Rita, and a ten-bob note. While you're doing that I'll get meself sorted out. And when the men come in from work, will yer ask one of them to go to the corner pub for the drinks? I'd say a bottle of port, six bottles of milk stout, and whatever beer the men drink. The pound I've got left should take care of that.'

Rita helped Aggie to her feet. 'Come on, sunshine, just listening to Bessie has me head in a whirl. She can have things done while you and me are thinking about it.'

'I'm expecting Evelyn to bring Milly in any minute, so I'd better get this table cleared.' Bessie only had to mention Milly's name and her spirits lifted. She'd have the girl for nearly three days this time, and they'd both love every minute of it.

Bessie shone the small torch she kept by her bed, and the light from it told her it was nearly half-past six. She hadn't slept well, she was too excited. She'd never had a child in the house for Christmas and didn't know whether they woke up very early. She had heard that some children woke their parents in the middle of the night, wanting to know if Father Christmas had been. But what time Milly would wake she had no idea. Perhaps she should go down and light the fire so the room would be nice and warm. She'd hung a few decorations last night, with Milly's help, and draped silver and gold tinsel over the pictures and mirror so at least the room looked a bit Christmassy. After the girl had gone to bed, Bessie had hung a pillowcase from one end of the mantelpiece, in which she'd put some fruit and nuts, a Christmas stocking filled with chocolate bars, a new dress she'd made for Daisy, a book of drawings and coloured pencils to colour them with. The green dress with its pretty white lace-trimmed collar was hanging on a coat-hanger at the other end of the mantelpiece. The presents from her mother, which Evelyn had brought in already wrapped in Christmas paper, Bessie had left on the table so they would be the first thing Milly saw when she came into the room.

Clicking her tongue with impatience, she swung her legs over the side of the bed. She'd be better off downstairs lighting the fire instead of lying in bed. She never could stand being idle. She felt for the fleecy dressing gown which she'd had for so many years she'd lost track, and slipped her arms into the sleeves. Then, careful not to make a sound, she crept down the stairs and into the sitting room which was still warm from the fire she'd had roaring up the chimney last night. Once she'd raked the ashes out, it wouldn't take long for the sticks of firewood to catch because some of the coals were still glowing. Moving at the double as she always did, she soon had the ashes in the bin and fresh coal laid on top of the sticks which were crackling into life.

'Now for a hot cuppa,' Bessie told the grate. 'It's flipping freezing outside. I was only in the yard for a few seconds and I'm shivering, I'm glad I don't have to go to work.' Five minutes later she was sitting at the table with her hands around a cup, watching the flames dancing up the chimney. In the peace and silence of the room, her thoughts drifted. Would this be the last Christmas she'd see Milly? If her grandparents took her to their heart, as they surely would, and if they were very rich and could give her anything her heart desired, then it would be churlish not to be happy for her. But, human nature being what it is, Bessie couldn't help feeling sad.

She was so wrapped up in her thoughts she didn't hear the tell-tale creak of the stairs. It was only when Milly jumped down the last two, and there was a slight thud, that she came out of her reverie. Putting her cup down, Bessie held out her arms. 'A very happy Christmas, sweetheart, and I hope Santa has been good to you.'

'Merry Christmas, Auntie Bessie.' Milly held her tight and rained kisses on her face. 'It's going to be the best Christmas I've ever had.' The girl's eyes had already taken in the large parcel at the end of the table, and the pillow case and dress hanging from the mantelpiece. Milly had been told from an early age by her mother that there was no such person as Father Christmas, and even though all the shops were decorated with pictures of him, and the girls in school talked of nothing else for weeks, she still didn't believe there was such a person. That is, until her Auntie Bessie had come on the scene. If her beloved Auntie Bessie said there was a Father Christmas, then there must be.

Bessie removed the girl's arms from her neck. 'Aren't yer going to see what presents yer've got, sweetheart? The big parcel on the table is from your mother, and she's wrapped it in pretty paper, so d'yer want to open that first?'

'Which do you think I should look at first?'

'Oh, your mother's, definitely. I bet it's something really nice.' When Milly hesitated, Bessie said cheerfully, 'I'll give yer a hand, shall I?'

'I think it would be best if you open it, Auntie Bessie, I'm afraid of tearing the paper.'

'Don't worry about that, sweetheart, 'cos half the pleasure is ripping the paper off to see what goodies are inside. Look, get hold of my hand and we'll do it together.'

The dress inside was in a deep red wool, with long sleeves. Very serviceable for winter days. The accompanying neat, tailored coat, in deep red and grey checked pure wool, was of the finest standard. 'Oh, aren't you a lucky girl, sweetheart, they're lovely! Oh, my, ye're going to be quite the young lady in these. Your mother has such good taste. Both the dress and the coat really are beautiful. Don't yer think so, sweetheart?'

Milly put her hand on the coat and stroked it, not because she wanted to but because she thought it was what was expected of her. 'Yes,

525

they are nice, I'll be able to wear them on a Sunday or if I'm going somewhere special.'

'We'll fold them up for now while you look to see what other presents Santa has brought for yer. Then I'll find a coat hanger and hang them in the wardrobe. We're going to have a houseful this afternoon, and I don't want them to get stains on them.'

'Is that green dress for me, Auntie Bessie?' Milly's heart was beginning to beat faster at the thought of the party. Just think, eighteen children, and one of them her friend Jack. 'It looks very pretty.'

'That's your present from me. I made it for yer, and I hope yer like it.'

Milly stood on tip toe to reach the top of the hanger. 'It's beautiful, Auntie Bessie. Can I wear it for the party? I promise I'll be careful and won't dirty it.'

'Of course yer can wear it, sweetheart, and it wouldn't matter if yer did make it a bit mucky, it's easy enough to wash.'

The girl's happiness knew no bounds. She threw her arms around Bessie's waist and cried, 'Oh, thank you, thank you, thank you! It's the prettiest dress I've ever had. You must be very clever to have made it.'

When Bessie smiled, she was once again hugged and kissed. 'You are the bestest auntie in the whole world.'

'I'll believe yer where thousands wouldn't.' Bessie stroked her hair.

'Now take the pillowcase down and see what other presents are in there for yer, while I make another pot of tea and some toast. And we'll have to have an early dinner, 'cos don't forget, today is going to be a very busy day and I'll need your help with the guests. After breakfast, you and me are going to have to move fast if we're to have everything ready on time.'

Bessie had worried herself to death when Reg and Sam carried Rita's dining table over. There wasn't enough room inside her house and the men had to stand in the street while the women made space for it by carrying the sideboard out through the kitchen and into the yard. 'I hope it doesn't rain or snow on me sideboard,' Bessie wailed. 'I must have been crazy to think we'd get eighteen children in here.'

'Calm down, sunshine, it isn't like you to panic,' Rita said. 'Once the table comes in, we can get everything organised. Give the men a shout, Aggie, then we'll have to move out of the way.'

'I'll go and get the chairs from our house.' Aggie saw the legs of Rita's table being manoeuvred round the door and decided to go out the back way. 'I'll carry them over two at a time and leave them under yer window until the men are finished.'

Rita had been right. When the men finally struggled down the narrow passage, they were quick to take in which way the new table and Bessie's should stand to give most space. Then, the job accomplished, they went out whistling happily. 'Ooh, that looks better,' Bessie said with relief, 'now we can get the cloths on and start bringing the food in. I'm glad Milly's over in your house, Rita, 'cos she'd only be in the way here.'

'She looks a treat in the dress yer made her, sunshine, yer did a good job on it. And, oh, boy, is she swanking in front of our Jack. There's a permanent look of disgust on our Billy's face. He's more determined than ever he'll never have a girlfriend. He looked horrified when Reg said he'd have daughters of his own one day.'

Aggie was dying to say that the day would surely come when young Billy realised there was more to girls than a mouth, but she thought better of it. It was Christmas Day, after all, and Bessie was on the religious side. Not that there was anything wrong with that, but being too pure meant yer missed out on a lot.

'Come on, Aggie, shift yerself,' Rita said. 'Start bringing the plates in, and a cracker to go on each one. And if ye're going to drop a plate, make it one of yer own, eh? I haven't got that many I can spare one.'

'Well, the bleeding cheek of you!' Aggie looked hurt. 'Another crack like that and I'll be telling yer to sod off and do the job yerself.'

Bessie puckered her lips and blew out. 'Will you two shut up and get on with the job in hand? I'm a nervous wreck without listening to you arguing.' She wiped the back of a hand across her brow. 'I'm sweating cobs and I'll be glad when it's over. I'm sorry I even thought of such a daft idea, I want me bumps feeling.'

Rita put an arm across her friend's shoulder. 'Yer won't say that when yer see the kids' faces when they set eyes on the table. Believe me, sunshine, yer won't regret it.'

Once again Rita was right. Bessie was paid back a hundredfold when she saw the wide eyes of eighteen children who had never seen such a well-laid table or the variety of food on offer. Jelly creams in red, green and yellow, a huge bowl of trifle topped with cream and tiny silver balls, fairy cakes iced on top, sausage rolls, and several plates piled high with sandwiches. Some of the boys were giving each other sly nudges to make sure their mates had seen the Christmas cracker beside each plate. They'd never had one of those before and were longing to pull them, but they'd been warned by their parents to be quiet and well behaved.

Milly wasn't quiet, though, she was so excited she couldn't stop chattering. 'Can we pull the crackers, Auntie Bessie?'

'Yes, of course yer can. As soon as Mrs Gordon and Mrs Wells have poured lemonade out for yer, we ladies are going into the kitchen and leaving you to it. Everyone is equal here, it's everyone's party, so help yourselves. But I'm relying on the big boys, like Billy, to see that everyone gets a fair share. And Kitty will see to the girls.'

Once the three women had retired to the kitchen and closed the door, the racket started. Free to talk now, the boys' voices could be heard above the girls'. 'Ay, this is great, isn't it? I never expected nothing like this. I wish me mam and dad could see how much is on this table.' His mate answered, 'There won't be this much by the time we've finished. Ay, can yer eat those silver things?' A girl had the answer to that. 'Yeah, yer can eat them, but they're hard so yer'd be better off sucking them.'

Rita moved from one foot to the other. 'Let's go over to mine for an hour, what d'yer say? Me feet are dropping off, I couldn't stand for much longer. The kids will be all right, I can tell our Billy to keep an eye on them, and none of them are bad kids.'

Aggie nodded. 'My feet have had it too! And don't forget we've got to wash all the dishes for our little party tonight. I won't be in good form if me corns are acting up. Tell our Kitty and your Billy to keep an eye on the others, they're both sensible. Besides, it's their party, for heaven's sake, leave them to enjoy themselves.'

'Put yer head around the door then, Rita,' Bessie said, her own feet playing her up. 'I'll have to sit down meself, I'm bushed.'

As soon as Rita opened the living-room door the racket stopped and there was complete silence. 'We're going over to mine for a cup of tea, and we're trusting you to behave yerselves. We want yer to enjoy yerselves, as long as nothing gets broken. When yer've finished eating, yer could play some games. I was going to suggest Blind Man's Bluff, but as there's no room to breathe in here, yer couldn't play that. So ye're going to have to use yer imagination, I'm sure one of yer can think of a game.'

Several heads nodded, and two boys said they knew loads of games. 'And we'll behave ourselves, missus.'

Rita smiled and said to herself, Ah, God love

them, they get very little in life. 'Yer better had behave yerselves, sunshine, or yer won't be asked back to next year's party.'

One boy piped up, 'How long can we stay here for, Mrs Wells?'

'Ooh, I'll have to ask the boss about that.' Rita backed into the kitchen and closed the door. 'They want to know when yer'll be chucking them out. But you go and tell them yerself, Bessie, and take a good look at them. That should tell yer whether it's been worth all the hard work yer've put in.'

Aggie gave her mate a dig. 'Ay, we helped as well. Let's all have a look-see at them.'

Eighteen children and eighteen happy faces. They were all wearing the cheap paper hats they'd got out of the crackers, some of which were too big and kept falling down over their eyes or hanging cock-eyed, giving the wearer the appearance of being drunk. On the older boys the hats were too small and looked like a pimple on a mountain. But who cared? The kids were having the time of their lives, and the sight was a tonic to Bessie. 'I'll have to throw you out at five o'clock, kids, 'cos I'm having visitors tonight. But the main thing is, are yer enjoying yerselves?'

The roar from eighteen voices must have been heard as far away as the Pier Head, and left the women in no doubt that Bessie's Christmas party was a huge success.

At eight o'clock that night, Rita and Reg Wells, and Aggie and Sam Gordon were enjoying a quiet drink with Bessie. Milly had gone to bed

531

without any coaxing, dead beat from all the excitement. For years she'd had no friends to play with, and now she had so many. And she had someone to kiss her goodnight and tuck her into bed.

'Well, it didn't take long to get the place back to normal, Bessie,' Rita said. 'No one would believe yer had eighteen kids here this afternoon for a party.'

'It's thanks to the four of yer that it is back to normal, I'd never have managed it on me own.' She took a sip of her milk stout. 'What with the table to be carried over to yours, the mountain of dishes to be washed, and the floor swept and mopped, I wouldn't have known where to start. In fact, I'd have probably thrown me hands in the air and gone to bed.'

'Well, yer can sit back and relax now, queen,' Aggie said with the permission of her chins. 'When my feller gets a few more beers down him, he'll entertain yer with a song. And after another milk stout, I might even give yer one meself. I used to be noted for me clear voice. I was once told I should try and get on the Empire, or the Metropole in Bootle.'

Sam looked sideways at his wife. 'Who told yer this?'

Aggie waved a hand. 'Oh, some bloke what heard me sing.'

'How old were yer?'

'Don't be so bleeding nosy!' Aggie bristled. 'I was eighteen, if yer must know.'

'Yer were eighteen when I met yer, but I've never heard yer sing like a lark.' Sam was winding his wife up. 'This bloke what said yer had a good voice, was he sitting in a chair or lying on the floor, blind drunk?'

'It was before I met you, smart arse, and he was a proper gentleman, I'll have you know.' Aggie's tummy was thinking if she didn't laugh soon, it would burst. 'In fact, you wouldn't have stood a chance if this bloke hadn't been bandy-legged and cross-eyed. It took a lot of thought before I decided I'd be better off with you, because I never knew whether this feller, gent as he was, was looking at me or the person next to me.' Their smiles and titters egged her on. 'Another thing, something me mam said got me thinking. She said he was so bandy he'd never be able to stop a pig in an entry. I thought he'd be no good to me then, so I turned me charms on to you instead.'

Rita's husband, Reg, was chortling. 'Yer mam was right, yer know. He wouldn't have been no good to yer if he couldn't stop a pig in an entry. Not with all the pigs we see down these entries.'

And so for the next hour, the five friends enjoyed jokes and banter which put them in a good mood. It was nice to have neighbours you got on well with. Then, after the glasses had been topped up a few more times, Sam started the singing off. He had quite a good voice, and sang Paul Robeson's 'Old Man River' as well as the great man himself. Well, after so many drinks, anyone could have sounded like Paul Robeson. The women opted for Marie Lloyd songs, and they sang with gusto. The two men tried to out-sing the women, but at three to two they didn't stand a chance. They did try, God love them, but they'd drunk so much beer, they spent most of the time running down the yard.

'Men can't hold their drink.' Aggie thought she would impart this information to her mates in case they didn't know it. Her words slurred, she said, 'Not like us women.' She hiccupped several times, then passed her glass to Sam to hold while she pushed herself up. Slightly unsteady on her feet, she felt her way around the table. 'Yer'll have to hexcuse me, folks, I need to spend a penny.' She lurched from the table to grab hold of the door. 'I'll sing yer another song when I get back.'

'I'll go with her, just to make sure.' Rita took her mate's elbow. 'Come on, sunshine, and I'll sing "Look For A Silver Lining" with yer.' A few seconds later, 'No, that's not the lavatory door, sunshine, that's the entry door. Oh, okay, if you say so, then it's the lavatory door. I'll just stand here and wait for yer. But don't sit down, will yer, 'cos there's no seats in the entry.'

Bessie fell back in her chair and, with Sam and Reg, burst out laughing. Her tired feet and all the worry forgotten, she said, 'Oh, what a wonderful day this has been.'

Chapter Twenty-Eight

'Two whole days, my lovely Evelyn, with no interruptions at all.' Philip sighed with pleasure as he pulled her closer. 'I could ask for no finer Christmas gift than that.'

'But you must go and see your parents tomorrow, darling. I would not like to them to think I was keeping you away on the one day of the year when families should be together.'

'I will be going to see them. I have their presents, and certainly would not let such an important day pass without visiting them. You were invited, remember, they're longing to meet you. Will you not change your mind and accompany me on a short visit tomorrow? They would be so happy to meet you, and then I would not feel guilty about leaving you here alone.'

'But I wouldn't be alone, would I? Isn't Annie coming in to prepare and serve our meal? I'm not very good in the kitchen, I'm afraid, but giving her a hand would make the time pass quickly, and I can always potter around and help if I can.'

'It won't be for long, my lovely, perhaps an hour and a half. There'll be no traffic on the roads as the buses and trams are not running, it will only be fifteen minutes' drive each way and an hour spent with my parents. Can you survive for so long without me?'

'I will try, my darling.' There was tenderness in

Evelyn's smile. She had never imagined a love such as she felt for this man, who was never far away from her thoughts. 'It will be hard, but I shall steel myself.'

'Let us forget tomorrow. We have the whole evening to ourselves and I can lose myself in your beauty and my love for you. I shall open a bottle of wine, and when you are slightly inebriated, I shall lead you to the bedroom and make passionate love to you.'

Evelyn stayed him with her hand. 'Don't get up yet, my love. I want to tell you about something which touched my heart, and which I think will please you.' With the scene still in her mind, she told him of the women she had seen coming and going with boxes of food. 'All those poor families helped, thanks to you, and of course there were the shoes for the boys. And if you had seen the looks on the faces of those women as they carried their precious boxes, you would certainly have been moved to tears, as I was. Those women, so thin and gaunt through lack of nourishment, will be blessing you. With your help they will be able to feed their families this Christmas.'

There was astonishment on Philip's face. 'How could so many families be fed for just twenty pounds? Surely that would give them very little in the way of Christmas fare?'

She stroked his cheek. 'You live in a different world from them, my darling, as I did until my husband died. I had everything I wanted, never knew what hunger and hardship were. These people are so poor they barely exist, yet they have much more spirit than I. They love their children,

536

and feed them while starving themselves. What I saw yesterday I found so uplifting, I thought I should tell you about the happiness you have put into their lives, your Christmas gift to them.'

Staring at the flames roaring up the chimney, Philip shook his head. 'You are making me see how very selfish I have been. I often drive past streets in the slums, but never think what life is like for people there. Oh, being a solicitor I find out many things, but never give a thought to the people who live in slums owned by clients of mine. I know many of them have no sanitation and must share an outside toilet with four or five other families, no running water in houses lived in by two or three families with children, and if they don't pay the rent on these hovels, they are turfed out on to the street.' He turned his eyes from the fire to look at her. 'I have acted for these landlords, but never once thought of the people I was evicting. And there are many other people, friends of mine, who don't give a thought to those who are less well off. We probably spend more in one day than these people earn in a year.'

'I only wished to tell you of the happiness you have given these families, my love, I didn't intend to make you sad. I certainly meant no criticism of your life-style or that of your friends. I am the last person to talk of selfishness, I have been selfish all my life.' Once again she stroked his face. 'It has taken two people to make me see myself for what I am. One is your dear self for showing me what true love is, and the other is a neighbour who has taught me humility.'

He squeezed her hand. 'This is the person who

wrote out the list you showed me, isn't it?' When Evelyn nodded, Philip said, 'I want to meet her. In fact, insist on meeting her, she must be a very good person. And, she's a friend of yours.'

'Perhaps in the New Year, my darling.' Evelyn's happiness was blighted by the knowledge that there was much for her to do before the New Year came in. Her future, and that of Amelia, very much depended on the outcome of her visit to her father-in-law. 'Anyway, let's not talk of sadness. We have two whole days before us, let us make the most of them. Open that bottle of wine, my darling, and let us forget the outside world.'

This brought a smile to Philip's face and he was quickly on his feet. 'Your wish is my command.' He grinned down at her, his eyes twinkling. 'I can't quite remember now, my lovely Evelyn, how many glasses you need to make you so endearingly loving? Is it one glass or two?'

'I do believe that at this moment I would not need a single glass of wine to make me endearingly loving, my darling. You only have to touch me and my whole body comes alive.'

'Then go through to the bedroom, my sweet, and prepare yourself while I open a bottle. I want to make love to you slowly and sensually, until you purr with pleasure. When our appetites are appeased, we will indulge in a glass of wine and playful behaviour until our need is once again aroused. Remember, my lovely Evelyn, you do not have to leave tonight, so let our love for each other have its way.'

When Philip entered the bedroom, Evelyn was in bed, her head raised on two soft feather pillows. He placed two slender glasses and a bottle of wine on the bedside table, then with his face wearing the boyish grin that Evelyn found irresistible, whipped the bedclothes back to reveal her nakedness. His eyes never leaving her body, he untied the belt of his robe and let it fall from his shoulders. Then he slipped in beside her and took her in his arms. 'Every time I see how beautiful you are, I can't believe I had to wait so long to find someone so perfect. For ten years I've floated from one woman to another, looking for the perfect one, while at the same time you were a widow, with no man in your life.'

'I was eight years without a man in my life, my darling, but we won't gain anything by thinking what might have been. Let's be grateful we have found each other. If your uncle hadn't retired, and you hadn't taken over from him, we would never have met. So let's say that Lady Luck was on our side then and brought us together.'

'You make me very happy, my lovely,' Philip said, stroking her breasts. 'But I would be much happier if we were married and I was sure you were mine and no one could come along and take you from me. When are you going to make an honest man of me?'

'Very soon, darling. I am as anxious as you for us to be united in wedlock. I have made you a promise that very early in the New Year I will have my affairs sorted and then you can set the date for our wedding.'

'But what affairs do you have, my love, that are important enough to keep you from me?'

Evelyn put a finger to his lips. 'Trust me, all will

be revealed in a week or so. Until then, we must both be patient.'

'I will try to be patient,' Philip said, moving his body to cover hers. 'But right now I have no patience, I can't wait to make love to you.' And as their two naked bodies met, both sighed with contentment and satisfaction.

The time passed quickly, far too quickly, and all too soon it was time for Philip to return to the office, while Evelyn had asked if she could have the remainder of the week off. 'I will ask someone to ring in and say I have a very bad cold and will be confined to my bed for the rest of the week.'

'I will not allow my future wife to tell lies.' Philip was adamant. 'I intend to tell them very soon that we are betrothed, and really have no interest in what they think. So do not bother making excuses, my love, you do what you have to do. The sooner your affairs are sorted out, the happier I shall be. But surely I don't have to wait for a week to hold you in my arms again? It is far too long, I shall pine away.'

'Give me two full days after today, my love. The day after that I'll meet you here in your lunch break. Perhaps you could take an extra half-hour to give us a little more time together?'

Philip pouted like a child. 'I feel as though someone has taken my favourite toy away and won't give it back to me.'

Evelyn kissed his cheek. 'You will soon have your favourite toy back, I promise. Anyway, when we are married you mustn't think you can always have your own way. I too can be very stubborn at times.'

He hugged her and grinned. 'You can be stubborn whenever you like, my love, but never in the bedroom. I am the master in that department.' After another hug, he said, 'I think you had better go before I change my mind and lock you in.'

'Yes, I must be on my way, darling, but the last two days have been heaven, and I thank you and love you. I'll see you very soon.'

Evelyn walked off in the opposite direction from the office, so she wouldn't be seen. It was quite busy in the city. For most people it was their first day back at work after the holiday. But she caught a tram without having to wait long, and the journey gave her time to empty her head of thoughts of Philip and her love for him, and concentrate on meeting her father-in-law after eight years. What would his reaction be? There was no point in trying to guess, she would have to meet him in person. She hoped he would be in the office today, so she could get it over with and not have to spend the day worrying. Amelia's school was closed so it would be an ideal time to try. If the office were closed, then she would have to wait until after the New Year holiday, but from what she remembered of Cyril Lister-Sinclair, he never missed a day at work. It was worth a try to put her mind at rest.

Rita opened the door and looked surprised when she saw Evelyn standing there. 'Hello, Mrs Sinclair, I wasn't expecting you until this afternoon. Bessie is at work so I'm minding Milly.' Too late she realised she'd slipped up on the name, then thought, Oh, blow it, why worry? 'Would yer like

541

to come in? She's playing a game with my son.'

'Would you mind if I didn't?' Evelyn didn't want to offend, but her tummy was turning over with nerves and she knew if she didn't act quickly, then she never would. 'I have an important call to make this morning, and want to take Amelia with me.'

Milly had heard her mother's voice and come to the door. 'Do you want me, Mother?'

'Yes, dear. I have an errand to go on, and would like you to come with me.'

She tried not to let her disappointment show. 'My best clothes are over at Auntie Bessie's, do you want me to get them?'

'I'll fetch them,' Rita said. 'You go home with yer mother, and I'll bring the clothes to yer.' She pulled a face at Evelyn. 'I'm afraid yer'll be going into a cold house, Mrs Sinclair. I would have lit yer fire if I'd known.'

Evelyn smiled, thinking what she had missed over the years by not making friends with this woman and her neighbours. 'We won't be in the house long enough to feel the cold, I want to be away as quickly as possible. But if you would light my fire later, when you have time, I would really be most grateful.'

'Consider it done.' Rita stood aside to let Milly pass. The girl was struggling into her school coat, and her downcast expression revealed that she was not happy to be taken away from her game. 'The house will be nice and warm for yer to come back to.'

'Goodbye, Auntie Rita,' Milly called as she followed her mother across the cobbles. 'I'll see you later.'

'Yer'll see me in five minutes, sunshine, with yer best clothes.'

As soon as they were in the house, Amelia asked, 'Where are we going, Mother?'

'Wait until Mrs Wells has been with your clothes, dear, then I will tell you.'

The girl could see her mother was a little agitated, and wondered why. Young as she was, she connected her mother's nerves with the important call she'd heard her telling Auntie Rita about. But why did she need to take her daughter with her?

When Rita knocked, Evelyn opened the door quickly. 'Thank you so much.' She took the clothes, adding, 'Please don't think me rude, or ungrateful for your kindness to my daughter, but we must hurry to be off.'

'No need to apologise, Mrs Sinclair,' Rita said, turning to cross back to her own house, 'it is a pleasure to have your daughter, she's a little angel.'

Back in the living room, Evelyn handed the dress and coat to Amelia. 'Rinse your hands and face, dear, then put on your dress and comb your hair. When I have changed, I will sit down and tell you where we are going.'

'Couldn't Jack come with us, Mother? He would like that and he's my best friend.'

Evelyn shook her head. 'Not today, Amelia. You will understand why when we've had our talk. Something may happen today that will change our lives completely, yours and mine, so I'm afraid I can't allow Jack to come with us.'

Amelia had changed into her new dress when

Evelyn came down the stairs wearing a dress she usually wore for the office. Her mass of dark hair had been brushed until it shone, but she wore no make-up apart from lipstick. With her flawless complexion, she didn't need to cover it with powder or rouge. 'Sit next to me on the couch, Amelia, and listen carefully. What I have to tell you will surprise you very much, and perhaps it was wrong of me not to tell you before this. But circumstances have changed, and I have no choice but to do what I am going to do today. A lot depends upon the outcome.' Evelyn crossed her legs and licked her dry lips. 'You know your father was killed in the war before you were born, don't you?'

'Yes, Mother, you told me.'

'But I didn't tell you that your father's parents are still alive, and you have a grandmother and a grandfather. After your father was killed, I had a falling-out with them. It is now nearly eight years since I have seen them. However, I think the time has come to make amends, if it isn't too late.'

Milly's eyes were like saucers. 'I have a granddad and grandmother?' She was finding it hard to take in, for she had often wondered why all the children in school had grannies and grandas and aunties, while she had no one except her mother. Now she would be like other children, with a big family and relatives. But there were questions in her head that dulled the happiness she was longing to feel. 'Didn't Granddad and Grandma want us? Did they send us away?'

'It's a long story, Amelia, and I can't answer it

in a few words. Things were said that hurt, but the fault was on both sides. Today I want to find out if there is any regret on the part of your grandparents, and ask if the rift can be healed.'

'Oh, I would love to have a granddad and grandmother! That would make me the same as other children. Will they like me, Mother, d'you think?'

'I don't think they could help but like you, Amelia, for you were not responsible for the harsh words that were spoken. But I have to be honest with you and say I can't promise that your grandfather will even agree to see us. I intend to take you to his office, and if he is working today we can take it from there and see what happens.' Evelyn averted her eyes. She had robbed this young girl of so much. 'I will tell you that your father came from a very wealthy family, and your name is really Amelia Lister-Sinclair. It was I who dropped the "Lister", perhaps out of spite, or perhaps because I didn't want them to find us. It doesn't really matter now, it is all in the past. I would like to start again with a clean slate.'

For the first time in her life that she could remember, Milly touched her mother's hand. 'Can we go now, and see if Granddad likes me?'

Tears were stinging Evelyn's eyes. Oh, she had a lot to answer for, ruining this child's life. Please God, Cyril wouldn't turn them away. 'Yes, we can go now. Put your coat on, there's a good girl.'

Cyril Lister-Sinclair swivelled his deep leather chair as he faced Oscar Wentworth across the desk. 'We had a very quiet Christmas, just a few close friends for dinner. Matilda isn't one for socialising these days. But it was pleasant enough. The food was good and the wine plentiful. But I can't forget the Christmases of years ago, when the house would be filled with Charles' friends and merriment. I know I shouldn't dwell on the past, but I can't help it. How was your Christmas? Did the children enjoy themselves?' He didn't mean to let a sigh escape but couldn't stop it. 'It really is a time for children. For the grown-ups it's just an excuse to buy new clothes and have parties.'

'You should have come to ours, Cyril, I did try to persuade you. You are right about children, though, it really is a time for them. Just seeing their eyes when they came downstairs and saw the presents under the tree was like magic. They are still too young to understand, and that is the beauty of it. They are so innocent they really believe Father Christmas came down the chimney and left the presents. Before Gwen had taken the boys to bed the night before, she had left a glass of wine and two mince pies on the table, telling them they were for Father Christmas as he got hungry working so hard.'

'Gwen is a wonderful mother,' Cyril said. 'Kind and loving, just as a mother should be. You are lucky in your marriage, Oscar, you should count your blessings.'

'I do every day, Cyril, believe me. I am the luckiest man alive.' Oscar was in two minds whether to tell his friend where he was off to when he left the office. He didn't want to build his hopes up, as he had done in the past only to disappoint him, but the lead he'd now been given in his quest to find Evelyn and Amelia, looked very hopeful indeed, and would put some interest back in the life of the man who appeared to have everything but was sad and lonely, with little happiness in his life.

'I have some news which I think will interest you, Cyril, regarding the whereabouts of Evelyn and Amelia. I was introduced to someone a few days ago who has quite a high position in the Department of Education. I pretended to let it slip that I was trying to trace an old family friend and her daughter. During the long conversation, I asked him casually how I would find out if a child attended a school in the area, and he said he could do that quite easily if he had details such as surname and date of birth. As this conversation took place at a party, I didn't like to monopolise the man's time, so I said I would call to his office some time this week. I'll be on my way there when I leave here. If I have any news I will call this afternoon. If not I'll see you tomorrow.'

There was a spark of interest in Cyril's eyes. 'That sounds very promising, Oscar, the best lead so far. I would appreciate it if you kept me informed of any news. My thoughts are never far away from them, and the dreadful way I cast them aside.'

'No, Cyril, I will not have you shouldering all the blame when Gwen and I were of the same mind as yourself. If there is blame to be laid, then my wife and I must share it. However, I do not believe it was all one-sided, Evelyn did herself no favours by adopting the attitude she did. I only hope the years have mellowed her, and she'll realise there were faults all round.' Oscar pushed his chair back. 'I'll get off, old boy. I want to get to the Education Office before the staff have their lunch break. You can rest assured I will let you know the second I have news for you. It would please me no end to put a smile on your face again and hear the laughter that has been missing for so long.'

'You don't know how much your friendship has meant to me over the years, Oscar,' Cyril said. 'You have been like a son to me, and that is something I will never forget. Now, go about your business, and my prayers go with you.'

There were six steps up to the offices of C. LISTER-SINCLAIR LTD, and Evelyn and Milly were on the second step when the door opened and a man dashed out. He passed them without a glance, but some instinct made him turn back. He saw a slender woman holding the hand of a young girl.

'Evelyn?' Oscar climbed the steps to stand beside the couple. 'I don't believe it, Cyril and I have just been talking about you!'

Evelyn had recognised him as soon as he came out of the door, and the sight of him had stopped her in her tracks. She told herself it was a mistake to have come. 'Oscar ... what a coincidence.'

'It is more than that.' He looked down at the little girl and Evelyn heard his sharp intake of breath. For a few seconds he felt he was looking into the face of his old friend Charles. Then he pulled himself together. 'And this is Amelia, I

548

take it?'

Milly looked up into the smiling face of the unknown man and smiled back. 'I'm going to see my grandfather. Do you know him?'

Evelyn's face flushed. 'We don't know that for sure, Amelia, he may not be in the office today.'

Oscar bent his knees so that his face was on a level with Milly's. 'I'm your Uncle Oscar.' He held out his hand. 'How do you do? I'm very pleased to meet you.'

She shook his hand, her pretty face aglow. 'Are you really my uncle?'

Oscar was tempted to hug her, but afraid it might frighten her. 'Let us say I'm a step-uncle who has been searching the city for you and your mother.'

Oblivious to the drama taking place, Milly asked, 'Do you think my grandfather will be pleased to see me and my mother, or will he send us away?'

'Far from sending you away, my dear, you will be welcomed with open arms. He will be most happy to see both of you.' Oscar stretched to his full height. 'Shall we go inside, Evelyn? It is far too cold to stand here.'

The entrance hall to the building was quite large with several doors off it, leading to the offices of the clerical staff. There was also an ornate winding staircase which led to Cyril's office, and those of his personal secretaries. 'Shall we talk here for a while before going upstairs?' Oscar asked. 'This is going to come as a shock to Cyril, and as his friend I care very much for his welfare. I am, therefore, concerned that the

549

reason for your visit is not such that it will cause him further anguish, for he has suffered greatly over the last eight years?'

Evelyn shook her head. 'I have not come looking for trouble, far from it. I have come to ask for Mr Lister-Sinclair's help.' She glanced down at her daughter. 'I do not wish to explain right now, it would be a little awkward, but I will explain in detail to him the reason for my being here. I am hoping for his understanding.' She looked directly into Oscar's eyes. 'I believe you married Gwen, I saw the announcement in a paper. I hope she is well and happy, and would like you to convey my best wishes to her.' Her eyes dropped. 'We were very good friends at one time.'

'And there is no reason why you shouldn't be friends again. You have never been forgotten, Evelyn, but I hope we are all grown-up enough to realise that each of us must share part of the blame for the turn of events. Don't you agree?'

'Yes, I am more than prepared to admit I wasn't the most easy person to get along with. But someone has come into my life who has changed me greatly from the selfish person I once was.' With her daughter in mind, she added, 'You will hear all, eventually, but for now please take my word that I come not to make trouble, but to make peace.'

Oscar held out his hand and Evelyn took it with a tremulous smile. 'Welcome back, Evelyn, you and Amelia are going to make a lot of people happy. For months I have been scouring the schools in search of your daughter, and was on my way out now to visit the Office of Education.

Now I am going to ask a really big favour of you. I would like to be the one to take Amelia into Cyril's office, without any warning. I have had to disappoint him so many times, I would like to be the one who unites him with his granddaughter. Would you allow me to do that, please?'

Evelyn nodded. Her heartbeat had slowed down now she knew she would be welcome. 'Of course you can, Oscar. I will wait here for you.'

'Certainly not! You must come upstairs and I will leave you in the capable hands of Cyril's secretary. He won't be able to see you, and Miss Williams is the soul of discretion so you need have no fear. She also makes a very good cup of tea.' Oscar gazed down at Amelia. 'You don't mind coming with me to meet your grandfather, do you? Your mother won't be far away and she will be in good hands.'

Milly felt as though she was dreaming. It was a lot for a young girl to take in, and she was afraid she was being shown something that would soon be snatched away from her. But the tall man looking down at her had such a kind face, she put her hand into his. 'I would like to see my grandfather now, please.'

When the rap came on his office door, without lifting his head from the ledger he was checking, Cyril called, 'Come in.'

'I've brought someone to meet you, Cyril, have you five minutes to spare?' Oscar was so happy, he could barely contain himself. He walked across the office floor with Amelia's hand held tightly in his, then pressed her close to the desk

551

while he took a step back.

When Cyril looked up, he was perplexed, until he found himself looking into a pair of green eyes. At first he thought he was going to faint. He held his head in his hands for a few seconds, until he heard a soft voice asking, 'Don't you want to see me, Granddad?'

Wiping away tears, Cyril turned his chair sideways and held out his arms. Milly, seeing his tears, walked round the desk and into the outstretched arms. 'Don't cry, Granddad. Have you got a handkerchief and I'll dry your eyes for you?'

Cyril tried to compose himself, but he was far too emotional. The girl reminded him so strongly of the son he had lost. Her colouring, the shape of her nose, most of all the green eyes. To think he had turned his back on this child from the day she was born, calling her mother a liar. He had wasted eight years of both their lives.

'Granddad, aren't you going to give me a kiss and say you are glad to see me?' Milly wiped away the tear that was rolling down his cheek. 'I didn't want to make you cry.'

'I'm crying with happiness, my darling.' Cyril hugged her close, raining kisses on her face. 'And now I've found you, I'll never let you go again.' Over her shoulder he asked Oscar, 'How did this miracle come about?'

Oscar cleared his throat, for he was very touched by the scene. 'I was going down the steps while Amelia and Evelyn were coming up.'

'Where is Evelyn?'

'She's having a cup of tea with Miss Williams. I

asked if I could bring Amelia in, I didn't want to miss the moment you found your granddaughter.'

Milly said quietly, 'I would like you to call me Milly, all my friends call me that. Except Mother, she always calls me Amelia.'

'Milly!' Cyril nodded his approval. 'Yes, I like that name, it suits you.'

'I'll have a cup of tea with Evelyn and Miss Williams while you two get acquainted,' Oscar said. 'I know Evelyn wants to have a serious talk with you later, Cyril, and I don't want to interfere so I think it would be best all round if I take Amelia ... er, Milly ... out for an hour or so. I could take her to meet Gwen, I know my wife would like that.'

'Then would you bring that chair around the desk so I can sit near my granddaughter for a few minutes first? We have a lot of years to make up.'

When a brown leather chair was placed next to Cyril's, Milly sat on it and giggled when she found she could swivel from side to side. The sound was like music to the two men listening, both of them remembering that Charles had been a giggler when he was a young boy.

'I'll leave you to it for a while. When Evelyn comes in, I'll take Milly to meet Gwen. I'll make it an hour, that should be long enough for you both to say what you need to, and to listen to each other.' As he was crossing the room, Oscar heard Milly asking, 'You do like me, don't you, Granddad, you won't send me away?'

'I don't like you, my darling, I love you. And I will never let you go now I've found you. And your grandmother will be so happy when she sees

553

you, she will adore you.'

'I'm a very lucky girl, aren't I, Granddad?'

'It is I who am lucky, to have found you after all these years. Come and give your granddad a big kiss and a hug.'

Oscar closed the office door quietly, swallowing the lump in his throat.

Chapter Twenty-Nine

Evelyn stood at the top of the staircase, hands resting on the highly polished rail, and watched Amelia going down the outside steps with Oscar. She could hear her daughter's infectious giggle as she hopped down each step, and Oscar's laughter. He had been very kind and friendly, never once asking personal questions about her life since they'd last met. She had found it awkward at first being in Miss Williams' office, for they had met when she was courting Charles and he'd needed to call to the office one day to see his father. But although Miss Williams must have been filled with curiosity, like Oscar she was friendly without prying.

Taking her hand from the rail, Evelyn let out a deep sigh as she turned. She was on her way to face Cyril now, and was feeling nervous and apprehensive. The atmosphere was bound to be emotional, it couldn't be otherwise, but she hoped her father-in-law's reception of her would be as friendly as Oscar's, for her whole future depended on his reaction to what she had to tell him. The sooner she went in and faced him, the sooner her tummy would stop churning and her heartbeat would slow down. So, after running a hand down her skirt to smooth out any creases, and patting her hair, she straightened her shoulders and made for the door that bore his name in gold letters.

When the knock came Cyril jumped to his feet. He was crossing the floor when he called, 'Come in.' His arms were outstretched when Evelyn came through the door, and he gripped her shoulders and kissed her cheek. 'You are very welcome, my dear, it has been such a long time.'

Evelyn was reduced to tears. She really didn't deserve this kind of welcome. It was her fault this man had been without his granddaughter for so long. She had spent the last few days reviewing her actions, and knew now she had been a selfish bitch. She hadn't cared for anyone but herself and her greed for a life of luxury. When this man had lost his beloved son and was devastated, she hadn't tried to console him or even say she was sorry. Neither had she shed a tear for the man who was her husband, too busy feeling sorry for herself and worrying about her own comfort. And she'd kept on feeling sorry for herself for over eight years. It was Philip who'd made her take stock of the person she'd been, and she didn't like what she saw. She didn't deserve this man's kiss or his warm welcome.

'Sit down, my dear.' Cyril cupped her elbow until she was seated. 'Shall I ask my secretary to bring in some refreshment?'

Evelyn nodded. 'Miss Williams very kindly made me some tea, but I'm afraid my mouth is dry with nerves so another drink would be most welcome.'

Cyril picked up the phone and rang through to his secretary. 'A pot of tea and some biscuits, please, Miss Williams, and then I don't want to be disturbed for the rest of the day.' He replaced the receiver, and smiled. 'There is no need for nerves, Evelyn, I hope we meet up as friends, with the past forgotten. I cannot tell you how I felt seeing my granddaughter. She is so like Charles. I did you a grave wrong, my dear, and hope you can find it in your heart to forgive me?'

Evelyn shook her head vigorously. 'I know you have asked that we put the past behind us, but I want you to know that I do realise the type of person I was then, and that was a greedy and selfish woman. All I thought about was myself and my own comfort, and when circumstances changed I blamed everyone else for my plight. I haven't been a good mother to Amelia because I saw her as the reason I lost my status in society. I can see myself as I was then, and I don't like what I see. I knew you would want your granddaughter if you saw her, for she is so like Charles, but because I wasn't happy, I didn't want anyone else to be either.' She leaned forward and gripped his arm. 'But I have changed, Mr Lister-Sinclair, and I regret those lost years. The reason for the change is that I have met someone I have fallen in love with. The only man I have even looked at since Amelia was born. He returns my feelings and wants to marry me, and that is the reason for my coming to you today. I want you to help me.'

They were interrupted then as Miss Williams brought in the tray. 'Shall I pour, or would you rather do it yourself?'

Cyril smiled at his trusted secretary. 'You pour, if you will. You are much more efficient and will have the job done in half the time.'

As soon as they were alone again, he bent forward. 'Tell me about this man, and how I can help you?'

'I work as a secretary and he is my boss. All anyone in the office knew about me was that I was a war widow and my name was Mrs Sinclair. I made no friends, and no one knew I had a daughter. It was my boss who broke down the defences I had wrapped around myself, and gradually I fell in love with him. He is kind, thoughtful, humorous, and very much in love with me.' Evelyn sighed. 'But I haven't told him about Amelia, he doesn't know I have an eight-year-old daughter. It wasn't intentional to begin with. I never thought our feelings for each other would lead to anything. Then, when he asked me to marry him, I didn't have the courage to tell him about her. To be truthful, I'm afraid it will change his feelings for me. He will think I am deceitful for not telling him sooner.'

'If he really loves you, it won't change his feelings. Why should it?'

'Because I'm afraid then everything will have to come out in the open. That my name is really Lister-Sinclair and I was married to Charles, but his name is not on the birth certificate. If you remember, you advised me not to put Charles' name down as the father. Which means my friend will jump to the conclusion you and Gwen jumped to: that my baby was illegitimate. I couldn't bear to face him and have him think I was a loose woman, so I've come to ask if there is any way this whole sorry mess can be put right? Can the birth certificate be made right, or is it too late now?'

'Of course it can be put right. I will see to that as soon as possible, if you will let me have the original certificate with all the details on. And I have to hang my head in shame when I tell you I had the marriage annulled, on the grounds it had never been consummated.'

'I had an idea you would do that, and dropped the "Lister" from my name so people would not connect me with your family. I don't blame you for doing what you did. Although I was too wrapped up in myself at the time to appreciate how devastated you and your wife must have been, I can appreciate it now. The word "sorry" is totally inadequate, but it is the only one I can think of right now, and it comes from my heart.'

'Let the past be erased from our memories,' Cyril said, 'and look to the future. I will attend to the birth and marriage certificates immediately, that will be no problem for me and no one else will be told. Except for Oscar and Gwen, who have helped me so much over the years and who have for a long time questioned their own attitude towards you. They will both be overjoyed to have you back as their friend.' He sat back in his chair and held his chin in his hand. 'Now, about this man you have fallen in love with. Am I allowed to know his name?'

'He's a solicitor – Philip Astbury.'

Cyril sat forward to rest his arms on the desk. 'Philip Astbury! My dear Evelyn, I know Philip well! His family have been friends of ours for years, and they're friends of the Wentworths. Oscar knows Philip particularly well. He and Charles used to be in the same class at school as

Philip.' He shook his head in disbelief. 'It's been such a marvellous day for me, meeting my grand-daughter for the first time and seeing your good self again. And now, on top of that, comes the news that you and Philip Astbury are to wed! He's a wonderful chap, very popular with everyone, and comes from a good family. I'm so pleased for you.'

'I think perhaps you are taking too much for granted,' Evelyn told him. 'I can hardly face him and tell him I've been living a lie and have an eight-year-old daughter. I dread seeing the expression on his face which tells me I have lied to him and he no longer wants to marry me.'

'Then you won't have to tell him, I will.' Cyril left his chair and rounded the desk to where Evelyn sat. 'I did you a great wrong all those years ago, practically saying you were no better than a woman of the streets and leaving you to do your best with my son's child. I can only say that I was distraught with grief, and wanted to hurt someone. Now I want to right that wrong, so please let me?'

Evelyn shook her head. 'Much as I am dreading facing Philip, I feel I must do it myself. What a coward he would think me if I allowed you to do my dirty work.'

'My dear Evelyn, I have known Philip Astbury since he was a toddler. I know his parents well, and his Uncle Simon. We are all good friends. I firmly believe Philip will be more understanding when I tell him of my role in all this, and how very much I wronged you. And if you will allow me to do this one thing for you, it will ease some of the guilt I have carried around for a such a long time. Please, I beg you?'

Evelyn sighed. 'My fear is he may not want to take on an eight-year-old daughter. He has mentioned that his parents keep asking when he's going to wed and give them grandchildren, and I know he will want to have a child by me as soon as possible, for I am not young, I am twenty-nine.'

'How would Milly feel about you getting married? Would she feel left out?'

'Good heavens, no! I have not been cruel to Amelia, but neither have I been a good, loving mother. She thinks more of the woman who lives next door who is very good with her. In fact, the pair of them idolise each other.'

'Who is this woman next door? And where in Liverpool do you live?'

'Amelia and I live in a small two-up-two-down house, and the woman next door is called Bessie. She minds Amelia for me until I get home from work. She has a job herself, though, so only has Amelia for an hour or so every night and every weekend. They get on very well together, and although I should be ashamed to admit it, my daughter would far rather be with Bessie than with me.'

Cyril stared at her for several seconds before speaking. 'We can discuss these things another time, don't you think? The best person to solve your worries and put your mind at rest is Philip, and we can't guess what his thoughts will be on the matter. So, do I have your permission to speak to him?'

Evelyn nodded. 'If you think it would be for the best.'

Cyril opened an address book which lay by the phone, and leafed through the pages. Then he lifted the receiver from the hook at the side of the telephone and dialled. 'May I speak to Mr Philip Astbury, please? My name is Cyril Lister-Sinclair, and it is a personal call.' After a few seconds, Evelyn could hear Philip's voice and her heart turned over. She couldn't hear clearly, but it sounded as though he was very pleased by the call.

'Do you have a busy day ahead of you, my boy?' Cyril asked. Then, 'I was wondering if you could spare me an hour? No, it's not something I wish to discuss over the telephone, I need to see you. No, nothing is wrong, I was just thinking it's a long time since I saw you.' He smiled. 'Two o'clock will be fine, Philip, as long as I'm not taking you away from an important client. I look forward to seeing you.'

Evelyn jumped to her feet. 'What am I going to do? I don't want him to see me here, but Amelia isn't back yet...'

Cyril waved her to her seat before picking up the phone and dialling again. When he heard Gwen's voice, he asked, 'Gwen, my dear, is Oscar still there with Milly? Oh, would you ask him to drive back here straight away and pick up Evelyn? I am sure you would like to see her after all these years. There is no need for him to bring Milly unless you are busy. I'm sure Evelyn will explain all about the events that led up to today when she sees you. But it would be best if you could find something for my granddaughter to do while the explanations are going on. She has no inkling, and it would be better to leave it that way for now.' He suddenly burst out laughing. 'No, you may not keep my granddaughter, even though you think she is delightful! My wife and I have priority, and I can't wait for Matilda to see her. But right now, will you ask Oscar to make haste, please?'

Cyril was so happy he couldn't keep the smile from his face. It was like a dream come true, to have part of his beloved son back in his life.

'I know I have no right to ask any favours of you, Evelyn, but it means so much having a granddaughter in my life. It's as if my son will always be with Matilda and me. Every time we look at her, we will see his dear face. Would you allow me to take her home with me some time later today, when other matters important to you are settled? I don't want to ring my wife with the news, I want to walk into the room and watch her face when she looks at Milly. I won't even introduce them, I don't think it will be necessary.'

'I would be very happy for you to take Amelia home. You have been so generous today, with warmth, friendship and understanding. But if Amelia...' Evelyn smiled. 'It seems I'm going to have to give in, or be the only one calling my daughter Amelia. If Milly isn't home when Bessie gets in from work, she and two other neighbours will be concerned about her. But we have several hours yet, so I'll worry about that nearer the time.'

'I shall have to meet this Bessie sometime. If Milly is fond of her, then I must make sure I become her friend. When everything is settled, would you take me to meet her?'

'Yes, of course.' Evelyn turned her head as the door opened. 'Oh, here's Oscar, I'll get my coat from Miss Williams' office.' She hesitated then said, 'Mr Lister-Sinclair, would you ring me at Oscar's whatever the outcome? I shall be a bag of nerves, wondering what is being said in this office.'

'I shall ring you immediately my meeting with Philip is over, or even when he is still here, if that is what he wants. Have no fear, my dear, I feel certain that everything will turn out well for you. Now, go with Oscar and renew your friendship with Gwen. You both have lots to talk about.' His smile was one of encouragement. 'Oh, and most of my friends, young and old, call me Cyril. And I would like you to look upon me as a friend.'

Philip didn't wait for an answer to his rap on the office door but threw it open and strode across the room wearing a beaming smile, his hand outstretched. 'Hello, old boy, it's quite a while since we met. I hope you and Matilda are well?'

Cyril waved him to the chair opposite. 'We are both in good health, thank you. And I don't need to ask you, for you look remarkably well. Would you like some refreshment – a cup of tea or something stronger?'

'I had tea and a sandwich before I left the office, I couldn't cope with another cup.' Philip rubbed his hands together, smiling. 'I can still remember where you keep your stock of the finest wines and malt whisky in the city though, so shall I do the honours?'

'Yes, my boy, a whisky would go down very

well.' Cyril watched as Philip opened the doors of the high cabinet which did indeed boast a fine selection of drinks. He was fond of Philip, and like all the people who knew him, had wondered why he had never married. It wasn't that the chances weren't there, for he was chased by every eligible female in their circle of friends. 'So, how is life treating you, my boy?'

'Life is excellent at the moment, Cyril, and I'm very happy.' Philip placed a glass in front of him, then sat down with his own glass in his hand. 'I'm delighted to see you, as ever, but rather intrigued by your telephone call. There is nothing I enjoy more than something with a hint of mystery to it.' He swirled the whisky round in the glass before taking a sip. 'Was there a reason for your call, or were you genuinely interested in my health?'

'There was a reason, Philip, and I think when you hear it you will be surprised.' Cyril was going to take things slowly and choose his words with care. 'I believe you know a woman called Evelyn Sinclair?'

Philip's brows shot up. 'Yes, I know her very well! We're courting! In fact, we will be getting married very shortly. It isn't general knowledge at the moment, except that my parents know of her though they have not met. Do you know Evelyn?'

Cyril sat back in his chair and drew a deep breath. 'I want you to listen without interruption for a short while, if you will. Evelyn Sinclair is really Evelyn Lister-Sinclair. She is Charles' widow.' He saw the shock on Philip's face and quickly went on, 'This is not to say she doesn't love you, nothing changes that, but there are things you should know. It is quite a long story, and I don't come out of it very well, but I think everything should be brought out into the open now and then you and Evelyn can start with a clean slate. So please be patient, dear boy, and listen to what I have to say.'

For half an hour Philip sat quietly, his expression changing at intervals. Cyril told him everything, kept nothing back. Except one thing, which was a little lie that would hurt no one: he told Philip that Evelyn conceived a child on the last day of her husband's leave before he was sent overseas. He was hard on himself, too, revealing how he had ordered Evelyn to leave the house in Princes Avenue, even though she was with child. The fact that she had a child brought Philip to the edge of his chair, but not once did he try to interrupt.

'Oscar and Gwen Wentworth were best man and maid of honour at Charles' marriage to Evelyn, which was held in a registry office because Charles only had a few days' leave and there was no time for the big society wedding my wife and I had envisaged for our son. Gwen was a friend of Evelyn's all those years ago, but lost touch with her just after the baby was born. Oscar has been trying to trace mother and child for a while now, without success. In fact today has been a day of coincidences and surprises. He was due to meet a man at the Department of Education this morning, in the hope he could pull a few strings and find the school Amelia attended. He was going down the front steps when Evelyn was coming up.' Cyril sat back in his chair. 'So there you have it, my boy, the full story.'

Philip sighed. 'Why didn't Evelyn tell me all this herself?'

'She wanted to. She loves you very much and is now terrified in case you think badly of her and walk away. She said you would think her a coward for not telling you face to face, but I talked her out of it. I took eight years of that woman's life by wrongfully accusing her of having another man's baby. I had just heard that Charles had been killed in action and was beside myself with grief. I couldn't believe she could possibly have been made pregnant by my son in that one day. I wasn't thinking clearly, Philip, and unfortunately Evelyn isn't given to showing any emotion. I thought her hard-hearted when she didn't grieve for Charles as I grieved.'

'I'm having a problem taking all this in, Cyril,' Philip said. 'I was hoping to marry Evelyn in the next month or so, even though I knew very little about her life. She wouldn't even tell me where she lived. None of that bothered me, I fell in love with her the minute I set eyes on her. Her being your daughter-in-law and the widow of Charles, I can live with. In fact, I would be delighted to be a close member of your family, and I know my parents would be pleased. They don't know anything about her really, not even her name. Evelyn asked me not to tell anyone until she'd sorted her affairs out. When I came here today I thought it was a friendly call, I certainly wasn't prepared for what you've told me. And, as I say,

567

I can live with most of it. But for her not to tell me she has an eight-year-old daughter … well, I find that very hard to take.'

'Evelyn knows that, and it is her worst fear. She said your parents were keen for you to marry and give them grandchildren, and she knows they would be unhappy for you to take on an eight-year-old girl.' Cyril couldn't keep back what was in his heart and mind. 'Even though Milly is the most beautiful child imaginable. I am completely captivated by her, and she is the image of Charles. Now, there may be a solution to this, but I haven't mentioned it to Evelyn. She was very nervous when she left here, knowing you were coming. But I will test it on you, to see if you agree with what I have to say. I am going to ask Evelyn to let Milly come to live with Matilda and myself. We would dearly love to have her, she would bring happiness back into our lives. Evelyn could see her whenever she wished, while you could be her uncle. That would leave you free to lead the lives of newly-weds. To have your own children, your own family. How would that sit with you, Philip?'

'Cyril, I love that woman so much I will marry her no matter what her circumstances are. I admit I would like to start a family of our own, but I wouldn't make that part of the bargain. I would never take a mother away from her child.'

'Even if mother and child agree, and it is best for both of them?'

'Ah, I could live with that. But I can't see Evelyn doing so.'

'Then we must wait and ask her.' Cyril didn't

want to mention the fact that there wasn't the closeness between Evelyn and her daughter there usually was between mother and child. Nor was he going to mention the neighbour, Bessie, whom he would very much like to meet.

'I am to ring Oscar's when you leave, and he will bring Evelyn and Milly back here.' Cyril was looking thoughtful as he tapped his fingers on the desk. 'Do you have any business to attend to, or would you like to see Evelyn today and clear the air? Or perhaps you'd like some time to think things through?'

Philip seemed to come alive. 'I don't have any clients, you know it is always quiet the week between Christmas and New Year. Even if I had, I would cancel their appointments. I desperately want to see Evelyn, tell her that no matter what obstacles are in the way, I intend to marry her as quickly as possible. My parents will no doubt be concerned, but when they get to know her, they will understand why I love her so much. When you said you were distraught when Charles died, and saddened that Evelyn showed no emotion, I could understand both sides. You see, from what little she has told me, her parents showed her no love. It took me a while to break down the wall she had built around herself, but it was well worth the effort. She is the most loving woman I have ever met. And in time, Cyril, you will find that out for yourself.'

He got to his feet and began to pace the room. 'I sound like a lovesick schoolboy, don't I? Who would ever have thought that Philip Astbury, the philanderer who attended every party with a different woman on his arm, would become so besotted, so head-over-heels in love, that he was prepared to do anything for the love of a special woman?'

'I should think all your friends will be very happy for you, Philip, for you are very well liked and have never spoken ill of any of your women friends.' Cyril was so happy he thought his heart would burst. This was one day in his life he would never forget. To see again the woman his son had married, and the granddaughter who was the fruit of that short marriage. Then to find out that Philip, the son of one of his best friends, was in love and wanted to marry Evelyn – well, it was like a storybook ending, where everyone lived happily ever after. But was he being over-optimistic?

Philip stopped his pacing and stood in front of Cyril's desk. 'Do you have a spare office where Evelyn and I could talk in private?'

'There is an office on the next floor which is furnished and comfortable, you are very welcome to use that. While I ring Oscar to ask him to bring Evelyn and her daughter, I suggest you help yourself to another whisky to steady your nerves.'

When Oscar answered the phone, he was asked to bring Evelyn and Milly back to the office. Cyril suggested that as soon as they arrived, Evelyn should be directed to the office on the top floor while Milly be brought into his office. 'It's been quite a memorable day, my boy, don't you agree? It is a long time since I have felt so happy and light-hearted. A great weight has been lifted from my shoulders.'

Oscar chuckled. 'It has certainly been a day of

surprises. Gwen's eyes have been as round as saucers since Evelyn arrived. I know a little of what is happening but not all. I have been keeping Milly amused and out of the way. What a treasure the girl is! She is clever, without a doubt, but what I find most endearing is her sense of fun. When she laughs, it's catching. You can't help laughing with her. If she were mine, I would love her to bits.'

'I can't wait for Matilda to see her. And, as you know I love her dearly, you will not think I am making fun of her when I say the bottle of smelling salts will definitely be needed.'

'The door facing you at the top of the stairs is the one you need,' Oscar told Evelyn when they entered the lobby. 'You can't miss it.'

She was shaking visibly. 'I know it's silly of me, but I'm scared.'

'I'm quite sure there is nothing to be afraid of, my dear, so take a deep breath and run up those stairs as though you haven't a care in the world, which I'm sure you haven't.' He held on to Milly's hand and together they watched Evelyn mount the stairs.

'Why is Mother scared, Uncle Oscar? There's no bogeyman up there, is there?'

'Now, you don't believe in bogeymen, do you? You're a clever girl, and if you are clever, you will know there is no such thing. Come along and ask your granddad if I'm not telling the truth.'

Milly pulled her hand free. Giggling, she said, 'I'll race you to Granddad!' With that she took off like a shot, flung the office door open and ran across the floor to the desk.

Cyril looked up when the door burst open, to see Milly running towards him, her face aglow and her childish laughter filling the room. 'Well, I never, what have we here?'

'I bet Uncle Oscar I could beat him to get to you first.' She turned to Oscar, who was leaning on the back of a chair pretending to be out of breath. 'I won!'

'Ah, but did you win fairly?' Cyril asked. 'That is what you should ask yourself. Did you give Oscar a start because he is older than you and is carrying more weight?'

Milly's brow furrowed. 'I never thought of that, Granddad, because I've only ever raced the girls in school. But you are right, it wasn't fair, and I'm sorry, Uncle Oscar. So shall we call it evens?'

He dropped into a chair, chuckling. 'You weren't behind the door when they were giving brains out, my dear. I must remember never to play cards with you.'

Now this remark was of interest to Milly. 'Oh, I can play cards, I'm getting very good at it. I win more games than Jack does.'

'And might we ask who Jack is?' Cyril asked, eager to know as much as possible about his granddaughter's life. 'And where do you play cards?'

'Jack is my best friend, he lives in the house opposite ours. He is one year older than me so he is nine. Because he's older than me, wouldn't you think he'd win more games than me, Granddad?'

'Perhaps he likes you and lets you win?'

'Oh, he does like me, but he doesn't let me win.

In fact, I have to keep my eye on him because if he gets the chance, he cheats.'

The two men exchanged glances. How refreshing it was to listen to a child who was too innocent to tell an untruth. 'Your grandmother is very fond of playing cards, Milly, so you would get along very well with her. Perhaps the games she plays are more grown-up than the ones you play, but she would love to teach you so you could play with her.'

Milly's eyes slid from side to side as she weighed up the situation. Then she asked, 'Does Grandma's table have a cloth on it that hangs right down over the sides?'

Cyril rubbed his chin. 'No, I don't think it does, my dear, but I'm not really sure. Why do you ask?'

'Well, if there was a cloth on the table that hung right over the sides, I'd have to keep my eye on her in case she tried to cheat.'

The hearty laughter of the two men reached the office of Miss Williams, and brought a smile to her face. She hadn't been told who the young girl was, but she didn't need telling. She remembered Evelyn from when she was courting Mr Charles, and as soon as she'd looked into Milly's face she saw the same features and the same green eyes as Mr Cyril's son. And there was the age of the girl. All the signs told the wise secretary that this was the granddaughter her boss had pined for for a long, long time. And because he was such a caring boss, and she had grown very fond of him over the years, Miss Williams was happy for him.

Chapter Thirty

Philip had pulled the two office chairs close together and, after holding Evelyn tight and smothering her with kisses, he pressed her gently down on to one of the chairs, still gripping her hands. 'My beloved Evelyn, why didn't you tell me all the things that were on your mind, and apparently worrying the life out of you? What sort of a man do you think I am, that you were afraid to confide in me?'

'I didn't think our relationship was going to become serious, and by the time it did, and I found myself in love with you, it was too late. I thought you would think badly of me, and couldn't bear for that to happen.' Evelyn stroked his cheek. 'I was afraid of losing you. If I had known your family were friends of the Lister-Sinclairs, then I would have been more open with you. But, as Cyril has probably told you, we didn't part on the best of terms.'

Philip nodded. 'He has been very open and honest, and I would expect nothing less of the man I have known and admired all my life. He wanted to be the one to tell me, so as to spare you. He has admitted that he did you a grave wrong, and by telling me of his involvement in your break from the family, is trying to put things right. He is so happy to have you back as part of the family, and his joy in seeing his granddaughter is beyond words. He is like a new man, now he has something to live for.'

'I would like to set the record straight, my darling, and tell you that all the fault does not lie on Cyril's shoulders, I was as much to blame. I wasn't a very nice person then. I was too selfish, and thought only of myself. Never once did I consider the anguish he and his wife must have gone through when they heard their son had been killed. As Charles' wife, I should have been a help to them in their grief.'

Philip raised her hand to his lips. 'It is all over now, my love, your worries are at an end. No need for any more secrecy, your life can be an open book.'

Still the frown was on Evelyn's face, for she couldn't believe life was going to be happy ever after. That would be too easy. 'What is going to happen now, Philip?'

'The only thing I am certain of at the moment, my lovely, is that you and I are going to be married as soon as possible.'

'I'm worried about your parents,' she told him. 'What are they going to think of me, and how will they feel about Amelia? I know they are longing for you to give them a grandchild, but I think it would be a great disappointment to them if they were asked to accept an eight-year-old child. It would be asking a great deal of them.'

Philip lowered his head. 'I'd be telling a lie if I said they wouldn't mind, for I agree with you that it would be a great disappointment to them. Given time, I'm sure they, and myself, would grow to love your daughter, but at the moment it is quite a lot to take in.' He raised his head, a half smile on his face. 'In any case, we don't have a house yet, and for a while after we marry we would have to live in the apartment which only has one bedroom.'

'Are you quite sure you want to marry me?' she asked. 'Is it not too much for you to take on? I would quite understand if you had second thoughts.'

'If there is one thing in my life of which I am certain, my lovely Evelyn, it is my intention to make you my wife. There could, however, be a short-term solution. Cyril has said he would love to have Milly living with him. He said it would be a joy for him and his wife to have Charles' daughter under his roof. I didn't make any comment on that, I was sure you wouldn't agree.'

Evelyn mulled this news over for a while then said, 'That could be a solution, darling. If Milly was with Cyril and Matilda, I could see her very often, and she would still be my daughter. And, quite honestly, I believe she would welcome it, for as I have told you, my daughter and I do not have a close relationship. That is my fault entirely, not hers, and something I intend to rectify now, if she will let me. It may take a while, but I have to make up for the years when I treated her like a stranger.' She squeezed his hand. 'You will like her, I know you will, and if everything turns out as we both wish, then it would be my hope that when we have children of our own she will be treated as their sister. I have left her out in the cold for so long, it has to end. I want to win my daughter's love.'

'Does she know about me,' Philip asked, 'or not?'

'Not until today, and not from me. Cyril said he would mention it to her casually, so it won't come as a surprise when she meets you.'

'And is that to be today?' Philip found himself wanting to meet the child who was born of the woman he loved and his old friend Charles. 'I am looking forward to meeting her, and I hope she likes me and we can become friends.'

'She is a very friendly girl, with winning ways. Which shows she has a strong character since I have done little to help her development. She will like you, and I have no doubt that you will like her. Would you like to go downstairs now and meet her?'

Philip pulled her to her feet. 'Let me hold you in my arms for a while, so I know you are real and our future together is sealed.'

Down in Cyril's office, Milly was entertaining Cyril and Oscar. A real chatterbox, with a keen sense of humour, she was telling them of the capers she got up to in school. When she mimicked her class mates and her teacher, her facial expressions and changes of voice had them roaring with laughter. Cyril wanted to hold her tight and never let her go, but was afraid of scaring her off. Then she surprised the men by asking, 'Who has my mother gone upstairs to see?'

Cyril cleared his throat. 'Your mother has met a man she has grown very fond of, and he is very fond of her. In fact, he would like her to marry him.'

Milly took the news very calmly. She had never really believed that her mother went to stay with an old school friend every weekend, but hadn't minded for it meant she could stay with her Auntie Bessie. 'Oh, I'm glad Mother has a friend. Will she bring him down to meet me, d'you think?'

'Would you like to meet him?' Oscar asked. 'He's very nice, I've known him since I was about your age and we were at school together, with your father.' He had given some thought as to whether he should mention Charles, in case it upset Cyril, but after careful consideration decided it was best to put the child in the picture.

Milly was standing at the side of Cyril's chair, and she put her arms around him. 'I didn't know my father, he was killed before I was born. But he was your son, and you must have been very sad.'

'I was, my dear, and so was my wife. And that is why I am so happy that you have come into our lives, for you look so like him, you will be a constant reminder. It will be like having him back again.'

There came a rap on the door, then it was opened and Evelyn and Philip came in. Oscar broke the silence by greeting Philip. 'Hello, old boy, it's a while since we met. Haven't seen you at any of the parties over the holidays.'

As they were shaking hands, Philip said, 'I have been off the social scene for reasons you have probably guessed. But it is nice to see you, and when you go home, please give my love and regards to Gwen.'

Milly watched the scene with interest, her hand

clasped in one of her grandfather's. Then she asked, 'Are you my mother's friend?'

Philip walked over to the desk and held out his hand. 'I am a very good friend of your mother's, I hope you don't mind?'

Milly pursed her lips while shaking his hand. There were thoughts going round her head, the main one being that if her mother married this man, would she ever see her Auntie Bessie again? But he looked a nice man, and he was smiling at her so it would be rude not to smile back. 'You can't be a friend of my mother's without being a friend to me, can you? That would make us enemies and we'd have to fight each other with swords, in the park at dawn.' Suddenly she giggled and her face was transformed. 'I'm fast asleep in my bed at dawn, and I haven't got a sword anyway, so we'd better be friends.'

Philip was captivated. 'I wouldn't fight you, my darling, you are far too pretty.' He grinned, and that won Milly over. He's nice, she thought. And I'll really like him as long as he doesn't take me away from Auntie Bessie. 'Besides,' Philip went on, 'my sword has been sent away to be sharpened.'

'Thank goodness for that!' Cyril said. 'I wouldn't like any blood spilt on my floor, the cleaner would be very upset and think I'd murdered someone.' He raised his eyebrows and looked at Evelyn. 'Have you and Philip had a good talk?' When she nodded, he asked, 'And have all the problems been sorted out to your satisfaction?'

She looked to Philip. 'Would you say they have?'

'Most of them. There was never any doubt on my part, but there are others to consider.' He took a deep breath and decided to take the bull by the horns. 'Milly, I have asked your mother to marry me, but she won't give me an answer until she knows that I meet with your approval.' He dropped down on one knee and put his two hands on his heart. 'Please, Milly, will you allow me to take your mother's hand in marriage?'

Peals of childish laughter rang out and brought smiles to all those in the room. Even to Miss Williams in her office, but no one could see that. 'Oh, you are funny!' Her laughter turned to giggles, and her green eyes sparkled. She whispered to Cyril, 'Granddad, I do like him, so shall we let him marry Mother?'

'I think we should say he can, my dear, so he can get back on his feet. The wooden floor isn't very comfortable for his knees.'

Milly put a hand over her mouth and spluttered, 'It won't be very comfortable for his trousers, either, I bet they're not very happy.' She skipped round the desk and took hold of Philip's elbow. 'I'll help you up, then you can say sorry to your trousers.'

He was chuckling as he dusted his knees. 'Am I to take it that I have your approval to marry your mother?'

Milly nodded. 'I suppose so. Uncle Oscar has a very big house, and it's full of lovely things. Do you have a big house?'

'I don't have a house yet. I live with my parents part of the week, then spend some time in my apartment. But I will be buying a house when your mother and I marry.'

'Will it be as big as Uncle Oscar's?'

Evelyn gasped. 'Really, Amelia, it is rude to ask such questions.'

But Philip brushed her objection aside. 'It's only natural she should be curious. And to answer her question, I hope we will eventually have a house as big as Oscar's. But if you want to see a really big house, my dear, then you should see your grandfather's. It is probably the largest house in Liverpool.'

Milly's mouth and eyes widened at the same time. 'Is that true, Granddad? Do you live in a castle?'

'See what you have done now, my boy?' Cyril said, chortling. 'The child will expect to see a throne, and Matilda with a tiara on her head. The only thing I can do now is take her to see for herself. Would you like that, Milly?'

Evelyn spoke before her daughter could answer. 'I'm sorry, Cyril, but I have to be getting home soon, or our friends will worry about us. Could we not leave it until tomorrow?'

Oscar saw the disappointment on Cyril's face and stepped in. 'I can run Milly and Cyril there in ten minutes, and that would give you and Philip time to talk some more. I promise to have Milly back here in an hour, then I could run you both as near to your home as you want me to. Does that suit you, Cyril?'

'It would be wonderful. I want to surprise Matilda, and couldn't keep this myself until tomorrow.'

And Milly added her voice, because she wanted

to see the house that was bigger than her Uncle Oscar's. And, most of all, she wanted to see her grandmother. 'Go on, Mother, give in, please?' So much had happened today, it was like being in a dream. She didn't want to go home to bed, wake up in the morning and find it had all disappeared. 'I want to see my grandmother.'

A few minutes later she was sitting on the back seat of Oscar's car, with her grandfather sitting next to her. 'It's been a lovely day, Granddad, the best I've ever had.' Then she remembered her friends, Aunties Bessie, Rita and Aggie. She must never forget how good they'd been to her. 'Well, one of the best, Granddad, 'cos I had a wonderful Christmas.'

When Oscar turned into the long drive, and the house came into view, Milly lost her tongue all of a sudden. It wasn't a palace, but it was nearly as big as one. 'Is this where you live, Granddad?'

'It is, my darling, and I hope you will spend many happy hours here with me and your grandmother. And I can tell you that this is going to be a shock to her, so we must be very careful now.'

Oscar opened the car door for them. 'I'll come in with you, Cyril. It might take the edge off the shock, don't you think?'

A maid in a black dress and white starched apron opened the door, and smiled when she saw the trio standing there. 'You're early, Mr Cyril, Madam will be surprised to see you. And you, Mr Oscar, shall I take your coat?' She looked at Milly with curiosity. 'Shall I take your coat, miss?'

Milly moved closer to her grandfather. 'This is

my best coat, and my mother wouldn't like it if someone took it from me.'

Cyril and Oscar managed to hide their smiles. 'I wouldn't blame your mother for being annoyed if someone took it from you, my dear, but Maisie only wants to hang it up until you are ready to leave. Then she will give it back to you.'

'Oh, that's all right then.' Milly slipped off her coat and handed it to the maid who was having difficulty keeping the smile from her face. Then Milly remembered her manners, and said, 'Thank you very much.' But she still wasn't happy when she saw the maid walking away with the three coats over her arm. 'Will you hang it up by the tab, please, 'cos if you just hang it on a hook, it will put the coat out of shape.'

'Yes, miss,' the maid said, 'I will take really good care of it for you.'

The hall was massive, with a beautiful wide curved staircase. There were highly polished tables, gilt-framed pictures on the walls, several vases of flowers, and the most beautiful chandelier hanging down from the ceiling, its drops sending out flashes of colour. Milly's eyes were everywhere, she had never seen anything like it. But it was all so strange, she felt shy. 'Granddad, you won't let go of my hand, will you?'

'Of course I won't, my dear, and you have no need to be afraid or shy, for this is the house your father was born in. I'll show you his room later, but first I want to surprise your grandmother. She will be in the drawing room at this time of day, and I am not going to tell her who you are at first. Oscar will come in with us, and I want to see if your grandmother can tell who you are by looking at you.'

Milly had been looking forward to seeing her grandmother, but this house was so big it frightened her a little. 'You won't leave me, will you?' She looked up at Oscar. 'You'll stay with me, won't you, Uncle Oscar?'

'Your granddad and I will never be more than a yard from you, darling. In fact I will hold your hand all the time, I promise.' Oscar raised his brows and asked, 'Is that all right with you, Cyril?'

Milly didn't want to leave her granddad out though, 'cos he might be sad if he thought she didn't want him. She looked from one to the other. 'You can hold a hand each, then I'll have two men to protect me if there are any dragons hiding in cupboards.'

So it was a laughing trio who entered the drawing room. Matilda looked at them in surprise, it was far too early for her husband to be home. 'We've brought a visitor to see you.' Cyril let Milly's hand drop, and Oscar looked at him with a frown. But Cyril nodded as if to say, You go ahead, I want to see my wife's reaction from here. And Oscar understood. It was going to be a very emotional scene.

Matilda smiled at Oscar when he stood before her, Milly's hand in his. 'I didn't know you had a daughter, Oscar,' she said, eyeing Milly with curiosity. 'I thought your children were boys.'

'Oh, Milly is not my daughter. You're right, Matilda, my children are both boys and much younger. No, Milly is a friend of mine I thought you might like to meet.'

584

She looked at Milly and smiled. 'I am very happy to meet you, my dear. If you are a friend of Oscar's then you are a friend of mine.' She leaned forward when Milly smiled, and there was a strange expression on her face. 'You are a very pretty girl. You remind me of someone, but I can't think who.'

Standing in the background, Cyril could feel a lump forming in his throat. He wanted to tell his wife it was her granddaughter she was looking at, but he had lost the power of speech. He would have to leave it to Oscar to break the news, he himself was feeling far too emotional.

However, neither man was given the chance. Milly, young as she was, knew this was a very important moment in her life. And she felt sorry for her grandmother. Taking her hand from Oscar's, she moved to stand closer to the woman who was staring at her as though she was a ghost. 'Can't you think who I remind you of, Grandmother?'

It was when his wife fell back in her chair that Cyril was galvanised into action. He was by her side in seconds, his arm around her shoulders. 'Be brave, my darling, this is a wonderful day for both of us. This is Amelia, or Milly as she likes to be called, and she is Charles' daughter.' He was expecting her to faint, or ring for the smelling salts, but instead she pushed him aside and leaned forward to draw Milly towards her. And as Oscar was to tell his wife that evening, it was the most wonderful, yet sad scene he had ever witnessed. For Matilda was crushing the girl to her as though she'd never let go. The tears were running down her cheeks, and she began to rock Milly from side to side. She couldn't bring herself to speak, but her mind was reminding her that this girl was born from the seed of her beloved son, and while she lived, so did Charles.

It took Milly to break the tension. 'Grandmother, don't cry, 'cos you're making me feel sad. I thought you would be happy to see me?'

'Oh, I am, my darling, more happy than words can say. But where have you been all these years?'

'Granddad will tell you that, he's better at saying things than I am. But can you stop crying now, Grandmother, 'cos you're making my dress wet, and it's my very best one.'

Matilda sniffed and let her arms drop. 'I'm sorry, darling, but I am so happy I can't help crying. Now you are here, you won't ever leave us again, will you?'

Milly looked bewildered, so Cyril came to her aid. 'She has to leave us now, darling, for Evelyn is waiting for her in my office. I have so much to tell you, but I don't have the time to tell you now for I need go back to the office with Milly. Oscar was kind enough to bring us here, and he has promised to run Evelyn and Milly home. But you will see your granddaughter again very soon, I promise you. However, no more news for now, all will be revealed tonight.'

Matilda wiped a tear away and Milly reassured her, 'I do love you, Grandmother, and you'll see me loads of times, I promise. But now I want to ask you and Grandfather a favour. All the girls in school, and my friends, they call their grandparents Granda and Grandma. It sounds much nicer, doesn't it? So, please, can I call you the same?' When Matilda nodded, Milly gave her a big hug and kiss. 'I am a very lucky girl having a grandma and granda, and an Uncle Oscar and Auntie Gwen. And my friends in the street where I live, I love them too!'

Then something happened that Cyril had never seen before. His wife walked to the front door holding on tight to Milly's hand. She waved the maid aside. 'I'll see my granddaughter to the door, thank you, you may go.' She even walked to the car, waited on the path until it moved down to the double gates, then stood waving a handkerchief as Milly knelt on the back seat and waved back.

Cyril tapped Oscar on the back and chortled, 'Who was it said that miracles never happen? I think a certain little person is going to give my wife a new lease of life.'

Back at the office, Evelyn was on edge. 'My neighbour will worry herself sick if Milly isn't there when she gets home from work. I do hope they're not much longer.'

'The neighbour you are talking about, is it Bessie? The one I said I would like to meet?'

Evelyn nodded. 'And you will meet her, I promise. But everything can't happen in a day, it may take a few weeks.'

Just then they heard laughter in the corridor outside, and Evelyn let out a sigh of relief. 'Thank goodness, we'll make it home in time.'

The door opened and Milly ran towards her mother. 'You should see the size of the house Granda lives in, Mother. It's nearly as big as a castle.'

'Yes, I know, dear, I have been there. Was your grandmother pleased to see you?'

'Oh, yes, she gave me loads of kisses, and wanted me to stay there.'

Cyril thought this a good time to broach the matter that had been on his mind for a while. 'Have you and Philip made any plans?'

Philip nodded. 'I'm going to see my parents tonight, I think they should be told the news before they hear it from a stranger. Then tomorrow Evelyn and I will set a date for our wedding in the very near future. We will have to live in the apartment for a while until we find a suitable home, and that is the only drawback. There is only one bedroom.'

'Then Milly can come and live with us,' Cyril told them, 'we certainly have plenty of room and would love to have her.'

'I'll live with Auntie Bessie,' Milly said, surprising everyone but Evelyn. 'She has a room there for me.'

'But you can live with us, my dear,' Cyril protested. 'Your grandma and I would love to have you, and we have rooms to spare.'

Milly's face was set. 'No, I want to live with my Auntie Bessie. She is my very bestest friend and she'd be sad if she couldn't see me. And I wouldn't be able to see Jack, either.'

Evelyn shrugged her shoulders at Cyril. 'Shall we leave it for now and talk about it another day? I'm sure Milly will change her mind when she's had time to think about it.'

'I won't change my mind,' she said with a nod of her head for emphasis. 'I want to live with

Auntie Bessie.'

When Evelyn tutted, Cyril held his hand up to silence her. He didn't want his granddaughter to be forced into living with him against her will. 'This Bessie must be a very fine person if you love her so much, Milly.'

'Oh, she is, Granda, she's lovely. And she is very funny when she talks to the door and the grate, she makes me laugh all the time.'

'She talks to the door and the grate, does she?' Cyril would have laughed if it hadn't been for Milly's expression, which said she didn't see anything wrong in talking to them. 'Do they answer her back?'

'Oh, yes, and she tells them off then for being cheeky.'

'Do you know, I would like to meet this Auntie Bessie of yours, I'm sure I'd like her. You see, I talk to my desk sometimes, and my paper basket if it trips me up.' He nodded. 'Yes, I'm sure I'd get on with her.'

'You are not the only one who wants to meet Bessie,' Philip informed him. 'Evelyn has told me a lot about her and I'm waiting to meet the lady I'm told is so kind and caring.'

Milly was delighted, for anyone who liked Auntie Bessie was a friend of hers. 'I'll ask her tonight when she can come to see you, Granda, shall I?'

Events were moving too fast for Evelyn. 'Miss Maudsley goes to work every day, Milly, don't forget. We'll have words with her tonight, and see when it would be suitable for her.'

Milly wasn't going to be put off so easily, though.

589

'She doesn't work on a Sunday, Granda, would you like to see her then?'

Cyril could see by Evelyn's face she didn't like the way the conversation was going, and guessed she was worried in case her daughter invited them all to her house. He knew from Milly that it was a two-up-two-down, and while that didn't bother him, it might bother Evelyn. So he found a solution which he thought would suit everyone. 'Why don't you all come to my home on Sunday for dinner? A sort of celebration. Evelyn, you could bring Milly and Bessie. And Philip is invited, of course, and Oscar and Gwen. You could make your peace with Matilda, who would love to welcome you back into the family. What do you say?'

Milly clapped her hands with glee. 'Oh, yes, Granda, that would be lovely.' She turned to Evelyn. 'Ooh, I can't wait until Sunday, Mother, we'll all have a wonderful time.'

Chapter Thirty-One

Evelyn lay in bed on the Sunday morning going over the whirlwind events of the last three days. So much had happened she hadn't been able to take it all in, but now, in the still of an early Sunday morning, with Milly fast asleep in the next room, her mind was able to catch up on events. Philip had taken her to meet his parents and they had welcomed her with warmth and friendliness, instantly putting her at ease. She hadn't been asked difficult questions or made to feel awkward, for Philip had already told them everything from start to finish. They discussed the wedding, and both his parents were pleased that at last their son was to settle down. They instantly got involved in planning things, when it should be, where it should take place, and where to hold the reception. And they were sincere in the pleasure they showed at their son's choice of wife. It was Mrs Astbury who first brought Milly into the conversation, by saying she must be looking forward to being a bridesmaid. Even though Evelyn wouldn't be wearing white, Philip's parents still wanted their son to have a wedding he would remember for the rest of his life.

Evelyn sighed, but it was a sigh of relief and happiness. All her fears about facing Cyril had been groundless. The meeting had gone so smoothly, with not a word of reproach from him.

As for Oscar and Gwen, it was lovely to see them again and renew their friendship. She had such a lot to be thankful for, and no one realised that more than herself. But the fears and apprehension she'd suffered before meeting all these people had taken their toll, with a constant headache and tummy taut with tension. And although she'd had a smile fixed on her face most of the time, the first real, genuine belly laugh had come last night, and Bessie was the cause of it. Evelyn stretched her legs and relived the scene in her head.

'Ay, Evelyn, let's be serious for a minute while I get something off me chest.' Bessie was sitting on the couch with Milly beside her, while Evelyn sat in the fireside chair. 'Milly tells me that her granda's house is nearly as big as a palace, and filled with beautiful things. And he's got a maid, a housekeeper, a cleaner and a gardener. Now is she pulling me leg or is she telling the truth?'

'She's telling the truth, Bessie, I did tell you that the Lister-Sinclairs were very wealthy. They have a beautiful home. Why?'

'Why! Because I can't go to a place like that, I'd make a holy show of meself, and you into the bargain. I'd be frightened to open me mouth in case I put me ruddy foot in it.' She leaned forward to poke the fire. 'No, you two go and enjoy yerselves, I won't bother. I don't know why I was asked in the first place, I'd be well out of me depth.'

'Oh, you've got to come, Auntie Bessie, 'cos Granda and Uncle Philip are dying to meet you. I told them you were my bestest friend, and they want to be your friend as well. You've got to come or I'll cry and I won't go either.'

Bessie returned the poker back to the companion set then leaned back on the couch. 'Listen to me, sweetheart, I don't speak posh so I'd be frightened to open my mouth, and I don't have fancy clothes so I'd feel uncomfortable.'

'They're not snobs, Bessie,' Evelyn told her. 'I used to be a snob, as you well know, but I was only pretending to be something I wasn't, which is what snobs do. People who really have money aren't a bit like that. You would be made very welcome, I can assure you, and wouldn't feel uncomfortable at all.'

Bessie snorted. 'Oh, no, in me home-made dress and me Marcel-waved hair, I'd be the belle of the ruddy ball! And I can't afford to go out and pay a fortune for another dress, even if the shops were open, which they're not.'

Milly was pouting, very near to tears. 'I'm going in the dress you made me, Auntie Bessie, so that's a home-made dress, and I love it. And I'll tell everyone that you made it for me, so they'll all think you are very clever. I bet none of them could make a dress.'

'That's different, sweetheart, 'cos you're family. If you turned up in a sack, they'd still love yer. But I'm not family, yer see.'

Milly folded her arms, her face set. 'If you don't go, then I won't go either, so there!'

'Don't start behaving like a baby, Milly,' Evelyn said. 'You can't always have your own way. If Miss Maudsley doesn't want to come, we can't make her. I'll be very disappointed, though, because

I've told Cyril and Philip so much about her they really do want to meet her.' She suddenly had a brain wave. 'It's a pity, Bessie, because you said you would like to thank the man who gave the donation at Christmas, and if you don't come with us tomorrow night, you'll miss the chance of meeting him.'

Bessie chuckled. 'Nice try, Evelyn, but it won't work.'

Milly had shuffled to the edge of the couch. 'Which man is that, Mother, do I know him?'

'Yes, dear, it's Uncle Philip, the man I am going to marry.'

Bessie's eyes narrowed. 'Are you having me on, Evelyn, 'cos if yer are, I'll set the poker on yer. In fact, I won't bother with the poker, I'll have a word with the front door and tell it not to let yer in any more.'

Evelyn let her head drop back and laughter filled the room. 'Oh, if you don't come, Bessie, you'll miss out on a lot. Milly's granddad is like you, he talks to his desk, and the waste-paper basket. You would have so much in common.'

Bessie viewed her through narrowed lids. 'Is this another try, Evelyn? If it is, yer must be getting desperate, sweetheart, 'cos I could do better meself.'

'Mother isn't telling fibs, Auntie Bessie,' Milly said. 'She is going to marry Uncle Philip, and Granda does talk to his desk and the waste-paper basket, he told us.'

Bessie stroked her cheek. 'It's no use, sweetheart, I'm sure they are the nicest people in the world, but it doesn't alter the fact I'm not in the same class as them, and I really would be embarrassed. My clothes wouldn't fit, me accent would go down like a lead balloon, and I'd be dead miserable. You and yer mother go, and have a nice time. You can tell me all about it after. It'll be a New Year then, nineteen hundred and twenty-six.'

But nothing would move Milly. 'If you don't go, then I'm not going. I'll stay with you.'

Bessie lifted her hands in defeat. 'Okay, okay! I'll go with yer and spend the night in the kitchen helping the servants. Are yer satisfied now?'

They were sitting in a taxi on Sunday when Evelyn said, 'You look very smart, Bessie, I must say. Your hair looks very glamorous.'

'And so it ruddy well should do!' she said. 'I've had dinky curlers in all night, and I haven't slept a flaming wink. I don't know, the things we women go through. If a burglar had broke into my house last night, he'd have taken one look at me and scarpered hell for leather down the ruddy street. The things we women have to put up with, it's nothing but flaming torture.'

'Well, I think you look lovely, Auntie Bessie. Nobody will look as nice as you.'

Bessie was feeling very nervous, and would much rather have been sitting in her little house, with a fire roaring up the chimney, than in a taxi on her way to a house as big as a castle. At least in her own place she could talk to the furniture without feeling embarrassed because it was used to her Liverpool accent. Another thing, this was the first time she'd been in a taxi in her whole life and she felt uncomfortable enough, so how was she going to feel in a house as big as a ruddy castle, with a maid and a housekeeper? She gave a sigh and promised herself she'd find a chair in a corner somewhere and sit out of sight for the night. Or else find the kitchen and give the cook a hand. That would be more up her street than sitting with a group of people who had more money than they knew what to do with.

'It's the next house, driver,' Evelyn said, leaning forward to tap on the glass partition. 'You can drive straight into the driveway.'

While she was paying the man, Bessie was taking stock of the house and gardens, and felt like either getting back in the taxi and asking the driver to take her home, or taking to her heels and running as fast as she could. This was no place for her, she should never have given in to Milly.

'Come along,' Evelyn said, taking Bessie's elbow, 'Maisie has the door open.'

Bessie took one look at the uniformed maid and her heart dropped even further as she asked herself what she was doing here. But when the maid smiled as she asked if she could take her coat, Bessie found she could smile back. And she was soon thinking to herself that she'd have a good look around the enormous hall so she could describe everything to Rita and Aggie. She had barely got as far as the winding staircase, with the gilt-framed pictures spaced at intervals on the wall, when by her side she heard a deep voice saying, 'So, this is the Bessie I've heard so much about?'

After nearly jumping out of her skin with fright, she turned her head to see a man who appeared to be about the same age as herself. He was holding out his hand. 'I'm Cyril Lister-Sinclair, Milly's grandfather, and she's told me so much about you, I feel I know you.'

Bessie looked at the outstretched hand, then at the smiling, kindly face, and her hand went to join his. 'I'm pleased to meet yer, er, sir,' she said, pumping his hand enthusiastically. 'But Milly exaggerates something terrible, so don't believe everything she tells yer.'

Cyril saw before him a woman who was small and thin, with a face as honest as the day is long and eyes full of humour. 'Ah, yes, I can well imagine my granddaughter has a very vivid imagination, but I don't believe she exaggerates her feelings for you. She tells me you are her bestest friend, and I find myself a little jealous of you. I'm hoping in the near future to become another of her bestest friends.'

Bessie looked around for Evelyn and Milly, but they had disappeared. She was alone in the hall with this man she found she was at ease with. 'Oh, Milly is your friend already, she has told me so. You are very lucky, she's a child anyone would be proud of. Clever, caring, loving and with a sense of humour. She's also a very pretty girl, and I have to admit I love the bones of her.'

'Here you are, old boy,' a man's voice boomed, 'Evelyn said I would find you here.'

'Ah, Philip, may I introduce you to Miss Bessie? She is a neighbour and friend of Evelyn and Milly's.' Cyril made the introductions, and

Bessie weighed Philip up as they shook hands. 'You are one of the reasons I came tonight, Mr Philip, 'cos I wanted to thank yer for being so kind. There are a lot of people in our street who would like to thank yer as well, so I'll do it for them.'

Cyril frowned. 'What is this about, Philip? I didn't know you knew Miss Maudsley?'

'I have never met the dear lady until this minute, Cyril, but I know a lot about her. And when the chance comes, I would like to have a private conversation with her.'

'This is all very mysterious,' Cyril said. 'Would I be allowed to sit in on this conversation? I am now very intrigued.'

The sound of childish laughter had three pairs of eyes turning towards the sound. They saw Milly pulling on her grandmother's arm, her face creased in laughter. 'Come on, Grandma, here she is. This is my Auntie Bessie.'

Cyril couldn't believe his eyes. His wife looked twenty years younger as she laughed while being pulled towards the group. 'Auntie Bessie, this is my grandma and I've told her all about you.'

Without a word being exchanged, Cyril and Philip stepped back. Both men were interested in how this meeting would go, for it could affect their own lives. Matilda was smiling when she stopped in front of Bessie. 'My granddaughter has never stopped talking about you. You have certainly made an impression on her.'

Milly dropped her grandmother's hand and reached for Bessie's. 'She's my bestest friend in the whole world, Grandma, and I do love her.'

She gazed up at Bessie, her green eyes shining. 'Aren't you my bestest friend, Auntie Bessie, and don't you love the bones of me?'

There was no need to say it, for it was plain to those watching that Bessie adored the girl, but she confirmed it by saying, 'Yes, sweetheart, ye're me bestest mate, and I love the bones of yer.'

'I was telling Milly how much I liked her dress, it is so pretty,' Matilda said. 'And she tells me you made it for her. Is this true?'

Bessie didn't know how to address these people, so decided to use no names. 'Yes, that is my job, I'm a seamstress by trade.'

'That is wonderful! Did you hear that, Cyril, Bessie is a seamstress. I have said for years we should employ a seamstress, it would be so useful.'

'I'm sure Bessie is already gainfully employed, my dear.' But while he was speaking an idea was forming in Cyril's head. Part of the idea had been there since he'd first known of Milly's love for this woman, and now his wife had given him a way of taking it further. 'Don't you think you should go back to the drawing room, my dear, and take Milly with you? Evelyn and our guests will think it rude of us to both disappear. Philip and I will be with you shortly, but we both wish to have a word with Bessie.'

'My husband is right, I should get back to our guests.' Matilda was not usually a demonstrative person but, wonder of wonders, she put her hand on Bessie's arm and squeezed it. 'We will talk later. My granddaughter said we should be friends, and I would like that very much.'

Milly escaped from her grandmother's hand

599

and put her arms around Bessie's waist. 'Aren't you glad you came now, Auntie Bessie? I told you they would love you.'

Bessie smiled and stroked her hair. 'Yes, I'm glad I came, sweetheart, but you run along with your grandma now, and I'll see you soon.'

'Can I have a kiss first, please, 'cos you haven't given me one today. And then I'll be a good girl and go with Grandma.' When Bessie bent down to kiss her, the girl's arms went around her neck, and those watching could hear her say, 'I do love you, Auntie Bessie.'

Bessie smiled. 'I know yer do, 'cos yer told the shovel, and the shovel told me.'

Milly put her hands on her hips and feigned indignation. 'I'm going to tell that shovel off when I see it, it had no right to tell tales.'

Bessie pushed her towards Matilda, who was watching with great interest. 'You go with yer grandma now, I'll see yer in a bit.'

Cyril turned to Philip. 'I wish to talk to Bessie. Would you like to join us, or would you prefer to join our guests?'

'I'll tag along with you, if you have no objection?' Philip winked at Bessie. 'I can't leave you and Bessie alone in the study, what would people think!'

The two men took an arm each, and led her in the direction of Cyril's study. When they reached the door, she burst out laughing. 'Two male escorts no less. Wait until I tell me mates, they won't believe me. I know what one of them will say. "Oh, aye, two bleeding coppers taking yer in for being drunk".'

Both men roared with laughter. And although they couldn't read each other's mind, they were both thinking it wasn't hard to like this little lady. 'Oh, are you known for getting drunk and being escorted by policemen to the nearest police station?' Philip asked.

'Oh, yes, every Saturday night without fail. I have me usual six bottles of milk stout, then the landlord throws me out for being drunk, and I sit in the gutter singing me head off until the local bobbies take me to sleep it off in a cell in the police station.'

Cyril looked at Philip and opened the study door. 'We've got quite a character here, my boy, I think we will have to go easy on the brandy and port. There are no gutters around here, and the nearest police station is a mile away.'

Philip winked. 'I will take responsibility, old boy, I'll keep my eye on her all night.'

'Which eye will that be, sir, so I can dodge it?' Bessie was beginning to enjoy herself. Okay, so they were rolling in money while she was as poor as a church mouse, but that didn't make them any different. And these two seemed happy enough, they were laughing their heads off.

Cyril pointed to a comfortable leather chair. 'Make yourself at home, my dear. What I have to say is very important to me, my wife and Milly.'

Philip stood up. 'Would you prefer I joined the other guests then, Cyril? I don't want to intrude.'

'No, you stay, dear boy. This matter concerns Evelyn, and as her husband to be, it also concerns you. I will try to make it as brief as possible, or if we're not back with our guests when the bell goes for dinner, my dear wife will not be too happy.' He waited until Philip had seated himself, then looked across the desk at Bessie. 'I believe Evelyn has told you most of the story, up to last week when she and Milly came back into our lives so I won't go over that ground again. What I have to say concerns you, and my granddaughter. While Milly appears pleased to have us in her life, to be part of a family, and seems fond of my wife and myself, it is you she loves. She talks of you constantly, you are her bestest friend and she loves you. Of course I would like her to love my wife and me too, but I am not stupid enough to think love is something immediate, that you can take for granted. You have to work at love, to earn it.'

'Oh, Milly will come to love you in time,' Bessie said. 'She is a lovable child, with a heart full of love to give. It just takes time, Mr ... er ... Mr Cyril.' Bessie shook her head. 'I'm sorry, I'm at a loss as to what to call yer. But don't worry about Milly, she'll come to love yer, I know she will.'

Cyril lifted a pencil from a stand on his desk and started to scribble on a large blotting pad. 'I've asked Milly to come and live with Matilda and me while Evelyn and Philip begin married life together. We want her so much, for after all, she is the daughter of our beloved son. But Milly was quite definite that it was you she wanted to live with, and I would never force her against her will. I want her to love me, not hate me. So I wondered if you would consider the post of nanny to her?'

'But I have a job, and me own little house. And

602

me two best mates are my neighbours, I couldn't leave all that to be a nanny. I don't know the first thing about being one, I'm not qualified.'

It was Philip who said, 'I don't want to interfere, but I think love is the best quality anyone can have. And you only have to listen to Milly, and Evelyn, to know love is something you have in abundance. I think it is a marvellous idea. I'm sure you want to be with Milly as much as she wants to be with you. If you were suddenly to be taken out of her life, she would fret dreadfully and be very miserable.'

'And I'd be broken-hearted,' Bessie said with feeling. 'I knew it would happen one day, it had to, for she wasn't mine to love and to hold. But I haven't the faintest idea what a nanny does! I'm not well educated or clever, so I wouldn't be up to the job!'

'Let me explain what it would entail, Bessie,' Cyril said, 'then you can take the idea home with you and give it some thought. All you would be required to do is be a companion to Milly. Accompany her to school and back, help with her clothes, take her for walks to the shops or to the park, do the things you already do together now. This is a huge house, far too big for Matilda and myself, but we will never leave it because our son was born here and it holds memories of him. There are many rooms which are not used, so you would have your own separate accommodation. Your own entrance, sitting room, bedroom and bathroom. And my wife and I would appreciate it if you had your meals with us, as a family. You would have days off, and could have your friends visit you whenever you wished.' Cyril smiled. 'One who would be very welcome is a young boy named Jack. Next to you, he is Amelia's bestest friend, even though he does try and cheat at cards.'

When he paused to consider his next words, he caught Philip's eye and was rewarded with a slight nod and a smile of encouragement. 'Of course you would receive a salary, to be mutually agreed, and would be treated by the staff as a member of the family. But what is most important, you wouldn't be parted from Milly, and she would have her bestest friend here all the time.'

For a few seconds Bessie bowed her head in thought. Then asked, 'But what if I give me house up, pack my job in, and then find the arrangement you talk of isn't suitable? I'd have lost everything, and at my age I can't afford to take a chance. Apart from me two mates in the street, I don't have a soul in the world to turn to.' Her voice thick with emotion, she went on, 'I love the bones of Milly, but what would happen to me if I didn't get on with yer wife and the atmosphere wasn't a happy one?'

Philip left his chair to sit on the top of the desk, where he could look her in the face. 'I hope Cyril will forgive me for butting in, but I have an idea which may put all your fears to rest, my dear. You see, your future is of great interest to me also, for Evelyn admires you very much and has told me she will never forget how you helped her and will always remain friends with you. So listen to my idea and tell me what you think.' He gave her a smile of encouragement. 'Why not take a week off work, move in here and take on the role of nanny, as Cyril sees it? We all know you get on like a house on fire with Milly, but you are worried you may not fit in with Matilda and the staff. A week of living with the family would help you make a decision on whether you feel you would fit in. How does that appeal to you?'

'Take a week off work? I've never taken time off in all the twenty-odd years I've worked there. What would I tell the boss?'

Cyril felt like slapping Philip on the back for coming up with such a good idea. 'You would not have to worry about that, my dear. I will ring your employer if you would give me the name of the firm. I think we should have a trial run, as Philip suggests. If you turn it down out of hand, you may come to regret it. Please give it a try.'

All that was going through Bessie's mind was the thought of never seeing Milly again. And that didn't bear thinking about. And it wasn't as though she would be going to people who would look down on her, for she had been treated with great respect and friendliness by everyone she'd met. And like Cyril said, if she turned the offer down she may live to regret it. She nodded her head. 'I'll give it a week's trial, as yer said. And I want to thank yer both for the nice welcome yer gave me, and being so kind.'

Cyril was beside himself with happiness. 'You will not regret it, Bessie, I promise you that. And Milly won't be the only one to be delighted when she's told, I believe you will be a valuable addition to this household. Now, if you will write

605

the name of your employer down, Bessie, and your full name and address, we can join our other guests. There are only two you haven't met already, that is Oscar and Gwen, but they know all about you.'

As Bessie wrote out her full name and address, and that of her employer, they heard her muttering through the side of her mouth, 'You two would charm the birds off a ruddy tree. I'm going to have to keep a close watch on yer.'

Rita showed her surprise when she opened the door the next morning and saw Bessie standing on her front step. 'My God, Bessie, the streets are not aired off yet! Why are yer up and about so early, and where's Milly?'

Bessie grinned. 'And a Happy New Year to you as well, Rita Wells. That's a marvellous greeting, I must say.'

'Well, I didn't expect yer so early, sunshine, I thought yer'd be having a lie in after being out late last night.'

'I've got something important to tell you and Aggie, and as Milly is still fast asleep, and me fire's lit and the kettle on, I wondered if yer were both decent enough to come across for half an hour?'

'I'm dressed, as yer can see, but I don't know about Aggie, I haven't heard her this morning, she might still be in bed.'

The next door opened and Aggie's head appeared, her hair tousled and a smudge of soot on her face. 'Yer might not have heard me, queen, but I heard you raking the ashes out.' She eyed

Bessie. 'Did I hear yer say yer had something to tell us, queen? I'll just slip me coat on and come across, seeing as yer've got the kettle on for a cuppa.' Her head popped out a bit further so she could see Rita. 'Get yer coat on, queen, and let's hear what she's got to tell us about how the other half live. I hope yer haven't gone all stuck-up on us, Bessie, and expect us to wipe our feet?'

Bessie started to cross the street. 'The tea will be on the table in five minutes, and don't make a sound. What I've got to tell yer is not for Milly's ears.'

Ten minutes later the three women were sitting around Bessie's table and she was telling them that Evelyn was getting married in four weeks' time. The man she was marrying was called Philip, and he was the one who had given them all that money at Christmas. They were getting married in a church in Mossley Hill, and Evelyn was saying she would be buying a wedding dress in ivory, with her being a widow. Milly was going to be bridesmaid, and a friend of Evelyn's called Gwen had been asked to be maid-of-honour. It sounded like a big posh affair, and she wouldn't mind going to see it. Then she told her mates a little about the Lister-Sinclairs' house. How they had carpets in every room, pictures and chandeliers. 'Yer might get to see it for yerselves one of these days, yer never know.'

Aggie huffed. 'A snowball stands more chance in hell than we ever do of getting inside a posh house like that! They'd think we were beggars and chase us.'

'Well, it all depends.' Bessie sounded mysterious.

'I've got something to tell yer, and I want yer to give me yer honest opinion on what yer think I should do for the best.' She raised her thumb to the ceiling. 'Keep yer voices down, for heaven's sake, or I won't be able to tell yer if Milly comes down.'

Bessie went over everything that had been said in Cyril's office, and as the story was unfolding the expressions on the faces of her two best mates changed every few seconds. Aggie nudged Rita so many times her side would be black and blue. But although there were gasps of surprise, they didn't once interrupt.

'So there yer have it, and I don't know what to do for the best. It's kept me awake half the night. First I think I should go, then the next minute I think I couldn't leave this little house after living here all me life. So what do yer think I should do for the best?'

'I'd give it a try,' Rita said without hesitation. 'Yer'd be a fool to turn down an offer like that, especially as yer say everyone was friendly and they treated yer like one of their own. I don't know why yer didn't agree right away, knowing yer'd be with Milly. Yer'd break yer heart if yer didn't see her every day, yer know that.'

'She's right,' Aggie said. 'Yer'd be living in the lap of luxury, with yer own rooms and a bathroom as well.' She hoisted her bosom and leaned her elbows on the table. 'Did they really say yer could invite me and Rita?'

'As often as yer want to come. Mr Cyril knew about yer, 'cos Milly had told him. Oh, and Jack as well.' Bessie sighed. 'I think it might be too

608

good to be true. Perhaps I wouldn't fit in. I can't speak posh, I don't know which knife to use first at the dinner table ... oh, there's all sorts of things to think about.'

'Yer had yer dinner with them last night, didn't yer?' Rita asked. 'Then yer didn't eat with yer fingers, surely, so yer must have learnt something.'

'I just followed what everyone else did. Nobody sat watching me, they're far too nice for that, and not a bit stuck up.'

'It's up to you, sunshine, but I think yer'd be mad to turn down an offer like that. Don't yer agree with me, Aggie?'

'Yeah, I do! And she'd be selfish, as well. I mean, like, how else are you and me ever going to get into a toff's house? And to be able to go to the lavvy without having to go down the bleeding yard! I bet they've got that posh toilet paper we see in rolls in the shops.' Aggie's chins swept from side to side as she told Bessie, 'I think it would be selfish of yer to turn it down. Ye're not thinking about us two, are yer? Don't yer think we'd like to swan up the driveway what yer told us about, in our best secondhand clothes? Don't be so bleeding miserable and grab the offer with both hands.'

'That's something ye're going to have to learn not to do,' Bessie said. 'Yer don't use any bad language when yer come to visit me.'

Rita smiled. 'So yer are taking the job?' When Bessie nodded, she said, 'I'm glad for yer, sunshine, I know ye're doing the right thing. Me and Aggie will give yer a week to settle in, then we'll pay our first visit. And I'll bring a gag with

609

me to stick in her mouth if she forgets to watch her language.'

Bessie had been living with the Lister-Sinclairs for three days. Although Matilda had told Cyril things were going very well, he decided on the fourth day to come home at lunchtime and see for himself. He knew his wife could be difficult sometimes, having been spoilt by him since the day they wed. He didn't tell her he would be back, wanting to surprise her and to see for himself how Bessie was fitting in. Milly had gone back to school, but would be leaving it the following week to go to a private school which was nearer her new home. She spent a lot of time in Bessie's room, and Cyril was hoping that would change when the trial week was over and she'd agreed to stay on. She seemed to be happy enough whenever he saw her and he was keeping his fingers crossed. He would be very upset if she told him she wanted to go back to her own house.

Cyril let himself in the front door and put a finger to his mouth when the maid came to take his coat. 'I will have some lunch, Maisie,' he said softly, 'a sandwich will do. This is a surprise visit to see how Miss Bessie is settling in.'

The maid grinned. 'She's settling in very well, Mr Cyril. Everyone likes her. She's very funny, always laughing.'

Cyril nodded and turned away, hoping Matilda appreciated Bessie's humour too. 'They're in the drawing room, are they?'

'Yes, they finished their lunch some time ago.'

He stood outside the door, listening, and heard Bessie's voice saying, 'My mother's name was Matilda.'

'Oh, what a coincidence!' his wife said. 'I'm surprised they didn't call you Matilda then, instead of Bessie.'

'I wasn't christened Bessie, my real name is Elizabeth. But my mam said it was too much of a mouthful, so from then on I got Bessie.'

Cyril was about to knock when Bessie spoke again. 'My mam didn't get Matilda either, she was always called Tilly. It suited her, too, like a pet name.'

'Tilly!' Matilda laughed. 'That's a funny name!'

'I didn't think so, I liked it. It was more friendly, 'cos all our neighbours had pet names for people they liked. Margaret was shortened to Maggie, Clementine to Clemmie, and so on.'

'Would I suit Tilly, do you think?'

'Ooh, don't ask me, sweetheart, I don't want yer husband giving me down the banks.'

Cyril smiled and turned away from the door. He wouldn't intrude, not when they seemed to be on such friendly terms. He'd have his sandwich in the kitchen and then go back to the office.

On Friday morning, Oscar called to see him. 'My wife is curious to know if Bessie has made up her mind yet?' He sat down in a chair facing Cyril. 'We are both of the opinion that you have a gem in her, and agree you should do your best to hang on to her. She is down-to-earth, honest, practical, and with a very sunny disposition. The very

611

qualities that will help Milly grow into a sensible girl with her feet firmly on the ground.'

Cyril nodded. 'She seems to have found favour with everyone, and I'm hoping we have found favour with her. Milly would be devastated if Bessie went back to her own house. In fact, I think she would pine and make herself ill if they were parted. But there's little we can do, it is up to Bessie. Tomorrow sees her week's trial over, and I am really keeping my fingers crossed. It's not only Milly, either. Matilda gets on really well with Bessie, and you know how hard to please my wife is! However, there is little I can do but hope.'

'Why don't we bring the matter forward and then you'll have your mind put at rest?' Oscar asked. 'I could come with you, on some pretext, so Bessie won't feel she's being ambushed. And if push came to shove, I could always add my plea to yours. I'm quite good at pleading. What do you say, old boy?'

'I think it would be a good idea, but it would have to be this afternoon after lunch. Evelyn will be there then. She's visited Bessie a few times this week, they seem to be fast friends. I'd be so glad if Matilda could be close to them too.' Cyril closed the folder he'd been going through and placed it at the side of the desk. 'Have you any business to attend to or shall we have a drink at the club and an early lunch? I'd say two o'clock would be a good time to arrive home. Bessie has to leave at three to pick Milly up from school.'

'So Evelyn calls to see Milly too, does she?'

Cyril nodded. 'Usually Philip is with her, he wants Milly to get to know him.'

Oscar smiled at him across the desk. 'Life has changed radically for you over the last few weeks, hasn't it? And all to the good.'

'I feel a new man, my boy, and a much younger man. My dear wife and I can't believe how lucky we are. The house has come alive with Milly and Bessie there. There is a homely feel about it, and when Milly's laughter fills the rooms, it's like music to my ears.' Cyril pushed his chair back. 'To the club, dear boy, we can pass an hour away talking of how life was, and how it is today.'

'Hello, Mr Oscar.' Maisie smiled as she took his coat. 'It is nice to see you.'

'Where are the ladies?' Cyril asked. 'In the drawing room?'

'Yes, Mr Cyril. They finished their lunch half an hour ago. Shall I bring a tray in?'

'No, my dear, Oscar and I have just come from the club.' He walked towards the drawing room with Oscar close on his heels. Cyril opened the door to hear Bessie say, 'I think a colour like hyacinth blue would suit Milly, and it would look nice with your ivory.'

The men had entered quietly, and the women started when Cyril said, 'Do you think I would suit hyacinth blue, Bessie?'

She shook her head. 'No, Mr Cyril, it wouldn't go with yer complexion at all. Far better stick with the grey top hat and tails that Matilda was saying yer'll be wearing.'

Oscar kissed each of the ladies in turn. 'Plans for the wedding going well, are they, Evelyn? Gwen and I are looking forward to it. Her parents have agreed to have the two boys for the day.'

When Evelyn smiled, he thought how much she had mellowed. All from her love of Philip, who clearly adored her in return. 'Yes, we seem to be organised. Invitations have gone out, the reception has been booked, flowers ordered and cars attended to. I have had a fitting for my dress, and you probably know that Gwen had hers at the same time. There is only Milly to worry about now. She is being very stubborn, insisting that Bessie should make her dress.'

'I don't mind, Evelyn, as long as you show me a pattern and get the same material as Gwen's. I'd need three yards, 'cos I wouldn't want to skimp it. And there's no need to worry, I'll make sure she looks as lovely as she is.' Then she said something that brought a smile to every face. 'I'll see if I can manage to get me sewing machine up here tomorrow so I can make a start as soon as I have the material. It's only a hand machine, I think I could manage it on the tram.'

'Does that mean you've decided to stay with us?' Cyril asked. 'To make this your home?'

'Of course it does, yer daft thing! There was never any doubt of that. I'm happy here, I get on with everyone. That is, if you're satisfied with me?'

There was a chorus of approval and Oscar said, 'I'll take you home tomorrow and help you with the sewing machine. And there must be other things you want from your home?'

'I don't need any furniture, seeing as my rooms here are already furnished, but there are a few things I must have, sentimental things that belonged to my parents. I wouldn't part with them. And I'll have to ask me two mates to give the rent collector a week's notice for me, and pay him the two week's rent. Oh, and they'll stop the coalman and the milkman too, and that's the lot.'

'What about your furniture?' Oscar asked. 'Won't you try and sell it?'

'I'll let my two mates do it. It isn't worth much, but they'd get a few bob for it and they'd be grateful 'cos they aren't well off. One of the local secondhand shops will empty the house so the landlord won't have any complaints.'

'That's something I'll have to think about, too,' Evelyn said. 'I'll come with you to meet Milly, and we can talk about it on the way.'

Cyril put his hand on Bessie's shoulder. 'We'll leave you ladies now, but I'm delighted you are going to stay with us. I shall go back to my office a very happy man.'

Oscar went as far as kissing Bessie's cheek. 'I'll pick you up at ten o'clock in the morning and we'll sort out your affairs then. And for now, welcome to our circle of friends.'

Chapter Thirty-Two

'I'll make us a cup of tea to warm us up,' Bessie said, 'it's freezing in here 'cos the fire hasn't been lit all week. Would yer rather just take the sewing machine and I can come back another day for the other things?'

Oscar shook his head as he looked around the small room. 'No, Bessie, this is a very warm overcoat, I don't feel the cold. We may as well get it all done in the one journey.'

She had seen his eyes going around the room, and chuckled. 'Bit of a difference to the Lister-Sinclairs', eh? But it was home to me mam and dad, and it's been home to me all me life. I'll miss it, for the memories it holds, but we can't have everything we want in life, can we? Being with Milly is the best thing in my life.' Bessie took a deep breath then blew it out slowly. 'The sewing machine is on the floor in the bedroom on the right. While you're doing that, I'll make us a drink.'

Oscar came down with the Singer hand-sewing machine, which was housed in a wooden case with a handle on top for carrying. 'You would never have managed this on the tram, Bessie, it's heavy.'

'I would have had a go. I might be little and thin, but I'm quite strong.' She grinned up into his face. 'I'm glad I didn't have to, though, 'cos it would have been hard going lifting it on to the tram. So thank you, Mr Oscar, I'm beholden to yer.'

He placed the sewing machine on the floor before asking, 'Why "Mr" Oscar? We're getting very formal, aren't we?'

Bessie scratched her head. 'To tell yer the truth, I don't know what to call anybody! All the servants call yer Mr Oscar, and they say Mr Cyril, and address Matilda as Madam. And I'm only a servant, so I should do the same, I suppose.' A picture came into her head and she put a hand over her mouth to try and keep the laughter back. But it didn't work and she began to chuckle. 'Can yer imagine it, Oscar. I'm sitting at the dining table, and as yer know it's a very long table, almost as long as from here to the Pier Head. Anyway, Cyril sits at one end, Matilda at the other, and I'm somewhere about halfway down. And I want the cruet set. Do I leave my chair and fetch it myself, or do I call, "Ay, Madam, would yer pass the cruet set down, please?" Or perhaps, "Shove the salt down, Matilda, there's a good girl". Or do I keep me mouth shut and do without the ruddy salt?'

Oscar was shaking with laughter. 'Oh, Bessie, you are absolutely priceless. I can quite see why Milly won't be parted from you. You are really going to be an asset to everyone in that house.'

'Ay, ay, ay! It's all right for you laughing, but that doesn't help me, does it? I want you to tell me how to address people, before I get the sack after only being there a week.'

'You are treated as one of the family, so you

617

address them by their first names. They don't call you Miss Maudsley or Miss Bessie, do they? And for friends like myself and Philip, it is the same, strictly first names.'

'Right, that solves that little problem.' Bessie's grin appeared. 'If I get the sack for being too familiar, I'll expect yer to find me another job, okay?'

He moved towards her and put his arm across her shoulders. 'I think you can safely say that your home will always be with the Lister-Sinclairs. They know how lucky they are to have you. However, if it will make you feel any better and put your mind at rest, you will always find a job with my family.'

The kettle began to whistle and Bessie made haste towards it, shouting over the noise of the kettle, 'Yer can always put an offer in, yer know. I'll go to the highest bidder.'

Thinking there would never be a dull moment in the Lister-Sinclair household while Bessie was there, Oscar followed her in to the kitchen. 'I'll put the machine in the car out of the way, then you can see what else you wish to take with you.'

Bessie poured the hot water into the teapot before following him. And, sure enough, there were dozens of kids around the car. It was so unusual to see one in the street, particularly a big posh one, they were curious. But they weren't touching it, and moved out of the way to let Oscar put the machine on the back seat. 'Ay, mister, that's a smashing car, what make is it?' one lad asked, eagerly eyeing the leather upholstery and the clocks on the polished wooden dashboard. 'I bet that cost a lot of money.'

Oscar noted the holes in the boy's woollen jumper, and the trousers which were far too small for the size of the lad. His shoes were well worn, and he was without socks. 'It's a Bentley, made in this country,' Oscar told him. 'And one day, when you're a man, you might have one.'

'I wish I could,' another boy said, wistfully, 'but I never will, 'cos I'll never have that much money.'

A front door on the opposite side of the street opened and Rita appeared. She'd seen the car, and her two sons were among the crowd of boys. 'Bessie, if my two are in the way, chase them.'

'They're not doing any harm, Rita, don't be worrying.' Bessie waved her friend over. 'Rita, this is Oscar, he's helping me take some of me things. Oscar, this is Rita, one of me best mates.'

Rita shook his outstretched hand. 'Pleased to meet yer. Yer'll have to excuse the way I look, I'm up to me neck in housework.'

Bessie tutted and huffed. 'Rita Wells, will yer stop making excuses for yerself? Oscar isn't a snob, and he's not daft either. He knows yer can't do housework without getting dirty. I was going to come over to see you and Aggie, 'cos I want yer to do me a couple of favours. But seeing as ye're here now, yer might as well come in.' Bessie's keen eyes spotted Kenny Gordon, and she called, 'Kenny, go and ask yer mam to come over too. Tell her not to bother putting an evening dress on, or her tiara, it's only an informal cup of tea.'

Oscar looked on with mixed feelings. All these

children were poorly dressed, it was a narrow mean street, yet not one of them had put so much as a finger on the car or been cheeky. It made him feel quite sad when he thought of his own children who wanted for nothing. He was deep in thought when he heard a loud voice shouting, 'Get out of the way, the lot of yer, anyone would think yer'd never seen a bleeding car before.' And crossing the street, he saw a woman with enormous breasts and stomach, untidy hair, and wearing a dirty pinny which had clearly seen better days. She pushed the children out of her way and stood before him with a beaming smile on her face. 'They won't hurt yer car, mister, they're not bad kids.' She nearly pulled his arm out of its socket with her hearty handshake, then she rubbed her hands together. 'Now, our Kenny said something about a cup of tea, and unless me ears were deceiving me, he said something about a custard cream biscuit too.'

Bessie smiled. 'I wish I had ears like yours, Aggie, they only hear what they want to hear. But ye're going to be disappointed 'cos I've only got ginger snaps. Anyway, come on in or I'll never get everything done I wanted to do.'

Oscar was given a china cup and saucer which brought knowing looks and nudges from Aggie. 'Blimey, she's only been living with the toffs for a week, and she's already forgotten herself. Another week and she won't even remember you and me, Rita.'

Bessie's eyes went to the ceiling. 'Aggie, if I live to be a hundred I'll never forget you. For ye're

620

one of those "once seen, never forgotten" people. And I wouldn't trust yer with a china cup 'cos yer'd break the ruddy thing with those ham shanks yer call hands. I've only got three china cups and saucers, they were me mam's and I treasure them. I don't even use them meself.'

'Take no notice of her, sunshine, yer know how she likes having yer on. If yer'd given her a gobstopper instead of a biscuit, it would have kept her quiet for an hour. So let's pretend she's not here and tell us what favour yer want from us?' Rita suggested.

'I'd like yer to tell the rent collector I'm giving a week's notice and he can take over the house from next weekend. I'll leave yer the money for the two weeks' rent.'

Rita pulled a face. 'I'm not half going to miss you, sunshine, after all these years of us being friends. It won't seem the same with a new family living facing me.'

'The same goes for me, too, queen,' Aggie said. 'We've had some good laughs together and we'll miss that.' For once Aggie showed her soft side, her voice full of emotion. 'And yer've been a good pal to me and Rita, always there to help out when we were stuck for money to buy food. We'd have been in Queer Street many a time without yer.'

'The three of us have helped each other, Aggie, it hasn't been all one-sided.' Bessie's heart strings were being pulled. It wasn't going to be easy to move out of this house and away from her two mates. 'Anyway, can we get back to business? I'm only taking a few small things with me, like photos, ornaments and pictures, things that belonged to me parents. So what I want yer to do is, have a look around yerselves and see if there's anything yer'd like. The beds and bedding should be worth having, but yer can decide that. I'm leaving the key with yer. Anything yer don't want, get the man from that secondhand shop on the main road to come and have a look at it, and ask him what he'll give for it. And any money yer get I want yer to share between yer.'

'Don't be so daft!' Rita said. 'We'll get the best price we can for it and we'll give you the money. I wouldn't dream of keeping it. We've always been the ones to take off you, and never been in a position to give you anything back, so the least we can do is help yer out now. But we don't want the money, we'll hand it over to you.'

Aggie's chins, which fascinated Oscar, swung up and down. 'Hear, hear! I'll second that, queen. It'll be our pleasure to do something for you. Especially after what yer did for us at Christmas, and half of the ruddy street too. A flipping hero, that's what yer are.'

Bessie swivelled round in her chair to face the visitor, who was sitting in the fireside chair, greatly interested in the goings-on. 'Oscar, if yer hear anything that's not meant for your ears, yer won't repeat it, will yer? Not that anything is a matter of life or death, and yer'd find out eventually anyway, but for now keep it to yerself.'

Oscar grinned. 'Bessie, don't you know I'm as deaf as a door post?'

She grinned back. 'Anything yer don't understand, I'll explain to yer on the way home.' She swivelled herself round again and leaned her elbows on the table. 'Now, ladies, listen carefully. Evelyn will be coming down this afternoon, and a van will be calling to pick up what she wants from next door. Milly will be with her, and she wanted me to tell yer to make sure Jack's in, 'cos she wants to see him. And now, don't say a word until I've finished, let me get it all off me chest – Evelyn wants to know if you would be kind enough, next week, to give her notice in to the rent collector as well as mine. She's given me the money to cover two weeks' rent, so I'll give it to yer before I leave. And when the man from the secondhand shop comes here, she would very much like you to get him to look at the furniture and bedding she'll be leaving behind and she wants you to share the money between you.'

Rita shook her head. 'Ah, come off it, Bessie, we can't do that! We hardly know the woman!'

'No one regrets that more than Evelyn. She knows yer used to call her all the stuck-up cows going, and says you had every right 'cos that's exactly what she was. But yer haven't heard it all yet, so will yer keep quiet and let me get on? What I'm going to say next might have yer thinking she feels sorry for yer and is giving you her hand-me-downs, but that would be far from the truth. She's getting married in three weeks, as yer know, and she'd like you to come to the wedding.' Bessie ignored their gasps of astonishment and carried on. 'Yer will be getting an invitation through the post in the next few days.'

'Huh!' Aggie's face was a picture. 'This is a bleeding joke, Bessie Maudsley, and I'm surprised at yer, playing a trick like this on us.' Then the table rocked as her tummy shook with laughter. 'Can yer imagine me and you at a toff's wedding, Rita? In a sixpenny dress from Great Homer Street Market, a scarf on our head 'cos ye're not allowed in church without yer head being covered. We'd be a laughing stock. Folk would move away from us in case they caught something.'

But Rita wasn't listening, she was studying Bessie's face. 'It's not a joke, is it, sunshine?'

She shook her head. 'No, it's not, and I'm surprised at yer for thinking I'd stoop so low as to pull a stunt like that. And another thing: if you two aren't good enough to be invited then neither am I! D'yer think because I've moved to be with Milly, I've suddenly joined the ranks of the well-off? I haven't changed, yer silly nits, and I never will. And, what's more, the people I live with now, and the likes of Oscar here, and Philip who Evelyn is marrying, they treat me as an equal. I get on like a house on fire with all of them. I don't try and be something I'm not, and I never will. So if I'm good enough for the wedding, then so are me best mates.'

Rita said quietly, 'I believe yer, sunshine, and it's very thoughtful of Evelyn. But we've got no clothes for a posh wedding, we'd stick out like sore thumbs and that really would be embarrassing for us.'

'You'd have enough money from the sale of the contents of both houses to buy yerselves some really classy clothes. There's a shop in a lane off Church Street where they sell good secondhand clothes. Yer'd get a smashing dress and hat from

624

there 'cos they mostly deal in wedding outfits. For the money yer get for the furniture, bedding and kitchen equipment, yer could doll yerselves up to the nines. And it would be a day yer'd enjoy, one to look back on.' Bessie looked from one to the other. 'Before yer say anything, there's another reason yer should give some thought to it. The groom will have all his family and friends at the church, while Evelyn will have very few sitting in the pews on her side. I'm not asking yer to feel sorry for her, like, it was just a passing thought.'

Aggie gave Rita a sly kick. 'What d'yer say, queen, have yer made up yer mind? Meself, I'd like to go 'cos I might never get another chance to go to a posh wedding. And I quite fancy meself in a big picture hat.'

Rita stared at her, straight-faced. 'You in a wedding outfit ... now that would be something to see.' She suddenly burst out laughing, 'I wouldn't miss that for the world!'

'Are yer both game for it then?' Bessie asked. And when they both nodded, she said, 'Thank God for that, one problem solved. So I'll give yer the rent money now for both houses, and my front door key. Milly will give yer next door's when the van has been and Evelyn has taken all she wants from there. But don't hand the keys over to the collector on Monday 'cos yer'll need them to let the man from the secondhand shop in. Give them to the collector the following week, we'll have paid up till then.'

Bessie closed her eyes and held her forehead in her hand. 'Is there anything else now? Oh, yeah,

625

two things. I'm expecting yer to come and visit me next week, so how would Tuesday be, say about twelve? Yer can have some lunch with me. Then I'll bring Milly down on Saturday, 'cos I know she'll have me motheaten, wanting to see Jack.' She rubbed her forehead again, but it was all a pretence. 'What else was there? Oh, yeah, on the day of the wedding, yer won't have to worry about how to get to the church, they're sending a car to pick you up. And that wasn't Evelyn's idea, it was Philip's, her fiancé's. That's because she had told him how good yer were helping me with giving the Christmas hampers and things out. He wants to meet yer so he can thank you himself.'

Aggie was so flabbergasted she didn't know what to do or say. She folded her arms, hitched her bosom and sat back quickly in her chair. Now the chair wasn't used to being sat on by a person of Aggie's weight, it was only used to Bessie and Milly, so it creaked like mad to let them know it objected. But Aggie didn't hear it, her mind was on other things. 'If we're going to get in a car, I'll have to make sure I don't buy a hat with a bleeding big brim or I won't be able to get through the door.'

Rita was excited inside but keeping it under control until she was in her own house. She looked at her neighbour now, put an arm across her shoulders and said, 'I don't think getting in the car with a hat on is yer biggest worry, sunshine, I'd be inclined to be more worried about yer blue fleecy-lined drawers and yer elastic garters. I mean, if yer hat fell off yer could always run after it, but if yer knickers fell down –

well, it doesn't bear thinking about.'

Oscar couldn't stop talking and laughing as they drove back to the Lister-Sinclairs'. 'What a pair of personalities your friends are, Bessie, I could have sat listening to them all day. You will miss them, for they are everything you need in friends. Warm, loyal and funny.'

She nodded. 'Yes, I will miss them, but I certainly won't lose touch with them. I have seen those two laughing their heads off when they haven't had two ha'pennies to rub together. It's when times are hard that yer find out what people are really like, and Rita and Aggie are the salt of the earth.'

'I'm intrigued as to where Philip fits in. How did he come to hear of these ladies?'

Bessie told him about the donation, Evelyn's part in it, and how she, with the help of Rita and Aggie, had been able to help so many poor people in the street. 'It was hard going, 'cos I worked every day, but it was worth it to see the faces of women who hadn't had a decent meal in years. Husbands out of work, kids to feed and clothe, they were really living on the breadline. Philip was very kind, and although those people will probably never meet him, they will be eternally grateful to him.'

Oscar was really moved by what he'd heard. 'I wish I had known, my father and I would have helped. Cyril too, he would have been the first to put his hand in his pocket. Well, we will all be there to help next year. Or even now, if your friends know of any families who are really in trouble, I can get help for them. My family and my friends are very fortunate, but I'm afraid perhaps we don't always appreciate it. This afternoon has been an eye-opener for me, and a lesson I won't forget in a hurry.' He took his eyes from the road for a second to glance at Bessie and to smile. 'I like your friends. Thank you for letting me meet them.'

It was a week before the wedding and Matilda was in her bedroom trying on one of three dresses brought for her inspection by an assistant from one of the best shops in the city. She was helping her client pull the dress down over her hips. It was a navy blue dress, in stiff shot silk, with full skirt, high neck and raglan sleeves. 'Would Madam care to look in the mirror?' the assistant asked. 'I think it suits you beautifully.'

Matilda turned several times to inspect her appearance in the full-length mirror. Then she looked over to where Bessie was sitting on a delicate antique chair. 'What do you think, Bessie, does it suit me?'

In the four weeks she had lived in the house, she had often felt like asking Matilda why she always wore such old-fashioned clothes that made her look much older. But she hadn't liked to be so forward. Now, though, Matilda wanted a dress for Evelyn's wedding, and that dark one didn't do a thing for her, only made her look old and faded. It wouldn't be truthful or fair if Bessie didn't say so. 'I wonder if the assistant would kindly leave us alone for ten minutes, to give you time to make up your mind? This wedding is an important occasion, and the choosing of a dress for it is not something to be decided in a hurry.'

Matilda nodded. 'I think that's wise. Would you go down to the drawing room for a short while, please? I'll ring for the maid when we have finished our discussion.'

When the young lady had left the room, Matilda asked, 'Do you not like the dress, Bessie?'

'D'yer want my true opinion?'

'Yes, of course. I would expect nothing less than the truth from you.'

'In that case, don't say I didn't warn yer. That dress makes yer look old, colourless and drab. In fact, most of your clothes don't do yer justice. Ye're not an old woman, Tilly, so why do yer dress like one? And yer've got beautiful hair, but yer comb it right back into a bun which makes yer look older and is a waste of such an asset.' Afraid she'd gone too far, Bessie said, 'I'm sorry, I'm maybe speaking out of turn. But I'm also speaking as a friend who thinks yer could be a knock-out in the right clothes and a different hair style. And I'm sorry I called yer Tilly, that was out of order too.'

Matilda bit the inside of her lip to keep a smile at bay. She was getting used to Bessie being outspoken, and really appreciated it. Most of the staff fawned over her, always saying what they thought she wanted to hear. 'What about the other two dresses? Do they not find favour with you?'

Bessie told herself she may as well be hung for a sheep as a lamb. 'No, they're the wrong colour

629

and style for you. Yer need something younger, so Cyril can see in you the young girl he fell in love with and married.'

Without saying a word, Matilda crossed the room and pulled on the bell cord. She waited for Maisie to come into the room then asked her to tell the shop assistant that unfortunately none of the dresses had found favour with her, and would she take them back to the shop with apologies? 'Tell her I will ring her supervisor to say she has been very pleasant and efficient, so she won't get into trouble. And now Miss Bessie and I are going to her room and I am to be shown how I should wear my hair so I look like a young girl again. That should be very interesting, I have never seen magic performed before.'

When Bessie brought Milly home from school that night, the young girl stood at the door of the drawing room and gazed at her grandmother with eyes and mouth wide. Then she ran to her. 'Grandma, you look beautiful! Have you been to the shop to have your hair done? It makes you look very pretty.'

Matilda took the girl in her arms. 'As pretty as you, would you say?'

'Oh, yes, Grandma, much prettier than me. Have you been to a hairdresser's?'

'I have my own private hairdresser, my darling, and that is your Auntie Bessie.'

Milly ran to fling her arms around Bessie's waist next. 'Oh, you are clever, Auntie Bessie. My dress for the wedding is the most beautifulest dress in the whole world, and now you've made

630

Grandma look beautiful. I love you, love you, love you.'

'And guess what?' Matilda asked, looking very self-satisfied. 'Your Auntie Bessie has offered to make me a dress for the wedding.'

'Ay, Tilly Mint, I didn't offer, I was talked into it.'

Cyril happened to walk into the room at that moment. He often came home early now there was something for him to come home to. 'What were you talked into, Bessie?'

She knew he hadn't looked in his wife's direction yet, and she also knew Matilda was anxious to know what his reaction would be to the change in her appearance. 'Ask yer wife, she's the one who causes all the trouble around here.'

Cyril was speechless when he glanced at Matilda. It was a few seconds before he could move. 'My darling, you look wonderful, about twenty years younger. You look like you did the day we got married.' He kissed her on the lips. 'I have told you often you should visit a hairdressing salon. They have worked wonders.'

'I haven't been over the door, my darling, and the wonders were performed by Bessie. Who, incidentally, didn't like any of the dresses Cripps sent for my inspection, and sent the girl packing with them. She said they made me look old and staid, so I worked my charms on her and now she is to make me a dress for the wedding. She hasn't been given much time, but she said as soon as she gets the material, and a pattern I like, she will have it cut out and tacked in no time, ready for me to try on. Oh, and I am to be called Tilly from now on, and that is also down to Bessie.'

Milly's giggle joined Cyril's hearty laughter and the two women smiled at each other, knowing in that moment they had each found a friend for life.

It was the day of the wedding, and the Lister-Sinclairs' house was all hustle and bustle. There was excitement in the air, smiles on every face. Evelyn had spent the night there before leaving for the church with Cyril, who was giving her away. She had written to her parents telling them she was to be married and hoping they would make an attempt at a reconciliation. But if they were to be reconciled, it had to be because they wanted to make amends to her, not because she was marrying into a very wealthy family. So in her letter she hadn't said who she was marrying, just told them the name of the church and the date and time. She had asked if they would kindly reply to Philip's address within the week. But there had been no reply. Evelyn knew if she had told them who she was marrying they would have been to see her the day they received the letter. She was sad, but it proved they had never really loved her. Their only love was for money.

'Evelyn, ye're miles away!' Bessie said, coming into the dressing room. 'But I'm glad to see ye're not a nervous wreck, I'd hate to have yer fainting on me.'

'I was thinking how lucky I am, Bessie. My life has changed so much I sometimes wonder if I'm dreaming.'

'Yer've got the rest of yer life to dream,

632

sweetheart. Right now it's time to put your dress on. I've just finished getting Milly ready – she was so excited she couldn't stand still, and I have to say she looks a picture. I know I'm biased when it comes to your daughter, but she looks good enough to eat.' Bessie stopped to draw breath. She'd been on the go since she got out of bed, seeing to herself first, then dressing Matilda and doing her hair. And, wonder of wonders, Matilda had even asked her to put some powder and rouge on her face. She was a different woman these days, preferred to be called Tilly, laughed a lot and was more outgoing. And she looked a real beauty today in a dress of soft silk which fitted her to perfection. She had allowed Bessie to choose the material and colour, and not been disappointed. The dress was a pale beige, and she'd bought a wide-brimmed hat in a deeper shade, with gloves and shoes to match.

'Well, that's my bit of dreaming done, sweetheart, so let's get you ready.' Bessie reached for the dress which was hanging outside the large wardrobe. 'Lift yer arms up so I can get it on without creasing it.' Five minutes later, Bessie stood back and sighed with pleasure. The dress was a dream of beautiful ivory-coloured soft silk. There were yards of it in the skirt, and the nipped-in waist showed Evelyn's figure off to perfection. It had long sleeves which tapered off to the wrist, and the low round neck was set off by the link of pearls Philip had bought her as a wedding present. Bessie filled up, and a tear trickled down her face. 'Oh, sweetheart, you look lovely, and I'm so proud of yer. If it weren't for mucking yer dress up, I'd squeeze yer to death.'

'Will you do my hair, please, Bessie? You're much better at it than I am. And then all I need is a touch of rouge because I look a little pale. I'll leave the hat until it's time to leave for the church.'

The door opened and in came Matilda and Milly. The girl was hanging on to her grandmother's hand until she saw her mother. Then she ran forward. 'You look like a fairy, Mother, really beautiful.' She did a twirl. 'And hasn't Auntie Bessie made me the most lovely dress? I wish Jack was going to the church so he could see me.'

Bessie's mind flashed back a few months, to the day Milly had dressed in her mother's clothes and had the street out. 'There's nothing to stop you putting it on for him one day, sweetheart. Remember, yer like getting dressed up?'

Milly smiled, knowing right away what her Auntie Bessie was talking about. 'Mother, what have you done with the trunk that was in your bedroom? I often wondered what was in it.'

'It's in Philip's apartment at the moment, I had nowhere else to put it. Why do you ask?'

'If you don't want it, could I have it, please?'

'Of course you can, dear, but why would you want it?'

'Because then I'll have something of yours, and I'd like that.'

Bessie turned her head so she couldn't see the tears that welled up in Evelyn's eyes. It wasn't sadness the two women felt, it was happiness, for although Milly might never again live with her mother, she had now let it be known she would always think of her as her mother.

'Come on, let's get moving,' Bessie said, 'we've got a wedding to go to.'

Philip sat in the front pew with his best friend Clive, who was acting as his best man. 'She's late, isn't she?'

'Calm down, old boy, we were very early, at your insistence. Anyway, it's a bride's prerogative to keep the groom waiting.' Clive glanced sideways at his friend. He'd never thought to see Philip as nervous as he was today. Mind you, having met Evelyn he could understand why. Clive was happy his friend had found the woman of his dreams and was settling down.

Philip turned in his seat to see the church was filling up. He was about to turn back when he saw two women sitting in a pew at the very back of the church. They were on Evelyn's side, but he had never seen them before. Then a thought struck him. 'I've just seen someone I want to speak to, Clive, I won't be a minute.'

Clive frowned. 'This is most unusual, old boy, the bride could be here at any moment.'

'I'll be back before then, I promise.' With that, Philip walked towards the back of the church, surprising guests who were already seated. All heads were turned as he walked into the next to last pew, where he bent to talk to two women who were strangers to everyone except Bessie.

'Would I be wrong in saying you are Rita and Aggie?' Philip smiled when he saw the women look at each other, surprise on their faces. 'It's all right, ladies, I'm Philip.'

In a daze Rita and Aggie shook his hand. 'Ay, lad, shouldn't yer be down by the altar?' Aggie asked. 'Yer don't want to miss yer own wedding, do yer?'

'I have wanted to meet you for some time now, and I was hoping I could talk to you at the reception. However, Evelyn said she had a feeling you might not come to it, that you may sneak away from the church after the service.'

'I won't say we didn't think about it,' Rita said, truthfully. 'Yer see, me and Aggie would feel like fish out of water, not knowing anyone and ... well, we wouldn't fit in.'

'What nonsense,' he said. 'You have been invited as our friends and I would be disappointed if you let me down. In fact, I won't go back to my best man, who will be tearing his hair out by now, until you promise faithfully you'll come to the reception? A car has been booked to take you with Bessie.'

Rita heard one car draw up outside just then. 'Here's Evelyn! Quick, get down to the altar. We'll come, cross my heart and hope to die.'

Oscar waited until Philip was standing by his best man, then whispered, 'Are they coming to the reception?'

Philip nodded just as the organ started to play and all eyes turned to see Evelyn on Cyril's arm, walking down the aisle. She looked so elegant and beautiful. Cyril felt proud as he smiled at his friends. Gwen followed behind with Milly, looking very pretty in matching dresses, their bouquets of pink flowers matching the floral headdresses.

Milly was smiling, not in the least shy. She was happy, and proud that her mother looked so beautiful. And she was glad her mother had Uncle Philip, 'cos he was nice. Then she saw her Auntie Bessie and waved, mouthing the words, 'I love you,' and blew a kiss to her grandma. She was a very lucky girl having so many people to love her.

Philip thought his heart would stop as he saw the woman he adored walking towards him with a faint smile on her face. She was the picture of perfection and he felt he must be the luckiest man in the world to have won her love. He stepped from the front pew as the couple came abreast, and took Evelyn's elbow when Cyril smiled and released her arm before taking his seat next to his wife and Bessie. 'My darling Evelyn, you look so beautiful,' Philip told her quietly. 'I will love you for the rest of my life.'

There were tears shed, but once the service was over and the guests spilled into the church yard for photographs there was much jostling and laughing. The first to be photographed were the bride and groom, standing in the arched entrance to the church and looking the very picture of happiness. Evelyn was a radiant bride, Philip a very handsome groom. Then there was another photograph of bride and groom with Milly standing between them. This was followed by close family, then a group photograph which Rita and Aggie were pulled into by Oscar at the request of Evelyn. Then Oscar asked for one to be taken, away from the crowd, of the three friends, Bessie, Rita and Aggie.

'Ooh, er, I wasn't expecting that, Oscar,' Aggie

said, her bosom rising high with pride. 'Thanks very much.'

'I'll make sure you all get a copy,' he promised them, 'and that they're framed for you.'

'Yes, thank yer, Oscar,' Rita said, 'it'll take pride of place on me sideboard.'

Aggie and her chins were thinking ahead. 'We'll get all the neighbours in to see us all dolled up. But they better hadn't pick the photie up, though, and get all fingermarks on it, or I'll marmalise them.' The day had been one that she and her mate would never forget, and it had all been down to Bessie.

The reception was beautifully laid out, the food delicious. Poor Rita's side must have been sore with the constant digs she was getting from Aggie. In the end, she said, 'Aggie, I've got eyes in me head, sunshine, I can see what you can see.'

As the meal progressed there was a lot of laughter, most of it provided by Bessie, Rita, Aggie and Milly. Many friendships were formed that day. As Rita and Aggie realised, not every toff was a snob. And Milly reminded them some friendships would go on forever when she said to Rita, 'Don't forget to tell Jack how nice I look.' Then she grinned. 'I'll tell him myself next Saturday.'

This Large Print Book for the partially sighted, who cannot read normal print, is published under the auspices of

THE ULVERSCROFT FOUNDATION

PATHFINDER

PATHFINDER
THE UNTOLD SECRET MISSION IN IRAQ

The inside story of
the Pathfinders,
bastard son of the SAS

CAPTAIN DAVID BLAKELEY

This edition first published in Great Britain in 2012 by
Orion
an imprint of the Orion Publishing Group Ltd
Orion House, 5 Upper St Martin's Lane,
London WC2H 9EA
An Hachette UK Company

1 3 5 7 9 10 8 6 4 2

A CIP catalogue record for this book is available
from the British Library.

Hardback ISBN: 978 1 4091 4409 0
Export Trade Paperback: 978 1 4091 4410 6

Designed in ITC Charter by Geoff Green Book Design, Cambridge
Printed in Great Britain by Clays Ltd, St Ives plc

www.orionbooks.co.uk

For my mother and father,
for always being there for me.

'It is not the critic who counts, nor the man who points out how the strong man stumbles, or where the doer of deeds could have done them better. The credit belongs to the man who is actually in the arena; whose face is marred by dust and sweat and blood; who strives valiantly; who errs and comes short again and again, because there is no effort without error or shortcoming; who knows the great enthusiasms, the great devotions, who spends himself in a worthy cause; who, at the best, knows in the end the triumph of high achievement, and who, at the worst, if he fails, at least fails while daring greatly, so that his place shall never be with those cold and timid souls who know neither victory nor defeat.'

PRESIDENT THEODORE ROOSEVELT
Speech at the Sorbonne, 23 April 1910

'Happiness shall always be found by those who dare and persevere; wanderer – do not turn around, march on and have no fear.'

ANONYMOUS
Unofficial collect of the Pathfinders

ACKNOWLEDGEMENTS

A very special thanks to my sisters Anna and Lisa, for all your support over the years and especially when I was away on operations with the military: I love you and you continue to inspire me.

I would like to thank Damien Lewis, the master of jack brews, for the time spent searching for inspiration while staring into the blanket fog of a southern Irish rain; publishers Rowland White and Alan Samson, for their inspiration, vision and guidance from the very earliest stages; Jillian Young and all at Orion who did so much to make this book a success. Thanks also to Annabel Merullo, literary agent, and her assistant, Laura Williams, for their support.

Thank you to: my steadfast friends Ewan Ross, Gareth Arnold, David Green, Azim Majid and Stefan D'Bart. To the most loyal friend Jimmy Chew – thank you for being there. Also thank you to Lara Fraser, Alice Clough, Rob Mussetti, Francesca Mussetti, Matt Taylor, Andy Jackson, Sabina Skala, Janice Dickinson, Sophie Ball, Laura Pradelska, Olivia Lee, Bonnie Gilmore, Josh Varney, Emma Rigby, Richard Allen, Charles Towning, Luke Hardy, Andrew Chittock, Patrick Hambleton, Katie Rice, Charlie Birch and Katerina Konecna. And thanks of course to Eva, Chubbs, Logs and Podge, for putting up with my repeated impositions upon your hospitality.

Very special and heartfelt thanks to the men of my patrol, *Mayhem Three Zero*, with whom I shared so much and as is depicted in this book, and especially Tricky, who saved my life on more than one occasion.

To the Pathfinders (PF): many great men have put huge amounts of effort into developing this elite unit. The PF are the best in the world at what they do because of your efforts. To the fallen; we will remember you. To the current and future Findermen – move fast, stay low and enjoy it while it lasts.

'FIRST IN'
Pathfinder Platoon Motto

David Blakeley
March 2012.

Find out more about David Blakeley at:
www.davidblakeley.co.uk

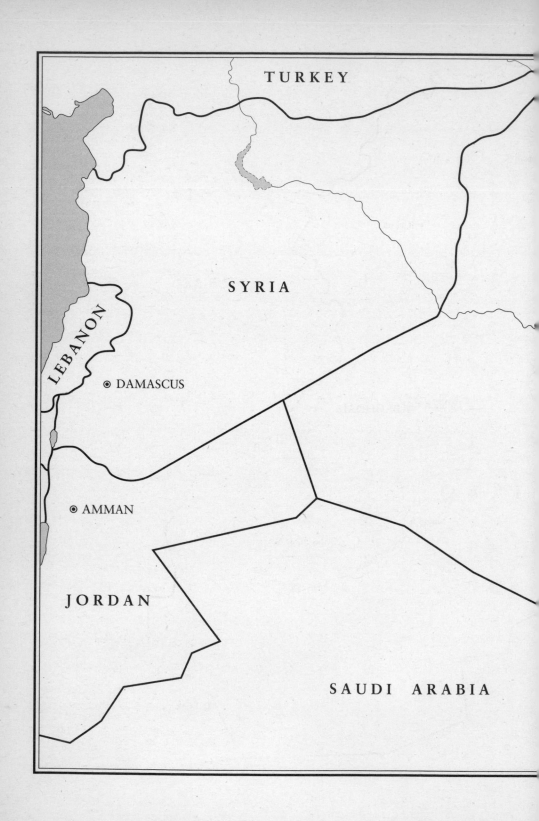

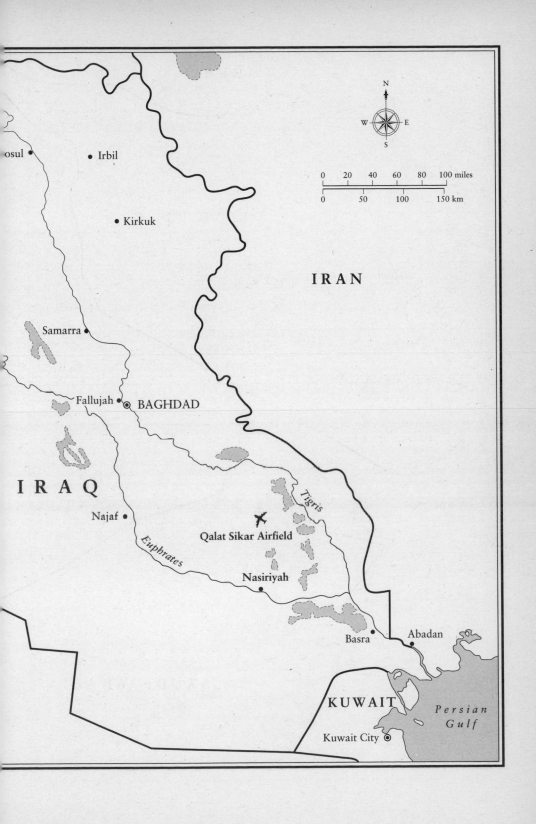

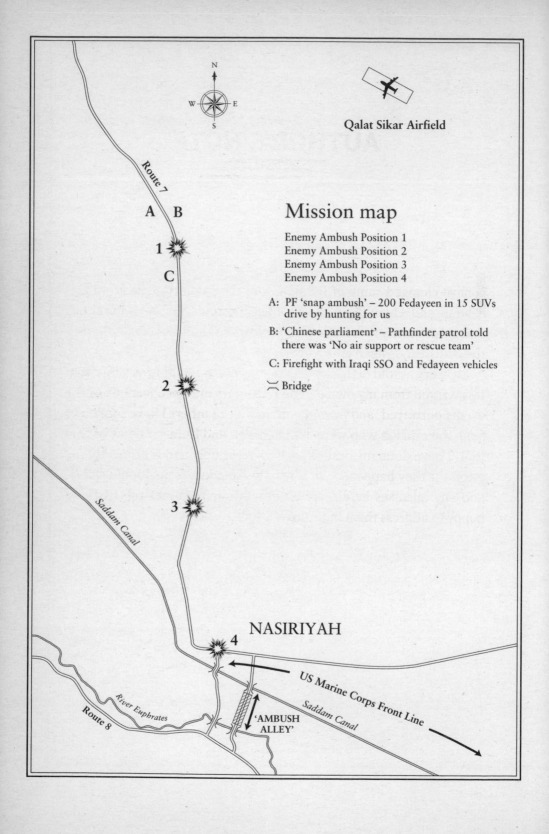

Qalat Sikar Airfield

Route 7

A   B

1

C

2

3

Mission map

Enemy Ambush Position 1
Enemy Ambush Position 2
Enemy Ambush Position 3
Enemy Ambush Position 4

A: PF 'snap ambush' – 200 Fedayeen in 15 SUVs
   drive by hunting for us

B: 'Chinese parliament' – Pathfinder patrol told
   there was 'No air support or rescue team'

C: Firefight with Iraqi SSO and Fedayeen vehicles

⌣ Bridge

Saddam Canal

NASIRIYAH

4

US Marine Corps Front Line

River Euphrates

Route 8

Saddam Canal

'AMBUSH
ALLEY'

AUTHOR'S NOTE

I have changed some of the names of the soldiers depicted in this book, and a handful of geographical locations, for operational and personal security reasons, and to protect the identities of members of the British and Allied elite forces.

My story as told in this book concerns my tour of Iraq as I fought it. It is written from my own personal memory and recollections of the events portrayed, and from the memories of others I have spoken to from the mission who were able to assist, and from my notes of that tour. I have done my best to portray accurately and realistically the events as they happened. However, my memory is no doubt fallible, and any mistakes herein are entirely of my own making. I will be happy to address them in future editions.

PROLOGUE

It was last light, almost time to load up the C130 Hercules and take to the darkening skies. I strolled down the deserted runway to get a little space to myself. The sun was sinking below the rumpled, grey mass of the mountains several kilometres to the west of us, with the vast expanse of the great semi-arid desert lying beyond.

The airstrip was deep in the shadows of a sunken valley and well out of sight, which was just as we wanted it. From high above me an eagle emitted a lonely, high-pitched screech. A dust devil came swirling across the bush, whipping up dry grass and debris as it skittered across the runway. The scene was so utterly deserted, it was hardly possible to imagine all the hidden men-at-arms making their last-minute, fevered preparations.

You can mount an airborne mission from just about any serviceable length of tarmac – from London's Heathrow to a battle-scarred Baghdad International Airport, or a disused airfield in the middle of the bush. Mostly, conventional military operations go out from one of the big airbases, with little need to keep them hidden. With missions such as ours we needed to be well away from the public gaze, and the prying lenses of the media.

With this airstrip we'd got exactly what we were looking for. It was so ancient it didn't even possess a working control tower. There was just a ragged, sun-bleached, dull-orange windsock hanging limp in the air, plus a couple of semi-derelict hangars. Since its arrival the previous night under cover of darkness, there was also the fat, powerful form of a C130 Hercules transport aircraft squatting on the apron, looking well out of place next to the pitted runway, half-overgrown with weeds.

One of the two hangars housed our vehicles, a pair of cut-down Land Rovers bristling with machine guns, which we affectionately referred to as the 'Pinkies'. The building dated from the 1950s, with brick walls topped by a sagging corrugated-iron roof. The rust-red metal had been patched with scores of repairs, like dull silver sticking plasters. Still, it served our purposes fine. From there we could load the Pinkies aboard the C130 for deep insertion missions, or on to a Chinook heavy-lift helicopter for shorter-range operations.

In the wild, empty quiet I took a moment to reflect upon what lay ahead of me. It was only recently that I'd taken over as second-in-command (2IC) of our unit, the Pathfinders, and here we were poised to jump into the darkness and the unknown. A number of the guys had many more years' experience than me: no doubt about it, I was going to be tested as never before.

They say that war is long periods of boredom interrupted by intense periods of action. We'd waited a good few days for this one to get the green light. But even now, two hours away from brakes off – the aircraft take-off hour – we could still get stood down. In fact, we could get called back at any moment before we dived off the Hercules aircraft's open ramp, high above hostile terrain.

Once we were out of the aircraft's hold we had reached the point of no return. No one could call us back. You can't use a radio on a HALO (High Altitude Low Opening) jump, which was how we'd be inserting. There was no way to hear a radio message, or to speak into a mouthpiece, when freefalling from extreme high altitude and plummeting to earth at speeds in excess of 100 mph. In any case, the slipstream would rip any earpiece or mouthpiece away.

We'd be incommunicado as we fell. Once we were on the ground we'd be in the midst of hostile territory, so radio silence would be paramount. The earliest we'd have communications would be at our first 'Sched', one of the two daily radio reports we had to make to mission HQ. Our first would be at 0800 the following morning, by which time we'd have reached our objective and completed our CTR (Close Target Recce), so what were the chances of getting called off then?

If we could just get our arses out of that Hercules and into the air, then we'd be free-running to target. It was an awesome proposition, and I could feel my pulse thumping just at the thought of it.

I made my way across to the Herc. Tom, the C130 pilot, served with the RAF's 47 Squadron, their Special Forces wing. I knew him well from previous jobs, and we'd been out on the piss several times together. He was a big drinker and a larger-than-life character, plus he was a superlative Special Forces pilot – a king at what he did, which was flying guys like us deep behind enemy lines.

At my approach he slid back a side window in the giant aircraft's cockpit, and poked his head out. 'Latest MET report is all good, mate. No change to weather conditions at the IP, and no change to the flight path we'll take in.'

The IP was the impact point, the exact landing spot that we'd pre-identified from the maps and sat photos.

I couldn't suppress a grin. 'Looks like we're on then?'

He glanced at his watch. 'Wheels-up minus ninety. I reckon this one's a go.'

Wheels-up meant aircraft take-off time. I felt around in the left-hand breast pocket of my smock, and pulled out a CD. It was AC/DC's album *The Razors Edge*. I tossed it up to him.

'Track three mate …'

He rolled his eyes. 'Not bloody "Thunderstruck" *again*? How many times am I going to have to listen to that racket as you guys pile out of my backside. Can't we have something a bit more classy – like Wagner's "Ride of the Valkyries" maybe?'

'RAF wanker,' I cut in. 'Anyway, you know the form. We always jump to "Thunderstruck". It's PF tradition.'

He shrugged and turned to the co-pilot beside him. 'Pete, can you get this crap racked up on the CD and test the Tannoy system's working?'

I hurried over to the hangar. There was still one hell of a lot to get done before we got airborne. As I approached the building I could hear music blaring out. Tricky most likely had revved up the Foo Fighters' heavy rock on his portable CD player. Out here in the midst of the deserted bush it didn't matter how much noise we made: about the only things that we were likely to disturb were the local ostriches.

This bone-dry mountainous region was renowned for its herds of ostrich. We'd seen them running in wild confusion across the valleys, their fat legs pumping and their plumed tails flapping, as they tried to get away from one of our Chinooks flying at 180 knots and at treetop level. Over the past few weeks our quartermaster had got very adept at flipping ostrich steaks on the makeshift barbecue we'd rigged up at the rear of the airbase. Tasty they were, too.

I stepped into the relative darkness of the hangar. The lads were busy doing their last-minute preparations. I made one final check of my weapons, my mags of ammo, the pouches on my smock and my webbing. The last thing you wanted was one of those falling open during the jump, and a vital bit of war-fighting kit spinning down to earth. I stuffed my belt and chest webbing kit into my bulging rucksack and shut the flap, tightening the straps to the max.

To one side of me Jason Dickins, the second-in-command of my six-man patrol, jammed his massive rucksack into a large canvas coverall. He turned to speak to a tall, awkward-looking figure standing next to him. We'd been tasked to parachute an extra body in on this mission. He wasn't a Pathfinder. He was some sneaky-beaky mystery type, whom we'd nicknamed 'The Ghost.'

'You got your bergen ready, mate?' he demanded.

None of us had particularly warmed to The Ghost. Ever since he'd joined us a few days back, he'd treated Jason and the other rankers as if they were one step removed from the mice and other vermin that infested the hangar. He'd managed to exchange the odd civil word with me, but only once he had realised that I was a Sandhurst graduate and an officer. Pathfinders wear no marks of unit or rank, so it had taken him a while to do so.

His attitude had gone down like the proverbial turd in a punchbowl. In the PF, as our unit is known, each man is treated as an equal regardless of education, class, background or rank. No one can enter the Pathfinders without passing the brutal selection course, which rivals that of the SAS. Selection is the first great leveller. And once in the PF, patrol command goes to the most experienced and capable soldier for the mission in hand.

Jason was one of a tiny number of operators in the British Army who'd qualified as a military tandem master. As such, he was able to freefall another human being from extreme high altitude into target. I'm not permitted to reveal from what height exactly we jump, but suffice to say it is from far above what any civilian parachutist would ever do so.

On this mission Jason would be parachuting with The Ghost strapped to his torso. Jason was the last person the guy should ever have treated with disdain or disrespect. Pretty shortly his life would be 100 per cent in Jason's hands, when they jumped out together into the dark and howling void.

'Erm, I imagine I've got everything I need,' The Ghost remarked, gesturing at his bulging pack. It wasn't our need to know what was in there, or what he'd be using it for exactly. Our mission was just to get us, and him, to target.

'Hand it over then, mate,' Jase prompted, impatiently.

Jason stuffed the guy's rucksack into the canvas coverall alongside his own, and laced the whole tightly closed. He'd freefall with The Ghost strapped to his front, and the canvas sack hanging on a strap suspended below him. Not counting his own body weight, he'd be steering some 130 kg into the IP. It was one hell of a tasking.

Being the most experienced parachutist amongst the six of us, Jase would lead our stick out of the C130. As 2IC Pathfinders and a well-experienced high-altitude parachutist myself, I'd follow.

Jase turned to me. 'Wheels-up minus sixty,' he grunted. 'Best we load up the bergens.'

It took the three of us – myself, Jase, plus The Ghost – to man-handle the canvas sack containing their two packs the 200 metres or so to the waiting aircraft. We staggered up the open tail ramp and dumped it in Jason's place, nearest to the rear. We ferried the rest of the bergens across the apron, mine going next to Jase's, then Dez's, Steve's and Joe's, with Tricky's last of all. You'd always put one of your most experienced operators last in the stick, for he'd have no one to watch his back.

You placed those with the least experience between your better guys. So, Dez Vincent would come after me, for he was a bit of a meathead and not long with the PF. Steve Knight, the Pathfinders' armourer, came next, so Dez was sandwiched between the two of us. Between Steve and Will 'Tricky' Arnold – an unbeatable PF opera-tor – we had Joe Hamilton, who at twenty-three was the young pup on the patrol. No one could quite figure out if Joe had done enough soldiering to qualify for the PF, but he'd passed selection and that made him one of us.

With the bergens loaded we headed over to the second hangar. We paused for a nervous piss outside, before strapping ourselves into our HALO gear.

Inside, the lead PD (Parachute Dispatcher) greeted us with a crink-ling around the eyes. 'Ready, lads?' he queried. 'Parachutes on?'

Alfie was a warrant officer with the RAF. His one and only role in life was to serve as a parachute dispatcher, ably assisted by the two other PDs who made up his team. Our state-of-the-art BT80 chutes were lined up against one wall in the order that we were going to jump.

There were a couple of the RAF's parachute packers to the rear of the hangar. It was their job to ensure that our chutes were stored, repaired, checked and documented properly. They'd unpack and re-pack them at regular intervals, to check they were in good order and free of tangles. They were hanging around the hangar just in case one of us had a problem with our chute, not that it had ever happened.

Those guys were consummate professionals and we had absolute faith in what they did, which was fortunate, because our lives depended upon it. We couldn't keep our chutes with us at all times, for often we'd deploy far behind enemy lines on foot-mounted or vehicle-borne operations, and we couldn't lug our BT80s on those. They remained under the care of the parachute packers until the very moment that one of us strapped himself into his parachute harness.

The BT80 is effectively a massive oblong of silk, one that is finely engineered to carry 90 kg of bloke slung beneath it, together with another 60-plus kg of kit. It's a hugely durable yet delicate piece of equipment, and it needs to be treated as such. We each flipped open the top of the para-rucksacks in which our chutes were packed. Inside were two wires, each of which was encased in red cotton thread. We checked that they were present and correct, which meant that the seals hadn't been broken since the chute last was packed.

That done, Jason turned his back to his BT80 and Alfie stepped up beside him. His para-pack was noticeably different from ours, for it had been specially configured by the parachute packers to enable him to strap The Ghost to his front.

'Here you go then, lad,' Alfie remarked with a grunt, as he lifted the heavy pack.

With Alfie's help Jason slipped his squat, powerful form into it. He straightened up and took the weight, the shoulder straps pulling tight as he did so. He bent down and began to fasten the loops that go around the top of the thighs. By the time he was done Jason was standing there with the equivalent of a sack of coal strapped to his back, but showing no visible sign of the weight he was carrying. Jase was always one of the last on PF training runs, but on a tab over the hills carrying serious weight he was unbeatable.

Alfie helped him tighten his para-pack until it was immovable. To one side of us The Ghost was standing around looking lost. It was quite possible that he'd never done a jump before. He'd certainly never have done a HALO. He wouldn't be getting strapped on to Jason until the last possible moment, for trying to shuffle around a C130 at altitude whilst bound tightly together wasn't any fun. It looked as if the reality of what he was about to do was starting to dawn on him, and that he was shitting his load.

I was next to load up. We'd only had the BT80s for a couple of months now, and the harness felt stiff and hard, like it still needed to be properly worn in. At six foot four I'm not small, but the shoulder straps were large enough to half-cover my chest. As I fastened the heavy titanium chest buckle – *Kerthunk!* – I felt my torso being tugged into a stoop by the pressure of the harness. By the time I'd clipped the chunky leg-buckles together and pulled the straps tight, it was like I was in a straitjacket.

I could well remember the agony of getting my tackle caught on a previous jump, and even now the leg straps were cutting into my groin area. But it was vital to strap on the BT80 until it was tight as a vice. The last thing you wanted was a loose harness. You'd start the freefall and it would immediately shift and saw its way into you. By the time you reached the ground you'd have rubbed your shoulders and groin raw, which would bugger you for the next stage of the mission – the long tab under a crushing bergen through hostile terrain.

The BT80 was exactly what we'd needed to replace our previous kit, the GQ360. The GQ360 was strapped to your back with your bergen below it, which meant that you were backside-heavy when you jumped. If you caught a fierce air current it could send you into a violent spin, which could render you unconscious. The GQ360 would be triggered by the altimeter to release automatically, but if you were lying on your back it would open under you. You'd fall through it, the chute wrapping itself around you, and you'd be toast.

By contrast, with the BT80 you had the weight of the bergen hanging from your chest, which meant it was all but impossible not to fall front-first. Even if you were unconscious, the chute would open on your back and should still function properly. We'd joined forces with the SAS in order to get the BT80. Together, we'd managed to sidestep the MOD's laborious procurement system, and had gone straight to the parachute's French manufacturer. And thank God we'd done so: it was a fantastic bit of kit to have in service right now.

The BT80 Multi-Mission System is made by Parachutes de France. At £50,000 a throw it's no snip, but it's arguably the best military parachute in the world. It has the best glide ratio, which means it can cover great distances in relation to its rate of descent. When dropped from extreme high altitude we could glide an enormous distance, crossing borders and infiltrating deep into hostile terrain. It was also designed in such a way that when you pulled the chute it released more or less silently, so we could descend unnoticed and unobserved.

Having got myself into my chute, Alfie helped me fix my personal oxygen canister pack to my front. It went on with a series of straps, which Alfie looped below and behind the BT80's harness, before pulling them tight so my stomach felt it was being crushed. He passed me the oxygen mask, and screwed the black, ribbed rubber tube into the nozzle on the oxygen pack. I placed the mask over my mouth and nose, and fastened the metal clips to either side of my helmet. Pathfinders use light, open-faced fibreglass helmets, a little like you'd see a Hells Angels biker wearing.

I pressed the oxygen mask into my face, and breathed hard. If the latex rubber of the mask wasn't making a proper seal with my skin, I'd feel air leaking around the sides. I gave Alfie a thumbs-up, and he switched the oxygen cylinder valve to the 'on' position. I breathed in and felt the cold, clear burst of oxygen entering my lungs, and an instant later I got the rush to my head. We weren't breathing pure oxygen, but pretty close, and it was fantastic. There was no better way to clear a hangover if you'd been on the piss the night before.

Prior to doing the HALO course every PF operator has to undergo a hypoxia test, to check his ability to function under conditions of lack of oxygen to the brain. You're placed in a compression chamber, which to start with replicates the atmosphere at sea level. Gradually, the chamber takes you up to 10,000 feet, where the oxygen level is noticeably lower. You then have to take your mask off, and yell out your name, rank and serial number, plus do some clapping games to demonstrate your co-ordination is still okay.

It kept taking you higher, until everyone in the chamber was pretty much scrambled. Human beings react differently to hypoxic conditions, just like individual mountaineers on a high-altitude climb. The aim of the hypoxia tests is to prove that you can operate for a few minutes at such extremes of altitude on little or no oxygen, in case your mask fails.

Alfie switched off the valve and moved on to the next bloke in line. I grabbed my main weapon – my battered M16 assault rifle – and slung it over my left side, barrel pointed at the floor. My 13-round Browning pistol was in my rucksack, for if I strapped it to my thigh I'd risk it getting in the way during the jump. My grenades and most of my spare mags of ammo were in there too. But you'd always jump with your main weapon strapped to your body, just in case you lost your bergen during the fall.

We all carried a knife, usually strapped in a sheath on our left shoulder. You needed it within easy reach, in case one of the many lines from your chute got tangled and you had to cut it free.

Lastly, I pulled on a pair of thin leather gloves. When freefalling from high altitude it can get bitterly cold, but the gloves were more to protect your hands. The handles with which you steered the canopy were made of a tough canvas material, and you'd often have to do a good deal of work with the chute as you fell. Even a blacksmith's hands could still get cut to shreds, which would be the last thing you'd ever want at the start of a mission.

I had my altimeter strapped to my left wrist, to tell me the distance I was from the ground during the fall. I'd set it to zero before take-off, with an adjustment for the height of the terrain we were jumping over. If you didn't account for that change in terrain, your altimeter might indicate you had bags of height still to go, when actually you were about to smash into the earth. We'd each be checking our altimeters as the C130 climbed to altitude, to ensure they were working properly.

With all six of us strapped into our HALO gear we made our cumbersome exit from the hangar, looking like a bunch of astronauts about to board the Shuttle. As we did so I heard the whine of the starter motors on the C130's four turbines, followed by the cough and splutter of the first firing. Tom was getting the big bird ready for brakes-off. We stepped towards the Hercules as it began to spool up to speed, and I felt the first flush of goose pimples.

I reached up and pulled down my HALO goggles, which were strapped around my helmet and secured at the rear. They were much like a scuba diver's mask, with a glass eyepiece and squidgy rubber sides. I checked to make sure they made a good airtight seal. If not, the goggles would get torn off my face during the freefall. Our terminal velocity would be approaching 150 mph, and it would be impossible to see without goggles. It'd be like riding a motorbike at that speed with no visor.

Ahead of us, Alfie and the two other parachute dispatchers were waiting. We were so heavy and cumbersome that it would be easy enough to take a fall, and they helped each of us up the C130's open ramp and into our places. Alfie lowered me into a red, fold-down canvas seat, the third from the rear, and buckled the safety strap across my knees. The last thing he did before moving on to Dez was to plug my mask into the C130's main oxygen tank.

As the aircraft climbed we'd be breathing 100 per cent oxygen, to flush any nitrogen from our blood stream. We'd breathe from the C130's on-board tank, to save our own supply. At higher than 22,000 feet a rapid ascent or descent can lead to decompression sickness, more commonly known as 'the bends'. By breathing pure oxygen on the way up we hoped to minimise that threat.

The C130 was completely dark, and we'd be flying into target on black light. Outside the aircraft the runway was also devoid of illumination. There was a faint glow emanating from the cockpit, and the parachute dispatchers had broken out Cyalume light sticks to help show us to our seats. But otherwise all was in shadow, my fellow jumpers presenting a dark silhouette to either side of me.

– 11 –

The dispatchers plugged into the C130's intercom, so they could talk to the aircrew. Tom would be doing his last checks by now, as the four-bladed propellers spun at speed in the darkness. There was no soundproofing in the Hercules, so unlike in a commercial airliner the noise from outside was deafening. There was the roar of the turbines pulsating in my ears, plus the odd whine of hydraulics as the aircrew tested the flaps, and the scream of the fuel injectors.

I was acutely aware that if we were going to get stood down, this was the most likely moment. It had happened to us before. We'd been pumped up with adrenaline and waiting for the take-off when the engines had powered down, and the mission had been postponed for twenty-four hours. The deal was never done until the money was in the bank, as they say.

All of a sudden the aircraft jerked forwards, and we began the taxi to the far end of the runway. I turned to Dez and shouted a couple of words of encouragement into his helmeted ear, but I doubted if he could hear me. There was a flurry of gripped leather fists between the six of us, as we realised we were that much closer to making the jump.

We reached the end of the darkened runway and I felt the Hercules doing an about turn, as Tom spun it on the spot through 360 degrees. There was a momentary pause as we waited for the final go. I could feel my heart pounding in my chest as the engines revved up to take-off speed, and the familiar smell of the exhaust seeped into the C130's interior.

A fleeting thought flashed through my mind. I remembered being jammed with ninety men in a C130 during my days with 1 PARA, as we headed into Sierra Leone. We'd done this low-level insertion through horrendous turbulence, and there were guys puking up to the left and right of me. Now, we were six soldiers – plus The Ghost – about to climb for an hour or more to the still and silent heavens, whereupon we were scheduled to do an epic freefall into the unknown.

Needless to say, there was nowhere else that I'd rather be right now than here in this aircraft with these blokes. There was a massive boost to the roar of the engines outside, the sound of which tore into my thoughts, and suddenly the C130 was surging forwards. It had hardly gone more than 500 metres before the aircraft lifted off and began to climb steeply.

I reached under my chin and unhooked my helmet strap. I yanked it off, and pulled on a set of intercom headphones, so I could listen in on the chat. I heard Tom's voice giving a running commentary to his co-pilot and the navigator to his rear, plus the parachute dispatchers in the aircraft's hold.

'Airspeed 700 knots. Altitude 1500 feet. Rate of climb …'

Tom was speaking so calmly he sounded as if he was some kind of British Airways pilot addressing his civvie passengers. I was waiting for him to say: *We're about to start our in-flight entertainment, but first the hostesses will be serving you some complimentary drinks and snacks. Our expected flight time to New York's LaGuardia airport is eight hours and fifteen minutes …*

The only threat to the mission now would be a drastic change in the weather conditions at the IP. If severe winds blew up we could still have the jump canned. It wouldn't matter much what the wind speed was at altitude, for we'd plummet to earth like stones. But at the IP anything over 20 knots could prove fatal. You'd come in to land under your chute, the wind would knock you sideways like a battering ram, and you could break a leg or an arm, or even get yourself killed. We just had to pray the weather stayed good at the target.

'Altitude now at 10,000 feet,' Tom's voice announced over the intercom. I felt a surge of adrenaline as we kept climbing toward our jump height. 'P-Hour minus sixty.'

P-Hour (Parachute Hour) was the moment we'd jump from the C130's hold. We had sixty minutes to wait and we'd be gone. I turned to Jason and mouthed 'P minus sixty'. Jason was a taciturn individual at the best of times, so all I got in return was a barely noticeable nod of the head. Sandwiched between Jason and me was The Ghost. He was staring at the Herc's cold metal floor seemingly in a daze. Reality was sinking in big time, I figured.

'P minus forty,' Tom intoned. 'MET conditions and flight path unchanged.'

Even with the C130's ramp closed there was still an icy draught seeping in from the rear. I stamped my feet to force some life back into them, then I leaned forwards and glanced left, towards the back of the plane. Tricky caught my gaze, and there was the barest hint of a smile in his ice-blue eyes.

A hard-as-nails Jason Statham look-alike, Tricky was the operator that no one ever tried to mess with. To de-stress from operations he'd go sparring with Lance Green, another PF stalwart. During his weekends off Lance used to bare knuckle box in a cage in front of mega-wealthy London bankers, and to see him and Tricky going at it you'd think they were trying to kill each other. Tricky and I were dead close, and I took huge comfort from having him back-stopping my patrol.

'P minus twenty,' Tom announced. 'P minus twenty.'

It was the moment we'd been waiting for. I removed the headphones and pulled on my helmet, as the three parachute dispatchers started to help us on with our bergens. You couldn't lean back in your chair, due to the BT80 strapped to your back, so you had to stand and heft your bergen on to your seat. Then you had to squat down and clip the bergen on to the two titanium D-rings set into the front of your para-harness. There was no way we could manage this on our own, so the PD boys were really earning their pay now.

That done, the six of us were left standing by the C130's starboard side, with one hand grasping the top of the bench seats in an effort to steady ourselves. We each were carrying 30 kg of parachute gear and a 30 kg bergen, plus weapons and oxygen weighing another 15 kg or more. Fortunately, there was very little turbulence at this altitude, and Tom was keeping the C130 steady as a rock. Even so my back felt like it was bent double, and it was starting to ache like hell.

My mind blanked the pain as Alfie reached out to grab the tube of my mask, whilst signalling with his other hand that he was going to swop over the oxygen supply. This was the single most dangerous moment prior to making the jump. One gulp of the rarified atmosphere at this altitude and I'd get a burst of nitrogen into my bloodstream, which could balloon to dangerous levels. If that happened I'd get the dreaded bends as soon as I jumped.

I took a massive in-breath and held it, and as quick as a flash Alfie plugged me out of the C130's tank and into my personal oxygen bottle.

'P minus ten.'

I couldn't hear Tom's announcement any more, but Alfie's hand signal compensated: ten fingers held up in front of each of our faces, to make sure none of us had missed it.

'P minus five.' Five fingers were waved in front of our begoggled eyes.

Alfie held up a closed fist and blew into it, spreading his fingers as he did so, like his breath had blown them apart. This was the signal for wind speed at the IP. Having blown into his fist like that, Alfie next held up five fingers. Wind speed was 5 knots at the IP. Perfect for making the landing.

Above the roar of the C130's engines I suddenly heard the first guitar riffs screaming out of the aircraft's speakers. AC/DC's 'Thunderstruck': the signal for three minutes to P-Hour. High-pitched, fast, crazed; each whine of the guitar was punctuated by a mad, breathy, spooky chant, which built and built to a climax.

Thunder! Wahahahahahahaha.
Thunder! Wahahahahahahaha.
Thunder! Wahahahahahahaha.
Thunder! Wahahahahahahaha.
Thunder! Wahahahahahahaha.
THUNDER! WAHAHAHAHAHAHAHA.
THUNDER! WAHAHAHAHAHAHAHA.

Drums started crashing and more guitars kicked in, howling and echoing down the C130's hold, as the chant kept building in volume

– 15 –

and intensity.

> *THUNDER!*
> *THUNDER!*
> *THUNDER!*
> *THUNDER!*

Then the lyrics proper kicked in, deafeningly loud over the Tannoy system. In spite of his earlier comments, Tom, God love him, was cranking up the volume.

> *I was caught in the middle of the railroad tracks.*
> *THUNDER!*
> *And I knew, I knew there was no turning back.*
> *THUNDER!*

To the rear of the aircraft there was the hollow *thunk* of a seal breaking, and the whine of the tail ramp starting to lower. To our left and right the PD boys were helping us as we shuffled towards the rushing void. The nearer we got the louder grew the noise of the aircraft's slipstream, the wind howling above the music and threatening to drown out the lyrics.

> *Sounds of the drums, beatin' in my heart.*
> *The thunder of the guns tore me apart.*
> *You've been thunderstruck ...*

The icy blasts of air were mixed with the powerful, heady scent from the engines, a combination of burning oil and aviation fuel. It was the kind of smell you'd only ever get when you were about to jump, and it set my pulse racing like a machine gun. I saw Alfie and the other PDs strap themselves to one side of the ramp, to prevent themselves from getting torn out of the opening by a sudden blast of wind.

I glanced towards the void. Nothing. Swirling darkness. I took a step closer, and gazed up into the massive expanse of the starlit heavens. We were on the very roof of the world here. During the long ascent our eyes had adjusted to the gloom. Our natural night vision had kicked in, which meant we'd have as good a chance as any of keeping sight of each other as we began the freefall.

There was no way you could use NVG (Night Vision Goggles) when doing a HALO: the slipstream would rip them from your face in an instant. In any case, NVG tended to channel your vision into a narrow corridor of artificially boosted fluorescent light, which meant you lost your spatial awareness, and that was the last thing you ever needed during a HALO jump. The NVG were stashed in the bergens, along with all our other gear.

We were seconds to the 'go' now, eyes glued to the red bulbs glowing faintly to either side of the open ramp. We each did a final check on the bloke in front of us, making sure his BT80 hadn't managed to snag on anything.

To one side Alfie was strapping The Ghost to Jason's front. Jase's squat form held the bloke upright and jammed up against him, as he shuffled him closer to the ramp. I could see from the guy's expression that he was screaming, his eyes wide with panic, but not a sound was escaping from his oxygen mask. In spite of the massive adrenaline high we were feeling, we couldn't help exchanging exultant looks. *Payback time.*

Then Alfie, yelling: 'Tail off for equipment check!'

At the rear, Tricky whacked Joe on his right shoulder. 'SIX OKAY!'

Tricky's oxygen and chute were all good. Joe repeated the move and the shout, and it rippled down the line. It reached Jason, who was face-to-face with Alfie, and the old hand just gave him a thumbs-up: *Good to go.*

We shuffled tighter together. Too much space between blokes would result in too much separation in the sky, and we mightn't find each other. As we steeled ourselves for the go, I felt this incredible high coursing through my veins. We might have done this a hundred times before during training, but still nothing came close to the buzz of doing the jump for real. *Nothing.*

There was no way down for us now but the freefall, and we all knew the dangers involved. Too many good men had died doing exactly what we were about to do now. We might have total trust in our kit, our ability and each other, but still any one of us could perish out there. And who knew what might await us on the ground? The intel said the IP was clear of hostile forces, but how often had the intel been wrong?

We stood on the edge of the ramp, cold air buffeting and rocking us. The green light flashed on. Alfie stepped back, and yelled: 'GO! GO! GO!'

I saw Jason forcing The Ghost towards the void, and suddenly he was diving forwards, the two figures plummeting as one into the darkness. I dived directly after him, hit the C130's slipstream, and felt the powerful blast flipping my legs over my head, and twisting me around. I ripped out of the slipstream, stabilised my dive, and began searching below me for Jason and his jump-buddy.

I pushed my weight forwards on to my bergen, and felt myself accelerating into a headfirst dive. I felt like a giant shuttlecock plummeting directly towards earth. There, right below me was the form of my stick leader, a black spot against the darkened terrain far below. All I could make out of the landscape we were dropping into were the different shades marking out the mountain ridges and valleys.

To increase my velocity I got my body into a delta shape, arms by my side, legs streamlined behind me. Jason had turned to the right as he began his freefall, and I brought myself down beside him so I was facing the opposite direction. I steered myself by moving my arms and my head gently in the direction I wanted to go. I'd done over a hundred HALO jumps, and I'd learned that if I stuck an arm or leg out sharply I'd flip myself over and be well messed up.

I got to within 50 feet of Jason and brought my arms and legs into more of a star shape, to slow myself down. I stabilised at that distance, so I could maintain this position for the duration of the freefall. Then I turned my head gently into the roaring slipstream, so I could check on Dez. When I caught sight of him he was maybe 80 feet behind me, but catching up fast. I counted four other dark human-shaped blobs strung out behind him. So far, so good.

We were falling in a staggered line formation. Keeping eye contact man to man was vital. If I lost Jason we'd all lose him, and we'd get scattered across the ground, which would be a nightmare. Having made sure the line was complete I did a quick check of my altimeter. Even when jumping from such height we'd be just ninety seconds in the freefall. If you didn't keep one eye on your altimeter you could easily lose track of time, and crash through your release height.

Release height was set at 5000 feet above ground level, and we were going to manually open our chutes. You could opt for automatic release, but the auto systems can and did fail. Manual was the fail-safe. As we hammered towards earth I kept checking on the position of the blokes to either side of me. At the same time the mission plan was running through my mind at lightning speed.

We'd set the release point almost directly above the Impact Point (IP), and the IP was set some 30 kilometres back from the target. That way we should hit the IP undetected, but should still be able to make the target on foot before sunrise.

As the stick leader, Jason would choose the exact spot to put down. There was no way you could read a map when doing a HALO, so the only way to select a landing spot was by visual means. He'd be scanning the ground as it rushed towards him, trying to choose a spot devoid of trees or other obstructions and away from any obvious danger.

The key responsibility for the rest of us was to stick on his tail, and not to lose him. If you lost one guy during the jump, it was all but impossible to find him again. You couldn't radio each other to try to work out where you were and you couldn't afford to show any lights, for obvious reasons. Keeping the stick together was the absolute number one priority.

Below me Jase hit the 5000-foot mark. I saw the flash of his canopy blossoming grey in the darkness, before I reached my right hand down and grabbed for my own release. The 'throwaway' release is a mini-parachute-shaped piece of material that deploys your main chute. You have to grab it out of its pouch on your right thigh, and throw it into the air. The mini-chute opens and drags your main chute into the void behind you.

Trouble was, as my gloved hand flailed around my right thigh, I couldn't seem to get my fingers on the throwaway. I plummeted past Jason, and made a second grab for it. *Still nothing.*

My right leg strap must have shifted slightly and trapped the throwaway. I'd tried to grab it twice now, and lost 1000 feet in doing so. Every second brought me 300 feet closer to a pulverising impact with the earth. There were just seconds before I hit, and the adrenaline was bursting through my system like a massive punch to the head.

Instinctively, I reached my right hand up and ripped away the emergency release strap from my left shoulder strap, so jettisoning my main chute. I slid my left hand into the wire handle on my right shoulder strap, and ripped it forwards, so triggering my emergency chute. An instant later I felt as if some giant was reaching over me and yanking me violently upwards by the shoulders. A second after that it was like I'd driven a car into a wall at 150 mph, and the air bag had just gone off.

I'd gone from deafening wind-noise and the sense of death rushing towards me, to total silence and quiet. I counted in my head: *one thousand, two thousand, three thousand.* I looked up to check my reserve canopy was good. Then I reached up with my hands, grabbed the steering toggles, and gave them a sharp series of pumps, which forced more air into the chute. Thank God it felt and looked perfectly okay.

I'd gained a good 1000 feet on the others, so my priority now was to slow myself down. Fortunately, the BT80 reserve is more or less a carbon copy of the main chute, with the same glide properties. I knew the rest of the stick would be trying to catch me, steering sharp left in a series of turns that would make them descend more quickly. I kept trimming my chute with the toggles, making small adjustments to steer it and slow myself, as I waited for the guys to appear.

I sensed a faint swish of air beside me in the darkness, and there was Jason, two-up with The Ghost. He didn't even bother looking over to check I was okay. If there was a problem he knew I'd let the blokes know about it. We had barely a couple of thousand feet to go, and Jase's priority was getting us down safely. We formed up in line, and began serpenting after Jason as he led us into the IP.

After chute-opening, this was the most dangerous moment. If we were spotted from the ground we had no way to defend ourselves. It's impossible to operate a weapon when under a chute and still in the air. Jase had to get the landing just right, bringing us in so that we touched down into the wind, to help break our momentum and ease the impact. Plus the poor bastard had to get his passenger down safely, on top of everything else he was doing.

I checked my altimeter: 1600 feet to go. I reached forwards and pushed the two metal levers together on the bergen attachment system. I felt it drop away, as the pulleys let it fall to 80 feet below me. Like this the bergen would hit first, so taking its own weight. I concentrated on my steering, trimming the chute with the left and right toggles, to mirror Jason's line of approach.

I saw the dark terrain rushing towards me, and a moment later I heard the soft plop of the bergen hitting the ground. That was the signal to pull back hard on both toggles, which flared and slowed my chute. I hit the ground running, and did a few steps to keep pace with the chute and burn off the speed. I came to a halt and stepped to one side, the chute going past me and coming down like a bundle of washing.

I dropped down on one knee and scanned for Jason's position, then did a visual check that Dez wasn't coming in to land on top of me. Reassured that all was good, I unclipped myself out of my chest and leg harnesses and dropped the para-pack. I unslung my M16, grabbed a magazine out of my smock pocket, and slipped it into the weapon with a faint click. I cocked it, closed the dust cover, and I was locked and loaded. If we had been spotted by anyone I was good to fight.

I slipped my Silva compass out of my smock. I found north and lined it up with the dark silhouette of a distant mountain peak. I now had us oriented. From studying the maps I knew exactly in which direction was the nearest known threat. I grabbed my webbing and belt kit out of my bergen and slipped it on. I worked myself into my backpack, bundled up my parachute and made my way over to Jason's position.

Jase was our pre-arranged RV (Rendevous Point). By the time I got there he was still busy trying to sort out The Ghost, who was clearly in bits. We were in deadly earnest now and under huge time pressure to get to the target. With a 30-kilometre night march ahead of us we wouldn't use our NVG kit, for it'd be too much of a strain on the eyes. Our vision was well adjusted to the darkness, and there was just enough ambient light from the moon and stars by which to navigate.

As the lads came in to the RV they went into silent, all-around defence. I did a quick map check, then scanned the surrounding terrain. I detected a shallow ditch about 100 metres or so to the north. It was a good spot to stash the chutes.

'We're here,' I whispered, indicating our exact position on the map. 'We'll head out on a bearing of 060 degrees, heading northeast. We need to cache the chutes. Dez and Joe, go check out that ditch.'

Without a word the two guys disappeared into the gloom. I felt around inside my bergen and pulled out the smooth steel form of my SOPHIE thermal imaging system. The SOPHIE was an outstanding piece of kit. Via its optics any warm object would appear as The Predator sees it in the movies, outlined by its heat signature. A fire, a warm vehicle engine, or a living being would appear as a distinctive hot white heat blob.

I grabbed the SOPHIE, switched it to 'on', and started a 360-degree scan of the terrain. Apart from the rhythmic chirruping of the crickets in the dark bush, it was utterly silent out there. My sixth sense told me that our landing hadn't been observed, but one sweep with the SOPHIE would prove it either way.

I'd completed about half the sweep when I stopped dead. There was the distinctive form of a standing figure due east, and it appeared to be looking directly at us. For an instant it shifted, and I froze. Then it went down on all fours, took a few bounds across the earth, and stood again. I knew from the intel briefing what the main big game animals were, here in the mountains: gazelle, leopards, baboons. No guessing which this was then.

I finished the scan. Nothing.

'It's all clear,' I whispered.

Dez and Joe were done stashing the chutes, and Jase had got The Ghost pretty much sorted. I checked the map again. 'Our grid is 457395. Repeat: 457395.'

I glanced around at the faces before me, making sure everyone had got it. We knew in what order we'd start the march.

'Okay, let's go.'

We moved out, heading into the hostile darkness and the unknown.

CHAPTER ONE

We'd deployed to Kuwait sanitised. We wore no insignia or marks of rank – nothing to betray what unit we were from or who was in command, and nothing from which the enemy could gain the slightest advantage if we were captured or killed. Prior to crossing the border into Iraq we had to sanitise ourselves still further – removing all family photos, wallets, keys, tearing out any notes from notebooks, removing any marked-up maps, and snipping out manufacturer's labels from our clothing.

We couldn't afford even to miss a brand name. If we got captured and one of us had a Berghaus label in his jacket, it would give the enemy a clue, an edge. It would give them the nod that we were most likely Brits, and that would give them the chance to get inside our heads and break us. Do that and they could extract vital information, and that could compromise any of our unit still going forward to achieve the mission. That in turn would impact upon the wider war effort, jeopardising the ability of the British and US forces to bring about a quick and decisive end to this conflict.

It was March 2003, and some eighteen months since I'd had to pull my reserve whilst HALOing into the night-dark African bush. Now, we Pathfinders were the first British boots on the ground in what was to become known as the Iraq War. We had jetted into the gleaming, space-age terminal of Kuwait International Airport in an ageing RAF Tristar, a fleet of which operates out of RAF Brize

Norton. It said a lot about the British military's can-do, make-do attitude that its airmobile vanguard was sent to war in a converted Pan Am passenger airliner dating from the 1980s.

We were here as part of 16 Air Assault Brigade. The Brigade consists of 1, 2 and 3 PARA, 1 Royal Irish Regiment (1 RIR), 13 Close Support Regiment (Loggies), Army Air Corps, 9 Squadron Royal Engineers, 23 Engineer Recce Squadron, 5 Battalion REME (Royal Electrical and Mechanical Engineers), a Javelin Battery (hand-launched missile operators) and a few other bits and pieces tacked on.

16 Air Assault Brigade was the airmobile hammer of Britain's armed forces, one that was scheduled to spearhead the push into Iraq. All told, it consisted of some 5000 men and women at arms, and it was us – the Pathfinders – who were to be the eyes, ears and cutting edge of that force.

Twelve years earlier, in January 1991, a coalition of thirty-four nations backed by a UN mandate had gone to war against Saddam Hussein's forces, to drive them out of oil-rich Kuwait. The Iraqi military had invaded Kuwait on Saddam's orders. The First Gulf War had been a race to liberate Kuwait, then 'home for tea and medals', as we say in the Pathfinders. Mostly, there was an expectation that this conflict – the 2003 Iraq War – would go likewise. The Iraqis were expected to surrender in their droves, leaving us little chance of getting any trigger time.

But my gut instinct told me otherwise. This war was a wholly different prospect from its predecessor. Firstly, we would be invading the Iraqis' territory proper, not driving them out of a foreign country like Kuwait. Second, the case for doing so – that Iraq had weapons of mass destruction that threatened global security – was far from cut and dried. If we were sent across the border, we'd be going deep inside Iraqi territory on either reconnaissance (recce) or sabotage missions. That's why the Pathfinders exist, and those are the kind of tasks that we live and breathe for. And somehow, I reckoned there was going to be real war-fighting to be done out there.

The Pathfinders is an incredibly tight-knit unit. It consists of six patrols, each containing six men – so thirty-six fighting men in all. Each patrol has two vehicles – open-topped Land Rovers specially adapted for PF (Pathfinder) operations. Together with support staff – engineers, signallers and the like – that makes ours a sixty-strong unit.

Whilst we may be small, we're perfectly formed. Pathfinders are widely regarded as the most highly-trained and specialist mobility troops in the world. Unlike the SAS (Special Air Service) and the SBS (Special Boat Service), who are trained in all facets of anti-terrorism, anti-insurgency and irregular and regular warfare, we train relentlessly for one thing only: insertion deep behind enemy lines on recce, capture, demolition and kill missions.

We are experts at HALO (High Altitude Low Opening) and HAHO (High Altitude High Opening) parachute jumping, our usual means of ultra-covert deep penetration airborne insertion. HAHO enables us to open our chutes at extreme high altitude and drift for many miles silently towards target. HALO and HAHO are the bread and butter of what we do, and it's what we're renowned for. But we're equally highly trained for insertions via foot or vehicle far into hostile terrain.

We'd been warned that the British press would be waiting at Kuwait airport, to get the first photos of 'our boys' arriving in theatre. We'd been asked to tone it down as much as possible. Apart from the long hair and beards, we were not to make like a bunch of Mad Max mercenaries in front of the British media, which is what we Pathfinders have a tendency to look like at times of war.

We were whisked past the press pack via the VIP Arrivals Area, then bussed out of Kuwait City heading north into the desert. Although we had our personal weapons and kit with us, we were yet to be issued with any ammo. We were here fully expecting the war to happen, but we had little idea what the road ahead would be like for our unit specifically.

As we headed north I gazed out of the air-conditioned cool of the coach. There was the baking heat of a flat, featureless desert outside, burning sands stretching either side of the tarmac to the shimmering, pencil-thin horizon. Here and there we passed the odd mosque or dusty village, places peopled by men with sun-blackened skin, and wearing white desert robes and dun-coloured waistcoats. These were the Bedouin nomads of the desert – the same tribes that Lawrence of Arabia had galvanised into a fighting force to harass the enemy, during the First World War.

It struck me that whilst the camel-riding Bedouin might be able to move around this empty, billiard-table surface pretty much unnoticed, we were going to have serious problems trying to do so. We just had to hope the terrain on the Iraqi side of the border was very different, and would offer us some cover and the chance to advance without being compromised. Or better still, we'd get to go in via HALO or HAHO parachute-drop, which is the Pathfinders' preferred means of insertion.

The Kuwait motorway petered out into an A-road, a B-road and finally a desert track heading into nowhere. Eventually, the track ran out completely, and the coach driver began crossing the open desert. He was clearly no Bedouin. Within minutes he'd lost his way, and we were driving around in circles. The other PF lads and I couldn't help but find this highly amusing: here we were, the vanguard of Britain's armed forces, and we were riding the road to nowhere with a clueless Kuwaiti coach driver.

'Fucking typical,' Tricky piped up, from the seat next to me. 'Lost, even before we go to war!'

Tricky is an excellent bloke and an outstanding soldier, and he was one of the two real jokers on my patrol. I'd happily have followed him to the ends of the earth, and fought back-to-back with him when we got there. In fairness, the poor Kuwaiti coach driver was trying to find a blob of open, featureless rock and sand, amidst a world of such terrain. But an important lesson had been learned already: it was very, very easy to get lost here, even for the locals.

Eventually, the driver managed to locate a unit of US Marines setting up camp amongst the sand dunes. He stopped and asked for directions. I couldn't help noticing how different we looked from your average US marine. The younger grunts were these buzz-cut, clean-shaven clones. They were fresh out of the factory, and they kept wrestling each other and 'hoo-aah-ing', and 'yessir-ing' the whole time. Your average PF operator was older, and more wiry, grizzled and battle-worn.

This massive, barrel-chested Marine Corps sergeant pointed our coach driver in the direction of the British base. Half an hour later we reached 'Camp Tristar', as someone had affectionately nicknamed it. We dismounted and took a look around. There was absolutely nothing but rock, sand and more rock. We knew that the Iraqi border was just a few kilometres to the northeast, but there was nothing to mark where Kuwait ended and Iraq began, and certainly no noticeable change in terrain. It was a godforsaken flat and featureless desert in Iraq, just as it was here.

Over the coming days the Royal Engineers would use their giant bulldozers to construct massive sand berms all around Camp Tristar. They would provide a little protection against blast, should Saddam Hussein decide to start lobbing SCUD missiles our way. But right now we were some of the first on the ground here, and no one had so much as scooped out a bucket-load of sand.

We were allocated a patch of bare desert as Pathfinder Central. It was tucked away to the rear, adjacent to where the brigade commander would establish his headquarters. The Pathfinder Platoon would work to the brigade commander's orders direct, so he needed us close at hand. Invariably, we'd be tasked with sensitive and urgent missions, and Brigade HQ and our own unit would be quarantined off from the rest of the camp, to prevent any curious journalists from wandering our way.

It was a fact of life that media ops had become a part of any war effort, but we were one element of 16 Air Assault Brigade that wouldn't be having any journalists embedded in our unit. We could see why reporters needed access to the front line: the British public deserved to know exactly what our soldiers were doing when they were fighting wars far from home. But we couldn't risk a journalist going far behind enemy lines with a PF patrol, especially as our kind of missions were far too unsuited to the glare of publicity.

It was last light by the time we got our tent pitched. The entire sixty-strong PF Platoon was housed in a large, green canvas affair. The clever bastards amongst us had brought their own fold-up camp beds as part of their personal gear. As yet little of the Pathfinders' 'comfort kit' had been shipped into theatre, so the rest of us had to bed down on the hard desert. We'd been a good thirty-six hours deploying from our home base on the east coast of England, flying out from Brizers and then transiting across the Kuwaiti desert. We were dog-tired and we crashed out early, each of us quietly hoping that this time the Pathfinders really were going to war.

Whilst it may have looked pancake-flat from a coach window, one night's kip proved the desert to be rocky as hell. Come morning, there was a bunch of grumpy Pathfinders at Camp Tristar who hadn't slept that well. As second-in-command of PF I decided remedial action was required. There was one military force that always had all the kit you could ever wish for in theatre: the Americans. We needed to beg, borrow or steal some camp beds off the nearest friendly Yanks.

The Americans had a permanent base down in Kuwait City, dating from the First Gulf War. It came complete with a bowling alley, plus a Burger King and a Ben & Jerry's. But the nearest American base to Camp Tristar was several kilometres to the south of us, back where the Kuwaiti bus driver had asked for some directions.

The Americans proved to be as typically forthcoming towards their poor British allies as they always are. We managed to blag enough rugged canvas US military cots to sleep most of the Pathfinder Platoon, and with a good few left over – which only served to remind us what Gucci kit the Yanks always seemed to manage to bring to war.

We decided that as soon as we had a moment free we'd pay a visit to their PX store at their Kuwait City base, and stock up on cheap, subsidised American cigarettes and scoff. I just loved the little bottles of Tabasco sauce the US Army did to accompany their MRE (Meals

Ready to Eat) ration packs.

Whilst there, we'd also score a job lot of US Army T-shirts. They were far better than our British Army ones, which were thick winter-cotton issue, and totally unsuited to the Iraqi desert. As soon as we'd stepped off the air-conditioned coach we'd started to sweat bucket-loads. The thick cotton soaked up the sweat, and when the sun set and the desert turned freezing cold the sweat-soaked T-shirt chilled you to the bone. The US Army T-shirts were made of a thin, breath-able fabric, one that wicked away the sweat.

The American PX store would also have racks of DVDs that were cheap as chips. Here in Camp Tristar we were feeling the lack of the Pathfinders' favourite movie: *Things to Do in Denver When You're Dead*. It's about a group of ex-cons, some of whom are ex-forces, who come together for one last job. The movie had achieved iconic status amongst the PF lads, but somehow in the mad rush to deploy it had been forgotten. So we were on a mission to go score a copy.

We were unsure as to when we might get the green light to pile across the border into Iraq, but by the time we did so we wanted to be fully tanned-up and bearded. When heading behind enemy lines – the core function of PF – we would make like locals. A full growth of facial hair, plus a deep tan, would help disguise the fact that we were a bunch of British soldiers not long out of rainy mother England.

The brigade commander intended to use us to scour the ground for the enemy, recce numbers, positions and strengths, and attack, seize or destroy vital terrain or installations. And like every man Jack in my platoon I sure hoped we'd get used. I say 'my' platoon, for I was the 2IC (second-in-command) of the Pathfinders, which as far as I was concerned was the best job in the world.

I'd come to the Pathfinders from 1 PARA via the murderous PF selection course. In the PARAs – itself a crack unit – I'd served in Northern Ireland, Kosovo and Sierra Leone. When on operations with 1 PARA I used to long to have my 'dream team' around me, men who were totally dedicated, exceptional soldiers, with the psy-chological strength to deal with whatever the enemy might throw at them. Now, in the Pathfinders, I'd got it. The problem was that there were those in the PF who didn't see me in quite the same way.

There was no tradition of military service in my family. Both my parents had been teachers, and I'd found my way into the Army by sheer chance. I'd been going badly off the rails at school when an Army careers officer had offered me a chance of a sponsored place at military college. It was the draw of the outdoor life and the adventure that had hooked me. With the Army paying my fees, I'd gone to Welbeck College and managed to stay the course. I'd done well in my A-levels, and gone on to do officer training at Sandhurst.

At the age of nineteen I'd been commissioned into the British Army, and at twenty-one I was made a captain, the youngest for decades. At the age of twenty-five I'd passed PF selection, and I was doubtless the youngest 2IC the Pathfinders had ever had. By contrast, many of the blokes had been in the PF for a decade or more and were 'rankers' – they'd worked their way up through the ranks. Once in, PF was often a job for life. You might move on to the SAS or the SBS, but most would choose to stay with the PF. Understandably enough, some of the old and the bold looked on newcomers like me as upstart officers they could well do without.

I'd been with the unit for fifteen months, and I loved what we were about. I wanted to spend the rest of my soldiering days in the PF, but Iraq was the first time that I'd taken the unit to war. I was commanding men who in many cases had years of elite soldiering on me. It was one hell of a challenge. The PF works on the basis that patrol command goes to the most suitable soldier, regardless of rank. It's a meritocracy.

I was on a massively steep learning curve, and there were those in the unit who were just waiting for me to fail.

CHAPTER TWO

Whilst John – it was all first name terms in the PF – our OC (Officer Commanding), would remain at Brigade Headquarters to command operations, as 2IC I'd get the best of both worlds. I'd be closely involved with mission planning, yet I'd get to go out on the ground leading my fighting patrol. As 2IC I had a specific role to fulfil on ground operations. Once all six patrols were out on taskings, my patrol would act as a forward HQ. That way, if we lost comms with Brigade Headquarters I could orchestrate missions in the field.

The old and the bold were hugely protective over the PF pedigree, and rightly so. The unit traced its lineage back to some of the most iconic units of the Second World War. If the Pathfinders have a predecessor, then it is the 21st Independent Parachute Company, the original Parachute Pathfinders. Formed in June 1942, the Parachute Pathfinders made up part of the British Army's 1st Airborne Division. One of their tasks was to land at the DZ (Drop Zone) some thirty minutes before their comrades, and to pinpoint it by means of a Eureka radio beacon. They were then to clear it of obstacles and beat off any counterattacks by the enemy, so the main drop could be made in relative safety.

As with the PF, the men were all volunteers and had passed exacting physical and psychological tests, which foreshadowed the current Pathfinder selection process. The original Parachute Pathfinders saw action in Algeria, Tunisia, Sicily, Italy, Norway, France and Holland, and finally Greece and Palestine, although Arnhem was the most testing operation in which they took part. On the night of 17 September 1944 they led what was then the largest airborne force ever into German-occupied Holland, as part of Operation Market Garden. The plan was to seize bridges across the Meuse River and two arms of the Rhine, so enabling the Allied forces to outflank the Germans and encircle the Ruhr, Germany's industrial heartland.

But at the Dutch town of Arnhem actual events proved the intel picture hopelessly wrong. The British 1st Airborne Division ran into far stronger German resistance than the intelligence suggested was present, and only one end of the Arnhem road bridge could be taken. On 21 September the small force holding the Allied end of the Arnhem bridge was overrun by German forces, the men fighting to the last bullet and beyond. The remainder of the Division was trapped in a small pocket to the west of the bridge, and had to be evacuated.

As a result of the failure of Market Garden, the Allies were unable to cross the Rhine in sufficient numbers to achieve the mission objective. That in turn ended the Allies' expectations of finishing the war by Christmas 1944, and the Rhine remained a barrier to their advance until ground offensives in March 1945. The Arnhem raid was immortalised in a book and a film, both entitled *A Bridge Too Far*.

The Parachute Pathfinders were seen to have accounted for themselves well in Market Garden. 'Your unit is unsurpassed by any other in the world,' wrote General Browning to their commanding officer, Major Wilson, after it was all over. General Alexander commented that the Parachute Pathfinders had shown 'all the true qualities of good soldiers – high morale, dash and fighting efficiency'. Bravery, *esprit de corps* and professionalism were the hallmarks of the unit, even when it was deployed on what was ultimately an abortive mission.

The main difference between the Parachute Pathfinders and us was that in addition to para-insertions, we were exhaustively trained in vehicle mobility operations, enabling us to drive vast distances behind enemy lines. That side of the PF pedigree was inherited from the LRDG (Long Range Desert Group) of the Second World War. From December 1940 until April 1943 the LRDG operated alongside David Stirling's SAS in the North African deserts, driving fleets of Chevrolet trucks and Willys Jeeps. Their function was deep penetration behind enemy lines on recce, capture and sabotage missions, hitting enemy supply lines, fuel dumps, airfields and ammunition stores.

During the seventeen months of the North African campaign there were reportedly just fifteen days when the LRDG weren't operating behind enemy lines. In September 1942 the LRDG undertook Operation Caravan, perhaps their best-known mission. Seventeen vehicles carrying forty-seven men travelled 1859 kilometres across the desert. On arrival at the Italian-held Libyan town of Barce the patrol split, one half attacking the Italian barracks, the other the airfield. During the airfield assault, some thirty-two aircraft – mainly Cant Z.1007bis three-engined bombers – were damaged or destroyed.

By the time the attack was done the LRDG had lost ten men, three trucks and a Jeep. But the epic withdrawal would cost the LRDG dear, because they were repeatedly hit from the air, losing all but two of their Jeeps and one Chevrolet truck. The surviving vehicles continued with the wounded, whilst different groups set out to escape on foot, most making it out of there alive and linking up with other LRDG patrols.

The Commander of the German Afrika Korps, Field Marshal Erwin Rommel, admitted that the LRDG caused his forces 'more damage than any other British unit of equal strength', during that war. The LRDG was disbanded in August 1945, when its function was supposedly amalgamated into the UK Special Forces. But somewhere within that amalgamation a lot of the specialist capabilities of the LRDG had been lost, and eventually that led to the founding of the Pathfinders.

The Pathfinder Platoon was formed in the 1980s to fulfil a very specific role – that of an air and land mobile recce and sabotage force, one seen as missing from the British Special Forces. It was the SAS blokes who first established the PF, and for many years its existence wasn't even formally recognised – hence our nickname, the 'Ghost Force'. As with the SAS in its early days, the men of the Pathfinders were pulled together from various units, so forming a small handful of specialist soldiers.

The Pathfinders became known informally as 'the bastard son of the SAS', and while on paper the men of the PF were still serving with their parent units, in reality they were members of this ghost force. We felt a close affinity with our fellow elite operators – the SAS, plus their sister regiment, the SBS. Our kit was begged, borrowed and stolen from wherever we could find it, but mostly it was passed to us by the SAS or the SBS on the QT (on the quiet). The Pathfinders had fought for many years to be properly equipped to do the jobs that they were tasked to do, a battle that was ongoing.

During my first week with the PF I sensed the difference with this unit and its men. From day one the Pathfinders felt like a pack to me – like a living, breathing organism rolling forward with its own life-force and free will. The guys were totally self-motivated. No one was sitting around waiting to be given orders or to be told what to do. They were busy refining skills and knowledge to improve themselves, and for the good of the entire unit. When not on formal training, they'd be sharing skill sets. Each PF soldier brought his own experience and expertise to the party, and the unit would let him grow into his ideal role.

At the end of my first week in the PF we'd gathered in the NAAFI for a Platoon Drinks Night. It was one of the lad's birthdays, and there was this PF bloke called Smudge on stage, microphone in hand and sporting a full Elvis rig. This wasn't cheap Elvis gear. He had a real-hair wig, glossy sideburns, thick, gold-framed Aviator sunglasses, white skin-tight flares, platform shoes, and a tight, open-chested shirt. The Pathfinder lads kept calling out Elvis and Neil Diamond numbers, whereupon Smudge would croon away like a good one.

This Platoon Drinks Night struck me as being pretty outrageous. These guys were way out left-field. I came direct from the PARAs and I was in at the deep end, getting my first taste of the über-confidence and individuality that the Pathfinders nurture. It was such a contrast to my previous life in the Regular Army. I can't sing for Adam, but the lads kept telling me that it was a sacrosanct PF tradition that the new guy – *that was me* – had to sing. They wanted me up on stage with Smudge, shirt unbuttoned to the waist, hips gyrating and crooning away.

I was fresh out of the trial by fire that was Pathfinder selection, but to me being forced to sing was far more daunting than any physical challenge. Singing and dancing are two of the things at which I am genuinely, utterly crap. During officer training at Sandhurst I'd been taught what to wear when at a casual function like a dance. The standard rig for an officer was red cords, pink-collared shirt and a blue blazer with brass or silver buttons. That, according to Sandhurst, was the acceptable dress code, and jeans were the 'devil's cloth'.

I never could go there, and thank fuck that at my first Pathfinder function I'd ignored the Sandhurst dress code. Early on in the evening a PF veteran called Jock came over to talk to me.

'I like your shirt, Dave,' he remarked. 'Where did ye get it?'

I was wearing this ill-fitting Levi's shirt, one that I'd picked up in town that day. I was happy to talk to Jock about pretty much anything, as long as it wasn't about me getting up on the stage to sing. We were five minutes into a conversation about my denim shirt – *Really Dave, is that right?* – and whether Jock should get one himself, when I realised that he was quietly ripping the piss out of his new 2IC.

Jock's verbal wind-up was a far more effective test than an arm-wrestling bout or a fist-fight would ever be. We ended up having a good laugh about it, and Jock figured I was all right as far as officers went. I'd passed that first major test, and I hadn't freaked out too much at the Elvis carry-on. And God was I relieved when it came to the end of the evening without me having to dance or sing. But it left me thinking what a bloody weird way this PF lot went about letting their hair down. It wasn't exactly 'normal' squaddie behaviour. I was more accustomed to the get-naked-and-drink-a-pint-of-piss-and-have-a-punch-up PARA way of partying.

My first few weeks in the PF continued to prove a total eye-opener. The unit had an entirely different way of operating. At that time John's predecessor, Lenny, was in command. One morning a female officer cycled over to our end of the base, to have words with him. She was based in the Regimental Administration Office, which provided admin support to the Pathfinders. A lot of the admin clerks were female, so Steve was forever volunteering to take the paperwork over there to get some face time with the office girls.

The lady officer explained to Lenny that she had a serious problem with the way the PF soldiers were behaving. They were failing to salute her, or to say 'Good morning, ma'am', as a junior rank should do. Lenny gave it to her straight: *They don't salute me, so they sure as hell aren't saluting you!* That lady officer had been in the Army for three years commanding a bunch of clerks. Many of the PF lads had been in for a decade or more, and were decorated combat veterans. It was hard for them to see why they should salute her: many believed the PF had no need for officers.

Camp Tristar was a flat, featureless moonscape of rock and sand, without a scrap of natural shade in any direction. It was burning hot, pushing 40 degrees centigrade. During the first few days we were ramming water laced with rehydration salts down our necks, in an effort to acclimatise as quickly as possible. Gradually, we started sweating less and then needing to drink less, as our bodies adjusted to metabolising at this kind of temperature.

We started building fitness training into our acclimatisation regime. We put together a home-made gym, using ammo boxes, jerry cans of water and scaffold poles as makeshift weights, plus we began running circuits around the base perimeter.

More of our kit started arriving. Big steel shipping containers were dumped at our end of the base, stuffed full of PF-essential gear, including our HALO and HAHO parachuting equipment. It was the dream of every PF operator that we'd get to do an airborne insertion behind enemy lines, and secretly we were all hoping that Iraq might offer us the chance to do so.

We established a logistics base and an armoury next to the accommodation tent, and started ticking off all the mission-essential kit, which included at least one full set of Elvis gear. It was SOP (Standard Operating Procedure) that Smudge's Elvis kit got deployed on all operations. It went everywhere we went, and for good reason: it was a crucial element of Pathfinder morale.

We'd also got issued with a new piece of kit, the L17A1 UGL (Under-slung Grenade Launcher), one that slotted on to the underside of our assault rifles. We rehearsed weapons drills with the 40 mm UGL, and as soon as the Camp Tristar ranges were up and running we'd be out there test-firing the weapon. We studied the maps of southern Iraq, and recced potential routes across the border and north towards the prize – Baghdad.

During all such activity, Steve was acutely aware that just across the sand from us was the Army Air Corps camp, which meant female pilots. Whenever he got a chance he'd have his top off and his shades on, and be out there catching some rays while posing in front of the girls. I'd have expected nothing less of Steve, but there was one member of my patrol who disliked him for it: Jason.

Jason was the Pathfinders' platoon sergeant and my second-in-command. He and Steve were like the proverbial chalk and cheese. I could feel the tension between them bubbling away just below the surface, plus I feared that Jason had issues with my command.

With only thirty-six fighting men in the Pathfinders we were an extraordinarily close, tight-knit unit. We knew each other intimately, even more so within each six-man patrol. As with all families, personality clashes could cause real problems. We were on the verge of going into Iraq, and my patrol absolutely needed to have its shit together. It was crucial that we started to function as one well-oiled, war-fighting machine. I feared that we were not, and that these kinds of tensions could end up tearing us apart.

We were a week into Kuwait and we'd tuned into our environment well. We'd acclimatised to the heat, and had grown seriously unshaven, dirty and hairy. It was obvious the war was going to happen now, and we were chomping at the bit to get across the border. We killed time doing intensive mobility training in the desert terrain around the base. This wasn't only about learning how best to use the vehicles and weapons in such a hostile environment: it was also about getting us working as a team in such conditions.

We headed out one evening for an extended stint of night driving. I flipped down the night vision goggles from my helmet-mount, until the twin leather cups were resting on my eye-sockets. The NVG resembled a small pair of binoculars, and they weighed about the same. They worked by amplifying ambient light from the moon and the stars. That night there was little or no cloud cover and the sky was star-bright above us. The NVG functioned exceptionally well under such conditions. Every way I looked they painted the desert in this weird, foggy-green glow, which was almost as good as driving in daylight.

But with the NVG down it was impossible to wear sand goggles – plastic safety glasses similar to those a welder uses, which are designed to protect your eyes during sandstorms. You couldn't fit them over the NVG. The weather in Kuwait had been pretty much the same every day: blistering hot during the daylight hours and bitterly cold at night, plus a good number of sandstorms. Some were minor flurries that you could drive through. Others were monsters, piling up like dark thunderclouds on the horizon and dumping half the desert on your head.

The only choice when you were hit by one of those storms was to go firm, which meant searching for some suitable cover. Our standard operating procedure was for Jason's vehicle to take the lead, and for us to follow him to whatever LUP (Lying-Up Point) he could find. We'd remain in the LUP until the storm had blown over, at which point the air would clear and we could see to navigate once more. But on night mobility exercises we didn't have the luxury of being able to use the sand goggles.

We'd been driving for a couple of hours when a storm hit. It wasn't a monster and I figured that we could keep going. Then I felt something hammer itself into my eye. I could sense my eye starting to close up, and then it began to weep liquid into the shemagh – the Arab headscarf – that I had wrapped around my face. We followed Jason's lead into a patch of undulating terrain and went firm. By now I could only see out of the one good eye, and I was losing my spatial awareness – my ability to judge distances and bearing by sight.

I was dead worried. If the injury proved to be at all permanent, then that would be me out of action for the coming war. It was also a sharp reminder of how vulnerable we were. Pathfinder or not, I'd suddenly become a liability to my team. Worse still, it was my trigger eye that had been damaged. There was no way that I could fire a weapon, or go to war, in this state.

Steve was the patrol medic, which meant that he'd done advanced first aid training, and was also responsible for the medical kit that each vehicle carried. He'd volunteered for the role, because it provided ample scope for liaising with medical staff wherever we might be – *and that meant nurses.*

He took a look at my eye, but he couldn't see much in the dark. Then he grabbed a bottle of eye-drops from the medical kit and squeezed a few drops into my damaged eye, but I still couldn't get it to open. There was an American field hospital not so far away, and Steve suggested we navigate our way there to seek help. But Jason started pulling a face like a dog pissing on a patch of thistles. He clearly thought it was all a lot of fuss over nothing.

'It's only some bloody grit in his eye,' he started muttering. 'We should bloody well crack on.'

In truth, I did feel like something of a big girl's blouse, with my hand clutching my eye and tears weeping out of it. Being the patrol medic Steve overruled Jason, and we headed for the field hospital. After a short drive we reached the American base. Whilst I waited to be seen by the doctor, Steve was doing his thing with the American nurses, so no surprises there.

The doctor gave my eye a good sluicing out with an eye bath, and a desert-load of sand came out. He inspected the eyeball, and told me that it was badly scratched. He gave me some prescription eye drops, and told me to keep treating it hourly with those. Do that and avoid any more sandstorms, and it should recover, he told me. But if I didn't look after it, it would turn septic, and that would be the end of me going to war in Iraq.

Steve wasn't the hottest medic in the Pathfinders, but he'd done all right by my injured eye. When push came to shove, he'd delivered. It had been Jason who to my mind had wanted to ignore it and 'crack on'. Yet I knew that Jason had a unique set of skills to contribute to the team, and we had to try to make it work. A lot of life was like that, trying to pull teams together, trying to make them work. The difference was that when you were in the Pathfinders you were in a pressure cooker, being in such close proximity to each other 24/7.

Plus we had the added stress of fatigue, dehydration, exhaustion and war-fighting to come.

CHAPTER THREE

Jason 'Jase' Dickins was a squat, short, compact kind of soldier. He was around five foot seven, and at some stage he'd had his two front teeth knocked out whilst playing rugby. He was supposed to wear a plastic plate with two false teeth in it, but he rarely did. As a result, he looked like a Bedouin version of Popeye the Sailor when he was all done up in his desert warfare gear. He also had this Popeye high-pitched strangled-chicken chuckle, which I figured the blokes found fucking annoying, as I did.

He had sandy hair, which was receding, and he was somewhat awkward-looking – hardly one for the ladies. But he was a battle-hardened operator, and he was possessed of a blind, brute strength and courage that demanded respect. He was also an extremely capable sergeant, with widespread demolitions and other specialist experience. He'd been in the PF for nine years, for many of which he'd commanded his own patrol. It was hardly surprising that he didn't exactly love it when he was put under my command in Kuwait. I was several years his junior and a relative newcomer to the PF, and I knew that Jason would far rather be leading his own patrol into Iraq.

Jason was the only married member of our six-man patrol, and Steve's suave, womanising ways really wound him up. Steve would taunt Jason about it, just to wind him up still further. But Jason couldn't seem to nail anything on Steve in terms of wrongdoing, and as far as I was concerned we were all big boys, so I was hardly going to intervene. Jason was big enough and ugly enough to fight his own battles.

No one could fail to respect Jason's military experience and expertise. As a tandem master, he had reached the ultimate in military parachuting. He could HALO from extreme high altitude with a fellow jumper strapped to his body. There are only a handful of soldiers in the world who are that jump-capable. There are very few tandem masters in the entire British military, and Pathfinders boasts a good number of them.

Jason could carry a non-parachutist – an intelligence officer, or an electronic-warfare or language specialist – deep behind enemy lines on operations. He could do the same with specialist stores – sensitive electronic-warfare devices for example – the kind of delicate kit that needs a human jumper to shepherd it to earth. Jumping at extreme high altitude strapped to another person, or a massive tube of stores, is extremely physically demanding.

The training was so intensive that you'd only ever get selected to do it if you were staying in the Pathfinders for several years, so the unit could reap the long-term benefits. Jason certainly wasn't going anywhere outside of the PF any time soon. He loved the unit, and I guessed that was the one thing that united us – Jason, Steve and me. We were Pathfinders, and we were intensely loyal to the PF family.

Of all the lads in my patrol I was closest to Will 'Tricky' Arnold. Tricky rode in my vehicle as the rear gunner, manning the 50-calibre heavy machine gun, our punchiest weapon. He was in charge of Pathfinder communications, and he was also the Platoon's most senior JTAC (Joint Terminal Attack Controller), the soldier who calls in the battle-winning air power. With Tricky embedded in my team we could act as a normal PF fighting patrol, but switch to being a forwards HQ element as needed, orchestrating comms between all patrols and conducting air strikes.

The nickname 'Tricky' suited him perfectly. It had a non-aggressive, cartoon character kind of ring to it. Whilst he smoked forty tabs a day, Tricky was still one of the fittest and hardest men in the entire unit. As with all truly handy blokes, he rarely had to show it. Tricky was like Jason Statham in looks and build, but he was a calmer, surfer-bum version, and more raggedy and battle-worn. He'd be well at home on a Californian beach, but he'd have a look in his blue-grey eyes that told you that if he levelled it at you in a beach bar, you wouldn't want to challenge him.

Tricky was three years my senior and was the living, breathing example of what a PF soldier should be. Whatever shit we might get into, I knew I could rely on him to keep cracking the jokes and cracking on. Nothing ruffled him. He didn't tend to love the 'officer class', but he and I had a special bond. He'd been my DS (Directing Staff) – akin to an instructor-cum-examiner – on Pathfinder selection, so he'd brought me into the PF. He was well aware that Iraq was the first time I'd be leading my patrol into action, and he was hugely supportive of me.

Tricky had come to the PF from the Royal Signals, which meant he'd spent a lot of time around headquarters and officer types. He was best placed to judge a relative newcomer like me. It didn't matter if you had all the ability in the world: in the Pathfinders, if you didn't get your hands dirty you wouldn't win respect. That was what Tricky saw in me, that I was a doer and a trier.

It was working in a Signals Squadron headquarters that had given Tricky such an in-depth understanding of warfare: the people who fight it, the command structures, the interpersonal relations, and the situational awareness that is needed if you are to make sense of a fast-moving battlefield. He commanded universal respect from the men, and in many ways he was ideally placed to be the Pathfinders' platoon sergeant. That position had fallen to Jason by virtue of his seniority, and because it was seen as more suitable for a PARA Regiment bloke, but I'd have preferred Tricky as my second-in-command any day. He was no sheep. He could be challenging at times. Yet from day one he and I had gelled.

Tricky had this smooth Edinburgh burr, which was soft and gentle on the ear. He used that – plus his looks – to devastating effect with the ladies. It was another point of bonding between us. Whether we were HALO jumping in California or doing vehicle mobility training in Sweden, 'The Findermen' – as the PF are known – worked together when on the pull. As long as you were fit for duty the next morning all was good, and we were none of us greedy. My PF nickname was 'Dave The Face', and the lads used to rip the piss out of me for what they said were my 'chiselled good looks'. Whenever we were out in a bar it was always: 'Let Dave The Face go first.' I was the eye candy. The lads would order me forwards, with the instruction to act gorgeous and shut the fuck up ringing in my ears. Once the women were in tow I had to let Tricky or Steve take over. Let me open my mouth, they said, and it'd all be over.

Steve was the bloke in the patrol that I was next closest to. He and I had soldiered together in A Company, 1 PARA. I may have been an officer, but I was still one of the fittest men in the company and I'd led by example. I'd earned Steve's respect back then and he hadn't forgotten. Steve wasn't an 'officer hater'. In fact, Steve didn't hate anyone. It was love – particularly the love of women – that was his major undoing.

A Scouser, Steve had toned down his accent because he'd figured out that the women preferred it that way. Whenever we were out on the town there was a touch of Enrique Iglesias about him. He'd wear a black shirt, sleeves rolled up past the elbows, and buttons undone to show off a bit of chest hair, plus lashings of aftershave. He was classically handsome in the dark-haired, dark-eyed Italian way, and he was forever telling the women that his family hailed from Italy, which was complete bullshit. That epitomised Steve: never one to let the truth get in the way of a good story.

As the Pathfinders' armourer, Steve got every chance to indulge his love of weaponry. Back at our base in the UK we had a purpose-built, impregnable underground armoury, equipped with a state-of-the-art alarm system. That was Steve's domain. It would take time to oil, issue and make an inventory of all the Pathfinder weaponry, and Steve had it down to a fine art. He'd stretch a two-day job into seven, and all the while he'd be down there in the Kingdom of Steve, his laptop hooked up to the Internet, surfing cyberspace for chicks.

If there was a training job going down with Jason in charge, Steve would suddenly discover a shed-load of armourer's duty that needed doing. He'd find a dozen 50-cals requiring urgent maintenance. No one was going to argue with the armourer, because your weapons were key to your survival.

Being PF armourer was about as much responsibility as Steve ever wanted in life. Some saw him as a shirker, but whilst I knew he'd take the easy path he'd never do so at another patrol member's expense. He was bird happy in the PF, and didn't give a fuck about progress-ing his career or sucking up to anyone. He was an excellent soldier, and I liked his calm, chilled exterior, and the fact that he was always – *always* – talking about women. Steve was the driver on my vehicle, and no matter where we were he'd turn to me and start philosophis-ing about the fairer sex. He was a thirty-year-old, single, smooth-talking, chilled Scouser, and a total Casanova.

Dezmond 'Dez' Vincent was the fourth member of my patrol. He was a sergeant, but he'd been with the PF less than a year, and he hailed from the Engineers, so he had little infantry experience. As a REME (Royal Electrical Mechanical Engineers), he'd deployed to the First Gulf War, but he'd spent his time fixing tanks. He'd decided to go for PF selection because he'd been in the Army for years and had never seen any combat. He was bored, and wanted to be truly tested.

You can go for PF selection from any unit in the British military. There are only two rules: one – to Steve's eternal regret – you can't be a woman; two, you have to have served at least three years in the armed forces. Coming from the REMEs, Dez loved his wagons and he was a vehicle mechanic par excellence. He was a great asset for a unit like ours that relied on vehicle mobility much of the time.

When planning ops the blokes were always saying: 'Dez, just worry about the Pinkies, mate.' Ever since David Stirling's SAS ran riot amongst German commander Erwin Rommel's forces, during the North Africa campaign of the Second World War, pink has been the colour of choice for British Special Forces desert vehicles. Pale pink was found to be the colour that best blended in with the desert sands, and – no doubt about it – Dez loved looking after our Pinkies.

The Army was Dez's life, and he was covered in tattoos from the various units that he'd served with. He'd got a Commando REME tattoo; another with a dagger-type motif; and a REME cap-badge tattoo depicting a horse. Directly before coming to the Pathfinders Dez had been attached to the Royal Marines and spent a lot of time at sea. Marines are known for washing themselves the whole time, and Dez had got into the cleanliness habit big time. In the closed confines of a ship cleanliness was crucial, for disease could quickly spread, but in the PF this was anathema.

Long before deploying to Iraq we'd have stopped washing completely. There was no point going sneaky-beaky far behind enemy lines, if the scent of soap or deodorant gave you away to the local stray dogs. There are strays everywhere in Iraq, roaming the night in packs of a dozen or so. The more you smelled like a clean human, freshly bathed in shower gel, the more alien your scent would be to the dog packs, and the more likely they would be to raise the alarm. Conversely, the more you smelled like an animal, after taking on the odour of your environment, the less likely you were to be detected.

Once we had crossed the Iraqi border we were also fully expecting to be hunted by their military. Whereas the US Marine Corps and most of 16 Air Assault Brigade would be taking on the Iraqi forces in open warfare, our role would be to penetrate the enemy lines undetected. Just as soon as the Iraqi forces suspected we were there they would try to track us. They'd do so from the air, using surveillance and spotter aircraft. They'd do so from the ground, using EW (Electronic Warfare) devices that tracked our radio and satphone signals – and we knew that the Iraqi military had a fine EW capability. They'd do so by sight, using night-vision and thermal imaging kit to pick up human body heat. And they'd do so using tracker dogs trained to pick up the human scent, which was perhaps the single most difficult thing for an elite force like ours to evade.

Since reaching Camp Tristar we'd stopped shaving completely. Shaving wastes precious water and can cause infections. We wouldn't be washing on operations, so our skin would be dirty and smeared in old camo cream. Shaving causes cuts, which lets the dirt and gunk leak into the bloodstream. It also produces waste water full of human hair and soap, the scent of which is a dead giveaway. We needed to blend in with our environment as much as possible, looking and smelling like the wild.

We also needed to tune in mentally to that environment. If you were trying to move through the Iraqi positions, but you were worried about getting your hands or your uniform dirty, you'd never make it. We needed to fuse with our environment, becoming at one with it. Dez found all of that a bit of a challenge.

Whilst out on ops we'd be on hard routine, shitting into plastic bags and carrying it with us. If you left any behind it was easy for a search dog to detect, and then it could pick up your scent and track you. Shit could also provide vital intel to the enemy. If you'd been in a hidden OP (Observation Post) behind enemy lines, and you left six turds in six holes, the enemy could figure out there were six on your team. If you were compromised and forced to go on the run, the enemy would know how many they were hunting.

They could count the number of craps you'd had, and estimate the number of days you'd been there. From that, they could make a good guess as to whether you'd secured the intel that you came for. There may have been a SCUD missile delivery four days back, and your shits might indicate if you'd been in position long enough to have witnessed it.

Being on hard routine was brutal, and it could lead to some horrendous problems. Prior to deploying to Iraq we'd been on an exercise on Salisbury Plain. Inserted by Chinook helicopter, we'd been tasked with a night march to an objective where we'd carry out a close target recce. As soon as we hit the ground Leo, one of the most senior blokes on the patrol, had run into problems. He'd got the shits real bad. He hadn't been ill beforehand. It had just hit him from out of the blue.

All of a sudden we had to stop every fifteen minutes, so Leo could squirt into a plastic bag. It's quicker and easier if your mate holds the bag for you, but Leo's problem was proving so bad that it needed a plastic bag *and* some cling film. Each time he needed to crap we had to go firm in some kind of cover, whilst Leo struggled out of his massively heavy pack and dropped his trousers. We were under huge time pressure to recce the enemy position and report back to HQ, but we had to keep ripping off the cling film so Leo could let rip.

If we didn't keep catching and carrying his crap, we'd make ourselves a piss-easy target to track. We were stopping every five minutes by now, so this was seriously slowing us down. Taking his bergen on and off repeatedly was proving exhausting for Leo, and he was getting seriously dehydrated from all the shitting. Eventually, we took Leo's heaviest kit and shared it around our own bergens. That done Jason took point, and set a blistering pace to try to make up time. But we were bent in two by our loads, as we tried to move fast at night across punishing terrain, so our knees and ankles were getting hammered.

We were doing a forced march that was tougher and faster than PF selection, and one of our blokes was seriously ill with the shits. In spite of the cold the pace got us sweating, but each time we had to halt so Leo could crap we'd quickly freeze. We were hot-cold-stop-go for hours on end, but Jason never let the pace waver. I thought about how he'd come last on a PF training run at the start of the week, but out here on the moors and under a punishing load he was unstoppable.

We helped Leo as best we could, and we each knew that if we'd been in Leo's sorry position the lads would have done the same for us. We made up the time and managed to recce the objective, but by then we were plastered in Leo's shit. And all of this really wasn't Dez.

At Camp Tristar water was supposedly strictly rationed, but Dez was forever in the showers. He was full of nervous energy and permanently jiggling and jumping about. He was either running and doing press-ups, or in the showers scrubbing away at the sweat and the dust. There was the equivalent of a giant paddling pool on the roof, one that fed sun-warmed water into the showerheads. The showers were open plywood boxes, which left the head and shoulders free.

Tricky took the piss the whole time. 'Dez, what're you doing now, mate?'

Dez would worry that he'd done something wrong. 'I'm just having a wash, aren't I?' he'd answer, defensively.

Tricky would raise one eyebrow. 'But you had one this morning, mate.'

'Yeah, but I just did some more phys, so I'm sweaty again.'

'Dez, there's nothing wrong with being sweaty. You're not with the Marines now mate. You're with the PF.'

'Yeah, I know, mate, but it's hard to break the habit, and I have been in the Army for thirteen years, and I just like to keep in shape and keep clean.'

Tricky would exhale a long plume of cigarette smoke. 'Dez, take it easy. Once we're across the border there'll be no washing for weeks on end.'

I figured Dez was a bit of a misfit in the Pathfinders, but deep down the blokes liked him. He'd joined the Army at sixteen and worked his way up to being a REME sergeant. He'd thrown away any chances of further promotion, and all the pay and perks that went with it, because being a PF operator was the one thing that he hungered for. He didn't want to be in charge of a hundred engineers fixing tanks. He wanted to be part of a six-man patrol on operations behind enemy lines. Dez wasn't particularly bothered that he had the least combat experience in our team. He'd do any job asked of him and was keen to learn, and that demanded real respect from the rest of us.

The last man in the patrol was Joe Hamilton. Joe was twenty-one years old and he'd been in the Army for barely three years, which made him the runt of the pack. He sounded as if he hailed from the southeast of England. Like Tricky he had transferred from the Royal Signals, so Tricky had become like a big brother to him, which made him pretty much untouchable. Joe was keen and hyper-fit, but very, very quiet. He knew he was here to listen and to learn. He was skinny and boyish-looking, with wide blue-green eyes and brown spiky hair. On top of that he was puppyish, with gangly, bandy legs, and there was something slightly Fraggle-ish about him.

Whereas Steve could chat up anyone, Joe would be totally tongue-tied with the ladies. Like Tricky, he smoked like a chimney, and by rights he shouldn't have been as fit as he was. Joe and school hadn't worked out, but he was actually incredibly sharp. The Pathfinders was the alternative school in which he'd truly started to spark and come alive. The teachers here were people like Tricky and Jason, blokes he respected enormously, and he had no choice but to learn, for our lives depended upon it.

My guess was that Joe came from a tough home background. Something about him told me that, but we rarely got to learn each other's personal stories. The past was the past in the Pathfinders, and blokes generally didn't bleat about it. He'd passed the rigours of selection and completed the basics of PF training, and he was about to go behind enemy lines as the machine-gunner on one of the wagons in our patrol. We were Joe's family now.

Still, there was a part of me that was concerned about Joe. He was the youngest and the least experienced on our patrol, and if we had a weakest link I figured Joe was it. Technically, we were unsure if he had done enough time to qualify for PF. A soldier had to have served a minimum of three years in the military, and he was unlikely to get in without having served closer to six.

Still, we were in Kuwait and about to go on combat ops, so no one gave a toss about that now. We needed every man we'd got.

CHAPTER FOUR

Tricky was the guy that I'd choose to go back-to-back with if we were on the run behind enemy lines. Dez could out-bench press and out-run Tricky, but it was mental hardness that mattered most when on PF operations, and Tricky's psychological stamina was second to none. He'd keep going no matter what had happened and what parts of him were blown off and missing. Tricky would share his last mouthful of water with you, but he'd also be able to outwit the enemy.

After Tricky, I'd choose Jason as the guy to go on the run with, because of his experience and his solidity under fire. Jason would get you out of there, but it'd be less personal. After Jason, I'd choose Steve. You'd have a laugh with Steve even when you were dying: 'What d'you reckon those Army Air Corps chicks wear beneath their flight suits, Dave? I always was a lover not a fighter, mate!'

Next, I'd go for Dez. If you told Dez to go and attack an enemy position with his bare hands, he'd do so without hesitation, and regardless of whether it was the right or the wrong decision. He was a fearless military machine. And finally, I'd go for Joe. Joe would look to me to lead any decision-making, because my experience and skills were better than his. But I was certain that even young Joe wouldn't be found wanting if and when the shit hit the fan.

Breaking down the six of us between the two Pinkies was a bit like picking a football team at school. Tricky came with me automatically, for he was the platoon signaller, and he had the TACSAT comms system with which I could talk to PF headquarters.

Dez volunteered to be Jason's driver, because the two of them were real close. Steve jumped at being mine, and I figured there was no way that he and Jase could be in the same vehicle. That would be utter misery for the two of them, and could spell disaster for the patrol.

It was young Joe who drew the short straw. He got lumped with the last available place, on Jason's wagon as his rear gunner. He'd have been far happier on our vehicle. He'd have been with his mentor, Tricky, and no one would speak down to him. Steve would have made him laugh his tits off, and I'd have been able to keep a close eye. But there was no other way to configure the patrol to make it work.

When not practising night driving we've been doing mobility exercises by day, using the mark one eyeball. We've moved from point to point navigating across the open desert using compass and maps, and relying on the GPS only as backup. In the Pathfinders we only use our GPS as an emergency navigational aid, for it can and does fail. Batteries get drained in the blistering heat; desert-blown dust works its way inside; electronic circuits malfunction and go down. Navigating on GPS also tends to make you horribly disorientated. It gives you no sense of your geographical position or what the surrounding terrain is like, and you don't know where to run if you're compromised. We never use a GPS close to a target, or a recce tasking, for the glow from the screen could give your position away.

We practised desert driving and contact drills relentlessly, but we had to move carefully, especially when ramping the Pinkies across the Kuwaiti sand dunes. The wagons are top-heavy when loaded up with ammo, water and fuel, and they're vulnerable to rolling. During my days in the Parachute Regiment I'd had one of my best mates roll one. He'd been doing contact drills and had been turning across a slope when the wagon had flipped. He was a monster of a bloke, but still the accident had ripped his shoulder apart. He was very lucky to have survived.

At times we'd been taking a break from our Kuwaiti mobility training and having a brew, and Steve would be slouched against our Pinkie, lost to the world. To the casual observer he'd look like he was sunbathing or half-asleep. Jason would get so wound up by it, he'd practically have steam coming out of his ears. But what could he say? He couldn't exactly have a go at Steve because he was too chilled out.

Over the brews Tricky and Steve would share a ciggie between them. Just as soon as he got the faintest whiff of smoke, Dez would stagger back like he'd been punched in the face.

'Fucking smokers,' he'd mutter. 'Don't you know how bad it is for you? It takes three weeks to get one cigarette out of your system. D'you know how many people die of smoking every year?'

That I guess was the divide between the two teams in our patrol: the chilled, and the distinctly un-chilled. As we trained relentlessly for going across the border, I wondered just how we were going to pull together once we were deep inside Iraq and under fire.

One thing became crystal clear as a result of all the mobility work: we needed run-flat tyres. We were using standard cross-country tyres complete with inner tubes, for they were easier to repair if punctured. We hadn't opted to fit specialised sand-tyres – which have a special tread pattern and run at a pressure designed to float across dunes – for we expected to be operating across a mixed terrain: tarmac road, dirt track, hard plateau, and trackless rock and sand.

But driving un-armoured Land Rovers like we were, all the Iraqis had to do was shoot out our tyres and we'd be well and truly buggered. I put an urgent request through to our UK headquarters for twelve sets of run-flats. With run-flats you could keep driving, even when they'd been shot out by small-arms fire. But right now any number of British soldiers in Kuwait didn't even have body armour, they were that under-equipped, and it came as no great surprise when the request for run-flats was denied. We'd just have to make do with what we'd got, and hope the Iraqis couldn't bloody shoot straight.

There was only so much training we could do in the heat and dust of Camp Tristar. Frustration was on the rise as we waited to go to war. Sand seemed to work its way into every crevice, and it stuck to every sweat patch. We worked off some of our pent-up tension by sparring with each other. Tricky trained with his mate Lance, the champion bare-knuckle boxer. He would hold the pads as Lance smashed the fuck out of them, and then they'd swop around, each egging the other on.

There was nothing cosmetic about the six-packs, or the neck and arm muscles on these guys. They were the real deal: highly trained and carefully honed fighting and killing machines. They weren't like most guys you'd see in the gym, where appearance meant so much. With Tricky and Lance, every ounce of muscle was there for functionality. They could run over long distances carrying serious amounts of weight, even in arduous conditions like the Kuwaiti desert, and at the end of it they would still be ready to fight relentlessly hard.

As for me, I was spending more and more of my time with John McCall, the Pathfinders' OC, dealing with the planning side of things. I'd rather be training, or better still out on ops, but the command side was crucial to what I did in the Pathfinders, and I had never wanted anything more than to be 2IC of this unit. I didn't want to get promoted, for then I wouldn't be doing HALO jumps from the roof of the world as part of a six-man patrol. I didn't want to get my major or colonel, for then I'd have hundreds of lads under me fresh out of the factory, and I'd be dealing with red tape, court cases and all that crap. I wanted to remain as 2IC of the Pathfinders, and to enjoy it and do it well, for it could never get any better than this.

But all work and no play makes Jack a dull boy, and we all needed some downtime at Camp Tristar. Music plays a big role in the Pathfinders' unique *esprit de corps*. A mixture of timeless sounds had become associated with the Platoon: Johnny Cash, Neil Diamond, Kenny Rogers, and AC/DC for when we were about to jump off the rear ramp of a Hercules. New blokes picked up the classic tunes as the veterans faded into the dying light. Often you'd hear Kenny Rogers' 'The Gambler' blaring out on someone's speakers, before the whole Platoon would start to sing along.

DAVID BLAKELEY

Recently, Tricky had broken the mould a bit and got big into Pink, and he kept blaring out her girly, punky rock tunes. Anyone else in PF would get real stick for playing Pink, but no one was going to tackle Tricky. That all changed when the American SOF (Special Operations Forces) pitched up at our end of camp.

We were three weeks into Kuwait, and going stir crazy waiting to go to war, so it was a welcome distraction when the American SOF guys came along hoping to do some joint training with us. But it seemed that a bunch of unwashed, hairy, bearded, scruffy weirdoes blaring out Pink at top volume wasn't quite what they'd been expecting from this infamous Pathfinder ghost force.

In the PF it's every soldier's choice what gear he wears, and we'd culled bits of kit from just about every armed force in the world. Almost no one wore standard British Army issue gear. The British Army's desert boots had a hopelessly flimsy sole, and we knew that if we went in on foot we'd be man-carrying ridiculous amounts of kit for days on end. Instead, most Pathfinders wore Alt-Berg desert footwear. Alt-Bergs have a proper, mountain-wear Vibram sole, and they're made of a light and breathable material, which wicks perspiration away from the foot and into the desert air.

Alt-Bergs are manufactured by a tiny, specialist factory in Richmond, Yorkshire. That factory just happens to be next door to Catterick, where selection takes place for the Parachute Regiment. With PARAs fast wearing their boots out on selection, business at the Alt-Berg factory had boomed, and it was PARAs coming into our outfit that had brought Alt-Bergs to the Pathfinders. Steve just happened to know one of the girls who worked on reception at the factory, and just as soon as we'd heard we were off to Kuwait he'd got her to fast-track a bulk order.

A lot of the lads had brought a windproof smock with them. They were made of rip-stop cotton, and provided a shield from the cold desert night. We'd got them oversized, so we could wear a down jacket underneath, and so that the smock didn't ride up when marching under a heavy load. A few of the die-hard ex-PARA blokes insisted

– 56 –

on wearing a PARA smock – a slightly more modern version of those worn by the Regiment at Arnhem. I wasn't one of them. In my view the windproof smocks were far superior.

As with boots, webbing was a deeply personal choice as a piece of kit. If we were forced to go on the run, we'd be living out of our belt or webbing kit, and blokes had that down to a fine art. A normal, rucksack-style belt clip makes a sharp click when opened or closed. It can even open by accident when crawling on your stomach. Instead, the PF lads used an old-fashioned roll-pin belt made out of canvas. Once it was pulled tight it wouldn't come undone, and it was silent to fasten or remove. On to that was sewn whatever tried-and-tested collection of pouches each bloke favoured. The priorities were ease of use and access, and making sure that nothing in your belt clip rattled when you were moving fast on foot.

Some guys preferred chest webbing, so they wouldn't be sitting on their belt kits when in the vehicles. Some had SADF (South African Defence Force) webbing, which was a hybrid belt-and-chest kit. The SADF had masses of combat experience, and their kit was generally first class.

Jason was a belt kit man, as was Tricky, and theirs was more battered and seasoned than most. I was also a belt kit bloke, but I combined it with a compact set of Soviet Army chest webbing, which gave me the best of both worlds. Dez was a chest-webbing guy. He'd often be lying on his back tinkering away under the vehicles, and he could do so in comfort with his chest kit on. Joe wore chest kit because that's what he had done in the Royal Signals, and Steve had SADF webbing because it was a damn good pose.

Every piece of kit was tailored and modified to suit a bloke's personal experience on the ranges and in combat. It was also heavily worn-in. Pouches had been flipped open a thousand times to grab magazines; pistol holsters had been sprayed with DPM (Disrupted Pattern Material) paint, to better camouflage them; combats were patched, faded and worn. As a result, we tended to resemble a bunch of action-figure hobos.

Just prior to deploying to Kuwait we'd been on a training exercise in Scotland, doing a high-altitude para-insertion. On the drive back we'd called in at a motorway service station. We were dressed in our usual motley selection of gear, and we had long matted hair and greasy beards from being out on exercises for days on end. Not a pretty sight.

A little kid was passing with his mum, who was really quite tasty. The kid pointed to us and yelled excitedly: 'Look, mum, cowboys!'

Tricky kind of let out this half-grunt, half-laugh: 'You dunno how right you are, lad.'

We had that same kind of look when the US Special Ops guys pitched up at Camp Tristar. For the Americans there was already something odd about the lack of any insignia that marked us out as being something *special*, but then Smudge came out wearing his Elvis wig just to wind them up, and there was Tricky singing along to Pink at top volume. The American Spec Ops guys didn't seem to know what to make of us. The more macho amongst them were giving us these looks like we were all gay, or mad or both.

'Say, pal, d'you mind turning down the music?' one of them remarked to Tricky. Tricky lowered the volume a fraction, but upped his singing to compensate. 'So, how much can you bench press?' the guy asked him.

Tricky stared at the bloke for a long second, wondering how to respond to such a bone question. 'How many ciggies can you smoke in one day?' Tricky finally countered.

'I don't smoke,' the guy replied. 'And I can bench press 150 kilos.'

'Well I smoke forty tabs before breakfast,' said Tricky, 'and I'm not even trying.'

'So how many press-ups can *you* do then, mate?' Steve chipped in.

The Spec-Op guy took the bait. '*Man, press ups?* I hold our unit's record for press-ups done in one day: *4,500*. I do them knuckles on the deck, 'cause it's harder and it works the wrists and fists too ...'

It was now that Bryan Budd, ones of Steve's best mates from a sister PF patrol, pitched up. He pulled this mock, but extremely snappy and formal-looking salute, and the Spec-Ops guys stiffened their backs and pulled salutes in return. 'Sir!'

'To all of you who've done well, well done,' Bryan announced, in this perfect impersonation of a stiff, plum-in-the-mouth English officer's accent. 'And to all of you who've not done so well, well… well done anyway!'

The Spec-Ops guys were staring at him like he was cracked. He had no rank insignia, so for all they knew he could be a general. As for the rest of us, we were trying desperately not to laugh. In an effort to avoid the weird General Bryan Budd, one of the Spec-Ops blokes turned to have words with me.

'So, man, like where d'you come from in the UK?'

'London,' I told him. 'Have you heard of it?'

'Yeah, man, I know London,' he enthused, completely missing my sarcasm. 'I've been there once and don't you just love Leicester Square?'

He pronounced it 'Li-ces-ter', and before I could reply Steve cut in again.

'Yeah, I love Li-ces-ter Square. Next time you visit London go to this bar there – it's full of these chicks and they'll just love you American guys with all your muscles. It's called The Shadow Lounge.'

I had to kick myself to stop the laughter. The Shadow Lounge is London's number one gay bar. Me and a couple of the PF lads had stumbled in there one evening, after a 'Leo Sayer' – an all-dayer drinking session. As far as party atmospheres went, The Shadow Lounge rocked. We figured if you could survive a night as a straight bloke in there, you could survive just about anywhere.

The chest-puffing from the Spec-Ops guys and the piss-taking from us was over pretty quickly, and they asked us if we'd be willing to do some cross-training. They figured we had things we could teach them, and vice versa, plus it would break up the monotony of waiting to go to war. We headed for the ranges to have a go on their M4 carbines, whilst leaving them to try to figure out how to use our SA80s.

Recently, we'd been forced to give up our favoured weapon, the superlative M16A2 assault rifle. The M16s we'd been using were old and combat-worn, and we'd lost the battle to get replacements. Instead, we'd had the SA80 foisted on us, and we hated it. The M4 being used by the Spec-Ops guys was a fine weapon, being a lighter and more versatile version of the original M16 assault rifle.

We slammed through a few mags of ammo on the Camp Tristar ranges, putting the M4 through its paces. It was clearly well engineered, reliable, accurate and easy to clean and reassemble. It was also simpler to use, lighter and less prone to stoppages than the SA80, and you didn't have to reach one arm over the other to cock it. We wished we had the M4, and from the looks on the American operators' faces we could tell what they thought of our SA80s!

The guys were keen to show us what their Humvees could do. Like everything American they were massive – like a 4x4 jeep on steroids. They were better across country than the Pinkies, and they were up-armoured, providing far greater protection for the vehicle's occupants. By comparison, our wagons were Mad Max dunemobiles with the tops open to the sun and the air. But we still preferred them: they had better all-round vision, and vastly superior arcs of fire. They weren't low, claustrophobic and cramped, which was how the interior of a Humvee felt. Plus the Pinkies were easy on the gas, which meant they had a far greater range.In contrast to the SA80, which was a shit piece of engineering, we were proud of the Pinkies. The Spec-Ops guys could tell it, too. They were more than a little intrigued as to why we were so attached to vehicles that clearly offered so little protection from fire. They kept expecting us to show them a secret lever, which when pulled changed the Pinkie into something entirely more James Bond-like.

'Keep it quiet, lads,' Steve told them eventually, lowering his voice to a whisper. He pointed out the bonnet release catch. 'When the going gets tough – but only *real tough* mind – that is the special button you have to press, and hey presto! Of course, I can't tell you exactly what it does, 'cause it's classified.'

The guys were lapping it up. They didn't know that the Pinkies were basically the same piece of kit that the LRDG had taken to war some sixty years earlier.

CHAPTER FIVE

It was during the aftermath of the Second World War that the Land Rover was conceived by the late lamented Rover Company. Rover's Coventry car plant had been destroyed by German bombing, and it had been forced to move production to a 'shadow factory', where it was only able to make cheap and simple vehicles. The original Land Rover concept fitted the bill completely: it was basically a cross between a light truck and a tractor.

The first Land Rovers were built on a Willys Jeep chassis, using the engine and gearbox from a Rover P3 saloon car. The bodywork was handmade from an aluminium–magnesium alloy called Birmabright to save on steel, which was closely rationed after the war. The Land Rover was designed to be in production for only two or three years, in order to gain some cash flow for the Rover Company, which would enable it to restart car production.

But the Land Rover proved so wildly successful that it outsold Rover's cars, so leading to the birth of the iconic brand that the British Army would come to rely on so heavily. The Pinkies that we were showing off to the Spec-Ops guys in Kuwait were based upon the sturdy box-section chassis of the original 1947 design, with the same flat, lightweight alloy body panels that were used then. Compared to the HUMVEE the Pinkie was an arcane piece of kit, but we in the PF loved 'em.

Of course, we knew this was an American-led war, and that we were here as the Yanks' poor cousins. The US Marine Expeditionary Force had a full division – that's 10,000 marines, plus warplanes and heavy and light armour – poised to punch across the border. There were tens of thousands more marines here to back them up, plus massive teams of SOF (Special Operations Forces). The American SF community was somewhat different from our own: for a start, there were some 60,000 active duty and reserve SOF in the US armed forces. There were no more than a few thousand Special Forces troops – active and reserves – in the entire British military. The relative level of training, and the calibre of the recruits, was reflected in those numbers.

Yet we in the Pathfinders dug the US military. Big time. They had all the Gucci kit you could ever wish for, and they were hugely generous with it. Plus they seemed to love poorly-resourced, yet exceptionally highly-trained and resourceful, British Army blokes like us. Once we were done showing the guys the non-existent secret weapons systems on the Pinkies, we headed off to the ranges to fire their Javelin missiles, which at $40,000-a-pop was absolutely fabulous.

The Javelin is a man-portable system, and all you basically had to do with the thing was load a rocket into the launcher, crouch with it on your shoulder, aim and fire. After it had been ejected from the tube, the missile travelled a good distance before the rocket motor ignited, so there was less chance of the launch team's position being spotted by the enemy, and less danger from the back-blast. A fire-and-forget missile, it would lock on to the target prior to launch, and use an automatic self-guidance system to home in. It was a compact, simple and highly effective tank-killing weapon.

We in turn initiated the Americans into the joys of the LAW-90 (Light Anti-tank Weapon-90), which was the nearest equivalent we had. The LAW-90 was British-made and supposedly man-portable, but at 2 metres long in the unarmed position it was like lugging a roll of carpet around the battlefield. If you were on foot, the only way to carry it was strapped crossways to the top of your bergen, which was a Laurel and Hardy-esque way of going to war if ever there was one.

Whilst carrying a LAW-90, there was every chance you'd turn around and knock someone out with it, or get stuck fast when tabbing through thick bush. When you're first taught to use the weapon, you have six sessions in the classroom before being allowed to try one out on the ranges. Here at Camp Tristar, Steve offered the Yanks a bit of background and a quick lesson on the weapon's capabilities, with me doing the demo of how you operated the thing.

'The LAW-90 was designed in the late '80s by a British Army engineer called Sid Vicious,' Steve began. He just couldn't resist slipping a couple of priceless wind-ups into the lesson. 'It's got a range of 500 metres to effect a mobility kill, and 300 metres to stop enemy armour dead. It's a short-range weapon, so it's best to engage an enemy target that isn't driving directly towards you.'

A 'mobility kill' means immobilising enemy armour, as opposed to destroying it. Steve explained the series of moves required to get the LAW-90 armed, whilst I demonstrated with the weapon at hand.

'It takes ten separate operations to arm the LAW-90,' Steve announced. 'Watch carefully as Dave demonstrates, for I am not about to repeat myself. First, remove your tube ends ...'

I removed the hard black protective covers from either end of the 2-metre tube.

'Second, extend the tube.'

I tried concertinaing the thinner tube out of the thicker one, but predictably it was jammed. From experience I knew that only brute strength would shift it. I got the LAW-90 vertical, with one foot on the bottom end of the tube, and yanked hard. The top end shot upwards, until I had it extended to about 4 metres in length. The lads were in fits of laughter, as they imagined me doing this with a Soviet tank charging towards us, which was the kind of target the LAW-90 was originally designed to kill.

'As you can see, the LAW-90 is a perfect low-profile and concealment weapon,' Steve quipped. 'Now, Dave, slide forward the pop-up sight please ...'

I flicked the slide and up popped the sight. On Steve's instructions

I folded a lever around to activate the trigger, dropped the safety catch to off, mounted the tube on to my shoulder, and checked the area to my rear, for anyone up to 30 metres behind me would get badly burned by the back-blast.

'Now, what crucial move has Captain Blakeley forgotten?' Steve queried.

The Spec-Ops guys gave a collective shrug: *How the hell would we know*?

'Oooh! Oooh! I know! I know!' Dez was jumping around and eager to dump on me from a great height.

'Okay, Captain Blakeley, what have you forgotten to do in order to fire your LAW-90?'

'Well, Steve, I need to fire a spotter round from the magazine before switching to main armament.'

Steve set about explaining to the guys the incredibly long-winded process of getting the LAW to make a kill. You had to select a target, then fire a spotter, a small tracer round that once fired would show you if your aim was true. After firing between one and five spotter rounds, you shifted to a main charge and prepared for the big blast.

'This is all very well in theory,' Steve continued, 'but with a moving target who can tell me the disadvantages of using a spotter round? Americans only to answer, please.'

'Well, seems kind of dumb to me,' one of the Spec-Ops guys volunteered. 'By the time you've hit the target with the spotter round, the damn thing will have moved!'

'Bravo!' said Steve. 'Anyhow, you try to keep yourself cool under pressure having just given your position away by firing the spotter round, and then you unleash the main charge. Now, have you all got that? Who wants a go?'

Two of the Spec-Ops guys volunteered to have a try firing the LAW-90. I figured they were true sports. It seemed to me we'd been ripping the piss out of the Americans' hospitality something chronic: first we'd blagged a load of their camp beds; then we'd fired off a shedload of their missiles and ammo; and now we were going to make them look like complete idiots with the LAW.

Steve pointed out a couple of wrecked trucks lying towards the end of the ranges. The first guy took up his firing position, sighted the weapon and let rip with the spotter round. It was bang on target. He flicked the magazine over to the main charge, and sighted again. He had to know that every one of us – PF and Spec-Ops alike – was dying for him to miss, so we could give him the biggest ever slagging. He pulled the trigger, a massive jet of flame spurted out of the launcher's rear, and a moment later the truck was engulfed in a powerful explosion.

He'd hit it first time, having had only a five-minute Monty Python-esque demo from Steve and me. It was some shooting. His buddy followed and did a repeat performance. Two shots with the LAW-90: two kills. Those guys had years of soldiering behind them, and that cumulative experience gave them the confidence and aptitude to fire even our most eccentric of weapons. All credit to them.

The LAW-90 was a heavy piece of firepower, but we'd have far preferred the Soviet-designed RPG (Rocket-Propelled Grenade). With the average speed of a tank over rough terrain being around 30 kph, the key qualities you wanted in a man-portable tank-killing weapon were light weight, plus speed and ease of operation. The RPG had those qualities in bucket-loads.

By contrast, the LAW-90 was a seriously inept piece of weaponry, but it was all we had and we'd never refuse the opportunity to take such firepower into the field. If nothing else, unleashing a few LAWs might buy us the time to extract from battle, if we were facing serious amounts of enemy armour. But what we wouldn't have given to be able to take a handful of the American Javelins to war.

Together with the Spec-Ops guys we burned through over a million dollars' worth of rockets, missiles and grenades on the Camp Tristar ranges. There was no doubt in our minds that we were going to war now. If we weren't, we'd never have been allowed to have so much fun at the expense of the British and American taxpayers.

Before heading back to their desert camp, the Americans suggested we trade some of the food in our ration packs with theirs. We jumped at the chance. We managed to offload a bulk load of stodgy treacle pudding in exchange for several dozen bottles of Tabasco sauce. None of the Yank operators had a clue what treacle pudding was, so we managed to convince them that it was ideal hot weather food.

All day every day there had been US aircraft howling through the skies above Camp Tristar. An endless series of UAVs (Predator Unmanned Aerial Vehicles) – a pilotless drone – would go buzzing overhead, flying recce missions into southern Iraq. Recently, we'd got news that two Predators had been shot down by Iraqi ground-to-air missiles, the first concrete sign of the looming war. That had been followed by the first wave of SCUD missile launches. Early one morning we'd heard this enormous rushing roar, like a tidal wave going over our heads. As a series of SCUDs streaked across the sky, we saw the US fast jets screaming overhead in an attempt to find and hit the launchers. There were scores of US and British bases here in the Kuwaiti desert, so one lucky shot by an Iraqi SCUD could cause carnage.

When he wasn't listening to Pink, Tricky had his radio tuned to the BBC World Service. It was a great source of information in this weird bubble that we were living in. The BBC reported that the UN was still trying to get Saddam to comply with its resolutions, in an effort to prevent war, but we knew Saddam wasn't about to do so and that we were going in. We heard news that the Iraqi commander nicknamed 'Chemical Ali' had moved down to Basra. Chemical Ali was responsible for gassing the Iraqi Kurds, back around the time of the First Gulf War, and he was the architect of Iraq's chemical warfare programme. His arrival in Basra put him 50 kilometres or so from us, so well within SCUD range.

We started practising our NBC (Nuclear, Biological & Chemical) warfare drills, donning NBC suits, gloves and respirators as soon as the NBC alarm sounded around Camp Tristar. But pretty quickly it became clear that it was impossible to wear all the NBC kit and operate properly as a Pathfinder. No way could we recce enemy positions and remain covert and functional when dressed in full NBC gear. We'd just have to hope that Chemical Ali's cartoon-character bad-guy name reflected the cut of the man, and when it came to it he'd baulk at unleashing any mustard gas or sarin on us.

As the drums of war upped their tempo, I was given the task of drawing up our EPs (Emergency Procedures), should we get compromised in Iraq. I picked Jason to help me do so, in an effort to give him some of the responsibility that he craved, and to try to forge a better bond between us. We went to visit the Army Air Corps, who were marked down to fly Lynx and Gazelle helicopters in CSAR (Combat Search and Rescue) missions on behalf of 16 Air Assault Brigade.

The Lynx is a British aircraft manufactured by Westland Helicopters. It is agile and fast – a Lynx broke the helicopter speed record back in 1986, flying at 249.1 mph. It's operated by a pilot and a co-pilot/navigator, and it can carry nine fully-equipped troops in the rear. That made it more than large enough to accommodate a PF patrol. But the AAC pilots were pretty blunt about the Lynx's capabilities out here in the desert. In the burning heat of the day its engines threatened to overheat, which basically meant it was unable to fly except at night.

In addition to the Lynx they also had a handful of Gazelles in theatre. Manufactured by the French company Aérospatiale, and in the UK under licence by Westland, this light helicopter was designed chiefly as an anti-tank gunship. Unfortunately, it's only capable of carrying five people, including aircrew, so it would take two Gazelles at least to rescue one PF patrol. The AAC lads had to keep cannibalising the few Gazelles they had in theatre, in order to keep a bare minimum operational, and there were no guarantees as to how many they'd have flying if and when we might need rescue.

In short, the Army Air Corps didn't have the spares or the supply chain to keep the right airframes reliably airborne. They promised to do their best to get us out if we did have to go on the run in Iraq, but there were no guarentees. It was hugely frustrating being in a so-called 'Air Assault' Brigade that didn't have the bare minimum of air assets, especially when those few airframes that we did have were dodgy as fuck.

We didn't have anywhere near the air assault capability the American military had had during the Vietnam War, and that was over thirty years ago. But you always want more and better kit in theatre, and there always comes a time when you just have to crack on. The selection and training we did in the Pathfinders were all about self-reliance: it was about depending on yourself and your small team to get you out of the shit, no matter what.

As we couldn't rely on the Brigade's own air assets for CSAR, Jason and I looked at other options. On our TACSAT comms systems there were two main nets: one was the British ground forces net, the other the air net. The air net was monitored by US AWACS (Airborne Warning and Control System) aircraft, which meant that US air assets should be able to pick up an emergency call from a PF patrol. The American military had a massive CSAR capability, and the potential to get lifted out by them was very real.

The Americans operated the Sikorsky MH-53 Pave Low, a state of the art CSAR helicopter. It had been designed to fly by day or by night, in all weathers and over all terrain, with unrivalled navigational aids and armour. It also boasted an in-flight refuelling probe, external long-range fuel tanks, a rescue hoist, and three gun mounts, equipped with two 7.62 mm six-barrel Gatling-type machine guns, and a single Browning 50-calibre heavy machine gun. If you had to be rescued, that was the boy you wanted flying in to pluck you out of harm's way.

Our default CSAR procedure would be to rely on our own forces – the Army Air Corps boys. But we also drew up plans for two RAF Chinooks to fly in a company of PARAs trained in CSAR techniques. We'd be at a designated HLS (Helicopter Landing Site), fighting off whatever force was pursuing us, as the PARAs hosed down the enemy and lifted us out. And as a third option we'd use our TACSATs to call up the American AWACS, and get patched through to one of their shit-hot CSAR teams.

We briefed the Army Air Corps lads, the American AWACS and the RAF aircrew on our call-signs, just in case we needed to speak to each other. The Pathfinder call-sign was *Mayhem*. My patrol had the specific call-sign *Mayhem Three Zero*. The AWACS aircraft were call-sign *Magic*, the British Chinooks were call-sign *Lifter,* and the Army Air Corps were call-sign *Rookie*.

At least we now knew how to talk to each other.

CHAPTER SIX

Jason liked getting involved in all of this big picture stuff, but at the same time he struck me as being a little out of his depth. We were liaising at officer level with the RAF, and with senior American aircrew. This required a bit of charm and diplomacy, and Jason's rough-and-tough soldier ways didn't always cut it. I figured he was starting to see a bit of the value-added of having an officer around. We weren't surrounded by the blokes here, so Jason could drop his anti-officer façade, and I was seeing a different and far more likeable side of him.

We'd been in Kuwait for the best part of a month, when finally we got the orders that we'd been waiting for. We were out in the desert doing mobility training, with a temporary field headquarters tent pitched amongst the dunes. John, the OC, would call for his patrol commanders whenever there was an important briefing. Jason, being an ex-patrol commander and now 2IC of HQ patrol, normally got included. But this time, when John called us in by name – 'David, Geordie, Lance, Gall …' – there was no request for Jason.

We gathered in the ops tent and were given the H-Hour, the time to cross the border into Iraq. We were making an 'Army move', with the whole of 16 Air Assault Brigade plus the 10,000 warriors of the US Marine Expeditionary Force moving through. All times were calculated down to the last minute, or else we'd fuck up the roll-through. Pathfinder Platoon would cross the border at 0300 on 16 March, and make for a FOB (Forwards Operating Base) deep in the Iraqi desert.

This meant that we had little more than twenty-four hours to get ourselves fully sanitised, get our shit together, and get the vehicles packed and mobile. And there was a shedload of stuff to do before then. I returned to where our patrol vehicles were gathered in the desert, to give the lads the good news. We'd parked in a shallow wadi – a dry riverbed that would only run with water when it rained – which provided the only scrap of cover for miles around.

As I descended down the rough, rocky slope, I could see the distinctive forms of our wagons parked up in the sliver of shade provided by the wadi's side. The heavy 50-calibre machine guns were sunk back on their mounts, the muzzles pointing skywards like the necks of some fearsome birds of prey. I came out from behind our Pinkie and Jason was holding forth. He'd got his back to me, and I was just about to interrupt when I heard what he was saying.

'Fucking Dave The Face!' Jason spat out. 'He's just passed his 21st birthday and thinks he knows …'

I didn't catch the rest, but I could see by the looks on the blokes' faces that Jason had been gobbing off. Steve, Tricky and Joe were facing me, and their expressions said it all. They knew that I'd just caught Jason backstabbing me, and Jason had twigged from the looks on everyone's faces that I was right behind him.

I figured I had to do something immediate and decisive, or I'd be seen as being weak. But I also knew that I couldn't lose my rag or tear him apart verbally. That would only serve to belittle him and make his resentment fester. The lads knew I wasn't some wimpy officer type who'd never been in a scrap. Prior to the Pathfinders I'd spent six years in the PARAs, before which I'd been in the boxing team at Sandhurst. Even so, I had to kill this now, before it blew up big time.

I spoke into the silence: 'Jase, let's go have a private chat.'

He turned slowly and rose to his feet. I led the way into the open desert, heading for an area where we wouldn't be overheard. I was keeping my pace slow and even, and Jason was following me in a tense silence. He knew he'd been caught red-handed. He knew he was in the wrong. He knew I'd never have done the same to him. I'd read all of that in the quick, guilty flash of his eyes as he'd turned to follow me.

As we walked the two hundred yards or so I was rehearsing what I was going to say in my head. In the past I'd had PARA corporals and others be difficult under my command, but I'd always made it work. The difference was we were about to go to war, and Pathfinders like Jason were as strong-willed as they came.

I stopped, Jason stopped and we turned to face each other. In a way, we were polar opposites. I was tall and wiry whilst Jason was squat, solid and meaty.

'Tell me, Jase, what's the problem?' I asked.

He paused. He was quiet, staring at the sand for a long moment.

Then: 'Dave, you just got to know there's a lot of senior blokes here in the patrol, and I'd just like you to know to use the blokes … Just use the blokes, that's all …'

I was in no rush to reply. I knew he'd lost face on this one. I had to try to be magnanimous here, and give Jason a way out of the confrontation that he'd got himself into. I offered him a simple route out of there.

'Jase, if you've got any more problems or issues with me, I want you to come and speak to me first, and be direct about it. Don't let it fester amongst the lads, okay?'

Jason nodded: 'Okay. Fair enough.'

There was no shaking of hands. No man hugs. Nothing corny like that. It was just a few stark words spoken in the open desert, and we were done. I hoped we'd got it sorted. We were about to go to war, and it was high time we buried such rivalries.

Jason was 'a ranker' – he'd worked his way up through the ranks – and I was sure that he saw me as typical 'officer class'. He figured I was from a posh, moneyed background and here by dint of privilege. He saw me as baggage that he'd have to carry, and rules that he didn't need. He was wrong on several counts. First, *no one* gets into the PF without passing the gruelling selection. *No one.* Second, I was brought up in Middlewich, a town on the outskirts of Manchester and I grew up on a boring 1970s housing estate.

My dad taught kids with learning difficulties and behavioural problems, many of whom came from troubled backgrounds. He had the patience of a saint with those who had been written off by the system. He managed to listen to them and treat them as human beings, and he turned many of their lives around. A few of those lads went on to join the Army, and on their first leave they'd come back to visit, and they'd thank him for what he'd done for them. I didn't think I could do what he did, and certainly not with the same kindness or effect, and I looked up to him enormously.

I'd gone to St Nicholas's, the local state school, and it was an accident of fate that got me into Sandhurst. I'd started to mess around at school, and at the age of sixteen I'd signed up to join the Army on a whim. When a visiting Army recruiter had noticed the grades that I'd been getting, he suggested I try for a sponsored place at Welbeck College. I'd go to Welbeck to do my A-levels, and if I stayed the course I'd go on to do officer training.

Welbeck is this top-notch private school, set in the magnificent former home of the 5th Duke of Portland. As far as my parents were concerned, this was a golden opportunity to get me a private boarding school education, one subsidised by the Army. It was something they could never have afforded. They were concerned that I was going rogue, and about to follow in the footsteps of some of my mates, who were getting banged up for dealing drugs and other crap.

The nearest we came to having any military tradition in the family was one of my grandfathers, who'd been conscripted into the Second World War. On my first day at Welbeck we had to do a 1.5 mile run. It was the longest distance that I'd ever run, and I came in second from last. I didn't like being at the back of the pack. I did well at Welbeck and by the time I made it into Sandhurst I'd turned my life around. I was one of the fittest officer cadets, and I was recruited into the Sandhurst boxing team.

But the one thing I couldn't abide was all the pomp and snobbery that seemed to go with being 'officer class'. My closest mate was a guy called Matt Bacon. He was ex-Army Air Corps and he'd served in the First Gulf War. He was also a corporal who'd worked his way up through the ranks. Matt organised a secret birthday party for me, which epitomised our time at Sandhurst and how we went against the grain. We had 200 blokes there. James Blunt – then an officer cadet himself – played guitar and sang, and Matt smuggled in a bunch of strippers.

It was definitely not 'officer class behaviour', and it was the kind of thing we would have got kicked out of Sandhurst for, if anyone had caught us. Matt was the oldest recruit in our year and I was the youngest. A lot of officer cadets would cruise into easy placements, ones that their schooling and family background somehow 'qualified' them for. Matt and I were the opposite. We kept ourselves at the same level of ultra-fitness and we trained together relentlessly.

It was Matt who encouraged me to go against the Army's intentions, which were to make me an officer in the Royal Engineers. I had zero interest in being left in the rear with all the gear. Instead, I opted to try for PARA selection. I saw the PARAs as a classless regiment where I could properly fit in.

In due course it was Matt who would encourage me to try for selection into the one unit that eschewed all the status-obsessed Army bullshit – the Pathfinders. Many of the blokes came to the PF to get away from the rules and regulations of the Regular Army. I was one of them.

One of my favourite movies is *The Wild Geese*, in which a group of veteran soldiers get recruited to carry out a crazed do-or-die African coup. I saw the Pathfinders as a similarly maverick force, a bunch of rebel warriors going behind enemy lines to spread mayhem and carnage. As with *The Wild Geese*, we were a small group of very determined men setting out to achieve the seemingly impossible.

The Wild Geese includes a HALO jump, which very few movies do, another reason why blokes in the Pathfinders rated it. We also rated *Heat*, the Robert De Niro bank heist movie. Again, the guys in

Heat were a small team working together as a band of brothers. The common theme of an unbreakable bond coupled with the honour of thieves – the one last job – ran through much of the PF.

It was another reason why the press has to be kept away from us. A PF bloke had once been asked by a reporter if he could ever see himself working in a bank.

His reply: 'Yeah, maybe with a balaclava and a shotgun.'

It didn't matter – or shouldn't matter – what your background was, especially in the Pathfinders. In my rulebook, you treated everyone as a human being and you didn't seek popularity at the expense of others. I appreciated Jason's soldiering skills, and his dedication to the PF was unquestionable. But I was buggered if I was going to start justifying myself to him. I wasn't about to start jumping through any hoops for Jason, or anyone.

As we made our way back to the Pinkies, I resolved to do something more to bring him onside. Jason had commanded his own PF patrol, so I'd been expecting a power struggle. I'd seen him chomping at the bit for more responsibility, so I decided to give it to him. I was going to hold out the hand of friendship and show him that I valued him. It was the counter-intuitive thing to do: after being caught slagging me Jason expected to get punished. But from past experience I'd learned that coming up with the unexpected could have an amazing effect on difficult blokes under my command.

In Sandhurst I was taught to lead by authority. 'You might run with the hounds, but you should never *be* a hound' was one general's view. Familiarity breeds contempt, I was told. You had to keep yourself apart. It didn't make a lot of sense to me back then, and it made even less in the PF. John Keegan, the head of leadership studies at Sandhurst, had written a book called *The Mask of Command*. It studied the ways of Alexander, Wellington, Grant and Hitler, and broke command down into a scientific kind of formula. But command wasn't that: it was human, personal, individual and instinctive.

In fact, leadership was largely intuitive. And a study that dealt with four such towering commanders and generals dealt with men whose very position meant that they would rarely, if ever, be disobeyed. They were commanders by right, not true leaders. I was far more interested in how a lance corporal managed to get his men to follow him over the top, in order to assault a German bunker during the Second World War. How did he get his men to follow when leading a charge to almost certain death? And how did a private take over command, when all the senior ranks around him had been put out of action?

Those were the true marks of leadership, for only via such a man's instinct, character and example would he get his men to follow him. One of the best things I ever learned at Sandhurst came from the writings of one of the most gifted, yet underrated generals of the Second World War. Field Marshal Bill Slim masterminded the brilliant Burma Campaign, leading a multilingual army composed of many races, and turning defeat into victory against the Japanese. He was fearless in combat, plus daring and maverick in designing missions that often struck deep behind enemy lines. He was also universally loved by his men.

Slim wrote: 'Leadership is simple – it's just plain being you.'

I'd never forgotten those words. If I had tried to adopt *The Mask of Command* here in the PF I wouldn't have lasted five minutes. The blokes would have quickly seen through the façade. With the PF I had to lead by instinct and example, and use the lads to help me do so.

I'd not tried to pull on 'The Mask of Command' to upbraid Jason. Instead, I'd talked to him man-to-man. I'd made it clear that everyone's experience counts, as did their opinion. As Slim advised, I'd just plain been me. I hoped Jason recognised that, and that he would react to it accordingly, and help me lead my patrol and the platoon into war.

I gathered the lads, and explained the game plan that John had briefed me on. We'd cross the border and establish an FOB inside southern Iraq. From there we'd be airlifted deeper inside the country, to seize targets of vital strategic value. We'd not been briefed on those targets yet, for it was all done on a need-to-know basis. But our deep penetration missions would be backed by 16 Air Assault Brigade, with crack units like the PARAs and the Royal Irish Rangers flying in to capture terrain that we'd recced, secured and marked on the ground.

The battle plan was designed to enable the US Marine Corps to outmanoeuvre and outflank the Iraqi forces. A series of lightning air assault and airborne advances would leapfrog the Iraqi positions, in a wave of *Apocalypse Now*-type strikes. We'd render the Iraqi front lines redundant via our speed and our reach. Or at least, that was the plan.

There had been a great deal of talk about doing parachute drops. It made perfect sense, for there were so few airframes available to put troops on the ground. We just didn't have the Chinooks to move an entire Brigade forwards, but we did have the C130 Hercules aircraft to do a series of massive air-drops.

A single battle group – 16 Air Assault Brigade consists of four battle groups – requires fifteen C130s (a 'fifteen ship') flying in formation, to air-drop into theatre. That's ninety men per aircraft, so 1350 men in all. I couldn't wait to be at the spearhead of that force, as the PF parachuted in behind enemy lines to find the way.

We broke down the planning for the move into Iraq, so each man got a sense of ownership. Tricky did the air plan (how to use any airpower we had on hand to support us); Joe did the comms plan; Steve and Dez used the maps to recce the route across the border. In spite of our altercation in the desert, I gave Jason responsibility for 'actions on' – the patrol's set procedures should the mission go pear-shaped at any stage – a vital tasking. I knew he was hungry to be valued, and I figured that would bring him onside.

When I was a kid my mother realised her lifelong dream of owning and riding horses. She'd grown up in Liverpool, where the only way she ever got a chance to ride was by looking after the steeds of wealthy people. She was determined that horses would be a part of our family life, so she and my dad scrimped and saved to make that dream a reality.

I was six years old when she'd first given me the chance to learn to ride, and I took to it like a fish to water. I learned that when you were riding a particularly troublesome steed, it was often better to do the counter-intuitive thing and loosen the reins. The horse realised it could have its head, and it would be more responsive and faster. That was my philosophy with Jason: give him some rope.

It was a gamble, but time was short and it was all I'd got.

CHAPTER SEVEN

Finally, 16 Air Assault Brigade's commanding officers were getting their men keyed up for the move across the border. In front of the massed ranks of 1 Royal Irish Rangers, Colonel Tim Collins did his epic 'We go to liberate, not to conquer' speech, the one that the then American president, George Bush, would hang on his wall in the White House.

The media were there in their droves, so we kept our distance and listened in from the sidelines. Colonel Collins was ex-SAS, and we had a great deal of respect for him. We'd been bumming around in Kuwait for approaching a month now, and Colonel Collins' speech reinforced the sense of anticipation we felt. We were going in.

The BBC reported that the speech had gone down a storm at home and in the States. We figured it was no bad thing that the American leadership knew and appreciated that we Brits were here alongside them, ready to get our hands dirty. After all, we pretty much depended on them for air logistics and air power, not to mention camp beds!

We checked and rechecked our wagons in preparation for the move. The pinkish paint of our vehicles was specially engineered to reduce the vehicle's thermal signature. The Pinkies were open to the elements, so the interior dash units were sealed and ruggedised. The seats were made of a tough plastic, with a gap between the back and the bottom where water could drain through.

Our ethos in the Pathfinders was that 'skin is waterproof'. It was better to have an open-topped wagon and risk getting wet, than do without all-round firepower. When moving at speed in the driving rain we'd put goggles on, and we had shemaghs to protect our faces, although we didn't exactly expect such problems when moving into the blistering heat of the Iraqi desert.

Each Pinkie had a GPMG (General Purpose Machine Gun) on the front passenger side – my side – mounted on an arm, so we could swivel the weapon around. The pivot was well balanced and manoeuvrable, and had a gliding, *Star Wars* kind of feel to it. It basically took all the weight of the weapon, leaving the gunner free to control, aim and fire. Once practised, we could fire accurately, even at high speed. The GPMG gave a 180-degree arc of fire – so from Steve's head in the driver's seat around to Tricky, stood at the 50-cal behind. With Tricky's 50-cal being in a raised turret, it had a 360-degree arc of fire.

Strapped to the roll bar behind me were three bergens, each packed with sleeping bags, bivvie bags and specialist clothing, plus water and rations for ten days. Most Pathfinders used the standard British Army short-backed bergen, as it sat better on your webbing, with extra pouches sewn on for quick access to ammo. But a few of the old and the bold used ancient SAS-issue bergens, complete with metal frames.

Under the straps of the bergen you stuffed your grab bag. If you were compromised and you had to go on the run the bergen could be ditched, and you could leg it just with your grab bag. Each bergen could hold 80-plus litres, and weighed in the region of 30 kg when fully loaded. When on foot we'd be carrying all of that, plus our webbing kit and our personal weapons.

Ammo tins were piled between the front passenger and driver seats, including six 200-round boxes for the GPMG, so 1200 rounds in all. Each box was stacked the same way around, rounds facing forwards, and with the seals broken. That way if I needed to change an ammo belt I simply lifted the breach on the weapon, flicked open an ammo tin, flipped the belt across, closed the breach, pulled back the cocking handle and I was good to go. I'd drilled so heavily for it I could do it in two seconds at night and working simply by feel.

Stacked in the vehicle's rear were 1000 rounds for the 50-cal. There was an SP-GPRS – a specialised military GPS unit – fitted into the dash of the Pinkie. The SP-GPRS is encrypted, so that the enemy can't trace the GPS signal. It works to the military's dedicated satellite network, as opposed to the civilian network that normal GPS systems use. The Americans are able to shut down the civilian network, which they might do if the enemy were using the civvie network to target them. The military satellite network would always be kept open.

To the front, on the bonnet, we had a couple of the cumbersome LAW-90s strapped crossways, right in front of the dash. A bundle of camo netting was strapped on top of the LAWs, with the camo poles wrapped inside. Once we were out on the ground in hostile territory, we'd erect the camo nets in such a way that we could drive the Pinkies into and out of their hides.

A couple of the vehicles had machetes in them. The lads would use the big knives to clear vegetation, or to make camp. We weren't Samurai and they weren't for fighting. If you saw a soldier with a huge knife strapped to his waist then generally you knew to give him a wide berth. We had a standing joke in the PF if ever we saw a guy dressed like that: *Yeah, but what's he like in a dark room with a knife?* It was a piss-take: if ever it came to close-quarter combat, you'd be far better off shooting your adversary in the head with a pistol.

Every other vehicle had a winch fitted to the front, just above the sump guard. It was a vital bit of kit for hauling out bogged-in vehicles, but it was heavy, hence fitting it to alternate Pinkies. That way, every two-vehicle patrol had a winch should it need one, and it kept the weight down.

Two jerry cans of fresh water were loaded aboard each wagon, plus a dozen ration packs, claymore mines and grenades. When we were done packing our Pinkie was jammed so tight you couldn't fit anything else in. Well, all apart from the Marlboro Lights. Tricky

Right Early days in the
Parachute Regiment, before
I became a Pathfinder. Those
around me are all PARAs, some
of whom would go on to become
Pathfinders.

Below Myself, left of photo,
during High Altitude Low
Opening (HALO) parachute
training in Nevada, USA. Only a
handful of Special Forces units
do this highly specialist training,
which enables us to drop from
very high altitude and plummet
to earth undetected.

Above Myself, far left, with fellow Pathfinders preparing for an epic HALO descent in Nevada. We're jumping with our M16 rifles strapped to our sides, which was then the Special Forces weapon of choice. The guys in shorts are RAF Parachute Dispatchers and they're checking that our oxygen breathing equipment is working properly before we jump.

Above Same Nevada drop zone. Myself to right of photo, with jump suits, parachute harness and helmets. We specialise in using HALO and HAHO techniques to penetrate enemy terrain covertly, to seize drop zones and bring in conventional forces.

Right Dressed in full oxygen equipment, state-of-the-art BT80 parachute with full Bergen, prior to a HALO descent and feeling like James Bond in *Tomorrow Never Dies*! With our parachute kit, M16 assault rifle, Bergen full of food, water, weapons, ammo and survival gear, we'd be carrying 100 kilogrammes of kit.

Above Pathfinders about to jump out of a C130 Hercules at extreme high altitude. At three minutes to P-hour – parachute hour; the moment to jump – the pilot would crank out AC/DC's 'Thunderstruck' at top volume over the aircraft's tannoy system. If the adrenaline wasn't already pumping in bucket-loads, that really got it punching through the roof.

Below P-Hour plus . . . We've walked the plank to the edge of the Hercules tail ramp and the wind is tearing like a hurricane around our ears. The lead Parachute Dispatcher stands strapped to the side so he doesn't get torn out by the wind. He's giving 'GO! GO! GO!' and we're diving headfirst into the howling void.

Above Nothing beats skydiving at sunset with the distant horizon a flash of burning fire. We're on a jump over the North Sea to practise flying under our parachutes so as to carry out a covert border crossing. A stick of six Pathfinders drifting silently under their chutes is all but invulnerable to detection by the enemy. We trained relentlessly for using this highly secretive method of penetrating enemy airspace in preparation for operations in Iraq.

Below Patrol in freefall. Terminal veloclty Is about 150mph. You need goggles to shield your eyes, otherwise it would be like riding a motorbike at that speed with no visor. It's vital to keep visual contact with the blokes in your stick so as not to gain too much separation in the air and lose each other during the descent.

When doing a HALO jump, we dive out of the aircraft on the roof of the world, but we only pull our chutes at very low altitude. This enables us to plummet into enemy territory with minimum time from jump to hitting the target – so giving the enemy the least chance to see and kill us. The most experienced parachutist always leads the stick into the Impact Point (IP).

Top right Yours truly in freefall over the desert, feeling like a giant shuttlecock plummeting to earth. To increase your speed you go into a delta shape, with arms by your side. Conversely, to stabilise speed and maintain your position in the stick, you get your arms and legs out beside you, in the starfish shape.

Centre and below right Still images taken from a video we filmed of one of our sunset HALO jumps. The camera was strapped to your helmet and reviewing the footage after the jump was a great way to learn and perfect the jump technique.

Below Pathfinders, with trusty M16 assault rifles slung over their left side, barrel pointed downwards. You'd always jump with your main weapon strapped to your body, just in case you lost your Bergen during the fall. 13-round Browning pistols are packed in the rucksacks, plus grenades, Claymores and most of the spare mags of ammo, so as to prevent weapons snagging in the parachute when it releases, which could prove fatal.

We're put through highly-realistic conduct after capture and resistance to interrogation training. Here Pathfinders are dragged out of the rear of a truck after being 'captured' by an 'enemy force'. The aim is to get us accustomed to how an enemy will likely treat us when captured on a mission behind enemy lines, and on the physical and psychological pressure we will be put through.

Bound and degraded; after hours of such treatment you either crack or you learn to find your inner peace and to zone out your captors. We were given talks by famous captives, one of whom, General Anthony Farrar-Hockley, had been captured and escaped several times during the Korean War. I will never forget his words: strength of mind was the key to surviving capture, and those who kept faith with their fellow POWs would make it through.

wasn't going anywhere without his forty smokes a day. When out on ops I'd share a ciggie with Tricky. It was a bonding thing. Joe and Steve too. Ciggies were a valuable currency, especially when the shit went down, so we loaded our Pinkie with a few extra crate loads.

The Pinkie is basically a cut-down Land Rover with a strengthened chassis. With three men to each wagon, plus all the water, fuel, weapons, ammo, comms kit and food, we were at the very limit of what it was designed to carry. We couldn't afford the extra weight of ballistic matting, which would provide protection against small arms fire and explosions. On the upside, we had an awesome amount of all-round firepower. On the downside, we had zero protection from incoming.

Needless to say, there was little room for personal kit, either. I had one problem with this: my girlfriend, Isabelle. Or rather, her generosity. She was a sultry French beauty; tall, leggy and with these large breasts that for some reason I was drawn to. Plus she'd got this gorgeous long, curly, dark hair. As a mate of mine remarked, she was a walking wet dream. She also had fantastic taste in French lingerie. She was a lawyer working for a top city firm, so I guess she could afford the best.

I'd seen her just before we'd deployed to Kuwait, and we'd had drinks and dinner in la-di-dah Hampstead. I'd only met her a few times, but I was still hopeful of cracking it that evening. It was what we in the Pathfinders called a 'trap or die' date. I had nowhere else to stay in London but her place, so unless I scored big time I'd be walking the streets until the morning.

I'd worked out the attraction on her part: I was Isabelle the high-flying lawyer's bit of rough. She had all these super-wealthy guys chasing her, but not so many rough as fuck soldiers. I knew that the more I talked that evening, the more chance I had of blowing my chances. So I played the still-waters-run-deep card and kept quiet, leaving Isabelle's imagination to fill in the blanks. It was amazing what a woman would dream up to explain a man's silence.

We ate and drank and she took me back to her swanky Hampstead apartment. It sure beat my one bed basher at Pathfinder camp with the mattress thrown on the floor. She put some slinky jazz music on the stereo, dowsed the lights and lit some candles. No Smudge crooning Kenny Rogers or Elvis here then. I forgave her when she started to dance for me, although I didn't join her for obvious reasons.

Then she asked me if I wanted some cheese. I thought: *For fuck sake, don't start eating garlic cheese whatever you bloody do!* She moved towards me, put down her glass of red wine and kissed me. Then she reached over and turned down the dimmer switch to zero. I guessed the cheese had been postponed until afters, then.

The lovely Isabelle had just sent me this care package out to Camp Tristar. Along with the melted chocolate and the wet wipes, there was a thick tome of a book. The wet wipes were much appreciated. With limited water, there would be days go by when we couldn't wash. They were perfect for getting rid of bacteria and grime around the mouth, so you could eat without getting sick.

But the book wasn't useful. Not at all. It was an appallingly bad novel about some future alien world laid waste by space-age warfare. In her letter she told me the book was especially precious, for her father had given it her on her twenty-first birthday. She asked me to carry it with me wherever I went, and to bring it and me back safely. Isabelle may not have had the greatest taste in literature, but hell, English wasn't her first language, and she did boast the finest French lingerie.

I figured I had to take the book with me into and out of Iraq. It got stuffed into my grab bag, along with the basics for escape and evasion. I hung the grab bag on the exterior of the vehicle, within easy reach of the passenger door. That way if I had to abandon the Pinkie and go on the run, I'd just grab it and go. And if we did have to do a runner, I could always use Isabelle's crappy novel as bog paper.

In the Pathfinders, you treated your vehicle as something extremely special. It was like you were a guy who'd worked all his life and finally managed to buy that dream vintage Ferrari. When not on ops we would barely use the wagons at all. We'd keep the mileage down, and carefully maintain and cherish our steeds. The vehicles were kept in a special hangar, and only once they'd been cared for would a bloke look to his own comforts. *You look after your vehicle – it looks after you.* Even more so when out on operations.

In many ways it was like the experience I'd had with horses as a kid. My mum taught me that you should always put your steed before yourself, for you were dependent upon it. Get the horse groomed, fed and watered first. So I'd give them their mixture of oats, molasses and corn mash, before ever I'd settle down to my own meal.

In an effort to prevent blue-on-blue (friendly fire) incidents, the Pinkies were fitted with BFT (Blue Force Tracker) panels, which were designed to send a signal making us instantly identifiable from the air. All NATO aircraft were supposed to be able to see Blue Force Tracker on their radar screens. At Brigade level they had this computer system that supposedly allowed them to see where all their callsigns were, via BFT. The Pinkies were also fitted with these visual recognition flashes, which were your back-up in case the blue force tracker system failed.

With the Pathfinders operating deep behind enemy lines we were most likely to be at risk from friendly fire, for we would be where the enemy were. We'd be sneaking about on minor roads, tracks or the open desert. We were also painfully aware of how different our Pinkies looked from the American HUMVEEs. From the air, an American pilot would most likely see them as enemy vehicles.

It was the first time that we'd had blue force tracker when on combat operations, and we thought it a fine idea – *that's if it worked*. We knew how easily computers crashed and electronic gizmos malfunctioned in the heat and dust of Iraq. BFT was also a new system that was untested in combat, so it was bound to have its teething problems. There was a lot of scope for it to go wrong.

We packed our NBC kits, as the threat of nuclear, biological or chemical attack was seen as being high. Our NBC detection devices looked a bit like metal detectors. You had to attach this special indicator paper, which would turn a certain colour depending on which NBC agent was present in the air. As far as we were concerned, the NBC kit was just more shit to cram into the wagons, which were already horribly overloaded. If we were to carry more weight we'd rather have had extra ammo, but we'd been ordered to carry the NBC kit.

Over the last week most of the lads had been doing an 'Op Massive' – that is, pumping themselves up in the makeshift gym. They'd piled on extra muscle, largely to put on weight that they could afford to burn when out on operations. When deployed into the field we were unlikely to get enough food. We'd be burning a lot of calories due to stress, pressure, the climate and sheer physical exertion. We'd burn muscle as well as fat, and we'd lose weight rapidly, hence the need for the Op Massive.

A few hours short of H-Hour, John asked the brigade commander to come and have a few words with us. Brigadier 'Jacko' Page had commanded several elite regiments, and his reputation went before him. He spoke to us in the mess tent, tucked away in one corner of the camp. He wasn't the biggest bloke in the world, but he had this ultimate confidence that shone out of him. The atmosphere was electric with anticipation, but Jacko remained measured and calm as he started speaking, as if he was having a fatherly chat with his lads.

'So, Pathfinders, finally we're going across the border. I'm sure all of you are more than ready. As we know this is a US-led war, and I know some of you wish you were deploying ahead of the US Marine Corps and their main force. All I'm going to say to you is that this is very early days. There's going to be a lot of surprises to come and you will get used, so be patient.'

Jacko wasn't bigging it up, like a lot of senior British officers tended to do. His talk was absolutely pitch-perfect for what we were about to do.

'You've done a cracking job during exercises,' he continued. 'Once we're in Iraq I want you to push the boundaries of what's possible. But just because we'll be war-fighting deep inside enemy terrain, that doesn't mean you'll get air cover all the time. You'll need to survive on your wits. I'm expecting the extraordinary from the Pathfinders, and I have every confidence that you will deliver.'

He gave us this steady look. 'Any questions?'

Jacko was a man of few words, and he'd said exactly what we needed to hear. If it had been some pompous speech, someone – most likely Steve – would likely have piped up with: 'Why didn't Chew Bacca get a medal at the end of Star Wars?' But Jacko commanded ultimate respect. John asked the first question, after which I figured it was time to raise the issue that was on the mind of every man in the room.

'Sir, if there is a need for us to insert by parachute, and that is the most tactical way to deploy, will we be jumping in?'

I'd just posed the million dollar question. I hoped I'd put it as diplomatically as I could, but what I was asking was did the will exist within the British military and their political taskmasters to allow us into Iraq by a para-insertion? I could see the blokes eyeing me, their expressions saying it all: *Balls of fucking steel to ask that one, Dave.*

It was more than sixty years ago now, but the British Army remained scarred by the loss of thousands of parachutists at Arnhem. Ever since then detractors had used that example to argue against airborne operations. I'd studied Arnhem at Sandhurst, where it was used to demonstrate the dangers of such a mission. They'd dropped the main force after relying on the intelligence given, and with disastrous consequences – but it was the intel that was at fault, not the method of insertion. Even so, Arnhem was still cited as an example of how many men could be lost when parachute operations went wrong.

The last time the British military had done a para-insertion into combat was almost fifty years ago, during the 1956 Suez Crisis. On 5 November a Pathfinder element of the 3rd Battalion the Parachute Regiment had dropped into El Gamil airfield, in Egypt, which made them the first British soldiers on the ground. The 'Red Devils', as they were called, were unable to return fire whilst parachuting, but as soon as they were down they'd used their Sten guns, their 3-inch mortars and their anti-tank weapons to deadly effect. Having taken the airfield with a dozen casualties, the remainder of the battalion was able to fly in by helicopter.

This was the first in a series of airborne landings. In spite of facing strong Egyptian resistance, and fierce street-to-street fighting, they largely achieved their objective. Working closely with French and Israeli elite units, the British seized the Suez Canal, which was the key military objective. But by then the international political battle was all but lost, and public opinion at home had turned against the war. Facing intense domestic and international pressure, the British and allied forces were forced to withdraw, and the entire Suez campaign was branded a failure.

In fact, Suez had demonstrated the effectiveness of parachute-borne operations in post-Second World War conflict. It embodied the very reasons that the Pathfinders were formed – to enable a small, elite unit to go in first and establish ground truth, so as to allow the main force to follow in some safety. It showed how you only needed to risk a small body of men to prove how things were on the ground. But the perceived failure of Suez had enabled the detractors of parachute-borne operations to brand them overly risky and prone to disaster.

It was that which we were up against now, as we prepared to deploy into Iraq. Jacko eyed me for a second. He was clearly thinking carefully about my question – whether the British military had the guts to send us in by parachute drop.

'You've raised a fair point,' he remarked. 'All I'm going to say is that we do have C130s in theatre. Your parachutes are here. If that is the best or the only way of inserting, and it's possible to do so, then you will be doing it that way.'

Each of us was aware that Jacko had commanded elite units at the time that the Bravo Two Zero patrol went on the run in Iraq, during the First Gulf War. As that patrol had discovered, going in by air and then on foot meant you had far less firepower than inserting by vehicle. But air insertions have a much longer reach, and are far more covert and rapid. Jacko's was an honest answer. It wasn't a firm commitment, but he wasn't shying away from the issue either. His message was that we stood as good a chance as anyone of doing a para-insertion.

After Jacko's talk was done we were issued with our silk escape maps. They covered the whole of Iraq and the neighbouring countries in great detail. But as a result they were absolutely fucking enormous. Spread out, each was the size of a large blanket. Rolled up, each was like a thick cloth belt. The upside was that the scale was superb, and they would be fantastic for navigating hostile terrain. The downside was that we had no idea where to hide them.

Tricky held one open above his head. 'At least now we've been issued with bloody parachutes.'

Steve pawed at his map and started doing a pompous officer impression: 'Now, men, we are here,' he jabbed the map with a stubby finger. 'I want you to go around here, up here, then over here and to take this entire area.'

Whilst he was doing so his finger was covering half a grid, and the map was blowing about in the wind. In the PF you never point with a finger when giving directions – it's far too inexact. You use the tip of a pencil, or something equally fine.

Eventually, we decided to roll the escape maps tight and thread them twice around the waistband of our combats, like a belt. There were no gold sovereigns issued to us, as there had been to the SAS in the First Gulf War. Then, they were for paying off local Iraqis to help the men of the Regiment escape from Iraq, if needed. Steve joked that due to the defence cuts the Army couldn't afford them any more.

In the final hours prior to crossing the border the lads were tinkering with the vehicles. They were checking the tyres for pressure and wear, and for thorns and sharp rocks; they were cleaning, greasing and oiling anything that might creak or squeak over rough terrain; and they were strapping down ammo tins and making sure the stowage cabinets were firmly latched shut. As he went about his work, Dez was mad enough and mince enough to talk to the vehicles.

'Right, so there we are – that's there, where it should be, in its place. Okay, nice and tight and looking good.'

Steve and Tricky took the piss relentlessly. But Dez was the equivalent of a horse whisperer with the wagons – *he could talk to his vehicles*. It was a real comfort to have him with us.

Even at this stage, when we were poised to head into Iraq, Steve was still playing the fool like a good one. He took an NBC early warning device and started tracking back and forth across the sand making this weird bleeping noise. He brought it close to Dez, and the beeping increased in pitch and tempo ten-fold.

'Emergency! Emergency!' Steve announced, in this metallic robot voice. 'Contaminated! Contaminated! This man needs another shower!'

Having alerted Dez to how he was 'contaminated', Steve took the NBC detector unit and attached it to the front of our Pinkie, with some gaffer tape. He stood back proudly once he was done.

'There you go lads,' he announced. 'All we have to do is get the beast up to 88 miles an hour and we can travel back in time.'

I was trying not to laugh. I couldn't be seen to be leading the messing, but I wouldn't ever want to stop it. As far as I was concerned, such larking about was a vital part of unwinding the tension of the coming mission.

With H-Hour fast approaching we grabbed a few minutes of our favourite movie – *Things to Do in Denver When You're Dead*. Steve had scored one from the American PX store, and it was playing on a laptop in the accommodation tent. The old sweats were back together for a final job, and each man had a compelling reason to be there. It wasn't just for the final pay cheque, so they could retire in the sun: each man had a personal reason to do the one last mission.

Andy Garcia plays the lead in the movie, a gangster with his heart in the right place and a whole host of problems. When one of his team is in prison Garcia goes to visit him. The two men touch hands on the dividing glass, and then mouth the phrase 'boats drinks'. It refers to how one day they'll have made their millions, and be on the

French Riviera sipping cocktails on the yacht of their dreams.

Having got a good hit of the movie, we wrapped up with our she-maghs. It was partly practical: they'd keep the dust out of our hair and faces. It was partly for disguise: at a distance we could pass for an Iraqi commando unit. And in part it was psychological: we were easing ourselves into a new skin. We'd have to think and act like the enemy now, if we were to outwit and defeat them.

We slipped on our goggles, because of the dust thrown up by the vehicles in front, and in case we hit a sandstorm. We weren't wearing gloves for the drive in. It was a night move, so it was going to be cold, but if it was any warmer than freezing it was best not to wear them. You needed skin on metal when you were in the fierce heat of a contact and operating all sorts of weapons systems.

By the time we were ready for the off, we were like a convoy of Mad Max lookalikes. As the first of the Pathfinder vehicles moved out into the pitch darkness, I turned to Steve and Tricky: 'Boat drinks.'

They gave me the thumbs up: 'Yeah, boat drinks it is, mate'.

CHAPTER EIGHT

We crossed the night-dark border, heading for the FOB (Forward Operating Base) from which 16 Air Assault Brigade would push further into Iraq. We'd barely got our wheels spinning when the sky before us dissolved into a sheet of flame. There was a massive firestorm on the horizon ahead, like a vast nuclear cloud. We'd been warned that the Iraqi forces might fire the oil wells in an effort to prevent us advancing through the desert. This was the result.

Away from the inferno, the terrain was pitch black and still. It was a vast, featureless sea of nothingness. But right ahead of us was this series of fierce glowing fountains. As we drew closer it became obvious how huge the angry orange eruptions actually were: each was a mountain of fire gushing up from below the earth, some several hundred metres high, and each was slightly mushroom-ish in shape, as if a cluster of atomic bombs was going off in slow motion.

As we got to within a few hundred metres of the first fiery geyser we were no longer cold. Instead, the burning heat was roasting the exposed parts of our faces. Five minutes of driving followed in the scorching heat, a deafening roar in our ears as the fire spurted high into the air, and then we were past that first torched well.

We pushed onwards, further wells gushing fiery volcanoes of oil all around us. For twenty minutes or so the heat was burning our faces and our backs, and then we finally found ourselves heading into the cold blankness of the night. It crossed my mind that each fiery eruption represented millions of dollars' worth of oil going up in smoke. But this was exactly what the Iraqis had done during the First Gulf War, back in 1991. When they were driven out of Kuwait they made sure to leave nothing of value behind them. They left only scorched earth and burning oil, the oil well fires being declared an environmental catastrophe.

I found myself wondering how long it was since the Iraqis had torched these wells. And where had the perpetrators gone? There wasn't the slightest sign of any locals anywhere, let alone the Iraqi military. In 1991 the Iraqi soldiers had largely run away, leaving only abandoned positions and burned-out wreckage behind them. It looked as if they might be planning to do the same this time.

We surged ahead on one of the main tarmac roads that penetrated into southern Iraq. At some stage we veered on to a minor track, and then we were heading into the open desert. We pulled into the location of the FOB, which was isolated from the main highway. It consisted of rocky terrain interspersed with the odd tuft of grass.

First light was at 0500 hours, and by that time we were stationary in our desert leaguer. We'd been on the road for a good few hours, it was freezing cold and the first priority was to get a brew on. As the day dawned it didn't seem to get a great deal warmer. The sky was strangely grey and overcast, and it looked as if the weather might be changing.

We'd been up all night driving, but we were still very much awake, for we've just crossed into a hostile war zone. The 1991 Gulf War had been a race to drive the retreating Iraqi forces out of Kuwait, then home for tea and medals. So far, it looked as if this war was going to go the same way. But even so we were now in a platoon leaguer in potentially hostile terrain, with the vehicles in all-around defence.

A half-hearted sunrise revealed an expanse of featureless rock and sand stretching as far as the eye could see in all directions. It was a flat-as-a-pancake stretch of bare nothingness. In the centre of the leaguer a couple of tents were being thrown up for the Brigade's forward HQ, and above and behind us in the distance we could still see the fiery black clouds of burning oil.

As the dawn light painted the desert a weird, sandy grey, we were doubly alert, and crouched over our weapons. For all we knew there could be Iraqi forces dug in a few hundred metres away, watching and waiting. With the sun well up and no sign of the enemy, we got sentries positioned on a rolling watch, and so began the preparations for whatever operations might be pending.

There were reports coming into the HQ thick and fast. Overnight the Royal Marines had staged a daring helicopter assault to take the Al Faw peninsula – a neck of vitally strategic land that gives Iraq its only access to the sea. The Marines had faced minimal resistance, but the sad news was that they had lost eight men when a helicopter had gone down in a sandstorm. We were also receiving reports that the US Marine Expeditionary Force was steaming north to take the town of Nasiriyah, 200 kilometres inside Iraq. Nasiriyah sits astride the Tigris River, so it was a vital crossing point for forces advancing upon Baghdad.

We now knew that the Royal Marines had seized territory with little resistance, and that the US Marine Corps were moving ahead seemingly unopposed. We also knew that there were SAS and SBS units on the ground in Iraq, doing covert operations. They'd gone in from the northwest of Iraq across the Jordanian border, and they would be recceing Iraqi lines of communications and cueing up air strikes. Plus they'd be hitting suspected SCUD missile sites, to prevent them being used on allied forces or being fired into Israel, as the Iraqis had done during the First Gulf War.

We were starting to wonder when our hour of action – the Pathfinders' moment – was going to come. I thought back over Jacko's words: *I'm expecting the extraordinary from the Pathfinders ... There's going to be a lot of surprises ... and you will get used, so be patient.* Jacko was right. We needed to be patient, and await the right kind of missions for PF. We had US forces ahead of us, but it wasn't our role to advance up roads to clear and hold ground. Our key role was to be air-dropped ahead of the enemy forces, and to recce and seize terrain deep inside their territory.

We didn't establish a tented camp at the FOB, for we didn't intend to be there for long. Instead, we bivvied up beside the vehicles and tried to catch some rest. We were hoping to get bounced out on ops when the brigade commander got recce taskings that he needed doing. Sure enough, John started calling in the patrols to get their orders. Need-to-know is the foundation of OPSEC (Operational Security) in the PF, and individual patrols often have no idea what the others are up to. You can't tell what you don't know if you're captured.

As 2IC Pathfinders, I sat somewhere in the middle of that need-to-know pyramid. If I was to take over command of patrols on the ground I needed to know the basics of what each of them was up to, without knowing too much to endanger lives. Over the space of the morning all patrols apart from ours got taskings. Three were being projected into the dead ground between the US Marine Corps and us. Their orders were to observe NAIs (Named Areas of Interest) – a series of major road junctions to the north – and cue fast air strikes if they spotted enemy forces.

We watched, enviously, as those patrols left the FOB. Two headed off due north driving into the open desert terrain, whilst a third loaded their Pinkies into a Chinook heavy-lift helicopter. They were to be dropped deeper in the desert somewhere to the northeast of us. We sat around drinking brews and trying to remain positive. We could see for miles in the flat grey light, and there wasn't a thing moving in any direction apart from British soldiers and vehicles. Yet our patrol didn't seem to be going anywhere.

Apart from the British forces on the move, it was eerily empty and quiet. There were no sheep, no goats, no Bedouins and no civvie vehicles. It was like we'd landed in a ghost land, or on a dead planet. Clearly, the Iraqis knew we were coming for they had torched the oil wells, but where on earth had they got to now?

*

Around midday I was called in to the HQ tent, to get briefed on the mission being given to two of the three remaining patrols. Hundreds of kilometres to the north of us lay an Iraqi airfield called Qalat Sikar. It was around halfway between where we were now and Baghdad. The two patrols were being warned-off to recce and mark an HLS (Helicopter Landing Site) at Qalat Sikar airfield, so 1 PARA could insert by Chinook and secure it.

Qalat Sikar had to be a good 150 kilometres inside the Iraqi front lines. Once seized, it would become the stepping stone that would enable 16 Air Assault Brigade to punch far ahead of the Iraqi forces. The British forces, plus the US Marine Corps, would use Qalat Sikar to launch airborne assaults deep into Iraq. In short, seizing Qalat Sikar was the key to the allied advance and to seizing Baghdad, and it could literally win us the war. It was the mission to die for.

One of the two patrols slated for the mission was led by corporal Kurt 'Geordie' Martin, a veteran PF operator who was viewed with massive respect. The other was led by Lance Green, Tricky's sparring partner. We watched enviously as those twelve men rushed around preparing for the mother of all missions. As Pathfinders we all wanted to face the ultimate test, like a pro footballer who was itching to play in a cup final. But right now it looked as if we were going to miss out on the Pathfinder mission of a lifetime.

It struck me that Qalat Sikar was the kind of operation in which all six PF patrols could easily get used. My lot would be the HQ patrol, co-ordinating the others on the ground. One patrol would recce the airfield and then mark an HLS, into which the PARAs could be landed by Chinook. Another would find a suitable DZ (Drop Zone), in case the PARAs inserted by parachute from a C130 Hercules. Other patrols would be positioned to the east, north and west of the airfield, covering NAIs like major road junctions. That way, when the PARAs were inbound we could keep a look out for Iraqi reinforcements, and hit them as required.

During the months of training back in the UK it was always HQ patrol – my boys – that went in to co-ordinate the marking of any crucial DZ and HLS. Other patrols would be out finding the enemy and calling in air strikes to smash them. I felt like we'd earned the Qalat Sikar mission, like we deserved it. I went to have a quiet word with the OC. John and I knew each other well from 1 PARA days, and in a way my relationship to him was like Tricky's to me.

During John's PF selection I had been his DS (Directing Staff) – akin to being his instructor-cum-examiner. At some stage during his selection I was tasked with giving John a 'gypsies warning' – the nod that he was close to failing selection due to what many saw as his over-confidence. As a result, I felt as if John and I had something of a special relationship – just as Tricky and I did – and I wanted to support him in making the right decisions in command.

John was busy on the radio-telephone, so I went to join Jason and Geordie at the ops planning table. Jason and I were hoping that somehow we were going to get a slice of the action on this one. If it turned into anything bigger than a two-patrol mission, John would have to send us, for we were the only other patrol at the FOB.

Jason and I scrutinised the maps and the satellite photos. Qalat Sikar was hardly Heathrow's Terminal Five. It was a minor airfield even by Iraqi standards. But the assessment by our intel boys was that it wasn't heavily occupied, and the airstrip was still usable.

'Can't be driving up to the airfield,' Jason remarked. 'Have a look at the ground – it's wet as fuck up around there. There's no way to get access cross-country in the Pinkies.'

'Too right, mate,' I agreed. 'Para-insertion is the only sound way to go in. We need to warn-off John to get Brigade cueing up the C130s, and to make sure our chutes are ready. Or what about Chinooks, flying in to drop the vehicles?'

Jason studied the map some more. 'Yeah, but they'd have to drop offset from the airfield, from where you'd still have the same problem driving across country. Plus there are outbuildings and there'll be shepherds and goats and shit. They'll hear the helos landing and that'll give the game away before it's even started.'

I turned to Geordie: 'What's your thinking, mate?'

'It's gonna have to be para-insertion,' said Geordie. 'Question is, have they got the balls to let us do it?'

'I'll go speak to John,' I told him. 'Any other way and you're fucked.'

I caught John as he came off the radio. I asked him if the Qalat Sikar mission was a definite. He told me that it was looking pretty damn likely. I asked him if those going in were going to jump. John said it all depended whether the Army high command had the guts to let them do so. The risks of a HALO insertion so deep inside Iraq were real, but we all knew it was the only viable way to make the Qalat Sikar mission happen.

'John, we've got to para for this one,' I told him. 'Can we at least get the Hercs allocated, and make sure they're getting the chutes ready?'

John gave me a grin. 'What's with the "we", Dave?' He paused for an instant to let the point sink in: *Your patrol's not going*. At the moment, it's Geordie and Lance's mission. I need to keep you in reserve, as you're the only spare team I've got.'

I shrugged. 'We live in hope, mate. Either way it still has to be a para-insertion, and the Hercs are back in Kuwait, as are the parachutes. It's one hell of a lot to organise.'

'Maybe you're right,' John conceded. 'But either way I'll have to go speak to Jacko Page first.'

'If they try sending us in by vehicle we're constrained to use the roads,' I told him, "cause the terrain up around Qalat Sikar is boggy and impassable. That means we'll be vulnerable to ambush the whole way. And that means we might not even get there. If we want the patrols to get to the airfield without getting compromised and recce and mark it, they need to go in by air.'

John eyed me for a second. I could sense his reluctance. 'Yeah, maybe. But remember Arnhem. Everyone's going to be flapping about the first British para-insertion in sixty years.'

'Yeah, but this isn't Arnhem. It's not dropping thousands of soldiers into an unknown area with bad intel. We're talking a dozen guys. We've trained and practised for this a thousand times, and you know we'll hit the IP.'

The IP is the impact point – the exact spot on which a force doing a para-insertion is supposed to land.

John shrugged. 'I know, but people will still be flapping that once the lads are there they'll be on foot with no vehicles if it all goes Pete Tong.'

Jason appeared at my side. 'Dave's right, boss: there's only one workable route in, and that's by air. It's the only way to do it.'

It was great to have Jason's support. 'We're at war, John,' I added, 'and people can't expect us to do missions like this without any risk. Right now if we don't go in by air, we're …'

'But this war is far from being popular,' John cut in. 'You guys know that. And the last thing the politicians and the generals want is to have another Bravo Two Zero on their hands.'

'Yeah, obviously,' I countered, 'but this is a game of chess, and we have to make the right move. If they want us to recce and secure the airfield they've got to get us there in the most tactically sound way possible. Once we're on the ground the risk is minimised, 'cause 1 PARA comes in on the back of us. We have to do a para-insert. There's no other way.'

There was silence for a second, before John announced that he'd go speak to Jacko about the options for an airborne insertion. As I watched him go, a part of me felt sorry for him. He'd been OC Pathfinders for less than four months and now he had to call this one. No doubt about it, the poor bastard was in at the fucking deep end.

Jase and I went to get a brew. By now Dez, Joe, Steve and Tricky knew there was something big going down, and they pitched in to the debate on how best to do the mission. We were all of the same mind: a para-insertion was the only way to do it. Qalat Sikar was over 300 kilometres to the north of where we were now, and far beyond the Iraqi front line. No one was going to make it in there overland and stay undetected.

If we parachuted in and found the enemy in significant numbers, then we'd radio in their positions and use our air power to smash them. But we would need the PARAs to come in rapidly on the back of us, for a dozen-odd Pathfinders couldn't hold that airfield indefinitely. The runway might be damaged, but we had Special Forces pilots who could fly the first wave of Chinooks in and land the PARAs just about anywhere.

The Special Forces Flight of 7 Squadron RAF had been formed in 1982, in the direct aftermath of the Falklands conflict, and in response to the need for specialist helicopter support to the UK Special Forces. Its pilots operated the Chinook HC2, which had improved avionics, electronic countermeasures, crew protection, fuel tanks and range, plus in-flight refuelling capabilities. If anyone could get the PARAs into Qalat Sikar safely, then the 7 Squadron aircrew could.

Depending on the state of the runway we could even call the PARAs in by C130 Hercules, in a TALO (Tactical Air Landing Operation). I'd orchestrated a TALO before, when the PARAs flew into Lungi Low airfield, in Sierra Leone, at the height of the civil war. The C130s put down with their ramps already lowered, and the PARAs drove off as the Hercs taxied along the runway, and took off again. We could para-insert under cover of darkness, recce and secure the airstrip using night vision kit, then clear the PARAs in for a Chinook insertion or a TALO. And that'd be it – job done.

We'd have leapfrogged the Iraqi front line by hundreds of kilometres. The enemy could then be hit from all sides, which would mess up their command and control, not to mention their supply lines. This was also about force projection: from Qalat Sikar we'd be within striking distance of the prize – Baghdad. This kind of mission was exactly what we'd trained for: the airfield was away from major settlements, it wasn't heavily guarded and it was relatively easy to defend. It was a peachy mission, and we all of us desperately wanted in on this one.

There was another big advantage to seizing Qalat Sikar. An army at war has a very heavy logistics chain – ammo, food, fuel, water. The only way to resupply forces here in Iraq was to drive up by road from Kuwait. Our resupply convoys were massively vulnerable to ambush, and if the enemy blocked the route the logistics chain would be buggered. That in turn would mean the war would take longer, and we'd take more casualties. But if we seized Qalat Sikar, that would open up an air bridge for resupply. Any way you looked at it, the Qalat Sikar mission had to be a winner.

Whichever PF patrols were sent in, they'd most likely go in by HALO as it is the quickest way to penetrate enemy territory, and land a body of men as a patrol, or a group of patrols. The IP would likely be offset a few kilometres from Qalat Sikar airfield, in case enemy forces were present in numbers. From there the patrols would infiltrate on foot and begin their recces.

However, if there was an air-to-air or ground-to-air threat – hostile enemy aircraft or missile batteries – then HAHO (High Altitude High Opening) would be the preferred means of insertion. Likewise, if there was a chance of the enemy detecting the Hercules by radar, which might alert them to parachutists being dropped into their territory, you'd again opt for a HAHO insertion. Saddam's forces were known to have good surface-to-air missile batteries and radar.

In HAHO your canopy would open automatically as you jumped off the aircraft, as each man was attached to a static line. You could be released many, many kilometres from the target and glide in. Each jumper would be wearing a specially insulated suit and mask, as protection against the freezing temperatures at high altitude. That would keep them warm as they drifted into target, the patrol floating to earth together with all its combat and survival gear.

On the front of your HAHO suit was a metal plate with a compass and an SP-GPRS, or 'spugger' as the lads call it. You plotted a course on the GPS to a waypoint – your IP – and the GPS would also tell you what altitude you were at. If there was reasonable ambient light, you'd use your naked eyes to scan for landmarks that you'd memorised from the maps, and to make sure you didn't collide with other parachutists.

HALO and HAHO are very specialist skills, ones reserved exclusively to military parachutists. The greatest height a civilian will normally jump from is 14,000 feet, and even then he won't be carrying anything like the amount of gear that we do. He won't be doing so at night, in difficult weather, and having been on missions already, and so feeling fatigued, and he won't be facing hostile forces.

I'd been on training exercises, and stood on an IP at night, and not heard or seen the parachutists until they had started landing right next to me. The canopy had opened so far away and at such altitude that there wasn't the slightest chance of me detecting it, and the glide in had been steady, stealthy and silent. It was like the parachutists had appeared from out of nowhere, and it reminded me of James Bond's para-descent in *Tomorrow Never Dies*.

You can do both HALO and HAHO in daylight, but doing so at night gives you greater protection from view. Most armies don't have decent NVG kit, and they don't like to operate in the dark. As Pathfinders, we're the opposite: we feel most comfortable deploying and fighting in the darkness.

The main drawback of para-insertions is the limited firepower you can carry. We HALO and HAHO with our personal weapons only, so assault rifle and pistol. We also have a sniper rifle and a Minimi light machine gun within each patrol. That is the kind of firepower that would enable us to find and fix the enemy at Qalat Sikar, and take out their command and control elements, but we'd be lacking any heavy weaponry if we came up against armour.

In PF, the decision to go in via either HAHO or HALO is the choice of the patrols. As a parachutist, you are horribly vulnerable: to bad intel; to equipment failure; to gusting wind; to your aircraft being shot down; to injury or death upon impact; to compromise or capture upon landing. But it's also the quickest, most direct and covert way to reach your target.

HAHO and HALO training is extremely expensive, and we'd recently brought a new parachute rig into PF – the BT80 – plus a new high-altitude breathing system called HAPLSS (High Altitude Parachute Life Support System). HAPLSS consists of an oxygen mask and a protective suit that enables you to survive in extremely low temperatures and at very low oxygen levels. If you were doing a HAHO jump you might be in the air under such conditions for up to forty minutes, whereupon HAPLSS is a lifesaver.

Qalat Sikar was the perfect opportunity to prove that all the investment ploughed into the BT80 parachute system and HAPLSS was worthwhile. But a part of me was worried whether John would win the argument with high command for us to do a para-insertion.

John hailed from a Scottish family, and he'd been to Robert Gordon's College, in Aberdeen. He was tall and distinguished-looking, and whilst he seemed proud of his Scottish heritage he spoke with a pukka southern English accent, which went down well with the generals at cocktail parties. Like all small, elite units the PF needed someone like him to fight our corner, and to keep getting us the resources and training we needed to stay at the top of our game.

John had charisma and a big physical presence, and if he believed in something he could charm and cajole it for the Pathfinders. But he was in a very tough position right now. He'd only been with the PF a short while, and now he was caught in the conundrum that if we para-inserted and it all went to ratshit, he'd be the guy in charge of the next Arnhem/Bravo Two Zero.

But if they tried sending us in by vehicle and we all got captured or killed, that would be equally disastrous.

CHAPTER NINE

John was showing all the signs of being under strain, and in a way it was hardly surprising. But for the men of the Pathfinders, Qalat Sikar was a dream mission. It represented the zenith of what we train for. Even the Hereford boys had never done an insertion as daring as this one, and it was the kind of tasking that the British military would talk about for years to come.

As soon as we had been warned-off to deploy to Kuwait, we'd started doing masses of HAHO and HALO continuity training. Time after time we'd jumped over the North Sea at night, and infiltrated into the UK on NVG (Night Vision Goggles) and using our GPS to navigate. We'd never be better prepared for a mission such as this one.

We were still waiting for the word from John, when I saw H, one of the true legends of the PF, approaching. H was this massive, moustachioed tandem master. Prior to coming to the PF he'd been a farmer in the northeast of England, and by anyone's reckoning he was hard as nails. He and Jason were the best parachutists we had, and amongst the most experienced in the world.

H started chatting to Jase. There was a whole lot of gesticulating, and they were clearly cooking up some kind of plan between them. They came over to me to have words. H could be very abrupt and abrasive when he wanted to get a point across. He said exactly what he thought, and as a bloke he did exactly what it said on the tin. I liked and respected him for it.

He waded right in. 'Dave if there's people bloody flapping about us parachuting, if they haven't got the balls for a couple of patrols to para in, then me and Jase can go in tandem with two others. That way we only risk four blokes and there's no way anyone can say we won't hit the IP.'

'They can drop the two of us and they know we'll hit the target,' Jason added.

'Jase's done shed loads of JTAC-ing,' said H. 'He can call in all the bloody air strikes we need. Job sorted.'

'H, Jase – I know,' I told them. 'I know you blokes could do it. Let's go speak to John and make the offer. But I reckon they'll flap even more about just four blokes going in.'

'Remember Ron Reid-Daly,' said Jason. 'The Selous Scouts. They did scores of two-man HALO insertions into Mozambique, and time and again they proved they worked.'

'Yeah, lads, I know. I hear you.'

The Selous Scouts were the Rhodesian Special Forces at the time of that country's civil war. They were some of the most experienced and battle-hardened elite soldiers in the world. They'd pioneered the technique of using small, two-man HALO teams to penetrate far behind enemy lines and call in air missions, which is exactly what H and Jase were now suggesting they do.

Recently, we'd started doing HALO and HAHO training in South Africa. It was more cost-effective than training in America, our normal venue. We'd done scores of jumps over the deserts and mountains, honing the kind of techniques used by the Selous Scouts to perfection (and similar to the mission described in the prologue to this book).

And right now I had to admire Jason's can-do attitude in suggesting they use such skills to get around the naysayers, and get into Qalat Sikar. I didn't doubt for one moment that he and H had the balls to do it, either.

The three of us went and found John outside the HQ tent. Jase and H hovered whilst I had words. I told John that if Brigade Command was worried about a load of blokes getting scattered all over the Iraqi desert, H and Jase were willing to jump in tandem and guarantee 100 per cent to hit the target.

We left John to mull it over as another of his options. With the approach of last light Geordie and Lance's patrols remained on standby for Qalat Sikar, although their method of insertion was undecided. But that evening we had some highly disturbing news radioed into PF headquarters. In the far north of Iraq a full squadron of SBS – the sister regiment to the SAS – had got compromised. Their entire mission was rapidly going to ratshit, leaving some sixty elite soldiers on the run up near the border with Syria.

The SBS squadron had flown in by Chinook, and had been dropped with their vehicles deep in the Iraqi desert. But over several days hundreds of Fedayeen (Iraqi irregular forces) had hunted down the British force, converging on their positions. The Iraqis had jeeps sporting DShKs (Dushkas) – a Soviet-era heavy anti-aircraft weapon, which is devastating when used against ground forces – plus they had Iraqi army regular units with heavy armour in support. The SBS were driving Pinkies, so they were totally outgunned.

The elite British force had made a fighting withdrawal, but during many hours of intense combat the patrol was split into smaller and smaller groups. Vehicles had got bogged down, and the SBS lads had been forced to blow up their Pinkies to prevent the enemy from seizing them. Yet several charges had failed to detonate. Under cover from allied air power, the main body of the squadron had been airlifted out. But by first light we still had at least two groups on the run, and the word was that the Iraqis would shortly be parading the captured Pinkies before the world's media.

Having those SBS blokes on the run in the north of Iraq was deeply troubling. A force of brother warriors was out there being hunted, and at the enemy's mercy. What had befallen that SBS squadron was the kind of fuck-up that could happen to any small group of elite warriors, when going far into hostile territory. It was a powerful reminder of the dangers we faced here, and of what we wanted to avoid happening to any of our patrols.

But most of all it was God-awful timing for the Qalat Sikar mission. Just as soon as the Iraqis started parading the captured Pinkies on the media, the world's press would be on to the story, so making our superiors doubly sensitive to the risks of small, elite units getting sent far behind enemy lines.

That morning we got the word that everyone had been dreading: John announced that the Qalat Sikar mission had been stood down. No reasons were given, but we figured it was due to the SBS squadron getting smashed and scattered across the deserts of northern Iraq. The two patrols slated for Qalat Sikar were immediately re-tasked. It made sense to get them out on ops, to dampen their sense of disappointment. But still, we were chomping at the bit to get used.

Finally, we were called in for our own mission briefing. It was late afternoon by the time the six of us gathered in the HQ tent. We were hoping for a tasking similar in scope and daring to Qalat Sikar. Instead, we got ordered to go recce two road bridges some 40 kilometres north of where we were now positioned. The bridges spanned a large man-made canal, and our tasking was to confirm or deny if the bridges were intact and crossable by military vehicles. The concept behind our mission was unstated, yet easy to guess at: we were recceing a potential route of advance for 16 Air Assault Brigade. With Qalat Sikar having been called off, command had to be searching for alternative ways of pushing forwards.

The Iraqis had blown the oil fields pretty comprehensively, so there was every chance they'd have blown vital infrastructure too. Our satellite imagery wasn't real time, so you couldn't take it as a given that what was shown on those images was actually there. And less still with the maps, which were even older. So it was our job to go in and prove it on the ground – a classic PF tasking. If the bridges were intact we were to hold them for forty-eight hours, to allow 16 Air Assault Brigade to move through.

This mission was hardly a Qalat Sikar – penetrating deep behind enemy lines – but it was still a potentially important tasking, one that could enable the British war effort to advance significantly. And at least we'd got a mission. We could finally get started.

We set out at last light, heading northeast and driving without lights on NVG. The weather conditions struck me as looking highly abnormal: it was overcast and chilly, and there was little ambient light, for the moon and stars were obscured by scudding cloud. It was totally different to how it had been over the few weeks in Kuwait, and it wasn't good for driving on night vision.

We were using cross-country tactical driving skills to navigate to the mission objective. We stuck to open desert terrain wherever possible, driving as fast as we could in such poor visibility. But there were large areas where rocky outcrops and wadis channelled us on to desert tracks, where we struggled to find a way through.

As we pushed onwards I thought back over our drills for getting a bogged-in vehicle moving again. Back in Kuwait we'd deliberately got one of the Pinkies stuck in soft sand, spinning the wheels until it was down to its axles. Standard operating procedure was for the team from the mobile vehicle to provide a security screen, whilst the team from the bogged vehicle worked to get it free. Folding spades just didn't provide enough digging power, so each Pinkie carried a full-length shovel strapped to one side. It was wrapped in hessian sacking to stop it glinting in the sunlight, or rattling. The slightest reflection or noise could give your position away.

Strapped to each of the vehicles were four lengths of steel sheeting with holes punched in them. Once the wheels had been freed from the worst of the sand by hard digging, the steel sheets were jammed under each of the wheels, to act as 'sand ladders'. The free vehicle was then manoeuvred into position, just ahead and on some firm ground. A reinforced baggage strap – the kind of thing used to lash cargo containers to an aircraft's hold – would be strung between the two wagons. The lead Pinkie would then drag the rear vehicle over the sand ladders and on to solid terrain.

There was never a good time to get the wagons bogged down on a mission such as this one, but at least we had it down to a fine art when it came to getting moving again. I glanced forward to the shadowy form of Jason's wagon. Jase was picking the route, whilst we kept the command wagon 100 metres or so behind. If we stuck closer together and the enemy ambushed us, both wagons were likely to get malleted in the one attack.

The lead vehicle was arguably the one that would get hit first. That was the reason the patrol commander's wagon went at the rear. We had all the comms gear with which to communicate with headquarters, plus the JTAC and his kit to call in air support. If the lead wagon came under attack, we'd use the 50-cal to give Jason covering fire while his wagon moved back beyond us, whereupon it would give covering fire to us. In essence, we'd do something similar to foot soldiers performing fire and manoeuvre drills, but by vehicle.

The further we pushed away from the FOB the worse the terrain was proving in terms of cover. It was a mixture of sparse tufts of grass, rock, some sand, and the occasional small mound. Other than that it was billiard-table flat. It was a nightmare for concealment, but fortunately we hadn't seen a single Iraqi vehicle anywhere. The entire area seemed utterly devoid of life. It was weird. Eerie. Spooky.

We approached the first bridge, whilst all the time trying to make sure we'd got a clear field of view and could fire all around us. In the thick, ominous gloom of the overcast desert night our visibility was down to a few tens of metres. We went firm and closed up the vehicles, so we could talk to each other. We ran through our options, and decided to skirt around to the south and recce a couple of kilometres beyond the bridges. That way we'd scan the terrain for any Iraqi forces, before revealing our actual objective.

We drove this wide, sweeping recce through the open desert, but the entire area seemed utterly deserted. We moved in closer and did a quick recce of the first and then the second bridge, each of which appeared to be undamaged. They were both of an iron girder-type construction, and they were clearly strong enough to take military vehicles. In fact, the canals they spanned were some 50 metres across, and each bridge was as wide as a two-lane highway.

I radioed in a sitrep (situation report) to John: 'Bridges intact. No other crossing points in immediate area. Intention to recce further afield.'

That done, we started driving north to scan for enemy presence, and prove the entire area clear of enemy forces. We did as much as we could do when the terrain all around us was obscured by a thick wall of darkness. The weather showed no sign of lifting, and we'd need to repeat our recces at first light, just to make sure we didn't bring the Brigade into a massive enemy ambush.

As we headed north there was a brooding stillness to the terrain, like the calm before the storm. We'd made about a kilometre when we were hit by the powerful blast of a chill, biting wind, gusting out of the east. It felt icy cold, and it carried with it the distinctive dirty-wet-dog smell of rain falling on baked earth. It had been burning hot for a month now, and we couldn't believe it when the wind was followed by a blast of rain. In no time the rain had turned to sleet, and then to a whiteout of snow.

Suddenly, we were in the midst of a howling winter's gale.

The Pinkies were open to the elements, but it wasn't necessarily a major drama. Recently, we'd been issued with HALO Gore-Tex jackets, which were designed specifically for high-altitude freefalling. They were manufactured from an ultra-thick Gore-Tex layer that was windproof and waterproof, and which provided a good degree of warmth. With that on over my North Face down jacket – designer labels snipped out, of course – I'd be fairly toasty despite the weather.

We'd got similar HALO Gore-Tex over-trousers. We'd only ever wear them when freefalling from altitude, or when the weather turned abysmal, because they were noisy to walk in and could give your position away. We'd also been issued with several pairs of gloves, including leather ones for driving in the cold (they dry out quickly when placed on a warm engine), plus Gore-Tex gloves for para-insertions, or for adverse-weather. Now was most definitely the time to use all our adverse-weather gear.

Jason pulled over and we pulled up alongside him, so we could break out our bad-weather kit. We were halfway through getting suited and booted, when Steve noticed that Tricky wasn't bothering with any of his cold-weather gear.

'So what's with you not bothering with your Gore-Tex?' he asked. 'You waterproof or something?'

Tricky shrugged. 'Nah, but I'm all right without it, mate.'

I glanced behind me to his position on the rear: 'What d'you mean, *you're all right without it*? It's been pissing down and now it's blowing a blizzard.'

Tricky was looking distinctly uncomfortable. He was trying to ignore it, but he was soaked to the skin and getting wetter and colder by the minute, and his position on the rear of the wagon was by far the most exposed.

Finally, he admitted his problem: 'The thing is, lads, I left all my Gore-Tex gear back in the FOB.'

'*You did what?*' Steve and I demanded.

By now Tricky was practically cringing with embarrassment. I'd rarely if ever seen him in such a state, and I was amazed that he could have got himself into such a predicament. Still, he was only human, and if I was honest with myself it had crossed my mind to leave my wet weather gear behind as well. I'd opted to squeeze it into my bergen just to be on the safe side, but I'd been that close to doing otherwise.

It was impossible not to see the funny side of his predicament, and Steve and I started laughing. Jason glanced across at us and smiled. It was rare to get a laugh out of Jase when on ops, but there was real warmth to his smile. He jerked his head in Dez's direction, as if to say – *Get some of this!* Dez was hunched over the steering wheel without a scrap of wet-weather gear, looking soggy and frozen.

'Dez, mate, where's your Gore-Tex?' Jason demanded.

'I left it in Kuwait,' Dez muttered. He looked like a child who knew he'd been naughty and was just getting found out.

'Why d'you do that?' Jase needled him.

Dez shrugged. 'Well, 'cause Tricky left his, so I thought it'd be okay.'

Both wagons were rocking with laughter now, Jason's Popeye cackle kicking in alongside ours. Even Joe was chuckling, though he was trying not to be too obvious about it, in deference to Tricky. That had Steve and me in tears.

Every patrol member could choose what kit to take on operations. After a month sunning ourselves in Kuwait, Tricky had clearly decided to stuff in a few more mags of ammo and throw out his cold weather gear. Dez must have seen him do it and followed suit. It was a bone decision if ever there was one.

Tricky tried a smile and a laugh, but it had a sheepish ring to it. As for Dez, it was like he was sulking. It was coming down in stair rods now. A howling gale of sleet mixed with freezing rain was battering all around us. There was no more recceing to be done with the weather like this, plus the two of them in such a shit state. Beneath the humour, we were all of us aware of how quickly this could turn nasty.

Jase voiced the obvious: 'We've got to go find some cover and get those two into some shelter.'

After twenty minutes' driving we came across a small road bridge crossing a wadi. It was a solid concrete construction that offered us more shelter from the elements than the iron girder canal bridges. We took cover by driving the wagons into the wadi, which got them and us out of sight and below ground level. It also got us out of the worst of the wind. It wasn't a moment too soon. It was around midnight by now, and Tricky and Dez were shivering like fuck. They were clearly into the early stages of hypothermia, and whilst we were sheltered from the worst of the storm it was only marginally warmer down here.

We got the vehicles parked up so we could make a rapid exit if need be. Jase put Steve out on the first sentry duty with his Minimi light machine gun, whilst I sent a sitrep to PF HQ. We'd seen no sign of any Iraqis, and we reckoned the weather was now our greatest enemy. Tricky and Dez didn't seem particularly aware of it, but they were starting to slur their words, as the hypothermia kicked in.

Soaked through to the skin, they rapidly lost body heat. Dez looked to be the worst. His face had an icy tinge to it, his teeth were chattering with the cold and his hands were shaking uncontrollably. Even though we were in some shelter he didn't appear to be getting any warmer. The only option was to break standard operating procedure by brewing up, to get some hot liquid into him.

'Nothing for it,' Jason grunted, jerking a thumb in Dez's direction. 'Let's get a brew on. Joe?'

Joe grabbed a hexy stove – a simple fold-up metal cooking stove about the size of your average book – and dug a scoop in the rocky earth to make a fire pit. He folded the stove into its cooking position, and pulled out a couple of opaque, whitish fuel blocks much like household firelighters. He held a lighter to the first one, dropped it into the stove, and soon had a brew going. He laced the tea with spoonfuls of sugar, then poured it into the patrol mug, an aluminium monster with fold-out steel handles and a pint capacity.

We always shared the one brew mug when out on operations, in case we had to move out quickly. We might get spotted at any moment by the enemy, so we kept it simple and passed the brew around from man to man in the one mug. This time we made sure that Dez and Tricky each got a good half pint of the steaming liquid down them. Joe brewed up a second time, and as we shared that around the chat got going.

I gestured at the storm raging all around us. 'Fucking unbelievable. Just when we get a mission, this shit has to come down.'

'Murphy's Law,' said Steve. 'If it can go wrong it will.'

Jase gave an affirmative grunt. 'Expect the unexpected.'

In the back of each of our minds was the Bravo Two Zero mission, from the First Gulf War. In 1991 eight SAS blokes were airlifted into Iraq and forced to go on the run, whereupon the weather did exactly as it had done now. Those without adequate cold weather gear quickly went down with hypothermia. The weather proved to be the one enemy that they couldn't defeat. Three men died, four were captured and only one escaped. The long shadow of Bravo Two Zero has hung over Special Forces soldiering ever since then. But no one seemed to want to give voice to this, not whilst Dez and Tricky were still in such a bad way.

Steve turned the chat to food. 'You know what, I bet those Yank Spec-Ops guys are loving their treacle pudding, now the weather's turned to shit.'

'Yeah, well they probably need it more than us,' I remarked. 'They're the only ones who seem to be heading for where the enemy are right now.'

It felt to me that once Qalat Sikar had been stood down, we'd been pretty much sidelined in this war. Steve started banging on about some girl he'd been seeing in the UK, while the rest of us tried to get some kip. I burrowed into my sleeping bag fully clothed and with my boots on, my roll mat spread below me. I curled into a ball but I was still cold.

There was a gale howling beneath the bridge, and I couldn't imagine how Tricky and Dez had to be feeling.

CHAPTER TEN

By first light it was still blowing a blizzard, and it was murderously cold. Tricky and Dez were slurring their words, and they were growing noticeably listless. We broke SOPs for a second time and brewed tea, plus we heated up some food. Joe whacked a job lot of Lancashire hotpot into an old ammo tin, chucked in a load of the Tabasco sauce that we'd got off the Spec-Ops boys, and bunged it on to the hexy stove. None of us had ever dreamed of eating Lancashire hotpot in Iraq. It is a thick meat stew with balls of dough swimming in it, and it was the perfect scoff for these kind of conditions.

With the weather continuing to batter us there was no way we could do any more recces. With Tricky and Dez in such a bad way *and worsening*, I put the call through to PF HQ. I explained our predicament to John, and he made the decision to call us back in. There was little more we could achieve here, especially not with two guys fast going down with hypothermia.

Crawling along at 45 kph in a raging storm the wind-chill factor was deadly, and the drive back was freezing and bitter. It felt never-ending, even for those of us with every part of our bodies shielded by Gore-Tex. Tricky had refused to swop his position on the 50-cal for somewhere more sheltered. We stuck to the main roads to speed things up, and get him and Dez back to the FOB as quickly as possible. By the time we reached it their faces had turned horribly puffy and blue.

We stuffed them into dry, warm clothing, then into sleeping bags and bivvie bags and into one of the tents. We forced them to eat some more hot food, and to drink endless brews. In the shelter and the warmth they slowly started to thaw out and come to life, and it was clear that the worst was over. It was now that we felt able to give the pair of them the slagging they deserved.

'Didn't you blokes ever read B2Z?' I ventured. B2Z was the slang we used for Bravo Two Zero.

'Yeah, that lot hit the worst snow storms in decades,' Steve chipped in. 'Remember? Just like we've done!'

All we got from Tricky and Dez were some sheepish looks. Still, I guessed they'd learned their lesson. I was amazed that Tricky could have gone out on operations without his cold-weather kit. He was an old hand. The ultimate PF soldier. It was almost unthinkable for him to have made such a basic error.

I'd first run into Tricky back in 1999, in Sierra Leone. I'd been there with 1 PARA, and Tricky had been there with the Pathfinders. I'd witnessed him and the other PF lads in combat in the jungle, smashing the murderous Sierra Leonean RUF rebels, and it was that experience that had made me decide to go for PF selection.

It was an SAS veteran – Aidey Warren – who first devised PF selection. It works on the SAS model, but it is shorter – six weeks, as opposed to six months. Basically, the salient tests of physical and mental fitness were pulled out of SAS selection, with the same times required to pass. Some claim that PF selection covers the same ground as SAS in less time, which makes it more intense and challenging. Others argue that is bollocks: it is quicker, which lowers the attrition rate. Most of us in the Pathfinders don't particularly care either way. It's PF selection. It's unique. It does what it says on the tin.

I'd pitched up for selection in the Brecon Beacons in the midst of a bitter winter. There were thirty-five of us, and we knew only a handful would make it. We were straight into the 8-miler forced march, which had to be done in one hour sixteen over the hills. We started losing guys in the first ten minutes, with knees or ankles gone, or simply from exhaustion. But it gave me a massive confidence boost when I recognised that my DS for that 8-miler was Tricky.

From the start Tricky made it clear that we had to really, really burn for it if we wanted to get into the Pathfinders. If you didn't truly burn for it, you were welcome to start VWing (Voluntary Withdrawing) yourself at any time. Tricky was taking the fitness and communications modules of selection, plus he was one of the six guys demoing how to go down the ranges. It was awesome watching him work his weapons. It was like the final scene from the movie *Heat*, when the bank robbers have to fight their way out of this trap set by US law enforcement agents.

Tricky also got up on the hills with us. He led the most extreme tabs in the worst possible weather, showing by example how to deal with the atrocious conditions on the mountains. In the Pathfinders you had to be able to operate in all kinds of climates, so on group exercises you'd pretty much go out in any kind of weather. You were more likely to get hypothermia or be injured on the individual test marches, but even then the DS would only pull you off the hills in absolute extremis.

We'd come off the Brecon Beacons into the showers, then we'd be straight on to tests in navigation, mountain safety, cold-weather kit and survival. Too many guys had died on SAS selection, so you had to prove you knew how to survive before they threw you alone and unaided on to those unforgiving peaks. All of which made it doubly surprising that Tricky had been caught out so badly by the weather in Iraq.

PF selection is run from the same camp over the same routes as the SAS. I can remember the times I dragged myself out of bed at an exhausting 0300, to shovel down a massive breakfast, and then clamber into a four-tonner truck for the long drive to the Elan Valley. You'd huddle together to share body warmth, because the thin canvas let the cold air come streaming in. I'd find my mind playing tricks on me. *Do I really need this?* I'd be thinking. *I could opt for an easy life with the lads back in my unit.*

By the time we'd reached the Elan Valley one guy or more would have decided to VW. They'd be left sitting on the truck as the rest of us set off into the hills. And occasionally someone would VW right after the tab was over: 'Staff – I'm not doing that again.' Ever more extreme forced marches followed, interspersed with weapons drills, and medical, comms and demolition skills lessons. And every day your pack was filled with more and more gear.

The starting weight of your bergen was 35 pounds, not including water and food. It was increased in 10-pound increments, all of which weight was necessary for military or mountain survival. No one carried any dead weight just to make up the load. Your kit included a GPS beacon that enabled the DS to track you over the hills. It was a bulletproof way of stopping people from cheating. If they noticed your tracker beacon was suddenly moving at 80 kph, they'd know you'd hitched a lift and you'd get binned immediately.

There were random checkpoints along the routes, where the DS would weigh your bergen, to make sure you hadn't filled it with water at the start and then emptied it out. You had to carry a deactivated SLR assault rifle, which you had to keep gripped in your hands at all times as you marched. On PF selection you're forbidden to use any roads or tracks that a vehicle can navigate, plus you're forbidden to use your weapon as a walking stick, which at times of sheer exhaustion was hugely tempting. If you got caught doing any of those things you were made to run up and down the nearest peak, and then told to carry on.

We were all dressed in combat fatigues with no markings, but a DS was set apart by wearing the distinctive maroon top of the Pathfinders. It sports the PF cap badge – a directional arrow, superimposed over wings, with a parachute in the middle. Even though you're totally fucked after the first week, and your feet are sore and blistered, and you're permanently dizzy from dehydration, you have to try to be reasonably together when you reach the DS manning the checkpoints. You were free to leave selection and return to the unit you came from at any time. All you needed to say was: 'Staff, I want to VW.'

There was one guy on my selection who was an Army ultra-marathon runner. He was extremely fit, and he had a 'No Fear' tattoo on his right shoulder. I'd spotted it early on when we were in the showers. We came to the final, 64-kilometre endurance march, the ultimate test in PF selection. We hit the 2-kilometre mark, where the route starts to climb this massive, all but sheer mountain. I was one of the last to set off, and I was part way up that horrendous cliff face when I spotted that bloke doubling back and coming down past me. I never did see him again. Incredibly, he'd fallen at the final hurdle and VWd.

I passed PF selection, although an injury on that final endurance march came very close to killing me. And once I was into the Path-finders proper the real challenges began. It was then that I had to learn the craft. Invariably in a PF recce unit the maximum force you'll ever reach is a six- or twelve-man patrol. You needed to be happy operating as a small group of very determined individuals. In the regular infantry it was all about going forwards and attacking as a company or a battalion – so 100 or 700-plus strength, and with the might of the Army and the Air Force behind you. In PF you'd be a tiny, isolated unit far into hostile terrain.

If you came across an enemy position it was likely to be a company at least, and you'd expect to be heavily outnumbered and out-gunned. Your skills were all about how to break contact, extract from the kill zone and disappear. That had to be slick and instinctive if you were to have any chance of survival. You practised to death how to respond to contact from front, side or rear. The IA (Immediate Action) drill was that whoever was contacted put down rounds, and shouted 'Contact front left!' or whatever. As a unit you'd concentrate fire on that target.

Whoever spotted a piece of cover to retreat to would shout 'Peel left!' or 'Peel right!' Any individual could then nominate a rally point: 'Rally on me!' You practised with full bergens and day sacks, and you rehearsed your 'man down' procedures for getting an injured bloke on to your shoulders and out of there. In the Mobility Cadre of PF training you repeated that process, only this time with your vehicles. You also did your specialist comms and recce training.

You learned how to find, assess and report the info that the brigade commander needed – the recce mission objective. You learned to report via long-distance HF radio, bouncing signals off the ionosphere, and by data-secure cryptographic means. You learned how to make rapid sketch maps of enemy positions, whilst wearing surgical gloves so that your reports remained clear and legible, despite the fact that you were filthy dirty.

But as much as Pathfinders were challenged physically, we were also challenged mentally. We were taught to operate in a different reality, to embrace what others feared. We were taught to possess the night, to inhabit the darkness. We were taught to be totally at home under moonlight, in starlight and in sheer black. Darkness was the cloak with which to hide our operations. We learned to love the darkness and make the night our own.

We were taught to seek out bad terrain, margins, arid desert and remote bush – anywhere abandoned by humans. And we were taught to seek out the worst, shittiest weather imaginable – conditions within which covert operators like Pathfinders could thrive. Or at least, where we were *supposed to thrive*.

After our first Iraq mission, I didn't hold Tricky's failure to bring his cold-weather kit against him. After all, we were all human. Whilst Tricky and Dez recovered from their ordeal, the rest of us wrote up the patrol report on the bridges mission. I read it back to the lads before submitting it, just in case I'd missed anything. We had no idea if the Brigade would use the route across the bridges to advance further into Iraq. It wasn't our need to know.

In spite of the appalling weather conditions we'd accomplished our mission, and we were expecting to get rapidly re-tasked. But we hadn't slept properly for several nights now, and were badly in need of some kip. It had stopped raining and snowing, but it was still bitterly cold. There were no tents available, so we wrapped up well and crashed out beside the vehicles, which did provide a little shelter from the wind.

The other patrols were all out on missions, so we could only presume that they'd got far sexier taskings than our bridges recce. The one consolation was this: if any mission did come in to PF HQ it would have to be given to us, for we were the only patrol left in camp.

At first light – 0500 – I was woken by the PF sergeant major, Ray Oldman, AKA the 'White Rabbit'. Ray looked almost albino in appearance, with his snowy hair and blue eyes tinged with red. He had a wild intensity about him, which made it all the more appropriate that he'd earned the White Rabbit nickname. Like many soldiers who'd seen a massive amount of combat, he had a wired look about his eyes that's also known as the 'thousand yard stare'.

Ray warned me off to prepare for our next mission. He had this weird gleam in his eyes as he did so. He gave me the nod. This was the big one.

'Better get your arse into the ops tent,' he told me. 'Qalat Sikar is back on …'

From being in the midst of the deepest sleep, I was instantly wide awake. This was the equivalent of being pulled off the reserve benches, and being told you were on for the world cup final. I was fucking buzzing. I told myself: *Fuck having a brew!* I needed to see John soonest and find out what exactly he'd got in store for us.

I'd taught myself to be good at coming instantly awake. I needed to be able to snap out of a deep sleep and make immediate decisions. One of the tricks of doing so was to eat well and to drink bucket loads of water before going to sleep. You might need to piss in the night, but you'd wake up with good energy levels and feeling well hydrated.

I woke the lads: 'Boys, orders in fifteen minutes.'

Jason grunted: 'What for?'

I said the magic words: 'Qalat Sikar.'

As soon as Tricky heard that he was up instantly and into action. Jason wasn't an early morning person, and he always took a good few minutes to get fully active. But even so the words 'Qalat Sikar' had got him crawling out of his doss bag and rubbing the sleep out of his eyes. As for Steve, he lay there for a second grinning like an idiot.

'Just give me a mo' while I deal with me semi,' he remarked, dreamily. There was this horrible, rhythmic rustling from within his sleeping bag. I hoped to hell he was bluffing, the dirty bastard.

I glanced at Joe. 'Joe?'

Joe shook the sleep from his young head. 'Qalat Sikar – wicked.'

I turned my gaze on Dez. 'Best you pack your Gore-Tex,' I joked.

Dez gave a sheepish grin. 'Just got to hope the sun keeps shining on us lot, eh?'

Inside the HQ tent it was buzzing. John had the PF signallers rushing around gathering documents, comms equipment and sat photos.

He nodded at us as we entered: 'All right guys? All good? Slept well?'

As the six of us took out seats John gathered his shit together, laying out the mission folders on the briefing table. He took a stand out front, the White Rabbit on his shoulder.

He gave us this warm smile: 'Right, lads, you got it: Qalat Sikar is back on.' He paused, letting the words hang in the air. 'But we need to wait one before I can do the briefing proper, 'cause you've got a three-man Engineer Recce Team coming with you.'

John could read the reaction on our faces. We were about to go far behind enemy lines and we'd got this dumped on us: we were getting a unit of Engineers tacked on to our patrol. The Engineer Recce Teams were exactly what they sound like: Royal Engineers trained-up for recce taskings. They were a newly-formed unit, and the reasoning behind having them was so that they could come in on the back of a mission like Qalat Sikar and repair the airstrip.

There was no selection process prior to joining an Engineer Recce Team. Needless to say, they weren't supposed to do the actual recce insertion and be the spearhead, which was the *raison d'être* of the Pathfinders. We'd never worked with the Engineer Recce blokes, but we knew they weren't para-trained and that they didn't know our SOPs. On a mission such as this one it was the very last thing that we needed.

John held up his hand to silence any objections. 'Guys, *I know*. It's far from being ideal, but mostly this is politics. You'll need to trust me on this one and go with it, okay, 'cause those are the orders.'

The CO of the Engineer Recce Teams was an ex-SAS bloke that I knew well. We Pathfinders had long been nurtured by the SAS, and he was clearly calling a favour back off us, by inserting his Recce Team on to our mission. We had to presume that he'd selected three of his best, in which case it was a fair one. Either way this was an order from on high, so we had no choice but to crack on. John told us to ready the patrol so we could deploy in three hours' time. He'd brief us fully on the mission once the Engineer Recce blokes had arrived.

We got busy refilling water bottles, and double-checking the wagons. Dez had never once stopped tinkering with the vehicles, and they were pretty much shipshape and ready to go. But I figured we wouldn't be needing the Pinkies on this one. We were going in to take Qalat Sikar and that had to mean parachuting in, and maybe with the Engineer Recce Guys tandemmed to us.

With Qalat Sikar being a good 300 kilometres away we clearly couldn't go in on foot. If we tried to drive in, we'd be risking the same fate that had befallen that SBS squadron that had got so badly compromised in northern Iraq. The fate of those sixty elite operators had to play to our advantage, and make the chances of getting cleared to go in via parachute that much higher.

At 0545 we gathered in the HQ tent for John's briefing. The atmosphere was electric. The three Engineer Recce guys joined us and took their seats at the back. Typically for Engineers, they were big, beefy blokes.

'Right, guys, as you know, Qalat Sikar is back on,' John announced. He was clearly excited, but he was trying not to show it. 'The situation is that 16 Air Assault Brigade, along with the US Marine Corps, wishes to seize the airfield and use it as a base from which to mount attacks into the rest of Iraq.'

Because we were the only patrol left at the FOB, the mission had fallen to the six of us, John explained. As Qalat Sikar had been originally tasked to two PF patrols – a dozen men – it made sense to have extra blokes with us, and so the Engineer Recce team had been asked to make up the numbers. John went on to outline the one major downside to the Qalat Sikar mission as it was now constituted: when push had come to shove, high command had baulked at an airborne insertion.

Instead, we were being ordered to go in using the vehicles, which meant that we had a massive drive ahead of us into the heart of hostile territory. If we were to attempt this mission overland, I figured that having one extra vehicle mounted with two GPMGs – the Engineer Recce Team wagon – might well prove useful. But either way, switching from a para-insertion to a vehicle insertion was about as close to madness as ever you could get in the British military.

It was a golden rule of soldiering that you never interrupted the OC's orders. At the end of his brief was the time to get vocal, if you needed to. And for sure I had several issues I needed to raise with John on this one.

'The mission is being led by your patrol, David,' John continued, 'with the three guys from the Engineers in support. What's your names, guys?'

'Ian Andrews.'

'Simon James.'

'Stephen Altry.'

'Okay, Ian, Simon, Stephen – welcome to the party,' said John. 'This is your collective mission: move by vehicle to Qalat Sikar airfield. Recce and mark the airfield in order to facilitate a 1 PARA battle group SH insertion.'

SH stood for support helicopters – Army-speak for Chinooks. Once we reached Qalat Sikar we'd need to mark an HLS (Helicopter Landing Site) for the Chinooks to put the PARAs on to.

'Timing,' John continued. '1 PARA battle group L-Hour 24-0400 Zulu.'

This meant that the Landing Hour for the PARAs was 24 March, at 0400 Zulu – local – time. I was immediately thinking: *Fuck me, that's less than twenty-four hours from now!* In the meantime we had to work out a mission plan and the possible routes in, decide actions-on, plus get ourselves to the airfield.

Once we reached the airfield we'd got to do a 360-degree recce, and clear and mark an HLS. Plus we'd got to get the Engineer lads checking for any obstacles and making good the runway, so the airfield could be made usable as quickly as possible. In short, it had all the appearance of a race against time on mission bloody impossible.

John moved on to the intel brief. 'The intel picture is as follows: the US Marines are advancing towards Nasiriyah, 150 kilometres to the north of us. They're expecting to encounter limited Iraqi resistance, so there will be contacts, but nothing overly significant. There is assumed to be "no significant enemy threat" in Nasiriyah.'

'Between Nasiriyah and Qalat Sikar there are no known Iraqi positions,' John continued. 'The intel assessment is that the area is "relatively benign". There's an intel pack in the Ops Box with satellite imagery, humint [human intelligence] reports and other bits and pieces, plus Geordie and Lance's patrol planning file.'

John finished with this: 'Brigade absolutely needs you to make 1 PARA's L-Hour, and so you need to reach and secure that airfield urgently. That's the deal, guys. Any questions? And keep 'em short ...'

'The obvious one: why by vehicle?' I queried. 'Why can't we para-insert?'

'I forgot to say,' John replied. 'There are no air assets available for this mission.'

'What, no air support at all?' asked Tricky.

'Nope. Nothing,' John replied. 'There is nothing available for this mission.'

'Isn't there even any SH?' Jason asked.

I knew what he was thinking. If we couldn't para-insert, at least we could go in by Chinook and get dropped with the vehicles, so we weren't channelled on to roads the whole way there.

'There's nothing available,' John repeated. 'The first time any air is coming online is at 0300 tomorrow, to get 1 PARA inserted for their L-Hour. That's it.'

Fuck. Hugely frustrating didn't cover it. The cash-strapped British military didn't have the airframes available to drop us over target, even if the will existed to do so. But in a way it was hardly surprising. We'd seen for ourselves how short was the supply of air assets to support the Brigade. In any case, we'd always known that Qalat Sikar was going to be dangerous whichever way we went in.

In the Pathfinders we have an unofficial collect – a poem that defines the ethos of our unit: 'Happiness shall always be found by those who dare and persevere; wanderer – do not turn around, march on and have no fear.' If they'd ordered us to insert by swimming up the Tigris we'd probably have done so, we wanted the Qalat Sikar mission so bad.

We weren't going in by air. We were going in overland. So be it.

CHAPTER ELEVEN

'I need you to get moving as soon as possible,' John prompted. 'Are your vehicles ready?'

'They're good to go,' I confirmed.

'David, I need you to back-brief me as soon as you're ready to depart. Can you do that by 0730 at the latest?'

I looked at the guys. They gave me the nod. *Sure we can.*

I said. 'Yeah. Can do.'

'And David,' John added, 'you'll need to use your charm and charisma with the US Marines to make sure they let you break through their lines and get to Qalat Sikar well ahead of them.'

I told John no problem. I sensed what he was driving at here. The US Marines had an H-Hour of 0800 this morning to start their push into Nasiriyah, 150 kilometres or so to the north of us. Up until their front line we could assume that the terrain was pretty much clear of Iraqi forces, and so secure. But once we reached Nasiriyah we were going to have to push ahead of the Marine Corps' front line, and break through into enemy territory. We were in one hell of a rush to make Qalat Sikar, and it was likely going to take some careful persuasion to convince the US Marine Corps commanders to let us through.

The mission was moving so quickly that we had little time to liaise with the US military on this one. We had a US liaison officer co-located within Brigade Headquarters, but even if we did get to brief him on our mission, the message might never make it out to the US front line. We were going to have to rely on our wits to convince the Yanks to let us push on through.

The briefing broke up. Jason grabbed the maps and started to scrutinise the ground between us and Qalat Sikar. I grabbed Geordie and Lance's patrol planning file, and started ploughing through the intel reports. Tricky headed off to Brigade signals to sort out the comms. He needed to grab the frequencies for the various TACSAT nets, which were changed regularly, and especially those for the air cover and the CSAR (Combat Search and Rescue) teams, if we ended up in the shit.

Tricky left Joe to sort comms with the Engineer Recce wagon, so he could patch them into our net. Steve scrutinised the sat images to find the best route in, whilst Dez started triple-checking the vehicles, plus I gave Jason actions-on.

The only way we'd be able to communicate directly with the US Marines was by routing a radio call via our HQ to theirs. Even then they'd have a different kind of crypto fill to ours – the software that scrambles signals to make them immune to intercepts – so we'd only be able make contact using insecure (unencrypted) means.

The US Marines would be running 300-odd radio nets out on their front lines, so each platoon could speak to its own men. They'd be changing their frequencies every twenty-four hours or so, as a precaution against enemy intercepts. Getting comms with the US Marines on their front line was going to be very, very challenging, and probably next to impossible.

From the sat photos the Qalat Sikar airfield looked like a small, military-use airstrip. The resolution was good enough to reveal a small control tower, plus a couple of hangars, but there were no aircraft or military vehicles present as far as we could tell. Normally, known enemy positions would be marked on the sat photos, and there were none shown. The date and time of the sat photos was to within a few weeks, so no more recent than that. The intel brief was hugely long-winded and full of waffle, but it boiled down to the fact that there were no known Iraqi forces present.

The first blindingly obvious thing from the maps and sat photos was that the area north of Nasiriyah was a lot wetter and more vegetated than where we were now. The sat images revealed canals and thick patches of undergrowth. At first it looked as if there was no way through off-road. But the more we studied the images, the more we were drawn to a couple of dirt tracks that looped northeast from Nasiriyah. They seemed to skirt the marshland all the way to the airfield.

We settled on a two-stage plan. If the intel picture held up when we reached Nasiriyah we'd take the main road – Route 7 – direct to Qalat Sikar. It would be the quickest route in, plus the intel picture said that it should be doable. We'd prefer to go off-road. That was always our first choice when on a vehicle-mounted mission. But the dirt tracks criss-crossed scores of canals, so all it would take was for one bridge to be down and we'd be buggered. However, if the intel picture proved badly wrong once we were past Nasiriyah, our fall-back option would be to take our chances and use those tracks.

From the maps, Jason figured it was a drive of some 290 kilometres to Qalat Sikar. We could average 50 kilometres an hour if we did it all on the main highways, so it was a six-hour drive minimum. That meant that we should be able to make it with ample time to recce, secure and mark the airfield, but it all depended on how well the intel picture held up once we hit enemy territory. If we ran into serious resistance, all of that would change.

From being an ultra-covert insertion, jumping from a C130 Hercules at high altitude, this had now become a mad dash up the main highway with a serious Charge of the Light Brigade feel about it. But there was no other way of getting in. In any case, ever since my time in 1 PARA we'd always been asked to do crazy operations with minimal kit and support. We'd done as much in Kosovo, Sierra Leone and Afghanistan. It's what the British Army is renowned for.

It was the intel that worried me most. We hadn't seen a single Iraqi soldier in the entire time that we'd been here. We knew that the

Yanks were moving towards Nasiriyah full steam ahead, and meeting little or no resistance. So maybe the intel picture – 'relatively benign' – was accurate. But somehow I doubted it. Relatively benign meant that no hostile forces were known to be present in the area. However, there was always a time lapse between intel being secured and the here and now. Plus we knew that the Iraqi Fedayeen – militias fiercely loyal to Saddam Hussein – weren't stationed in permanent bases as such. The Fedayeen were mobile, irregular forces and they were hard to pin down.

But we were where we were. We were being sent in with the best information available, and we were being asked to discover the ground truth. If the intel was wrong, it was only the six of us – or nine with the Engineer Recce blokes – that were at risk. And that was exactly the role for which the Pathfinders had been created.

The Engineer Recce Team consisted of a sergeant and two lance-corporals. We'd made it clear that they were free to chip in if they wanted to, but they'd seemed happy to defer to our expertise. With the mission plan pretty much done, Jase explained to Ian, their vehicle commander, the order in which we would proceed.

'Ian, this is the orbat [order of battle]: my vehicle in front, Dave's vehicle to the rear, yours in the middle. D'you want to send your blokes away so you can be ready for the off as soon as? Dez: go with them and help them get their wagon sorted.'

We began checking and rechecking our gear, especially our personal belt and webbing kit. A lot of care and attention went into it, for that was the one set of equipment we'd always have on us, even if we were on the run and had lost everything else. First priority was ammo. Each man had six thirty-round mags for his assault rifle in his webbing, the first facing forwards and the right way up, so it would slot directly into the weapon. Every few days we'd de-bombed our mags, getting rid of any dust and grit, then check and oil the spring and reload it. Some guys only loaded up twenty-nine rounds per mag, so as not to overstress the spring.

Second priority was grenades. Each bloke packed four HE (High

Explosive) grenades into two pouches. The side you carried them on depended on whether you were left- or right-handed. The primers were kept separate from the grenades, and screwed into them prior to going into combat. Third priority was food. Each man packed enough scoff for a normal twenty-four hours of operations, but not a full twenty-four-hour ration pack. Generally, we'd carry two boil-in-the-bag meals, which would likely be eaten cold. Food was stuffed into a rear pouch, for it was the last thing we'd need to reach for in a hurry.

If we did go on the run we might allow ourselves one boil-in-the-bag meal every three days – so just enough to keep us alive. With the food went a key piece of kit, the spoon, generally attached to our webbing by a length of para cord. If we lost our spoon we'd be forced to eat with dirty hands, which was asking to get sick. Fourth priority was water. We each packed two plastic one-litre bottles, one of which sat in our plastic mug to save space. Some of the blokes also carried a fold-up mountaineering water bag, which could be used for gathering extra drinking water.

Fifth priority was survival kit. This included steritabs for making dirty water potable; a personal first aid kit; a penknife; matches; plus a lighter (usually the cheap disposable kind). One emergency field dressing would be taped to the front of our webbing with green Army tape, where we could easily rip it off and slap it on to a gunshot wound. Sixth priority was a PRC-112 radio. This was an emergency UHF ground-to-air comms system. It was a Walkman-sized piece of kit, with an antenna that folded out so as to talk to the air. It provided line of sight comms only, and like a lot of our kit it was archaic and frequently broke down.

Seventh priority was our position-marking gear. We had classified and secret tactics, techniques and procedures, plus specialist equipment, which we used to covertly mark our position and to call in a search and rescue team via helicopter.

We each also carried a DZ marking kit in our webbing, consisting of a pop-up cone of fluorescent material that would be used for marking a DZ (Drop Zone) – a safe and cleared area for parachutists to drop into. Lastly, each man might opt to carry a hexy stove and some fuel tabs. It was relatively heavy kit, and we could survive on cold rations, but a hot brew was great for morale and it could be a lifesaver. Again it was personal choice.

At 0715 we back-briefed John on the mission plan. What we were attempting to do was complicated and a lot could go wrong. It was an isolated, unknown area deep behind enemy lines. The back brief complemented the patrol file, leaving headquarters with a clear picture as to our intentions, plus actions-on in the event of trouble. It also gave a clear sense of our route, in case John had to send in a CSAR team to find us.

I briefed John that our intention was to be at the airfield by 2200 hours latest, leaving us five hours to recce, secure and mark the HLS. We'd stop short with the vehicles, and do an initial recce on foot. We'd then use one vehicle to cover the others, as we did a 360-degree check of the runway. We'd do the first 360-scan using our SOPHIE thermal optics, which were outstanding pieces of kit.

SOPHIE has a 2000-metre effective range as we would be using it, and you can zoom it in to get up close and personal with whatever you are viewing. We used it primarily as an optical aid for CTRs (Close Target Recces), but it could also be used as a targeting aid to take out whatever enemy forces had been identified. If there was heavy activity at the airfield we might not be able to do a 360-degree sweep on foot. In that case we'd make clear to PF HQ exactly where we'd found Iraqi forces, and recommend that they put the PARAs down offset from the airstrip.

We'd mark the HLS using torches with IR filters (only visible by night vision), and our purpose-made IR markers. We'd radio through GPS co-ordinates of the exact spot for the helos to put down. There were only enough Chinooks available to do a company-level insertion, so 1 PARA would arrive in three waves, each consisting of three helos and some ninety men at arms. The rest of the battle group would follow on later. I finished back-briefing John on our plan, and Jason started to outline the actions-on.

'Enemy pre-seen: we go firm, report enemy location, and ID alternative route to avoid them. Contact: we return fire, break contact, send contact report, then carry on with the mission. Ambush: we return fire, drive through ambush and carry on with the mission. If the patrol gets separated, we go firm, wait thirty minutes, then return to the last ERV, of which we have three north of Al Nasiriyah.'

As we couldn't mark-up ERV (Emergency Rendezvous) points on the maps, each of our ERVs had to be an easily recognisable and memorable feature. I'd picked an electrical relay station as our last ERV point, en route to Qalat Sikar. It consisted of a forest of pylons lying just off the main highway a short distance down a dirt track. It was unmissable.

There were two more ERVs between there and Nasiriyah, each of which was a prominent road junction. Each ERV was calculated with a set stand-off distance and bearing, to reduce the risk of a blue-on-blue (friendly fire) incident. The ERV point was set 200 metres to the east of the landmark, and we were to approach it from the east.

On approach you'd go firm outside the ERV, which you scanned with your NVG kit and SOPHIE sight. You'd only actually go into the ERV point when you were certain that it was clear of the enemy, civvies and stray dogs. And you made sure that any friendlies present were aware that you were coming in. If the ERV was unusable for any reason, you'd move on to the next one.

If we had to call in CSAR, we'd mark a HLS for the CSAR aircrew to come in on, with a pre-arranged lay-out using either stones or IR markers. We'd adopt a non-aggressive posture as the CSAR helicopter came in – weapons on the ground, hands on our heads and kneeling. We'd be treated like the enemy posing as British soldiers until proved otherwise, for obvious reasons.

Jason rounded off the actions-on. 'Presence of enemy forces at airfield: conduct CTR, report enemy strength back to PF HQ, and neutralise if necessary. Blue-on-blue: do not return fire, take cover, and ID patrol as friendly forces.'

Tricky did a comms brief, which was short and sweet. We had two Scheds daily, one at 0800 and one at 1600. If we missed one or more Scheds John would presume we may have been compromised and were on the run. If we got into a 'lost comms' situation, where we couldn't contact friendly forces, we'd move back to the US Marine Corps and beg, borrow or steal some comms kit. There was no point in securing a HLS at the airfield if we couldn't communicate that it was all clear for 1 PARA to come in and land.

Finally, Tricky reminded everyone of our call-signs: 'Patrol call-sign is *Mayhem Three Zero*. Dave's call-sign is *Maverick One*. And the mission code name is *Operation Death or Glory*.'

His last comment lightened the mood. Everyone laughed. The mission didn't have an official code name as such, but as unofficial ones went Tricky had hit the nail on the head with that one. At the end of the mission briefing we synchronised our watches. When out on operations we needed to ensure that every member of the unit was working to the exact same minute and second. This is crucial for many reasons, and particularly for the air picture.

The Pathfinders' communications specialist, Pete, stepped forward. He held out his left arm, and gazed intently at his watch.

'In approximately two minutes it'll be seven-fifty-seven Zulu,' he announced.

We each of us moved the hands of our own watches to one second away from 0757. We now had two minutes to kill before the synchronisation second, and we spent it checking over the maps and sat photos of Qalat Sikar.

'Sixty seconds,' Pete warned. 'Thirty seconds. Seven-fifty-seven Zulu in fifteen seconds. Five, four, three, two, one. Mark!'

On Pete's call we each set our watches running, and were synchronised. Pete would have done the same thing himself earlier that morning, getting his time-synch from the RAF HQ in Camp Tristar. What was going on here was much bigger than simply a ground war in Iraq. The British and US forces had air missions flying in from all points of the compass: from carriers steaming off the coast, to fast jets flying out of Jordan, Saudi Arabia and Cyprus, and even B52s launched from bases in the UK.

You'd never run an entire air campaign from one location, for that would make it highly vulnerable to having its airbase attacked. But co-ordinating the air campaign across so many different countries and time zones was a complex and challenging task, hence our time-synch coming down from RAF headquarters. One air vice-marshal – British or American – would be in charge of the entire air campaign, and his timing would be co-ordinated directly with the Pentagon and PJHQ (Permanent Joint Headquarters). The air vice-marshal would delegate time synchronisation to his chief of staff, who would filter it down the chain to every ground unit, including ours.

Pilots would be flying in from a myriad of time zones, while having to co-ordinate their actions with ground troops down to the second. If you were on the ground you might get close air support allocated to you for a very tight time window – a few minutes or seconds even – and you needed to be one hundred per cent certain you were working to exactly the same local – Zulu – time. The same would go for a HALO jump over target, or for a CSAR extraction. Military precision was the key here, as was wearing a reliable timepiece!

I wore a Bvlgari watch, and had done for several years. Few people realise this, but cheap watches tend to lose a few seconds every day. Over time that mounts up. My Bvlgari had cost me £2000, money that I had had to scrimp and save for. Each Bvlgari is individually numbered, and I took pride in its fine, simple lines and its precision Swiss engineering. It had no flashy features – just a ruggedised black strap and an elegant, clean face that told the time precisely and accurately, which was exactly what I needed it to do.

It also had a sapphire crystal glass face, which was pretty much indestructible. Sapphire crystal is the hardest oxide crystal known to man, so up there with diamonds on the hardness scale. (Diamonds are at ten on the Mohs hardness scale, sapphire crystal at nine.) Sapphire crystal has the qualities of extreme strength, hardness, heat resistance and corrosion resistance, which meant my watch face wasn't likely to fall apart mid-mission.

A lot of soldiers tended to wear so-called 'military' type watches, ones that sported a button for every eventuality. The trouble with those was that as a Pathfinder, you'd often find yourself crawling through the undergrowth on your belt buckle. And whilst you might have turned off all the bleeper and light functions, it was all too easy to lean your weight on your watch or catch it on some undergrowth and reactivate them. Imagine being within yards of a hostile position, when suddenly your watch started to flash or to bleep.

The Bvlgari had no light function whatsoever, just a gently luminous dull silver dial. It had no bleeping functions either. During my officer cadet days I used to box for Sandhurst. I'd been forced to wear that Bvlgari on my right arm, because my left arm had been left swollen and bruised after I'd knocked out an opponent. I figured wearing the watch on the right had brought me good luck, for whilst I was doing so I was one of the few officers selected to join the Parachute Regiment.

I'd decided to wear the Bvlgari on my right wrist ever since. It didn't run on batteries, so there was no room for Murphy's Law coming into play: *If it can go wrong it will.* There was no danger of the battery giving out just as we were approaching Qalat Sikar airfield.

'It's 0758 and we move out in twelve minutes,' I announced to the lads on my patrol. 'Right, let's go.'

As we exited the HQ tent I spared a fleeting thought for John. Shortly, he'd have all six PF patrols out on operations. Over the past forty-eight hours he'd given orders and received back-briefs from all of us, and he'd been on the radio net 24/7 liaising with his patrols. He was also supposed to be present during the Brigade orders groups, and to have a view on what the Pathfinders could contribute. He was on information overload and had to be close to burnout. It struck me again that as PF 2IC I had the best of both worlds.

Before we set off I did a final verbal check with the other wagons. 'Jase, good to go?'

He nodded: 'Yep.'

'Ian, good to go?'

The big Engineer bloke gave me a thumbs-up: 'Yeah.'

At precisely 0810 we got our wheels rolling.

CHAPTER TWELVE

Barely had we pulled away from the FOB when Steve turned to me. 'Dave, are we there yet?'

He repeated it a few times, like Donkey does in the movie *Shrek*, until eventually I cracked: 'Steve, fuck off will you, mate?' But I was pissing myself laughing.

The weather had done an about-face. It was calm and sunny and without a hint of rain. We had smocks on with shirts underneath. That was all. In the dawn light the terrain looked cinematographic: it was a sea of flat, open plateaus, dotted with patches of yellow rock and rolling, golden sand.

The Pinkies picked up speed across the hard ground and I began to feel euphoric. *Finally, we'd got Qalat Sikar.* It may not have been a para-insertion any more, but it still promised to be epic. *We were underway on the mission of a lifetime.* I glanced around at the other lads and I could tell that they, like me, were lit up.

With the dawn light sparking off the glittering desert, I grabbed my sunglasses. They were Persol Havana 714s – hand-made glasses with arms and lenses that collapse in on themselves. When folded they were basically the size of a small compass, and they fitted perfectly in the top left-hand pocket of my smock, which made them great for operations.

As we drove across the empty desert a thought struck me from out of nowhere. Maybe Tricky had forgotten his cold weather gear on our first mission *for a reason*. If he hadn't done so and we hadn't been called back to base early, we'd still be out there minding those bridges, and we'd likely never have got Qalat Sikar. Maybe that was why Tricky had decided not to take his Gore-Tex kit. Maybe he'd had a premonition. I'm a big believer in fate: maybe Tricky had dumped his Gore-Tex so we could get Qalat Sikar, this peach of a mission.

After twenty minutes, driving through the open desert we hit Route 8, the tarmac road that stretches all the way to Nasiriyah. Route 8 is a four-lane highway with a metal barrier running down the centre, a lot like a British dual carriageway. We began to speed along it in line astern at 65 kph. The sun was beating down, there wasn't an enemy in sight and it felt like a road movie, like driving to Vegas. When Jason pulled over in the desert sands for a map check, we pulled up in line abreast, each vehicle covering its arcs of fire. But still there wasn't an Iraqi to be seen.

Jason had got his hands on some munchies, and was having a good scoff as he pawed his map. Food: that was Jason's vice. Dez was hovering near and trying not to ask too many questions. In the wagon's rear Joe was trying to have a quiet ciggie without blowing smoke on the others. Jason was the vehicle commander and he'd got to lead the crack, which was pretty much non-existent in their wagon. I could see Joe glancing over enviously at us. Steve and Tricky were taking the piss out of everything – especially the US Marine Corps grunts that had started to thunder past us in this long line of wagons.

A massive convoy of American military vehicles was doing the road move north. There were HUMVEEs, 4-tonne trucks and hulking great M1A1 Abrams main battle tanks. We felt tiny and puny beside them. Part of the American convoy went static nearby, young buzz-cut marines jumping down and deploying in all-around defence, flat on their belt buckles and assault rifles levelled into the distant glare. One glance at us lot and they could tell that we weren't US forces, but thankfully we did have the recognition flashes on our vehicles.

We shot past the static US convoy and were making good progress – nine Brits in three Land Rovers overhauling the thousands of troops and hardware of the mighty Marine Expeditionary Force. We were moving through the US armoured fist that was punching into the soft underbelly of the enemy, or at least that was our understanding. And we knew that our tiny team constituted the vanguard of the British advance into southern Iraq, which was a fantastic feeling.

There wasn't a lot of chat possible as we drove, for the wind rushing past the open-topped Pinkies was deafening. But I could see by the expression on the other blokes' faces, and the look in their eyes, that they were loving being on the move at last. We had VHF radios to communicate between the vehicles, with a handset that sat on the side of the Pinkies. We also had Cougar personal radios for secure comms between individual members of the patrol. Each of us had an earpiece stuffed in one earhole, and a handset the size of a massive 1980s mobile phone hooked into our webbing. But even with those radios, the noise of the wind rushing past made comms next to impossible.

Over time the Pathfinders had developed a series of hand signals to get the basic, vital information across when on a vehicle move: speed up, slow down, enemy seen, stop. A lot of the US vehicles we were passing were loggies – supply trucks and the like – and it was clear how enormous and ponderous the US resupply chain was. It was also clear how vulnerable it was to ambush or disruption, as there was only the one road – Route 8 – heading north into Iraq. It was a reminder of the urgent need to make Qalat Sikar happen.

We had this supreme sense of mission now. The minutes were ticking down towards H-Hour, and we had less than nineteen hours in which to get to Qalat Sikar and clear the PARAs in to seize it. Every now and then we were forced to a halt by a broken-down US Marine Corps vehicle choking up the traffic. We couldn't just go screaming past through the open desert to one side, for then some trigger-happy marine might decide to unload on us. It was very likely their first operational tour and they'd be jumpy as hell. Instead we had to wave and smile and thread our way through carefully – Her Majesty's finest coming through.

We slowed to a halt at one of those choke points, and this figure emerged from between a couple of HUMVEEs. He was dressed in the distinctive blue flak jacket of the press. He'd got a battered blue baseball cap jammed on to his head above mad professor-style hair, and these bizarre glasses propped on the end of his pointy nose. There was only one thing that this guy could possibly be: an American journalist embedded with the Marine Corps.

After making a beeline for our stationary vehicle he stopped right by my door. He had a tape recorder clutched in one hand and I'd seen him press 'record', although he'd done his best to hide it. He looked me in the eye, and fired off a first question in this self-important manner that just demanded to be answered.

'Hi, Matthew Johnson, CBS News. So where are you guys going?'

I pointed north: 'Thatta way.'

I figured it was pretty obvious really, as everyone was heading north. At that moment Jason pulled away, the RE vehicle followed, and Steve gunned our engine.

'Hey, wait up …' the reporter shouted after us. Then, when he realised we weren't stopping: 'Okay, see you guys next time in Hereford!'

I felt like yelling back: *We're not SAS, we're Pathfinders. Can't you tell the difference? That's like confusing a BMW with a Ferrari!* But if I did I figured he'd have an even bigger story.

We pushed onwards up the main drag. On open stretches we were making a good 80 kph now, but we were forced to a crawl whenever we hit the US convoys. I figured our average speed had to be around 30 kph, at which rate we should still hit Qalat Sikar within ten hours. That left us plenty of time to do the necessary.

Visibility was great, and we could see for several kilometres in any direction. We'd yet to see a single Iraqi, civilian or military. It felt really weird, for here we were driving up this massive fuck-off highway into the heart of Iraq. If it wasn't for the US Marine Corps it would have felt as if we were moving across the Planet of the Apes post the Apocalypse, it was that devoid of any human presence.

At 1100 we'd been on the road for a good three hours, and we stopped for another map check. We figured we were just a few kilometres short of the southern outskirts of Nasiriyah. It was now that we detected the distant signs of battle. Stationary in the desert as we were, we caught the first crump of explosions. I glanced northwards, and on the far horizon I could see thick, oily plumes of smoke drifting with the wind. Cobra helicopter gunships were circling and whirling in the air, pounding targets below, and there was tracer arcing skywards in return.

We moved forward a few hundred metres, and there was a shattered HUMVEE plus an LAV-25 APC (Armoured Personnel Carrier) lying by the roadside. It seemed as if the Iraqis were putting up some kind of resistance after all. The LAV-25 was a big hulking beast of a machine. It was still burning fiercely, a thick cloud of acrid smoke billowing across the highway. We slowed to a crawl, and there were the distinctive puncture marks of what looked like RPGs (Rocket Propelled Grenades) torn into the side of its thick armour plating.

There was no sign of any American casualties, so we figured that whoever had been in the APC and the HUMVEE must have got out pretty much unscathed. And there was still not the slightest sign of any Iraqis. We presumed that a small, mobile force had mounted a snap ambush here, before melting away into the desert.

Weirdly, we were almost relieved to see some sign of an enemy presence, concrete evidence that we were at war. We were almost a third of the way into Iraq, and we had yet to see a single Iraqi fighter. But equally, we'd yet to see a single Iraqi soldier surrendering, and they were certainly not laying down their weapons in their droves.

Nasiriyah is a Shiite town, as opposed to being Sunni. We'd learned as much from the intel briefs. The Sunnis were the traditional allies of Saddam Hussein, and the local Shiite inhabitants here were expected to be friendly. That contributed to the 'relatively benign' intel assessment that we'd been given. For the moment at least the intel seemed to fit with what we were seeing on the ground.

We pushed onwards for a further 5 kilometres, alert to the slightest movement around us. But apart from the Cobra gunships wheeling above the horizon, which had to be somewhere over the centre of Nasiriyah, there was nothing. Finally, we spotted what looked like a US Marine Corps command post some 200 metres ahead of us. To one side of the road was a cluster of tents and vehicles, plus scores of radio antennae fingering into the air.

The command post was surrounded by a line of US marines, lying on their belt buckles in all-around defence. None of them had dug in yet, so we figured they'd been here for only a matter of hours, and that there was no immediate threat. We could see for several hundred metres in all directions, and there was no sign of enemy forces. We figured the US Marine Corps commander would have units stationed 360 degrees around his command post, which meant we could be fairly relaxed around here, although we knew we had to be approaching their front line.

Under the watchful eyes of the Marine Corps grunts we pulled up on the roadside and dismounted. Tricky set up the TACSAT to send a LOCSTAT back to HQ – a report on where we were and what we were up to. Jason and I moved forwards on foot, heading for the command post. We were looking to secure some concrete intel on what might lie ahead of us, what kind of resistance the US Marines had met in Nasiriyah, and our best route through.

I'd grabbed my SA80 from where it was lodged between the driver's seat and mine, alongside Steve's Minimi light machine gun. Jason had also grabbed his, plus we'd got our pistols in our thigh holsters. There was the solid bulk of an Amtrak (Amphibious Armoured Tracked Vehicle) protecting the command post from the road. We skirted around it and approached the first tent. It had a curtain-like flap that shielded the entranceway. It was there so that light didn't leak out at night, revealing the tent's position to the enemy.

I reached forwards and lifted the flap. A big, square-shouldered Marine Corps orderly sergeant glanced up. He was clearly surprised as hell to see us. He stepped forwards and held out his hand, palm towards us, blocking the way. He had these massive, thick-rimmed sunglasses shielding his eyes, so there was no way of reading his expression. He didn't say a word, but he clearly wanted some kind of explanation as to what planet we'd just jetted in from.

'Hi, I'm David, a British Pathfinder,' I told him. 'This is Jason, my 2IC. Is your Ops Officer around? We have a mission to go north and I need to speak to him.'

He gestured for us to step forwards into something like a tented reception area. He seemed slightly less daunted after I had spoken – *and in English* – but I figured that about the last thing he had been expecting was two Lawrence of Arabia-type figures turning up out of the blue and stepping into his domain.

He gestured to a side table. 'Sirs, please put your weapons and your webbing down and leave them here.'

He got us to dump our longs and our pistols, plus our webbing. It was less that he was disarming us, and more that there wasn't the room in the ops tent for war-fighting gear. We followed him inside, and immediately we could sense the tension in the air. You could cut the atmosphere with a knife in there. Things were clearly in deadly earnest, and we sensed that the US Marines had taken casualties.

This was the Marine Corps' Regimental Combat Team 2 (RCT-2) HQ. They were part of the 1st Battalion, 2nd Marines, which made up Task Force Tarawa (TFT) – the force spearheading the assault into Nasiriyah. The guys here looked shocked and exhausted, and we realised it had to be proving pretty heavy out there. Our escort gestured towards this big, beefy Marine Corps major. He was positioned to one side in a vehicle that opened into the ops tent, and he was busy mouthing into a radio telephone.

'Ops Officer is on the net, sirs,' the Marine Corps sergeant told us. 'Figure he may be busy for some time.'

The Ops Officer was chewing tobacco and spitting in between issuing orders, and he looked as if he'd been on the go since well before dawn. He had his chair pushed back and his feet on a desk, and he was clearly having a tough time trying to control whatever was going down with his front line units. He was totally focused upon what was going on up ahead of him, and only marginally aware of us.

There was a moment when he nodded in our direction, and he looked as if he was about to break off from what he was doing to have words. But then some urgent message must have come in over the net, and he was yelling into his hand piece again. The delay was frustrating, but the longer we were here the clearer it became that things weren't going to plan in Nasiriyah.

With the major still yelling into his radio, one of his deputies pulled us to one side. He confided in us that they'd got three Marine Corps companies pinned down in the centre of the city. They'd lost a lot of blokes already that morning, and Nasiriyah was proving far from being the pushover that everyone had predicted.

Finally, the major dropped his handset and turned our way. As rapidly as I could I explained our mission. In response he just stared at us in exhausted silence. He had this expression on his face as if Jason and I each had our tackle hanging out, or something.

'Listen, guys, all I can say is there's no fuckin' way you want to be going north any time soon.' He eyed us in silence for a few seconds. 'You go pushin' north into all of that,' he jerked a thumb over his shoulder in the direction of Nasiriyah, 'then you gotta be on some kind of a freakin' death wish or something.'

Before I could respond there was a burst of static on the net, and he grabbed his radio to take another call. Jason and I had no option but to return to the Pinkies, and await developments. Back at the wagons I briefed the guys on where we were at.

'Right, the US front line is 1000 metres to our north. The Yanks are in heavy contacts, and they've taken casualties. They've got war-fighting to do and casevacs [casualty evacuations] ongoing, and that's what's holding us here. They're saying it's not secure enough for us to move forward. I'll keep checking in with their HQ, so be ready to move in half an hour, an hour, whenever. Okay?'

The lads seemed pretty relaxed about the hold-up, which was good. We broke down into groups and started studying the maps, trying to figure out if there were any better routes through. But with the time available to us rapidly shrinking, straight up Route 7 looked like the only way we were going to make it.

This was the problem with going in overland: it made the patrol highly vulnerable to hold ups. With time fast running out, I tried to figure out if there was any way we might beat the clock. It might well be that we would reach Qalat Sikar with only enough time to do a rushed recce, and that we'd have to clear 1 PARA in with minimal security. It was far from being ideal, but it could be the only way to get this thing done.

There was a part of my brain that couldn't help thinking: *Fuck me, if only we were stood on the tail ramp of a C130 right now, with AC/ DC's 'Thunderstruck' playing at top volume and a HALO jump ahead of us. 'Sounds of the drums. Beatin' in my heart. The thunder of the guns. Tore me apart. You've been thunderstruck ...' We'd be on the ground in a matter of minutes and getting the job sorted.*

Jason was obviously thinking the same. 'You know, if me and H had tandemmed in from a C130, we'd have recced that bloody airfield by now.'

I nodded my agreement. 'I know. But we are where we are, mate.'

The more we got into serious operations mode, the more I saw that Jason was rising to the challenge. I reckoned we were going to work fine together now that we were at war, despite the previous tension between us. Faced with the relentless, overriding pace of this mission all those petty rivalries had been left behind us, or so I hoped.

Tricky had managed to raise PF headquarters on the radio. It can be frustratingly hard to raise HQ, so I was relieved he'd got through. There was no watchkeeper on the HQ radio, so it relied on one of the signallers picking up our call. And with six patrols out on the ground, everyone at HQ would be running to stand still. Half of the time John and the White Rabbit would be in Brigade briefings, so even when we did get through there was often no one there who could make any decisions.

Thankfully John was present, and I proceeded to brief him on where we were at. I told him we were liaising with the US forces, and I gave him our grid, beyond which we were unable to move. I warned

John that it might take us some time to get through Nasiriyah. I asked if it was possible to roll back 1 PARA's H-Hour, as we'd got held up. I told him again we were static, and could be held here for some time.

But John reiterated the urgency of getting to Qalat Sikar for 1 PARA's 0300 insertion.

CHAPTER THIRTEEN

We waited an hour, during which we could see and hear more of the battle raging over Nasiriyah. It was fierce. The tension and shock on the faces of those in the ops tent had said as much to us – that right here and right now something was fucking with their shit. Now we were starting to get a real eyeful of it. In Nasiriyah at least, the Iraqis certainly weren't rolling over and giving up for dead.

While Joe got a brew on, Jason and I decided to pay a second visit to the US command post. If anything it was more tense and chaotic than ever. I didn't even try to bother the major. Instead, I got a heads-up from one of the Marine Corps lieutenants as to what kind of trouble they'd stumbled into. He spoke to Jase and me over a map of the city that they'd got pinned up in the centre of the ops tent.

The vital strategic importance of Nasiriyah was that it straddled the Euphrates River plus the Saddam Canal, he explained. These were the two major waterways that would block any further advance northwards into Iraq. In downtown Nasiriyah a pair of bridges carried the main highway – Route 8 – over those watercourses, opening up the road northwards to Baghdad.

The Marine Corps' present mission, codenamed *Timberwolf*, had been meticulously planned and timed to seize both bridges intact. The short length of highway linking the two bridges had been nicknamed 'Ambush Alley', for it was such an obvious place to hit the advancing US forces. So instead of heading directly up Ambush Alley, the Marines had planned to loop eastwards through open ground, moving fast from one bridge to the other and taking any enemy by surprise.

However, *Timberwolf* had gone to ratshit before it could even get properly started. The previous night a convoy of supply trucks from the US Army's 507th logistics battalion had somehow managed to pass through the US Marine Corps' front line positions unchallenged. The convoy threaded through the final screen of M1A1 Abrams main battle tanks, and carried on driving. It then headed into the centre of Nasiriyah, without anyone from the 507th realising they'd crossed the US front line.

At 0600 hours they'd crossed the Euphrates River bridge and entered Ambush Alley. It was then that they realised their mistake, and tried to make an about turn, so they could retrace their route. But by then it was too late. The Iraqi forces had been alerted to their presence, and they proceeded to unleash all hell upon the lightly armed convoy. Truck after truck got hit, and the 507th took horrendous casualties. Scores of drivers, including Private First Class Jessica Lynch, a female soldier – were variously killed in action, posted missing in action or presumed captured.

The dark, oily columns of smoke that we'd seen hanging over the centre of Nasiriyah marked the burning remains of the trucks of the 507th. In the process of blundering into the city, the 507th had blown any element of surprise that the Marine Corps might have had. Instead, the Marines were forced to advance into a raging firefight. Worse still, they'd had to race into the city at breakneck speed, in an effort to try to rescue the trapped soldiers of the 507th. They'd headed directly down the throat of Ambush Alley and had got torn to pieces in the process.

Dozens of US soldiers had been lost that morning, either wounded or killed in action. They'd faced regular Iraqi forces armed with T55 main battle tanks, self-propelled anti-tank guns, mortars, RPGs and smaller weapons. Plus they'd been hit by irregular Fedayeen-type

gunmen, who had been hiding amongst the city's civilian population. It sounded like sheer hell out there, and I could well understand
the major's reluctance to let us proceed.

We left it another hour, then visited the command post for a third
time. The atmosphere seemed calmer. It was now more like brute
shock and exhaustion. The Marines had secured their objectives –
the bridges over the Euphrates River and the Saddam Canal – so
opening up a road route through Nasiriyah. But in the process they'd
been hammered, those two bridges costing them dear.

Whilst we waited to speak with the major, the captain briefed us
again. Their forces were split, one company around the northern
bridge, and one around the southernmost crossing, with a third
sandwiched somewhere in the middle. They kept trying to send
troops forward to relieve the northernmost positions, but they were
getting shot-up all along Ambush Alley. It was anyone's guess as to
how the fighting would shake out in there.

Finally, we got to speak with the major. 'My radio net's overloaded
big time,' he told us. 'I don't have proper comms with all my units. It's
very, very confused out there right now, there's a shit load of fighting going on, and we're still evacuating our casualties. You go north,
that's what you're heading into, and I'd very strongly advise against
it.'

'I hear what you're saying,' I told him, 'but we've been waiting here
for three hours, and we've got our mission's L-Hour fast approaching. We can move ahead, speak with your forward company commanders, and scope it out from there.'

He eyed me for a second, weighing what he was going to say next.
He knew he couldn't order us to stay put, for we were British soldiers
not under his command. But it was obvious that he could make life
very, very difficult for us if he chose to.

He gave this resigned kind of shrug. 'Okay, guys, it's your call. You
wanna move forwards, you've been warned. I've strongly advised
against it, but it's your call, guys.'

I nodded. 'Thank you, sir, I appreciate your support. We'll move forwards to your first company, and liaise with them. We'll then move on to the others, and do the same. I'd appreciate it enormously if you could radio a warning that we're coming through.'

'I'll do my best – that's if I can get comms with my guys on the ground.' He paused, running a hand exhaustedly across his features. He brought his fatigued, bloodshot eyes up to meet mine. 'You know, guys, we got this one APC blown on to its side, and we've not managed to get anyone to it yet. We presume they're all dead, but we just don't know. When you move ahead could you guys push through to that APC, and check for survivors?'

I considered this for a moment. He was a Marine Corps commander with the armoured might of the US Marine Corps behind him. I was a Pathfinder captain with nine blokes and three soft-skinned Land Rovers. We'd got a mission ahead of us that could turn the course of this war, and time was running out. You could say it was taking the piss, what he was asking of us. But I could tell that he was in shock, and that his men had taken a real mauling.

'I'll speak to my blokes and see what we can do when we get there,' I told him. 'What we can do, we will do, of that you have my word.'

We returned to the vehicles. Before moving out we had a quick 'Chinese parliament' – a group discussion amongst all on the patrol. We figured that if we could just get through Nasiriyah, we could do the drive to Qalat Sikar under cover of darkness on NVG, and that would be our best chance.

It got dark around 1600, which left us a good eight hours to get to the airfield, do the recce and get 1 PARA in for their H-Hour. But we all knew there was only one possible route through the city. We had to cross the first bridge that was being held by the US Marines and run Ambush Alley.

At 1300 we mounted up the Pinkies and moved out. We took Route 8 north into Nasiriyah, heading first for the Euphrates River bridge. We were moving away from the Marine Corps command post, when Steve turned to have words with me. I figured maybe he'd seen something of significance.

He leaned over and yelled into my ear: 'Dave, I need a wee.'

'Steve, will you just shut up for one minute!' I yelled back at him, in Shrek's broad Scottish ogre voice. 'Just for one bloody minute!'

But in spite of myself I was laughing. You had to love him for the sheer bloody torment he could deliver, anytime, anyplace, anywhere.

We'd each forced several litres of fluid into our bodies before setting out again, for maximum rehydration. We'd only sip sparingly now. On a mission such as this one the last thing you needed to be doing was stopping all the time in order to rehydrate, or so Steve could take a piss!

We'd spent hours studying our maps minutely, and memorising the roads that we needed to follow into Qalat Sikar. The entire route was clear in my head, as it would be with each of the other PF blokes on my patrol. That way, if we somehow got split up or separated from our mapping, we'd still be able to navigate our way to the mission objective. With one eye on the milometer, it should be easy enough to steer a way through the various road junctions.

Word was that the blokes from the US 507th logistics convoy had no maps with them when they blundered into Nasiriyah. That in part explained how they had ended up getting so hopelessly lost, and stumbling into the mother of all ambushes.

We pushed ahead at a dead slow, scanning our arcs of fire and alert to anything suspicious. Wherever any one of us PF gunners looked, our weapon would be pointing, for we moved the barrels of our machine guns in synchronisation with our heads and eyes. That way, as soon as we spotted a threat or a target we could open fire and mallet it.

The terrain changed quickly, and soon we were passing through a network of irrigation canals plus dense palm groves. This was the biblical area of Babylon and the Garden of Eden, and suddenly it had turned very green, closed in and claustrophobic.

Before we were into the city proper we stumbled upon the first signs of battle. Four khaki-coloured wagons were skewed across our side of the road, their gutted shells spitting orange fire and spewing out great gouts of oily black smoke. These had to be the remains of some of the 507th trucks that never made it out of the cauldron of Nasiriyah. Flaming tyres were pouring out thick clouds of acrid black smoke, which was barrelling into the air.

The way ahead was all but obscured by the drifting, oily darkness. Our forward visibility was down to near-zero, which made this the perfect place to ambush us. As we pushed ahead we were hyper-alert to any enemy presence. We crawled past the first wagon and we could see that the paint was blackened and blistered from the scorching heat, the truck body riddled with bullet holes.

Here and there great rents had been torn in the soft-skinned vehicle, as RPG and other large calibre high explosive rounds had torn into it. The heat was scorching on our faces, and the sickly-sweet smell of burning flesh made me gag as we passed by. We heaved up our shemaghs to shield our exposed skin, and I said a quick prayer for the poor bastards who were caught in all of that.

A couple of kilometres further on we hit the deserted streets of the city. There was an eerie, brooding silence in the place that did not bode well. Now and then we caught a dog's distant howling, or a half-glimpsed figure flitting down a side alleyway. Otherwise, there was bugger all moving out there.

Two kilometres into the city proper the first bridge reared up ahead of us like a giant, humpback whale. All around the massive concrete and iron structure there was this scene of absolute carnage. There were wrecked Hummers and the armoured hulks of Bradley Fighting Vehicles strewn along the roadside, spitting angry smoke and flame.

We reached the first group of marines. They were positioned at the bridge, and they'd gone firm in all-around defence. But they seemed glazed and shaken, as if they'd just seen a terrifying ghost. These were the men of Alpha Company, the first into Nasiriyah that morning, and they'd lost a dozen men as they had taken the bridge, maybe more.

Bravo Company had moved through them to storm Ambush Alley – the stretch of road leading from the first bridge to the next – and to relieve the trapped soldiers of the 507th. There they were likewise smashed, their Abrams tanks and APCs getting bogged down in the mud of a swampy, sewer area to the east of the highway.

Bravo Company had regrouped in an open patch of waste ground, before going in to assault Ambush Alley for a second time. Charlie Company then came through in an effort to relieve Bravo, and seize the second bridge. They had taken a real hammering before they had managed to force a way ahead and take the bridge over the Saddam Canal.

The scene at that first bridge was surreal. A US Marine Corps battle group had been fought to a standstill here. Its vanguard had been hammered to such an extent that blokes were wandering about pretty much lost and confused. I wondered how these guys, the cream of the US military, could be so shocked and so frozen. It was as if they had come in here not expecting a shitfight, and had then suddenly realised – *Oh my God, we're being ambushed and attacked!*

I guessed the answer had to be pretty simple, really. Their intel was likely appallingly bad; way wide of the mark. They'd probably sat through highly inaccurate briefings, telling them that Nasiriyah was going to be a pushover, and that the Iraqis would throw down their weapons and run. Instead, they'd stumbled into a veritable shit-fight.

I sensed that the fighting was largely over now. There were still Cobra helicopter gunships circling overhead, and loosing off bursts of cannon fire. But it wasn't as if my sixth sense was screaming at me that it was all about to kick off. This felt like the exhausted, brutalised stillness after a big, ugly, bloody battle had gone down. Still, when the guys of Alpha Company heard that we were pushing on across the bridge, they warned us to take it real careful. It was bad up ahead. *Real bad.*

We spotted the massive form of an Abrams main battle tank creeping forwards, and we pulled the Pinkies in behind it. Using the cover provided by its massive armoured bulk, we crawled towards the apex of the bridge. We went firm just as we reached the downward slope, from where we had a panoramic view over the battle-torn city and directly forwards into Ambush Alley.

Smoke was pouring out of buildings to either side of us, and the nearest palm grove had been stripped bare by whirlwinds of shrapnel. There was the rhythmic '*thwoop-thwoop-thwoop*' of a helicopter gunship above us, and a Cobra came barrelling through the distant smoke, unleashing a long, deafening burst of cannon rounds as it went. Then it circled high above us.

A group of figures emerged from the shot-up palm grove. They were males dressed in local dish-dash robes and turbans. They moved towards us – lean, tanned and sure of foot in their light leather sandals. These were the first Iraqis of any sort that we'd seen since our arrival in their country several days earlier.

They pointed over their shoulders and started gesticulating. Then they yelled out in guttural, broken English: 'Soldier Americani! Soldier Americani!'

Is this where the major back at RCT-2 headquarters had lost his APC? Is this where he wanted us to check for any survivors? Or were these Iraqis trying to lure us into some kind of a trap? We looked where they had indicated. I could see a Bradley Fighting Vehicle lying on its side, half-sunken in the river mud. The back door was hanging open, and I reckoned I could see a dead or injured figure in there. But to confirm it either way we'd have to cross over the bridge and turn east on to the riverbed.

My instinct told me to stick with our mission. But still I wanted to do something at least to help. I opted for a halfway house. Whilst Tricky tried to raise Pathfinder HQ on the TACSAT, so we could file our 1600 Sched, Jason and I headed off on foot to find the Alpha Company commander. We asked a couple of marines where to locate him, but they were like zombies. All we got were a series of indistinct grunts and gestures. I guessed it was a fair one. It was like a champion boxer had taken on the underdog and got knocked to the floor. They'd been left reeling.

By luck rather than their directions we stumbled on to the Alpha

Company HQ. It was situated at an Amtrak, forwards right of the northern end of the bridge. The company commander was a Marine Corps major. He was out on foot a few paces away from the vehicle, gazing north into the cursed city and mouthing into a radio. We identified ourselves, and alerted him to the whereabouts of the Bradley and its grim cargo. It was adjacent to Alpha Company's right flank, so easy for them to investigate. Or at least it should be. I couldn't quite tell if he'd registered what I was saying. He seemed frozen; shell-shocked; all over the place.

There seemed little chance of getting any usable information out of him about what lay ahead. I tried asking, but he'd got dead, injured and missing marines scattered across the battleground, and he had his own shit to deal with. A focused briefing for the nine of us just wasn't happening.

We returned to our position on the bridge and I gazed up Ambush Alley. It was there that we needed to go. There was movement down there now. I pulled out my Nikon binoculars, a civvie purchase that I'd made just prior to deploying. They were compact and semi-waterproof, and they boasted low-light intensifier lenses. Via the binos I pulled Ambush Alley into sharp focus. I could see young women wearing dull black and beige headscarves scurrying this way and that, plus a couple of old biddies bent double with bags. Kids too. It looked as if the civvie population had broken cover to make some last-minute moves before nightfall.

There was no way the locals would be out and about if it was still Murder Central down there. It was a sure combat indicator when civvies disappeared from a city's streets. Conversely, when they reappeared you could pretty much conclude that it had all gone quiet. It was almost dusk now, and I figured it was time we pushed on.

For some frustrating reason Tricky couldn't raise PF HQ, but we couldn't afford to delay any more. It was 1530, and we'd likely miss our 1600 Sched, for we couldn't make the call on the move. But we could try again just as soon as we got into a static position with some security. In any case, I'd spoken to John just about every hour whilst we were halted at the Marine Corps command post, so he knew in detail what we were doing.

I asked Jason what he reckoned. He figured it was okay to move ahead. We'd press onwards and make the final call on the mission at the northern bridge. With the light fading fast we needed to move. Out of everything we do, operating at night is our absolute area of expertise.

We owned the night, and right now we had to get moving.

CHAPTER FOURTEEN

I'd been forward, speaking with Jason, and it was only when I went to return to my vehicle that I noticed what was happening with the Engineer Recce guys. They were flapping like they were about to take off. It turned out that their Land Rover had suffered a puncture. They'd been twenty minutes trying to change the tyre, and they couldn't seem to work out how to use the jack properly.

The Pinkies use a high-lift jack system, one that resembles a big chunk of steel pipe and levers. It consists of half a dozen parts, which you click together like a Meccano kit. With the arm under a jacking point, the high-lift can ratchet up the wagon to some considerable height. It's far lighter than a trolley jack, and it allows you to get right beneath the wagon if you need to, for repairs.

In the PF we kept our high-lifts strapped to the left-hand side of the wagon, right next to the spare wheel. Unbelievably, the Engineer Recce guys didn't seem to know where the various pieces of their jack were, or how to assemble it properly. As I watched the cluster fuck they were making of trying to change a tyre, I was boiling up with frustration.

We spend several months of every year training for vehicle-mounted mobility operations. The very basic first rung of such training is learning to deal with a puncture. We'd been refused the option of a para-insertion for the Qalat Sikar mission, and instead we'd been lumbered with an overland insertion, plus three guys who couldn't change a tyre. Right now they were putting the lives of my blokes in danger by their ineptitude. It would have been bloody laughable if it weren't such a fuck-up, and that was the root cause of my anger.

Perched on a bridge over the Euphrates in the midst of war-torn Nasiriyah was hardly the time nor the place to teach those guys how to change a tyre. We had little cover, and I wanted to get us moving pronto. Not a hundred yards away was a blown-up Amtrak, so the Iraqis had clearly been unleashing some big pieces of weaponry on the Yanks. Those Engineer Recce blokes had been bolted on to us to up the numbers, but right now it felt as if a massive ball and chain had been tied around our ankles.

By now Jason had also clocked the tyre-changing charade. The Engineer Recce blokes had yet to get the jack fitted together properly, and he was staring at them in utter disbelief. I saw him jab Dez in the ribs, and then Dez was staring at them in utter bemusement.

I caught Jason's eye and gave a nod in Dez's direction. 'Jase, get Dez on to it will you?'

In a flash Dez was off his wagon and over by the Engineer Recce vehicle. He was like a Tasmanian Devil: bam, bam, bam and it was done. Puncture sorted. From the sheepish looks on the Engineer Recce guys' faces, I guessed they knew how badly they'd messed up here. Had their vehicle got bogged down in the sand, and they'd not known how to free it properly, we might have cut them some slack. But this was so basic it was outrageous. *A recce team who couldn't change a tyre – in my book it was beyond fucking useless. It was ama-teur hour.*

That tyre-changing crap had wasted us a good twenty minutes, and it was 1600 dead when finally we moved off. We'd wrapped our faces in our shemaghs and dirtied ourselves up as much as possible. In the semi-darkness, and from a distance, I hoped very much that we could pass as locals. Bravo and Charlie Companies were 3 kilo-metres ahead of us, so that was how far we had to go.

We were driving on NVG, and up ahead Ambush Alley was bathed in a sea of fluorescent green brightness. There was good ambient light from a clear sky and we could see well to drive. We left the bridge and moved on to the flat, empty expanse of the darkened highway. We were alert and manning the weapons, whilst at the same time trying to make like we were some kind of local Iraqi militia. We were so used to patrolling in vehicles that we could have the weapons in a relaxed pose, but very quickly bring them to bear and put down murderous fire.

Ambush Alley seemed totally deserted now that it was dark, and we were the only thing that appeared to be moving out there. There was the odd, bullet-riddled, shitty white estate car abandoned by the roadside, and here and there light leaked from a cracked door or a window, but no one seemed to notice our passing. It was a tense, ten-minute drive before we reached the rear unit of the American forces. We'd asked the Alpha Company commander to radio Bravo and Charlie that we were moving forwards: *Beware, British Path-finders coming through.*

I spotted a group of Amtraks to the left of the road, in an expanse of flat, open ground. The road was elevated, and we could see further armoured vehicles to the right of us, in all-around defence. We stopped beside the first vehicle that had radio antennae. I went to introduce myself and to ask if this was the Company HQ. The guys here appeared more than a little surprised to see me, and I figured no radio message had got through. They also looked shell-shocked, and were clearly on the alert for further attacks.

One of the marines made a vague and exhausted gesture into the gathering darkness, pointing me in the direction of the Company HQ. We moved on and reached the second bridge, the one that crossed the Saddam Canal. It was smaller than the Euphrates River bridge, consisting of a flat concrete structure about 200 metres long. We crawled across it and at the northern end we located the Charlie Company HQ. Looking west I could just make out the lowrise silhouette of the city, about a kilometre away. To the east there were no buildings of any significance except for a few scattered huts.

We were on the northern outskirts of the city now, and as far as our intel briefings had told us there was only empty rural terrain ahead. It was 1700 and almost completely dark. All seemed quiet. Jason stayed with the blokes in the vehicles, as I moved forward on foot to speak to the Charlie Company commander. We were right on the front line, and it was best that Jase stayed with the wagons in case anything kicked off.

I moved through the men and vehicles of Charlie Company, the most forward unit of the US Marine Corps in Iraq. The grunts seemed hugely battle-fatigued, but they weren't as totally finished as their comrades from the Alpha and Bravo Companies. I found one of the Charlie Company commanders in his vehicle, and I made my introductions.

'Hi, I'm David, a British Pathfinder. We've got a recce mission 120 kilometres north of your front line. Have you seen any sign of the enemy north of your positions?'

'Yeah, I just got a radio message you Pathfinder guys were coming through,' he confirmed. 'But no,' he shook his head. 'No contact ahead of here for the last couple of hours.'

'And is your intel the same as ours – that there's nothing significant north of here in terms of the enemy?'

The guy eyed me for a second. 'We don't *believe* there's anything much out there.' He was choosing his words carefully. 'We don't *believe* there is. But, you know, we don't know for sure.'

'So as far as you know it's relatively benign?'

He nodded. 'That's the intel picture all right. But then again, there weren't supposed to be any significant hostile forces in Nasiriyah, and look what Alpha and Bravo got hit by, plus my boys. Lord only knows what might lie ahead of us.'

'Okay, but your best guess is that it's relatively benign?' I persisted.

'Yeah, right now we got nothing better to go on. So, I figure it's still relatively benign.'

'Okay, then we're going to press ahead and proceed with our mission. Where is your last vehicle?'

For a moment he stared at me. He seemed lost for words. It was like the idea of the nine of us pressing onwards into the unknown just didn't compute.

I repeated the question: 'Where is your last vehicle?'

He glanced at his map. 'It's around 300 metres to the north at the next road junction, a T-intersection where the main highway makes a sharp turn eastwards.'

I knew the road junction well from the maps: it was burned into my memory. 'Okay, and thanks,' I told him. 'We'll be seeing you.'

'Good luck with your mission,' he called after me. 'And one more thing, buddy: you'd best keep a watch out for any US warplanes, as much as you do the enemy. Two of our AAVs were hit by A10 tank-busters, and I lost a lot of good guys. So you'd best keep one eye on the skies.'

He asked me if we had Blue Force Tracker. I told him we did. He told me it had done little to safeguard his guys, so we'd best keep checking the skies. At the height of today's battle, two A10 Warthog tankbuster aircraft had pounced upon Charlie Company's AAVs (Amphibious Armoured Vehicles), as they tried to push through Ambush Alley and take the northern bridge. In the fog of war, the A10s had made several strafing runs with their 30mm cannons, before they'd realised what a horrific mistake they'd made.

By that time one marine from Charlie Company was dead and seventeen were wounded. The warning of the threat of friendly fire was ominous, but there was little I could do about it now. I thanked the Charlie Company commander for it, and returned to my patrol.

'Okay, guys, this is the sketch,' I told them. 'They haven't seen anything, or been in contact for the last couple of hours. Their intel picture echoes ours: north of here, relatively benign. Let's move forward to their last vehicles, which are at the T-intersection, and ask them what's what. If there's no change, I say we crack on.'

There were murmurs of agreement all around. We took a momentary pause, whilst each of us heaved on our Kevlar body armour, which until now had been sat in the rear of the vehicles. If we felt the situation warranted it we'd opt to wear the stuff, and now was as good a time as any to put on the Kevlar.

We checked that all the vehicle-mounted weapons had a round in the chamber, and we did likewise with our personal weapons. We'd been locked and loaded from the very moment of setting out from the FOB, but it never hurt to double-check.

Safety catches would be left on until the moment we were engaged or had to open fire. They needed to be, in case the vehicle hit a rut and you had a negligent discharge – the shock of the impact making the gun go off of its own accord. Your finger remained resting on the safety at all times, so it could be flicked off and you could open fire in one fluid movement.

But right now I was feeling fairly confident that we could push ahead without being compromised. I figured the drive along Ambush Alley had proved one crucial thing: a tiny force like ours could pretty much slip through undetected, if making like locals and driving at night on no lights and NVG.

I leaned forwards and flicked a switch on the dashboard, which cut all the circuits to the wagon's lights. Having done so, none of the Pinkie's lights would come on, not even the brake lamps. We pulled our shemaghs – our chequered Arab headscarves – up over our faces, until only our eyes were showing. We then roughened up our combats, our assorted rag-tag of uniforms.

We checked our weapons one last time: our personal assault rifles and pistols; magazines; ammo; grenades; grenade launchers; rocket launchers; plus the four GPMGs (General Purpose Machine Guns) and the two 50-calibre heavy machine guns mounted in the wagons. Finally, we flipped down our NVG, and waited for our eyesight to adjust to the smudgy, fluorescent-green alien-world glare.

We moved off and skirted around the US command wagon, pushing ahead until we were 2 kilometres north of the Saddam Canal bridge. As we approached the road's T-junction we slowed, searching for the last US Marine Corps vehicles. But there was nothing that we could detect in any direction.

We scanned the surrounding terrain first with our NVG, and then with our SOPHIE thermal imaging sights, but there was not a single Amtrak, Bradley or Abrams tank that we could make out. We figured that either the Charlie Company commander was mistaken about the location of his last vehicles, or the platoon had moved.

We paused for a few minutes to have a collective heads-up. We'd seen no sign of the last American positions, but equally we'd seen no sign of the enemy. Nothing had changed about the intel picture or the state of play, as far as we could tell.

If we'd got any concrete warnings from the Americans that there were Iraqi positions up ahead of us, then we'd have had to re-visit the mission plan. Maybe we'd have opted to try the tracks that looped eastwards, keeping off the major roads. But as it was, Charlie Company had been here for several hours and seen nothing. We figured we must have entered some kind of no man's land – that we'd pushed past the American front line and were into uncharted territory – but still I felt reasonably confident about moving ahead.

The American forces were driving HUMVEEs, Amtraks, Bradleys or Abrams tanks, all of which were hulking great armoured monsters, and unmissable. They dwarfed the Pinkies. We were in open-backed wagons wearing shemaghs over our faces, and dressed in a motley collection of uniforms. We reckoned we could flit past any Iraqi positions that might be out there, and those that did see us would take us for an elite unit of the Iraqi Republican Guard, or something similar. The vote was to crack on.

It was 1730 when we made the turn at the T-intersection heading eastwards, the start of a short dogleg that would take us from Route 8 to Route 7 – the freeway leading all the way to Qalat Sikar. The airfield was 120 kilometres north of here, and we had nine hours in which to make it, and get the PARAs in for their H-Hour. It was all doable.

In the confusion of trying to locate the last friendly positions, and get some usable intel off the Americans, Tricky and I had forgotten to send our 1600 Sched. Not sending it would trigger a process which would force PF HQ to consider us compromised and on the run, and to cue up the CSAR teams. But we didn't realise that we'd missed our Sched.

We moved out, heading north into the darkness and the unknown.

CHAPTER FIFTHTEEN

Almost unconsciously, our senses had become hugely height-ened as we moved forwards. We'd left the protective screen of the US Marine Corps, and we were out here on our own. But we were not here to recce this area. We had the draw of Qalat Sikar airfield pulling us forwards, and that was our focus.

We headed eastwards, the road passing through open, rural ter-rain. All around us there were thick palm groves, and the dense undergrowth was interspersed with the shadowy forms of low, mud-walled huts and farm-like structures.

We were hyper-alert to the presence of any US vehicles, in case they'd pushed ahead of the T-junction. The last thing we needed was a Bradley Infantry Fighting Vehicle opening up on us. The Bradley boasts an array of fearsome weaponry that could chew our Pinkies into shreds in seconds. But there was no sign of anything. No Ameri-can armour. No Iraqi military positions. No civilians. Nothing.

My brain felt unusually calm, quiet and clear. There weren't a hun-dred different thoughts crashing through my mind, as there often are when out on exercises. It was like a form of meditation, this tun-ing in to the night environment and our surroundings. I opened up my mind and my senses to any changes in the atmosphere and the setting, and I was hyper-alert to any sense of threat. But there was nothing that I could detect.

We approached the second T-junction, where Route 8 ran into

Route 7. It was here that we'd take the turning heading north, and that would complete the short dogleg around the outskirts of the city. We'd then leave Nasiriyah behind us. We slowed to a crawl as we swung around the junction, and as we did so I caught sight of the first substantial building that we'd seen since leaving the US front-line positions.

Just to the east of Route 7 there was this large, mud-walled compound. It was dark as the grave, and it seemed to be utterly deserted. But still there was something ominous about the place, and I sensed that it represented real danger and ... evil almost. It was weird, but the sense of blackness that emanated from the place was more than just visible. I could feel it.

A chill went up my spine as we began to sneak past at a dead slow. We were puttering along at 30 kph, our 2.5-litre diesel engines purring softly in the still night air, our tyres making just the faintest hum on the tarmac. We'd drilled and drilled and drilled for this kind of noiseless driving. The secret was making no sudden movements with the Pinkies – no noisy acceleration, or engines growling, or gears grinding, or the scrunching of tyres on the road. All was smooth and silent, and we were as soundless as the wind. A soft gust would cover our passing.

And then I heard it. *Voices.* It was just the faintest snatch of Arabic hanging in the cool desert air. I tuned in, my ears hoovering up the sound. The voices seemed louder than they really were in the night-dark quiet. I could tell that these weren't raised voices, that this wasn't someone shouting in alarm. This wasn't someone yelling: *What the fuck are those vehicles?*

I swivelled my head and my weapon about, trying to catch the chatter, so I could pinpoint what direction the voices were coming from. And then, in the periphery of my vision, I caught sight of the figures. I swung my eyes directly on to them, and as I did so I was sighting down the barrel of my gun. At one end of the dark compound a group of seated men were chatting away, and each was cradling a weapon in his hands.

They were 50 metres or so away from us, but I could tell by the cut of their forage caps that they were Iraqi soldiers. I figured it had to be a platoon-strength position, so maybe thirty men in all. I didn't know if Jason had seen them, for his wagon was 250 metres in front of us. All the Iraqi soldiers needed to do was glance towards the road, and they'd see me sighting them down the barrel of my GPMG.

The Gimpy as we call it – pronounced 'jimpee' – has a very simple set of metal sights, and the stark iron 'V' was outlined in the glow of my NVG. I was poised to flick off the safety, and open up on those figures, at the faintest sign of any trouble. I knew that the moment I did so the GPMG would spit out a funnel of fire, annihilating the figures before my eyes.

I didn't need to check that Tricky had clocked where I was aiming, and that he'd got the 50-cal ready to drop thunder if they spotted us. Even though there might be thirty enemy soldiers, we could easily outgun a platoon of Iraqi troops, especially when we had surprise on our side. We had the 50-cal and the GPMG mounted on a very stable fire platform. They had thirty hand-held AK47s.

As we crept forwards my heart thudded in my ears, but no one seemed to notice our passing. Within seconds we were leaving that sinister building and its occupants behind, apparently without anyone spotting us. Breathing a long sigh of relief, I swung my weapon and myself back to face the way ahead. The road looked flat and straight for several miles. It was dark and deserted as far as I could see, and devoid of any movement or headlights.

We were running along a raised embankment. To the west, the ground dropped away. To the east it rose to a low ridge, which was dotted with a scatter of outbuildings. There wasn't the slightest glimmer of light, or any sign of life anywhere in all directions. We gathered speed, and all I could hear was the hum of tyres on tarmac, and the rush of the night wind. I presumed that we were through the Iraqi front line positions now, so from here on it was a straight drive to Qalat Sikar. We were free-running all the way towards the mission objective.

Up ahead were the reassuring forms of Jason and the Recce Engineers' Pinkies. I had no doubt that we could still pull off the mission. For a moment I reflected on what we'd learned whilst passing through Nasiriyah. If the intel could have been so hopelessly wrong about that place – which by anyone's reckoning had spawned the mother of all battles – maybe they'd got it equally wrong about the area running north to Qalat Sikar airfield.

It was hardly a pleasant thought, but it was one worth considering. Maybe it wasn't relatively benign out there at all. Maybe the airfield wasn't largely unoccupied. But if so it wouldn't be the first time that the intel picture had been so hopelessly out of kilter. Either way we were at war, and as Jacko Page had told us back in Kuwait, he was expecting the extraordinary out of the Pathfinder Platoon.

The reason why the British Army had formed the Pathfinders was to take the risks required on the intel available, and to go forwards. That way we risked six, and not 600 or 6000 men. We might lose a couple of vehicles, and a few good blokes, but not an entire battalion. What we were doing now defined the PF: it went with the territory.

We were a kilometre north of the T-junction when for an instant I thought I caught the sound of voices again. We'd upped the speed to 40 kph by now, so I had to strain my ears above the roar of the wind to hear. Sure enough I could just make out the faintest gabble of Arabic. The night vision goggles tended to channel your sight into a tunnel of green light wherever you were looking, and your vision went dark and foggy towards the periphery. I glanced left, in the direction of the voices, and suddenly I spotted the source of the chatter.

There was a pair of soldiers strolling towards us on our side of the road. They were sporting smart forage caps, and each had an AK47 slung across his right shoulder. There was a slight hesitation in the step of the guy in front as his eyes met mine, and I could tell that there was a momentary freezing of his mind. I knew for sure that he'd seen us, and it was as if he was thinking – *What in God's name is that?* He was no more than 5 metres away as we rolled silently past him, and I was gazing right into his eyes.

Everything seemed to wind down to ultra-slow motion. I could see the Iraqi soldier's mind scrambling for some kind of comprehension, some sliver of understanding, some clue as to what this dark vision that had emerged silently from the night might be. My face was covered by my shemagh, my eyes shielded by the night vision goggles. All that he could see of me was the faint, other-worldly glow that the NVG threw off, making two pinpricks of fluorescent light, like frog-green alien eyes.

An instant later we'd shot past. I had to force myself to resist the temptation to swing the GPMG and myself around. That wasn't the ruse here. If we were a unit of elite Iraqi troops – say Republican Guard Special Forces – we were hardly going to pay those two Iraqi soldiers much heed. We would thunder on regardless, Saddam's elite treating those two Iraqi conscripts with the scant regard that they deserved.

The psychology here was a lot like kids out vandalising a car, when the cops drive by: *Don't look, or they'll know it's us*. We just had to carry on as if we had every right to be here. We wanted to leave those Iraqi soldiers with the firm impression that Saddam's finest were coming through. We'd got to hope we could bluff our ticket, and slip away silently into the night.

Once we were past them I concentrated on covering my arc of fire – from 8 o'clock to 2 o'clock in front of the vehicle. For all I knew there might be more enemy troops ahead of us on the road, and that was what I was searching for in the darkness. I knew that Tricky would be watching the rear. If it looked as if those two Iraqi soldiers were going to open fire, Tricky would mallet them with the 50-cal.

My thoughts as we sped onwards into the night were these: *Fuck me, that was outrageous!* I'd just passed an Iraqi soldier at arm's length, whose brief it was to kill me, and I'd looked him in the eye man-to-man. He was close enough to reach out and strangle me, or for me to reach out and grab him. I'd never heard of anything like this happening, not in the PF or any other unit. Whenever we got to the airfield and got the PARAs in, the blokes on my patrol would sure have some stories to tell.

The image of the Iraqi soldier that I'd eyeballed was burned into my mind. A lot of the Iraqi conscripts tended to look like a sack of shit, but not that guy. He was neat and professional-looking, his drab olive cap matching his drab olive uniform, and his weapon slung on a smart, polished leather sling. The bloke was lean and clean-shaven, with a neatly-trimmed moustache. He had one hand stuffed in his pocket, and his right hand resting easily on his slung weapon.

His buddy was smoking a ciggie. I'd seen the glow blooming green and smudgy in my night vision. I was struck by how relaxed they both looked as they strolled along Route 7. I compared their appearance to that of the US Marines, just a few kilometres to the south. The Iraqi soldiers appeared calm but ready. Compared to the US Marines that we'd encountered during the day, they had an air of cool about them. They certainly weren't flapping that the US Marine Corps was massed just to the south of them, and on the warpath.

Those two soldiers were so close to Nasiriyah that they had to be part of the unit that had been engaged in battle with the US Marine Corps that day. I figured that they were part of a company that made up a battalion, one that had been ordered by Saddam to repulse the US Marine Corps' advance. Their easy self-confidence had surprised me, and it was strangely unsettling.

It was the right decision not to have opened fire. Our job was to get to the airfield and facilitate 1 PARA's insertion, not to start brassing up the first enemy that we came across. If we passed by unnoticed, or were gone too swiftly for them to challenge us on our identities, then all the better for the mission.

An elite Iraqi Republican Guard unit would most likely be driving GAZ jeeps, a Soviet-era four-by-four used widely by the Iraqi armed forces. The Gorky Automobile Plant (GAZ) started manufacturing their jeep in the 1940s, so it hailed from a similar era to the Land Rover. At first glance the GAZ was not dissimilar in appearance to the Pinkies. The GAZ jeep was an open-backed four-by-four, with distinctly rugged, Second World War lines. You'd have to study our wagons carefully to be certain that they weren't

GAZs, especially when they shot past from out of the darkness.

I'd read confusion in that Iraqi soldier's eyes, plus real surprise, but there was no sudden realisation there that we were the enemy. I had to presume that for now at least the bluff was working. I knew instinctively that Steve and Tricky had also seen them. We'd lain in OPs (Observation Posts) for days on end, shitting into bags and hearing each other's life stories. I'd known instinctively that we were all on to them, and that each of us had clocked exactly what the others had seen.

When we went firm as a patrol we'd compare notes, just to make doubly sure that we'd all seen the same things. Any one of us was free to open fire, if he judged that he had to. But we'd only do so if we were being engaged, or if we were about to be engaged. The rule was to wait, wait, wait, because we might get through unchallenged and get away with it, just as we seemed to be doing right now.

We pushed onwards in a tense silence for another kilometre. A small building appeared on the left-hand side of the road. Clustered around it I could see a dozen Iraqi soldiers lounging around with their weapons. At the minimum this had to be a platoon-sized position, but it was a hundred metres or more away from the road, and I reckoned we could slip past unnoticed.

The nearer we got the more details I could make out. There were five guys sitting outside the building, and I figured there had to be more inside. They were not so much on sentry duty as hanging out and shooting the shit. Maybe it was some kind of checkpoint, but it was too far from the road to be effective. Still, I found myself thinking: *Jesus, more fucking Iraqis!* I had hoped we were through the main concentration of their front line positions by now.

A couple of the enemy soldiers got to their feet, but still they were chatting away unconcernedly. They clearly hadn't seen Jason's vehicle, or the Engineer Recce wagon. I saw a head flicking in our direction, but by the time the soldier thought that maybe he'd heard something we were flitting past, onwards into the night. I told myself that maybe that was it. Surely by now we'd pushed through the Iraqi front line, and more or less without being seen. I sure bloody hoped so.

We pushed onwards for another 5 kilometres. Nothing. The road up ahead was reassuringly dead. Dark. Deserted. It was great for using the night vision, for there were no man-made lights visible anywhere to flare it out. There was little limit to what we could see range-wise in this kind of ambient light. The terrain was totally silent. There wasn't a human voice, nor a dog barking, nor a farm animal bleating, nor an engine grunting anywhere, and all I could hear was the roar of the wind above the quiet purr of our vehicles.

I was starting to hope that the intel picture would hold up now. I was hoping that we'd sneaked through the Iraqi forces, and that we were in the clear. I glanced to the rear of our wagon and there was not the slightest sign of anyone in pursuit. We'd bluffed our way through at least three groups of Iraqi troops, which in itself was amazing going. I allowed myself to relax a little, as I shifted my weight behind my weapon.

We hit the 10-kilometre mark – 110 still to go – and there were some outbuildings to the east of the road. They were set back on a ridge some 500 metres away, and mostly they were dark. From one or two I got the occasional glimpse of light, as if a candle had been left burning behind a partly-shuttered window.

Jason's vehicle started to pick up speed. We followed suit. Soon we were barrelling along at 70 kph. It was a good call. There was no point hanging around in utterly deserted territory for any longer than we had to. Then I spotted a lone pair of headlamps far ahead of us.

I studied them closely with the NVG. The lights were close to the road, so it had to be a car, as opposed to a jeep or a truck. As the vehicle got closer I could make out that it was some kind of white sedan. It looked like an Iraqi taxicab. We'd been told to expect the occasional civvie vehicles on Route 7, for it was the main highway to Baghdad.

If we pulled off the road to avoid this vehicle we might have to do the same all the way to the airfield, especially if there was a lot of civvie traffic about. In any case, that wasn't the deal here. The bluff was that we were an elite Iraqi unit, and if we were spotted skulking about by the roadside we'd have blown our cover. As the vehicle drew closer, Jason made the call to carry on driving north up the highway. It was exactly the right thing to do as far as I was concerned.

I saw the car pass Jason's Pinkie, and it visibly slowed. As the Engineer Recce wagon neared, the driver momentarily flicked his headlamps on to full beam, fully illuminating the wagon. By the time we were approaching the sedan it was barely crawling along, and there was this face pressed close to the windscreen and peering up at us.

Tricky, Steve and I flipped up our NVG, to prevent the car's head-lamps whiting out our night vision and blinding us. As the vehicle got nearer, the driver flicked his lights from dip to full and back again. He had our Pinkie fully illuminated in his headlamps, so he could get a real good look at us. We shot past and I could see the driver star-ing up into my face. He was a fat, moustachioed geezer dressed in a dish-dash. He looked like some Iraqi version of Ron Jeremy, the fat American porn star with a droopy moustache. I guessed he was your typical Iraqi cabbie, one who used his taxi to drive to the local corner shop he was that flabby.

But whilst he was overweight and paunchy, his brain appeared to be pretty sharp. He took this great, long look at us, and I could see this expression of total consternation spreading across his fea-tures. There was alarm and disquiet in those pudgy eyes, like he was suddenly on to the fact that we were far from being his fellow Iraqi brothers in arms.

A thought flashed through my mind: *Never take the third light*. It's an old Army saying from the First World War. In the trenches, the guy who struck the match would alert the enemy to your position. The second light would give the enemy something to aim at. And with the third light … he'd pull the trigger. Hence you never accepted the third light.

We were the third vehicle in our well-spaced convoy. I figured with

Jason's wagon the Iraqi cabbie had thought – *What the fuck was that*? With the Engineer Recce truck he'd slowed down and asked himself – *Are those Iraqi vehicles*?

And with us his eyes had started bulging with disbelief – *Who the hell are those guys*?

CHAPTER SIXTEEN

As we pushed onwards into the night I was not sure exactly what the fat cabbie's facial expression had meant. He'd seen these weird alien warriors steaming out of the night, but did that mean that we'd been compromised? And would anyone listen to him if he tried to raise the alarm? If the cabbie knew what was best for him he'd keep quiet, for who was ever going to believe his story?

We carried on driving, and it was Steve who broke the silence. 'Did you see fucking Ron Jeremy giving us the once-over?'

'Yeah, what d'you reckon?'

'I pity the poor Iraqi bird that's married to that one.'

That was Steve's way of saying that we had no choice but to crack on. Of course we could always turn around and shoot up the enemy forces that we'd seen behind us, but that wasn't our mission. We had to presume that we'd had another lucky escape with Ron Jeremy, and continue with the mission.

We'd got 15 kilometres under our belts since Nasiriyah, so 105 left to go. From the sat photos of Qalat Sikar we figured it was pretty much open desert some 30 kilometres this side of the airfield. Once we hit the 30 kilometres to target mark we could leave the road and head overland, which meant all we needed to do was get near enough to that open terrain.

I felt a sudden sharp whack on the shoulder from Tricky. 'Dave! Dave! Lights coming up fast from behind!'

For a moment I went to check my rear-view mirror, before remembering the wagon didn't have one. At night, wing and driver's mirrors can reflect street lamps and car headlights, so giving your position away. During the daytime, if the sun caught a mirror it could flash a blinding reflection across enormous distances, and directly into the eyes of the enemy. In fact, small mirrors are often carried by SF units as a last resort, to signal a position to a rescue party. I had one stashed in my grab bag.

I turned my head and gazed backwards along the length of the Pinkie. I could see this dazzling light beaming out of the darkness, and bleaching out my night vision. It was a lone pair of headlights coming up fast from behind. The nearer the headlamps got, the more I was convinced that it was the same vehicle as before – Ron Jeremy's taxicab.

As we were the last in line it was with our vehicle that the fat Iraqi cabbie first pulled level. He had one hand on the wheel while the other was fiddling in the pocket of his dish-dash, and he was staring up at us in total amazement. He pulled out what looked like a mobile phone, and started gabbling into it. I spotted the distinctive flick of an antenna poking out of the top of it, and realised that it was some kind of radio.

Suddenly, Ron Jeremy was no longer just a run-of-the-mill Iraqi cabbie. They didn't carry those kinds of radios. But if he was Iraqi military, he was well out of shape and far too old to be a junior-ranking soldier. So maybe – just maybe – he was some kind of Iraqi commander heading back to his front line positions. If he was, and if he was radioing through our presence to headquarters, that was seriously bad news.

Still, he needed to know exactly where he was on the road to give our position accurately. It was night, and there had been no noticeable landmarks in the last 10 kilometres or so. It wasn't going to be easy for him to pinpoint our convoy, even if he had pinged us. For a moment, I considered blowing the guy away, but he was driving a civvie vehicle and he was dressed like a civvie, and I couldn't see any weapon.

If I brassed him up I'd have to live with that for the rest of my life, and PF or no PF, I wasn't up for murdering civilians. In any case, we'd been given very specific rules of engagement for Iraq. We knew that we had to be able to positively identify an Iraqi with a weapon, one who was a clear and present threat to us, before we were permitted to open fire.

The car dropped behind us, overtook again, then pulled in behind Jason's Pinkie. I was certain that he was 'dicking' us – a phrase that we had used in Northern Ireland when we had an enemy disguised as a civvie spying on our patrols. I was equally convinced that he was reporting back all that he could see to some form of higher control. But I had no proof that this was so.

I'd seen no weapon, he'd not opened fire on us, and he wasn't causing us any physical harm. Even though we'd seen him dicking us, unless we were under heavy and accurate fire it was best to stay covert for as long as possible when on a mission such as this one. In short, I couldn't find the slightest excuse to blow his brains out, which one part of me was very tempted to do. One other thing was absolutely clear. Whoever the hell the guy was, he had balls of total steel to do what he was doing. He was getting eyes-on with our vehicle, then the next and the next, and all the while he was a sitting target. *Balls of fucking steel!*

I wondered what it was that had fingered us as a non-Iraqi unit. Our wagons had military number plates on them, but they were non-reflective and I doubted that he could see them. With the amount of kit hanging off the Pinkies they could easily be GAZ jeeps, for their shape was all but totally obscured. We were probably physically bigger than most Iraqi soldiers, but we certainly wouldn't look like any US marine did in the video games that Ron Jeremy played.

Finally, his vehicle dropped behind us again, and his lights disappeared. All I could think was – *Thank fuck he's gone.* We were 25 kilometres in now, but I could sense that the net was starting to close. Yet there was still no sign of any Iraqi forces on our tail, and we had to hope that we'd got through the worst.

We were a good quarter of the way to Qalat Sikar, and the worst we'd had was some ballsy Iraqi cabbie-cum-fat-controller fucking with our shit. It was a lot of ground to have covered without a single shot being fired, and I figured that we were getting there. I could see a long, long way in front, and there wasn't a vehicle or a building in sight.

Even if the net was closing, they still had to find and catch us, plus there was no way we could ever go back the way we'd come. I could guess at the size of the Iraqi force that was positioned behind us, which had to be a couple of companies at the very least. I'd got a sense of their calibre too. They were going head-to-head with the US Marine Corps, and they were hardly running away or throwing down their weapons.

We had to presume that Ron Jeremy had alerted the Iraqi force commanders to our presence, so they'd be waiting for us, and that meant the element of surprise was totally gone. There was no option but to keep pushing north. Still, I couldn't shake off this creepy feeling that we were driving into a trap, and that in turn got me thinking about how to survive if the enemy did capture any of us.

We'd recently attended a talk by the British general Sir Anthony Farrar-Hockley, who was then a living legend in elite forces circles. Some generals had one medal earned on peacetime ops, but Farrar-Hockley was the real deal. During the Korean War he'd been taken prisoner by the enemy, and had escaped and been recaptured several times over.

It was amazing that he was still alive after all he had been through, let alone so pin-sharp in his presentation. He had to be well into his eighties, and it was a true privilege for every bloke in the PF to hear his stories from the Korean War, which was still the fiercest conflict fought by British forces since the Second World War. What he had been through – the repeated hell of capture and torture and interrogation – was very much what we dreaded happening to us on our kind of missions.

The general looked robustly healthy, and he was unlike any man that I'd ever seen of that age. He told us that the secret to staying youthful was to keep the mind busy and occupied. He talked about how he'd kept himself mentally strong under duress as a prisoner, and how strength of mind was the key to surviving such horrors. During one escape attempt he'd made it all the way back to his unit, only for it to get attacked again and for him to be recaptured.

He told us how they were fed very little in captivity, getting a few bowls of rice between many prisoners. There were two types of people who emerged at those times: those who shared a bowl of rice with you, and those who did not. He stressed how the more selfish prisoners who didn't share tended not to make it, whilst those who were generous with their fellows somehow had the strength and the will to survive. Against the odds it was the good guys who made it through, reflecting how mental fortitude was the absolute key to survival.

As Farrar-Hockley had talked us through all this, I'd wondered whether Jason was the type to share his bowl of rice with you. Back then, just a few months ago, I'd figured that he most likely was not. But right now on this mission, and heading into the heart of enemy territory, I was changing my mind fast on that one.

At Sandhurst I'd been taught to lead autocratically, by right and by rank. When I joined the Pathfinders I'd realised very quickly that was the wrong approach completely. I had to give the lads on my patrol far more respect than that. I'd done so to the ultimate degree with Jason on this mission, and he'd risen to the challenge. He was leading from the front, making a lot of command-type decisions on the fly, and I'd yet to fault a single move that he'd made. I guessed if I were prone to insecurity I'd see this as threatening my role, and seek to rein him in. Thankfully, I wasn't. As much as ever we could be, we were a team of equals.

The other thing that Jason was showing in bucketloads was sheer bravery and raw courage. There was a simple rationale behind putting your command vehicle in the rear: it meant the patrol leader and your command communications had greater protection. By taking pole position Jason's wagon was going to be first into any ambush. He knew that, and he'd never once baulked at it.

I was torn away from my thoughts by a distant crackle of gunfire. I turned my head and way behind I could see tracer rounds arcing high into the wide, starlit heavens. The fire was coming from somewhere back near the US Marine Corps' front line, and I had no idea who was firing at whom or why. But it sounded as if a firefight of sorts had sparked off again.

I had little time to dwell upon it. Up ahead the road was no longer a clear run through. Instead, there were two sets of headlamps bearing down upon us, pinpricks of light in a sea of blackness. They were larger and brighter than Ron Jeremy's cab lights, and they showed up like massive, smudged green frog-eyes in my NVG.

I could ID the lead vehicle pretty much right away, for the lights of the rear wagon were shining through and illuminating the one in front. It was a white minibus, and I could see by the silhouettes inside that it was packed full of women wearing burka-type head coverings. The vehicle behind looked to be a similar vehicle carrying a similar load.

It seemed as if some form of civvie transport – the local Nasiriyah bus service? – was bearing down upon us. We'd got to be doing a combined speed of 130 kph, and the distance between us narrowed rapidly. We rushed past the first minibus, and no one seemed to pay us any heed. Within seconds we were past both vehicles, and the road was clear again.

One thing occurred to me when we were passing, something that I hadn't really noticed before. Those minibuses had shot by on our left-hand, passenger side, because here in Iraq we were having to drive on the wrong side of the road for British vehicles. The Iraqis drive on the right, and it suddenly struck me that maybe that had been the giveaway to Ron Jeremy. How could we possibly be Iraqi Special Forces, if we were using right-hand-drive vehicles – *those that are driven by the foreigners*?

Steering wheel on the wrong side: it was glaringly obvious when you thought about it. He'd certainly spent long enough staring up at our wagons in the full illumination of his headlights to clock the fact that we were driving foreign vehicles. Up until now I'd just presumed that we could pass as an elite Iraqi unit. Suddenly, I was convinced otherwise. Ron Jeremy had clocked us: the question is, what would he and his Iraqi brethren do about it?

I flicked my eyes across to the milometer. We were 40 kilometres along Route 7, with 80 more to go. I checked my watch. In addition to the Bvlgari's indestructible black leather strap, it has a faintly luminous dial, which makes it easy to read. It is also waterproof to a depth of 600 metres, which made it all but bulletproof in terms of the kind of soldiering we did in the PF. It was approaching 1800 and it was as quiet as the grave out there. We had to press on.

All the satellite images and intel reports had suggested that there were no major Iraqi settlements along Route 7, the whole way from Nasiriyah to Qalat Sikar. The maps showed a couple of minor villages and a scattering of oil wells, but no major towns, and certainly no Iraqi army bases. Yet we were just 50 kilometres in when we hit our first major obstacle. Up ahead we could see the distinctive orange halo-like glow of street lamps. Street lamps had to mean a significant Iraqi settlement of some sort, for the smaller villages didn't even have them.

A kilometre in front of us and closing fast the road was bathed in a sea of orange light. As we drew closer I could see a dense cluster of buildings to the right, eastern side of the highway. These were the first street lamps that we'd seen since Nasiriyah. They reared above the highway like a long row of dinosaur necks, heads poised to strike downwards at their prey. Our convoy would be illuminated for the entire length of the highway on which they were situated.

We were a good 500 metres out when we were forced to discard our NVG, due to the blinding orange glow. We flipped up the goggles on their brackets, before the street lamps whited out our vision completely. Even so, it took several seconds for our eyes to adjust to the new light levels.

To the east of the road I could make out more of the buildings. There were groups of flat-roofed structures two or three storeys high, running for a good 300 metres along that side of the highway. Most were totally dark, but from the odd window a sliver of light spilled out from behind a curtain. This was a substantial human settlement, and it was clearly occupied.

The land rose up to a ridgeline several hundred metres high, and about a kilometre to the east. The buildings were set on the slope running up to that ridge, so they were higher than we were, with good views of the road. It looked as if this was some kind of a purpose-built settlement, and just about every building covered a huge killing area on the slope below, stretching down to the highway – Route 7 – itself.

It was an ominous proposition having to run this stretch of road in the full glare of those street lamps, and being so visible. I glanced to the left – western – side of the highway, to see if there was a way through off-road. But there was a wall of vegetation looking thick, dark and impenetrable. There was no point heading off-road that way, and going east would only take us directly into the built-up area. There was only one possible way through and that was dead ahead.

I saw Jason's wagon speeding up, and Steve pushed his pedal to the metal to keep up with the lead Pinkies. We hit 90 kph, and I figured Jason's plan had to be to run the street lamps at top speed and hammer on through. It made total sense to do so. There was no point trying to be all sneaky-beaky and creeping along, when we were going to be 100 per cent visible. That would make sitting ducks out of us.

We hit the pool of light beneath the first street lamp, and the instant we did so I felt horribly exposed. It was like being in the pitch black of night, and suddenly having a police helicopter put a massive searchlight over you. I could see the vegetation to the left-hand side very clearly now. It was a thick, tangled mass of bush, with palm trees arching over it. We were right keeping to the road.

Steve was gunning the engine, which was screaming and revving hard. I could feel the Pinkie weaving about as he fought for control over the steering. The wagon was painfully overloaded with all the weight in the rear, and it handled like a complete pig at anything like this speed. All we needed now was for one of the Pinkies to suffer a blowout, and we'd be fucked.

I held my breath as we barrelled through, the street lamps beaming down on us like fizzy orange daylight. I felt horribly naked, deprived of the cloak of darkness. As Pathfinders we shun the light, and running this stretch of road bathed in the glow of the street lamps felt like we were asking to get smashed. There was a shoulder-high wall along the eastern side of the road, one that provided a little cover from view, but still we were sticking out like a pair of dog's bollocks.

The tension was fucking horrible. Surely, someone had to see us. Jason's wagon hit a gap in the wall, and a series of sharp, staccato shots rang out into the air.

'*Crack! Crack-crack! Crack!*'

When the Engineer Recce wagon reached the gap, exactly the same thing happened: shots punched the night. '*Crack! Crack-crack! Crack!*'

As we came upon that same opening we heard a dozen-odd rounds tearing into the air. '*CRACK! CRACK-CRACK-CRACK! CRACK!*' The fire was close: it had come from somewhere on the far side of the wall, but no way were the rounds aimed at us. There wasn't a lot of difference in the noise made by our own 5.56 mm (NATO) rounds and a 7.62 mm short – the bullet fired by an AK47. They both made the same, distinctive sharp crack. And in these calm, cool, dry, desert conditions we could tell how close the gunman was.

Often, it was hard to tell where a round had come from exactly, but you always knew if you were the target. You saw tracer zipping past, the sound was amplified by the punch of pressure waves, and you might see bullets hitting the road or your vehicle. The bursts of fire from behind that wall had been squirted high into the dark night sky. But I didn't kid myself for one second that they weren't linked to our presence somehow.

The bursts of rounds had been synchronised with each wagon's passing. Whoever the gunman was, it almost felt like he was signalling that we were on our way. *But who was he signalling and why?* Again, I had that horrible, creepy feeling. Ice running down my spine.

We're driving into a trap.

CHAPTER SEVENTEEN

We sped out of the area lit by the street lamps and onwards into the welcoming blackness up ahead. I locked eyes with Steve. He leaned across to have a word.

He had to yell into my ear to make himself heard: 'See, mate, the thing about women is …'

At least it burst the tension bubble.

I flipped down my NVG, as we pushed onwards for another few minutes. Nothing. Blank darkness and an empty silence. I checked the milometer. We were 75 kilometres in now, so over halfway to Qalat Sikar airfield. Whoever the gunman may have been signalling, there didn't appear to be anyone out here, so maybe it wasn't a signal after all?

I got the answer to my question at the 85-kilometre mark. Up ahead a massive settlement emerged from the gloom. It straddled both sides of Route 7. By rights – and according to our intel and sat photos – it shouldn't even exist. But here it was, squat and dark and menacing, bang in front of us. This settlement was far larger than the first. It was more built up, with dozens of buildings three or four storeys high. But the strange thing was that it was completely dark. There were no street lamps, and barely a window was showing any light.

For a moment I wondered if it was deserted. Maybe it was a not-yet-finished town, or maybe it had been abandoned. I wasn't left in doubt for very long. As soon as the approach of our vehicles could be

– 186 –

heard from the settlement, we started taking incoming fire. It was pitch dark all around us, but we could hear these long bursts of fire come rolling in. '*Brrrzzzt! Brrrzzzt! Brrrzzzt!*' Whoever was trying to hit us, they were loosing off on automatic, and from the sound of the gunfire it was coming from a good half a kilometre away.

The hot, green slug-trails of tracer arced through our night vision, going way above us in the sky. Our attackers clearly couldn't see our wagons to aim at. We held our fire. If we opened up on the source of those tracer rounds, all it would serve to do was give our position away. We train and train and train for being under fire. We do so in the wagons, driving under fixed gun positions that squirt rounds over our heads. We do so on our belt buckles, crawling beneath barbed wire over which machine guns are pumping bullets. It gets you used to the terrifying noise and feel of being under attack.

The natural human reaction to being shot at is either fight, freeze or flee. We had taught ourselves to ignore such instinctive responses, so we could assess how best to deal with any combat situation – like now, when Tricky and I held our fire and Steve drove on through. It would be a cardinal sin in the PF to get a flap on. We needed to be able to think calmly and clearly when under intense pressure and danger. Anyone prone to panicking would've been deselected at an early stage, most likely when poised to jump off a C130 Hercules' tail ramp. But all the training in the world doesn't make you any the less shit scared.

There was more fire coming from the eastern side of the road now. There were maybe half a dozen AK47s squeezing off wild bursts, plus a heavier machine gun had opened up. But there was no way that they could see us. They were aiming at a speeding chimera, at ghosts.

As we hit the heart of the settlement the fire started to get more and more concentrated. I heard the unmistakable '*tzzzinnnggg-tzzzinnnggg-tzzzinnnggg!*' of rounds cutting through the air barely yards from our vehicle. Someone had to be spotting our progress, and calling through our position to the gunmen, to better direct their aim.

– 187 –

Whilst few of the Iraqi gunmen would have NVG, it would only take one commander with such kit to be doing the spotting. He would radio through our movements to his forward positions: *Enemy vehicles passing by the green mosque now.* That would give them a specific enough target area to aim for.

A couple of bigger, GPMG-type machine guns had joined in the one-way firefight. I could hear their throaty growl echoing around the darkened hillside, amongst the sharper crackle of the AKs. They were most likely Kalashnikov PKMs, Soviet-era belt-fed 7.62 mm tripod-mounted weapons, accurate up to 1000 metres or more.

As with the GPMG, the PKM is an area weapon, and it doesn't take pin-point accuracy to smash an adversary with one of those. It was a horrible feeling knowing that the PKM would be spitting out some 650 rounds per minute, and that every one of those bullets was trying to find us and smash us. Standard ambush drill is always to keep driving. It was far better simply to speed on through. If you tried to stop, fight or turn your wagons around, you made yourself a sitting target and you'd likely get killed. But still, I couldn't help wondering how the other lads were faring up ahead.

Just as we were almost through the settlement, I saw the fiery trail of an RPG (Rocket Propelled Grenade) streaking out from the ridge-line. Whilst I couldn't make out the warhead in the glow of the NVG, the exhaust trail appeared like a massive green comet roaring across the sky. In the thing came. It was heading right towards us. From the trajectory of the flaring green rocket trail, it looked as if it was aimed right at mine and Steve's heads. Instinctively I ducked, and the warhead thundered across the bonnet of our Pinkie, missing it by a bare couple of feet.

Targeting a vehicle moving fast at night and showing no lights is extremely difficult, even with a machine gun. To do so with an RPG from over 500 metres away was next to impossible. But that rocket had been horribly close – a one in a million shot. We thundered onwards and out of the built-up area, Steve gunning the Pinkie like crazy into the welcoming embrace of the night. Gradually, the fire started to fade away behind us. There was the crackle of gunshots and the odd crump of a powerful explosion in our wake, but they were firing into the space that we'd just vacated.

I was searching in the darkness up ahead with the GPMG, scanning my arcs, half expecting there to be a follow-up attack, or maybe a blocking group placed upon the highway. But all there seemed to be was open, deserted road stretching as far as the eye could see. Steve turned to me. I was readying myself for another wisecrack about women, or a peachy line from *Shrek*.

'That was small arms, HMGs, RPGs,' he yelled above the road noise. 'It's getting closer. Best we pull off the road and assess the situation.'

It was standard operating procedure in the Pathfinders that if any man saw something of crucial importance, he had the authority to call a halt to the patrol. It was the same as when you were in a contact, and you called a spot of ground to retreat to. Steve had made the call that we should stop and get a heads-up, to try to assess the state of play and see what exactly was happening.

Being in the PF was like being in a football team: anyone who saw the break or the opportunity to score could call it, and Steve's was a good call to have made. I sensed Tricky leaning forwards from the rear of the wagon. He was raised up on the 50-cal turret and he would have the best all-round view.

'Dave, they lobbed a load of mortars after us,' he shouted. 'They were creeping nearer, until we managed to outrun the fuckers.'

I nodded an acknowledgement. I hadn't even realised we were getting mortared. Those mortars had to have been called in by an enemy spotter – one who could see us, and was tracking us as we speeded north. I had this horrible feeling that the net was closing on us big time. We needed a plan – something to allow us to escape from whatever trap had been set for us.

My mind groped for some kind of inspiration. I was the leader of this mission, the Pathfinders' 2IC. If anyone was supposed to come up with the brainwaves at times like this, it was me. I glanced all around me, desperately trying to detect the source of the threat. I smelled the faint scent of burning diesel from the engine of the Pinkie up ahead, the reek of oil burning on a hot exhaust. There was the muffled rattle of ammunition in one of the crates beside me, and the ghostly hiss of the wind in the trees. Otherwise, there wasn't the faintest sign of life out there.

We were a long way from home now, and a good distance from Camp Tristar and the relative security of our FOB, just this side of the Kuwaiti border. Wherever the enemy might be, there was no way I was going to flush them out of hiding. But I was convinced they were out there, somewhere in that darkened landscape, watching, waiting and preparing to strike. If I couldn't think of a plan, it was now more than ever that I needed the lads. We needed to get our heads together, and pool our thoughts, and maybe that would lead to something.

I leaned over to Steve. 'Pull up abreast of the Engineer vehicle.'

He accelerated until we were next to their wagon. I gestured at them to prepare to stop. I shouted across to Ian, their sergeant: 'Get ready to pull over, mate.'

He gave me a thumbs-up, and we moved forwards and did a repeat performance with Jason. It was easier to do it physically and verbally than to try to use the radios. That way, you got the clarity of face-to-face communication, plus the earpiece on the Cougar was flimsy, and not well-shielded from the wind noise.

Up ahead Jason slowed and started searching for a place to stop. We dropped back again into our original position. The golden rule was that you never broke the order of march, not unless you came under fire and you were doing a vehicle-based fire-and-manoeuvre drill. It was crucial to know where the other vehicles were at all times.

Jason's wagon was positioned around 200 metres in front of ours, with the Engineer Recce wagon sandwiched in between. We figured that our wagon had been targeted by the worst of the incoming fire, and that Jason might not be aware of how fierce and heavy it had been. A light mortar has an effective range of around 1000 metres. Jason's vehicle would have been 300 metres or more ahead of where those shells were landing, to the rear of us. It was highly unlikely that he even knew that we'd been mortared.

Half a kilometre further on Jason's wagon slowed, then pulled off the road. The Engineer Recce wagon followed suit, and us with them. We nosed into a patch of dense palm groves and undergrowth. Jason pushed ahead some 50 metres, until he reached a position where he figured we were hidden from the highway.

The thick vegetation provided cover from view only. Cover from view stops you being seen, but it doesn't stop a bullet. We'd need a ridge, a thick wall or a deep wadi to provide cover from fire. But we couldn't push any further into the undergrowth, or we'd get stuck. There was a wall of tangled palm groves to the west of us.

Jason's wagon did a U-turn, until it was nose-on to the road. The Engineer recce vehicle did the same. We looped around the back and pulled up alongside Jason's wagon, likewise facing the highway. Joe, the top gunner on Jason's wagon, automatically covered his arcs to the west, away from the road. Every other weapon – that was four GPMGs and one 50-cal – covered the direction east, towards the main threat, Route 7.

We cut the engines.

We were now in a snap ambush.

It was dead quiet. We were close enough to have a Chinese – a group heads-up – without moving from the vehicles. We flipped up our NVG. Whenever we were talking to each other like this we needed to have genuine eye contact. For a few moments everyone was silent and listening for signs of the enemy, but it was ominously quiet and still out there.

Jason and I began checking the map. First priority was to work out exactly where we were. We nailed our position, then compared notes on what we'd seen since leaving Nasiriyah, some two hours earlier. It turned out that Jason had no idea of the weight of fire that had been levelled against us. Being the front vehicle he'd got through well before the worst of the shit had kicked off. He'd missed the RPG and the mortar rounds completely.

'I had no idea it was that heavy,' Jason whispered. In the quiet hush we were alert to making the slightest noise.

After the drive thus far north from Nasiriyah nothing seemed to make much sense to us. The Iraqi front line positions somehow seemed to stretch all the way up Route 7. We'd hit two company-strength positions at least, directly as we left Nasiriyah, and we'd just been fired upon by what had to be another company-strength position. Jason added one crucial bit of info to the overall picture.

'Did you see the fat cabbie in the Datsun trying to take us on?' he asked.

I shook my head. 'No, mate. What happened?'

'He pulled off the road just ahead of us, drew this pistol and started waving it out the window. He loosed off a few wild rounds into the air as we charged towards him, the fucking idiot.'

Jason gave this Popeye gap-toothed smile in the darkness. I couldn't help letting out a chuckle.

'I swung the Gimpy on to him,' Jason continued, 'and he soon stopped waving the shooter about. That fat Iraqi cabbie's been watching too many cowboy movies.'

There was a part of me that was surprised that Jason hadn't mal-leted the guy, but I guessed that would truly have blown our cover. Jason had just finished telling me about the fat cabbie attack, when I caught the faint snarl of an engine breaking the night's stillness. It was far to the south of us, and I was unsure at first if I'd heard it. I strained my ears and I could hear it again, deep, throaty and powerful.

I locked eyes with Jason and I could tell that he too had detected it. We swung our heads away from the Pinkie's dash, where we were gathered over the map, and gazed southwards, towards the direction from which the sound was coming. Our sight was still adjusting to its natural night vision, as opposed to the artificially boosted luminos-ity of NVG. We strained our eyes in the darkness, trying to work out what it might be that was moving on the road out there.

From out of the flat blankness of the desert there came this vision, like a bloody great mirage. Gradually, the entire length of the road to the south of us came alive with the glare of vehicle headlights. The convoy approached, headlamps glaring like the eyes of a swarm of angry insects.

We had no idea what the hell was coming out of the night.

But of one thing we were certain: they were coming for us.

CHAPTER EIGHTEEN

A s the lights drew closer they disappeared from view, for the vehicles were passing through the slight cover of a natural depression. By the time they reappeared, the silent night was being torn apart by this deafening rumble, one that was shaking the very ground at our feet.

I could make out the lead vehicle in the convoy now. It was a smart Toyota-style pick-up truck. The open back of the wagon was crammed full of fighters, plus there was the unmistakable form of a tripod-mounted DShK (Dushka) HMG (Heavy Machine Gun) poking ominously forwards from the rear.

The convoy thundered towards us along the highway. It was moving fast, with the vehicles closely spaced, the drivers making no effort to move tactically. With a strength and firepower such as theirs, I reckoned they didn't feel the need to. In the rear of each truck there were ten to fifteen Iraqi fighters, perched on bench seats. Those who were closest had their backs to us, but those on the opposite side would be staring right at us over their fellow warriors' shoulders.

I counted fifteen sets of lights, and still there were more coming. Each wagon was an identical white Toyota pick-up, crammed full of fighters. The convoy was bristling end-to-end with Dushkas, so I guess Saddam must have purchased a job lot off the Russians. Fucking nice one. The Dushka is the Russian equivalent of our own 50-cal heavy machine gun. It can only fire on automatic, and it unleashes its big, armour-piercing, high-explosive rounds at the rate of 600 a minute.

The Dushka's 12.7 mm bullets can chew their way through walls and trees. Body armour or no body armour, a direct hit from one of those would rip an arm or a leg from your body, and take your head clean off. It was a devastating weapon when used against aircraft, or lightly armoured vehicles, and it'd make mincemeat out of our soft-skinned Pinkies. One round into the diesel tank of our wagon, and that'd be Tricky, Steve and me nicely torched and done for.

The convoy was so close by now that I could lob a cricket ball into it, with a good hefty throw. As the first Toyota drew level I could see that the guys on the back weren't regular Iraqi army. In contrast to the smart soldiers in forage caps that we had stumbled across earlier, these guys were dressed in white dish-dash robes, and they had red and white checked shemaghs on their heads. This, we knew from the intel briefs, was the trademark dress of the Fedayeen.

The Fedayeen were Saddam loyalists recruited into a specialist paramilitary militia. They were able to rove around in fast, highly-manoeuvrable vehicles doing guerrilla-style hit-and-run operations. They were mobile, they had an organic, flexible command structure, and their purpose was to engage us in unconventional warfare. And from the looks of these guys they were well-disciplined, plus they were very well-armed.

We were here in Iraq expecting to face conscripts lacking in morale. That's what the intel briefings had told us to expect. We were expecting to confront soldiers who didn't want to fight and who couldn't think for themselves. Instead, we were up against Fedayeen in brand-new SUVs actively looking for a scrap, and packing some serious firepower. They looked and felt hardcore.

They were passing so close that no one dared breathe a word. We had cut our engines as we went into the snap ambush, so they were unlikely to hear us. But just to the north of our position there was one small area devoid of any vegetation, where we had zero cover from view. All it would take was for one Fedayeen to glance our way as he passed that gap, and he'd see us. We just had to hope that with all the light their convoy was throwing off, none of the enemy had attained any great degree of natural night vision. Hopefully, they'd be blinded by their own headlights, and with our wagons being totally dark the night would shield us.

These Fedayeen had to be a hunter force sent to find us. It was clear that there was no way that we could outrun them. A Toyota four-by-four is faster than a Land Rover, plus with all the weight we were carrying we were bound to be far heavier than their vehicles. We were part-dismounted from the Pinkies with the engines turned off, which was hardly great for making a getaway. And we were boxed in by thick vegetation to the west, so the natural route of escape was closed to us.

If they saw us we'd have to open up with everything we'd got. There was just a chance that with the element of surprise we'd be able to mallet the lot of them. They were too bunched up to avoid being hit by our firepower. But still, I didn't exactly rate our chances.

The first few encounters with the enemy, plus the one sustained contact just south of our position, hadn't really made me feel threatened. We could have been killed, but equally we could have taken on and smashed the enemy, and we had escape options. This felt very, very different, and it made my gut drop like a stone.

They were right on top of us, wagon after wagon pounding past, and we knew in our hearts that they'd been sent out to find, fix and kill our patrol. Playing hide and seek with these guys wasn't going to be fun. I had to fight off this strong sense of nausea that was rising within my throat.

It didn't escape my notice that this was exactly the same kind of hunter force that had gone after the squadron of SBS in northern Iraq – those sixty-odd lads who had been forced to go on the run. That entire squadron of elite soldiers had been torn apart and scattered across the desert by a similar number of Fedayeen. We were nine. The SBS had been sixty. The odds were horribly stacked against us.

After what felt like an age, but could only have been a matter of a couple of minutes, the last Fedayeen vehicle thundered past. I had this anxious, sickly feeling as I waited to see if its occupants had spotted us. I was well in control and my head was still together, but my larynx was tight and dry with all the tension. I breathed a long sigh of relief as that last Fedayeen vehicle proceeded north at full speed, and without faltering. They clearly hadn't seen us.

That was a mobile force of some 200 hunting for us, with scores of vehicle-mounted Dushkas. It was clear now that we must have passed through a couple of major enemy positions to the south, if they'd managed to rustle up a convoy of that size and lethal power. You never made a hunter force more than 25 per cent of your main body of men, so we had to presume there were anything up to 1000 Iraqi troops positioned to the south of us, and possibly far more.

We remained silent and observed the situation. For five minutes we watched the tail-lights growing ever smaller in the distance. Those five minutes felt to me like fifty. And then, some 3 kilometres ahead of us, we saw a row of brake lights blinking on, red and angry in the night. We watched as the Fedayeen vehicles slowed and pulled off the road to the eastern side. There was a bit of shunting backwards and forwards, dust shining golden in the beams of their headlamps, then all lights were extinguished.

Darkness.

Engines killed.

Silence.

I figured they had to know that we were headed for Qalat Sikar airfield. They must have known that they were moving faster than we were, and that they had passed us somewhere on the road. And now, their ambush was set. Everyone was silent, staring at the spot where the enemy convoy had gone static. I knew what the rest of the lads were thinking: *How the hell were we going to make it through to the airfield, with that little lot sat bang in our way?*

We had to make the airfield for 1 PARA's L-Hour, so that the first airborne forces could come in. By now they'd have the 1 PARA lads positioned somewhere near the Brigade HQ, where they'd marry up with the Chinooks and move out. They wouldn't get airborne unless they got a signal from us giving the green light, and they wouldn't get the Chinooks in unless we'd marked the HLS, that was for certain.

The Chinooks would have been bouncing around from one air mission to another, and they very likely only had a specific time slot available to get the boys into Qalat Sikar. It was vital that we made the H-Hour. The Chinooks cruise at no more than 10,000 feet, as they have no oxygen for the troops they carry. From the FOB to Qalat Sikar it'd be around an hour's flight. So from us giving the green light it'd be an hour minimum prior to the PARAs coming in, with attack helos in support. Getting the timing right was critical.

But I had this growing feeling that time and fate was fast turning against us. If we pressed on up Route 7 we'd doubtless take a lot of the Fedayeen with us. We had the advantage of NVG, which gave us some stealth and surprise, but there was little doubt that we'd get annihilated. Our only chance of achieving the mission was to remain covert, and we couldn't do that any more if we stuck to the highway.

I turned to Jason, and nodded for Ian, the Engineer Recce sergeant to come closer.

'That's it – enemy ambush set,' I whispered. 'There's no way through on the main road north.'

It was stating the obvious, but someone had to say it.

'Enemy ambush bloody set,' Jason hissed, in confirmation.

'Yep,' Ian, the Engineer Recce sergeant, muttered. 'Looks like they've gone well firm up there.'

Ian had a face like death, and he clearly wasn't relishing the thought of those several hundred Fedayeen being so close on our tail. For that matter, I didn't figure any of us were.

Jason grabbed the map and we placed it under the tiny, hooded map light set in the Pinkie's dash – one specially designed to beam a tiny cone of illumination downwards, whilst allowing the minimum of light to escape from the vehicle. We figured the airfield was 45 kilometres away, no more. *It was so fucking close – less than an hour's drive on good roads.*

We couldn't head south to box around the Fedayeen ambush, because south lay the settlement and the main body of the enemy. We couldn't go further west, for the vegetation was impenetrable that way. The airfield was north-northeast of us. It was obvious that we'd got to try to cross over the road and box around the Fedayeen by going east, and then hooking around northeast.

'Only one thing for it,' I ventured. 'Cross the highway and see if we can link up with those dirt tracks.'

'Yeah,' Jason agreed. 'We've cracked most of the distance on the main road. We'll do the remainder cross-country.'

We knew the rest of the lads would have overheard what we were saying. Their silence meant they were in agreement with us. We were deep behind enemy lines, we'd been compromised and now we were being hunted. In situations such as this making the slightest noise could end up getting you killed, so we kept the chat to an absolute minimum.

The ground we were on was slightly lower than the road. Jason's vehicle led off, its engine whining horribly as it hauled the heavy Pinkie up the shallow incline. In the deadly quiet the noise sounded deafening, like a bloody great jet aircraft taking off. We just had to hope there was no way the Fedayeen could hear us from 6 kilometres away.

Jason halted by the roadside, did a careful visual check both ways, and then crossed over. Once he was over he waved the Engineer Recce vehicle forwards, whilst providing cover with the weapons on his Pinkie. As their wagon nosed on to the road, we were covering it with our weapons from the rear. Ian went firm on the far side, from where they provided cover for us, as we moved across the deserted highway.

At a dead crawl we pushed into the humped and jumbled shadows to the east side of the road. We were back on NVG now, and the vegetation was clearly sparser here, but the going seemed rough as fuck. The Pinkies were cannoning into potholes and kangarooing off ruts, as the suspension struggled to cope with the weight and the terrain.

We dropped our speed to 5 kph, and at that kind of a dead crawl it was just about possible to keep pushing ahead. But still it felt like we were three sick camels stumbling through the darkened desert. For a moment I considered what would have happened if we hadn't followed Steve's suggestion, and pulled off Route 7 when we did. Presumably, the Fedayeen would have caught up with us, and we'd have been in the battle of our lives.

We'd been incredibly lucky to have evaded them as we had. I could barely believe that those hundreds of Fedayeen had failed to see us. Even so, the whole game had changed now. I could sense it from the tense, strained atmosphere on our wagon. In an instant we'd gone from being the hunters to being the hunted.

All around us there was the intense '*rubbittt-rubbittt-rubbittt*' of frogs croaking in the bush. Somewhere nearby there had to be water, and the frogs were beating out an eerie rhythm. Somehow, it seemed to reinforce how, with each passing moment, the trap was fast closing. It was a struggle even to think straight, with all the racket they were making.

One thing was clear: far from being the Charge of the Light Brigade, this was all about stealth and concealment now. If we were to have any chance of making Qalat Sikar we had to remain undetected. We were nine men in three overloaded Pinkies, trying to evade 200 Fedayeen in dozens of fast pick-ups. Staying hidden was infinitely preferable to facing all of that in a full-on firefight.

What made it all the worse was that we didn't know how the three Engineer Recce guys would hold up under serious fire, for we'd never been to war with them. They could prove to be rock-steady; or they could lose it and crumble under the pressure. Either way we just didn't know, and it was that lack of shared combat experience which made them such an unknown.

When driving across rough, heavily-vegetated terrain as we were now, we had to bunch the vehicles closer together. It was easy to lose sight of one another in an environment like this, and the last thing we needed to be doing right now was making radio calls, and trying to locate lost wagons. We'd got maybe 25 metres between each Pinkie and were crawling along at a dead slow, when I noticed both Jason and Ian's vehicles come to a juddering halt.

Jason's wagon was most forwards. Ian's had stopped alongside it, but set a little way back. We pulled up on the opposite side of Jason's Pinkie, so together our three vehicles formed a shallow 'V'. I jumped down and went to cross the couple of metres to Jason's wagon. As I did so, I caught the faintest glimmer of moonlight on a stretch of water just to the front of us.

I peered through the undergrowth, and as I did so the noise hit me. Jason's wagon had halted on the very lip of a canal, and the frogs were going nineteen to the dozen down there. The waterway looked about the size of a normal British canal, the type that carries barges full of holidaying families. I glanced across the water, and I could just make out the dark silhouettes of a clutch of low hut-like structures on the far side. They were set back 300 metres or so from the canal, and they looked like some kind of agricultural outbuildings.

I turned to the lads and made a signal like a knife-cut across my throat – PF talk for 'cut the engines'. We needed to take a view on where we were heading, now that we'd hit the first Iraqi waterway. All three wagons powered down. Once the engines were cut, the only noise from the Pinkies was the whir of the fans trying to cool the hot engines, and the weird, rhythmic click-click-click of cooling steel. It sounded as loud as gunshots in the eerie night stillness, and I wished to hell it would quieten down.

Jason pointed towards the glimmer of moonlight on the water, and spoke into the silence.

'Dave, there's no fucking way the wagons are getting through that.'

I rubbed my hands across my face, trying to massage away some of the tension. 'Don't I know it, mate.'

Standard British Army Land Rovers have a breather tube fitted to one side, the end of which pokes above the driver's door. The diesel engines can suck in air through those tubes, which gives the wagons a good couple of metres of wading capability. But the Pinkies don't have them, for the cut-down open-topped design means there's nowhere to bolt the tube on to. In any case, the water in front of us had to be deeper than that, and we had no idea what the canal bed was like. The water looked more or less stagnant, and below it was very likely soft, clinging mud.

'I'll tell you something else,' Jason hissed. 'We fucking well nearly drove the Pinkie over the edge and into the drink. We didn't see the canal bank until the last bloody moment, what with all the under-growth. And with all the weight we're carrying, the wagon most likely would've flipped over. That would have been the lot of us head down in the water. Fucking nice one ...'

'I know mate,' I cut in. 'The going's fucking horrendous.'

Jason pointed north. 'Plus there's fucking that one too, and God only knows how many more.'

From his vantage point in the vehicle he was a little higher than I was. I had to crane my neck to see where he was indicating. Just to the north of us there was what looked like a side canal coming in from the direction of the road. The canals had to form part of an irri-gation network, and we were effectively boxed in. It wasn't looking very good. Those two waterways barred our routes east and north, the very directions in which we needed to go.

Apart from Jason, the lads on the wagons were silent, peering into the dark wall of bush all around us and scanning their arcs. We were clearly going to be here for some time, as there was no obvious way through. It was good that we had the wagons in a snap, silent ambush, especially with that hunter force just to the north of us.

I caught Steve's eye, and nodded eastwards: 'Steve, mate: sentry.'

Without a word he removed his Minimi from the wagon, and moved off stealthily on foot. He stopped some 30 metres away on a slight rise overlooking the canal, and then he went firm, his weapon held at the ready but not in the aim. Once he'd stopped moving his form faded into the background darkness, until he was all but invisible.

'Jase, maps,' I whispered.

We gathered over the dash of my Pinkie, and we got the map

under the hooded light once more. We figured we'd gone no more than 500 metres east and were moving away from the main highway. There were no waterways marked on the map at the point where we now found ourselves. Either the maps were bang out of date, or the canals were too small to be marked. Whichever, it was a complete gang fuck.

From the maps alone we had no way of knowing what other canals might be out there, and no means of mapping a possible route through. Jase and I didn't need to give voice to this. We both knew it. And we were racking our brains as to what to do next.

'What about the sat photos?' I whispered.

The images from Qalat Sikar airfield were burned into my mind, with the level of detail revealing individual control towers and vehicles. They were more than detailed enough to show watercourses the size of the canals that we'd run into. It was standard operating procedure not to carry sat photos with you, for they constituted too sensitive a source of intel to fall into enemy hands. But I was hoping that Jase might have spirited a couple on to his wagon, knowing how crap the maps might prove.

I heard him give a snort under his breath. 'Sat photos – I fucking wish. Back at the FOB.'

I felt a hand on my shoulder. I turned around. It was Tricky. He motioned towards Steve on sentry. I looked over, and I could see that Steve was standing tense and motionless, his Minimi hard in the shoulder and in the aim. He'd clearly seen something. I reached for my SA80, and moved off, ghost-walking, to join him. As I did so, I saw him glance over his shoulder.

The expression on his face said it all: *We've got fucking company.*

CHAPTER NINETEEN

Steve turned back to whatever it was that had spooked him. His stance was fire-mode, eyes down the barrel of his weapon pointing northeast. I picked my way through the undergrowth, silently feeling a route through, my weapon in the aim. I came to a halt just behind and to the left of Steve. It was the position his shoulders had presented to me.

He gave me the signal to keep silent, then gestured towards where his barrel was pointing. I heard them before I saw them. Voices speaking Arabic, drifting across to me on the cool night air. Whoever it was, they were speaking loudly and animatedly, and moving ever closer to our position. I presumed it had to be a search party, a follow-up from the Fedayeen hunter force. Maybe they were checking both sides of Route 7 on foot, back from their ambush position. Combing the ground to flush us out of hiding. If so, we'd have to open fire and break contact without having a clue as to where we were going.

The voices grew louder. There was dense undergrowth all around us, so we couldn't yet see them. Plus there was a thick mist rising off the canal and curling into the vegetation, which added this weird horror-movie feel to things. We were both of us working without NVG, for we'd flipped up our units when we stopped to get the heads-up. If we changed to NVG now, it'd take too long for our vision to adjust properly, especially with the enemy right on top of us.

In the eerie silence and stillness the guttural Arabic of the voices was growing deafening. Figures appeared on the far side of the canal. We could see their feet below the thick bush, their heads above it. I could see the dull glint of gunmetal reflecting off whatever weapons they had slung over their shoulders, and the smell of cigarette smoke reached me clearly across the still water.

They were 15 metres away, and it seemed impossible that they wouldn't spot Jason's Pinkie, the nose of which was poking out into the mist-shrouded canal. Steve and I were frozen, following the Iraqis in slow motion with our gun sights. My finger was achingly tight on the trigger, a hair's breadth away from opening fire. My heart was racing, pounding in my ears. It felt so loud, like it alone was going to give us away.

Steve whispered: 'Dave, I'm gonna slot 'em.'

I motioned for him to hold his fire.

'Dave, I'm gonna slot 'em.' Steve's voice was tight with tension.

Again, I signalled for him to hold his fire. We had to try to remain covert until the last possible moment. I was convinced that the success of our mission – not to mention the chances of our getting out of this alive – depended on it.

Slowly, so slowly it was physically painful almost, the figures drew level with us. Slowly, their voices faded away into the thick mist and the tangled, brooding bush. Unbelievably, they didn't appear to have seen us. For five minutes we remained totally still and silent, just in case there were more of them, or they were doubling back to attack our position.

With the urgency of our mission, and the God-awful situation that we had found ourselves in, those five minutes felt like an absolute lifetime. Finally, Steve lowered his weapon. I gave him a nod, then crept back to the vehicles. In a whisper I explained to the others what we'd just seen. Then I was back to studying the map, and trying to work out just how we might keep pushing ahead towards Qalat Sikar.

It was Jason who finally broke the silence: 'Dave, there's no way through.'

All eyes turned to me now, apart from Steve who was out on sentry. Everyone was waiting for my response. Between the six of us, we had more than sixty-five years of military experience. On exercises we'd covered every possible eventuality, *or at least we thought we had*. Likewise, we reckoned we'd done so on operations in Sierra Leone, Afghanistan and elsewhere. But in truth, none of us had ever been in this kind of situation before – with no route through on all sides, and surrounded by a massively superior enemy force.

We prided ourselves on being cunning and audacious, and on thinking the unthinkable. Yet I was racking my brains and I couldn't seem to see any way through.

The distance between the eight of us on the vehicles was a few metres at most. In the pitch darkness I could hear the lads' quiet breathing, interspersed with the rhythmic '*breep-breep-breep*' of the insect life all around us. Otherwise it was deathly quiet. This silence, coupled with the crushing indecision, was fucking horrible. I hated being trapped like this.

For an instant my mind flashed back to the last time I'd been hemmed in like this, with the enemy on all sides. It was Afghanistan and my very first mission with the PF. I was a captain back then, but I'd been allocated a place as the top gunner on the rear of one of the wagons commanded by one of the old and the bold. He was mentoring me through my first PF combat mission, to ease me into becoming the Pathfinders' 2IC.

It was late 2001 and we'd flown into Bagram air base, tasked with being first into a Kabul freshly liberated from the Taliban. After the decades of fighting, Afghanistan's capital city was shot to fuck. I'd never seen anything remotely like it. It was a ghostly wasteland. Our mission was to establish some ground truth, because no one had a clue what was going on there – which clans controlled which areas, who the key warlords were and what were the chief threats.

It didn't take us long to realise that Kabul presented a very fast-moving, fluid situation, one replete with shifting allegiances and treachery. We drove out to meet a warlord at his base on the city limits. The closer we got to the rendezvous, the more nervous and frightened our Afghan interpreter became. It was a sure sign that the guy we were about to meet was seriously badass.

We pitched up at his base, which turned out to be a mini-fortress with watchtowers, gun emplacements and walkways around the walls. Upon arrival we suddenly found our two wagons surrounded by skinny Afghans sporting Pakuls – their traditional rolled woollen caps – and toting guns. A group of around twelve surged around us. At each corner of the fortress there were guys on the watchtowers smoking these massive hash joints, and the air was thick with the sickly-sweet, heady smell of burning grass.

A guy stepped up to me and offered me his RPG. It was a bizarre kind of a gesture. I feigned interest and accepted it. As soon as I did so he reached inside the wagon and grabbed my SA80, from where it was strapped to the vehicle's side. A second later the guy had it pointed at my head. We'd come in here in 'non-threatening' mode. That meant we hadn't dismounted with our longs – our assault rifles. Now I had a wild, stoned-looking Afghan with my own weapon levelled at me, and his finger white with tension on the trigger.

One glance around the place had been enough to show how totally outnumbered we were. We were surrounded, trapped and outgunned. It had taken some kind of epic standoff to get us out of that warlord's domain alive and unharmed. The memories of that Afghan stand-off triggered a sudden flash of inspiration. It was true that on the face of it we were trapped here in Iraq. We couldn't go north, south, east or west with the vehicles without hitting insurmountable obstacles, or a vastly superior enemy force. *But what about if we did so on foot?*

I checked the faint fluorescent dial of my watch. It was 1900 hours, and the airfield was less than 45 kilometres away. We'd got eight hours until 0300, H-Hour for 1 PARA's insertion. I reckoned it was just about doable. I thought back over the final, endurance stage of PF selection, which involves a 64-kilometre night march over mountains. You had to do it carrying 80 pounds in your bergen, plus your weapon, and you had to achieve an average speed of 6 kilometres an hour.

It was 45 kilometres to the airfield, it was flat terrain, and we'd be carrying far less weight than we do on endurance. I calculated that 45 divided by 6 made it an eight-hour march. *We could make it.* In fact, we might well make Qalat Sikar in under eight hours, maybe even as little as six, if the terrain held good. We might not have time to do a full 360-degree recce of the airfield, but we could secure a HLS, mark it and green light 1 PARA in.

It'd be a beast of a march through the unknown, but moving forwards on foot was the one way that I could see us getting out of here. If we stuck with the vehicles, we were boxed in on all sides by impassable terrain and the enemy. We had to presume that the Fedayeen hunter force had radioed through that they'd lost us. They would know that we'd gone cross-country, which in turn meant that they'd be alert for any vehicles moving off-road. Dumping the wagons and proceeding on foot was the last thing the enemy would be expecting.

It was time to voice what I'd been thinking. I glanced up and my eyes met Jason's. I could tell that he was looking to me for some kind of leadership here and a sense of what we could do. In a hurried whisper I outlined my idea to the guys.

'You're right, Jase, there's no way through *by vehicle*. The only way left for us to achieve the mission is to blow the vehicles, and go forwards *on foot*. That's the last thing they'll be expecting, and it's our only way out of here without heading into a massive contact. If we leave everything but our weapons and grab bags, we'll be travelling fast and light. We'll leave one-hour fuses on the charges, so we're long gone by the time the wagons blow.'

We'd have to blow the vehicles, so as to deny them to the enemy. But we'd leave hour-long fuses, to give us the time to get well away from where they were by the time they exploded. Otherwise, we'd bring the enemy down on top of us. We'd rip out any top secret kit, wreck it, then chuck it into the canal.

For a couple of seconds no one responded to my suggestion.

It was Jason who broke the silence. 'We could try and make it through on foot. Trouble is, we don't know what the fuck lies between here and Qalat Sikar. So far, there's been Iraqis all over the place. We've seen a 200-strong hunter force, plus they've got positions all along the road, and they've been taking a good pop at us. There's no way of knowing what we might be walking into if we push ahead on foot, and we'd be doing so without our heavy firepower.'

'Tricky?' I prompted.

Tricky shook his head. 'I just don't think we'll make it on foot for H-Hour. We could make the distance, but not in time to get the PARAs into a cleared and marked HLS. We'll need to avoid local habitation, dogs, canals, marshes, main roads. Plus we'll have to box around Iraqi army positions and maybe Fedayeen. And all of that will slow us down.'

Tricky was one of the most experienced and positive operators in the Pathfinders, but he was also a realist. Along with Jason, he was the most battle-tested operator that we'd got. If the two of them were against what I was suggesting, maybe going ahead on foot wasn't an option. But still I wasn't ready to let it go.

'Maybe you're right,' I conceded, 'but we've come this far, and we're 80 per cent of the way there. I reckon we can press ahead on foot, and if necessary we can get 1 PARA to delay their H-Hour. If it takes longer on foot to reach, recce and secure the airfield, we can get them to come in later, and we can still make the mission happen.'

'What do we do if we're on foot and we get pinned down by Iraqis?' Jason asked. 'We'll be lacking the heavy firepower provided by the wagons.'

'We do what we always do: we put down fire and try to withdraw from the contact and escape and evade.'

'But what happens if there's no way out?' Jason persisted. 'If we're pinned down and trapped?'

'If that happens we go into a hide, and we call in a CSAR team to pull us out. We call up the Army Air Corps, and if that fails the RAF with a Chinook, or if that fails the Yanks with an MH-53 Pave Low. Either way we get a machine in with some serious firepower, and we get ourselves pulled out.'

There was silence again. I could almost hear people's brains racing. No one else was voicing an opinion now, or even making any suggestions. It was like we were frozen: *was going forwards on foot really an option, or was it a bridge too far?*

Eventually, Jason said: 'Tricky, what d'you reckon?'

Tricky was a combat-hardened soldier and very battle-space aware. That was why Jason sought his opinion.

Tricky said: 'I think we've got to keep the vehicles for as long as we can. We can always end up on foot, but they are our firepower, our speed and our mobility.'

There was one glaring problem with keeping the vehicles: we couldn't drive west, because the terrain was impassable; we couldn't go north due to the Fedayeen ambush, and east we'd hit the canals. The only route open to us was south, and that meant abandoning the mission and heading back through the Iraqi forces that we'd just avoided.

For several reasons we figured there were at least two battalions – so anything up to 2000 Iraqi troops – to the south of us. The Fedayeen force had numbered 200, minimum. We figured there were 1000-odd troops in the last settlement that we'd driven through. South of that, we figured the Iraqis had to have another battalion at the very least, to stand against the US Marine Corps.

Those troops would be stood-to and alert to our presence. They would be more than ready to hit us if for some bizarre reason we came driving back through their positions. Driving south we'd have zero element of surprise, and we'd be heading into a series of ambushes. And we might well have the Fedayeen hunter force bearing down fast on our tail.

Going south was asking for a world of trouble. We'd be facing thousands of Iraqi troops, and most likely we'd get slaughtered. But so too was any other bloody direction. It was crunch time, but it was clear that no one had a fucking clue what to do.

Tricky broke the quiet: 'The constant is the vehicles. Remember Bravo Two Zero? They were fucked 'cause they didn't go in with vehicles.'

'Dez, what d'you think?' asked Jason.

'Same as Tricky and you, mate: we keep the vehicles.'

I asked the Royal Engineer sergeant, Ian, for his take on it.

'Keep the vehicles,' he said. 'Remember what happened to those SBS lads up north: they lost their vehicles and they were fucked.'

'Joe?' said Jason.

'Keep the vehicles,' said Joe.

I called Steve over from sentry. This was everyone's decision. Had to be.

I outlined our predicament to him. 'Steve, we can't go east, north or west with the vehicles. We either blow them and go forwards on foot to the airfield, or we keep the vehicles. Everyone else so far wants to keep the vehicles. We'll have speed, fire and mobility, but we're likely to get malleted big time.'

'I still think we can go forwards on foot,' I continued, 'and that way we can achieve the mission. But there's obviously a high chance of being captured or killed. So, it's like I'm offering you a fucking great boot in the bollocks, or a massive punch on the nose? Which is it to be, mate?'

Steve grinned. Shrugged. 'On balance, I want to keep my bollocks. So I guess we keep the vehicles.'

In life I've always believed that acceptance is a virtue. Sometimes, you just have to accept the shit you're in, and try to see the opportunity that can come out of it. Otherwise, it was your own head and your own fear that would mess you up. But this was still the hardest decision that I'd ever made in my life. What determined it for me was that I would never go against the blokes, especially not when it was a life-or-death choice like this one.

I took a long in-breath and exhaled. 'Okay, so we keep the vehicles. But that has to mean heading south and fighting out way through to the American front line.'

Jason nodded. 'We use the wagons to get as far as we can towards the Americans. When we can't get any further with the wagons we fight on foot, back-to-back if it comes to it.'

I glanced around the rest of the faces. There was a series of grim nods from all. The decision was made, but I didn't kid myself that somehow we were okay now that we'd made it. The reality was that we had *nowhere* to go. North, east, west, or south, we were all but certain to get smashed.

At best some of us might get wounded, captured and tortured by the Iraqis, and I reckoned I'd prefer a bullet rather than that.

CHAPTER TWENTY

There was no time to linger on any of this. We couldn't afford the time to think, or to freeze. We only had one option now and that was to fight. And if we were to do so to the maximum of our ferocity, we had to get up and at 'em pronto and get scrapping.

'Dave, if we're making the run south we could do with some fucking air,' Tricky suggested. 'If we can get some air above us I can call in air strikes on both sides of the road as we drive down it. It'll open up a tunnel of escape and smash the enemy positions as we go.'

It was hardly a subtle or a covert plan, but Tricky's suggestion was a mark of pure genius. It was classic PF. We could turn our presence here to everyone's advantage by calling in air strikes to mallet those enemy positions that no one but us knew were here. In doing so we might not have achieved our mission, but we sure as hell could annihilate a whole lot of hidden enemy units – ones that had just given the US Marine Corps a seriously bloody nose.

Take a totally shit and murderous situation and turn it into a battle-winning opportunity: it was the kind of maverick, lunatic thinking that defined the men of Pathfinder Platoon. As a PF JTAC, Tricky was one of the most experienced air war operators in the British Army. If we could get some serious firepower orbiting above us, I had no doubt that he could pull it off.

I raised a smile. 'Cracking idea, mate. Let's get some fucking air.'

Tricky set up the comms, so we could put the call in to PF HQ.

'*Mayhem Three One*, this is *Mayhem Three Zero*,' Tricky intoned. 'Fetch *Sunray*, over.'

Amazingly, there was an instant response. Within seconds we had John – call sign *Sunray* – on the radio. Tricky passed me the handset.

'*Sunray*, this is *Maverick One*,' I told him, using my personal call sign. 'We're 80 kilometres north of Nasiriyah and we're trapped behind enemy lines. Our exact location is grid 937485. There are enemy forces to all four points surrounding us. We cannot proceed with the mission.'

There was a moment's silence on the net, then John's response: 'Roger. What's your intention?' From his voice it sounded to me like he was tired and shocked.

'We intend to move south on Route 7,' I told him. 'We'll engage enemy forces as we go, and link up with the Americans. Enemy are positioned in significant numbers all along Route 7. The area is not, I repeat not, relatively benign.'

John's voice came back to me echoing over the static: 'Roger.' Pause. 'You need to get back to the American positions.'

I thought: *No shit, Sherlock. What's the point in repeating what I've just said?*

'Tell him about the air plan,' Tricky interjected.

'Request air cover,' I told him. '*Sunray*, we can call in air strikes on heavy enemy positions all along Route 7. The area is not relatively benign. It's crawling with enemy. With air cover we can smash 'em. Requesting air to do so.'

John's voice came back to me instantly, flat and mechanical: 'There's nothing available.'

It was my turn to pause now. *How could there be no air?* We were on a battle-critical mission deep behind enemy lines, and we'd got the might of the British and American militaries depending on us. We'd just discovered scores of enemy in hidden defensive positions, and we were ideally placed to whack them. In those circumstances there had to be a way to find us some air.

I glanced at Tricky. He had this look of total disgust on his features.

How could there possibly be zero air available, especially when we had a golden opportunity to strike such a killer blow? It made no sense at all.

'Ask again,' Tricky mouthed at me.

I tried explaining to John that we'd uncovered the hidden positions of thousands of Iraqi soldiers, and that with air on hand Tricky could direct it in to hit them. I tried explaining that those troops were waiting to ambush the US Marines, as they advanced out of Nasiriyah. I argued that this needed to be made an air mission priority. There was a momentary delay in the comms, and I guessed John was checking with higher command.

'There's no air available,' was his response again.

Of course, we'd been told in the patrol briefings that it was highly unlikely air would be available to us. Air cover is never in limitless supply. But we weren't asking for air to somehow come in and rescue us. We were simply saying that if they gave us air assets we'd smack it into the enemy in all their hidden positions that we'd discovered, and rout them.

'If there's no air, is there a CR capability available to us?' I queried. I was going to push it as far as I could go now. 'Is there a team on standby, in case we need one?'

I wasn't asking if there was CSAR available. You only get Combat Search and Rescue when you're on the run, have zero comms and HQ doesn't know where you are. CSAR gets called in to find you and get you out. I was asking if there was a CR capability that we could call on, if we reached a suitable area where we could clear it in. You call for Combat Recovery when you're at a known location, one where you're able to remain static for long enough to get a rescue force in.

A Combat Rescue force would likely consist of two Chinooks, packed full of infantry, with helicopter gunships in support. I figured that right now 1 PARA must be stood-to for the Qalat Sikar airfield insertion, with Chinooks available and ready to get airborne. So presumably John could get a bunch of those lads re-tasked to fly a Combat Rescue mission for us lot, if needed.

The lads on my patrol knew what CR was, and we'd trained for it relentlessly. I figured the Engineer Recce blokes probably hadn't, but we could nurse them through it anyway. They'd all heard me ask John if CR could be made available. Without any air cover, it was almost inevitable that we were going to need it, because in truth we had *nowhere* to go. North, east, west, or south, we were all but certain to get smashed, and especially without any supporting air strikes.

John came back on the air: 'There's no air cover available. There's no rescue team.'

He told us we would need to extract ourselves. To my mind that meant that we were in effect on our own. For a moment I was totally lost for words. We all knew that forces such as ours could get left to find their own way out of the shit. But we were in a position where we could rain down fire on to a series of enemy positions, ones that no one knew were here until we'd stumbled into them. We'd flushed the enemy out of hiding, and they were clearly here to fuck up the US Marine Corps when they moved north out of Nasiriyah. But there was no sense me arguing this any further over the radio. We didn't have the time for this shit.

I told John: 'Roger. Out.'

I turned to the blokes: 'There's no air. We're on our own. We need to get moving.'

On the few occasions in my life when I've felt I have been really left in the shit, I have prayed. All I had time for now was a quick: 'God, if you get me out of this one, I *promise* I will screw the nut.' We were so deep in the shit that it was only a fleeting thought. We had no time to linger on anything now that was not directly related to getting us the hell out of there, and preferably alive.

We'd just had this massive shit sandwich rammed down our throats. In spite of this, we started sparking. Sometimes in life when you were dealt a shit sandwich you just had to squirt a load of ketchup on it, and get it down you.

Jason started to reel off the actions-on. 'I'll lead us off. Keep the space between the vehicles. Only engage the enemy when we're taking accurate fire. Keep covert and hold fire at all times otherwise …'

Over the past forty-eight hours I'd totally changed my opinion of Jason. He was fearless, and nothing seemed to knock him back. Like now – when he volunteered to take the lead position on the coming suicide run south towards Nasiriyah. For none of us were kidding ourselves any more: it was a death run that we were facing here.

Jason was right: fire discipline would be everything. We could be fighting for days here, especially if we were forced at some stage to go on the run on foot. We needed to conserve our ammo, and use it only when we were forced to fight and could be sure of making kills.

'I'll lead, throwing smoke,' Jase continued. 'That'll give the two rear vehicles cover from view. If there's a roadblock, I will lead us off the road to try to box around it. If a vehicle gets taken out, every-one else gets the fire down and extracts the blokes from the fucked wagon into the two that remain.

'If all vehicles are taken out or blocked and we're pinned down, then we get the rounds down with the vehicle weapons, break con-tact and move off on foot. At all times our aim remains to head south, whether by vehicle or on foot, and to make the US front line.'

'What about when we get to the American positions?' Tricky asked.

It was a fair question. If we did make it through against all odds, crossing back over friendly lines was likely to be our most danger-ous moment. The Marines were tired; we didn't have comms with them; they'd lost dozens of men; they'd been fighting brutally hard for the last twenty-four hours; and we would have to approach and cross their front line positions from the direction of the enemy. The chances of getting torn to pieces by our own side were all too real.

'When you see me put on my hazard warning lights you put yours on too,' said Jason. 'Lower your weapons. Put your IR Fireflies on. If the Yanks engage us do not return fire: get away from the vehicles and into cover.'

Tricky turned to me. He had this hard, determined look in his eyes, like he was steeling himself for what he was about to do.

'Dave, I'm going to flush the Crypto,' he announced.

I paused. This was horribly fucking ominous. Tricky knew how deeply we were in the shit, and that it was only going to get a lot worse from here on in. The Crypto was the encoded messaging software that enabled us to speak with PF HQ and air cover. If the enemy got hold of the Crypto, they could hack into the comms net of the entire British war effort. By flushing the Crypto Tricky would wipe it off all of our radios, and that would be it – comms gone.

Flushing the Crypto was a pretty terminal move. You only ever did it if you thought you were about to get captured or killed. But I figured Tricky was right on this one. We'd just been told by our OC what our situation was. We were pretty much facing certain capture or death here.

'Yeah, mate, fair enough,' I told him. 'There's no one fucking listening anyway, so flush the Crypto.' I turned to the rest of the lads. 'And whilst Tricky's at it, better ruin any other top secret kit that's in the wagons. You know the form. Tear it out, rip it to shreds and dump it in the fucking canal.'

'How about we drive lights-on?' Steve suggested. 'They'll expect us to be dark. Three vehicles, lights off – they'll know it's us lot right away. All their wagons were lights on, even the Fedayeen hunter force.'

'Let's see what ground we can cover first on black light,' said Jason. 'But if I flick my headlights on you lot follow suit, okay?'

There were murmurs of agreement all around.

I mounted up our Pinkie. I saw Steve laying out a neat line of grenades on the Land Rover's front dash, within easy reach, and then I glanced around at the lads. At that moment I realised how close I was to each and every one of these blokes. If I was going to go down fighting, I couldn't choose to die in better company.

In spite of my gut-churning fear, I forced a smile. For an instant, I found the Pathfinders' collect running through my mind.

> Happiness shall always be found by those who dare and persevere; wanderer – do not turn around, march on and have no fear.

In the bars we frequented, on exercises and on ops, it had been short-ened over the years to one word that we all understood: *happiness*. The lads had their eyes on me now: steady, firm, unwavering. They were men of courage. They were showing no visible signs of fear. They were waiting for me to give them the go.

I gave it with that one word: 'Happiness.'

There was a moment's silence, then the lads returned the gesture.

'Yeah.'

'Fuck it.'

'Happiness.'

We started the engines. I checked my watch, cupping it in my palm to shield the faint glow of the hands. We'd been here for twenty minutes – that was all the time it had taken to make the decision of a lifetime.

After the quiet and stillness of the night, the purr of the diesel motors sounded deafeningly loud. The rhythmic beat of the cicadas – '*breeeep-breeeep-breeeep-breeeep-breeeep*' – seemed to falter for a moment, as the engines fired. It had been the constant companion to the silence here, the beat of a million tiny insects marking time as first we considered the impossible, and then accepted it as being the only option left open to us.

Jason led off, the other wagons following. We bumped and kan-garooed over the rough terrain back towards the road. We checked right – north – where we knew the Fedayeen hunter force was lying in wait. It was dark and silent up there, and there wasn't a thing to be seen. Then we turned left and hit the tarmac heading south. I still couldn't quite believe that we were doing this, but we were.

It is what it is.

We picked up speed with the wind in our faces, and I felt strangely, oddly calm. I held on to this moment – a few seconds of peace and stillness before the storm of all storms – for myself. I was sure the lads were feeling the same fear that I felt. We all felt fear – it was how we controlled it that mattered. We kept it real, controlled the adrenaline as it burst and burned through our system, and used it as fuel for the coming battle.

Our speed increased to 70 kph. *Soon now.*

We were on the road speeding through the night, when a line from Monty Python's classic comedy *The Holy Grail* came unbidden into my head. When facing the Killer Bunny the knights of King Arthur's Round Table had opted to 'Run away! Run away!' I told myself there was nothing wrong, or cowardly, about the decision that we'd just made. We weren't bulletproof. We didn't stand and fight Rambo-like when to do so was sheer suicidal stupidity.

Instead, we'd opted to make a tactical retreat, and we'd be fighting all the way through the heart of enemy territory. It was either a moment of complete and utter madness or a mark of sheer genius: *maybe they won't be expecting us.* Either way, I wished we had that air power on hand to really smash them.

But there was no point dwelling on that now.

We'd been on the road for 5 kilometres when I felt a tap on my shoulder. It was Tricky. He leaned forward from his position atop the 50-cal turret.

'Car headlamps,' he yelled above the wind noise. 'About a klick ahead of us, flashing on and off.'

He pointed in the direction of what he had seen. I raised myself up in my seat, and scanned the dark horizon. And then I saw it, just to one side of the road up ahead: a pair of lights like two devil's eyes, going flash-dark-flash-dark-flash-dark.

'You see it, yeah?' Tricky yelled. 'That's it: enemy ambush set.'

Shit: so they knew we were coming.

CHAPTER TWENTY-ONE

If you want to know where the enemy are and what they're planning, you have to try to think like them. You have to take on their mindset, and second-guess what they're up to. You've got to figure out where you would choose to attack a three-vehicle convoy moving south down the main highway. In any other context, a car flashing its headlights wouldn't be so unusual. But Tricky had seen it and read it for what it was: a signal to the Iraqi forces lying in wait that we were coming.

As if to confirm what he'd just been saying, there was a burst of sporadic shots from out of the southeast. It was some 500 metres forwards of Jason's vehicle, and the tracer rounds went arcing high into the night sky. This wasn't aimed at us. It was signal fire to back up the message of the flashing headlights.

They're coming.

We were approaching the large settlement where a short while earlier we'd got mortared, and where the RPG round had skipped across our bonnet. For a moment I wondered whether we shouldn't try going off-road, to box around the enemy. But just as soon as I'd entertained the thought, I'd dismissed it. Now they knew we were on our way they were sure to have radioed through an alert to the Fedayeen hunter force.

Any delay, and that hunter force would be on our tail. The Fedayeen wagons were swifter than us, and more manoeuvrable, and we had to presume they knew the ground here intimately. Our only chance was to keep heading south at full whack, and try to outrun them on the main highway.

Seconds dragged by in a tense silence. The only noise was the rush of the wind. For any soldier there is nothing worse than speeding into a known ambush when you're outnumbered and outgunned by the enemy. But right now any fear that I might be feeling was buried by the pure animal aggression of the coming fight.

I pulled the hard angular steel of the GPMG closer into my shoulder. It felt comforting. *Bring it on.*

We sped past the location from which those warning shots had been fired. Suddenly, the night ahead of us erupted into a volcano of tracer fire. The enemy had opened up from positions 600 metres to the east, high on the ridgeline. From there the fire rippled downwards towards our convoy, until the entire hillside was awash with flame. From out of the flat, empty blankness of the night it was suddenly as if a laser-gun battle from *Star Wars* was being re-enacted on the eastern side of Route 7.

A few hundred metres ahead of our speeding vehicle I could see tracer rounds sparking and ricocheting off the tarmac. There was a wall of fire right to the front of us. I flipped up my night-vision goggles as I clocked the size of the ambush, and the amount of fire we were facing, which would dazzle us. I saw Steve and Tricky do likewise.

The enemy gunners must have got their weapons zeroed in on the highway, for they were hosing down that stretch of tarmac with a murderous rate of fire. This was a well-co-ordinated, concerted ambush, and we were going to have to run 400 metres of solid fire. It was fucking terrifying.

Silhouetted in the harsh glare of the enemy's muzzle flashes I could see row upon row of buildings up on the hillside. They looked a lot like army barracks, and they were alive with stick figures darting in and out of them. Fuck knows where they'd all appeared from, because this place had been pretty near deserted when we had first driven through it.

After our drive north, the enemy must have been placed in their stand-to positions, ready and waiting. We had one small advantage. They obviously couldn't see us, and so they were firing at static points on the road.

As I studied the approaching enemy positions, I could make out purpose-built sandbagged bunkers set amongst the larger, barrack-like buildings. There were thick walls running up and down the slope, providing rat-runs with ample cover between the various positions. We'd missed all of this on the way through, and it was only the weight of fire and the muzzle flashes that were illuminating it for us now.

First time around this had been a dark hillside running up to a ridge with a cluster of dark buildings. Now we could see that it was the perfect defensive terrain from which to hit us. I pulled the GPMG tighter into my shoulder, and flicked the big clunky safety catch to 'off'. I raised myself up on the balls of my feet, so I was ready to swing the weapon from side to side in smooth, killer movements. But still we held our fire.

The enemy tracer groped its way towards our hidden convoy. The roar of belt-fed machine guns joined the staccato crackle of small-arms fire, as more and more weapons opened up. Then I caught the fearful, rhythmic 'chthunk-chthunk-chthunk' of a Dushka heavy machine gun. The road ahead of us was being hosed down by Iraqi gunmen firing AKs, heavy machine guns, and 12.7 mm armour-piercing rounds.

The roar and thump of the approaching fire punched over us in a pounding, crushing shockwave. It was a shooting gallery out there, and I figured we had half a kilometre or more to run before we would be through to the far side.

A thick cloud of grey smoke billowed up from the road ahead. For a moment I feared that the lead Pinkie had driven into the fire and taken a direct hit. Then I realised that it was Jason throwing a smoke grenade, to give cover to the wagons behind. *Jase: what a fucking hero!*

Just as his vehicle disappeared behind that curtain of smoke, I spotted an enemy bunker position up ahead, close by the roadside. We were in amongst them now, which is why Jason had started to chuck the smoke. Fire erupted from that bunker. It was less than 100 metres from the highway, and rounds went tearing into the Engineer Recce wagon. The Engineer lads opened up at the very same instant, angry tongues of flame spitting from the pair of Gimpys mounted on their vehicle.

We were under direct and accurate fire now, and I didn't waste a millisecond. The enemy bunker was a low dugout with a thick, sand-bagged roof. I could see the silhouettes of gunmen in there, hun-kered over muzzle flashes. I was already in the aim, and as I pulled the trigger with my right hand I'd got my left gripping the top of the weapon, to give extra stability.

I sensed Tricky behind me, spinning the 50-cal around, and then it was thumping away above my head, booming deafeningly in my ears. He was firing right across the top of my scalp, and it felt as if the rounds were about to take my head off. Being 'area weapons', both the 50-cal and the GPMG spray out a cone of rounds to saturate the terrain immediately surrounding a target.

I aimed at the central point of the bunker, knowing the Gimpy would plaster all around it with death. At the distance that I was smashing rounds into the bunker, I'd be hitting at least half of it with fire. I saw bullets from my weapon striking sparks from metal, and ripping into the sandbagged walls, kicking up plumes of dirt as they tore the walls to pieces.

Then the bigger rounds from Tricky's 50-cal were blasting the bun-ker apart. I saw sandbags exploding under the impact, and bodies being thrown backwards into the shadows. Finally, we were smash-ing the enemy back. *And man, was it a fucking wonderful feeling.*

It's standard operating procedure in the PF not to use tracer rounds, especially when on a night mission behind enemy lines. It helps you stay hidden, but still our muzzle flashes would eventually give us away. For several seconds we tore that bunker apart, and then we were in amongst the acrid, choking cloud of smoke from the grenade that Jason had thrown. For a further couple of seconds we were rushing through this dark, eerie tunnel of smoke, lit orange and white by muzzle flashes and explosions from the outside.

We held our fire. There was no point trying to engage and kill the enemy when you couldn't see them. *Conserve your ammo.* But still the noise from all around us was deafening. We thundered out of the cover of the smoke, and there was a wall of tracer before us. The enemy would have packed their mags with one tracer round per four or five bullets. What we could see now was only a fraction of the weight of enemy fire. It was only a matter of time before we started taking hits, and got torn apart.

I was dancing the Gimpy around, engaging target after target after target. Every inch of the hillside was awash with fire. I was hitting muzzle flashes, silhouettes of gunmen, windows spitting bullets at us. Everything was instinctive now. All hopes of stealth and concealment were gone. It was fight or die.

A short burst and I was on to the next target, doing what we'd all learned so well during the months of training and exercises with PF. Tricky and I were on our feet in the vehicle, ramping the guns left and right, fighting for our lives. I was back-to-back with the lads, seeking to kill as many of the enemy as I could. And for sure we'd take a lot of them with us, before we were smashed and bleeding out our last.

Every man in our convoy was doing the same. He was doing it for his life, but more importantly for his mates' lives. If we fought with total ferocity for each other, we had a small chance that some of us might make it through. We didn't have to think about this much. There were few conscious thoughts. That was the beauty of the training.

The barrel of the Gimpy juddered and rocked with each burst of fire, the smooth, gun-metal-blue steel of the weapon reflecting the latticework of tracer rounds tearing past above us. Already, the barrel was burning hot to the touch, and I figured I had to be a hundred rounds into that first 200-round belt.

I had to conserve my rate of fire. *One burst, one kill*. If we made it to halfway through this ambush and I pulled the trigger and got an empty click, then we were well and truly fucked. I'd have to change the ammo belt, and this really was not the time to stop getting the rounds down, even for the couple of seconds it'd take me to do so.

A wall of smoke like fog engulfed us for a second time, as we sped into the cover of the second of Jason's grenades. I remained hunched over the Gimpy and in the aim, finger on the trigger, for when we came tearing out the far side. All around the wagon the dull, opaque whiteness was threaded with the fiery trails of tracer rounds. I could sense that the vehicle was getting hit, though the overall noise was too deafening to be able to hear the individual bullets strike. I hoped and prayed that a round didn't take out a tyre, or something equally terminal. If we got a puncture here we were as good as dead.

As we thundered out of the smoke, an RPG round came flaming out of the darkness. It tore towards our convoy from 600 metres up on the ridgeline, and straight towards the Engineer Recce wagon. It hit the road to the left-hand side of their Pinkie, then skipped up and shot beneath it, going between the front and the rear wheels.

I couldn't believe it when the RPG round emerged on the far side and exploded in the bush. The white-hot heat of the detonation lit up a wide stretch of the highway in this eerie, smoke-filled halo of light. It had passed clean beneath the Recce blokes' wagon. *How the hell had it missed?*

RPG teams are often positioned in units of three. You have one shared re-loader between two blokes operating the launcher tubes. It crossed my mind that there was probably a pair of launchers up on the ridge, so I could expect another RPG.

I swung the GPMG around and engaged the location from which the RPG had been fired. As I did so there was the blast of a second RPG launching. It was a violent burst of orange-yellow from within the darkness. It was like a mortar flash, only horizontal and aimed right at us. The flame of that second RPG lit up the billowing cloud of exhaust smoke still hanging there from the first launch.

Above Our arrival in Kuwait by C130, several weeks prior to the war in Iraq starting, as the advance British contingent. I'm standing second from right. Small teams of Pathfinders like us were kept well away from the prying lenses of the media, who were soon to descend on Kuwait in droves.

Below Kuwait, March 2003, making preparations for our move into Iraq. Note all vehicle-mounted machine guns are in dust covers, to protect them from sandstorms. I'm to the right of the photo, along with the five fellow members of my patrol, call-sign *Mayhem Three Zero*: Steve, Tricky, Dez, Jase and Joe.

Right Just prior to crossing into Iraq, March 2003. All weapons uncovered and ready to rumble.

Above Pushing deeper into Iraq, there was almost zero cover provided by the flat desert terrain. My patrol was tasked to drive some 300 kilometres through such terrain to reach an airfield deep behind enemy lines. As Sod's law would have it, once we set out temperatures plummeted and snow and sleet began to fall.

Below The Euphrates bridge at Nasiriyah, the front-line of American forces in the war. Thick palm groves and rivers meant that this was difficult ground to cross. Nasiriyah became the focal point for the Iraqi resistance, and the battle to take the city became known as the 'battle that America nearly lost'.

Top We sported *shemaghs* (Arab headscarves) to help disguise us as locals and wore a personal choice of uniform and kit culled from half of the militaries around the world. Driving at night with Night Vision Goggles, our aim was to slip by Iraqi positions unnoticed.

Centre The cut-down Land Rovers we used on the Iraq mission were nicknamed 'Pinkies'. Ever since David Stirling's SAS ran riot amongst German commander Erwin Rommel's forces in the North Africa desert, pink has been the colour of choice for British Special Forces desert vehicles.

Below Two Pathfinder Pinkies using a wadi – a dry, seasonal riverbed – as a Lie-up Point (LUP) in which to hide from the enemy. Two vehicles, each carrying three men – a driver and two gunners – is the basic Pathfinder patrol unit.

The Iraqi Fedayeen – a militia fiercely loyal to Saddam Hussein – were a mobile, irregular, and very well-armed hunter force.

The intelligence we were given prior to our mission proved hopelessly wrong: whilst we were told the area we had to penetrate was relatively benign – devoid of enemy – it was actually teeming with hundreds of Fedayeen and thousands of other hostile forces including Iraqi Republican Guard, the Iraqi SSO (the feared Secret Police), and regular troops. Many of these units were preparing to fight their last stand in Iraq, for if Saddam's regime fell these people would lose their stranglehold on power.

Above My patrol, *Mayhem Three Zero*, passed through scores of Iraqi positions undetected before the enemy finally had us surrounded. As ferocious battle was joined, Tricky, the rear gunner on my vehicle, used the heavy .50-calibre machine gun to smash through the walls of enemy bunkers and to tear apart their vehicles.

Centre We were outnumbered several hundred to one, but at least we had a serious amount of firepower. On the three Pinkies we had a .50-calibre heavy machine gun (like the one pictured here), five trusted General Purpose Machine Guns (GPMGs), rocket-launchers, personal assault rifles, pistols, and a whole stack of grenades.

Right We train relentlessly for mobile operations and firing accurately from fast-moving vehicles – one of the hardest of combat skills to master – and it was that expertise that kept us alive during hours and hours of full-on combat.

Left Yours truly, in the 'local' gear that we wore in Iraq.

Below Having a much-needed scoff and a brew back at the American front line the morning after our patrol finally fought its way through a series of massive Iraqi ambushes. Steve was the Pathfinder's armourer, and he managed to lob a grenade one-handed into an enemy bunker whilst he was driving through a murderous ambush. Tricky is setting up comms in the background. He was the .50-calibre gunner on my wagon, and more than once on this mission saved my life.

Right Myself, on stretcher and oxygen, having been Casevaced from Iraq into a field hospital in Kuwait. My patrol had been on our second night mission when our Pinkie rolled down a ravine. It was a miracle that I had been pulled out of it alive.

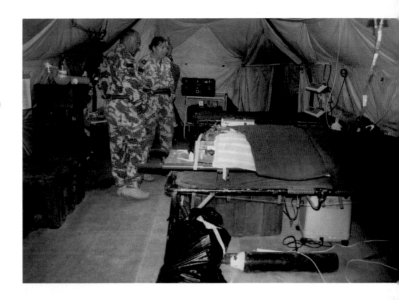

Above My military medals. From left to right; Kosovo, Northern Ireland, Sierra Leone, Afghanistan, Iraq, Queens Jubilee.

Right Myself, with HRH Prince Charles, the Colonel-in-Chief of the Parachute regiment, at Copehill Down Urban Warfare Training Centre, on Salisbury Plain. I'm briefing him on an 'urban warfare' demonstration – fighting through built-up areas.

BIRKHALL

6th April, 2003

Dear Jane,

I heard of the terrible accident that befell you in Iraq and just wanted to write and send you my very best wishes for a speedy recovery. I am relieved to hear that you should be able to leave hospital soon.

My spies also tell me you had a narrow escape from a carefully aimed Iraqi bullet, just the other day before your crash and that you were saved only by a lucky pair of trousers! The good Lord is obviously still smiling on you...! I hope that, despite your setbacks, you remain in good spirits and that the enclosed "medicine" might help to raise them a bit...

I know you will be desperate to rejoin your comrades in the Pathfinder Platoon as soon as you can but, in the meantime, I hope you are able to enjoy some time for recuperation with your family.

Yours most sincerely,

Charles

The letter HRH Prince Charles wrote to me after I was injured. He refers to me being shot through my trousers by a 'carefully aimed Iraqi bullet', which happened during our mission to seize Qalat Sikar airfield. The 'medicine' he mentions sending me is a bottle of whisky from his personal cellars.

In that instant I spotted the RPG team crouched behind a sand-bagged barrier. I unleashed a burst of rounds from the Gimpy, which went tearing into them. There was this massive flash and the bang of secondary explosions, and shredded sandbags went flying in all directions. I figured my bullets must have touched off their spare RPG rounds. *That was one very dead RPG team.*

The very same instant that I'd smashed them, the RPG round that they'd fired went screaming over our bonnet. It wasn't as if it was in front of us, or near us: it was right over the Pinkie's bonnet, like metal scraping metal, a great big fuck-off rocket before our bloody noses.

Instinctively Steve swerved, and started yelling: 'FUCKING HELL! FUCKING HELL! FUCKING HELL!'

I glanced at him in surprise. I figured he must have been hit. But he was eyes front still and doing the drive of his life, as he fought to control the careering wagon.

I was instantly back to my arcs, picking targets and hammering rounds into them. The ground to the east was 500 metres of solid muzzle flashes sparking right to the ridgeline. There were rakes of buildings up on the high ground, and I could see figures on the rooftops, loosing off whole mags on automatic at us.

Their aim was shit, but a lucky bullet was still a lucky bullet. And nearer to the road there were yet more bunkers and dug-in positions. Those had to be my priority. I picked a target, focused, sighted and fired; picked a target, focused, sighted and fired. On and on and on it went, until I was sure the Gimpy had to be down to its last round. And then the next billowing cloud of smoke engulfed us.

I had no idea how many smoke grenades Jase had brought with him. We went thundering out of the far side of that one, and for a moment I sensed that the fire was mostly behind us now. I swivelled the Gimpy around, to engage the last of the enemy positions, but they were too far to my left and behind us. The bonnet-mounted GPMG could cover to the front and side of the vehicle, but not to the rear.

Behind me Tricky swivelled the 50-cal around until it was pointing rearwards, and for several seconds he kept malleting rounds into the enemy positions. Then he too ceased firing. The enemy guns were still trying to hit us, but there was no point making us an easy target by revealing where we were. Somehow, miraculously, we'd made it through that first ambush alive.

I could sense Tricky searching in the darkness of the road behind us. I knew instinctively what he was looking for. *Vehicles in pursuit.* This had become a crazed dash south before the Fedayeen hunter force could catch us.

Acting on automatic I reached forwards and unhooked the ammo belt from the GPMG. I hefted its weight in my right hand, and I could feel that it was all but empty. I chucked the used belt into the footwell and slotted on another 200 rounds of link.

I'd just finished changing the ammo belt when Steve leaned across to have a word. The tension on his face dissolved into this crazy kind of smile. 'Dave, we fucking made it through! Boat drinks, mate!'

I gave him the nod back. 'Yeah, boat drinks it is. But if you want to make it home to all those lovely Scouse girls, there's more of that to come, mate.'

'Scouse girls? I'm making straight for the bloody Shadow Lounge. You with me, or what?'

I bared my teeth and let out this crazed kind of laugh. We were high on the adrenaline, and the sheer knowledge that we were still alive.

We pressed onwards on a dark and deserted stretch of road. I flipped down my NVG and scanned the terrain ahead. Apart from us, it seemed utterly devoid of life out there. After the insane intensity of that ambush, the silence was deafening. Fearful. I had no idea if any-one had been hit on Jason's or the Recce wagon. I couldn't radio to check, because we'd flushed the Crypto and had no comms between vehicles.

I checked my watch. It was 2100 hours. First light was around 0500. We had eight hours in which to complete this death run. If we were to stand any chance of surviving it, we had to get it done during the hours of darkness. With sunrise we'd lose the cover of the night, and we'd be finished. From the drive up here I reckoned that the settlement we'd just driven through was the largest this side of Nasiriyah. I was hoping that we'd just managed to run the biggest force the Iraqis would be able to throw at us.

Maybe they just presumed that we'd never make it through that first ambush alive. We pushed onwards for 7 kilometres in silence. I was hunched down behind the GPMG, continuously sweeping my arcs, the steel sights seeking targets amongst the night terrain all around us. *Nothing.* Just empty bush, with the skeletal silhouettes of palm trees piercing the darkness. The tension was unbearable.

As my senses tuned into the environment, I realised there was a new scent in the air now: the reek of burned gun oil. The barrel of the Gimpy before me was still hot from the battle. The GMPG is a fantastic weapon. It's been tried and tested over many years, and whilst you do get stoppages they're rare. The barrel does get red hot – by which time you have to change it – but only after unleashing a few thousand rounds. I'd got a good way to go before that happened.

I'd freshly oiled the Gimpy when we'd been waiting to move forwards at the Marine Corps command post, just south of Nasiriyah. Some of that gun oil had cooked off during the firefight. When I'd oiled my weapon I'd done so almost subconsciously. It was one of those automatic drills hammered into us in the PF: *Look after your weapon, your weapon looks after you.* And when I'd done so, I hadn't the slightest idea what shitfight we were driving into. *Relatively benign my arse.*

As I scanned the empty night with my NVG, I couldn't help but wonder what it was that had kept us alive during the frenzy of that firefight. My mind drifted to one of the key lessons learned by our predecessors, the Long Range Desert Group, during their epic feats of soldiering in the North Africa deserts. At first, along with their sister regiment, David Stirling's SAS, they had sneaked on to enemy airfields and planted their Lewis bombs, melting away again quietly into the night.

But on one mission they'd decided to change their means of attack.

The favoured weapons of the LRDG were the Vickers 50-cal heavy machine guns, plus the Vickers .303 inch K machine guns, mounted on pivots and often in pairs. In December 1941, the LRDG and the SAS had carried out two raids on the airfield at Sirte, in northern Libya. But this time they decided to drive their trucks right on to the airfield and between the rows of parked aircraft, using their fire-power to shoot them up. The raid was so successful that this became their standard means of attack, and that December they destroyed 151 aircraft that way.

The LRDG operators were skilled at manoeuvring at high speed and making their vehicles difficult targets, whilst putting down accurate and heavy concentrations of fire. They also relied upon the fact that their enemies – more often than not Italian conscript troops – were taken by surprise, and their fire was wild and inaccurate. I figured it had to be the same kind of mobility skills and fire discipline that was keeping us alive.

But as I scanned the empty Iraqi night, the difference with this mission struck me with the force of a speeding truck: the enemy knew we were coming, so we had zero element of surprise; and we were being forced to speed down a main highway, which left us bugger all room for any manoeuvre.

Our turn-around point had been some 80 kilometres north of Nasiriyah. I figured we were around 15 kilometres south of there by now, so we had some 65 kilometres of enemy territory to run before we reached the American front line. That was more or less the distance of the endurance stage of PF selection, which you had to complete in a twenty-hour night march, or fail. That was how far we had to run the enemy gauntlet, before we reached comparative safety.

I was scanning the darkness, and checking for any sign of headlights in pursuit. But the road seemed dark and totally deserted behind us. It was from way out in front that I spotted the next threat.

There was a line of vehicles speeding towards us, lights on full beam.

CHAPTER TWENTY-TWO

Headlamps probed the darkness, catching on the dust thrown up by whatever was coming at us, and creating a weird glowing halo of light. As the convoy drew closer, I began to make out the details. There were a couple of minibuses in the lead, the headlamps from the wagons behind glinting off their dirty, white bodywork. From the silhouette of the third vehicle, I figured it had to be a Toyota-type pick-up of the type driven by the Fedayeen. There were further pick-ups behind.

After our experiences with Ron Jeremy – the fat Iraqi cabbie-cum-spy – we'd woken up to the fact that the Iraqi military were using civvie vehicles as their key means of transport. In fact, it made perfect sense for them to move around in non-military vehicles. With the coalition forces having total air superiority, our warplanes would be able to blast their convoys from the air, as long as the aircrew could positively identify them as being Iraqi military. However, our air power was far less likely to hit the Iraqi forces if they were buzzing about in minibuses, pick-ups and taxicabs, and making for all the world like civvies.

We had to figure that this was an enemy hunter force. Jason must have reached the same kind of conclusion as I had. With the gap between the Iraqi convoy and ours closing fast, I saw our lead wagon opening fire. Bullets hammered south across the distance between Jason's vehicle and theirs.

The lead pair of headlights suddenly went dark. The minibus slewed wildly across the road before righting itself. I saw muzzle flashes spark from all along the speeding vehicle's windows. It was packed with Iraqi fighters. From the rear the pick-ups joined in the firefight, and all of the enemy wagons began to engage us as we hammered towards each other at a combined speed of over 100 kph.

It was now that a curve in the road opened up a clear line of fire. The guns on the Engineer Recce wagon started pumping out bullets, and an instant later I unleashed fire from the GPMG. I saw my rounds falling just short, sparking off the tarmac to the front of the lead enemy wagon. I leaned my shoulder harder into the GPMG, raised the muzzle a fraction on its pivot mount, and fired another long burst. Rounds tore along the length of the front vehicle, punching out the windows, and sending fountains of glass into the air. The shattered glass glinted momentarily in the light thrown up by the following vehicles, as if trapped in slow motion.

I could feel every one of those windows getting smashed to pieces. Further bursts of fire tore through the bodywork, chunks of metal spinning off in all directions. Finally, the lead minibus swerved violently to the right, left the road completely and careered into the bush. It rolled over several times, and I followed it with the sights of the Gimpy until it stopped moving. It came to a rest on one side, and then there were no more muzzle flashes coming from the wreckage.

I ramped the hot, smoking barrel of the Gimpy back towards the road, and as I did so the second minibus came juddering to a halt. For some reason it wasn't engaging us any more. It looked as if it may have given up the fight. I decided not to mallet the fuck out of it. But in the third and fourth wagons – the Toyota pick-ups – I could see kneeling figures silhouetted in the glare of their muzzle flashes, as they sprayed off long bursts and tried to smash us.

As one, the six machine guns on our three Pinkies swung on to target and opened up. As we sped towards the enemy convoy we concentrated our combined firepower on those two wagons, and within seconds they were riddled with 50-cal rounds. Bullets shredded the lead pick-up from end to end, punching jagged rents in the white bodywork. There was a lick of red and angry flame from the second wagon, and it looked as if the diesel tank had taken one of the big, armour-piercing rounds.

We roared past the wreckage of the first vehicle. It was lying in the bush with the roof crumpled in, and the window struts buckled outwards. Bodies were hanging out of the shattered windows, with others lying face down in the dirt amidst spreading pools of blood. It was too dark to make out what, if any, uniforms they'd been wearing, but their discarded weapons were everywhere.

We roared past the second minibus. It was parked up on the road-side more or less intact, and it seemed to be totally abandoned. There weren't even any bodies that I could see. Maybe its occupants had done a runner, once they'd seen what our vehicle-mounted machine guns had done to the lead wagon. They must have decided discretion was the better part of valour, and made themselves scarce.

We came level with the pickups. The cab of the first one was a shattered mess. I caught the flash of a red-and-white chequered headscarf tumbling out of a half-open doorway. Sure enough, they were Fedayeen. There were more dead and dying Fedayeen in the rear of the vehicle, but it was half-obscured by a thick blanket of choking smoke. The rear pick-up was a mass of seething flame, oily black fumes from the inferno barrelling into an even blacker sky.

We shot past the wreckage with the hungry roar of the fire in our ears, the pick-up's burning tyres popping and exploding as we went. I glanced at Steve, his face lit up tense and ghostly in the searing heat as he focused on the driving. Behind me the fiery orange light flickered across Tricky's features, as his hands gripped the 50-cal and swung it around to cover the enemy to our rear.

Then we were heading onwards into the cool darkness of the night. Those vehicles had been packed full of Iraqi fighters, mostly Fedayeen. I guessed they were a mobile reception party sent out to hit us, or maybe reinforcements heading north to bolster the enemy positions. Either way we'd managed to smash them first, before they got to ambush us.

We drill and drill and drill for how to fire accurately from fast moving vehicles. It's one of the most difficult skills for a soldier to master, and it's one of the key specialisms of the Pathfinders. And right now, it was those skills that were keeping us alive.

We'd rehearsed those drills repeatedly back in Kuwait, just to make sure we were 100 per cent ready and that our vehicle-mounted weapons were properly zeroed in. During transit, sights tend to get knocked and a weapon's zero can go out of true. It's also the case that rounds deliver to target via a different trajectory depending on atmospheric conditions. The hot and baking desert air was very different from the soggy damp of the UK.

Out on the Camp Tristar ranges we'd got ourselves accustomed to how bullets fly in such burning, bone-dry conditions. Tricky and Joe had had to zero in the Thales Kite sights on their 50-cal machine guns. The Kite sight has times-six magnification, plus low-light image enhancement, which means it doubles as a night sight. Under starlight illumination alone it can detect a standing man at 600 metres. We'd been engaging the enemy vehicles of the hunter force from well within that range.

We'd practised firing the weapons from the Pinkies moving at speed, using human cut-out targets, which are radio-controlled to pop-up and pop-down again. They give you just seconds to spot and kill the target.

We'd started by firing single shots from stationary vehicles, with a buddy spotting our rounds to see if they were falling short or long. That way, we'd got the weapons zeroed in. All three of us – Tricky, Steve, me – had rotated around the 50-cal and the GPMG, to ensure we were up to speed on the weapons, and the sights were true. Anyone could get killed or injured when in combat, so we all needed to know how to use the weapons. If we got the vehicle bogged and Tricky was put out of action, Steve would need to be able to operate the 50-cal.

We'd moved on to firing from single vehicles to firing from pairs of wagons, as a patrol. Targets would pop up randomly on the Camp Tristar range, and we'd yell out warnings so as to co-ordinate our fire. Then we'd graduated to both vehicles being on the move, and engaging the targets across all types of terrain. The targets would fall when hit, so it was possible to see if you were aiming too far in front or behind, in an effort to compensate for your speed.

We'd drilled for firing from the Pinkies when moving at speed by day and by night, and hitting targets that only appeared for a split second. We knew that if we were compromised behind enemy lines, it would be the speed, accuracy and lethality of our fire-and-manoeuvre skills that would keep us alive.

As we pulled away from the shattered wreckage of those pick-ups and the minibus, Tricky leaned forwards. 'Remind me to always take the train.'

It was the perfect comment to break the knife-edged tension of the moment. Steve and I cracked up.

'Well, at least until we're old enough to get us a free bloody bus pass,' Steve quipped. 'Did I ever tell you about that Aussie chick I met once on a train ...?'

'Will you ever shut the fuck up about women,' I cut in. Now wasn't really the time for another of his shagged-her-in-the-toilet stories.

By now we'd pushed 25 kilometres south, which meant we had more than twice that distance still to go. I was tensing myself for the next fight. No doubt the enemy commanders were radioing warnings ahead, and all along the road. They had to know that we were coming. The distance to the next settlement – the one that we had driven through under the fierce orange glow of the streetlamps – was 15 klicks away. At the speed we were travelling at, it would take us less than fifteen minutes to reach it. That was when I figured we next had it coming – that's unless they sent out another mobile force to try to hit us.

In the down time and the silence, I swept the night with my weapon. As I did so I reached forward and stroked the barrel momentarily. It was burning to the touch, but not glowing red-hot so that I'd have to consider doing a barrel-change. Reassured, I settled back to sweep my arcs. I couldn't quite believe that the three of us in my wagon were apparently unscathed. I couldn't speak for the other vehicles: maybe they had taken casualties. Maybe they'd lost someone even. There was just no way of knowing unless Jason called a halt.

Jason. How my impression of him had changed. I'd found him difficult, and at times even divisive, when back in Kuwait. A part of me had been dreading having him on my patrol when we went to war. Now, he'd more than made good. He was leading our charge south with lightning-fast reflexes and an instinct that was proving close to infallible. As a soldier in combat, he was pretty much second to none. I had to accept that I'd got it badly wrong about him. When it came to war-fighting, he was an invaluable asset to have on the patrol.

Despite the early challenges with the lads, I knew now that these were the blokes to be fighting back-to-back with. I wouldn't change a single one of them for the world. Class, background, rank, personal rivalries – it had all gone out of the window. Here, in the midst of this death run, we were all on a level, and not a man amongst us had been found wanting.

Driving into almost certain death had got me brimful with fear. I had felt the tension and the terror gnawing at my guts. But the brave man was the man who channelled that fear, and used it for the fight. Knowing that we were all in this together, that we were a brotherhood of equals, had given me something incredibly powerful to help conquer that fear. I presumed it was the same for the others: we all felt the fear, yet it was tempered by the brotherhood.

I was torn out of my thoughts by a jab in the ribs. 'Up ahead,' yelled Steve. 'Roadblock!'

I looked forwards, straining my eyes to spot whatever Steve had seen. In the glow of my NVG I could just make out a pair of hot engine blocks a kilometre or so ahead of us. A couple of vehicles had been parked up sideways on to the highway. They formed a makeshift roadblock. Their motors were still warm, and it was that heat which had been picked up by the NVG.

As we drew nearer I could make out more details. The vehicle on the left looked like an empty Toyota minibus parked arse-end on to the highway. It was similar to the two that we'd just shot to pieces. The vehicle on the right looked like a Datsun-type taxicab of the kind that our old friend, Ron Jeremy, had been driving.

They'd left a gap between the two vehicles that appeared to be just about large enough to squeeze the wagons through. It didn't make a great deal of sense to have thrown up a roadblock with a bloody great gap in the middle of it. Or, thinking like the enemy, *maybe it did*. Maybe they'd got that gap covered by a couple of great big Dushkas, zeroed in and waiting for us to poke our noses through. Maybe if we took the bait and went for the gap, that was going to be a sure kill for those waiting Dushka gunners. A dead cert.

Or maybe they'd got a series of hidden explosive charges rigged to either side of the gap and linked to a detonation wire. As we went to pass they'd trigger the detonators, and blow the lot of us sky high. Or maybe they'd got some strands of razor wire strung across the gap at neck height, in an effort to rip our fucking heads off.

Or maybe they'd thrown some tyre-busters across the tarmac, which at their most basic were planks of wood with nails driven through them and pointing vertically upwards. We wouldn't see them until the last moment, if at all. Without the run-flats that we'd asked for back in Kuwait – and been denied – we'd be finished. We'd go roaring over the tyre-busters and they'd blow out our inner tubes. It'd be a crude but very effective way of stopping us.

If they blew out our tyres they'd fucking have us. Images flashed through my mind of what the Iraqis had done to the Bravo Two Zero boys, once they'd captured them. The B2Z lads had claimed to be from a CSAR team sent in to rescue some downed British pilots. The Iraqis hadn't believed them. They'd locked them isolated and alone in cells plastered with shit, and used beatings, mock executions and worse to try to break them, so they would admit what unit they were from. The torture and abuse had lasted for days on end.

From those images my mind flipped into a powerful memory of being in a torture chamber myself for real. 1 PARA were the first troops into Kosovo during that conflict, and I'd led my company into the war-torn capital, Pristina. We were a couple of days into the city and were out doing a day patrol. We had bergens on our backs, our personal weapons in our hands, and we were moving fast through the streets on foot. We came across this building with a bonfire of burning documents outside. I asked our interpreter what was happening here.

It turned out to be a Serb police station that had just been abandoned. The bonfire was intended to destroy all the evidence of their wrongdoing. But there was no hiding what they'd been up to down in the basement. There was blood spattered all over the place, baseball bats studded with nails, bed frames with straps on them to hold down the victims, and even photos on the walls of those they'd tortured. But most disturbing were the heaps of extremely vile vampire-type pornography lying around the room.

That place had reeked of pain, dark perversions and evil. If the Iraqis captured us alive, I guessed they'd have something similar in store for us. Maybe this roadblock was the ultimate trap, and everything up until now has been just some gentle kind of prelude. *Who fucking knows?*

There was little point me worrying about it, or what we should do about it. Jase was leading the convoy of wagons, and it was his call. In any case, we all knew the actions-on for encountering a roadblock. Pretty soon Jason should pull off the highway, so we could box around the roadblock off-road and rejoin the tarmac further on.

Yet Jason's wagon just kept hammering forwards at full speed ahead. The Engineer Recce vehicle and our own had no option but to follow Jason's lead. The PF golden rule number one is not to break the line of march. Do that, and with no radio contact we'd lose each other pretty damn fast.

The roadblock was growing closer and closer by the second, and I just knew that Jason was going to try to run it or die trying.

Balls of fucking steel, Jase, balls of fucking steel.

CHAPTER TWENTY-THREE

The great thing about the Land Rover is that it sits upon a solid hunk of steel, a ladder frame chassis, the solid, chunky build of which hasn't changed much since it was first put together back in 1947. On top of the Land Rover's natural robustness, our Pinkies were specially strengthened. The chassis had been engineered to massively increase load capacity, with fibre webbing encasing all of the welded joints and stress points. So whilst they might not be able to outrun a Toyota SUV, they'd smash one up in a head-on collision every time.

As we careered onwards, muzzles started sparking amongst the shadows between the Toyota and the Datsun taxicab. As one, our guns opened up and tore into the thin metal skins of those vehicles. We were almost upon them, driving down the enemy's muzzles, when the minibus exploded in a blinding sheet of flame. The fuel tank had gone, the massive blast throwing the vehicle half out of our path.

I saw Jason's Land Rover going for the gap, smashing into what remained of the minibus, punching the wreckage out of the way and careering through the scattered debris. Meanwhile, the Recce wagon and us lot were pumping rounds into what was left of Ron Jeremy's taxicab, at very close range. *I fucking hoped it was his vehicle and all.* It was Ron Jeremy the fat cabbie who'd compromised us in the first place, and brought this world of shit down around our ears. There was nothing better than seeing 'his' sedan getting chewed into small pieces of shattered glass and bullet-punctured steel.

We sped past the remains of that roadblock, leaving the twisted wreck of the burning minibus on one side, and the bullet-torn carcass of the Datsun on the other. I felt this crazy blast of euphoria as we did so. *Fuck 'em!* They'd had us at that roadblock. It was there that they should have stopped us, and killed or captured us all. Instead, Jase had smashed the minibus out of the way, and led us through from a totally unexpected direction. If they did have their guns zeroed in on the gap, we'd neatly side-stepped them.

Still, I couldn't quite believe that we'd made it through. As we emerged from the smoke and the flames I caught sight of two bunkers close by the roadside, up ahead of the lead Pinkie. An instant later they opened up, pouring fire into Jase's wagon. It suddenly struck me that maybe the roadblock had been a ruse, designed to screen us from the real threat – our arrival at the second big settlement that straddled Route 7.

Those two bunkers were the trigger for the full-on ambush. As the gunners there unleashed on Jason's wagon, so the entire hillside behind them erupted into a massive wave of fire. For whatever reason – *they know we're coming; we're nearer the Iraqi front line (though we're approaching from behind it!); they're a better calibre of soldier here* – the gunfire was more accurate than ever, and there was even more of it. It was total fucking murder.

There was no smoke being thrown by Jason any more, so I figured either he was all out of grenades, or he was seriously wounded or dead. As the last vehicle, we had no choice now but to run this ambush, and with zero cover from view. I forced myself to concentrate my fire on the closest positions, because they had to present the greatest threat. I swung the GPMG into the aim, and started to hammer the bunkers that were 100, 200, 300 metres forwards of us, all down the roadside, in one long burst of aimed, accurate fire.

I saw the empty cartridges spewing out of the Gimpy's breech, as I kept my finger on the trigger, churning out the rounds. They went tumbling into the Pinkie's footwell in one long cascade of hot, smoking brass. It was a sea of spent bullet cases down there, and I had to keep kicking them out of the way so as to maintain a good foothold. I could only imagine that our wagon was getting riddled with enemy fire, but the noise from the Gimpy, plus that of the 50-cal thumping above my head, was so deafening that I couldn't tell where we were getting smashed.

I was on my feet ramping the GPMG from side to side, those spent cartridges scrunching underfoot. Time had wound down to a slow, dragging, agonising loop, in which I figured I could all but see the bullets rocketing out of the barrel of my weapon. I was locked into the slowmo, adrenaline-fuelled, tunnel-vision of full-on combat, where a second seemed to last for a whole hour.

My mind felt crystal clear, as it processed sight, sound and smell at the speed of light, and with seemingly all the time in the world to do so. My brain pumped out a million thoughts a second, my body responding instantly to each one: *threat; target; fire; threat; target; fire; threat; target; fire; threat; target; threat; target – FIRE!*

My shoulder muscles were burning from the pain and tension of swinging the weapon from side to side, as I poured rounds into those targets. But as much as I might be smashing those enemy fighters, the fire against us just kept coming. I saw this wave of bullets slamming into the road right in the path of our vehicle, and ricocheting high into the air. I could feel the harsh jab of the shockwave punching over us. I was half-blinded by the tracer flaring like an angry bonfire right before our wheels.

I was used to seeing and hearing tracer on exercises, but I'd never known anything like this. It was like we were driving into the heart of a volcano of solid fire. I sensed the bullets tearing metal all around me, and punching into steel. I figured they were making mincemeat out of the Pinkie, and I just prayed that she fucking kept moving. *We stop here, we're instantly dead.*

And then it just got worse.

High on the ridge, a good 800 metres away, was the silhouette of something truly terrifying. There was this big, multi-barrelled weapon swinging towards us – the kind of thing that should be pointed at the sky, to bring down allied warplanes. Instead, it was being depressed to its lowest trajectory so its four gaping barrels could point right at our vehicles.

The muzzles reached horizontal, and then they started to throw out long gouts of flame, one after the other after the other. Rhythmically: 'Kaboom! Kaboom! Kaboom! Kaboom! Kaboom!' Big, long dirty spurts of smoke accompanied each burst, as if the squat, ugly weapon was some kind of primeval monster that ate and vomited smoke and fire.

It had to be a ZPU-4 or something similar. The ZPU-4 is a towed, quadruple-barrelled anti-aircraft weapon, which throws out a devastating barrage of 14.5 mm armour-piercing shells. It is accurate up to 2000 metres when used against ground targets. We were well within its range. If it hit us, it'd shred us.

I aimed in on the ridgeline where those four muzzles were spouting smoke and fire, and I sprayed and prayed. Rounds from the GPMG groped towards the target, but 800 metres is approaching the limit of the Gimpy's accurate range, and it was like a duel to the death between me and the ZPU's gun crew.

I saw rounds from the ZPU tearing into a palm grove just ahead of us, ripping trunks in two as if a giant chainsaw was going to work in there. I figured the ZPU gunners were over-compensating for the speed of our wagon, and firing just a fraction too far to the front of us. But they wouldn't keep doing so for very long. Sooner or later they'd adjust the fall of their fire, and nail us.

I held the GPMG steady, readjusted my aim to account for the distance, and saw my first bullets tear into the four-wheeled weapon. Rounds went sparking off the metal armour, ricocheting high into the dark night sky, and I knew that I'd found my target. I kept my finger hard on the trigger and poured in the fire.

Just at that moment I felt something punch into my leg with a frightening power and violence. It was at the level of my left ankle, so on the side of the enemy guns. With all the weight of fire slamming into us, I guessed it was inevitable that someone on my wagon would take a bullet. We'd probably got wounded blokes up and down the vehicles. And now it was me that had taken a hit.

I tried putting all my weight on the left leg, but I had to be so high on adrenaline that I couldn't feel the pain. I just hoped that it wasn't a round from the ZPU, or it'd be my foot and half my leg that was gone. For an instant I wondered if that was it for me: that I'd be hobbling around for the rest of my life on one peg. Would I ever be able to lead my daughter down the aisle? That's if I lived to have kids of my own...

Either way, I forced myself to ignore whatever injury I'd taken, and keep my weapon churning out the rounds. I'd deal with it later, that's if we ever got out of this shitfight. Through the stark metal sights of the Gimpy I saw figures bailing out of the sandbagged gun emplacement to either side of the ZPU. I followed them with the steel 'V' of the weapon, finger hard on the trigger, and I saw them stumbling and going down hard.

The four-barrelled monster had stopped spitting its lethal, 14.5 mm rounds at us. Finally, unbelievably, we shot out of the far side of the ambush. I could barely believe that we were still moving, and that I was still on my feet and alive. I risked a glance away from my weapon, and I could see Tricky hunched over the 50-cal covering the rear, and Steve hard on the steering wheel.

Steve had been 100 per cent focused on the road, and he'd not once been able to return fire. Being the driver meant that you were prevented from being able to use a weapon to defend yourself, which must have been a totally fucking horrific way to go to war. I saw Steve lift his one hand from the steering wheel and punch high into the air.

He let out this crazed yelp. 'YEAAAHHHH! WE MADE IT! YEAAAH-HHH! DAVE! DAVE! THIS IS FUCKIN' MEGA!'

It was wildly inappropriate what he'd just said – *This is fucking mega!* – but somehow it felt just right. Steve was a total pro, and I couldn't imagine how fucked up it was to have his job – to have to drive through that wall of death, and not be able to lift his weapon and fight – so why not enjoy it now and let rip?

As we sped away from the kill zone Steve was grinning and laughing like a lunatic, and he kept punching the steering wheel in sheer exhilaration. I knew exactly how he was feeling. He was on the pure, incomparable adrenaline high of not getting killed. *Not yet, anyway.*

No one was kidding themselves that this was all over. We were 35 kilometres south of our turn-around point: less than halfway back to the American front line. The truth was we'd got the majority of the death run still in front of us.

It was now that I remembered my injured leg. On previous ops in Sierra Leone and the Balkans I'd seen what horrific damage even a small-calibre round can do to the human body. A 7.62 mm short – the standard AK47 round – hits human flesh at a velocity of 715 metres per second. The bullet ricochets off bone, and rips an erratic course through the body, tearing a ragged exit hole as it leaves.

Fearing the worst, I reached down and felt around my ankle gingerly. The first surprise was that the drawstring of my combats seemed to be undone, leaving them hanging loose over my boot. It was an old habit from PARA Regiment days that I never left my combats unfastened.

I fumbled underneath, trying to find where the bullet had hit. I was sure that my fingers would meet blood, pulverised flesh and shattered bone. But I couldn't seem to feel any damage. No slick of blood. Nothing. I lifted my hand to my face to check. There was no sign of any warm sticky liquid, but it was pitch dark so maybe I'd missed it.

I checked the Pinkie's floor for anywhere a pool of blood would have congealed, but it was thick with bullet cases. I touched my hand to my face, and my lips, but all I could taste was the barest hint of blood. There was just the faintest smear of red on one of my fingers. I knew for sure that I'd been shot. I'd felt the fucking impact. I couldn't understand what had happened. *Where was all the damage and the carnage?*

There was bugger all that I could do about it now. We pressed onwards, Steve gunning the heavily-laden Land Rover, and all of us praying that the vehicle's battle damage wasn't terminal.

In the empty, windswept silence of the night I found my mind wandering. The PF exists as a recce force to prove what's on the ground in enemy territory. We'd done that. It was clear now how totally, hopelessly wrong some idiot had got the intel picture here. *Relatively benign it was not.*

A great deal of our intel had come down from the Americans, and we'd already seen the mess they'd made of predicting Nasiriyah. I didn't blame the Yanks though. As far as I was concerned we were all in this together. The US Marine Corps and the nine of us just happened to be at the harsher and brutal end of things.

If it wasn't for the Yanks, we'd probably be left without any sat photos or proper mapping at all. Nevertheless, the intel picture had proven a total fuck-up. The Marine Corps had expected to face minimal resistance in Nasiriyah. In reality, thousands of Iraqi regular forces and Fedayeen had converged upon that city for the mother of all battles.

And tonight, we'd blundered into the heart of them.

We pushed on for a good 10 kilometres on an open, deserted road. With every turn of the wheels I could feel my heart thumping in my chest, as the adrenaline coursed through my veins. There wasn't a sniff of the enemy anywhere, but it was pretty obvious that sooner or later our luck was going to have to run out. It always does for everyone some day.

Yet right now I was feeling pretty indestructible. You could almost say *bulletproof.* Whatever round it was that had punched into my left leg, it seemed to have bounced right off of me. *Incredible.*

As we thundered onwards the first lines of the poem 'Invictus' – Latin for 'undefeated' or 'invincible' – came into my mind. Almost without noticing, I found myself mouthing those words into the dark void of the Iraqi night.

Out of the night that covers me.
Black as the pit from pole to pole.
I thank whatever gods may be,
For my unconquerable soul.

That last line was whipped away by the vehicle's slipstream. But just as I'd uttered it, I'd heard a voice echoing mine, or at least I thought I had. From out of the corner of my eye I fancied that it was Steve, and that he'd started to mouth the immortal lines of the second verse

In the fell clutch of circumstance,
I have not winced nor cried aloud.
Under the bludgeonings of chance,
My head is bloody, but unbowed.

I figured I caught a third voice joining us now – Tricky, from the wagon's rear – as together we hammered out verse three, and moved into the enduring final lines.

It matters not how strait the gate,
How charged with punishments the scroll.
I am the master of my fate:
I am the captain of my soul.

Those final words were torn out of my mouth by the wind, yet still they sent a shiver up my spine. Or maybe in the heightened, trance-like state of combat that I was now in – the red mist of battle all around us – I'd just imagined it all. Who knows?

Either way, reliving those lines had taken me back to the warm familiarity of the PF Interest Room, and my very first day in the Pathfinders. As soon as I'd stepped into the Interest Room, the difference between this and any other unit that I'd served with had hit me in the face. Here, there were men of all ranks sharing a brew and a chat together, as equals.

I guess the closest analogy to the Interest Room would be a common room at school or college. It was in the Interest Room that the men of the unit gathered, to socialise and share the essence of the Pathfinders' unique *esprit de corps*. As I'd glanced around the room I'd spotted the glory wall, which displayed the mug-shots of those who'd died on past PF operations, and the mementoes brought back from the furthest theatres of war. Finally, my eyes had come to rest on a framed poem, one of several hanging on the wall. They were ones that individuals from the PF had gifted to the unit when leaving, often to move on to the SAS.

The poem that drew my eye was by someone that I'd never heard of before, William Ernest Henley, and it was entitled *Invictus*. In between getting introduced to various members of the PF, I'd read and re-read those lines: '*Out of the night that covers me ...*' I'd sense in them the defining feature of this unit that I had fought so hard to be a part of. It was a unit defined by an individualistic, maverick bravery and cunning, and a singular determination to win through.

And it was defined by the kind of action we were now involved in, wherein a small group of determined men could face death together, *bloodied but unbowed*.

CHAPTER TWENTY-FOUR

I'd glanced around the PF Interest Room, and I'd realised then that I'd never seen a group of soldiers with such a tight-knit sense of purpose, or who were so relaxed in their own skins. These were guys who'd spend nine months of the year away from barracks, on PF training and exercises. And then, during their weekends off, they'd volunteer to go do some extra HAHO or HALO jumping, just to keep it knife-sharp.

But in spite of the confidence that shone out of them, there was real humility too. There was a lack of arrogance and bullshit that was palpable. It was around then that Tricky had asked me the million-dollar question.

'Dave,' he'd said, 'if you cut a Pathfinder's legs off is he still a Pathfinder?'

I told Tricky that I reckoned he was.

'You're right,' said Tricky. 'He is. He can't walk at 6 klicks an hour for 60 kilometres, but he's still got the Pathfinder's state of mind.'

It was David Stirling who'd first said of SF selection that most people failed themselves. They failed themselves due to their lack of self-belief: they just didn't believe strongly enough that they were good enough. Yet a good number also failed themselves due to over-confidence bordering upon self-delusion. They'd never had the humility to make it through. For sure, it was a hard balance to get right. I didn't know if I'd always managed to do so, but

I hoped at least on this mission I was getting there.

I understood now what it meant to experience the ultimate thrill of combat, whilst standing shoulder to shoulder with men like these. More than likely, we were all going to die on this mission. In the wagons up front we may already have lost some. I couldn't but think that we had some seriously injured. But I wouldn't want to be anywhere other than in this battle with these blokes, fighting for our lives.

If against all odds we did make it out of this alive, I would try to do better. I'd try never to hassle Steve because of his crappy jokes. I'd try to stop teasing Dez over his bone questions, and Tricky for forgetting his wet weather gear. I'd never think the worse of Joe because of his youth, and I'd forgive the Recce blokes for not knowing how to change a tyre.

But most of all, I'd never again look askance at Jason because of his insecurity, or his dour ways. We were the team. *We were the team that I'd always been searching for.* I was privileged to be amongst them.

As all these thoughts were rushing through my mind, tumbling over each other to be heard, we had pushed a good 10 kilometres past the roadblock-cum-ambush. But I could feel the tension rising again now, like a vice gripping the pit of my guts. I could feel it pressing down upon Steve and Tricky, like something dark and suffocating that I could almost see and touch.

We knew another attack was coming. We could sense it, animal-like, instinctively. In the ferocity of battle, when soldiers face all but certain death, their sixth sense is said to reach a hugely heightened state. I guessed that was what we were experiencing now – the ability to sense the enemy, and to know when the bullets were coming. And it was the wait – the unbearable tension of anticipation – that was killing us.

It was almost as if we were willing the next attack to come. Almost as if it was easier to fight, than to be poised and waiting and dying for the next battle to start.

'Where the fuck are the enemy! Fucking bring it on! Come and hit us!'

I didn't know whether I'd actually yelled those words out loud, or if they were just screaming inside my head. In a sense it didn't matter. I knew the lads had heard them, and that their minds were screaming out exactly the same kind of challenge.

This time, I saw them before they hit us.

I can't explain how, apart from it being the unknowable power of the sixth sense. Something – something beyond human understanding – directed my eyes to exactly where the Iraqis were waiting in hiding to smash our patrol. And in the moment that I saw them I ramped the Gimpy around and opened fire, my screamed words of warning drowned out by the flaming roar of its muzzle.

'AMBUSH 11 O'CLOCK!'

The darkness ahead of us erupted into fire. There were three hidden bunkers right by the roadside. I could see them more clearly now, the enemy faces being illuminated by the harsh yellow-white thrown off by their muzzle flashes. They were hammering rounds into our lead wagon, ripping them across Jason's exposed flank, then back towards the Recce vehicle. As they did so I felt myself burning up with this blinding rage. *They're trying to kill my fucking team!*

I aimed in with the GPMG, pouring fire at silhouettes of heads and shoulders, squirting ten-round bursts into each. I saw figures go down and bodies jerking under direct hits, as bullets tore into them. I swept the Gimpy left and re-aimed, and as I did so I saw this massive figure rear to his feet just to the front-side of our wagon. He'd appeared seemingly from nowhere and he was hefting the unmistakable form of an RPG-7.

The RPG-7 is the old faithful – unmissable, with its unmistakable bulbous warhead and flared exhaust. He'd got it on his shoulder, and he was pretty much on top of us. I swivelled the GPMG around as he levelled the tube, both of us racing to be the first to open fire.

As I did so, the words from a lecture I'd attended at Sandhurst flashed through my head. The speaker was a veteran of numerous battles against irregular forces, and he sure as hell had known his onions.

'Don't be fooled by its brute simplicity,' he'd announced, in this cut glass officer's accent. 'In the hands of a skilled operator the RPG-7 grenade launcher is a formidable weapon. It is rugged, easy to use and packs a lethal punch. It is one of the most common and brutally effective infantry weapons in contemporary conflict. Whether used against a US Black Hawk helicopter in Mogadishu, or a British Land Rover in Oman, it is the weapon of choice for many militia. It is a weapon for all seasons, and it will haunt the battle-fields of tomorrow.'

No shit. Or how about the battlefields of today?

This operator wasn't going to need a great deal of skill: he was going to hit us at point blank range if I didn't get him first. I tried to swing the Gimpy's sights on to him, but he was too far to my left and beyond my arc of fire. I was screaming out a warning when the 50-cal from behind me thumped out a deafening burst. The bullets blasted the guy off his feet and hurled him backwards, but not before he'd unleashed the RPG.

There was the blinding yellow flash of the rocket motor firing right beside us. A millisecond later the grenade streaked across the wagon like some giant firework, barely inches from Steve and me. I felt the pressure wave punching into my face as it tore past, leaving a cloud of choking exhaust gases in its wake.

Steve wrenched the steering wheel to one side, the sharp swerve made by the wagon almost throwing me off my feet. I figured the smack of the RPG-7's shock wave must have thrown him. But then he reached forwards with his one free hand, the other still gripping the wheel, and grabbed for a grenade. An instant later he'd torn the pin out with his teeth, and was lobbing the grenade forwards and to the left-hand side of the road.

'FUCKING GRENADE!'

I didn't have a clue what his target was. I followed the trajectory of Steve's throw with my gunsights, and the grenade landed just in front and to the side of us. There was a fourth and final bunker posi-tion at the very roadside – more like a small, sandbagged checkpoint

– but I'd been so focused on smashing the RPG gunner that I'd completely missed it. I hadn't even realised it was there.

The grenade curved in gracefully under the sandbagged roof. First there was the blinding flash of the detonation, and then a blast-wave of shrapnel tore through the position. The roof lifted slightly, bodies were thrown into the air, and a thick cloud of choking smoke billowed out of the open sides. An instant later the heavy, sandbagged roof collapsed in on itself, crushing the bunker's occupants.

A few seconds later we were speeding past that last enemy position, and out of the other side. As we powered ahead the surviving enemy fighters fired off wild bursts into the darkness behind us, but we were fleeing invisible into the black embrace of the night. We were through ambush number three. *Fucking unbelievable. How on earth had they failed to nail us?*

In the PF we have an expression: *to use The Force.* Of course, it's a piss-take from the Jedi Warriors in the movie *Star Wars*, but it still encapsulates much of the ethos of the unit. If you opened up your mind to your soldier's sixth sense, it could enable you to win through the seemingly unwinnable. We had sensed the enemy threat, and that had enabled us to get the drop on them. That was using The Force, and maybe it was that which had saved us.

We pressed onwards, but by now Jason was pushing his wagon to the very limits. Steve increased his speed to keep with him, and soon the convoy was careering along at pushing 100 kph. I kept wondering what it was that had made Dez put pedal to the metal. Maybe they had someone badly wounded, and bleeding out. Maybe it had become a race to get to the American front lines to save him. Or maybe it was the Engineer Recce wagon that had taken the casualties. With no comms between vehicles I had no way of knowing. All I did know was that their wagons, like our own, must have taken an unbelievable hammering.

Steve was wrestling with the steering wheel as the heavily-laden rear of the wagon kept trying to overtake the speeding front, and send us into a horrible, careering tailspin. The only way to drive a Pinkie this heavy in any safety was to do so slowly. It didn't matter greatly that you had four-wheel drive. It didn't make it safe. Whether you were on snow or ice or hard, dry tarmac as we were now, if two of your wheels lost traction you might as well be driving a Nissan Micra.

I kept checking for any sign of the Fedayeen hunter force. Maybe they were catching us, and that was what had made Jason go for maximum speed. But there was no sign of any lights anywhere to our rear. Unless the Fedayeen were like us, driving on black light, they'd got to be way behind us still.

I slapped a third 200-round belt of ammo into the breach of the GPMG. Two boxes down, four to go, including the belt now on the weapon. I figured I was doing fine on the ammunition front. The real miracle was how all three of the wagons were still apparently drive-able. *Or maybe I'd spoken too soon.*

Up ahead, Jason's vehicle began to slow noticeably. From career-ing along at 100 kph Dez decelerated the lead Pinkie to little more than a crawl, using the gears to break the wagon's momentum more than he did the brakes. It was the quietest way to bring a wagon from high speed to a dead slow, for the brakes would emit loud piercing squeals and squeaks.

The Recce wagon slowed in turn, and we slowed with it, and all the while I was wondering what the fuck was the problem with the lead wagon. If we lost one vehicle we could cross-deck Joe, Dez and Jase on to the other two. But if we lost two wagons, we either split the patrol so one wagon carried on alone, or we abandoned the vehicles. That would leave the nine of us on foot and depleted of our heavy firepower, and with the enemy knowing pretty much where we were.

I figured we'd got around 25 kilometres to go before we hit the US front line positions, and no way did I want to be losing the wagons at this juncture. We were creeping along at less than 10 kph, and I had no idea what the hold-up might be. I was dying to get us moving again, for I could almost sense the Fedayeen hunter force breathing down our necks.

I kept scanning my arcs to the east and the south. On the horizon I figured I could just make out the warm, domed-orange halo of street lamps – what had to be Nasiriyah city. It was like an impossible promise of hope. I told myself that we weren't there yet. Nasiriyah might as well be a whole world away.

And then I saw it – the reason why Jason had slowed to a dead crawl. Outlined against the faint orange glow of the city there was what had to be yet another Iraqi army base. I could see vehicles parked up in formation, plus here and there a figure standing sentry and silhouetted against the night sky. Jason must have sensed the enemy position first – *he was using The Force* – hence slowing the convoy.

No one had opened fire yet, or called out a challenge, and Jason had to be trying to sneak past undetected. We crept forwards at 5 kph, tyres humming gently on the road, engines purring softly. I saw a momentary flare in the darkness, but it was only the spark of a match. It was followed by a faint, glowing pinprick of light, as an Iraqi soldier drew in a deep lung-full of smoke and nicotine.

I was dying for a cigarette myself. The Iraqi soldier was almost close enough for me to reach out and grab one. At that moment our wagon hit an unseen bump in the road, and one of the sand ladders banged against the wagon's metal side. The body panels of the Land Rover being aluminium, as opposed to steel, the ladder made a soft, dull, muffled thud, as opposed to a clang. Still, in the harsh stillness of the night it felt to us like a powerful drumbeat. *Booooom!*

I had my gunsights glued to that smoking soldier. I held my breath, as if merely by breathing I could alert him to our presence here on the road. I was praying that none of the Iraqi sentries had heard the thump of that sand ladder, or if they had that they wouldn't recognise it as the noise of a passing vehicle.

We crept past that enemy position without a shot being fired, and with no challenge in Arabic ringing out in the darkness. It was a fucking miracle that we'd done so. We hit open, empty terrain and gradually we picked up speed again. We thundered south, desperate to eat up the miles.

Up ahead, for whatever reason, Jason suddenly flicked on his vehicle's headlights. I saw the driver of the Recce wagon follow suit. After operating for so long on black light it seemed weird and wrong – shocking almost – to be able to see the leading Pinkies. I turned to Steve, and raised a questioning eyebrow.

'Are we nearly there yet?' he quipped, reaching forwards to flick on our own headlights. 'I guess we are … And that's why Jase's putting the fucking lights on, to warn the Yanks we're coming in.'

I felt this rush of excitement. 'What else can it be, mate?'

Steve grinned. 'Dave, I have never loved the US Marine Corps as much as I do right now!'

I grinned back at him. 'First shaven-headed grunt I see I'm going to hug and fucking kiss him!'

Jason's vehicle slowed. I saw it start to make a sharp turn east. I took it he was going off-road, in which case I guessed we had to be facing a major roadblock. Maybe the Americans had moved forward during the hours of darkness, and set up a new front line position here on the road. Maybe Jase was trying to get past their most-forward – and potentially trigger-happy – troops so we could come in to some more relaxed, and hopefully less lethal, Yank positions.

But it was nothing of the sort. As Jason's wagon turned I spotted two bunkers to the right-hand side of the road, and a dark, sinister-looking building behind them. All of a sudden I knew exactly where we were. This was the first compound that we had driven past after we had left the US front line, in which we had seen our first Iraqi soldiers.

We were at the T-junction on the northern edge of Nasiriyah itself. *I couldn't believe that we were this close.* But in the wash of Jason's headlights I could see now that this was no ordinary compound. It was like a bloody great big fortress, with watchtowers and bunkers and sangars (temporary fortifications) all over the place.

Groups of Iraqi soldiers were positioned within each of them, and Jase had to be trying to bluff his way past, headlights-on.

CHAPTER TWENTY-FIVE

The lead Pinkie was side-on to the bunkers, and Jason couldn't use his GPMG, because Dez was directly in his line of fire. They'd almost made it past when one of the figures in the nearest bunker yelled out a warning in Arabic. He must have realised who it was that was trying to sneak past. An instant later the first AK47 opened up on Jason's wagon, with a dozen more following suit.

Joe sparked up his machine gun and began thumping rounds into the bunkers to the side of them. I saw Jase swing the Gimpy around but he couldn't bring it to bear. We couldn't provide covering fire, for fear of hitting Jase's vehicle by mistake. For a moment I was convinced that they were going to get hammered, and then I saw Dez lift his pistol from the dash. The next moment he was firing it one-handed into the bunker, whilst ramping the wagon around with the other.

It was like a scene from some Wild West movie. I couldn't believe it was for real. Dez emptied what looked like a whole 13-round Browning mag into the enemy bunker, and then they were through. Normally, you'd use your pistol for close-quarter combat on foot. One thing we'd never ever drilled for was firing a 13-round Browning handheld from a speeding vehicle! The Pinkies were bristling with machine guns on state-of-the-art pivots, so in theory you'd never need to use a pistol.

An instant after Dez had unloaded with the Browning the Engineer

Recce guys started malleting the bunkers, and both wagons were speeding past. It didn't matter any more how many showers Dez might have had during his time in PF, he was the fucking boy now. In spite of being the driver, he'd got his moment of glory, and what a Hollywood moment it was.

We were last in line, and as we headed towards the enemy positions I opened up with the trusted Gimpy. I saw bodies blasted backwards, as a whirlwind of lead pounded into the enemy position. When we went to make the turn, I couldn't use the GPMG any more, because Steve was in my line of fire. I gazed into the last bunker half expecting to get smashed by Iraqi fire, but all I saw was a heap of bloodied bodies. The occupants of that position had been torn to pieces, and they weren't about to do us any damage any time soon.

Muzzles sparked from windows set back in the darkened building, but they were a good distance away. In no time Steve had made the turn, and we were speeding away from them. Steve leaned forwards, clicked off the headlamps, and put pedal to the metal, the night-dark terrain swallowing us. Just another few kilometres and we'd be there, at the American front line.

Some instinct made me glance behind. Suddenly, I realised there was no Tricky. The 50-cal was swinging around in its turret completely unmanned. *Fucking Tricky's gone!* For an instant my heart stopped beating. I was gripped by this all-consuming panic. We were a man down and we didn't know where we'd fucking lost him!

I started yelling, my voice cracking with panic: 'TRICKY! TRICKY! WHERE THE FUCK'S TRICKY?'

I had visions of us having to turn the wagon around and go back the way we'd come. Either Tricky had been hit at that last enemy position, or he'd somehow tumbled out of the wagon as Steve had made the turn at the T-junction. Whichever, there was no way in a million years that we were ever leaving Tricky.

Steve clocked where I was looking, and then he started yelling too. 'Tricky! Tricky! WHERE'S HE FUCKING GONE?'

All of a sudden a head popped up from behind the big machine gun. Tricky kind of rolled his eyes at us. Grinned this dead cool smile.

'What's all the flap, lads? I was just changing the ammo box on the 50-cal.'

Steve and I cracked up laughing, but it was mostly with relief. He and I exchanged a sheepish glance. For a moment there we'd both been close to losing it. Tricky was the picture of unruffled calm. It was like the last few hours of full-on combat were no big deal, like he'd done it all a thousand times before.

The moment of lightness passed, for now we were approaching the Marine Corps' front line positions. We knew well the state of the Marines stationed here: they were pretty much exhausted; they'd lost a lot of their guys; they were thirsting for revenge. And worst of all, as far as we were concerned, they were maxed up to the eyeballs with some serious firepower.

I looked front and saw Jason's wagon pulling over into the darkness by the roadside. I saw his hazard lights blink on, off, on, off. A couple of American Bradley Infantry Fighting Vehicles loomed out of the distant gloom. As we pulled over behind the Recce wagon, I couldn't help but remember the friendly fire incident that had torn apart the marines of Charlie Company, during the previous day's fighting.

The A10 tankbuster ground-attack aircraft had pounded Charlie Company's armour with their fearsome, seven-barrelled 30 mm GAU Avenger Gatling-type guns. One of the most powerful cannons ever flown, the GAU Avenger fires depleted uranium armour-piercing shells, and Charlie Company's AAVs had barely stood a chance.

The Bradleys up ahead of us were packing a cannon of only a slightly smaller calibre – an M242 25 mm chain gun – one capable of taking out Iraqi T55 main battle tanks. Crossing back across our own front line could well prove the most dangerous moment of the death run so far. If we got opened up on by those Bradleys, we were toast.

We stripped off our shemaghs, and buttoned up and smartened ourselves as best we could. We were dropping the Iraqi disguise, and trying to make like 'proper' soldiers. I grabbed an IR Firefly from out of my webbing, switched it on and placed it in front of me on the bonnet. Anyone using NVG would now be able to see it flashing away, and should recognise that as a signal that we were friendly forces.

We closed up the space between the vehicles, lowered all the weapons, and Jason moved off. With our hazard lights flashing we crawled towards the US front line position, marked by the Bradleys forming a block across the road. As we drew ever closer my heart was beating like it was going to burst. We'd fought our way through some 200 kilometres of enemy terrain. How ironic would it be to have run a series of massive ambushes, evaded hunter convoys, and smashed the enemy's roadblocks, only to be blown away by our own side?

As we crawled closer to the Bradleys, Dez started honking the horn – Peep! Peep! Peep-peep! Peep! Peeeeep! Peeeeep! *The Brits are coming through.* The Recce wagon's driver and Steve started doing likewise. It struck me as being vaguely ridiculous, the six of us doing this whilst sandwiched between two armies that had been tearing each other's throats out. But what other option did we have?

There wasn't the slightest response from the Bradleys. We presumed they had to be occupied, but not a soldier there seemed to see us or hear us, or acknowledge our approach. We reached the two hulking great armoured vehicles, and drove through apparently unseen. On the US front line, in the aftermath of the battle for Nasiri-yah, we'd managed to slip through whatever Marine Corps sentries had been posted here, without being challenged.

We pressed on at a crawl until we reached the area where I figured the US command post was situated – the last Americans that we had spoken to before commencing the mission of a lifetime. Then we cut the engines.

We bailed out of the wagons. For a moment we were standing there in stunned silence, staring at each other in complete disbelief. And then I grabbed Steve and I was hugging him, and Tricky was bear-hugging both of us, and we were practically dancing with joy. We simply couldn't believe it. *Fucking hell! We'd made it out of there alive!*

There were serious man-hugs going on all around, and this really wasn't us. Pathfinders, PARAs, whatever unit we hailed from – we didn't generally go in for man-hugs. But today, after the death run south from Qalat Sikar, all that had changed. All our macho attitude and bravado had gone out of the window.

Because, fucking hell, we were alive!

I pulled out our Thuraya satphone, part of our lost comms kit. It's an open, insecure means, and so we'd only ever use it as a last resort, if all other comms were gone. It was the kind of thing that we'd use to call in a CSAR helo, if we were about to get captured or killed. The satphone was about as easy to intercept as your average mobile phone signal. But that didn't particularly matter now that we were in amongst the American lines. My first responsibility had to be to report in to PF HQ.

As I was waiting for the call to go through, I spotted a couple of US marines wandering over to stare at us. It was like they couldn't get their heads around where the nine of us had just appeared from. I guess it was fair enough really. It was pushing 0300 hours, and we'd just emerged from the darkness of the night with our vehicles half torn to pieces by enemy gunfire. And there we were hugging each other like a bunch of schoolgirls.

I spoke to the Pathfinders' signaller and gave him the good news: 'This is *Mayhem Three Zero:* urgent sitrep for *Sunray.* Patrol is back in friendly lines and with no serious casualties. Will send locstat and further details once we have comms on secure means.'

I was speaking on insecure comms, so I couldn't afford to say any more than that short message. I'd yet to check what injuries the blokes might have, but I could see from the way the nine of us were celebrating that no one had lost any limbs, or was about to die out here.

I came off the line, and went to ask the nearest marine for a smoke. I felt ready to hoover up a whole packet of twenty in one long inhalation of sweet, calming *nicotine.* The marine passed me a ciggie, and cupped a lighted match in the palm of his hand. I took the light, and as I did so I realised that my hands were shaking. I inhaled, sucking in a first, deep, greedy drag. *Fucking paradise.*

The marine gave me this look. 'Uh, say buddy, where did you guys just come from?'

I pointed north. *Out there.*

He stared at me, like it didn't compute.

I was past caring.

The lads gathered as we shared around the smokes. Tricky, Steve, Joe, plus Ian, Simon and Stephen from the Recce wagon, sparked up. Jason was down on his knees by his Pinkie and rummaging in his grab bag. I knew instantly what he was after. He was searching for some scoff. I knew from experience that he didn't like to be disturbed when he was eating. God knows he'd earned the space to stuff his face fuller than a fat girl's shoes, if that was what he fancied doing right now.

Dez wandered over to join the smoking party. For an instant he looked a bit uncomfortable, kind of shifting from one foot to the other nervously, and then he said it.

'Tricky, mate, any chance of a drag?'

No one could quite believe it. We were speechless. We watched him take a couple of awkward puffs, then he was honking and coughing his guts up. He was jerking about like a guy riding one of those electric rodeo horses in an amusement arcade.

Tricky was crying with laughter. 'Yee-hah!' he gasped. 'Ride 'em, cowboy!'

'Yeah, we all saw your Hollywood moment on the Browning, mate,' Steve added, 'but you'll never make a proper cowboy if you can't handle a Marlboro!'

We'd all been in contacts before. All of us, even Joe. But none of us had ever known anything remotely like what we'd just been through. We'd been repeatedly ambushed far behind enemy lines, with thousands of hardcore Iraqi soldiers and Fedayeen trying to rip our heads off. We'd never expected to get back alive. And now here we were pissing ourselves laughing as Dez choked his lungs up over a Marlboro.

Jason chucked some food down his neck, and got a hexy stove

going for a brew. Whilst he was waiting for the water to boil, he pulled out his map. We spread it on the bonnet of his Land Rover. There was a sense of urgency about the two of us now, for there was work to be done. We started comparing notes, working out exactly where the main Iraqi positions were. We configured a series of six-figure grids. The biggest surprise was how close the last ambush point had been to the US front line. As the crow flies, it had to be less than a kilometre away.

I asked one of the marines for direction to his CP (Command Post). He pointed out a group of vehicles 300 metres to the east of us. As I started walking, I realised how totally and utterly exhausted I was. The adrenaline was pissing out of my veins now, to be replaced by a crushing, leaden fatigue. I made my way silently through the sleeping positions, and stepped inside the US command post. It was little more than some canvas sheeting strung between two Bradleys, but even at this hour the place was buzzing.

There was one figure that I recognised instantly. It was the Charlie Company CO. He stared at me like I was some kind of apparition. He'd got a couple of blokes on his shoulder, and they looked equally mystified.

'David, the British Pathfinder patrol,' I announced. 'Remember? We've been having a bit of fun north of here ...'

'Yeah, got ya.' He cracked a smile. 'Good to see it's not just us Americans gettin' down and dirty out there. So what's cookin?'

'Well, we've just been on a long drive north on Route 7, pretty much all the way to Qalat Sikar airfield. We hit a bit of trouble, and fought our way back again. I thought I should report to you what we found.'

The entire place had fallen silent. You could hear a pin drop. These guys made up the US Marine Corps' most forward positions in Iraq. They'd spent the day fighting for their lives in Nasiriyah and pretty much getting hammered. Then night had fallen and it all had gone quiet. But a little over an hour ago they'd have seen this massive shitfight erupt on the night-dark horizon to the north of them. Now

I'd walked in and told them that it had been the nine of us, fighting through the Iraqi lines in three open-topped Land Rovers.

'We got to within 40 clicks of the airfield,' I continue in a tired, but matter-of-fact way. 'We ended up being surrounded by the enemy, Iraqi regulars plus Fedayeen. There was no way of pushing further north, so we decided to head back the way we came. En route we were hit by a series of ambushes, each of which corresponds to a major Iraqi position.'

The marines had eyes like saucers. They clearly thought we were some kind of Mad Max bulletproof James Bond lunatics. Either that, or we were on some serious drugs. They couldn't seem to get their heads around the fact that we got that far north and back again, without getting annihilated. One of the guys passed me a brew, another some Hershey's chocolate. But mostly, they were staring at me in stunned silence.

'You advance any further from here, that's the force you're going to run into,' I told them. 'They're in good, dug-in and sandbagged defensive positions. They've got bunkers, trenches, rat-runs, the works. They're got light arms, HMGs, RPGs, some big four-barrelled anti-aircraft cannon and God only knows what else we didn't see. We figure that each of those positions corresponds to a company strength force, maybe more.'

I glanced at the major and his men, and I could read the thoughts in their eyes. This was some kind of nightmare. The battle for Nasiriyah was far from over: just ahead of them lay thousands more fighters, in well-camouflaged, well-constructed defensive positions, and they were clearly ready to rumble. In terms of numbers that Iraqi force – regular soldiers plus Fedayeen – was far larger than the force that had halted the Marine Corps in Nasiriyah, and had cost them so dear.

I figured it was time to give the major the good news. 'Whilst we failed to reach our mission objective, we did identify a shed load of Iraqi positions en route. We can provide you with a series of six-figure grids for each of those.'

I saw the major's face light up. We went into a huddle over the maps. I talked him through each ambush point, and gave him my best guess as to what the enemy strengths were in each. At ambush point one – the most northerly attack point – Jase and I had figured there was a battalion of Iraqi troops, plus the 200 men of the Fedayeen hunter force.

At the second ambush point we figured there had to be a further battalion. At ambush point three we reckoned there was a company. Then there was the company that never saw us, plus the ambush point at the T-junction, just north of Nasiriyah. All told, we figured that made some 2000 Iraqi infantry plus militia at a minimum, and probably a whole lot more.

Our estimates were based upon the volume of fire that rained down upon us from those positions, plus what we'd seen of the hardware. I told the Marine Corps major that those numbers were conservative. Those 2000 fighting men would have an equal number of logistics, signallers, and reserve troops in support.

'My take on this is that you've got to get air strikes on to those positions fast,' I told him. 'Hit them hard before you move forwards, and that'll clear the way for you guys.'

The major looked at me. Nodded. I saw this glow of excitement lighting up his tired eyes.

'You betcha, soldier,' he growled. 'You're damn right we will.'

With that he started barking orders. I sat there savouring my coffee – a fine cup of Starbucks homebrew – as his men went scurrying about, getting those co-ordinates reported up the chain via their radio net. It was one of the best brews I'd ever had in my life, and I drained it to the last. Then I headed back to the wagons, where I found the blokes getting ready to crash out on the deck, next to the trusted Pinkies.

To a man we were all totally done in. But before getting comatose, there was one more thing that had to be done. We needed to organise sentries, for if we could drive through the US front line completely undetected, so we figured could the enemy.

I was too wired to sleep, so I took the first stag along with Dez. As I stared out from the island of light that was Nasiriyah and into the darkness to the north of us, I said a short prayer. I was born and raised a Catholic, although I guessed I was pretty lapsed these days. Still, I took a quiet moment to thank my God that both I and all the blokes in my patrol were alive.

And I offered up an apology for only ever praying when I was in the shit, and in desperate need of help.

CHAPTER TWENTY-SIX

Apart from my stint on stag, I slept the sleep of total exhaustion. At first light we were all nine of us up, and locked and loaded for stand-to. No one was going back to sleep, so Tricky and Joe set up our 319 HF radio. Although Tricky had flushed the Crypto on the TACSAT and the VHF radio, we still had the HF system via which we could in theory send secure, text-type messages, but only when it chose to work.

Long-range HF comms are a nightmare to establish, and it was a shit piece of kit anyway. We managed to get a short text message back to PF HQ, or at least we hoped that it had gone through: 'Sitrep: enemy grids at 937584 ... Our grid with US forces at 738295. No casualties.'

We got a brew and a scoff on, and the sun rose fine and bright. In the clear desert light we started to notice stuff. I realised that the pull string on my left bottom trouser leg hadn't come undone: it was missing completely. I took a closer look, and noticed that there was a hole punched through the material. I checked the leg, and there was barely a graze.

I inspected the puncture marks more closely. They consisted of a circular entry and exit hole of the type a 7.62 mm round would make. Somehow, I'd been shot through my trousers but the bullet had missed my leg. As my hands felt around those bullet holes, I noticed how swollen they were. I had fingers like sausages. It must have been from the hours spent gripping a juddering GPMG, as I ramped it back and forth across the targets.

Fingers like sausages. I kind of smiled to myself: that phrase took me way back. I'd always associated it with Prince Charles, the colonel-in-chief of our Regiment. On the day that I was due to be commissioned into the Army Prince Charles was scheduled to have lunch with us on our Regimental table – the PARA Reg table. My mum, my dad and my sisters had come down for the ceremony, plus my nan and grandpa from Liverpool.

Grandpa had told me that he'd got to meet Prince Charles once, and if I ever got to shake his hand I was to get a good look at his fingers. They were like little sausages. I didn't get the chance just then, but I'd always remembered what Grandpa had said. A while later the Parachute Regiment was scheduled to receive new regimental colours, for after twenty-five years in service our flags were well battle-worn. As one of the youngest officers in the regiment, I was picked to receive the colours from Prince Charles. Afterwards, there was a dinner in the marquee, and I shook his hand and made conversation with him.

Prince Charles didn't do meaningless 'small talk'. He was focused and involved, and I admired him greatly. He struck me as being genuinely interested in who I was and what I had to say. We met once more when I was on operations in Kosovo, and the PARAs were first on to the ground in that war-torn country. He flew out to meet and greet us personally, and to lend his moral support to the campaign. I did get to have a good look at his fingers, and Grandpa was right. Prince Charles did have fingers a bit like sausages.

Grinning stupidly to myself at the memory, I did a quick check of my Bvlgari watch. There wasn't a scratch on it. The thing was fucking bulletproof. I went to fetch my grab bag from where it was hanging on the door of our battered Land Rover. I unhooked it, and took a good long look. The grab bag resembled a bloody sieve with all the bullet holes torn in it. Inside, even my brew kit was shot to pieces, which pissed me off no end because I couldn't make a brew any more.

There was one upside to all the battle damage. My sexy French girlfriend Isabelle's crappy future-world alien novel had taken a round clean through it. I figured I'd lucked out here. I'd take it to her when I got home, and it had to be worth the greatest shag of my life. *What better reason not to have got myself killed?*

I pulled out my Persol sunglasses from my smock pocket. They were smashed to pieces. It was hardly surprising, and my fault entirely. I'd not bothered to collapse them, or put them away in their hard, protective case. Hand-made they might be, but even they couldn't survive the kind of punishment I'd put them through, when ramping the GPMG back and forth. It was 200 quid down the drain, but a small cost to still be alive.

I retrieved the medical kit from my grab bag. There was a neat hole punched through the middle of my can of Savlon antiseptic spray. It was a perfect round hole blown clean through it. I held it up for Steve and Tricky to admire, shaking my head in amazement.

In response, Steve pointed out the fuse box in the Land Rover. It was a black plastic rectangle the size of a shoebox and it sat in the centre of the dash, between the driver and the passenger's knees. Right now it looked like a bloody great Swiss cheese. But it wasn't nice neat bullet holes that it was riddled with: it had great rents torn in it by what looked like chunks of shrapnel.

I turned to the other blokes: 'Fuck me, have you seen our vehicle?'

No one seemed particularly interested. They were all staring at their own wagons, and checking out their own kit, which was like-wise shot to buggery. I heard Ian, the Engineer Recce sergeant, let out this low whistle of amazement. He held something up for all to see.

'Fucking check this out.'

Unlike us, Ian had carried his Browning 9 mm pistol strapped to his body in a chest holster. We PF blokes had ours strapped to our thighs. Ian's positioning of his pistol had been unbelievably fortunate, for it had quite simply saved his life. There was a big, fat ugly bullet embedded in the steel of the weapon. He rolled up his shirt, and there was a bloody great angry red and purple bruise spreading across his torso, where the pistol had taken the force of the round.

It was a sobering reminder of how we weren't bulletproof. We'd just been incredibly, insanely lucky.

Joe pointed to the 50-cal on the rear of Jason's wagon. 'Fuckin' take a look at that,' he muttered.

The circular, ring-like mount of the heavy machine gun was horribly bent and twisted, where it had been hammered by fire. When Joe had been pumping rounds into the enemy positions, they had been aiming in on the muzzle flash of his weapon. It was impossible to comprehend how the young lad could still be alive.

We were counting the numbers of bullet holes in the Pinkies, and taking bets on who had the most, when the distinctive form of a US Cobra attack helicopter came barrelling over the horizon. It circled once over the enemy position at the T-junction, just to the north of us, then gave it the good news. The Cobra plastered the target below with 30 mm cannon fire, flying strafe after strafe after strafe.

It was great to see the airpower coming in so quickly, to act on the intel that we'd provided. The Americans were bringing up the big guns. *Result.* We may have been prevented from JTACing in the warplanes, but this was the next best thing. It was our intel that had got this air strike in and bang on target.

A runner appeared from the Marine Corps Command Post. Charlie Company's OC wanted a quick word, if I was free. I wondered what was up. I strolled across to the CP. When I got there I was treated to this long, piercing look from him, one of awe mixed with disbelief. He offered me a brew – coffee again, being as he was an American – before getting down to business.

'We just got a recce flight over those co-ordinates you gave us north along Route 7,' he began. 'You guys are dead right: there are shit loads of Iraqi positions up there. But the aircrew says a lot of those Iraqi units have been smashed to fuck.' He paused. 'Just what the hell were you guys *doing* out there?'

I eyed him for a moment. I was unsure what to say. The truth would sound so totally absurd, so utterly far-fetched. *We were fighting for our lives. We thought we were all dead. Somehow, against all odds we made it through.* The truth just didn't add up, so I said nothing.

'I got it. Yeah.' He gave me a nod and a wink. *'Need-to-know, right? No worries.'*

I saw his eyes searching my combats for some indication of rank, or even the unit we hailed from. Of course, there was none.

'Captain,' I offered, as helpfully as I could. 'David. Pathfinder Captain.'

'Captain, Dave, Pathfinders, I want you to know this,' he announced, somewhat formally. 'Thanks to your intel we got air strikes racked up to go in all along the grids that you gave us. All along Route 7 there'll be US F15 fast jets, Cobra gunships, A10 ground attack aircraft and other warplanes giving those positions a seriously good hosin'. And Captain, we got you guys to thank for that. Hoooo-ahhh!'

I'd spent a deal of time with US Marine Corps types before, and I was used to their 'hooo-aahhhing'. It might sound strange to us, but it was their equivalent of 'Yes, sir!' We chatted away for a while longer, and the major kept stressing what an intel bonanza we'd delivered to them. If not for us, he figured his forces would have advanced right into those hidden Iraqi positions and on to their guns.

Then he had this for me: 'You know, Captain, I got dead bodies from Charlie Company that we've yet to recover. We're heading back down Ambush Alley this morning, and then east into the marsh area to recover the vehicles, and search for our dead. 'Cause we leave no man behind, you know'

'Yeah, that's important. Same with us.'

'Now, I got a favour to ask you Pathfinder guys.' He paused. 'Captain, you figure you guys could provide an armed escort as we do that recovery mission, and maybe give my boys some top cover?'

It struck me that this was a somewhat insane request. We'd got three open-topped, soft-skinned Land Rovers that were shot to fuck. His men were operating in heavily-armoured Bradley fighting vehicles, each packing an M242 25 mm chain gun. It'd be a little challenging for us to provide some top cover for them. But I told him that we'd do what we could, although we'd likely get re-tasked on to another mission any time now.

We said our farewells, and for a couple of hours me and the lads busied ourselves doing damage assessments and checking the vehicles, in preparation for departure. Our position kept coming under sporadic but inaccurate fire, but we didn't take much notice. We left it to the Marines to deal with.

At one stage a yellow garbage truck came thundering down the road towards us. It stopped a good distance away, and a couple of guys with long greasy hair leaned out of the window and unloaded AK47s in our general direction. It was all a bit laughable compared to the death run from Qalat Sikar, and we didn't pay it too great a mind.

The truck started moving again, and it built up speed until it was careering towards the US front line positions. One of the Bradleys sparked up and tore the truck to pieces with its M242 chain gun. It was only right that they'd malleted it. It could well have been packed full of explosives, those Iraqi gunmen being on a suicide mission.

At 0100 we received a response from PF HQ to our text message. We were ordered back to the FOB. Dez had spent the entire morning tweaking, talking to and patching the Pinkies, with the other lads helping wherever they could. As long as we took it slow, he reckoned they'd make it back to base okay.

At 0130 we departed, heading back into Nasiriyah and along Ambush Alley. As we did so, there was a long stream of US Marine Corps vehicles coming in the opposite direction. I guessed they were preparing for the big push north. We saw the Regimental Combat Team 2 (RCT-2) headquarters unit coming forwards – the same guys we had spoken to before first moving into Nasiriyah. We stopped to speak to their Ops Officer.

He gave us a flashing smile and a heartfelt thank you. The intel that we'd provided was dynamite, he told us. It was being used to find, fix and smash the Iraqi positions all along Route 7 to the north of their front line.

By the time we were through to the southern outskirts of Nasiriyah, we'd started to relax a little and enjoy the drive. This territory was owned by the US Marine Corps, and there was unlikely to be enemy for many kilometres in any direction.

Steve turned to me, and yelled a comment in this hammed-up American accent: 'Ya know what, buddy, a few weeks from now and we'll be in Li-ces-ter Square, meeting the loves of our lives in The Shadow Lounge.'

'Mate, I've never needed Smudge in his Elvis rig more than I do now!' I yelled back at him. 'Fuck it: I'm even going to fucking sing ...'

We were all three of us laughing.

As we headed south on Route 8 I found I'd got the lyrics from the song 'Hands of Time', by Groove Armada, running through my mind. It's a cool, mellow track, which kind of embodied my emotions right now. I was feeling the pure, total joy of being alive, and of having survived the unsurvivable.

Plus there was something else. We may not have reached the mission objective, Qalat Sikar airfield, but we'd been sent into a tsunami of enemy fire with no warning, and we'd ended up conducting a recce-by-fire through some 200 kilometres of enemy terrain. In doing so, we'd uncovered what amounted to two Iraqi divisions hidden in the desert north of Nasiriyah. We'd done our bit to mallet them, and now the American air power was going in to smash them big time.

The US Marines now knew what lay ahead of them, and they were forewarned with six-figure grids of each position. So whilst we might have failed in our mission, I reckoned we'd done something pretty extraordinary out there. I liked the American people and their military. I'd trained alongside them and served alongside them, and warmed to their generous, open-hearted spirit. I was thankful that we'd helped prevent some of those young US marines from getting the shit kicked out of them as they pushed north of Nasiriyah.

We'd been able to add something of incalculable value to their war effort – pinpoint-accurate intel. Plus I'd seen how much we'd boosted their morale by just being there. They'd taken the mother of all beatings in Nasiriyah. They'd had their arses kicked and their heads were down. They were licking their wounds, when suddenly us lot of lunatics appeared from out of the night. We'd been out there, way out front, taking the fight to the enemy.

Hoooh-ahh! as they say in the Corps.

As we sped south the chorus of that Groove Armada song, 'Hands of Time', kept running through my brain. The lyrics speak of the impossibility of turning back the hands of time. Well, I had no regrets. It had been a good mission. Not the one that we set out to achieve, maybe, but still the mission of a lifetime. As 2IC Pathfinders I was proud of what we'd achieved. And I was lit up that every man on my patrol was coming home alive. I wouldn't want to turn back the hands of time, even if I had the power to.

It was 2200 and pitch dark by the time we made it back to PF HQ. We hadn't slept much for several nights, and we'd been on the go for hours on end in the fight of our lives. We were totally and utterly chinstrapped. We said a quick, yet heartfelt goodbye to the three Engineer Recce lads, then bedded down wherever we could on the hard sand.

As I drifted off to sleep, I thought about those Engineer Recce blokes who'd been with us. They had come up trumps on this mission. There was the tyre-changing incident, which had set a bad tone at the start, but they'd more than made up for it in the heat and the fire of battle. Their wagon looked as smashed about as ours, and when the rounds went down they gave as good as they got. I was absolutely certain that the weight of fire they put down from their GPMGs was a battle-winner, and one that helped us break through in the death run from Qalat Sikar. It was good to have had them with us.

I slept the sleep of the dead. After stand-to and a brew the following morning, the lads from the other patrols gathered around. By now, word had got out about our murder run south from Qalat Sikar. Everyone seemed curious to know more, but that didn't stop the messing. Bryan Budd, Steve's best mate, was there, and as always he was playing the fool. He strutted around doing his best impression of a typical nose-in-the-air officer type.

'Hello, corporal, is everything all right?' he announced, to Steve. 'Mail getting through?'

Steve was trying not to laugh. 'No, it fucking isn't, and no, it's fucking not. I haven't seen a woman in days. I might as well be in the Shadow Lounge. Oh, yeah, and there's been a load of fucking blokes I've never met trying to kill me.'

After the Qalat Sikar mission, it was good to see the blokes having a laugh again, because by anyone's reckoning they'd earned it.

I felt an ominous rumbling in my guts. I headed over to the thunder boxes. I was sat there having the biggest dump ever, and really savouring the moment, when a familiar figure plonked down next to me. It was Brigadier Jacko Page, the CO of 16 Air Assault Brigade, and seemingly he needed a shit too.

I was tortured with embarrassment, because my enormous crap was polluting the atmosphere big time. Plus I was dehydrated and seriously constipated, so it was all taking one hell of a long time, but by all appearances Jacko didn't seem to mind.

He turned to me and gave me this half smile. 'Well, that all sounded rather interesting. Qalat Sikar: quite a mission. Bloody well done for getting everyone out of there safely.'

Jacko was a man of few words, and he was known for not giving praise lightly. He must have commanded countless covert operations whilst serving with elite units. I'd just had a well done on the quiet from the brigade commander, whilst we were sat together on the bogs. It didn't get much better than that.

But it seemed as if not everyone felt the same way as Jacko.

CHAPTER TWENTY-SEVEN

I returned to the vehicles feeling on a real high. It was then that I got called to have a one-on-one with one of the more senior officers in the Brigade. In theory there were eight or more ranks above me who might have a direct interest in the Qalat Sikar mission and in debriefing me, so I wasn't particularly worried.

I made my way over to his tent. He was sat at a makeshift wooden desk, and as I entered he didn't look up, which struck me as being somewhat odd.

He gestured to a chair: 'David, take a seat.' I could sense immediately that something wasn't quite right. 'So tell me, David, how did you end up being so far north pinned down by loads of contacts?'

I was immediately thinking: *What the hell is this*? Where was the small talk, the chat, maybe the offer of a brew? I tried to keep my cool. In fairness, it was important for high command to get as full a debriefing as they could and as soon after the mission as possible. That way, lessons could be learned which could be passed on to other PF patrols, not to mention the wider British military.

'There was only the one route in towards the mission objective,' I replied, 'one that we'd been ordered to make overland by vehicle.'

He scribbled a note on a pad on his desk. I realised then that he was effectively giving me a formal interview, what we in the military call 'an interview without coffee'. This was priceless. When missions went well and everyone on a patrol was bathed in glory, all wanted to claim they were involved. But when you were asked to achieve the impossible and the shit hit the fan, everyone began searching for a scapegoat.

He stayed silent for a moment. Then: 'I understand you missed your 1600 Sched?'

Up until that moment I hadn't realised that we had missed it, and neither had Tricky. I thought back to the first bridge crossing in Nasiriyah, where we'd tried and failed to raise PF HQ on the TACSAT. I guessed it was shortly after that we must have missed the Sched. But we were mobile and crossing enemy lines at the time, which must have been why we had forgotten to send it.

I could imagine what a nightmare that would have been. For several hours after we'd missed our Sched headquarters might well have feared that we were compromised and on the run. Having to list our patrol as 'missing in action' would have been one of the worst of all possible outcomes for the Brigade.

'We tried once, just before 1600, but couldn't raise PF HQ,' I told him. 'We must have forgotten about it in the heat of the mission. But we'd maintained constant comms throughout the day, and headquarters was well aware of our intent. In any case, we were mobile and moving through enemy lines. You can't send Scheds when you're mobile, because you've got to stop to set up the radio antenna.'

Again, he noted down my answer. Then he asked: 'Why did you move ahead of the Marine Corps' front line positions?'

'We did so because that was our mission – to move ahead and recce and mark a HLS at Qalat Sikar.'

'At Nasiriyah the US Marines were getting pinned down. Why did you think it was safe to move forwards?'

'I didn't think it was safe. We are at war. We work behind enemy lines. It's never safe. But the intel we were given said the area north of there as far as the airfield was "relatively benign". We checked with the most forward units of the Marine Corps. They'd seen nothing in terms of the enemy in front of them. We went forwards on the best available intel. It happened to be entirely wrong.'

It was only with great difficulty that I was holding myself in check. The point about us missing the Sched was a fair one, but this was feeling more and more like a Spanish Inquisition. My fists were starting to ball with pent-up fury.

'Why did you keep going north after the first compromise?' he demanded.

'It's standard operating procedure for Pathfinders to drive through ambush points, plus it was the only way to achieve our mission.'

'Why did you only send one basic text sitrep when you got back to the US frontline? Don't you think headquarters could have used more info?'

'That's because the comms guy on my wagon, Tricky, had flushed the Crypto, because we were surrounded by the enemy and thought we were all about to die.'

'Even so, why didn't you send a proper combat rep with ammo states?'

I couldn't believe this. It was akin to asking why I'd broken health-and-safety procedures, when I was convinced that we were about to get slotted. He was giving me shit because we didn't file a report telling him how much ammo we had left, when we'd just escaped from the fight of our lives.

'Funnily enough, we were more concerned about getting accurate intel to the Americans, so they could smash two divisions' worth of enemy with air strikes, intel for which the US Marine Corps were very, very grateful. Funnily enough, ammo stats just didn't seem that important at the time.'

I had nothing more to say. I got to my feet, dismissed myself and left the tent.

I went for a good long walk around the FOB in an effort to calm myself down. Why had I just had this crap dumped on me? An interview without coffee after all that we'd been through, and us saddled with a crock of shit as the intel. *What was his fucking problem?*

I reckoned headquarters must have got a massive flap on when the mission went tits up and they thought they might lose an entire patrol. Had we got up there unscathed and recced the airfield, and 1 PARA had gone in and secured it, then we'd all have been in clover. As it was headquarters must have presumed they'd lost us, and hence they were somehow trying to disown the patrol.

Instead, we'd come out of the death run from Qalat Sikar alive and with crucial intel, which had the potential to turn the tide of the war. As far as I was concerned we'd pulled off a crucial mission, one that we should all be proud of. I'd just had a quiet 'well done' from the brigade commander whilst sat on the shitters, so he clearly felt the same. I'd had similar and better from the US Marine Corps commanders. More the pity, then, that someone at headquarters couldn't share that sense of satisfaction in the mission.

As I stomped around the base there was one thought at the forefront of my mind. We'd gone forwards to carry out the orders that we had been given, but had we all been killed or captured out there, I wondered if there were those in headquarters who would have tried to distance themselves from the patrol?

I knew that as 2IC Pathfinders the final burden of leadership for field operations lay with me. If we fucked up, rightfully I'd be held responsible by Brigade Command, and that was probably what lay behind the interview without coffee that I'd just had. I'd been using the blokes by breaking down mission planning, and giving each a specific area of responsibility, but it was still my gig. It was me in command of my patrol. When the shit hit the fan, the buck stopped with me. But I felt we'd done good out there and I was proud of my team and of our mission.

When I tired of stalking the base perimeter I returned to the lads. I found Tricky resting by the side of our wagon, enjoying a cuppa.

'Just made a jack brew, have you, mate?' I quipped. Making a 'jack brew' was PF speak for brewing a cuppa for yourself only.

'Fuck off, you were in seeing the slipper city gang.' Tricky eyed me for a second. 'How did it go? You look like shit.'

'I was told to take a seat and given an interview without coffee.'

'What the f – !' Tricky spluttered, half spilling his tea. 'After a mission like Qalat Sikar, you get given that kind of crap?'

I did my best to shrug it off. 'Don't worry about it. They were just doing their job.'

I didn't want to make a big deal out of this, and for resentment to fester amongst the lads and for problems to escalate.

We spent most of that morning dozing in the shade by the vehicles. I felt demotivated and bitter, but my anger was tempered by what the brigade commander had said to me on the bogs. I knew that he had got it, even if there were others who hadn't.

As the day wore on my mood cooled. I figured this was what must have happened: at this stage of the war there had been few, if any, British combat casualties. There'd likely been a major flap on by senior officers and politicians, when it became clear that an entire Pathfinder patrol was missing in action behind enemy lines.

Very likely there were people higher up the chain than Brigade banging on about 'Britain's Black Hawk Down' – the infamous 1993 incident in which scores of elite US soldiers were trapped, shot up, captured and tortured by Somali gunmen, in Mogadishu. I ran that scenario through my mind a good few times, and I started to feel a little better about that interview without coffee. I was sure they had their reasons.

In the Pathfinders operations are fast-moving, and we'd shortly be onto our next mission, of that I had no doubt. If that interview led to lessons being learned that would improve future ops and save blokes lives, then maybe it was fair enough. But still, it had left me with a bad feeling.

All that day the lads from the other PF patrols kept wandering over for a natter. They'd heard about our mission, and were unable to comprehend how we had got out of there alive. They were welcome to join the party: I had no idea how we'd done so, either.

If there was one positive thing that came out of all this, it was the collective realisation of how unusable the intel was that we'd been given. Areas slated as unoccupied or benign were far from it, and the Iraqis were more than ready to put up a fight. An order came down from the brigade commander: all Pathfinder patrols would now deploy four-up in terms of wagons. That way, we'd double our firepower.

The following morning we did a Brigade move northeast towards Basra. We thundered through the open desert to link up with the Royal Marines, who'd air-assaulted into southern Iraq during the opening hours of the war and seized the Al Faw peninsula. Once there, we made for an abandoned Iraqi army camp, which would be our base for some weeks now. We found an old hangar where we could set up camp together with our beloved vehicles. We'd been kipping in the open up until this moment, so this was sheer luxury.

The camp was a big old compound, consisting of a cluster of stark concrete structures that looked to have been abandoned for some time. But the key thing was that it had a big solid building within which Brigade HQ could establish their ops room and planning cells. They had complex and sensitive computer and communications kit, and they were busy as fuck with a million and one moving parts relating to the war effort, including the air missions that were being flown. There was only so long they could operate in tents in the desert.

The Brigade engineers strung some razor wire around the compound's perimeter, and constructed sandbagged sangars at the entry and exit points. We soon had teams of blokes buzzing in and out for orders groups, including a group of lads from the SAS. They pitched up to brief the brigade commander on what they were up to in the area, and for an information exchange. A couple of the SAS lads were ex-Pathfinders, and they wandered over to our hangar for a natter.

The SAS blokes were dressed in civvies, and they were driving four-by-four Toyota-type jeeps. They were running operations in and around Basra, and although they loved what they were doing you could see just a hint of envy in their eyes when they heard about the Qalat Sikar op. They knew there was little chance of them getting HALO'd deep into Iraq, or of being sent on a mission to drive hundreds of kilometres behind enemy lines.

Hereford is a much bigger unit than the PF. It's less personal, and you could go for years without seeing the others in your squadron. Inevitably, you'd lose some of the feeling of togetherness we had in the PF, and the closeness and brotherhood. There was a phrase we used a lot in the PF: *Grip change by the hand, before it grips you by the throat*. For a lot of the blokes who moved on from the PF, only when they left did they realise what they'd lost.

When you leave the PF, you get given a statue of an operator doing a HALO jump. In return, one of the blokes had given the PF something for the Interest Room. It was a statue of an SAS bloke tabbing through foul weather across Pen-Y-Fann. Across the bottom was the inscription: 'To the PF: enjoy it while it lasts.'

But in truth, as we swapped war stories there was a bit of envy both ways. The SAS lads were at the top of their game, and they were doing their edgy, sneaky-beaky work relentlessly. The last time we'd seen them was at Hereford for a piss-up after a funeral, when another ex-PF operator had been killed on ops. There was a high mortality rate in the kind of work that we did, and none of us ever knew whose funeral it might be next.

Our hangar was actually an old agricultural kind of barn, with brick walls and a corrugated iron roof. It was fine for our purposes, and similar in size to our hangars back in the UK. All six of the wagons had been brought inside for much-needed maintenance and repairs. We knew for sure now that the Iraqis were going to fight – as opposed to surrendering in their droves – and we needed the Pinkies in tiptop condition.

We ignored the scores of bullet holes torn in the alloy bodywork. They posed no threat to ongoing operations. We taped the worst over with khaki gaffer tape, and they were good to go. A couple of fuel pipes had been damaged and needed replacing, and luckily we had the spares on hand to do so. Amazingly, the fuse box in our wagon was still just about working. We replaced the broken fuses and gaffer-taped it up, after which we figured it might well last out our war in Iraq.

As we worked on the wagons, we learned about what the other PF patrols had been up to, whilst we'd been busy on the Qalat Sikar mission. They'd been out observing road junctions and other NAIs, and some had cued up air strikes on enemy positions.

But the banter that flew was mostly about our own op, Qalat Sikar. It was in a whole different league entirely, and the other patrols were itching to get their teeth into something equally meaty. We were barely a week into the conflict, so there was every chance of them doing so, and we were excited to see how the next few days and weeks might unfold.

Qalat Sikar had changed things for me personally. It was the most outrageous operation that anyone here had ever heard of, including the old and the bold. As a result, the grumpy officer-hater types seemed much warmer now. I hadn't done any single-handed bayonet charges to save my men, but I had commanded a patrol that against all odds had come out more or less unscathed. I'd not been found wanting, and that hadn't gone unnoticed.

There was another factor at play too. Word had got around about my altercation with the senior officer. I'd not said anything other than the few words to Tricky, but everyone seemed to know. I hadn't tried to bring anyone else into the line of fire, or blame any of the others. I alone had carried the can, and in a way they respected me for it.

A day or two after our arrival at our new base I went to pay a visit to the Brigade HQ building, situated about 100 metres from our hangar. I was used to the hustle and bustle of the place. People were working feverishly hard, but still there was always some banter. This time I walked in and the atmosphere was like death. There was this horrible edge to the air, and people everywhere were flapping.

I spotted Josh, one of my longstanding mates from my Sandhurst days. I grabbed him by the arm. 'Mate, what's happened?'

'An American plane has just done a drop on one of the Household Cavalry vehicles,' he told me. 'We think they're all dead.'

He hurried onwards to the bank of radios. I glanced over at the air cell, where a handful of RAF blokes were tasked with co-ordinating ground and air missions. There was a horrible air hanging over those guys, and one in particular looked ashen-faced and in shock. If the air cell had failed to pass the right warnings to the US warplanes, that might have accounted for this blue-on-blue, but it was more than likely simply the fog of war.

There was nothing more that I could do, so I returned to the hangar. I'd been sat having a ciggie with the Household Cavalry lads just a couple of weeks back, in Kuwait. We'd been on a shake-out exercise together, in which we were practising moving in tandem with their Scimitar light tanks. They, like us, had the Blue Force Tracker gear, plus the friendly forces recognition panels, so what on earth could have gone wrong this time?

Over the next few hours further details started to emerge. A squadron of Scimitar light tanks had been moving north of Basra, at the vanguard of the British advance. They were trying to recce the road northwest of the Iraqi town of Ad Dawr. Once again, intel had suggested that they'd face little resistance. Instead, the lads of the Household Cavalry had advanced into a barrage of enemy fire.

During fierce gun battles with Iraqi armour, they'd discovered there were hundreds of Iraqi T55 main battle tanks dug in and hull-down in the desert sands. As with the Qalat Sikar mission, the Iraqi positions had been skilfully camouflaged and hidden from aerial view, and no one had had the slightest idea they were there until the Household Cavalry had stumbled into them.

The British Scimitars were heavily outnumbered and outgunned. They'd ended up playing a deadly game of cat and mouse with the Iraqi armour, as they tried to make a tactical withdrawal. The British forces had proceeded to take a hammering, just as the US Marine Corps had done at Nasiriyah. The Household Cavalry had called in air strikes, as they tried to break out of the trap set by the Iraqi armour. But a US A10 tank-buster warplane had shot up two Scimitars, killing one British soldier and wounding three.

This blue-on-blue had taken place some 40 kilometres north of

Basra. It had happened despite the giant Union Jack painted on the roof of one of the armoured vehicles, and their friendly forces recognition gear. It struck me that this was fast becoming our own Nasiriyah. Even with multiple intel sources – satellite imagery, human intelligence, Predator UAV overflights – you never knew what was on the ground until you sent men in up close to get eyes-on.

And that, of course, was the *raison d'être* of the Pathfinders.

CHAPTER TWENTY-EIGHT

It was hardly surprising when we got stood to for a rush mission. Our patrol was tasked to join forces with Geordie's, one of the two patrols originally slated for the Qalat Sikar para-insertion. We were to push ahead of the British front line, to recce and verify the strength of the enemy positions. Our orders were to move out almost immediately, and wherever possible we were to call in air strikes to smash the Iraqi armour, once we'd positively identified their locations.

There were hundreds of Iraqi T55 tanks out there, hull-down and perfectly camouflaged. Each was a 40-tonne beast, with 20-centimetre-thick armour on the turret. Each boasted a 100 mm rifled cannon as the main weapon, a direct hit from which would pretty much vaporise a Pinkie. As secondary weapons, they were fitted with either two 7.62 mm machine guns, similar to our trusted GPMGs or our old friend the Dushka.

We were twelve men in four, thin-skinned wagons. Nice one. Yet another peachy mission.

We loaded up the Pinkies with a couple of MILAN anti-tank rockets, newly arrived in theatre, in case we did have a close encounter with one of those armoured beasts. The MILAN Anti-tank Light Infantry Missile is the French equivalent of the American Javelin, and it is equally user-friendly and potent. It employs SACLOS wire guidance to target, being accurate up to 2000 metres. It was an Aston Martin Vantage compared to our LAW-90s, which were Citroen 2CVs. But even so, I'd prefer it if we avoided getting up close and personal with too many Iraqi T55s.

Geordie, a corporal, was small, wiry and hard as nails, and he punched well above his weight. A highly-respected member of the Pathfinders, he was seen as being a very capable patrol commander, and he was placed in overall command of the mission. After Qalat Sikar, everyone in my patrol was feeling pretty much burned out, and we were happy to let Geordie take the lead. Our role was to provide protection and support to his wagons.

The mission plan was for us to move through our own lines and cross into enemy territory, whereupon our patrol would occupy the high ground, so we could give covering fire to Geordie's lot in case they got compromised whilst probing the Iraqi positions. We were doubly aware of the danger of friendly fire now, and it was crucial that we liaised closely with 3 PARA, for it was their forces that were manning our front line in that area. We had to let them know we'd be recceing the terrain to their north, as well as where and when we'd be crossing over their front line positions.

As we weren't leading the mission we weren't involved in the detailed planning, so I spent a lot of time studying the maps and inputting waypoints into my GPS: the location of 3 PARA's front line units went in, plus their forward HQ; and I marked up any potential routes into and out of enemy territory. Late that afternoon Geordie gave his patrol orders. It was a rush mission, and he made it clear we'd follow SOPs if we hit any trouble.

At last light Geordie's patrol led off, our vehicles following. Fairly quickly we moved off the tarmac road and on to a small track, driving northwards on black light and using night vision goggles.

I felt Tricky lean forwards to have a word. 'So it's Operation Death or Glory again?'

'No, mate,' Steve cut in. 'It's Mission Impossible Two, this one.'

I smiled. It was good to see that the lads were still sparking.

It was sod's law that tonight of all nights the cloud base was low and glowering, and the ambient light minimal. I could see bugger all with my NVG, and I figured Steve was struggling to see the way ahead. After a half-hour's drive we passed through the last of 3 PARA's positions, which meant we were moving into enemy terrain.

We reached a small bridge, the far side of which was heavily-vegetated marshland. We knew that there were enemy units positioned in there, hidden amongst the thick swampland and the bush. It was our role to find exactly where they were, and to start smashing them. As we bumped across the rough bridge, the side door on one of the Pinkies popped open. In the rush to leave the base someone had forgotten to check the latches on their vehicle. A load of cooking kit fell out. It was deafeningly loud in the night-dark quiet.

Fuck. Nothing like signalling to the enemy that we were coming.

Not securing your stowage was a rudimentary error of recce patrolling, and it was the kind of mistake that happened when missions got rushed, and operators got tired. Over the past week Geordie's patrol had been bounced from one mission to another more or less without a break, and they'd got little proper sleep. We just had to hope and pray there were no Iraqi positions near enough to have heard anything.

We crept ahead for another 4 kilometres at a dead slow. The only noise was the swish of the thick undergrowth against our wagon's smooth alloy sides, plus the faint purring of the diesel engine. The Pinkies were fitted with a 300Tdi engine, as opposed to the civvie Land Rover, which had a more powerful but complicated Td5. The Td5 unit requires diagnostic computers to repair any faults, and there was no way we were going to have that kind of kit in the field. Plus there was always the danger that the Td5's electronic control systems could be scrambled by electromagnetic interference put out by an enemy.

We had Iraqi units to all sides of us now, and one of the few comforting thoughts was that they wouldn't have the means to mess with our engines. There was little chance of pinpointing exactly where those units were, for the darkness and the bush obscured everything. We were nearing the point where our patrol would head for the high ground, leaving Geordie's lot to probe the enemy terrain.

Geordie pulled over. I presumed this was where he wanted us to split up. We came to a halt in all-around defence, but I could see that Geordie was looking flustered, which was not like him at all.

'Fuck it,' he muttered. 'I've forgotten to warn 3 PARA what we're doing, and to give 'em the mission plan.'

He was angry with himself, and for good reason. Without us having given them a heads-up, 3 PARA wouldn't know that we'd gone past their front line, and more importantly where and when we'd be coming back in again. Geordie was an über-committed PF soldier, and a well-experienced patrol commander. But this was what happened when operations were thrown together hurriedly by men who'd been on the go for days on end.

Geordie knew he'd made a serious fuck-up here, one that could cost men's lives, and he was kicking himself. Geordie and I considered our options. For sure, 3 PARA were going to be hyper-alert and ready for any enemy forces trying to infiltrate their lines. If we tried to cross back blind we'd be asking for trouble. We couldn't radio 3 PARA, for we were not on their net, and even if we tried to patch a call in via PF HQ, using the radio might well compromise us.

We were in the midst of a mass of Iraqi infantry and armoured positions, so we had to presume they had the ability to intercept our comms. Also, we were on strict radio silence for this op, and for good reasons. The Iraqi military were known to have excellent DF (Direction Finding) equipment, from which they could pinpoint the source of any radio signal. To break radio silence might well prove the death of us.

I'd been surrounded and trapped once by the enemy in the past few days: I didn't fancy going through all of that again. Geordie figured he needed to study the maps, so he could work out the best route to get us back to the nearest 3 PARA position, whereupon he could give them a verbal heads-up as to our mission. But even the pinprick of light thrown off by his wagon's map-light might well compromise us.

Geordie and I gathered around the dash of his wagon. He pulled out the mini Maglite he had strung on some paracord around his neck. Light discipline was everything in the PF, especially when surrounded by unknown enemy positions. As with the rest of us, Geordie had wrapped some black gaffer tape over the end of his Maglite. He'd pierced that with a needle-sized hole, which meant that when he twisted it on it let out the barest pinprick of light.

I cupped my hands around the map, as Geordie shone his Maglite on to it, like a tiny laser beam. With my palms shielding even that tiny amount of illumination from any watching eyes, we did a detailed map check without having to worry about getting seen. We located 3 PARA's nearest position, which as a bonus just happened to be their forward headquarters.

I told Geordie that I'd got that location way-pointed into my GPS, along with most of the roads and tracks lying between them and us. I offered to lead the patrol direct to it, which would mean that Geordie wouldn't have to keep illuminating his maps every five minutes, to try to navigate our way there. In the circumstances, Geordie thought this a blinding suggestion.

We readied the patrol, turned the vehicles around, and my wagon led off with the others following. The thick cloud cover meant that neither the stars nor the moon were visible. The lack of ambient light made driving on NVG a total nightmare. I couldn't see more than 5 metres ahead of me, and it had to be the same for Steve. We moved at a painfully slow crawl in the opposite direction to that which we had driven in on, but the terrain was proving horrendous.

I was navigating along this network of narrow tracks, using the GPS as my guide. We pushed back 3 kilometres and were approaching the nearest 3 PARA position, which was the moment of maximum danger. It was black as a witch's tit out here. We hit the junction of two dirt tracks, and I reckoned from my GPS that 300 metres to the right of us we'd find 3 PARA's forward HQ.

As we made the turn right, a challenge rang out in the darkness. 'Halt! Who goes there? Identify yourselves!'

We'd practically driven into a 3 PARA sentry post. Luckily, we were crawling along at 3 kilometres an hour, so Steve managed to stop before we ran the sentry over. He was a young private with his weapon gripped tight in the aim, and he was on the verge of slotting us.

'Pathfinders!' I hissed into the night. 'Pathfinder patrol. We've been on a mission into enemy terrain. We need to liaise with your HQ.'

I saw his shoulders sag as he visibly relaxed. He lowered his weapon. 'Bloody hell, sir, I was just about to open fire.' He jerked a thumb in the direction of the track behind him. '3 PARA HQ is that way'.

With a few words of thanks we pulled away and pressed onwards in the darkness. We'd gone another 15 metres at a dead crawl when I felt this weird sensation. It was like a giant hand was lifting the Land Rover and flipping it over, and suddenly everything was spinning out of control. There was a horrendous falling sensation, then a tremendous, crushing impact.

A moment later my world turned black.

I came to and opened my eyes. There was a crushing weight on my chest. I was trapped in the pitch darkness with something massive lying on top of me. I sensed that I was upside down, but I couldn't seem to right myself. I was trapped. I had this horrible, piercing ringing in the centre of my head, screaming out towards my ears. It felt like the devil himself had been let loose inside my skull, and it was agonising and totally deafening.

I tried to free an arm, so I could press my fingers into my temples, to try to stop the pain. But I didn't seem able to move at all. I heard Tricky's voice from somewhere, echoing and faint, as if it was coming from down the end of a long tunnel.

'DAVE! DAVE! WHERE THE FUCK'S DAVE?'

I could only hear his voice. I couldn't see him. I heard Steve yelling the same.

'DAVE! WHERE THE FUCK'S DAVE?'

Then Jason: 'HE'S UNDER THE FUCKING WAGON! HE'S GOT TO BE!'

I tried to shout a response, to give some form of confirmation. *I'm here! I'm here!* But my mouth was blocked with mud, which was smeared in thick globules all over my face and nose. I couldn't speak and I could barely breathe. I realised that the vehicle must have rolled off the track. It had fallen down a massive drop, and it was upside-down on top of me.

Neither Steve nor I had noticed the precipice in the darkness. Now I was trapped in my seat and pinned under the Pinkie, with my face thrust into some kind of fetid Iraqi swamp. It was stand-ard operating procedure for Pathfinders not to wear seatbelts. It was pretty obvious why. They restrict your arcs when you have to spin the weapons around, and they delay you debussing from your vehicle. Just an instant's hindrance could prove fatal, hence the no seatbelt rule.

Tricky would have been stood behind me in the 50-cal turret as the vehicle rolled, and he must have been thrown clear. Steve was on the driver's side, and I figure it must have rolled over him, leaving him to tumble out unharmed. Which left just me. I was lying almost vertical beneath the upturned wagon, horribly twisted and unable to move.

I felt utterly helpless and totally alone. Terrified. Almost impercep-tibly, I felt the Land Rover start to settle, compressing my chest and my legs a fraction more. It was a horrifying feeling, like being sucked into the dark heart of hell.

Suddenly I heard Jason yelling orders. He was trying to work out how the fuck to get me out from under the wagon, or to get it off of me. I heard Dez and Joe arrive beside the upturned vehicle. I heard Steve's hurried explanation – *the Pinkie's rolled and Dave's trapped beneath.*

The pressure on my neck and back kept growing. I was short of breath. I heard blokes scrabbling to my left and my right, but I couldn't see anyone. I counted the minutes. Ten went by. It seemed like an eternity.

Another ten. With each minute the vehicle settled a little further into the quagmire, forcing my head deeper into the gunk, and twisting and crushing my neck and spine. I could smell the rotting leaf matter, plus whatever animal or human shit had been draining into the swamp. The stench was thick in my nostrils.

We were right on 3 PARA's front line. The enemy would be positioned in the darkened terrain to the north of us, and within visual range. The NVG were barely working in the pitch darkness, but no one could risk showing any lights. To do so would draw a whirlwind of enemy fire.

The Pinkie was full of all the usual heavy ammo, supplies and weaponry, and the weight was forcing it deeper into the mud. I'm a tall bloke at 6 foot 4. When sitting in the front seat my head would be up against the rollbar. That was all but submerged now, rammed into the swamp by the mass of the vehicle above it. Gradually, my head was going the same way.

I felt this nauseating tide of panic rising up inside me. *I'm going to fucking drown in this mud and shit down here!* And then I heard the guys start digging for me. Jason was at the front urging them on. But I was so far under the vehicle, and already it had sunk so low, that the more they dug with the shovels the more the Pinkie settled. It was a horrible, vicious circle, a zero-sum game.

I felt the muck and gunk seeping into my eye sockets, and then it was over my eyes. I was blinded by it. I could taste the acrid, metallic tang of blood in my mouth. I figured I had to have internal bleeding, as the wagon slowly but surely crushed the life out of me. It was clear that digging me out wasn't working.

I felt so alone. What a way to die.

CHAPTER TWENTY-NINE

I heard a body crawling beneath the vehicle. A hand reached out for me, scrabbling desperately, groping in the thick mud. Fingers touched my fingers; reached to hold my hand. Whoever it was didn't try to pull me out. The hand just held my hand, tightly. He knew there was no moving me.

A face wriggled nearer to mine, ghostly-white in the darkness. It was Tricky. He started talking to me. He wasn't asking stupid shit like – *Dave, are you okay?* All he was doing was chewing the fat, talking about the bars we used to frequent and the lines we used to pull on all the women.

'I never told you, mate, but when you met Isabelle, that gorgeous French bird, in the Backroom Bar. Remember? Well, you went for a slash and she said:

"Wow. Who's your mate – the tall, dark, silent one?" I told her the only reason you were silent was that you'd send her to sleep if you opened your bloody mouth.'

I was trying not to laugh through a mouthful of mud and blood.

'I told her you'd talk about PF lost comms procedures, or selection, or some such bollocks all night long. I told her I was the man she needed. You only managed to pull her, mate, 'cause she got you on to the dance floor, and she saw what a crap dancer you are. She took pity on you, that's all.'

I tried giving it back to him. I wanted so desperately to talk, to laugh, to share a little human warmth. But I could barely breathe. My words came in hoarse, rasping gasps. I couldn't really hear all that he was saying even, but I was glad that it was Tricky who was with me.

He never said any of the shit that you hear in the movies – *You're gonna be all right. We'll get you out of there.* He figured that was a lie, and how the fuck would he know, anyway. He was just there to be my brother and to show me that I wasn't alone.

The weight of the Pinkie was pressing on me more and more. It was squeezing the life out of me. I felt my lungs start to fill with liquid. I could taste the stagnant water as they flooded with liquid gunk from this rancid Iraqi swamp. I tried talking to Tricky, but the words came out as frothy gargles and spurts. It was terrifying. I could hardly breathe. I stopped talking.

The pressure kept increasing, until finally I started to feel this weird sense of peace and happiness wash over me. I started to have this freaky out of body experience. I was feeling euphoric, like I was stoned out of my brain. I realised this was what it had to feel like to die. I was glad Tricky was with me, and that I wasn't on my own. He was a good guy to be with when it was your time to die.

I started to have flashbacks to my childhood and my family. These weren't slow daydreams, but rapid flashes of all the good stuff and the joy. I could see myself on a summer camping holiday in Wales, with the family. I was around seven years old and my dad was taking me fishing. We hired a little chugging boat and caught eighteen mackerel. There were too many for us to barbecue and eat, so my mum sent me around the campsite giving the spare fish away.

I flashed forwards a year or two to another family holiday. Wales again. This time my dad and I were up at the crack of dawn, and climbing the sheer cliffs around Abersoch. He'd sussed out this great fishing spot, but we had to scale the rocks to get there. I felt a rush of fear – fear of heights and fear of falling – and my father's protective arm around me. We caught some mackerel, and then my dad hooked a dogfish.

A dogfish? What's a dogfish? Half a fish, half a dog?

He reeled it in triumphantly, and there was this mini-version of a shark on the end of the line. We took it back to the campsite, and my father taught me how to prepare it for the pan, by ripping off the tough, sandpaper skin. My dad was so proud of the job we'd done with the dogfish, he put me on his lap and let me drive the car from the campsite across the farm and up to the main road. My little sisters were in the back, giggling their heads off.

I flashed forwards to my mum training me to showjump horses. She'd drive me all around the country so I could compete at the best competitions. She'd worked so hard at her job, and to care for the family, and so she could provide horses for us all.

I jumped forwards again. My sisters were fourteen and eleven years old, which meant they'd been sent to the same secondary school as me. I was constantly looking after them, just as I have done all my life ever since. It struck me as being so sad that now, after this accident, I'd never get to look after them again.

I saw my family gathered around the Christmas dinner table, all laughter and joy and light. Mum had cooked a wonderful meal, for a second night running. My older sister Anna's birthday fell on Christmas Eve, so it was always like having two Christmases in a row. There were double presents. Double the celebrations. And double the cooking for Mum to do.

I saw my Mum and Dad in their beautiful, sunlit rose garden at home, their cottage pretty in pink, and my two sisters playing amongst the flowers. Weirdly, I felt happy as these snatches of memory spooled through my head. I loved my family, and I knew they loved me back. I'd got my patrol out of Qalat Sikar and I had brought every one of them out alive. It had been a good innings. I accepted that it was my time to go.

Then a thought occurred to me. My life was a room in the mess back at our base in the UK. My shit army mattress, a stack of books and DVDs, and a crappy video system. Plus my army gear. There was almost nothing in there that was personal.

When my room was emptied my life would be summarised by that. That was what my parents would get to see. I didn't really have anyone permanent in my life. No wife. No kids. I was going to leave no one behind me, no lasting human legacy.

I remembered then that there was a pile of porn mags in my room. *Shit*. That's what my mum was going to find. She'd be so disappointed in me. It was even worse because some of the other lads had dumped their porn in my room, whilst their girlfriends came to visit one last time before they went to war. All those mags were stacked up high in one corner, like a shrine to the gods of porn.

I tried asking Tricky to sanitise my room, to ditch the porn before my mum could get to it. I was desperate to get him to do so. But I couldn't seem to speak any more.

It was a nice and warm druggie feeling now. I'd got a head full of pink cotton clouds, and the pain started to fade away into rainbow shades of grey. I started drifting in and out of consciousness. I was halfway gone, and I felt pretty happy and complete. I didn't have a regular girlfriend or a wife. There was the lovely Isabelle, of course, but we'd only just started dating. I had no kids. This was my life – *the Pathfinders*.

I managed a whisper to Tricky: 'Mate, I love the Pathfinders.'

'What d'you say, mate?' Tricky asked, trying to wriggle his head even closer to me.

I was kind of annoyed that I had to repeat myself. I was dying here. Why wasn't he listening? I gargled out the same words – *'Mate, I love the PF.'* It struck me that it might be a stupid thing to be saying, but it was exactly how I felt right now. I was fading, floating and flying towards somewhere ethereal and fantastic. I was HALOing into the balmy sunlit heavens, Supertramp's 'Goodbye Stranger' on repeat full blast, as I turned and twisted in the golden slipstream. And all around me echoed sounds of chattering and laughter, as images from my family and childhood zipped past me.

Tricky started going crazy. He was scrabbling frantically at the mud with his bare hands, trying to dig out a scoop large enough for me to breathe. I heard him shout: 'GET ME A FUCKING MUG OR A MESS TIN!'

An arm reached in with a tin mug. Tricky started to shovel out water and mud and shit as fast as he could. I got a tiny bit of relief. I grabbed a breath or two. The euphoria started to recede. As it did, I could feel how crushed and twisted my body was. Every part of me was screaming in total agony.

I was making spluttering noises with each tiny intake of breath. I tried to move my legs, or my arms, or even wiggle my fingers. Nothing. I heard a commotion outside. I heard Jason dragging the high-lift jack out from its stowage place on the vehicle.

I heard his voice: 'Get jacks under it, as many as you fucking can! We got to lift it off of his chest!'

I heard grunting in the darkness. Muffled curses. Then Dez's voice, thick with tears and frustration: 'It's not fucking working!'

I felt Tricky disengaging his fingers from my own. An instant later he was gone. I didn't know why he'd left me. I figured he'd stuck with me until the last possible moment, before his arm got crushed beneath the vehicle and he got trapped with me. I was on my own down here again, and I hated it. I'd been abandoned.

A while later I regained consciousness. I sensed that the downward force of the vehicle had eased slightly. It was barely perceptible, but maybe the wagon had lifted just a fraction. I guess the jacks had to be working. I could hear a new voice now. It was an officer issuing instructions. Then whoever was speaking stopped yelling orders and crawled beneath the vehicle. He took up position where Tricky had left off, and started speaking to me.

'David, it's Andy Jackson, 3 PARA. Are you okay?'

It was a bit of a bone question. Of course I wasn't okay. I wished Tricky was still with me. I guessed he was outside, working on the jacks. I heard scores of voices all around the vehicle. It sounded like a gang-fuck out there. There were people trying to get chains under the Pinkie, and I guessed they had to have a REME recovery truck on the track up above.

There was this debate raging about how they were going to lift the vehicle off me. There were long patches where nothing seemed to be happening, and still I was drifting in and out of consciousness. But at least the Land Rover seemed to have stopped sinking.

The chains were on but the vehicle wasn't moving. I didn't know why. Water kept seeping back into the breathing hole that Tricky had dug for me. I was spluttering in mouthfuls of mud and gunge. I gave up struggling to breathe. I was so fucking tired. I just wanted it over with now.

I hear 3 PARA's RSM start yelling for his men to stand back, as they were going to lift the vehicle.

'Everyone back! Back! We're lifting now and I need everyone back, or you'll get crushed! The vehicle's going to swing left when we lift, and it might crush you lot if you don't bloody move. So everyone back now!'

With all the noise he was making I couldn't believe the enemy hadn't pinged us, and opened fire.

Andy Jackson yelled something at the RSM. 'I'm fucking staying with him!'

I felt him scrabbling with his hands, and then the tin mug, as he tried to bale out my breathing hole. He grabbed my arm and told me he wasn't going anywhere. The bloke was a fucking hero, but I still wished Tricky was there. It was just that I trusted my own blokes so completely.

I heard a winch start to whine, as it took up the strain. Finally, the vehicle jerked up a few inches, creaking and groaning horribly with every lurch. Hands reached in and dug me out and dragged me back, away from the Pinkie's crushing weight.

This bloke was straight on to me. His voice said: 'David, it's going to be all right. I'm a London paramedic out here with the TA, and I've got you ...'

I felt somewhat reassured. I'd come across some seriously dodgy Army medics in my time. At least this one was the real deal. I couldn't speak. I couldn't even think any more. I was barely conscious. Just flying. Gone.

I felt myself lifted on to a stretcher. I was carried up the bank and slid into the rear of a field ambulance. A mask went over my face. I felt the sweet release of gas and oxygen. The pain faded, as tubes and needles went into my hands and face. Everywhere.

One of the ambulance doors opened a fraction. I sensed someone leaning in. A hand touched my hand.

'Dave! Dave The Face. Boat drinks, mate.'

It was just a head stuck around the door and a couple of rushed words, but it did the world for my morale. I couldn't move my head to see who it was even. The voice was gone. The door closed and the vehicle moved off.

With those words running through my head – *'Boat drinks, mate'* – I drifted out of consciousness.

CHAPTER THIRTY

I came to in some sort of stretcher bed. I'd got blankets piled over me, but still I was freezing cold. I'd got a tube in my mouth, my neck was in a brace, and I was pinned down in some sort of strait-jacket. I couldn't see properly. My vision was swimming. I was doped up to the eyeballs.

A voice told me that I was still in Iraq, but I was about to be flown out to a field hospital in Kuwait. I heard a helicopter land. It struck me as being ironic that they could manage to get a helo in for one wounded guy, but there was no air available for my patrol when we were trapped behind enemy lines.

Shit happens.

I was loaded beneath a whirling set of helo blades, and I passed out again. I came to in some sort of field hospital. I guessed I was in Kuwait. I looked around me. There were military doctors every-where, in stiff white medical tunics and with clipboards. Plus nurses. It looked like a scene from *M*A*S*H*.

I spotted a figure out of the corner of my eye standing by the bed-side. This one was wearing a horribly mud-stained uniform of sorts, and was sporting a thick growth of stubble. It was Steve. What the fuck was he doing here, I wondered? Why the joker and the slacker? Why not Jason? *Or Tricky?*

A nurse came over. I saw Steve's eyes light up. They followed her every move. *Now I understood.* I knew exactly why it was Steve that was here and not one of the others. *Nurses.*

I saw the nurse start to slice my clothes off me, using a pair of scissors to do so. My combats were ripped and soaked in mud, blood and shit, and she threw what remained of them into a refuse sack by her side. She got to my trousers and I managed to signal that I wanted her to stop.

She lifted the oxygen mask so I could speak. 'I was shot … A few days back … Through the trousers.'

I managed to make her understand that I wanted to keep the trousers. Somehow, in spite of the total mess that I was in, it was important to me. They were the only memento I had of the mission of a lifetime – of the suicide run south from Qalat Sikar – plus I had my silk escape map sewn into the waistband.

I asked her to give them to Steve, for safekeeping. As I did so I could tell that he wasn't listening. He was gazing into her face with his most alluring, trust-me-come-to-bed eyes. *The bastard.*

Somehow, I just knew that I was never going to see those trousers again. If Tricky were here, I'd bet my life he'd bring them home from war for me. But not Steve. He was only there for one thing – the women. I didn't hold it against him. He was what he was.

Once the nurse was gone, Steve decided he could afford me a bit of attention.

He shrugged, uncomfortably. 'Mate, I'm dead sorry that I rolled the vehicle. I didn't see …'

I silenced him with a wave of my hand, and gestured for him to come closer. He brought his face nearer to mine.

'Not your fault, mate,' I murmured. 'We both missed the drop. No one's to blame. So, how's the nurses, you jammy bastard?'

A couple of specialists came to speak to me. They explained they were orthopaedic surgeons, here with the TA. They told me I'd be back in the UK in twelve hours. My lungs were full of blood and water, so I had to remain on the oxygen. They were here to drain the liquid out of my lung cavity. They inserted some big needle device under my right armpit, and explained that the water and blood would drain out over time.

Hours passed. I was put into some sort of cocoon. I couldn't move at all. It was really comfy and warm in there. I guessed I'd got a lot of broken bones, hence all the cushioning. I was carried out to the airfield. We hung around for a while. There was the scream and whine of jets taking off and landing. I killed time by watching Steve charm and schmooze the nurses.

Finally, we started to board a military aircraft with all the seats removed.

I didn't have to move a muscle, which was great because I couldn't. I was placed on a stretcher with tubes, bags and drips attached. There were two nurses with me, and they'd keep an eye on me until we reached the UK.

Steve left with a last joke and a laugh for me, plus a few choice words for the nurses. I figured I saw a scrap of paper change hands. Phone numbers. *Slick.*

We took off and I drifted into the sleep of the dead.

I came to lying on a bed in Taunton Hospital. I was at the back of a ward, and my body was full of tubes and needles. I was feeling a bit of culture shock, to put it mildly. I was classed as VSI (Very Seriously Injured), so they had decided to put me in a ward with the old and the dying. The average age must have been seventy-five plus.

Less than twenty-four hours ago I'd been in Iraq, on my second mission behind enemy lines. I was there with my mates, fighting for my life. I'd now been crushed by our Land Rover, so my war was over, and I'd been placed in a ward with those about to die. I figured they'd put me here because my prognosis was likewise.

A pretty young nurse came over. She perched on my bedside and asked if I needed anything. I started to cry. I didn't know why or what for, but I couldn't stop the tears. She held me and told me it was all going to be all right. She smelled good. Her skin was soft. I passed out in her arms.

When I woke again my mother was there. I felt this massive sense of relief just at the sight of her. I knew she'd get all over this and sort this shit out. Sure enough, she got me moved into a private room where I could be alone with my morphine drip and my addled, woozy brain, plus my dark thoughts.

Over the next few days I had dozens of X-rays. I had eight broken ribs on my right side. I had a badly dislocated shoulder. I had flooded lungs. But the main problem was with the right brachial plexus (a network of nerves). There was severe nerve damage to my right arm. In fact, it was so badly damaged that I might never be able to use it again. My right arm might remain withered and dead for the rest of my life, being left to flop by the side of my body.

It was my right arm. My trigger arm. And without it I had no reason to be a Pathfinder any more.

But at least I was alive.

A week in and I was released into my mother's care. I was wrapped in blankets and I was still on the morphine, but at least I was out of that place where people were sent to die. When I reached my parents' pretty Lincolnshire cottage, my dad helped me into the house and on to the sofa. It was so good to see him again.

There was a brown envelope on the coffee table. It looked official and it was addressed to me. My mum opened it. It was a template letter from the MOD. It stated that following my injuries I was posted away from the Pathfinders to the 'Y-List'. This was the Army's sick and injured list. I didn't have a unit any more. I was out of the PF. It was like a massive kick in the bollocks.

My mum explained how they had got the news that I'd been injured. She'd heard the garden gate go, and leaves scrunching underfoot. She'd glanced through the door to see a grim-faced man in a suit walking up the garden path. She dropped to the floor, screaming: 'No!' My dad fell to the floor and hugged her, crying.

The man in the dark suit had put his mouth to the letterbox, and shouted: 'It's okay! David's not dead! He's just injured.'

I'd only ever seen my dad cry once, and that was after his mother died. This was only the second time that I'd even heard of him being in tears. If I didn't know it before, I knew now how much my parents loved and cared for me. They lay me on a sofa in the lounge with a duvet over me. I found it impossible to sleep, the broken ribs were so painful.

The next day another letter arrived, plus a long, odd-shaped parcel. The envelope looked posh. It was a letter from Prince Charles, personally written on his Birkhall-headed paper. I read it, and it did so much to cheer my soul.

> *Dear Dave,*
>
> *I heard of the terrible accident that befell you in Iraq and just wanted to write and send you my very best wishes for a speedy recovery. I am relieved to hear that you should be able to leave hospital soon.*
>
> *My spies also tell me you had a narrow escape from a carefully aimed Iraqi bullet, just the other day before your crash and that you were only saved by a lucky pair of trousers! The good Lord is obviously still smiling on you …! I hope that despite your setbacks, you remain in good spirits and that the enclosed 'medicine' might help to raise them a bit …*
>
> *I know you will be desperate to rejoin your comrades in the Pathfinder Platoon as soon as you can but, in the meantime, I hope you are able to enjoy some recuperation time with your family.*
>
> *Yours most sincerely,*
>
> *Charles*

I opened the parcel. The 'medicine' Prince Charles referred to was a bottle of vintage Laphroaig from his own personal cellars. My dad told me we'd keep that bottle forever. He'd buy me the same Laphroaig vintage, and we'd drink that one together to toast my homecoming.

A few days later there was a bluey in the mail. It was from Tricky. He didn't ask how I was. Instead he chatted away for a while about what the rest of the PF lads had been up to, and then he asked after my two, beautiful sisters. *The cheeky fucker!*

After I'd been casevaced out of theatre, the blokes had been told that I was VSI, but that I would live. At that stage I was ripe for a slagging. That was when they had started the rumour that when I was trapped under the Pinkie, all they could hear me screaming was: 'Not the face! Not the face!'

Oh how I love 'em.

The bastards.

EPILOGUE

I spent many months in recovery in the UK, during which time my parents nursed me back to health. With time, many of my injuries would heal naturally – the broken ribs, the damage to my lungs. The chest drain worked well, and the bag soon filled with this nasty red and yellow fluid as my lungs drained.

During the time I spent in recovery I remembered that whilst lying in the Kuwait hospital I'd been visited by an Army mate. He'd told me that there was a friend of the family in the UK who was a specialist in treating arm and shoulder injuries. Get in touch with his girlfriend, he said, and she'd sort out an introduction between me and that medical specialist.

My mother got on the case and made an appointment. The specialist, Professor Rolf Birch, was a consultant orthopaedic surgeon, and I was taken by my mother to see him, with my right arm in a sling. There was severe nerve damage to my arm, and I'd been warned that it might never fully recover movement or feeling.

Professor Birch turned out to have wild white hair and a long, white walking stick. He really looked the mad professor part. After examining me, he told me that I would come under his personal care for several months, whilst he treated my arm. He told me how he hoped we'd get it working again, but with nerve damage there were never any guarantees.

Before leaving I asked him when I could start doing some fitness training again, even if it was simply some sit-ups. He gave me this look as if he thought I was bonkers. I was still on the morphine, and I guess I was quite high, but I was also deadly serious. I was desperate to get back to the Pathfinders, and I wasn't about to let my injured arm get in my way.

The professor told me that it was 'best just to rest for now'. Largely, I ignored his advice. I put in place my own training regime, based in part on the kind of gentle exercises we do in the Pathfinders after completing a proper workout. Over the weeks and months I built up my body strength and fitness again, and I began to sense the return of some feeling in my arm. But after periods where I progressed a little, then regressed, it became clear that I needed some serious shoulder surgery. Due to a mess-up within the NHS I waited eighteen months for the operation, by which time I lost patience.

I sold my car and used the proceeds to pay to have the operation done privately. Some six months later I rejoined the Pathfinders. It had been very much a triumph of mind over matter, but I'd managed to regain the full use of my right arm. I felt physically and mentally fit enough to rejoin the unit as a fully-fledged operator, but I was restricted to doing desk duties until I could be vouchsafed as such by the MOD. Eventually, I would rejoin the PF as a fully-functioning operator, and take up my post again as 2IC.

When I received the letter from the MOD on the day I returned home from hospital, being put on the Army's sick and injured list, the Y-List, was the cruellest blow imaginable. It was a computer-generated automatic mailing. Whilst I can appreciate the logic behind sending it, the MOD showed about as much sensitivity as a charging elephant in doing so.

The letter stated that if I had not fully recovered within eighteen months, the Army reserved the right to kick me out of the armed forces. It didn't even wish me a get well soon. Nice. I was a war-wounded soldier just a day out of hospital. I'd taken a look at the name of the MOD pen-pusher who'd signed it, and I'd memorised it. I resolved to meet up with him in a dark alleyway sometime in the near future, and get even. It's still on my list of things to do.

It was only the letter and the bottle of whisky that I had received from Prince Charles that in part made up for such insensitive and shoddy treatment. That personal, hand-addressed letter from Prince Charles – plus that bottle of single malt whisky – did the world for my morale when I was so badly wounded. It made me think that maybe the Army was a reasonable, humane force to serve with, after all.

One of the biggest mysteries surrounding our mission to Qalat Sikar airfield was why there was no air available for our patrol, when we had called for it *in extremis*. At the moment that we asked for it we had no idea what the rest of the British forces were up to. For all we knew there could have been soldiers fighting for their lives all over southern Iraq, and they could have monopolised the air power.

In reality, that wasn't the case. Apart from our unit of Pathfinders, very few if any British troops were at that time facing serious combat. With the benefit of hindsight, and having spoken to competent people within the UK armed forces, I believe that air could have been found from somewhere – or re-prioritised from a strategic tasking.

It could have been made available, because we had discovered a massive hidden Iraqi force that needed to be taken out, and it might have been the means of saving our lives. It is also a fact that the Americans had masses of air available to cover Nasiriyah, and they proved how swiftly it could be brought to bear once we'd passed over the co-ordinates of the Iraqi positions to them.

However, any rescue force sent in to try to lift out our patrol would almost certainly have flown into a barrage of fire, considering the concentration of Iraqi forces equipped with heavy machine guns all along the route north of Nasiriyah. That force would likely have consisted of two Chinooks carrying PARAs and with helicopter gunships in support, and to send them in may well have risked getting them shot out of the sky.

This may explain why John, the PF OC, felt he was unable to send in any kind of airborne rescue force. It doesn't however explain why no air cover was provided at the time we asked for it to call in air strikes on the enemy positions we had discovered.

The battle for Nasiriyah has been written up in several books, and is the subject of several TV films, including HBO's *Generation Kill*. The best account is perhaps Tim Pritchard's *Ambush Alley: the most extraordinary battle of the Iraq War*, named after the road through Nasiriyah along which the Marine Corps advanced, and along which we subsequently followed.

The book *Ambush Alley* recounts the story of the March 2003 battle for Nasiriyah from the perspective of the three US Marine Corps companies – Alpha, Bravo and Charlie – who fought to take the city and seize the two vital bridges. Those are the same Marine units with whom we liaised, both before crossing over their front lines and once we had made it back again safely.

The following words are quoted from the final page of *Ambush Alley*. They recount the reaction of one Charlie Company marine to seeing our patrol return from the Qalat Sikar mission.

> He couldn't tell if anyone was moving out there or not. *They might still be out there. They can kill us whenever they want.* Out of the darkness a group of figures did appear. They weren't Iraqis. They were British. They came over to Robinson and his buddies and asked for some cigarettes. In their strange accents they started saying that the Marines shouldn't go north, that it was heavy up there.
>
> Robinson was impressed by them. They were older, with beards and moustaches and shit. They were loaded with ammo and their all-terrain vehicle was bristling with rockets and M240s. And then they just disappeared into the desert with no support and no word of where they

were going or what they were up to. Robinson could
guess who they were, and in spite of what he'd just been
through he yearned for the romance of life in the Special
Forces.

Eighteen US marines died in the battle to take the Southern Euphrates Bridge and the Northern Saddam Canal Bridge. Some thirty-five
were injured. There were also eleven US Army soldiers killed in
Nasariyah that day, bringing total US casualties to twenty-nine. That
represents the single greatest loss suffered by the American military
during the taking of Iraq, reflecting the bloody intensity of the battle
for Nasiriyah.

Notably, every US Marine captured during the week of our mission north of Nasiriyah was executed by the Iraqi enemy. This was
very different from the 1991 Gulf War. One American Recon Marine
was reportedly crucified in the town centre where he was captured,
and left on display. Something similar would no doubt have been our
fate, had we been captured.

One of the reasons for the ferocity of the Iraqi resistance experienced at Nasiriyah and north only became clear to us long after
the war. Apparently, Saddam had sent his Special Security Organisa-
tion (SSO) forces – his 'most feared security forces' according to the
CIA – to defend Nasiriyah and routes north of there, along with his
Fedayeen.

Both the SSO and the Fedayeen consisted of die-hard Saddam
loyalists who understood that they would have no role in the
rebuilding of Iraq should Saddam's regime be defeated. Nasariyah
was their last-ditch stand, and the SSO and Fedayeen would have
believed they were fighting for their very survival. In retrospect, it
seems highly likely that 'Ron Jeremy' and others we blundered into
on the route north from Nasariyah were SSO operators.

The day after the battle for Nasiriyah, and following the air strikes
that went in north of the city, using the intel that we had gathered,
the Marine Corps 2nd Light Armoured Reconnaissance Battalion

spearheaded the 1st Marine Expeditionary Force's lightning push north of Nasiriyah to seize Baghdad.

It was several days before the last bodies of the US Marines KIA (Killed In Action) in Nasiriyah were found. They had been buried in shallow graves in some of the city's residences. On 1 April 2003 marines from Task Force Tarawa launched a rescue operation to free Private Jessica Lynch, one of the soldiers from the US Army's 507th Maintenance Convoy, whose capture in Nasiriyah had caught the attention of the world's media.

We were nine British soldiers tasked with the Qalat Sikar mission, and as far as I know we were the only British troops present in, and forward of, the battle for Nasiriyah. For the tiny, lightly-armed force that we were, I like to think that we played a vital role in enabling the Marine Corps to advance out of that city and take Baghdad.

Qalat Sikar airfield was never seized by an elite force along the lines planned in our original mission, and that of the PARAs who were to follow us. As events transpired, the lightning advance of the Marine Expeditionary Force north out of Nasiriyah pushed far into Iraq, and the airfield fell into coalition hands anyway.

John, the OC of the Pathfinders, submitted recommendations for honour and awards after our Iraq tour. Jason received the Military Cross for his actions during the Qalat Sikar mission. Deservedly so. He was a flawless, superlative operator, and in spite of the ups and downs in our relationship before the war he was solid in his support of me, and his bravery was second to none when leading the patrol out of almost certain death.

His clarity of mind while riding in the front vehicle and leading the convoy down Route 7 was incredible, and he was a fine example for us all to follow. He showed calmness and consideration for those behind him by throwing smoke grenades, which helped save the lives of all in the two wagons following, the Engineer Recce lads included. I have immense admiration for Jason as a soldier and an elite operator.

Though he was put forward for a medal, Tricky received no

decoration for his soldiering in Iraq, and despite the fact that the plan to move back south down Route 7 and link up with the US Marines at Nasiriyah arose from his insistence that we keep the vehicles. Tricky was a fearless, professional and cool operator, and the safety of the patrol was heavily dependent on his experience, not to mention his use of the 50-cal.

He was unflappable when handling that heavy weapon, despite the fact that he was the most vulnerable person on our wagon, for the 50-cal operator sits higher and is more exposed than the rest of the team in the Pinkies. At the end of the day I've no doubt that Tricky didn't particularly give a damn about the lack of medals he received from Iraq: he wasn't in the Pathfinders for the glory.

I will feel indebted to him for the rest of my life, for it was Tricky who was under the upturned wagon holding my hand, and trying to pull me out of there.

Sergeant Ian Andrews – the Engineer Recce sergeant – was also awarded the Military Cross. That was fair enough and well-deserved. When the shit went down the Engineer Recce lads delivered on that mission, and were not found wanting in the heat of combat. He was also allowed to keep the pistol that saved him from the Iraqi bullet that struck him on the side, as a souvenir. I hope he has it framed, and displayed in a prime position on his glory wall.

None of the other patrol members received an honour, including Steve, Joe, Dez and the other Engineer Recce lads, although a number of us were put forward for medals of one sort or another. Although I understand that honours given out are limited in the British Army, I firmly believe that every bloke on the Qalat Sikar mission deserved a Military Cross, or something similar.

After I was medevaced out of theatre John went on to command the Pathfinders exceptionally well for a further five months of operations deep in Iraq.

Each of us on the Qalat Sikar mission went through a baptism of fire, and came through a changed man. Consider Dez. Whilst he didn't get a medal, his modern-day Wild West gunslinger moment with the pistol has gone down in Pathfinder legend. He wiped John Wayne off the map, and in the secretive world of elite forces operations people will be talking about Dez's stunt for years to come. Half in jest, Pathfinders refer to battle-hardened blokes as having had 'more action than Chuck Norris'. I can't recall any Chuck Norris film in which he's trapped behind enemy lines, facing thousands of enemy forces as we were, and does a Dez and fights them off with a pistol.

Some senior officers have argued that as the patrol commander tasked with the Qalat Sikar mission, my decision to push forward beyond the US front line in an effort to complete the mission was the wrong one. I hope from the telling of the mission in this book it is clear why that decision was made – a decision which crucially was shared by every man of my patrol. As the patrol commander I know the buck stops with me: but I believed then and still firmly believe that we made absolutely the right decision to proceed with the mission, in light of the intelligence that was available to us, and the outcome of the mission in itself proves our decision the right one. I am sure the men of my patrol feel likewise.

In the final analysis, the immense sense of satisfaction that we got from being able to pass those enemy co-ordinates to the Americans meant a huge amount to every man on the Qalat Sikar mission. Apart from the blindingly obvious fact that it was vital intel – especially when satellite, aerial and human intel had already proven so disastrously out of kilter – it was fantastic to be able to contribute to the American war effort in such a crucial way.

Throughout my Army career I've been on joint operations and training with the Americans many times. I've been used to being their poor brother, and borrowing from them whatever we might need: airframes first and foremost, but other kit as well. More often than not we're the paupers, and it has been embarrassing at times. Our blokes have as much skill and can-do attitude, but never the right kit, or enough of it.

In Iraq, 16 Air Assault Brigade had initially sat in the rear with little or no air assault capability, and yet we'd seen thousands of Marine

Expeditionary Force troops advancing into combat, with massive air support. In Iraq two different wars were being fought by two very different militaries, and we were there to support the Americans with our hands tied behind our backs a great deal of the time.

We were doubly hamstrung by the lack of will, which made a para-insertion into Qalat Sikar somehow militarily and politically unacceptable. Had we been allowed to HALO into Qalat Sikar, I have no doubt that we would have achieved the mission we had been given, which might have shortened the length and lethality of the war. As it was, the ability of our patrol to pass vital intel to the Americans meant that the British forces added something of enormous value, and of almost equal import, in my view, to seizing Qalat Sikar airfield.

Nasiriyah held the key to the jewel in the crown of Iraq, which was Baghdad. The fight to seize Nasiriyah has become known as 'the mother of all battles'. The US Marine Corps had been fought to a standstill, and the losses on the American side speak for themselves. I believe we truly helped change the course of that battle, and that in turn was a decisive moment in the war.

The Americans have always been so respectful and supportive of us as British soldiers and Pathfinders, so to be able to deliver something back was returning a favour to them – a favour that was well due. Our patrol's achievements in gaining that intel, *and coming back alive to deliver it*, should have been something HM Forces trumpeted from the rooftops. Hopefully, this book will go some of the way to making known what was achieved by a small body of British soldiers in the opening days of the war in Iraq.

Pathfinders regularly train with American elite forces, and our relations with our American fellow warriors remain strong. I hope the Qalat Sikar mission – and its telling in this book – helps strengthen that relationship. In recent years we have started doing more HALO and HAHO training in South Africa, and the operation written about at the start of this book concerns a training mission undertaken by myself and other Pathfinders in South Africa.

The Pathfinders remain the most decorated platoon in the British Army. Pathfinder sergeant Stan Harris was awarded a Military Cross when fighting the West Side Boys, a rebel group in Sierra Leone. Bryan Budd was awarded the VC in Helmand province – sadly posthumously – and he'd just come out of the Pathfinders to join a regular unit. In his heart he was and remains a PF. Plus there are scores of MIDs (Mentioned in Despatches), and the 2 MCs awarded for the Qalat Sikar mission.

This tiny unit of men can justifiably stand proud. Rest assured that on the ground right now, in remote and hostile parts of the world, there are small groups of very determined men spreading chaos amongst the enemy.

If you ask them, you probably won't get any answers, but they're very likely Pathfinders.

GLOSSARY

Belt kit   *pouches a soldier wears on a belt to carry his ammunition, survival equipment etc.*

Blue Force Tracker   *military term for a GPS-enabled system that provides military commanders and forces with location information about friendly (and, despite its name, also about hostile) military forces*

Browning   *Browning 9 mm pistol*

C130   *Hercules aircraft used by many armies for troop, vehicle and logistic transportation. Also used to transport and dispatch parachutists*

CR   *Combat Recovery*

CSAR   *Combat Search and Rescue*

CTR   *Lose Target Recce*

DPM   *Disrupt Pattern Material – commonly used name for camouflage pattern*

EPs   *Emergency Procedures*

ERV   *Emergency Rendezvous*

HAHO   *High Altitude High Opening*

HALO   *High Altitude Low Opening*

HAPLSS   *High Altitude Parachut Life Support System*

HLS   *Helicopter Landing Site*

IA   *Immediate Action*

intel   *intelligence*

IP   *Impact Point (at which a parachutist lands)*

LONG   *slang for long-barelled weapon, i.e. rifle*

LUP   *Lie-Up Point*

M16   *US-made assault rifle once used by the SAS and Pathfinders*

NAI   *Named Area of Interest*

NBC   *Nuclear, Biological, Chemical (warfare)*

NVG   *Night Vision Goggles*

Op Massive   *soldiers' slang for undergoing an intense training regime whereby they bulk up in muscle*

OPSEC   *Operational Security*

PARA   *term for a Parachute Regiment Battalion of about 650 soldiers or an individual Parachute Regiment member*

PJHQ   *Permanent Joint Headquarters – UK headquarters which commands military operations*

Roger   *military speak for 'understood'*

SA80   *standard-issue British Army rifle*

Sched   *scheduled time for a patrol to send a radio update*

SCUD   *tactical ballistic missiles developed by the Soviet Union during the Cold War and exported widely to other countries, including Iraq*

SH   *support helicopters – usually refers to Chinook CH47 but can include Pumas, Wessex, Lynx, etc.*

Sitrep   *situation report*

Snap Ambush   *hastily made ambush to observe any enemy who can then be fired upon*

SOP   *Standard Operating Procedure*

SOPHIE   *thermal imaging system*

Watchkeeper   *an operational appointment in the army in which an experienced officer or non-commissioned officer has limited control over a headquarters or its radio operators while the commanding officer is resting or on other tasks*

PHOTO CREDITS

Author on stretcher (© David Blakeley)
Author's military medals (© David Blakeley)
Author and HRH Prince Charles (© David Blakeley)
Letter from HRH Prince Charles (© David Blakeley)